The Invisible Country

The Invisible Country

H. E. Francis

Frederic C. Beil
Savannah

First published in the United States by
Frederic C. Beil, Publisher, Inc.
609 Whitaker Street
Savannah, Georgia 31401
http://www.beil.com

This is a work of fiction. Names, characters, and incidents either are the product of the author's imagination or are used fictitiously, and any resemblance to actual persons, living or dead, is entirely coincidental.

Segments of this novel have appeared in different form in *The Literary Review, Virginia Quarterly Review,* and *Transatlantic Review.*

LIBRARY OF CONGRESS CATALOGING-IN-PUBLICATION DATA
Francis, H. E. (Herbert Edward), 1924–
The invisible country / by H. E. Francis
p. cm.
ISBN 1-929490-06-2 (alk. paper)
1. World War, 1939–1945—Fiction.
2. Brothers—Fiction. I. Title.
PS3556.R328 I57 2001
813'.54—dc21
00-031147

First Edition

This book is set in Adobe Warnock Pro OTF, composed by Nangle Graphics, Savannah, Georgia; printed on acid-free paper; and sewn in signatures.

Printed in the United States of America

To

My Son

Carlos Roberto Francis

We all live at least three different lives,
a real one, an imaginary one, and one *we're not even aware of.*

Thomas Bernhard

The mystery of life is not solved by success, which is an end in itself, but in failure, in perpetual struggle, in becoming.

Patrick White

Contents

The Invisible Country

Cory

He wanted to touch her.

She said, "It's the last time, the last, isn't it?"

"Vanna."

"Savannah."

"Listen—"

"*Savannah*, Cory."

"Savannah."

"Isn't it?"

He stared past her, out the window, over the trees and the fraternity houses, at the frozen lake and the dark far shore.

"I hate endings," he said, and knew—because she was suddenly eyes, alerted, pure eyes on him—he communicated nerves, tension, even apprehension.

"Beginnings," she said unconvincingly.

"Endings. End of university life, end of you. Endings."

"Not me," she said. "Never me. We were born—born, yes—at this place: friends, together."

"And died here."

"No, Cory." There was a cry in her hands rising. They encircled air and fell to her lap. "No. But you won't be back. You'll go and stay this time. You and that island. You love it so, you'll never leave it."

She must have known that was a lie, he couldn't stay on Long Island, he'd never stay. You hated what you loved, you loved what you hated, you didn't know, you just didn't know what to do sometimes, how to handle it, and no degree ever helped in that, no degree gave you wisdom. Besides, you had your work, your work called, no matter what else you loved you went where the work was.

"Endings."

"No. I want to think for now just our last hours together. I loved you, you know that. And I love you now. From the minute we looked at each other, I knew that. You've been closest of all to me from the beginning: all those nights in the greasy spoon, all the study, the madness together's been you."

Last sun made the branches dark. Between them, below, far, the lake burned with a last white. Mendota. All the years he had seen the lake across Langdon Street, three stories below, and from the Union and the dorms, and from every angle, and rode it and soaked in it. His friend the lake it seemed now, too familiar to leave it. The lake his womb.

He shuddered, standing before the window, though the room was not cold—if anything, too steamed from the radiator. He was damp, hands and armpits, and felt a sultry stick to his clothes. He could feel it all come together; in his tension he bit his teeth hard.

"And you won't write. You won't."

Far over the ice a lone sail streaked a white blaze against the dark ridge of trees, past Picnic Point. Gone, it left a blinding white thread across his vision.

"Will you?"

"You know *not* writing's impossible for me."

"But not to me."

"We've never been apart long enough." He had not realized it till he said it—through his bachelor's, day and day and day, years. He and Rod and she.

The lake was dark now, the far trees a dark wall, the sky a last sinking crimson cry.

My brother.

He turned from the water.

"But we will be now. Forever maybe. Will we, Cory?"

"Don't, Savannah."

For years you went back and forth between your rooms and classes; you sat in the Union over talk and talk, discussions, violent sometimes, night after night over beer in the Rathskeller and then in the Campus Grill, your clothes reeking of grease after and your head breeding a chaos of thoughts, vipers that you desired but which would not let you sleep.

He sat on the edge of the bed, facing the window.

Rod had been sitting on the edge of the bed facing the window.

The springs broke the silence. "This old thing." He might have said *I'll miss the damned creaking.* In his nervous moments, it would wake him. Rod had been a log.

From his own room, when he woke he could see the spires of trees, the peaks of houses, like lying on some crest of the world.

He dropped his head. Seeing destroyed. The bed fixed an image. Most of the time thought kept him from the image.

The image conjured up the old man lying on a daybed.

"My grandfather," he said.

"What?"

"My grandfather." And the familiar image made him laugh, giddy, aloud.

"Well, that's a welcome note. Your grandfather?"

"If there were ever a place, a thing, someone you could count on forever, it would be that old man. Did I ever tell you he had albino eyes but could see more than anybody? Did I ever tell you he had crippled hands from a fire at sea but could build? Did I?"

He could see his grandfather: the eyes were staring at him, tiny flecks of pink in that hard cold blue of some winter skies, and the eyes were quivering. He was standing very still in his old mismatched brown pants and black pin-striped suit jacket; and his hands, his crippled hands, were two hard claws jutting from the sleeves of his jacket. The hands were held up against his chest like two still cat paws; and his mouth, the lower jaw, was moving slightly from side to side pensively, that habit he had.

"Oh, Cory, you don't feel—you don't—that desperate?"

He heard her sit on the bed, behind.

He did not reply. He dropped his head.

She touched it.

"Do you, Cory? It isn't all over. Nothing's ever over, you know that. If we could say *how* it wasn't, but we can't. But it isn't over."

Silent, he let her hand touch his hair. He wanted the hand to burn him. Burned, he would become the image of his grandfather. Then he could let the image alone. All the world would let him alone, the way they did that old man.

"I hate this apartment." He stood up, feeling taut, pure wire.

"Hate it! But once—"

"Once!" He saw in the dresser mirror his own bitterness bite. He didn't like the look on his face. He saw Savannah's legs behind him.

He had seen her stretched on his own bed round and white, naked: when she'd caught sight of his face, she'd thrust her head into the pillow. A smear had made a quick glitter on her leg. He hadn't been able to take his eyes off it. Rod, his back to him, had been sitting on the other side of the bed by the window, naked.

Now when he turned around, Savannah was stretched full, but not white and not naked. He said to himself, *Not white and not naked.* In night, in any dark, he saw the smear glitter on her leg, clear and burning. He would be afraid to touch it.

Her hand, which had touched his hair, was still raised.

"It's all right, Savannah. I'll be all right. Why do I make such a fuss?"

For the first time she smiled. He felt even in his fingers he could give her now his smile, and touched her hand.

"These years," she said.

"Yes."

He felt her warm clutch. She drew her legs up, her stocking feet, raised herself on one arm, and leaned against him.

"Nothing in our lives could ever be so fine again."

"There has to be something left," he said.

"Your grandfather?"

"No. To cling to from all this—you." He rested the fingertips on her hair. Her short hair was parted perfectly. He stared into the part.

He laughed.

"Going's that funny?"

"I was thinking how, the first time we'd ever talked half the night and I'd gone home and couldn't sleep, I got out of bed and went out in the middle of the night looking for a phone to call you just to tell you I couldn't sleep."

She laughed. It was Savannah then, the hoarse choke of laughter in her throat followed by the quick little cough into her fist from smoking too much, chain smoking, her eyes closing briefly, and then her broad smile, which pulled her flesh back over her cheekbones and gave a neat firm shape to her fleshy face and pressed the eyes half shut into narrow glitters, a sudden softening that said tender, maternal, vulnerable. She couldn't hide her teeth then, the separations. She hated her teeth. "*Yes*, I hate them." "Everybody hates something about himself," he'd said. "That doesn't console me, Cory, but thanks." Maybe that was why she'd developed the habit of that initial grunt laugh and the hand over her mouth, to conceal especially the gap between her two large front teeth, maybe also the heavy nicotine that yellowed the enamel. She was an English major and her friends soon kidded her about being gap-toothed—*gat-toothed* like the sensual Wife of Bath, they'd say—easing her awareness, making her laugh with that intimate laugh-choke that conveyed a sexiness she'd never been aware of until Rod, who in the early days of their few accidental meetings would stare at her teeth, at the gaps, until she'd become confused, her thoughts sudden vapors. All her flesh, then, seemed to collapse; she sank into herself, shrank; she seemed to lose form and her body reflected the slack motion of her mind at that moment. Later, it was all Rod had to do to make her drop her eyes, and still later all he had to do to make her smolder.

Rod.

Cory stared now at the gap in her teeth.

She closed her eyes. "Don't, Cory." She sank onto the mattress as if shrinking from a slight, invisible thrust.

He hated the sight of sheetless beds, stripped rooms, empty drawers and cabinets, disappeared decorations, stains, the wallpaper virginal where pictures had hung. This Victorian room was suddenly soiled.

"I've lived here too long." He didn't say I can't leave it, though he didn't want to go, dreaded the moment that was coming, though he wanted that moment too, wanted to escape Savannah, wanted to leave her sitting there so he could imagine her sitting there forever, behind, *done with*, a monument he did not even want to be a monument to that past they had had together.

"Not long enough for me." She gave way to the mattress then, let herself slip back, her arms flop out in a cross, her head fall back, and talked to the ceiling. "You came, you saw, you conquered—you and your brother—and now I'm plowed up waste, a desert, deserted. Oh, I'm not blaming. What's to blame? It happened. Time moves. You don't know time. Suddenly, it seems, it's gone—over you, around you, through you? Time takes everything, but it has nothing. How do you like that? Nothing takes everything. You're here. I'm here. We never got that in any philosophy class, did we?"

"I don't know that we ever got anything from a philosophy class but a way to think."

"Even when you don't want to think. Yes."

Now all the lake was a dark glow, slate, dying into black. Below, up and down Langdon, the streetlights and lights in the windows warded off the dark. In the sorority opposite he could see girls moving and talking in the bay window below, and over the Union the lights began to mould the night.

"You can get into a way of thought," she said, "as visual and palpable and inescapable as any metal groove—okay?—and some days once you begin you can't turn back. You start and you say I can turn this back, I can control this, I *will* control this; but you're already on your way, you're thinking, and thinking's a roller coaster; and you realize what you've realized a thousand thousand times before, that the only way to control it is not to get on it in the first place, not to make the first movement of thought. But how do you stop, Cory? You're so smart, you with your degree now, tell me that."

"Don't, Savannah, please."

"Don't *Don't, Savannah, please* me! Oh, Cory!"

She turned on her side, slid her hand up under her head, and drew her legs up, almost a fetus. Like that, her hip rose emphatically from her small waist, what he'd first noticed about her when he'd seen her cross the Rathskeller in the Union, a fleshy girl very near his own height with an amazingly small waist. Her hips moved in an easeful rise and fall when she went back and forth to the counter—she liked beer—and her breasts over the taut waist quivered. On Monday, Wednesday, and Friday mornings he found—she must have just come from class—she was there just after eleven infallibly, and alone. She worked, her notebooks sloppily spread, breasts slumped over the table, head concentrating, sometimes with tortoiseshell glasses on—coffee after coffee. He could see the part down the center of her head; he could see, when she was staring straight at nothing the mouth, the thick wide lips murmuring, memorizing. All her features were large—thick brows, bold eyes, a broadish somewhat flat nose, thick neck. Her hair, not thick, was short around her neck, with a rather wiry look, the kind that split at the ends and could not possibly grow long, full, willowy. No beauty made her stand out, but he found himself on the way to the Union merely to see if she were there, betting with himself she would be. Maybe it was the dresses, full skirts, always of light airy stuff, that gave her freedom, played down the heavy hips but emphasized their motion, and the off-the-shoulder bodices; more, the ballerina slippers that were meant to shrink feet to Alice in Wonderland daintiness; most, she had a penchant for white. She knew about white. He could not explain why she impressed. He carried her away with him, she stood in his head, at the oddest times she intruded on his vision.

She gathered her white dress about her ankles now. Only her bare feet, looking helpless, protruded.

White. She would wear white for her graduation come spring. After, there would be the plethora of June brides.

But not Savannah.

She would wear her white alone. She would bed alone. Even if she fucked, she would be alone, because every man would be Rod. Or him. Some women who fuck are virgins, or the most indifferent sluts, because you can't really touch them; and you must be touched to the quick of you or there's nothing, it's nothing, you're nothing.

You're nothing, Cory, Rod had said. Here. In this room.

My brother.

Emptied except for the bare furniture, the rooms were forlorn, the wallpaper, the woodwork marred. The storm windows were streaked with smut. With the sun dead, the overhead light was dingy.

"You don't realize what muck you're living in till it's over, do you?"

The open suitcases he had tossed things into helter-skelter, clean and dirty mixed. The guts spilled.

When he kneeled to wrestle with them, he saw she was crying silently, staring at him, wet gathered at the rims.

"Savannah?"

"Was it such muck, Cory?"

"I didn't mean—"

"I know what you meant."

"No, you don't. You always think you do, and lots of times I guess you do. I meant this wreck of a place."

"But there's always an undertone in you, Cory. You want to blight—you *do*—what we had, you and I and, yes, Rod. Why *do* you?"

"How can I blight what's dead, Savannah?"

"Not! It's not dead, Cory . It's inside us, part of us, it always will be, and it won't die, I know it won't, and you know it won't. We're our own ghosts, but we don't have to feed on it, blight it, to keep it alive. It'll stay alive of its own accord, but you won't let it rest wherever things must finally lie so we can accept them and live with them. Why do you *gnaw* on things so?"

"Because I'm Cory Moorehead and not Savannah Goshen, that's why. Go ahead and say it—*That's stupid!*—but it's not so stupid as it sounds, Savannah."

"You always know what I'm going to say."

"Because you keep saying the same things. You won't get off them."

"Because *you* won't get off them. Rod did."

"Did he?"

"He never dwelled on things the way you do."

"Didn't he?"

"No."

"Don't fool yourself. Some people dwell on things in silence. Remember, he's a Moorehead too."

"Rod always spoke his mind."

Rod *had* kept some silence. That was the revelation, that Rod too could be secretive.

"No Moorehead ever spoke all his mind."

"Rod did."

"About what? About everything? Or about *your* things?"

"What was wrong with *our* things?"

He wouldn't look at her. He heard the tears, he heard the chafe of her legs along the mattress, he heard the thin constricted breaths.

"You have to answer that."

"But you know the answer?"

"Right now I don't know any answers, Savannah. Everything's a question."

"Why don't you ask *me* then?"

"Because they're questions that don't have answers."

"Come down to earth, Cory."

"How far down do you want me to go?"

"So far down that we can only go up—together. If I could only find the way . . ."

"You found the way with Rod."

"You've got it wrong, Cory. You know you have. It just happened."

Here. In my room. On my bed.

"And you, you never made a pass at me all those months before Rod came to Madison—and seeing me every day, and with Dalton. Were you leaving me to Dalton?"

"You knew Dalton at home. You felt comfortable with him. How'd I know what was going on between Dalton and you?"

"You never asked."

"I wouldn't. You knew I wouldn't. Besides, Dalton was your friend. Then he became mine."

The hundred nights after they had closed the Campus Grill, he and she and Dalton walked one another home, first to his place on Bowen Court, then to her room, then to Dalton's shared apartment, each not wanting to leave the others, and ended up at an all-night, drinking coffee and talking till class time the next morning.

Before Rod. Rod changed all that.

"And I knew you before Rod. So what does that prove?"

"Rod never asked either, about us."

"Don't play the fool, Cory. He didn't have to ask, he knew you, you're his brother."

You're nothing, Cory.

"But I didn't know him."

"Of course you did."

"I thought I did, I really did, but it was because—it sounds funny—I was vain. I thought I had insight. I thought I knew everybody—intuition, *you* know—because even as a kid everybody said, 'Cory knows.' It was Miss Sisson in PoliSci who said, 'I can tell by your bright look you see everything.' That's a laugh, isn't it?"

"You knew him better than I did, and who ever got closer to him physically than I did!"

Who?

"Besides—" She broke her fetal position, stretched her legs, stretched her arms and rolled over on her back, and stared at the ceiling. "To be honest, there wasn't so much to know in Rod. I can't lie about that. You've never believed me, have you?"

"You don't lie, I know that."

She knew only what Rod had given her. She couldn't know what Rod could not give, what Rod had concealed all the years from him too.

Savannah would never lie. That, he did know, had known, instantly. He knew the moment she spoke the first word to him. That came at one of his usual eleven o'clock arrivals at the Union, where always if she could get it she sat at the same Rathskeller table and where if he could get it he'd take one directly opposite under the same arch. You could hear a whisper from the other side, all the conversation, if you sat silent and ignored the other sounds; so already, though she had no idea he knew her sounds from the now-and-then talks to other students who sat with her, he knew her voice. He carried her voice inside him, startled that when alone he heard it sometimes, a voice somewhat deep, heavy for a woman, with a teasing huskiness in it, deeper when she gave that throaty, choked laughter. He sat, opened his Physical Geography text, but he was watching her. She looked up, caught his stare, and without setting her pencil down, rose, made her way through the labyrinth of round and square oak tables, light on her ballerina slippers, her fleshy hips accentuated as she dodged the table corners, and came straight to him. She swayed, he wasn't sure if nervously.

She said, "You've been watching me—a long time."

Her voice did not betray nerves. She smiled—those gaps between the teeth—and gave her head a shake as if sweeping long hair from her shoulders—a habit she had, and maybe *that* was nerves.

"I suppose you think I'm interesting. I look interesting, but I'm not. I look odd, I guess—I do, don't I? Oh, you don't have to answer.

I see myself. You can't lie about what you see, can you? Well, I guess some people can. It makes things a lot easier. But *I* can't. Anyway, I wouldn't fool you. I'm just a small-town girl from Black River Falls and all I ever wanted was a little cottage and a husband and lots of kids, so you'll wonder what I'm doing here at the university. It's my mother's fault, she named me. Oh— I'm Savannah, Savannah Goshen, and *that's* awful too, isn't it? She named me Savannah because she was religious and romantic, incurably romantic, and must have had all sorts of illusions about life in the South and the Beauregards and Ravenals of the Civil War world and the romance of Savannah and all that stuff; but I'm here because—oh, she was awful good, poor but awful good, and I wouldn't not have come for anything because of her, she's dead you see—the last thing she said was, 'Make something of yourself, Savannah.' She scrimped to take out insurances so I could be here. I didn't know that till she was dead. Coming here was the only way I know of to keep my word to her and try to make something of myself, I don't know what. It'll just have to happen if it's going to, the way things do, won't it? She did say get a husband who's educated, and where else can you find an educated man—well, one getting a degree anyway—but at the university? So here I am. You don't *look* interesting, but what *is* interesting about you, if you want to know, is you're so quiet, you're never with anybody, you never talk to anybody. *I* talk a lot, don't I?"

Nerves. Nervous talk.

He had to laugh. "I wouldn't say you were silence personified."

"You'd be a liar if you did, and I wouldn't like that. You don't look like a liar."

"What does a liar look like?"

"Now you've put me down. I should know better. Even Shakespeare taught me that: *There's no art to find the mind's construction in the face.* Yes, I talk a lot. Most women do. Men complain about that but it's their salvation; they'd really go crazy without it."

"Then you'll never drive anybody crazy."

This time she laughed, guttural.

"I like your voice. You should talk more. You want a beer with me?"

"I was hoping you'd ask me."

"You!"

Now, spread on the bare mattress, she held the years at Wisconsin in her, and Rod, and more of himself than she knew, maybe more than he himself knew. And he carried her, too much of her. He was afraid of her. If he could dare, he'd say, *I'm afraid of you, Savannah.*

Why are you afraid of me, Cory? *Because Rod.* But he couldn't say it. Why speculate? Rod was inside them, yes, but Rod was the wall between. Did she know the obstacle Rod was? When he saw her, he saw Rod. When he touched her, he touched Rod. You touched love and it was death. You touched death and it was love. How did you free yourself forever? Fool! He knew he couldn't. But how *far* free himself? And when? How long? How long . . .?

How did you make something of nothing?

"Why *do* you think there was so much to Rod? Oh, I know he was your brother, you loved him, but we can't distort our memories of what people were. We know what was there. Somehow what's in you *has* to come out in action sometime, doesn't it? Or you wouldn't be you otherwise, would you?"

"Maybe some things die with us."

"Then I think they never really existed. You need to live them or they're nothing."

"*Savannah—*"

"Now what'd I say wrong?"

"Nothing."

"I mean *doing's* the important thing. Life's *doing.* I can't help it if I'm so sensuous and practical, but I can't live without concrete things. You can't either, Cory. It's just that you see so much in concrete things that sometimes what you see takes over and you forget the solid thing it came from. You could live inside Alice's mirror, but nothing would come of it, you'd be in the land of magic or fantasy or death. You've got so much imagination you could live in it and that could kill you—it *could,* Cory—oh, I don't mean dead dead, I mean you could walk around dead, the worst kind of death. But you won't let things out, will you? You think I don't know? You think I've been with you years now and don't know my Cory?"

My Cory.

Don't, Savannah.

She rose on one arm. She raised a leg.

He sank down on his knees by the suitcases. He stared at her leg—there was a pulsing under her thigh, a regular regular maddening pulsing he could not move his eyes from.

"What, Cory? Have I got something . . ." She brushed her thigh.

He shook his head.

"Well, what I need to *do* is close these suitcases or I never will get to Long Island."

How the Island lured! If he closed his eyes, thicks of pines would loom, then thin out, the sea spread, and sand; there would be the white wings, the gulls' cries, the dank sea smell, strong, heavy, and the sound, sometimes light, sometimes heavy, persistent, of waves endless, endless. The apartment was abruptly too enclosed. He wanted to escape—to air, space, where there was no time; wanted to escape Savannah, Rod, and thought. But he knew: I'm going right *to* them.

And more.

Family. All of it. Generations. In the houses, on the land, in Stirling cemetery, in the very air.

And sea—that inescapable devourer, sea.

And my mother.

And my stepfather—him, German.

And Gramp.

And memory.

I have to go back or there's no way out ahead.

Both suitcases, spread side by side, were jammed.

"Your books?"

"I had them crated and stored for the time when." Until he could leave the Island, satisfied.

He pressed the clothes down—uselessly.

"Oh, come on, Cory. You've chucked these things in haphazardly. Where's all your famous Moorehead discipline?"

Gone. Nearly. To survive Rod, all he could shore against despair were the remnants of his discipline.

She slid off the bed, down on her knees, facing him. One by one she removed the stuffed-in clothes, folded them, replaced them.

She sank back on her haunches, facing him across the suitcase—"You could put *me* in it"—and gave her choked laugh—"all this blubber." Then she was crying, staring into the suitcase and sobbing, her head moving from side to side—no-no, no-no—like a mourner's.

"Oh, Cory. What are we going to do, Cory?"

He felt a great tugging. The floor would heave and buckle and like sand be sucked back by the waves.

Do.

"What did we ever do?"

But there had been Rod. She would not be asking if there hadn't been Rod, if Rod were here now, if she weren't grieving for Rod, if she did not want Rod, if when *he* left for Long Island it did not mean that Rod at last really left and she would have to admit that there was *no* visible connection with Rod, that Rod was gone because Cory was gone and Rod could not come back because Cory would not come back.

You! You think I don't know all that, Savannah Goshen?

Or you, Rodney Moorehead?

He felt such a sudden seething, such a sick churning, that for an instant Savannah, rocking from side to side now, her head going *no-no, no-no,* blurred in a wave that rippled the room, lifted and carried everything, then broke and the room toppled and everything fell into sudden sharp clarity.

"Nothing. That's our trouble—we let things ride, we just went on after Rod as if nothing had happened."

"We couldn't change that."

"We went on as if he were still alive, Cory."

"He *was* still alive, Savannah. Is. There are ways. It takes time. It's not for nothing people invented stories of spirits walking the earth till they can rest and you can live. You know that."

"Live, yes. Why didn't we? Why'd we keep putting it off—as if Rod wouldn't let us?"

Because he wouldn't. He was always there. Is.

"You wanted me to *be* Rod, Savannah. Is that it? Right away you wanted me to take his place. *Did* you? You wanted me to leap into bed with you because my brother was gone for good?"

"Oh, stop it, Cory—stop! You *know* it was you I always wanted. From the first day, *not* the day I went over and talked to you, no, but from the first time I *saw* you. I was turned on, if you want to know."

"Because I wasn't interesting?"

"Well, you remember that at least. You won't forget that."

"I won't forget anything, Savannah."

"Then *why*— Oh, Cory."

"Anything, Savannah. I told you. You don't forget in an instant. It's not just Rod. I'm Cory. I have to find my own way. I can't abruptly pick up where my brother left off."

"*I* know feelings don't vanish overnight. Wasn't Rod part of my life too? Cory, it's six months now since Rod . . . So that's *not* long, but you have to begin, you have to make a motion, you can't be mute, you can't be separate, you can't live this way forever. You've got to do something."

"I am doing something. I'm going back to the Island."

"Oh, come on, Cory, right back to—"

"No, away from—"

"Me?"

"You know better than that."

He was going back to her, his mother, and him, Gramp, and something in them which he had to face, wanted to face, wanted to make their presence explain and make him articulate to himself what he was responsible for, how much a man was responsible for.

He was trapped between this room and the Island.

Rod had been perverse. He had brought her here to their room. He had taken her on this bed. He had left the evidence. Had Rod wanted to make sure he would know?

He could not, could never, rid himself of the glitter, the smears of their *come,* semen. *He* had changed the sheets. All night he had slept on the other side of the bed. At the thought of rolling over onto *their* side his flesh burned.

On his knees he closed one suitcase and locked it, then kneeled on the other.

"Here, let me—" Savannah pressed as he snapped the locks in place. She remained, motionless, staring across the suitcase at him, her hair disheveled, a gleam of perspiration at the hairline. The white lapped low over her shoulders (Had she worn white deliberately? The meanness of the thought shamed him), her full breasts still, in her eyes his own image, two of him, as if she could not, would not, get enough of him. Her eyes were wet. She sucked at her upper lip.

"What will you do in June after graduation, Savannah?"

"Go back to Black River Falls. What else?"

"But you hate the place."

"And love it too. Hate it because there's no man there for me, love it because if there were it's exactly what I *would* want—the man, the small house, the kids, town. You've heard that enough. It would help if he could read Shakespeare like you. It would make all the difference."

"Those were good nights."

"No, great nights—the greatest. Sometimes I thought I couldn't live without them."

"You can live without anything." He saw his grandfather's face, the pinkish eyes squinting, saw the crippled hands with the fingers drawn up like crouched spiders.

"If you have to."

"Yes."

His mother had made all the difference. She had never let his grandfather go. She had been loyal. *Pa.* She had put him first, always, even before her men. She did now.

"I have to. There's no place else to go. It's the only place I know. At least there's that. It's important. You have to know a place. You taught me that. A place can make you. You can love it like a person; you can be tied to it like a person, like you and your Long Island, your

Greenport, your sand and wild roses and pines and ocean and . . ."

"If you're trying to make me feel sorry for you—"

"Oh, shit, Cory!"

"Then why don't you go?"

"You bastard!—"

"Well, what do you expect me to do, Savannah, weep and wail, take you in my arms and have a last minute reconciliation? For what, *what*? for Rod? for the time lost? for our long lost love? for the one thing we never had? for the missing link? for sentiment and Black River Falls and Greenport and the future and—"

It was all pressing up into his chest, his breath. His head throbbed with it, his eyes. His blood heaved, heaved.

"Don't, Cory. Don't cry, please—"

"You!"

He thrust the suitcase aside. He gripped her arm. He pulled her close. He drove his head into her neck. His hands pressed at her legs, quick to her thighs, rubbing. He mouthed, sucked at her neck.

"Is this what you want, Savannah? *Is* it?"

She groaned. He could feel the sound run through her, in his mouth against her throat. She cried out, "Yes. And it's what you want, what you've always wanted too, *it is*." But she thrust him. He latched his arms more firmly under her legs. "No, Cory—because you're not *Cory* yet. Don't you know you're not Cory yet?" She clutched his head, freed her neck, and pressed him aside. "Not this way. You *know* you're not Cory." When he caught at her neck to draw her close again, she slapped him and rolled free, and lay there an instant, the chokes in her throat clear now. *Rod*. "You'd never forgive yourself. You wouldn't. You'd end up hating yourself and hating me for letting you this way, blaming me because I could have stopped it but didn't."

Rod.

He tried to hold back the choking in his own throat.

"Maybe you don't even know you want that. It would make everything so easy. It would be the end, all very convenient. Then someday you'd wish it had never happened. There'd always be the blight—on both of us—that would make anything else, ever, impossible. And you don't want that. Do you? *Do* you, Cory? Tell me that. At least, give me that satisfaction."

Passion. What he knew but did not understand. What he wanted to understand. What had driven them all. My family. He knew, behind his mother's serene look, that turbulence. In his grandfather's stare was a blinding vision so encompassing that time and space grew meaningless. And Rod: he had restrained it till he could no longer control it, and passion overwhelmed *him*.

"No. I don't want that."

He did not look at her. He stood—and went to the window.

My last view.

Up and down Langdon the lights made tiny white fires. Beyond, Picnic Point, the pines, the ridges, Mendota had all gone into night's death.

He took the suitcases down the three flights to the front door and went back up.

She was still sitting on the floor. Against the old, soiled carpet, the white looked too clean. He stared down into the part in her hair, at the straggles along the back of her neck. The dress hung loose over one very white fleshy shoulder.

"Savannah, you'd better go."

"I'll go after a while."

"I've got to lock up."

"I'll give Mrs. Stockton the keys. Just leave them on the bed."

He tossed them onto the mattress.

He reached down and barely grazed the ends of her hair.

At the doorway he said, "I'm going."

She did not move.

His gaze made a quick flight over the room, the living room beyond, the bath—

These years. My life.

By the bed, Savannah sat sunk in a heap of wrinkled white that caught all the light and made the room look sordid.

He closed his eyes an instant.

Then he went down.

When he had set the suitcases into the trunk, he sat taking in the view in the dark, the long street, the fraternity and sorority houses near empty now between semesters, through the hollow areas of streetlight the few stragglers ambling. In the mirror the Union behind illuminated the whole area as usual, and the buildings on the hill were lit up, and the lights along the walk up made a trim design up toward the carillon. He would like to see Professor Sánchez-Barbudo once more, walk up the hill to Henry Mann's office, sit there while the bells were resounding; he would like to ride the lake once more, sail, sail into the far dark reaches between the points; he would like to sit with Savannah in the Union and wander to the Campus Grill or sit and watch her twirl pasta at the Spaghetti House once more, once more . . .

But the thousand or more miles ahead beckoned, the road, the eventual monotony of the turnpikes—and at the end his Island, that whale-shaped heap of sand, the end of the world thrust into the ocean, and Gramp and Ma. The silent utterance filled him with such desire, such dread, to see them, with such ambiguity, that he heard Savannah's choke in his own mouth, and Langdon Street wavered. He closed his eyes. Go, damn you, Cory. His mother's voice was urging him back: "Oh, then you *are* coming home." She almost never called, *he* did the calling, but the call had come. She had called simply to congratulate him. They would celebrate his graduation when he got home. He *was* coming? Actually he had not intended to make the trip; he had intended to linger and reconsider his acceptance of the postgrad scholarship to Brown or the editing job offer because . . . sometime . . . he must break with the Island, with home, with, yes, Rod. Was there a way? There must be, there must be a way he could *will*, and if there was, he would will it. And then the moment he had thought *will it*, the phone rang as if something out there was intentionally defying him, though he could not concede to such thought. At the sound of her voice, he waited. He was too trained not to wait, for all the past was in her calls. The calls meant Gram had died, uncle Ben and Reggie Webb had drowned, meant now a reminder of everything in his life, in theirs, that had happened to them on the Island or elsewhere. He listened: how proud of him she was, *they*—German and she—were. What a shame he had not finished his work in normal sequence to graduate with his friends in June. What would Wisconsin do, mail the degree to him? He listened with that intuition of the infallible, waiting. It was then he'd told her, "Ma, wait. Yes, I think I'll come. It may be the last time for a while. What do you think?" He knew, from the briefest interval, she must have understood what the water, the sight of the Gut, might mean to him without Rod. She said, "Oh, Cory, I'd so hoped—" And from the break, he knew. "Then I'll be there soon." "Oh, I'll be so glad. And German will be glad too."

He would have to reckon with Rod.

And that might reckon him with Savannah.

Mine.

Rod.

Savannah.

He had said nothing of this to Savannah. She would find one more reason to attack his weaknesses, though he knew her attack was love, was the desire for his fulfillment, his salvation, whatever she could do for that fulfillment and salvation because she loved him; so it would be her fulfillment and salvation even if she could not have him, if she never had him. That was Savannah, Savannah Goshen. She did not know her own gold. Unintentionally, she shamed him.

Savannah. For an instant he thought, I should go back up. But he could do nothing, they could do nothing, until he could see himself with some clarity. Now, after Rod, he still felt paralyzed. He had to face himself. And if he waited, Vanna would not come down—she was surely waiting for the sound of his car. *That old Buick, I'd know that sound anywhere.* She would not leave till he had gone.

He would like to see her come down the stairs, that sad look light up abruptly, hear her grunted laughter, see the rise and spread of white as she caught sight of him and began to run.

That white.

Go, damn it, Cory.

So he did, but kept on, straight—he couldn't help it—drove up the rise to the square, where the lights from the capitol dome cast a larger dome of luminous roseate haze, beautiful and ephemeral, over the heart of the city.

He drove round and round the square. *Here*, despite Hitler and the war, despite illusions and losses; meant all the grandeur of those words taught from childhood, attached to which were complexities not yet realized; *here*, the abstract words *beauty, honor, friendship, knowledge, responsibility, love, justice* in all their old idealism took shape and meaning though radically revised by his experience in the Army Air Force. Forever they would be embodied in this place. No matter what he did, however far his experience removed him from them, whatever part of him atrophied, the roots gripped down too deep into his blood roots to die. Though he clung to the sentiment of the moment, he knew too he was bolstering himself against home—them, and Rod.

He could put them off no longer.

Move it out, Cory.

He broke the circle and headed out.

Why was he here—in Wisconsin, in his Buick, on the road back?

In high school, he had intended to be a cost accountant. He was going to commute to Providence to study. He would pass the CPA exam and set up an office in his hometown and spend the rest of his life there in Bristol, happy, happy, though he could not then know his mother would one day make that impossible. Then he did not know passion, his mother's, his own, his grandfather's, Rod's, how indiscriminately passion could create and destroy.

Why was he here?

Because of Hirohito. The news over the radio had stunned. He'd stared at the photos in the *Providence Evening Bulletin* of the ships billowing smoke in Pearl Harbor, at the flames which inflamed the nation, and him. Men were enlisting in Providence. His stepfather had gone, but came home forlorn: flat feet and age kept him out. Thirty-five, too old! He had never seen Pete so anguished, red-eyed, ashamed too. He himself had not thought *war, go, enlist*; but he heard Roosevelt, the magic voice, the measured words, the words, words. And one morning on the way to work to his desk in the accounting department at the zipper factory, his first job (with the money he'd earn and the help from Pete he'd intended to go to business college in Providence), he got on the bus, lunch in hand; but he did not get off after the four miles to Warren; it was only at the usual stop that he knew he would not get off. The driver even held the bus up for a bit, eyeing him in the rear-view mirror, till he shook *No.* With no conscious forethought, it had erupted: I'm going to enlist. So it was Hirohito, but not directly. And it was Roosevelt. You, FDR. Father of my country. My father.

Our father, Rod said.

Ours, yes.

If he had thought, he would have been startled at Rod's including himself because Rod had never mentioned *father*, had never given him the least idea he missed the real father he had never known. Rod loved his stepfather. They both did. To them Daddy Pete *was* their real father, though for years Rod thought of Gram as his real mother because he was a baby when Ma sent him to live with Gram during the divorce. And Rod was an energetic kid when Ma went out to Long Island to bring him home for good, to live with her and him and Honor—Daddy Pete. They would never think of him as anything else.

When Cory came home from his physical examination in Providence, at supper he said, "I've enlisted in the Army Air Force."

"Whoopee!" Rod shouted.

His mother didn't say a word. She rose, stood there lost an instant, then went into the pantry and stood over the sink, staring out the window into the backyard. Her dress was trembling. The great pines beyond made her look tiny.

"What'll you be?" Rod said.

"I signed up for radio operator."

His mother went to the stove. "You want more ham?"

"No."

"When do you have to leave?"

"Monday morning."

"Monday morning! Why, that's not a week!"

Her eyes filled then.

"You're too young," she said, almost belligerently. "They wouldn't take you—"

"You'll have to sign for me."

"We'll talk about it when Pete gets home."

"You're my guardian, not Pete."

But he sat up, waited until Pete got home from the restaurant, till almost three in the morning, to tell him.

Pete stared at him, smiling, his eyes sentimental and wet, softened by a drink or two, and gripped his shoulders and pressed, pressed.

"The Army Air Force." Pete's voice tremored. He went into the bathroom.

So on that morning—November '42, the eleventh it was—on the bus to Providence again, he went to serve his father.

Who died on him during the war.

Roosevelt died.

All work stopped. The airfield died. It stood, skeletal, empty of personnel. He had never seen men cry. By the hundreds they cried openly. Our Commander in Chief. Because millions had elected him, three times chosen him—more, recognized him. The father of our country. He was.

Unum.

Of many. E pluribus.

Unum.

Then Churchill is my father and Hitler is my father and Stalin is my father and Haile Selassie is my father and Mussolini and Tito and Chiang-Kai-Shek and Petain and De Gaulle and Perón and Franco ("I believe in Franco, man almighty; creator of a great Spain and a well-organized Army; crowned with the most glorious laurels; liberator of a Spain which was suffering, and engraver of a Spain born in the shadow of the most rigorous social justice . . .") and Caesar and Octavius and Alexander and the gods immortalized on antique coins.

Because the E Pluribus world saw something undeniably Unum in each of them. Because the world fathered you too.

Then Harry Truman became his father.

But he had lived his whole youth with Roosevelt, as he had with Pete.

His fathers.

How many fathers did a man have?

What makes a father?

Surely the one father he did not know led somewhere directly. Blood led somewhere, flowed *from*, flowed *to*. It connected, but what?

He had not known he could feel so bereft. In England at the announcement of Roosevelt's death, he had taken a pass and walked the road to Hungerford, wandered over the heath like Thomas Hardy's Jude, thinking, *I'm back on your terrain, Jude,* for on passes he had traced Jude's footsteps from town to town, followed the choices and chance events of Jude's life, dreaming as Jude had dreamed of being a student at Oxford. It was only when he had stopped and sat on a milestone on the spot he was sure was described in Hardy's novel that he choked with sobs.

Roosevelt.

My country.

Which, after the war ended on V-E Day, had given him the GI bill.

For those three years of his life in the service, his father, Uncle Sam, had given him the way, freedom—Wisconsin, UW.

So he had no longer needed the help from Pete, who had done so much for him, or the eleven dollars a week he had been earning at the zipper factory before the war, though until the semester started he had gone back to the job, his veteran's right as the law allowed. They had been glad to have him back and proud to have an ex-serviceman, and at three times his old wages—thirty-three dollars! He had been shocked by what was to many still a pittance.

What shocked him the most on his return was Rod. The brother he'd left, almost three years younger than he, had just gone into high school, but the boy he returned to was taller than he, a three-letter athlete, the lead in the high school operetta, voted "the most popular" and "the most likely to succeed," the girls ga-ga over him, the boys always hunting Rod for a game, fishing, hunting, repairing their cars, weekend trips. The house was a whirlwind of activity.

Perhaps that was why nobody perceived what was happening to his mother. After, he would marvel at how he and Rod and Pete had missed it all. For his mother had blossomed, radiant—because of his safe return and discharge, he had thought. She *was* overjoyed and showed it. She'd stare at him, the man he'd become, though half in admiration, half in resentment when she said *the spit and image of your father*. She'd spend hours talking with him and Rod. He didn't know she was *hoarding* their faces, their words, moments. Otherwise, her activity left them with vertigo. "We'd have beaten the

Krauts twice as fast with your energy, Ma." But she didn't let up, and when he asked where the pongee curtains were, she smiled and said, "They always were your favorite, weren't they?"; and the fiberglass tulips in sand in a shiny green pot by the living room door, "You used to complain they gave you fine splinters every time you touched them. Besides, you always admired that Victorian cat playing with the glass ball I put in its place"; and the long painting of a mountain stream flowing between birches and boulders, "I thought the flowers in the maple frame went better with the Winthrop desk."

Perhaps he was detoured from his mother's zeal by Rod's shenanigans.

"Where are the mosquito boots I sent home from Brazil?" His squadron had flown the southern route to England. He'd lain for a couple of days on the black sands of Recife. In the city he'd bought his mother an alligator purse.

"Rod wore them. They're right here in his closet."

She showed them, disastrously done in.

"Where the hell's Rod? I told him these were war souvenirs, mementoes—mine. Rod? Rod!"

"Well, I didn't think you'd care. I'm your brother. Aren't they mine too?"

"No, they're not yours. There are limits."

"I didn't know that. What limits?"

"Oh, for heaven's sake, use your head, Rod."

The annoyances mounted when he found split at the seams the leather wallet he'd picked up when the squadron landed in Marrakech.

"The thing's just for show anyway, Cory."

"Show, my ass!"

But the one thing he treasured, sent home with the original coating of protective grease still untouched, was the machete. He found it in the cellar, the handle scored and its blade dented and battered.

"Jesus, what'd you do, try to chop down Bethlehem Steel?"

"Nothing but good old New England trees."

"Lined with what? I'll have your ass for this."

"Okay, so I'll get you a new one."

"You can't duplicate this."

"So you can't duplicate it. What's wrong with a different one?"

Their bickering blinded them to what was happening.

In September when Rod was ready to leave for the university, his mother made over him so, hugged, and said, "You'll come to me as often as you can? And you too, Cory, when you're at Wisconsin. It's such a change in our lives. Houses get so empty, don't they? I guess I got used to your being away in the war because Rod was here, but now that he's going it hits me hard, he's still my baby."

But Rod was not there to feel the emptiness of the house, an emptiness even she could not have known when she'd spoken of it. Only one emptiness was worse, to stare into spaces that would never hold your buddies again but still claimed them in your sight.

His mother did not die, though for an instant he had wished her dead—because he came home one night in December, went into the bathroom, came out into the living room, and abruptly something halted him—the emptiness. The house was full, but so empty.

She was gone.

The configuration was wrong in the bathroom, in all the rooms. Her things were gone. Now the changes assailled, as if hurled, one after the other—curtains, tulips, pictures, linens, and—he went into her room—yes, her cosmetics—and into her closet—yes, her clothes—and in the kitchen—dishes of all kinds from the corner cabinet, favorite pots and pans from the pantry. Then the incessant early lesser farewells, the nostalgia, the long hours of chat, the stares in which she fed so lovingly on Rod and him kaleidoscoped into meaning. . . .

Bit by bit, for months, she must have been packing, mailing, shipping possessions; must have had some plan; must have had some destination—

Did Pete know?

He could not bear to see Pete. He shut his bedroom door. When Pete came in as usual after his two a.m. closing, he heard him moving around inordinately—to bathroom, bedroom, kitchen, parlor.

Pete was wandering.

But how did Pete know?

He waited. He knew Pete would call him. And Pete did come to his door, stood there, listening no doubt, testing his breathing, went away—returned, waited—

Finally, Cory got up and sat on the edge of the bed.

"Cory?" Pete's usual soft voice was softer.

Cory opened the door. From his face, his stance, surely Pete could have told; but no, Pete was too distraught, his gaze wandered, his hands grappled at air.

"Your mother's gone."

He did not respond. Perhaps he himself was numbed by the loss. Perhaps he was too fascinated by the change in Pete, his floundering in a kind of silent mindless madness in which his hands, head, legs seemed to move with no coordination. Despite his own pain, his compassion for Pete, he found himself watching him as an alien body.

"How'd you know?" he asked.

"Know what?"

"Ma was gone."

"She called me at work. She said she was leaving me. I don't know where she was calling from." He gripped his head with both hands. He blinked. What was he seeing?

Then Pete awakened. "How did you know?"

"The house—it's different, things are gone."

"Gone?"

Pete gazed about, turned, went into the parlor, into his room.

"Gone?"

"Her things. Her Pond's cold cream, her perfumes, fingernail polish . . ."

"Gone."

"You know that. You've known it all day." He didn't say You could have called me. But Pete wasn't aware of what he was doing or saying. Yet *he* knew, and he hadn't called Pete.

Feeling Pete was suddenly the younger, he said, "I'm going to bed. Aren't you going to take your bath?" and without waiting for an answer, went to his room and, feeling he could not neglect Pete, left his door open.

There was a long silence before he heard Pete go to his room, sit on the edge of the bed long too—so long he almost got up to see if Pete was all right—and finally remove his clothes, put on his robe, cross the living room to the

bath.

After his bath, Pete went into his room and got into bed.

From his own room Cory could hear all that because for the first time Pete and his mother's bedroom door was open and the light was still on. Then Pete called him. He rose and went to Pete's door. They stared at each other. Pete's eyes filled with tears; he was crying silently. He threw back the covers and sat on the edge of the bed. He himself was standing by the bureau edge, his hand on the knob of the small right drawer where she had kept her scented handkerchiefs. When he glanced down where only her black and silver and orangy box of Coty's face powder still stood on the bureau, he felt Pete's hand touch his left arm. Pete stood and drew him close. He said, "I don't know what to do." His head grazed his neck and chest. He could feel then the quiet tremors of Pete's body as he sobbed, a man shorter than he was, now weaker than he was, he the son who had not cried once, indignant that she would dare leave them, proud against her action. He saw Pete wanted to be comforted. Pete in need. "I can't stand it, I can't sleep alone," Pete said, sobbing, sitting on the edge of the bed but not letting go of his left hand. "Please get in with me, please, I can't be alone." He himself felt a danger, the threat of falling into a ravine down which were jagged dangers which would tear, batter, destroy forever. He was afraid. He drew his hand out of Pete's. "No," he said. "You get in. You'll go to sleep eventually. Try," wanting but not daring to touch the poor man's head, his hair, but stepping back, beginning to leave. "No," he said to Pete's insistent "Please, please," withdrawing as Pete sobbed, perhaps even intentionally sobbed more emphatically to draw him into the bed, not to be alone, to clutch someone warm to allay the emptiness and isolation. "No," he said. "You"ll be all right, we both will, but it will take time," watching Pete shrink in his loneliness, his shoulders smaller in their desolation, feeling his own growing strength and a growing sense of detachment in viewing the weakness of a man who was now to him a boy whose growing up he himself was in charge of, assuring himself that time would enlighten Pete if not console him for her loss.

Things had never interested Pete. He had rarely noticed the house, furniture. But he loved *doing*. He never tired of the one thing they all did together, croquet Sunday after Sunday in warm weather. He loved sports, betting on boxing, the horses, especially the dogs. He frequently took her to matches or the races on his days off. "Buy what you want," he always told her. "Pete should have been a priest, we thought he would be," Pete's brother had said on his first visit to them. "Ma sure was disappointed." His mother was never sure of the approval or disapproval in that undertone—Guillaume liked her, but he loved Pete. Pete's face did suggest the saintly—and the soft honey-colored hair which when long fell in luminous waves over either side of his face, the soft gaze almost of adoration of something invisible, even the soft almost whisper of his voice. In childhood photos he was as radiant as the Madonna. Already Cory had sensed, from a high school Catholic friend who wanted to be a priest and later from some of his service buddies who were always trying to save his hide, what he would confirm in himself when he read the saints, that some men and women chose such isolated concentration to save themselves from their own sensuality, or perhaps to destroy themselves. He himself was capable of such isolated concentration.

Before he could call Rod, Rod called from Kingston.

"I haven't heard from anybody, not a call or a letter. *I've* written, and I'm the busy one. They sure keep you studying here every minute, and you know I'm no bookworm."

"Well, we've been busy, Gramp and Pete and I."

"And Ma, she broke a wrist?"

"Ma . . ."

He didn't want to tell him yet, didn't want to blight his studies.

"Yeah, Ma."

"Ma's taken a trip."

"A trip? She didn't mention any trip."

"It was sudden."

"Sudden? What's happening? Is it Gram? Something out there?"

"Out there, yes."

"What's *wrong* with you, Cory? Can't you talk straight today?"

"Ma's gone, Rod."

"Gone!"

"She's left Pete for good."

"Jesus!" There was a long hiatus.

"You still there, Rod?"

"Where the hell *would* I be?"

"Okay, Rod."

"I'm sorry, Cory. But *why*? Do you know why? What happened? What'd Pete say? How is he?"

"Whoa, Rod. I don't know a thing. Maybe Pete does—he hasn't said—but I don't think so. I think it's all Ma. I mean I think she has reasons she's not telling, whatever reasons between her and Pete. You know Ma never talks, and she's—it's a strange way to describe her after she's exposed herself to the whole town—always discreet."

"Discreet! Jesus, think what everybody's saying. We won't be able to show our faces. How do you and Pete stand it? Didn't she think? Couldn't she have used her head? I'm glad I wasn't there, though I should be with you and Pete. Poor Pete! Can you imagine how he must feel?"

"I don't know that anybody can."

"Listen, Cory— *You* won't do anything?"

"Me!"

"I mean you won't go anywhere till I see you? It's still on for Christmas? You'll be there. You won't be gone yet, will you? I'll be home soon. You can hold it together till then, I mean."

"I'm not going to Wisconsin till January, to enter for the spring semester. I'm already admitted."

"Then we'll have Christmas together."

"I'll be here, and Gramp. You all right, Rod?"

"I've still got you, Cory."

"Sure, Rod."

Rod came home for Christmas. Pete embraced him, stared at him, sentimental, tears almost spilling, clamping his lips taut, shaking his head—perhaps seeing Ma in him, perhaps even imagining Rod's return heralded hers.

Rod was out most of the time, visiting old high school friends, but returned always somewhat humbled, dogged by the looks, the fishings, of his friends' parents, but more by casual acquaintances, always bolder: "Haven't seen your mother in a while." "Miss your mother at bridge." "Your mother gone off on a vacation?" "Is your mother sick?"

"They're bringing the tree this afternoon," Gramp said.

"What tree?"

"The Christmas tree. I picked it out and chopped it down myself. The Smiths gave it to us. You can't have Christmas without a tree." He had raised peacocks, had worked for the Smiths on Ferrycliff Farm for years. Through the Depression and during the hurricane of '38 the Smiths had left great aluminum kegs of milk at their door three mornings a week.

As the days passed, Gramp went to and fro with his cart, an orange crate he had rigged, nailed to a long plank with small wheels on one end, a crossbar handle on the other. He could not carry much in those hands with their drawn tendons. He always came home with it loaded. He went from cellar to kitchen, tending the furnace, preparing for the holiday. For two days before Christmas he indulged all his lifelong energies and talents as a cook. They could hear the fork beating eggs, tins being greased, strange poundings, little grunts of annoyance, flubbings, "Oh, shit!" now and then, his "There you go!" of satisfaction, sizzlings in the black skillets he'd seasoned for her. The house filled with aromas. Green tomato pie appeared the afternoon before, and mincemeat and pumpkin and apple. "You feeding an army?" "Huh!" he said. "You never can tell who'll drop by." And on the holy day morning, they heard him up and moving around in the dark. They were forbidden the kitchen, he complaining like a woman, "Don't want anybody under my feet." He'd insisted on church: Cory and Rod must go to the special service as always or what was the day about? Or did *he* have to give the sermon? At that they scooted and dressed for church, hearing him mutter, "I thought that would do it!" And when he called the three of them—worn with wait, hungry, each reading different parts of the paper—and they entered the kitchen, the sight stopped them. "Wow!" Rod said. "Oh, godfrey!" Cory said. "Dad!" Pete said. For the table, extended, was spread magnificently, the fine white napkins, the lace, the silver, the "Sunday" dishes she'd left, all impeccably set as if he still worked as cook on Commodore Vanderbilt's yacht; an enormous stuffed turkey golden brown; serving dishes brimming with dressing and vegetables; the gravy boat steaming; the cranberry sauce a crimson glow; the sun-struck crystal water glasses quivering reflections that danced in myriad colors over the walls.

"Gentlemen, be seated." Gramp chortled. To match the elegance of the occasion, all he lacked was the dress uniform he'd wear whenever he left the ship. They'd never seen him dressed that way except in the great oval full-length photograph in the living room. The young Gramp was standing on the ship, handsome in full dress, one perfect hand holding a rigging rope, the other resting on the deck rail, hands they all marveled at because they couldn't imagine him without those hands burned in the fire at sea.

It was strange to see Gramp at the head of the table. Usually he ate behind them, at a little collapsible table he'd built under the north window, and most of the time after they'd already eaten, because a constriction in his throat made it well nigh impossible for him to keep his food down so he'd regurgitate at intervals into a bucket he kept beside him and emptied after each meal. On holidays he took his place with them for grace and then excused himself. Now, seated on the four sides of the table, the table so complete, they seemed to be waiting. There was a long silent moment as if, with the splendor of the meal, Gramp had set the scene up for a miracle: in a minute *she* would appear. *Why, Pa . . .*

Rod broke the spell. "You know what *I* want."

Gramp swelled as Rod heaped up dressing.

"This turkey's sure moist and tender, not dry like most, Pa," Pete said. But he hardly picked at his plate.

"You can say that again," Rod said.

"How'd you make such good cranberry sauce, Gramp?"

"All right, Cory!" Rod said.

Gramp squinted. "Did Cory say something, Rod? It's awful to be stone deef." He broke into a cackle—nothing, but nothing, was going to spoil this day. He was not the cook now. "You know, it was turkey that got my brother Gill into the jam of his life—" This time he was the captain himself, the host, the perfect amphytrion, oh, yes— "Gill took the ferry from Orient to Connecticut for a weekend on the town. He was an old man then." Gramp was off on a blue streak. "He met this pretty, sedate woman he told he had a cottage on the beach. She was propertied, sons in college, set up pretty well. Gill had himself a real catch. He was going to get in good and marry her—he did in no time—and cash in on her property. She was over every weekend, but couldn't leave her children, had to be in New London, wanted his place for the beach. He'd lied. She found out he was just the caretaker. That didn't bother her, but Gill got tired of going back to the mainland to see her, wanted her to sell and live with him or he'd divorce her because she wouldn't live with him seven days a week. He was a fool. The woman was only an hour and fifteen minutes away by ferry. But she wouldn't give in. Gill kept insisting, finally called her number, till he drove *her* away, lost the best thing he'd ever had, did himself in. She really loved him. He never forgave himself after."

"Where's the turkey come in?"

"Tough turkey!" Gramp struck the table with his bone palm and roared at his own joke, which set them all to laughing.

Recovering, Gramp said, "Hold your horses, Rod, don't stuff yourself so. Be sure you leave room for the special dessert."

"Special! With all those pies?"

"A cook won't do unless he has his—whatdoyoucallit?—chef-d'oeuvre. You, Cory, help me clear the table."

When the plates were gone, the dessert dishes on, Gramp said, "Now you just sit still, all of you." He was all smile.

A brief silence in the pantry, the strike of a match, a small whoof, then Gramp came in with a tray of blue fire—

"Plum pudding! God, look at it," Cory said.

Gramp set it ablaze in the center of the table. Very quickly the rum burned away, leaving a rich dark coating, filling the air with the smell of burnt sugar. "Now there's four desserts, plenty of choice, and here's the plum pudding sauce."

"First decent meal I've had since before Kingston," Rod said.

"You needn't fish, Rod. Once a year's enough. There'll be leftovers aplenty."

"I'll kiss the meals good-bye after a farewell meal like this," Cory said.

Pete scowled at his sliver of pumpkin pie. "Farewell?"

"Wisconsin. I'm leaving next week when Rod goes back to Kingston."

"Next week?"

"You knew that."

Pete nodded. "But you'll be back?"

Back? He hadn't thought that far ahead. With her gone, what would he come back to? But he couldn't say that.

Rod saved him. "Where else would he go?"

Or Rod?

Gramp headed for the pantry.

Cory intercepted. "Oh no you don't, Gramp! I'll do those dishes. You've done your week's work."

"Well—"

"Now that's what I call resistance, Gramp," Rod said.

Pete's hand rested on Gramp's shoulder. "Thanks, Dad." He seldom touched anyone, but he was sentimental. He appreciated them all, proud of Rod's athletic achievements and Cory's high marks (Rod had said, "Pete appreciates your brains and my body, Cory. At least we give him something for what he's done for us.") and grateful to Gramp for untiringly going at the chores.

"I'll go check the furnace," Gramp said.

"And me to the Common to see what's going on," Rod said. "Oh-oh, it's snowing."

Fine white flakes were falling straight down.

Gramp went down to his dark world. He would sit hours sometimes, staring into the furnace, musing, maybe attracted to that flame behind the isinglass, the moth to the mystery of its own destruction, that fire that had determined so much of his life.

In the other half of the cellar, his and Rod's territory, along the length of one wall was the long counter Gramp had built for Rod to assemble his models, at first balsa planes, and then the gasoline-run ones, twenty-two of them, which all through Cory's senior high year Rod would set going all at once till he would go down, wanting to pound him into the cement floor. But Rod would laugh with his perfect white smile in that warm, winning way that lured all ages—old Mrs. Merriman asking for Rod, only Rod, to do some odd jobs; or old Mrs. Rhett, Could Rod take care of the five dogs while she's off to New York for a few days, he's got just the right hand with them. The instant Rod casually walked into a room, his relaxedness, an almost rubber flexibility to his spontaneous body, a certain natural blasé indifference, drew people. Only when his voice was breaking, abruptly dropping into harsh scrapes, did he blush and laugh self-consciously. Rod was a magnet. Once anybody got his eye, his interest, he fixed his attention with such total empathy that nothing else existed—it was the supreme compliment—yet two seconds later his natural indifference freed them, they were not sure he'd even heard. That contradiction spellbound. *Your brother*— But they never finished.

"Cory," Pete said. "I'm going to Fall River. Ma and Pa'll be expecting me. And Guillaume and Peggy. I've just got time to make the connection in Warren. I'll spend the night. They'll be disappointed if I don't."

"You ought to."

Pete hesitated.

We got through the day, Pete. Don't.

Pete went into the hall closet for his overcoat and a moment later the front door resounded.

Cory did not want this—did not want Pete turning to him, did not want Pete to make him *her*, did not want them all *depending*. He was himself, he was Cory, he was not his mother.

He stood at the sink, gazing out the pantry window at the long yard, her dead and dormant plants, the vacant clothesline with its pronged pole, the giant spires of old firs against the sky, the wood fence, all the neighbors' yards already veiled by a fine white layer. Her view. All the years she'd stood here, morning, noon, night, staring out on this. Waiting. Waiting? *Had* she known she had been waiting all the years for Reggie Webb? Then what had his father and Pete been to her? She had known Reggie Webb since girlhood. Did the true go on living in the blood till some miraculous encounter made it leap time and insist on its life? So what happened between, in one sense, did not exist. In one life his father and Pete and he and Rod did not exist. They were now the other life, the life that might not have been at all *if*—if in the diphtheria epidemic that swept over the Island his grandfather, frantic, had not sent Stella with her sister Gladys to Bristol, where she'd met Reggie Webb; if Reggie Webb had not enlisted in the Army to escape his tyrant of a father and his uppity sisters; if then she hadn't met his, Cory's, father.

The house was dirty. He and Pete and Gramp tried to keep it going, but Gramp's albino eyes couldn't see much though he tended the furnace faithfully as always when, between renting a cheap tenement or house, he had lived with them. Pete worked long hours, so it fell to Gramp. Worse, the house had become for each of them a last resort, their rooms caves of silent lament. Besides, he felt guilty because, though he had lived with Pete all the years, now that she was gone, why should Pete support them all? The question haunted. Each time he saw Pete, he thought, With her gone, what life has Pete? What comfort are we to him? We're constant reminders of her.

"How's he going to live?" Rod said.

"You don't die of it, that's the trouble."

"Don't talk like that, Cory. There are other things."

"Not for Pete."

"How do you know that? You've heard them argue when he comes in too late. She may have had more reasons than we know."

"Well, she sure kept them to herself."

"Wouldn't you? And why would she tell us? Ma'd never talk against Pete."

"And Pete hasn't said a word about her, not one."

"He wouldn't. He hurts too much. At heart he's a gentleman, and he loves us. But you don't talk about her either. Why don't you?"

"Why would I, after what she's done?"

"Because she's your mother, Cory."

"She sure acted like one!"

"She loves you, Cory."

"It's not me she loves."

"You love her, Cory."

"Love!"

"You do, Cory."

"Shut up."

"You do."

"Shut up, Rod! Wasn't it *you* who talked about shame?"

Until Rod left for Kingston, he kept at him. Rod wanted to know: "Will you see Ma?"

"Now why would I see her? Uncle Ben's called. I won't talk to him. I won't talk to her."

"You're mean, Cory."

"Are *you* going to the Island?"

"When the time comes maybe."

"What's the maybe for if you're so hipped on my going?"

"You know I'll go, Cory. Why wouldn't I?"

"Because it would hurt Pete."

"Pete knows. He's got a mother. Don't be a fool, Cory. Why *are* you? You're supposed to be the levelheaded one, aren't you? *She* always said so."

My man in the family. From the time she had regained custody of him after the divorce, she had rattled on—"Don't you think so, Cory? Shouldn't I?"—till, yes, it was not Pete but Cory who was always consulted, Cory who really made the decisions, Cory who could be depended on . . .

"She wasn't wrong."

"Then for Chris' sake, show it."

"It'll be a cold day in hell before I go out to the Island to her." If he went, he'd betray Pete. If he stayed, he'd betray her. But she had betrayed them all.

But—it bit—she had been loyal to herself. Something he begrudged in her abandon, a courage he admired. That galled.

"Will *you* go to the Island then, Rod?"

"Why not?"

"You don't know Reggie Webb. We've only seen him a minute once when he was on furlough."

"I won't be going to see him."

"You won't be able to avoid him."

"Why should I? He's her business, not mine."

"And she's not yours?"

"Not anymore."

"But you're yours."

"And you."

"Me?"

"Yes. You're my brother. Remember she used to say, 'You and Rod are closer to each other than you are to me or your father because you share the same blood, half your father's and half mine.'"

"And you don't feel alone?"

"I'm not alone. I've got you, Cory."

"And Pete."

"Yes. But I'm ashamed to say it's not the same."

"I know. Do you think he knows that?"

"How could he help it. Because he's never said much, don't think he doesn't feel things. The silent ones sometimes feel more than the rest of us."

Rod was silent.

"Well, let's go." He took Rod's suitcase.

"I guess I'm no cripple."

"Oh, for once I can be—brotherly?"

"You're a bastard, Cory."

Cory laughed. "What would that make *you*?"

At their corner he waited with Rod for the bus to Providence; there he would take the train to Kingston.

"I'll see you in Madison sometime."

"Sure, Rod."

"You think I'm kidding!"

"Sure. It takes money."

"Big Daddy, thinking always of the money."

"Who else would if I didn't?"

"I might."

"Try it without Pete."

"I might have to."

"Well, when the time comes—"

"I'll see you in Madison."

Cory laughed. "You joker, you. Here's your bus." He embraced him.

"Remember—you've still got me, Cory."

He watched the bus, a great red creature making its way under the arch of maples along Hope Street. Rod reached in his pocket for change, his left hand supporting him on the vertical rail—he reminded Cory of that photo of Gramp in dress uniform gripping a rigging rope with a perfect hand—and then walked toward him, to find a seat. He watched till the bus disappeared and the street was empty.

Off and on snow came down, days of snow, as if preparing him for Wisconsin. The world turned white, virginal, and he bundled up in sheepskin, cap, galoshes, gloves, and walked to the edge of town, past the little green and white house he and Rod had been born in; past the meadow across the street and the brook, frozen along the sides, the water crystal clear running down its center; and into the dark woods, darker for the covering of snow, and up to Mount Hope—to Philip's Seat. He brushed the snow from the stone and sat as he had so many afternoons in his childhood, making King Philip his friend, making himself a Narragansett Indian, a true Wampanoag. He knew he had that gift of projection, of gradually slipping into the skin of another, or what he imagined was another, till he could *become*. It took him away from people at times. It made his everyday world isolated, too alone. But when he entered the other world, he—he could not tell anyone—lived. How he lived! Philip's spring was half frozen over too, and still. "The last time, Philip. I don't know when I'll come again." He spoke it to the spring, the sycamores, pines, elms, oaks, the air, the dark woods. For the first time since his mother had left, he wanted to cry. He wanted to throw out his arms and embrace all this, take it bodily with him—how?—and he *would*, inside him. He would never let it go because he knew this actuality was gone forever and nothing could restore it. This was for other eyes now. Somebody else would invade his King Philip world as somebody had invaded and destroyed the world at home. He stood—in the enclosure, dark under the trees, with no snow, it was almost warm—and then mounted to the crest of the great rock cliff. From here he could see only spires, chimney tops, edges of roofs, the windows of Tiverton, and imagine the far lights of Fall River, that city which he had always imagined as the dream city on the far side of the woods which he and Philip would one day reach, where all the agonies of his school years and all the meannesses of this town would no longer exist.

Back home, when he stomped the snow off his feet on the porch and went in, he heard his grandfather in the cellar.

He came upon him bent over under the bare bulb with his face pressed against a letter, squinting to see, mouthing word after word almost aloud.

"Is it you, Cory?"

His eyes quivered. Flecks of pink stained the light blue.

He casually folded the letter.

"Just a word from your mother."

Gramp had been receiving letters from his mother regularly, letters which he hoarded and read and reread by the furnace when he was alone. He'd come upon him like that frequently.

"She's getting along fine in case you want to know."

He said, "Rod's gone."

"I figured. He came to see me. I'll be going myself soon."

"I figured."

It must have chafed Gramp's puritanical conscience too to be somewhat dependent upon Pete, for on the verge of the new year, he came up from the cellar just before Pete left for work.

"Well, Pete, I'm going now."

Pete smiled, stoic.

"Sure, Dad."

He must have been expecting it. He did not ask where. He knew Gramp. Absolute as the Bible, his place was with her.

"Things are in tiptop shape downstairs. Cory can tend the furnace and bank it at night till he goes off."

"Fine, Dad."

"There anything you want me to do before I go?"

"Not a thing, Dad."

"Well . . . I'll be wanting to make the afternoon ferry to Orient." He went down for his things.

But when Cory went down to help him, and he bent over to kiss him good-bye, Gramp's quivering eyes were swimming wet, and his hug was strong and did not let go.

"What's wrong, Gramp?" He had never seen Gramp cry.

"I'm afraid I'll never see you again."

He felt the bone of those hands against his neck, cheeks. He gripped the hands hard. In his childhood he had hung from those hands, swung, twirled by Gramp. Gramp could break walnuts with his palm. He could hammer and saw and repair anything with them. In Greenport all year he collected toys, anything from dolls to bicycles, and repaired them so at Christmas there'd be something for every one of the horde of kids who poured in. He had built the house for himself on the rear lot of that century-old family house he was going home to now. To her. To be near his daughter. And to be near the woman next door, his wife, who had divorced him after the fire; after months in the hospital, wrapped in white, a living mummy; after the crippled hands, the bones. He still loved her. He had never stayed far away from her place for long.

"What makes you think that? I'm just going to college. I've survived a war, gone lots of places, and you never felt that way."

"This time it's different. I just know." He stood and gripped his bags. "No, Cory, I'll take them. Always did travel light. And you don't come to the bus. I know my way. I've been making this trip since long before your mother was born."

And longer even than that: Gramp had been born in Bristol harbor. Gramp's mother was on her way to visit her sister Jennie when she went into labor, so the boat docked at Prudence Island. She was too far gone to get her off in time. His first cry must have sounded strange over the water.

I was born at sea, the sea's my father.

He had on his mismatched suit, black jacket, brown pants, worn, and his perennial brown corduroy cap. His shirt was not pressed, and he'd managed to knot a nondescript solid brown knitted tie.

"You going like that?"

"What's wrong with me? I'm clean, ain't I?"

"Well, at least you've shaved."

"Humph! You think I'm going to the White House?"

Cory broke into laughter. "Well, they could really use a man like you there, but I don't think you'd get past the door, Gramp."

He kissed him.

"You come when you can, Cory."

He went out the back door and from the living room Cory watched him move along the side of the house and down the embankment steps to the sidewalk. He held himself as straight as he could, but he was slight and his shoulders sagged under the weight of the two bags. As always when he was outside, his eyes were nearly closed and his head shivered a bit with that inherited quiver of the eyes all his sisters and brothers were cursed with. For an instant Cory wanted to rap on the window, call *Stop, wait,* and then go out and talk him into staying. But what use? In a couple of days he himself must leave . . . and he envisioned Pete standing here, watching him, the last of them to go.

Then it *was* his day. Because of Pete's hours—Pete was always still sleeping when he got up in the morning—he went in to wake him. Pete was only half-asleep.

"It's time, Pete."

"Now?"

"The bus'll be here in a few minutes."

"You have everything you need? Enough money?"

"That's all taken care of."

"You want me to send anything?"

"Everything's shipped, the trunk, bags, all but the one."

"If you have problems—"

"I'll try not to."

"You can always come home."

"I know that, Pete. Well . . ."

He kissed him. Pete's hair reeked of restaurant, of rancid sweet grease, cigarette smoke, and drink. He did not want to forget that smell, anything. Pete gripped hard. He eased out of his arms.

"Do good now," Pete said. "You always have."

"I'll try."

"You'll do it."

"Good-bye, Pete."

"So long."

In the living room he listened for a moment: Pete took a deep breath and rolled over, the old electric clock on the living room mantel made its nervous hum, the hot air whispered through the ducts, the refrigerator clicked into abrupt motion; but over it all was a silence, and the silence made a great cry of absence.

He seized his bag and went the front way, not turning as usual to look at himself in the long mirror at the end of the hall. Though he wanted nothing more than to leave this house—it had become a charnel house of memories—he did not want to *see* himself go. Everything around him was cold, uncomfortable, sordid, and *he* felt sordid. He was ashamed of that feeling, and his shame made him feel more sordid, like walking on broken shells down an endless damp street, naked, in broad daylight. Poor Pete—in this house emptied of her and then Rod and Gramp and now him, everyone who was part of her, who could make it full to overflowing. How sudden emptiness was! And how often it repeated itself.

But he found his escape. At Madison he had his niches—his tiny room on Bowen Court only four blocks from classes and when lucky his choice place at the same library table, a choice place in the reserve reading room in the Nissan hut, and the same table under the Rathskeller arch where he parked and drank coffee and studied.

And observed the girl in white.

At first he did not know about Dalton, because, though stragglers stopped at her table in the Rathskeller, Dalton worked to put himself through. She saw him on his in-between hours. He was somebody from home, Black River Falls, and it was long before Dalton came one day to the Rathskeller and she introduced him.

Dalton Ames.

Dalton said nothing. He had a tight, spare body and a distant gaze, and these gave the impression of an inviolate space around him. Savannah's whole body veered toward him. Her hands seemed drawn to touch him each time she said Dalton, but some silent law refrained her: an invisible barrier, which her eyes and gestures made almost visible, rejected the hands.

Dalton appeared seldom. When he did, his presence governed her behavior completely. She was dependent on his every reaction. Flatteringly attentive, she stared at him, laughed with caution, her eyes alive to the subtlest motion of his hands, intonations, movements, her right hand poised with a cigarette, her left supporting it at the elbow, her gaze undeviating. She knew all his signals.

"Pretty, isn't he?" she said.

"Most things are if you get close enough—babies, puppies, insects. Did you ever see anything absolutely ugly?"

In singsong she said, "I can see you're going to be an absolute bastard, Cory Moorehead."

"Am."

"Are, then."

"Dalton's taking Business. You can tell, can't you—precise, every minute timed, efficient, and not a blink at the arts."

"Cold?"

"Depends on whether you get close enough, I suppose."

"I can see you're going to be a bitch, Savannah Goshen."

"Am." She laughed that guttural.

Abruptly, at odd times over the weeks after she'd approached him in the Rathskeller, she'd say nervously, "Oh, shit, I'm late. Dalton'll be mad as hell." Still, she'd sit finishing her cigarette, the smoke drifting up into her hair. After, she'd run her hand through it nervously, leaving it unkempt, shake her head hard as if to set it back in place. She seldom excused herself to go off to primp, and never made up in front of him. Lipstick slowly retreated over her thick mouth till she had two, one inside the other. He'd tease, tracing them.

Sometimes she came direct from Dalton's, nervous—and nervy—and sullen. "Pretty twitchy, aren't you?" And silent. The deeps of her brown eyes seemed to smolder.

"Something between you and Dalton?"

"I wish."

"Is he pushing you?"

"Dalton—push?"

"Do you?"

"That wouldn't do much good with Dalton. He's strong-minded. You'd have to wait. He'd let you know when."

"Would he?"

"Yes. You've seen enough of him now to judge that. Nothing much escapes your sensibility. There's no way a girl could push him. That, I suppose, is his attraction."

"He'd have to have more than that to begin with. Indifference isn't enough."

"Indifferent is the last thing he is. He wants to control. He demands. And he makes demands of himself.

"Not possible for long." But he sympathized. Something attracted.

"He's a pretty good choreographer."

"I can see you in ballet slippers!"

"You're a prick, Cory."

"We're not talking about mine."

"Fuck you, Cory."

"Wishful thinking, Savannah? I never go halves with anybody."

"Neither does Dalton."

"You'd know that?"

"I believe it. For me believing's the same as knowing."

"Now *that's* fallacious. Only a fool puts all his faith in another person. Faith you put in the invisible, whatever can't reply and can't fail you—because it simply isn't there, I suppose. If you let *him* represent that faith, then you endow him with all the weakness you have. And you know what you're in for then?"

"What I'd be in for, on your terms, with anybody."

"Not if you accepted him for what he is, what you know is in us."

"And you know?"

"That's what I'm trying to find out—what's in us."

"And not outside us?"

"If it's true. If there is truth. Truth can't be in one thing and not another, or something's wrong with the whole idea of truth, isn't it? You can't have lots of absolute truths. Maybe there are no truths. Maybe there's only change. Maybe there's something basic to a stone, a star, a tree, a cloud, a man which they haven't found out yet, though they keep reducing the components, they're getting there."

"They?"

"Science. You don't believe in it?"

"Believe?"

"Science is part of the same struggle, and half the scientists are coming round to feeling their business is as much the *why* of things as the *how*."

"It's not their province."

"If everything's connected, it is. Otherwise, it's all nothing."

"You mean I can't put anybody on a pedestal and make him my faith. I don't. No idolatry. I'm too down-to-earth for that. You're the one who's talking about faith. You're the one, if that's the case, who's hurting, or going to be."

"What would I idolize?"

"Art. You do, don't you? Shakespeare, Dostoevsky, the greats—and painters and architects and musicians. That's idolizing men."

"No, not men themselves, but what comes through them. There's a difference. There's something in them all, despite their differences, which has nothing to do with points of view or individual beliefs or religion. It's an impulse common to all of us which finds its expression in different forms, and it's there in every age of history, and it's always the same. It's like the voice you hear in poetry, an overvoice beyond the words, more than the words themselves, which the poet couldn't possibly know the source of. Perhaps he's a carrier who can't help carrying whatever it is. Perhaps simply the reverse of disease, like the good and bad bacteria which everything carries but which some creatures carry in concentrated lethal form because they're more susceptible, or even imbalanced, like great artists who carry one thing which we all have in some degree but which in them lives at the expense of other parts of their body yet makes the whole body live."

"Gee, I could listen to you talk all night."

"Shouldn't a down-to-earth girl like you save nights for something else?"

"You're a bastard, Cory. Maybe that something else is the same thing. Ever thought of that?"

She stared across at him, smiling, but her eyes wet.

"*Yes*, I've thought of that."

What he thought of, *it*, rose. That remembered image stood there very tall and dark, with thick animal hair on its head and a beard heavy and dark and hair burgeoning from its neck and chest and over its forearms and thick along the edges of its hands and on all its fingers. That was the unexplained thing. It appeared suddenly. It roused against all reason. It broke time. It broke order. Or it revealed an unknown order. Surely it did not know what it was doing. It was in the man, but it was not the man.

Reggie Webb.

It was in him.

And it roused *her*, his mother.

Passion.

"I've thought of it a lot, if you want to know, till it's driven me crazy: the artist can channel the thing he carries, but what do the others do when it comes to them in large doses and they can't keep it from spilling through them—despair? break? drown? They're carried in the flood and there's no control of the flood itself. You can stand against it. Sometimes you can control yourself in the flood but you can't control the flood. Or *can* you? Can you turn it your way?"

"Artists break too, Cory. They don't have a priority on other people's experiences, even though they use them."

"But when the time's ripe, they always have the means to channel their passion."

"You mean the rest of us don't. That's a little narrow, isn't it? How do you suppose the rest of us live? We reckon with it too."

"Not without Somebody with a capital S. Who created those stories we nourish ourselves on, too often only in our bad moments? If not the artists, who can do it for us? What would we do without the Bible or some kind of never-never savior but turn to other poetry or art for some image of Something that gives our experience meaning?"

"You care that much about them?"

"I didn't say that."

"But you do."

"I don't know which them."

"Now who's cryptic? But you hurt."

"I didn't say that."

"That's the point—when you hurt, *you* don't say."

"I don't?"

She was silent an instant, her face perceptive now. "Is it that bad?"

"*Yes*, it's that bad."

"I should be jealous then of anything that gets a hold on you that way. Most things don't."

"I'm cold, you mean."

"I didn't say that—no, never cold. You're passionate about—what you're passionate about."

He laughed. "And you're cryptic."

"Don't flatter my intelligence. You know I'm not."

"You can't be jealous of what's invisible."

"Oh? That's just what a woman *is* jealous of. She can't fight that."

"Maybe that's what we're all struggling with whether we like it or not, the invisible, maybe the struggle *is* the activity of the invisible in us, maybe it's in us all the time, and maybe at the least expected times it rears its ugly head."

"And you have to get your sword out like what's-his-name and cut your own head off—*you're* your own Gorgon?"

"Hercules. It would be easy, the easiest way, if you could cut your head off. But the thing rears its ugly head in *somebody*, and even if you cut *his* head off, the thing would go on in *you* only you might not be aware of it until it made itself known again through somebody else. Jesus and Judas were right here and nowhere else. They loved and betrayed each other—yes, each other—right here. Jesus should have stopped with the kingdom of God is within you, but should have included air and stone and roaches and weeds and crabs and crows in that *you*. *It* goes on forever, whatever it is that's in us, in everything—but here, now. Why'd he have to make false promises?"

"It sounds more like the Hell than the Paradise they taught me."

"It's got to be both. And it's got to be here, and nowhere else."

"Well, if you're looking for the Holy Grail, good luck. I'll be satisfied with a couple of kids in Black River Falls."

"And a man that will be satisfied with a couple of kids in Black River Falls? You think that? You really do? Wait till this place gets through with you, and you'll find out you want more, you'll find out you can't stop wanting more."

"Don't, Cory. You're beginning to get to me. You want to make me miserable? You want everybody to be miserable, thinking about such things?"

"It's more than thinking. Those who don't think about it or can't articulate it, or don't, feel it in their own way. They're not as exempt as you think."

"Don't put words in my mouth. *I* didn't say anybody was exempt."

"If you want to stop wanting more, you need the church. It was founded for that, to make *this* go on in another place. Even the most advanced ideas in the church are directed toward that; and if they're not, if they're simply modifications to help you live the good life in a social environment, then the church is a lie, it's moved away from its old purpose, to face the continuity of *it*, whatever *it* is. When it moved away from that, modernized, it became just a collection of town halls each for its own members. This is the church—" He threw out his arms; he embraced air; he touched the glass, table, her, the books. "And every one of them's a miracle. That's what the church has lost. That's what we've all lost, the sense of miracle. Every minute's a miracle. Everything you touch is a miracle. The world's a wonderful, dizzying place you have to live for. If you don't, you don't have any chance again, you've missed it all. And the church has made them afraid to give themselves up to life, all this life."

"Was it the war, Cory?"

"The war? The war. It made me love everything that could go in an instant—that means all this. It taught me my body. It taught me to love my body. Before that everything taught me it was filthy. I don't believe people *think* it naturally, but the conventions are so ugly and have been engrained so deeply in them that the littlest things become evidence of them. My mother was a good woman—"

"Is? I thought—"

"Is, then. But when I was a kid and suspected I was playing with myself, she took my hands and held them over the stove and said, 'If I catch you playing with yourself, I'll burn your hands on the stove.' Oh, she wouldn't have burned them for anything, but *she* didn't know what she was a victim of. She was trying to make me and my brother good, clean Protestant boys, to satisfy the world. She never connected the 'filthy habit' with her own passion for one instant. She didn't see in *me* what was so alive in her own body."

"You had all the war to think about that?"

"Not about that necessarily, but time to think, yes."

"And it changed you, the war I mean?"

"Radically. I won't say I grew up, simply that it made me sympathetic. I got along with everybody. I never thought I would or could; I was a little prig when I went in. Or maybe the capacity for sympathy was in me, but I had never become so aware of other people. In war all your relationships are intensified, even distorted. You're more than you knew. You find out how many things a man is. If it goes on long enough, men can become brothers and fathers and mothers and lovers to one another; subliminal at times, at other times overt. They argue and sulk, and stop speaking, and brood and make up, and love; and some fuck. It makes you doubt who you were before you enlisted. It makes you wonder whether or not that world which the photos by your bed or in your wallet or the images which spring alive when you receive letters are imagined, and whether or not the life you're living is the only real one. It's too intense, but then you can't imagine it any other way. Though you long for the war to end, when it does, you're scared shitless because it all ends in a sudden break, your buddies are gone, and there you are, released to go on with a life that went on without you and that you don't really know anything about in a world that even thinks differently in an environment you don't even recognize. You don't know how different *the same old thing* you go back to is. When you get home, you realize you've been inhabiting territory that you'd never have experienced otherwise. If you told that to people who've never been to war, they'd say you shouldn't have experienced it, or they'd be silent because when they talk *love, honor, sex, friendship, death, order*, all the *sacred* things people experience everywhere, they don't know that the same words can be two different languages, or many. There are dimensions you carry that no words could ever make them *feel*."

"Vanity of vanities! That's no reason you can't try. You're doing pretty well with me, Cory."

He laughed. "You'd think I had a gripe against the world, wouldn't you?"

"No. Against yourself, or somebody close to you. And close to you *is* you, isn't it?

My dear son Cory—

You're my father, aren't you?

For a long moment he stared out past figures moving black against the sunlight on the lake.

"I guess. Part of my mother's a part of me I hate, though I love her. She's the town, the part that intimidates. Town made her that way. They don't let you live otherwise, not since cavemen and pagan times, but thank God the world's breaking that. You've heard of the American Revolution, the French Revolution, the revolutions of 1848, Russia 1905 and 1917, the female vote, immigration quotas?"

"Never. You fool!"

"Those revolutions were all evolution, and you wait, next it'll be equal rights for the short and tall and fat and yellow and queer and housewives and people on welfare and in jail. Once a society starts on the right road to health, it's like all evolution, fits and starts, but fast, considering how one movement has mushroomed into another."

"Well, it can't be fast enough for some of us."

"Oh, we're always in a state of transition. That's everybody's doom, isn't it? The next step is always ahead, so we may miss it. But—*you* said it—then we haven't missed it because our children will experience it—no?"

"Go ahead, hit me in a soft spot. You win. Still, *I'd* like to have been one of those avant-garde kids for a change."

"You are but don't know it. I bet Oedipus thought that way, and Orestes, and Hamlet, and Macbeth; and think of Medea, a barbarian woman and a mistress with two children and abandoned by her mate in a foreign country and with no rights—and *you've* got problems? All you can complain about is that fate, chance, accident—*you* name it—has timed it so it doomed you to be sitting right here in white when I arrived—or doomed *me*."

"Am I that bad, Cory?"

"Well, you're no raging Medea, but I'll have to consult Dalton."

"Bastard!"

Dalton, he noticed, was careful not to violate their hours together. He would appear in the background, at the Union beer counter.

"Oh, it's Dalton." She waved to him. Was it planned?

"He doesn't like me?"

"Dalton? Don't be silly. It's probably because he does that he stays away. I think you make him self-conscious, maybe inferior—I mean you know so much, and he feels he doesn't."

"Know so much!"

"Well, you talk so well. Dalton goes right to the point—in business you can, or must—and I think he admires someone who can . . . expatiate like you. You must have been born with the golden tongue."

"It's in the blood. My grandfather had a farm and failed. He had a grocery store that went bankrupt during World War I because his mother and relatives and friends took advantage of his good heart and bled him, charged and never paid. He fished on all kinds of boats. He was a cook and nearly burned to death in a galley at sea. But all the years, through his tragedy, the one thing that never failed him was the call. He was an itinerant preacher who'd substitute on a minute's notice. All along the North Fork of Long Island he was known. Tom. Tom Verity. With his hands. They were a fearful sight. The fire curled his fingers back from the palms like crouched spiders ready to spring. The palms are bone. Whenever his hands leaped in the pulpit, clawed the air, and struck the Bible, they were as terrible to the congregation as the minister's black veil in the Hawthorne story. And when he squinted those albino eyes and his resonant voice rose and fell with his passion, you had to stare spellbound or drop your head and turn away from his eye, though you could not escape that voice which could evoke in you guilt or shame or sometimes laughter, because in the midst of it he could cast out the keenest irony or revelation. He never seemed small or burnt or crippled in any way then; he towered with the passion that seemed to enter and pass through him. When he was through, it was the voice they remembered, not the hands, as if the hands had led them to the voice and then disappeared. So maybe it's not what I know but my grandfather's voice in me that scares Dalton off."

"Or attracts him. When you're afraid of things, you're curiously attracted to them. I think he wishes he could talk the way you do. Dalton wants more than he'll let himself have, but he can't go after it because he has to concentrate on getting somewhere. He's driven to make it, he *won't* deviate, he's not going back at any cost. No more family for him, and no more Black River Falls. That's the way it is. He's told me."

"Why'd he tell you that?"

"So there'd be no misunderstandings or expectations—about anything."

"If we both attract him, then he's waiting for you to ask him over."

"I intend to."

Dalton cowed her. In his presence she fell into the eternal feminine, subordinate, humble, withdrawn, and something Cory, after Dalton had left, called sarcastically "that quiet sick look of adoration you put on when he's around. Why *do* you, Savannah?"

"To get to you—and make you ask that stupid question."

"What's so stupid about it."

"You know damn well what the answer is—that's what." She swallowed a laugh, hoarse. "Because I love you but want to sleep with Dalton."

"Are you sure you don't love Dalton, but want to sleep with me?"

"The truth is I want to love you and sleep with you."

"It's the Shakespeare you love in me, not me, Savannah."

"It is?"

"You don't believe that?"

"The Shakespeare helps."

"You don't believe that. You *know* I'm not the six kids and a house in the country type."

"You're what I want, Cory. You're what I came to the campus after. There's something in you—don't ask me what it is, who ever knows these things?—that works on me. I'm not talking about sex and I don't know *how* it works. It's not charisma, it's something more vital than that: you attract. You make me recognize something in you, and in myself. I'm not the only one aware of it; the other students are. It's some kind of emotional authority in you, something *I* need, and they recognize it as if they were talking to themselves through you. You can see that in Professor Buck. He's the most sensitive prof we havel in common, a great man, yes, and *he* knows you're . . . that rare thing."

"Don't, Savannah. I don't want to be that. I just want to be—"

"You don't know what you want to be, and I don't know what keeps you from knowing. But it fascinates me, if you want it straight. You don't realize what you are yet, do you?"

"Tomorrow, Savannah. I'll know tomorrow and tomorrow and tomorrow."

"You're so serious you're funny, Cory. I wouldn't be able to stand you if you weren't. I'd be crying all the time."

"Then between me and Dalton, you've got your comedy and tragedy. Pretty complete, I'd say."

"You won't give me an inch, will you?"

"Because now I know how much you'll take if I do. You shouldn't have told me how much you want."

"You've never told me what you want—"

"But you know." He spread his arms out. He would reach, if he could, through walls, ceilings, earth—to embrace it all. "This."

"Me and men. Dalton and money. You and God? One hell of a combination."

"Don't kid yourself. It's all one thing. Various forms of *it*, men, money, Big Daddy—real, perverse, imaginary."

"Poor Dalton!"

"Poor Savannah!"

"Poorest Cory! Men and money you can find plenty of, but Big Daddy? The golden egg but never The Goose. Ma always said settle for what is, because if you don't, you're forced to anyway—and if you resist, you make it all misery. I'm sure she was right, but I was young—that's what she forgot—and she'd had it, more or less. I want something solid I can touch. No images for me."

"Images are as solid to the eye and the memory as anything I ever touched. You have to live with memory all your life. There's no way you can cut it out of your head."

"Terrible thought."

"Depends on the memories."

"The flesh is enough for me. It *is* an image, you know."

"There you go. You can't get away from the Good Book. And the Word was made flesh and the flesh was Dalton Ames."

"I'll have your ass for that, Cory Moorehead."

"You wish!"

"Well, I *would* wish for that miracle, but I'm about to have another. Dalton, miracle of miracles, is going to row me around the lake, so I'll leave you to your images."

"*Elaine, the lily maid of Astolat.*"

"Pity poor Elaine!" she cried back.

He watched her amble off the terrace, dainty despite her comfortable roundness because her feet were small and she picked her path, light as a floating dancer, along the edge of Mendota and to the last dock, where Dalton was waiting. Something Dalton said made her laugh and she laid her hand against his chest and then her head fell against him only a brief instant before he steadied the rowboat until she stepped in and took her place in the stern. Then he lithely stepped in, sat, comfortable with the oars, guided the boat out of the stall; and with easy strokes in no time they were far out on the lake, almost unidentifiable in the horde of tiny dark figures drifting toward the black woods behind which the sun was falling. A cloud as thin as dusty frost over a pane formed a blurred face above the woods.

He bowed his head. He turned to his physics, but his concentration failed. All the figures had virtually disappeared in the rising dusk. The cloud had moved to the right edge of his vision, its form intact, still a hazy face.

Savannah was right about flesh. He hated, was even ashamed, to admit that to her. And he was right about image. She must see that. Maybe she did but did not want to seem to be intimidated into that admission. *In* him he knew they were one. They *must* be or what was the point of anything? Yet he could not master that unity. He could not understand unless he could *see*, and he could not *see*. As much as he tried, he could not penetrate that blur; it had haunted him, that face. It haunted now. Would it always? Suppose it never ceased, this random eruption of that blurred face associated with the father he did not know, had never known. Even if he did come to know his father, that part of the man he might have known all those gone years was dead to him and alive only in his father, carried by his father, never to be experienced by him as part of his living memory. Yet that face stirred not only the memory of the time before Daddy Pete, not only the memory of living with his father on Benefit Street after the divorce, a time which he would try so hard to obliterate, but something *like* a memory from before that time, something as ephemeral as frost.

His father would put him in a home.

But even with his father wasn't he in one? He had a cot, it was in the kitchen, and the woman (Louise, he would later tell his mother) had a room with his father, and the boy (Anthony, he would tell his mother) had the other bed in there with them. All he remembered from that time about inside was the cot jammed close against the wall near the kitchen stove, but about outside he remembered the face; or he did not so much remember the face as that the face insinuated. All the years it would insinuate, and at the oddest times; so it must never have left him, must have been floating, like so many other things, inside him. Perhaps it was the unsolved mystery of the face. The tenement in which he had his cot in the kitchen was in an enormous three-story wooden house next to another enormous house, both on a high embankment walled up from the sidewalk by bricks, with a narrow yard between, but that yard was far below with a high wall on his side which with the abandon of childhood he would jump from. His feet would strike the ground with such force that for an instant everything inside him stopped and then vibrated and his ears rang. Outside that immediate scene all, later, was black, as if there were a spot of light focused there and there alone. And at the center was not he himself but that face, which he first saw the first time he had jumped. Looking up, his legs still feeling that the bones had been driven right up into his shoulders and even into his head, he saw—and, afterward, almost every time that he dared to want to jump, that face would restrain him—in one of the enormous first floor windows, which were of course higher than the wall itself, a man's face. To him, at the time, the face was enormous with the suggestion of an enormous body; but he could not really see the body, only the face, and that not clearly. He could not tell whether it was black or white because the window was dirty with a dust much like frost, which when the sun struck it was almost white and blurred the image and when the sun did not strike it was gray and blurred the image; so he did not know and never found out whether that face was black or white, though he knew that in that run-down neighborhood there were blacks in the houses too big to be kept up by individuals during a time which was changing, his mother would later tell him, and that he couldn't remember, of course. Still, despite his fear, there were irresistible moments when his blood was violent and, no matter what, he *would* jump—and did—and then would dash on his trembling not yet dependable legs to the dilapidated gate to the sidewalk, always afraid the gate might be locked and he could not escape; and then hurling a lightning glance up at that window he would see the face undaunted, undeviating and not know, never know, whether it was there to protect or pursue. He came to think of it as a haunt in an empty house; but, his mother afterward said, the houses were all jammed close then on Benefit Street, where that tenement was, and many people lived there. There must have been lights on in the house next door at night, but he never saw it lit. He was always inside before dark and in bed in the house with Louise and Anthony, but never with his father. He never did see his father because he came home after he had gone to bed and was gone before he got up; so he only heard, as always, a voice somewhat quiet and resonant, and savored a scent of hair smoothener, stickum he called it, vaguely sweet, and of heavy tobacco, a scent dry autumn leaves would recall whenever he lay with them piled over him or went kicking them up in the gutter on the way home from school. But he never saw him, his father never woke him, he never touched him, he never said hello or good-bye. So why wouldn't he put you in a home, his mother said later, with that much interest in his son.

Yes, he could remember that place. He had, it was commonly acknowledged, especially by his teachers, a genius for place. He could build a place around an object, a glittering worn piece of glass, say, about which he could build a small world for himself, as he would when his mother took him from his father—"got custody," as she said, "because no son of mine is going to be put in a home, over my dead body."

Under the porch of the new home, he would make a paradisal world of the sun shafts pouring through the slats and the drifting worlds of motes and the silky sheen of spider threads and the spiders' stillnesses and dartings, the dry dust and clumps of dirt his little universe enclosed with its warm must or damp earthen pungence. Much later, he would trace his experience on the Island from the moment of the spiders. He and Agnes (his second mother as he called her, his mother's childhood and dearest friend, who had married at the same time she had) sat outside on summer nights, she trying to catch her asthmatic breath in the clear night air, and watched the spiders. He and Agnes would never forget when they saw two spiders do the mating dance on the clothesline—back, forth, teasing, back, forth—and Agnes suddenly said, "Ain't that somethin' though! You ever seen the like?" and burst into laughter at a world filled with such unexpected wonders. He had given the spiders names, Nidd and Doob, and always after, between him and Agnes, there was that place, concentrated and alive. Such scenes constituted his place, that house which would be forever that time in his life. And his places would never be confused. Even had he forgotten where one was located, that would not matter, for the place was itself, separate, not any other, and the whole time around it was clear and identifiable from such a moment as that of the spiders.

So, he remembered, came the place of the day of his leaving the cot world, the face world. This time it was a tiny restaurant with a counter on one side and a row of booths on the other. The man, the stranger—he could not be sure after whether it was his father except that his mother would not lie, she said later it had been—stood on one side, with him, his mother on the other with the lawyer and a policeman she had insisted be there both to witness the delivery and to prevent any words or violence between his father and her; and of course the counterman—the cook or owner—was also a witness. The act had evidently lasted only a few minutes, a legal transfer of him to his mother from the man he had virtually never seen and with time could not even be sure was his father, surely not, since he had not wanted him.

His father had written to his grandmother *I will have to put him in a home, that's all I can do*, without even a word to his mother, who would not have known about the home until the deed was a *fait accompli* had his grandmother not sent his mother that page and that page only from his father's letter.

That day in the restaurant in Providence he remembered for its fried smell, for the wafted sweet grease and dough scent from the new glass-walled doughnut machine where you could see the doughnuts being made and dropped perfect into the tray, a machine of glittering metal with a bright cleanness nothing immediately around it matched; and for the hang of stale breath and old bodies and breaking wind and worn clothes not clean which he would later associate with dozens of old men foully thickening the air of public libraries and above all with that rather farty smell of eggs.

The transaction—it was as cold as a transaction—was lightning quick. Of it there only remained over the years the conversation between him and his mother, who would never mention the business of *the home* to anyone he knew or at least never in his presence, as he never would despite his father's vile intention of putting him in a home and, worse, without having written directly to his mother about it (from indifference? vengeance?). He would never mention it though he'd often been on the verge, but he could never entrust to anyone what suddenly at the moment of speaking became somehow sacred or too intimate with the sudden sensation of shame and of physical filth he could not confess to, or could not actually attribute to his real or imagined father, never to tarnish a man whom he should not even be protecting and whose tarnishing might later also tarnish him in his son's eyes if he had one.

For his mother the detail that remained ineradicable from the day of the *transaction* was the startling sight of his legs. She would be knitting, or sewing at the Singer, or sitting on the lawn enjoying the sight of her Eisenhower roses when for some inexplicable reason, some random association, perhaps with color, perhaps with some past connection, she would mention that detail: "You had one brown stocking on and one blue." He did not remember, but he had been wearing knickers, so the blue stocking and the brown one must have stood out boldly. Mentioning it, she would at once burst into a kind of laughter which he would always observe would be confused ambiguously by the break in her voice and the abrupt sheen of her gray eyes, which though they always glittered so alive—she was known for it—would glitter doubly brightly at such instants. "One blue stocking and one brown!" She would settle then into a brief stillness, her gray eyes alien, as primordial, they seemed, as those of a praying mantis.

She took him home to a man named Pete. The man did not appear at once. In fact, it started that beginning next morning, in a ritual which would not be broken for many years, until his high school graduation, his mother said, "Shhh," and pointed to the closed bedroom door. "Pete's sleeping, he works nights, sleeps days." Was he then always to have a father behind closed doors whom he would never see in daylight? He did not yet know that boys had fathers like friends, like buddies, like heroes protecting them, like mothers whom they stood beside and who waited for them at appointed places like The Outlet or Buffington's Pharmacy, the Belvedere Hotel, The Lobster Pot, where they could be certain she would be. So his stepfather—Daddy Pete he and Rod would come to call him—had not been there waiting for his arrival, but asleep, and he was really not to see him except on weekends; though when he and Rod grew old enough to be left alone, then Pete and his mother would spend the day visiting friends, going to the city, to the Narragansett racetrack, taking the bus to Pete's parents and a brother and sister-in-law just over Narragansett Bay in the French colony of Fall River.

Mornings were the joy time—what surprise?—because in the icebox or on the kitchen table would be left miracles of pie, strawberry and raspberry jelly doughnuts, custards Pete had brought home from the diner, which with closed eyes he savored at breakfast, long slow tonguings, slushing from side to side of his mouth. "Swallow, don't suck and slurp, and don't wash your food down," his mother would say; but his mouth was his own—suck, slurp, savor, swallow.

The day—silence and sound—was built around Pete's rising, keeping the bathroom clear, in there the plunge of hot water, the almost stillness of shaving, the lingering Williams soap scent, so different from the pervasive night odor of his arrival, of grease, cigarette smoke, stale ashes thick as an invisible coating around him.

In the house his mother took him to, from his really unknown father to Pete, they lived in a small upstairs apartment. The spacious ell onto which it opened was unfinished, bare to beams and boards. In it was the toilet. All the ell space was for storage and, to him, for escape into sudden space, the actual space of his imagination forbidden most of the time to Pete and his mother, where both his self-created and book heroes and heroines lived their adventures. In spring the wisteria bush that grew and wound over the entire ell stunned with its lavender, drugged with its honey flow of scent along with the blue lilacs and white lilacs towering over the side fence. It created paradise from which he descended a long stairway from their apartment to a yard with a blooming apricot tree which would later drop golden fruit whose rich savor always after he would tongue on the least evocation. Like an overseer, when his mother was out and Pete was working, was the old woman, Miss Carey he called her, mother to the landlord's wife, who lived downstairs. He counted on her presence on the back stoop or under the apricot tree, a constancy in warm weather. She was very old. He had never been that long so constantly in another's presence. It was her head that interested—and, after, maybe it was the head that recalled to him, surely from memories his mother or grandfather or both had described, glimmers of times even before the interval he had lived briefly in the city with his father and that Louise and that Anthony. Miss Carey's remarkable immobility attracted his eye to her face. He'd watch and watch. He came without articulation to know that the raised head experiencing wind, shade, sun, sounds was the same as that of a lizard or snake or spider or praying mantis. The memory of his very early life before Louise and Anthony, a memory first given to him by his mother's and his grandfather's words, led to other associated memories which no words told him and which he did not realize until later were his own memories.

The house he had been born in was small, green with white trim on a green plot by a brook which ran under the road and under the low stone wall across the street and on its way to the harbor crossed a vast meadow bordered on one side by town and on the other by a forest of oak and elm and sycamore and birch and pine trees, where he imitated the Narragansetts who had once lived there, tempted where the light lured into a deep endless dark. The meadow sprang whole, rock and green, and enormous spreads of blue forget-me-nots running into glittery swamp with hundreds of wild iris, purple and large; and, beyond, into a harbor. It was in that meadow, beyond frail dew-laden lacey ferns by the north meadow wall, that he overturned rock after rock for the garter snakes he would collect in his pockets to take to his bed, to try to keep under his pillow, to his mother's terror. In the still pools were tadpoles he watched grow day after day into frogs, their tails shrinking to stubs. And there were the thousand times later when his feet would abruptly recall the pleasure of soaking—wet stockings and shoes, the suck and slurp and pull of muddy ground. But *now* what lived most in that remembered meadow was perhaps what he had never seen, for sitting in the midst of patches of forget-me-nots were three little girls. Always he *heard* them first, the bell-like tinkle of far-off laughter attracted his eye to them—in organdy dresses, one blue, one yellow, one pink, with enormous ribbon-rimmed hats covering faces which he had never seen but which he watched for with some strange premonition that if the children ever raised their heads what he would see would not be the faces of children. He associated the appearance of the three children in the meadow with Miss Carey's face and the heads of garter snakes and praying mantises, robins and chickadees and other birds; and a sense of anonymity like a feeling of fine thread ran tearing through him which he would like to grip and know and hold onto forever but which left his grappling hands empty.

He came to measure the time before they lived in the apartment with Miss Carey and the time after by the selling of his guinea pigs. The landlord had let him have a pen in the yard for two guinea pigs, which very soon became forty-four, so the sale was imperative because his mother said they were moving again. The cause was The Depression all the adults would speak and speak of till it seemed you ate The Depression and drank The Depression. To him it was an invisible unconquerable giant that loomed, cutting off sun and horizon and sky, in its wake witches with the laughter of those three children in the meadow and terminating in screeches and thunder which came from some far place and trembled the ground and, his mother would read, from a godman with muscles who hurled lightning from a great distance in the sky. "How far?" "Too far even to imagine." "Then how could he?" "He just can, he does," she insisted. "Then he's no man." "Of course not, we don't know what he is," she said. "Then how can you know he's there?" "We just know," she insisted. Where it came from was a place as invisible as where his father was, whom she never mentioned, who evidently did not exist for her except at those rare times when he'd look up and find her staring with intensity at his face and she'd say, "You're the spit and image of your father." He'd hear a kind of grind in her voice, not pleasant, not tender, though she would sometimes add, rarely, with begrudged admiration, "He was handsome, a lady-killer. Girls came right to the house after him. 'When you're through with him, I'll take him,' they'd say to my face. He'd have been fine if only he didn't have such a temper."

They did not stay long in the next house, an apartment upstairs too, where forever he had to be quiet, couldn't play—the owners disliked children—so he spent time on the long hall stairs or in his room, where once he spent a week in dark with measles, two with chickenpox. "Light may harm your eyes, it could blind you, we can't risk that." But always, for him, what the memory of the place gathered around was the shop whistle, for the house was across the street from the endless brick wall surrounding the U.S. Rubber Comany, where a good part of the town worked. "Your father—smart he was—had to master everything from the carding room up, in training for management, but since then," she said with what over the years he perceived as wryness, "he has found God, I wonder where, and has become one of His own. He now preaches the Word. Well, I wish him well, it's no easy row to hoe," at which he himself could imagine God's body battered. He had to assign it his own face because hadn't she said it was the spit and image of his father?

Nearer my God to Thee.

But to him that place was The Whistle, the company's gigantic tapered brick cylinder chimney which could be seen from almost anywhere in town. Driving straight up into sky, it gathered town, it governed the view. The Five O'clock Whistle the town called it though it hooted at other hours with a voice so deep its sound quivered even the sidewalk; he felt it in his feet and it seemed to jam its sound down into his ears. Later, with puberty, stretched flat on his bed, the first time his dick stood straight up, he called The Whistle the town dick; and much later he inescapably saw it as the man earth screwing the woman sky, a cosmic fuck in reverse.

In no time the apartment in Shaw's Lane was too expensive and they moved to the opposite side of town to the whole first floor of a three-story house with great spaces that in winter had to be closed off to save heat. For him all his experiences in that house would be gathered around the images of the Philco radio and the tiny dark hall that was the crossway to the bedrooms and kitchen and bath.

The Philco's wooden cabinet was grand, on legs, the facade intricately designed in wood over beige fabric. "Can we listen to Tom

Mix? Bobby Benson? The Wizard of Oz?" "Yes, but you must keep it low because Pete's sleeping." They knelt before the Philco god, their ears close: *Who knows what evil lurks in the hearts of men? The Shadow knows.*

But would never tell, never.

He would never tell about the soldier home on a month's leave from China, where that wall was which Cory longed to see. That man was a foot taller than his mother and dark with a stone face, with shag hair and brows; hair probed out of his shirt collar, hair covered his great hands; and he had a deep bass voice so resonant it vibrated. "Reggie was my girlhood sweetheart." His mother's younger sister was visiting, and Reggie Webb had brought a friend along. From his bedroom he heard them in the kitchen playing cards. Late came. The game changed to something they called *post office*. The door to the dark hall kept opening and closing. He got the idea. You bought stamps. You paid and you collected in the dark room. They sure bought a lot of stamps. Whispers went on, and kisses. Long. With changing partners. In. Out. "Our turn, ha-ha." And smudged laughs.

The games went on for a month. The men were gone when Pete came home. Neither his mother nor his aunt mentioned Reggie Webb to Pete. Pete never met him, but he would change Pete's life.

The Depression governed where they lived. It shrank the world. Pennies pinched, they moved. His mother could stand on a dime, and forever. Next, ten dollars a month went for a rear tenement, one of four on the third floor in The Block, which would normally have been a twelve-family building but half the first floor was Jack's Grocery.

There Pete went into the dark room—permanently, it seemed. Pete's and his mother's tiny windowless bedroom was between the kitchen and the parlor, its two doors forever closed because day was something Pete slept through. He arrived deep into dark morning. For years he was virtually invisible, and when the Great Hurricane of '38 washed the waterfront away, the restaurant he now worked for was carried off along with docks and ships and houses and shoreline and had to be rebuilt, and again Pete virtually disappeared.

Pete—there was so little to know about Pete—was kind to the point of self-effacement, yet actually uninvolved because he acted toward him and Rod through his mother. Pete gave her and them everything he could except his presence. To be fair, that wasn't his to give; he was not there because he worked for them. Pete satisfied his mother's desires for them—"My Rod and my Cory," she'd say—to have a place, an open spacious home, a lawn and a garden, to bring their school world to. They rented a high dignified house on a bank above the sidewalk on Hope Street, all light and air, serene, next to the quiet generations of old families living in austere and aristocratic dignity and only four houses from the high school. But Pete, except for the sometimes Sunday croquet he loved, was never there to enjoy, though, to be just, their joy was his joy.

All through "the Hitler war," as his mother called it, Pete was there; but his grandfather was the family mainstay, the forever motion behind things. His grandfather had always, of course, been *connected*, genuinely inspired by his direct line of descent from Adam, and during his varied jobs he was always spurred to itinerant preaching on the Sundays of his life in his alternate periods on Long Island. The living God flowed through him, emanated, at times radiated from him. His grandfather had never had to find. In his quivering albino eyes God shimmered permanently in all things everywhere. Who could doubt? He would give anything to see the view from inside his grandfather's head.

Or from Bernard Whitehouse's—because after the ennui of weeks of full-scale preparation for the invasion of Normandy, after simulating day after day the actual takeoff with the entire troop carrier group flying in formation, not knowing each day until they were in flight whether it was D-day. When on June 6 that man, his major, squadron C.O., flying straight for Normandy heard those words *This is it! D-day!*, at the critical moment his major broke formation and headed back to the base, landed with his crew and himself intact, and looking neither left nor right walked to his jeep and ordered Private Dinelli to drive him to the orderly room, where he waited to learn how one way or another those who would survive and show up one by one got back to England.

A hundred times he was reminded of Bernard Whitehouse. The major was tall, impressive, handsome, authoritative, respected, gentle. Often he was tempted to say, "You wouldn't have believed the major would have—" But no, that incident was the *other* moment he could never tell, even if one day he had a son. From love or fear the major had saved some of his charges, his sons, and it had cost his reputation. How could he tell anyone how, on the day the inevitable transfer came and Master Sergeant Rhodes called the squadron to assembly, the major stood there and thanked them for their work and wished them well, to what Bernard Whitehouse, *Bernie*, like any father to any son, must have known were mutters of *chickenshit, coward, traitor,* or *whispers of thanks* or lament or loss, or chokes.

No, he could not tell the shame which thrust up that other shame which he could never tell, *My father was going to put me in a home.* He could not blight that fall further. It was his own. He shared it. He might have told. His father's action affected only him, but the captain's affected the squadron, the entire group, and whom beyond? Did that single action become the foundation of the major's life forever after?

Unum.

E pluribus.

What makes a father?

At Wisconsin he missed Pete and her and Rod. A flurry of short notes came from Rod: What will you do this summer? You can't study all the time. If you must, can't you do it on the Island? Cory, go home. You *could* go. Ma wants you. Would it make it easier if we went at the same time?

To Rod, who as a child had lived with Gram and his uncles during the divorce, the Island was his true north, home. Something in him clung. In a now far past Gram had been his real mother. He had taken months to get used to his own mother. "I want Ma. Where's Ma? When's Ma coming?" At such moments, nothing, not the green metal grasshopper with the little well in its back to hide things in (the day his brother arrived from Greenport, Cory had pushed his giant grasshopper across the floor to him. "You can have it"), not his ball and bat or his cycle, no toy or food or run to the grocery or sousing with the hose in the yard, would console him.

But Cory squirmed, in his own way told himself Reggie Webb was beneath her. He shouldn't interrupt his studies. He would be isolated and not really on the Island he loved; and, though with shame he thought it, he *did* think it: he wanted to punish his mother, yes, for him and Rod and Pete. She deserved punishment. So did Reggie Webb.

Rod answered objection after objection:

"You're going to see Ma, not Reggie Webb. Besides, won't he be working all day? Why should you study your life away there? You'll be more efficient with a good break. And, Cory," Rod added, with the uncanny penetration which his oil-off-water presence always belied, "you can't play God. Don't. You'll hurt yourself as much as you hurt anybody else. You always do, Cory, because you don't know what's there, *we* don't, and we don't have to understand it or explain it either. Let Ma handle Reggie Webb, and let Reggie Webb handle Ma—they're out of our hands. We have our own lives to live. You'll be happy there. Don't tell me the scenery's any different. It's the same Sound and the same Gut, the same sand and wild roses and beach plums and pines, the same water to swim and fish and boat in; and we'll have Plum Island all to ourselves, the whole island. Ma says there's only the old lighthouse keeper and two young coastguardsmen on duty, and we'll have the jeep to drive. It'll be paradise. Even God has nothing like it."

We.

There was also that house of all their lives he could cross the Gut to, his mother's now. It's only, as his mother used to say, a hop, skip, and a jump from the Plum Island dock to Greenport harbor, and to Gramp in his house in the rear yard. Surely she would come weekends to see him and Gramp, for she never stayed away long without returning to check on Gramp. That way Cory could avoid Reggie Webb, but then he would not really be with her and there would be the problem of shopping for groceries, and he would be living virtually alone except for Gramp.

We. Without realizing it, hadn't he settled with Rod the day he'd enlisted? That day he had not gotten off the bus in Warren as on every workday. He had gone to Providence to enlist. Was that the day? Something had begun in him. He had felt the split. A tree had split; the trunk had divided in half, opened, bared its raw pith; it had to survive that way, and it could. He was free, wasn't he? You were, weren't you?

You're my father, Cory.

I'm not your father. Pete's your father.

You're my father, Cory. Your blood's my blood.

That doesn't make me your father.

You have to be.

I don't. I'm not.

But his mother would say, *Ask Cory. Do what Cory tells you to. Cory knows.*

Times, nights, in the days when they'd still slept in the big bed, Rod would choke breath, try not to cry, Rod would lay his head against his shoulder, Rod's tears were hot on him; but he would lie still. *I won't! I won't*! He felt Rod's head; asleep, he rolled against him, down into the crook of his arm, and one still hand over his side or belly or arm; but he would not yield. *I'm not his father! I won't be. I won't*!

Now from long distance, writing to Wisconsin from Kingston, Rod was fathering *him,* trying to, by urging him to a reconciliation with his mother. Did Rod know he was trying to save his *own* life? If he got Cory back to his mother, then Rod would have his father back too. Life would be restored, balanced. Rod could go on.

No, Rod. Cory was afraid. He would avoid if he could, but he would not lie to Rod. He would not hurt him, yet he went so long without replying that his delay misled Rod:

> You don't answer, you stay, so I'm assuming you're being stubborn and won't go to Ma. There's a chance here for special students to get an advanced look into some aspects of agronomy this summer, and as I'd been chosen and the answer had to be given almost at once, and you seem to be hedging, I've committed myself to the program. If you'd tell me *at once* you'll go to Plum Island with me to spend the summer with Ma and Reggie Webb, I can still withdraw. If you do break down in the next few days, go without your spartan breakfast and spend a couple of bucks for a phone call.

Consciously he eased out of it, let it slip. The day had gone by. He was safe.

But not. And not impervious. And this time not to Rod.

It was her hand: *My dear son.* The handwriting blinded.

> We are on Fort Terry—you know, Plum Island. We have an enormous house. You can work and study and swim. Nobody will bother you. Won't you come for the summer?

His eyes filled—for the loss of that old world, with relief that the rift was over, with remorse now for both his stubbornness with his mother and his disloyalty to Pete; but he knew—had known from the beginning—that his allegiance was to her despite his animosity toward her and Reggie Webb, that he and she were inseparably bound not only by being mother and son, no, but by the recognition, the intuition, of that silent irrational seething which no convention would keep them from immersing themselves in:

Passion.

The enemy. The friend. The friend enemy.

He heard passion. The house on Plum Island was enormous, eleven-foot ceilings, with transoms over the doors. His room was next to theirs, and because they had forgotten the high open transom between the rooms, at night for the first time passion awakened him. He was subjected to their rhythms, he rode their rhythms breath and breath and breath to breaking with the motion of his own mad hand (and, projecting, he was already warning himself *You'll have a son one day,* already planting every parent's dilemma, how to conceal, what barrier to place between his son and passion). Day after day he emerged not only conscious of their imagined nakedness but also with a new vision of her and Reggie Webb, somewhat detached, of two people living on a strangely edenic island. It didn't matter that their world was supported by the government, Reggie Webb the island's military caretaker, alone except for an old keeper and two young coastguardsmen living up at the lighthouse with whom they played cards, cooked up dishes, played the guitar, and the men who came on the cutter to deliver commissary supplies and mail, when they all converged on the government dock for news from the mainland.

What he never saw were the bowels of that island, where every morning Reggie Webb went—to the far end, underground, to maintain the hidden military machinery of protection and destruction that had pointed out to open sea during the war. But above ground all was a rage of honeysuckle and wild roses, lilies and irises and the myriad flowering weeds. Fragrances startled, shifting on the breezes. The island, its houses and military buildings a ghost town, was abandoned and the luxurious wild growth threatened to overgrow even the roads. Hurricane winds sent the sea over them.

Under passion his mother bloomed. Young, she had grown younger . . . and beautiful, a new creature. She had shed an invisible chrysalis. He caught himself staring at her, scrutinizing, speculating. The queen of the island, she entertained her little court, lush meals for him and Reggie Webb and whatever two of the three men did not have to tend the lighthouse high on the crest bordering the Gut between Plum Island and Orient Point, where the channel waters turned vicious at the change of tide.

She would cross the Gut to Greenport occasionally to keep up her house—Pa was living in his house in the rear and looking after hers—and to visit Ma next door. For one thing, his grandfather knew the lay of the land—Reggie Webb and his mother—for had she ever kept anything from Pa? He was discreet, respectful, as well as independent: his grandfather would not live in the big house, hers, with any of her husbands. Though when in need he'd lived in a corner, a room, a basement of their previous places, he soon scooted, saying, "You can't have two men ruling the roost anymore than you can two women." For another thing, you died someday, so he'd made up his mind that he'd end in this town. Nothing was ever going to move him out of it again—no, not death either. His place was in the family plot in Stirling Cemetery just over the rise. Wasn't he still on his own father's father's father's land back to 1636? That was it. No word more. Besides, his divorced wife, married again to a skimmer captain forever at sea, lived next door. Surely it satisfied him, knowing that when the woman he still loved looked out she saw him, knowing he would be a presence in her world till he died.

Mary.

Passion.

Silence.

Over the summer Cory crossed the Gut to Greenport to spend days at a time with Gramp and to visit Fatso García in his cottage, once a shed, on a small plot Fatso had bought at the edge of Gull Pond, looking across the breakwater to Shelter Island. The Coast Guard was not authorized to carry Cory, so the pilot always said, "I didn't see you come aboard." Though Reggie Webb was Army, the coastguardsmen liked him, his dark deadpan humor, his raised shag brows and the questioning glitter of his jet brown eyes when he almost broke into one of his rare smiles. They respected his dedication to his work, so alone on the far edge of Plum Island. You could count on him. Didn't a lifetime's loyal wait for the widow show that? Besides, they all wanted a glimpse of his new wife, a legend living on an island with four men and the direct opposite of the dark, towering Reggie—small, all energy, smiles, optimism, exuding the camaraderie he lacked; so as an unspoken favor to Reggie Webb and his mother they ferried him to Greenport and back whenever they had to make official stops.

Rod had claimed Greenport and Gram. He felt he'd been born there because after the divorce Ma had sent him to Gram. Ma could have custody of only one and chose Rod because he was the baby and sent him to Gram and his uncles. She could gain custody of him, Cory, when she proved she had a place and some means of support. So Gram was Rod's mother, Greenport his town, the uncles his fathers because Gram had divorced Gramp many years before he and Rod were born.

Cory was the novice admitted summers into the secrets of Rod's world—Moore's woods, the hidden paths and ponds, the mysteries of the town dump, of Gull Pond and Mill Pond, the tangles and undergrowth of shrubs thick as in ancient Indian country under close trees, and the great stretches of sand cliffs with their monolithic boulders running down into shores with a band of white stones polished by the eternal batter and chafe of waves.

The town was forced on him; he had to vacation there. He hated the place—the run-down two-story cottage, the black iron kitchen stove, the air vent cut in the ceiling over the stove, through which you could hear everything that was said downstairs and, from downstairs, what was said in the upper bedrooms. He hated the pump, the smelly outhouse in which he had to sit on cut-out holes where he could see the lime spread white over the mounds of waste below, fearing snakes or rats would bite his dick off or bees or wasps or hornets sting his ass. He scorned the relatives. They were beneath his mother, his own town, his house, his friends, and his father's family, which he'd never known but which now and then his mother dropped some hint of.

It was Rod who knew everybody in town. He was his uncles' paragon; he went everywhere the adults went. From the time he could carry a rake, he dug for clams; he dragged his basket through the water as he chased the swimming scallops; he rode the crick and then Peconic Bay in the rowboat with uncle Ben or uncle Bill or uncle Rich, his net poised ready to scoop up a crab, seagrass and mud and all. Sometimes he'd shout, "Look! It's a softshell," knowing his Ma loved them fried—you could eat shell and all. By six, Rod was already an ace mechanic. With Ben he was under cars, a little grease monkey, his hawk eye mimicking his uncles' labor at fixing scooters and wagons and bikes, and as he grew going on to model planes with buzzing, humming tiny gasoline engines, then to electricity when a wall switch, circuit breaker, or wire went faulty. "I can do it, Ma." When not fixing, he was sweating at games, putting every ounce of energy in the swing of a bat, throw of a football or baseball. "We can't play without Rod." There were always boys at the house after Rod to swim, boat, fish; or men wanting him to do a little job for them; or women who needed a thing repaired. They loved him. He went about with an ear-to-ear smile, his perfect teeth showing, his dark eyes squinched up to happy slits that gleamed like the quick reflections in his mother's gray eyes.

But he, Cory, could do nothing—no mechanics, no building, no games; and he hated fishing and scalloping and clamming. But he loved sea, walking the beach, his head hoarding gulls and the dying orange wild rose pods and the primordial boulders and horseshoe crabs and the white purity of the swans in silent motion on the pond concealed from the Sound between a sandbar and the woods beyond. When Gram took her cap and put on her sneakers and got out the buckets, he knew they were headed berrying. Hours later they'd return with a bucket or two of blackberries, huckleberries, raspberries, skin scratched and blood-streaked and clothes frazzled, at least his.

Their house was at the edge of town, but nothing in the town was far. Town spread over a narrow stretch of sand and rich black topsoil between the harbor and the Sound, no more than a mile wide. Bordered by Stirling Creek and the harbor, the town was virtually a tiny peninsula. The business district encompassed two blocks on Front Street behind the harbor docks, all the buildings low, making sky and sea and sometimes fog and rain and snow seem forever close, and Shelter Island like a mysterious green rock rising from the endless ocean.

Center Street divided the town. From Main at one end, you gazed at the García house at the other, like a very wide face that gazed blankly back at you from Third Street. The place was one of those low one-and-a-half story fishermen's with a porch running the length of the front, and a roof pitched gracefully forward, under which a row of four tiny windows indicating low upstairs bedrooms with sloped ceilings, surely the children's. The lot was bald. No grass grew, uneven dirt surrounded the house, no high green trees rose old and graceful as in most sections of town. The house stood on a bank backed by dusty shrubs barely disguising the town dump the yard ran into. Always the porch and narrow front yard were littered with broken bikes and fishing poles, an aluminum tub, a host of crippled or gutted chairs, rags, papers, refuse; and a flock of shouting and playing or lounging or talking children, and adults. For it was a full house. The Garcías must have had a dozen children from the look of the porch, a parking place for half the neighborhood. That end of Third, poor, ran almost unobtrusively into the white section on the downtown end.

Walking the shortcut back of town to carnivals and celebrations on the polo grounds, Cory had seen the house, but as a kid he was squeamish. The tiny mangy trailers, the blacks he didn't know, and unfamiliar faces that stared unfriendly at him from porches made him virtually run through it. Mostly, he took the long way around.

"Because you're scared," Rod would say.

"I'm not."

"Are too! Scared shitless." Rod laughed, raised his leg and farted. "Take that, Cory." He led Cory past the trailers and the painted up girls, niggers and white. "You know what they are, Cory?" Rod would laugh with the triumph of his knowledge. "Tooties. They fuck."

"Shut up, Rod."

"You're a snob, Cory."

He was jealous of Rod's intimacy with the town. He hated the town, but to compete he decided to possess it to the core, so he'd ask Rod, his mother, Gramp, Gram, relatives, visitors, or anyone about every house—who owned it, how old it was, how many lived in it, its history. He would gather. He would hoard. He would make town his body. It would be his, not Rod's.

"Who cares about that?" Rod said. "My friends live there. They're all I care about. You always care about *stuff*, Cory. You and your books and ideas!"

"That's us too."

"But the dump's real, and this street and these houses you think are so stinking."

Trailers on the corner of Third looked out on the town's old cemetery bordering the dump. Men, mostly white, hung around with booze bottles sticking out of their coat pockets or dangling by the neck from their hands. Now and then you could catch sight of a woman's face, white or black or high yellow, wearing a kimono. Those shambles were almost neighbors to the Negro church several houses from the García place on the opposite side of the road. The entrance to the dump was a great portal over the dead end of Webb Street, dark against the sky; it was fashioned of two telephone poles, one on either side of the road, the left tilted ominously, the right straight, with a foot-square crossbeam set on top of them, all black as tar.

He knew the dump. He didn't tell Rod. He kept it secret. Why secret? Because he would not have Rod violate it? No. He was always secret. *Why* was he?

The summer Rod turned fourteen—he was sixteen—he did serious clamming with Fatso for Claudio's and other restaurants in town. Staring after Rod's lanky loose frame, his mother was genuinely startled. "Why, he's a man now!" All summer, every morning before six, Fatso came for him. Fatso kept his boat at the crick, only a block from Gram's. The rowboat was Fatso's pride. He'd planned to own one. Obsessed, he'd worked at any job he could get, not breathing a word about the money he earned, hiding, hoarding. With a boat he could help his family more. The family didn't understand that. They railed violently at him, they needed money not later but now, but Fatso stood firm. They'd kept him out of school so much he couldn't pass; he was kept back, had to repeat, embarrassed because he was too big for classes; and he would never in a million years be able to pass any New York Regents' exam. He was older than Rod, Cory's age. His failing and his looks made Cory and the family at first think he was retarded. "Fatso's no fool," Rod told them, and Rod grew hot when they said Fatso was ugly, the ugliest thing in town, in *any* town. "You don't think so because you know him," his mother said, "but the first time you see him . . ."

Yes. You thought The Hunchback of Notre Dame. You thought Dracula, Jack the Ripper, Frankenstein. Don't look! You'll turn to salt or stone.

Fatso, Cory had seen a thousand times, but had never been with him. Fatso *was* ugly. Even far, you saw that wherever he was going, whatever he was carrying, oars, buckets of fish, clams, he walked fast with his head bent as if he were steadfastly pursuing a thing on the ground he would lose if he dared look up. If he did, teeth halted you. You saw nothing but that long jaw with big, protruding, widely spaced teeth. He could not close his mouth over those monstrous teeth in an upper jaw elongated as if some great hand had squeezed it out too long and narrow and it had stayed moulded that way. From his recessive lower jaw his tongue, always visible, could in no way reach his upper lip; it lapped over his lower lip, red, wet. To some people in town his dark skin meant nigger, what they called the hundreds of Puerto Ricans the farmers jammed into eyesore prefab barracks to work in the potato fields in summer. His hair so thick black was all forks when he wore no cap. And his brows shag. Gloom walking.

Just before sunset on an August night, Cory went home the "back way," lured by curiosity past the tooties' shacks and the blacks basking in last sun, men with glittering bottles. At the corner by the cemetery the sight through that portal halted: the dump was afire, the earth burned, the pond it bordered was flaming. Heaps and mounds were black against sun; and trails of smoke from real fires all over the dump made the earth a hell, dark, red, beautiful. He didn't move. What kept him there was a figure standing not far from Dewey the dump keeper's shed—not Dewey, who sometime back had been killed by his shed for some lottery money he'd won. Fatso. Cory watched for an instant. Fatso, facing the sun, didn't move. Then Cory went under the great arch, crossed the flat, stopped a few yards behind Fatso, and waited. Fatso had not heard. "Fatso?" Fatso swung around. "Cory!" Fatso was black against it. "What you doing here?" Cory went ahead so he could see Fatso's face. "The dump startled me. You'd think the world was burning up." "Yes!" Fires were smoldering all around them. "It's beautiful." Fatso laughed a warm laugh. "Ain't it! Every night this time I come back just to look." He turned a bucket over. "Sit." Fatso himself kneeled. "You got to watch. It slips down. In a minute it's gone." They watched, silent. Sun sank. It edged a sharp blood line. The pond and shrubs and trees and clouds and sky darkened, disappeared, dead to sight; but in the dark the mounds burned. Fatso was still; in a spell he seemed. Cory's breath caught.

Fatso's head was filled with fire. Cory was gazing into two windows. Mounds burned in Fatso's eyes. Then Fatso moved. "I got to get my junk together." Fatso never stopped. Since Huey the dump keeper's murder, Fatso made the rounds of the dump every day, picking over, collecting cans, bottles, silver foil, cartons, sometimes furniture. "You got to get here early before the rich people, you know that? Those ladies come, not just locals, but from Shelter Island and all around because they're looking for antiques. Lady sits in her big black car, watches, something good comes, she flicks her finger, that chauffeur piles it in the trunk or they drive away and right off a truck they sent drives off with it." He had a set of burlap bags to haul his treasure to Sol Golden, the junk dealer. "What do you do with all that money, Fatso?" "All!" Fatso laughed. "Hide it. Save." "What for?" "Pile it up to buy land. Then I build a house. I got all day to work all the jobs I can and hunt stuff now. I'm quitting school when I'm sixteen." "Quit!" "Because *them*. Ma hounds me, Pa does, and the kids. I don't have a minute they're not hounding me, all the time complaining. I want to help, I do; but they take my time, I can't learn, they won't let me; they tell me I'm stupid, I can't learn, I'm dumb; and me flunking. I can't get away without them after me—not to the skimmer shop, not Pell's, not the crick or Pete Neck to crab, no place." "Gramp says you're quick. And you can't fool him." "Not Tom. Tom's my friend. When I ain't got a place, it's Tom I go to, he takes me in. Tom'd take anybody in. And him with a houseful." Cory laughed at *houseful*—the mongrel Pal, and Shasta and the Whore of Babylon and the four other cats. "I got to wind this up, Cory. So long. Tell Rod I'll meet him at Pell's in the morning—at six." "Six!" "To clean fish. You got to do it early for the market." Fatso gathered his burlaps and disappeared down the slope into the deeps behind Huey's shed. Now night made the far roads a map of streetlights and Cory headed for Gram's, past the cemetery, where the lights whitened the tombstones along the stone wall. Opposite, the tiny cloth-covered windows in the trailers were lit up like blank stones too.

"Fatso's a worker," Gramp said. "Do Rod some good to keep up with him."

Work was almost a religion with Gramp. *Work for the night cometh when no man can work,* he'd intone. No grass grew under *his* feet. Night, day he was moving, catnapping at the oddest hours, his light on half the night as he worked, the neighbors used to his night noises. "Old Tom." "It's only Tom." "Tom's at it again." On Sunday the neighbors all around gave up: deaf, he always played the radio so loud that Bishop Sheen and Father Coughlin and Harry Emerson Fosdick (he didn't care which religion, it was all God) resounded in all their houses. "Listening can't hurt a body." Fatso brought him whatever he picked up from the dump, anything that could be repaired and made use of. "For sure Tom'll have it."

A night seldom went by that Rod and Cory did not drop in on Gramp, Rod usually with a pack of store-bought cigarettes. "Here's some Marvels, Gramp." Gramp knew they were from Ma. "Why, thank you, Rod." When Gramp happened to go short, Rod would get out the little mechanical roller, pour some package tobacco into it, set some cigarette papers in, and then pull the lever down and—presto!—a ready-made cigarette rolled down. "Don't make too many, Rod, they get stale and taste flat." Truth was, when alone he'd roll his own—pour a bit of tobacco in a paper, wet it with his tongue, roll it, and light up, and sit puffing, the cats all lazing, Pal at his feet, in his own seventh heaven. That was always the perfect time for Cory's "Want me to read to you, Gramp?" "That would be fine, Cory." Gramp's albino eyes didn't stop him from reading his newspaper or The Book. Cory would come in, unheard sometimes, and Gramp would be sitting at the kitchen table under the raw bulb he'd leave on day and night, his face pressed close to the page, his mouth going in a whisper as he read his daily verses. When he did hear, he'd look up: "Is it you, Cory?" Gramp recognized configurations, and some voices despite being hard of hearing. "Deef as a coot," he'd tell anyone. People would shout in his ear. "What you shouting for? I can hear you," he'd sometimes say. That would puzzle people. It was pitch. Rod's pitch was off so he'd talk loud, and Cory's at times fine. At the right distance Ma never had to raise her voice; he heard her every word.

A rainy night he said, "You in the mood, Gramp?"

"For the Word, always. I could do with the story of Joseph and his brothers. Genesis. Well, you know where. First, give me some hot tea."

Cory poured it steaming. Between his hands Gramp braced the 5&10 bowl he always drank from. Tiny Japanese men and women peered out from between his taut fingers. He sipped, crossed his legs and settled back in his rocker. Pal lay with his head on his paws, and the cats—The Whore of Babylon under Gramp's seat—were all so still they too seemed to be waiting for Cory to begin. He had no sooner read "*And Jacob dwelt in the land wherein his father was a stranger*" when something stopped him—*he* did not know what—and Gramp looked up, expectant. Then Cory caught sight of the face in the window, dark eyes staring. Fatso.

"What is it, Cory?"

The face vanished. Cory quickly rose.

"It's Fatso."

Since the night at the dump, he had glimpsed Fatso, whom he seldom saw except with Rod, passing the house alone, sometimes halted at the corner delicatessen, sometimes staring across at the house from under the green apple tree in Hinkelman's yard. From the little side entryway he shouted, "Fatso!"

Fatso halted and stared back.

"I didn't mean to bother you."

"Come in out of the rain, Fatso. Gramp's always glad to see you."

Fatso followed in, his hair matted, his drenched clothes clinging.

"No night even for fish," Gramp said. "Fatso, dry off and get yourself some clothes. You know where."

"Yes, Pa."

He came back in. He hung his soaked clothes neatly in the bathroom.

"Something wrong, Fatso?"

"Just my mother."

Was she at him again for money?

"Well . . . You just sit down and listen. Do you some good. Go ahead, Cory."

Fatso sank into the chair in the corner by the old maple china closet sent from Bristol, its glass frosted with dust and grease.

Cory read how Israel loved Joseph and made him a coat of many colors, how the jealous brothers hated him and plotted and cast him into a pit in the wilderness and dipped his coat in a kid's blood and took it back to their father and told him their brother Joseph was dead and their father rent his clothes and wept, and how Joseph was sold into Egypt and imprisoned and acquired fame for interpreting dreams and was raised up to the highest place in the land next to Pharoah, and how the seven-year famine came and his brothers went to him and did not know him, and how Joseph saved them twice and then revealed himself to his brothers, *I am Joseph your brother, whom ye sold into Egypt.* When Cory read "*Now therefore be not grieved, nor angry with yourselves, that ye sold me hither: for God did send me before you to preserve life, and to save your lives by a great deliverance. So now it was not you that sent me hither, but God,*" on *sent me hither* Fatso moved. He bent forward in the dark corner, and Cory looked up and hesitated the flash of a second. Fatso's eyes were black as uncovered pits. Empty. Endless. You could fall into them. Cory shivered. Quick, he read on.

When he finished, Gramp said, "That was fine, Cory. You'd make a great preacher," and laughed and his hand stroked the back of Shasta, who, always jealous of his lap, had slipped into it. Cory too laughed.

"What'd you think of that, Fatso?" Gramp said.

Fatso was still. His eyes looked vacant. Cory thought, They look so empty I could pour something into them. The look made Cory uncomfortable. Cold. Then Fatso moved, turned his head to Cory, and he saw the eyes did glitter. Fatso looked perplexed.

"Why'd He do that?"

"Who?" Cory said.

"God. Why'd He make the brothers do that to Joseph?"

"What'd he say?" Gramp leaned forward, and his right hand cupped his ear. Fatso's eyes were on the hand.

"You tell Fatso, Gramp. He says God was wrong to make the brothers cast Joseph into a pit."

"Wrong? Not that, Fatso." His hand fell to petting the Whore of Babylon again. "Anybody can use people wrong the way the brothers did Joseph and their father, but Joseph knew his brothers were part of him and had made a mistake and it would be wrong of him to make the same mistake and use his own good against them."

"But if Joseph was so good why'd God take him from his father and brothers all those years?"

"Joseph didn't realize the good in him till his brothers threw him into the pit. It tested his character."

"You mean we got to hurt people and then it'll be all right?"

"Not that, Fatso. There'll always be somebody to hurt the other, but the hard thing is to bring the one who hurts others back to life with the rest of us."

"You mean Joseph's special?"

"He could read dreams and the Hebrews believed dreams were sent from God to be read, so he had a way he could use for some good."

"Sure, special. And how 'bout everybody else?"

"Everybody's got some way. Depends on your capacities."

"Suppose you don't have? You mean what you do is just stand and take all the meanness. You got to be good with the meanness all round you and treating you like Joseph's brothers till you find a way to be good to them and show the meanness was fine after you made it all right, like Joseph? What's so good about that? Why's He have to trick you that way? You think that's fair?"

"Fair's what people drummed up to be able to live together, but there's got to be another, maybe a truer, way of thinking about what's fair or we couldn't stand all this. That's fair too. Justice. You see that?

Joseph could've chosen to be mean to get even with his brothers, punish them, but he didn't. We're the brothers. We're not Joseph."

"Why's God say He did it if they did? He sent the dream."

"It's a way to explain that there's something in us we can't see that's connected with things we can't see," Cory said.

"What's in us that we can't see?"

"I don't know."

"Then how can you tell me?"

"I can make up a story like Joseph's."

"Then it wouldn't be true."

"No, but what it's about might be."

"What it's about?"

"Yes. That people are good and bad, we know that, don't we?"

"We sure do."

"And we want to explain why we're both things. After all, it's all in one body. How can both things be in the same body unless they're one thing, maybe even the same thing and maybe come from one thing if we could figure out what it is."

"And God put meanness in you?"

"Gave you the choice to use yourself your way."

"But why meanness? Seems like he ain't God if he puts meanness in you."

Gramp said, "Well, Fatso, it's not meanness in you. Meanness is when you use your nature against somebody else. It's like stealing their good from them. Then it's evil."

"If it's good, then how can good be evil?"

"Because your mind can mistreat your heart and abuse itself too."

"Then God did. Why did God? Why'd He make the brothers do that? God did it."

Fatso's hands were wrestling.

"What is it?" Gramp said.

"Fatso still wants to know why God did that to Joseph."

Gramp said. "God doesn't do anything to anybody. Men do."

"Joseph said God did. He said so. You read it." Fatso clamped his hands between his knees. His eyes were glistening, wet. "He did. You read it, Cory. You did."

"We'll read the story again, together, Fatso—and we'll talk. Okay?"

"Cory?" his grandfather said.

"It's all right, Gramp?"

"I don't understand, Cory."

"Gramp will help us, Fatso."

"I don't understand. It's reading. Words. Them. Hounding me. I wanted to do my schoolwork, I *did*; but my family, they're always after me, hounding. And things, yes, things bother me, and I can't— Will you help me, Cory? I can understand. I can, can't I? *You* know I can, don't you, Cory?"

"Yes." Because Fatso did feel, deeply. Cory saw that. He had seen that the night at the dump. He saw that in how he behaved with the Garcías. Fatso loved his family, he worked for them, but he had learned that sometimes you have to help yourself first to be able to help them later. He had chosen his dream, a place of his own, a refuge; and he was sticking to that choice, working day and night. He would have his dream, he had promised himself.

"I want to know things, Cory."

"I know, Fatso."

"I can read, Cory—not like you, but I can. I want to read the way you do. I'm not dumb. Help me. Will you help me, Cory?"

"Yes. We'll read together."

"And you'll talk with me, you'll make me understand? I can understand things, Cory."

"We'll start whenever you want to, Fatso."

"You'll tell me what to read? I don't know what to read, Cory. I want to talk like you. I want to be able to think and talk like you and Tom when you're together. Nobody ever talks to me, just Rod fishing or cleaning fish with me. I'd die without Rod. Sometimes I think my tongue's dead. My throat gets dry and my voice sounds funny like it's drying up from not talking much to anybody but Rod."

"It'll take time, Fatso."

"I know that, Cory. I'm no dummy. I'll make time. You just tell me. Tell me, Cory." His teeth looked ready to chomp, masticate, swallow words, books.

"Tomorrow then. You come here to Gramp's and we'll start. From now on I'll do my books with you, and the math and science too, and what's important."

Fatso stared.

"You mean it?"

The room quivered in his eyes.

"Tomorrow," Cory said.

Fatso looked at Gramp, his eyes fleet then over Pal, the cats, the room; and he raised his arms as if to embrace everything. "Hot damn!" he cried and laughed. "Tom, you hear that! Tomorrow!"

"What? What is it, Cory?" Gramp set his knobbed hand behind his ear to catch the sound.

"Fatso and I are going to study together."

"Study? Well, a man can't get enough of that."

Fatso was laughing as they had never seen him laugh before, great chokes from his throat that could be crying too. His thick dark hair was dry now, looking like stiff forked tongues. He raked his fingers through it, laughing.

"You come back for your dry clothes tomorrow, Fatso," Gramp said.

"Tomorrow!" He laughed and ran out into the rain.

Fatso came all the days, never missing, and after the summer had passed and Cory had gone, Fatso wrote to him in Bristol and went on working with him all year round till Cory was eighteen and enlisted—and all through the war they read and wrote. Fatso was turned down, 4-F, so had all the war to correspond with Cory and read and read.

By the time Cory visited his mother and Reggie Webb in their almost solitary Eden on Plum Island, he and Fatso García had been reading or conversing or writing for almost seven years and Fatso the hermit scholar had become the town jest or wonder, or both, which were the same thing to some people. By then the teacher, old Miss Kellogg—who sometimes hired him to tend her lawn or paint or repair, whatever odd jobs she could save on by using Fatso—had grown curious about Cory. During the war she had even written a time or two to Cory—"doing her part for the boys overseas"—and had mentioned the mind he "had nurtured," as she put it, for Fatso had talked so much about him. Fatso had shown quite a profound interest in music, not "the stuff of the youth of today" but classical music, opera. Fatso's varied interests had made her curious about him, Cory Moorehead, who was related to the Veritys (she'd taught them all), Stella Verity's boy. She did not know him though he might be familiar on sight since he spent summers here, town was small, and sooner or later everyone passed the Kellogg house so prominently situated on Front Street, white with dark green trim, with a long gingerbread porch with otherwise austere lines.

By then Fatso not only worked for Pell's, cleaning fish, but had steady hours at the oyster factory, where he was an opener, and was also the sexton in old Emil's stead at the Protestant Cemetery, tending the lawn and bushes in season and digging graves, though still doing odd jobs.

Cory had not seen him since before the war. When the Fourth came, he took the Coast Guard cutter home to Gramp and looked up Fatso, for he hadn't seen Fatso's house, though he knew every inch of the terrain and the house and all its details. In Fatso's letters he had lived through land and boards and cement and drywalling and insulation and painting and furnishing and setting out maples and rhododendrons and around the house peonies and iris, then dahlias, asters, marigolds, and the inevitable winter mums, and "a lawn greener than all envy." He laughed at the remembered phrase when he did see the lawn, enviable green even in scorching July.

The house was not quite a mile from his own. In fact, from his upstairs bedroom window above the porch, he could see halfway to Fatso's. His bedroom window looked over the crest in the road that sloped straight to the entrance to Stirling Cemetery, where you turned on the road right and crossed a narrow wooden bridge over a rather stagnant meander of sea water from the crick that terminated in the cemetery. You passed between wild fields of head-high grass and the shipyard and St. Agnes' Catholic Cemetery. You went through a divide in the deep dark wall of pines, birch, elms, maples that cut off eastern light in the morning and western light in the afternoon. Suddenly you almost fell into space: the trees fell away, sky spread endless, Shelter Island rose green, and the sea moved alive as breath, endless, endless, and quivered with all the light.

It was a Friday night in July but bright yet when he walked to Gull Pond, though the wall of trees cast a deep dark shadow east, where Fatso's house was dark against the far gleam of evening sun on Peconic Bay. A faint light came through the house. He went round to the rear. A light was on in the kitchen. In the breeze the curtains fluttered like monstrous moths against the screens.

Fatso was bent over the table.

He rapped and called, "Fatso."

Fatso turned from his book and for a brief moment stared, startled. At once Cory saw Fatso's face, despite the overhang of upper teeth, was different—fleshed out, mature, manly.

"Cory!" he whispered in disbelief. He unhooked the screen. "Wow, what a surprise! When'd you come?"

"This noon. I'm at the house for the weekend. The Coast Guard brought me, an escape from my mother and Reggie Webb."

"Your favorite character?"

"Him."

Fatso laughed.

"Your life has sure changed, Cory."

"Yes."

"And mine. Look—" He took him through his bungalow. All the

rooms opened off the small hall that ran from the front door straight to the wall-to-wall kitchen. In front were a den on one side and a living room-study on the other; behind, a bedroom on either side. Books were everywhere—on endtables, in chairs, by the sofa, on the kitchen table.

Cory caressed the spine of *Nietzsche*. "I'm with you all the way."

What amazed was how ordered it all was, and how clean, impeccable.

Order.

"You have a woman, Fatso?"

"Ha!"

"You sure keep the place clean."

"What'd you expect? Nobody lives here but me. Sometimes Joey stays a night, but Ma gets mad I left. The family's down on me, been for years. They think it's nuts, the reading and music. They're jealous of me, their own brother. They even wanted me to sell and move home, for the money. I still give them what I can, but they don't speak, they cut me, Cory, because they think I'm so independent I stare down my nose at them—just because we don't like the same things. And people talk. Jealous, too. How could they be—of me? I'm not jealous. Haven't I got more reason than they have?"

"It's not in your nature, Fatso."

"They don't know that."

Fatso looked out across the bay to Shelter Island. Because his cheeks were fuller now, the eyes so dark and deep seemed set even deeper and gave to his head with its prolific hair a stature of crude, indignant strength.

"They don't know themselves. Most of us don't. It's the hardest lesson of all. It's the same with me, Fatso. Reggie Webb and I can live in the same house, but not for long. That's our salvation. I don't know what he thinks, but I think that."

"Even the ones the town's chucked don't let you alone. Even when they bandy together they're tearing the others up behind their backs or hacking at each other."

"In one way or another they're not educated, no sense and no books—it takes both."

"Those are just the ones who crucify you for reading books. You'd think I was a sneak coming out of the library, betraying somebody."

"You're the one who reads, so it's up to you to understand them. The secret's that. Gramp told you that. You can feel for them if you understand them. You can't change them but you'll know what they are. After all, you have to live with them."

"I want to. I try. But there's something in them don't let up."

"Doesn't," Cory finally said, gripping his shoulder.

"Doesn't. It's just that I hear *don't* all the time."

"I know."

"You have to watch yourself every minute, don't you?"

"Until you're so used to new habits that they're natural."

"What's so wrong with the natural ones?"

"Nothing—if you didn't live with the rest of the world. We'd be at each other's throats all the time."

"Aren't we? Still, most of us do control our impulses, don't we?" Fingers crouched, he kept tracing his thighs from his knees to his groin.

"We try to. Sometimes we fail."

"When we do let ourselves go, mostly we don't know what we're doing. Then we're in trouble?"

"When it concerns somebody else—"

"Like war."

"Yes."

"In war men don't just let themselves go. They plan it—around tables, at meetings."

"Yes, but their plans are about madness."

"So? Reason can be madness. They're crazy?"

"How you use it makes it madness."

"They're always preaching love." His fingers flicked, alive with dying sun. "They preach it but they don't know what it is?"

"Because love's irrational too."

"You!" Fatso laughed quick.

"It comes easy, but it's hard to keep up because every minute something stands in the way—"

"Something natural?" Fatso leaned forward, intent. The sea blazed in his eyes.

"You devil, you. You've learned to trap me."

"Touché. Then if what's natural is an obstacle, the natural can't be good or we wouldn't try to remove it?"

Fatso waited. The fire in his eyes moved.

"I wouldn't say that."

"Then what? What's natural's bad, the *evil* of old theology?" On his knees his hands were still.

"It can be negative. If enough of us gave way to our impulses, all hell would break loose."

"Ach!" His throat laughed. "Then you can be too reasonable and *not* act on impulse but make sure you direct other people's impulses even before their impulses come. You *make* them come?"

The falling sun left the sea dusky now, but the head of Shelter Island was a fringe of green fire. In the dim kitchen light, Fatso was still a shadow against the light of sky.

"Listen, Cory—" He stood, as if rising from the darkening bay behind him, turned and faced the water, dark against it. "All good things come from the irrational. You don't think about them, they're in you. One thing living on the water taught me is the sea's got everything in it. Nothing in it can live without it. It's all the same stuff, like us, only things have to be in the right place or they can't live, can they? It's the same with the body. The head's the same stuff as the rest of it and if it doesn't watch over everything else, some part of the body takes over; and if *it* takes on more than it's supposed to and atrophies another part, then the head's mad. Is that logical, or am I crazy, Cory?"

"Well, you don't give me much time to digest it."

"Cause I get excited. I should be reasonable!" His throat laughed, but his eyes were serious.

"Logical you are. And I see what you mean—a part of the self has to struggle up and order the rest."

"Exactly. The head has to be alert every minute or something might take over, but the head has to watch *itself* and not forget that it's a part of the body too or it won't let the rest of the body live."

Shelter Island was gone now, the yard and beach gone, the bay fused into sky, formless. The room—the maple table and chairs, the sink, the white cabinets, stove, refrigerator—took its own shape now as dark negated the world beyond. He and Fatso were reflections in the panes. Fatso gripped the back of his chair and stared down at him. He thought, *Fatso has become the professor. He's thinking out a lecture, with a vengeance.*

"But the head *wants* to give way to that sea too, like when we swim. We'd like to let go and lose ourselves in it forever. We *want* that. It's never happened to you, Cory?"

"Yes. Yes."

"When'd you feel that impulse?"

"Swimming, yes. And sailing. Listening to music. Sometimes speeding. In sex."

At that other table, theirs, in the Rathskeller, he and Savannah had spoken like this. They had tugged. "How can you find the right one if half the time you don't even see the real flesh your hand is on?" she'd said.

Wistful, he smiled. "You've got everything else. You need a woman, Fatso."

"Don't, Cory! *I* know what I need. You think I haven't had? You think there's not girls in town think a man's an animal. They're ready to fuck an animal anytime. You think I'd go to Madam Pam's or pick up a thing in Helen's?"

"I didn't mean *any* woman."

"You can't have it with any woman. *It. I know.* That's what I'm talking about. A thing comes. It's not a thing you *think* about. It happens. It takes you under, you want to go under. It's something never happened before. You can't hold back. You've got to let yourself go. You think you control it but you don't. You say *love,* but it's not love. Look at Tom's dog: you don't think it makes a difference *whose* leg he fucks when the impulse comes, do you? No. He can't resist—any leg, a towel will do, but he must, and *then*. And masturbating, it's the same, exactly. You think you control the hand, but the hand jacks off—must. And rape. You have to understand that about rape too. As if the *head* did it all! As if you *could* control *it*! In some people the impulse is a madness. That. What's terrible is *after*. You come back;. It didn't take you far enough."

"But, Fatso, if you go too far, you *do* die."

"And if you *don't,* you die too, don't you? *Don't* you, Cory?"

"I don't know."

"Well, you *do*. Listen, Cory— You remember that Raymond Lull?"

"The medieval philosopher who was converted?"

"Yes, him. His story's in that book—"

From the shelf above the table, beside the packaged sugar, he pulled it loose and lay down the familiar face—the white flame of hair around Schopenhauer's bald pate, the certain mouth, the lucid eyes.

"What sent you to *him*."

"It's from the Wisconsin reading list you sent me a long time ago, and you kept mentioning him when you took philosophy with what's-his-name—"

"Ah, Holzinger."

"You remember the story of that Raymond Lull? He fell in love with a beautiful woman, he wanted her, he had to have her, and he would. When the moment came, she let him see her body—her breasts were eaten up with cancer."

Fatso halted, staring. His raised hands, extended, could have touched something invisible. He kept staring, but talked, his head cocked, almost to himself now.

"And what did he do? He ran. And where did he run? To *God*. The fool! And why did he run to God? Because he didn't love her. He *couldn't* have or he'd have embraced her. He'd have taken her and loved her. He'd have wanted to give her joy. But *no*— You know what he did, Cory?"

"He became a convert."

"He *died*."

"No. He lived a long time."

"He died, Cory. When you can't love, you go to God. Because you can't love God, and God can't love you. You run away from love—that's death. Love's hard. He didn't love her, and he didn't love himself either. He didn't love anybody or anything."

"You don't know what goes on in somebody else."

"But you can know he didn't love—"

"How?"

"Because he didn't go all the way. We don't. Why *don't* we, Cory?"

Outside was pitch now, the room seemed shrunk. Leaning against the wall, Cory could see Fatso's still body reflected in the windows on three sides. His selves seemed to crowd the kitchen.

"Maybe we're afraid."

"Afraid?"

"Of ourselves."

"Yes!"

"We can't help that. We don't know how blinded we are by our own desires."

"No." He sat, as if the thought weighed, and clutched his hands; but his eyes darted, and quick he said, "So blinded by what people teach us that we're blind to our own *true* desires—we don't give way to them. If we don't, how will we find out who we are, Cory?"

"That could kill you."

His dark eyes were intense. What was he imaging?

"Think," he whispered, his voice filled with wonder. "*You'd know*. That would be worth everything."

"Not your life."

"Even that."

"That's too great a gamble."

"Gamble . . ." He seemed to savor the word. He smiled.

"You might learn nothing and lose everything."

"And if you learned *everything*!"

"That would be death."

"Still you'd know. Would it be worse than being alive but dead inside, walking around and not knowing you were a tomb—or what's worst, the most terrible thing, walking around and *knowing* you're a tomb—like the lawyer—"

"What lawyer?"

"—who tells the story about Bartleby the clerk, the scrivener."

"Melville?"

"Yes. I don't mean Melville, I mean the lawyer. *He's* the one. Listen, Cory— He's another case of what I mean. The lawyer gives Bartleby a job copying manuscripts and the clerk does the job to perfection—religiously, you might say! He's so conscientious he goes blind from copying. The other workers are cruel. They scorn him, make fun of him—you have to know what it is to be laughed at and sworn at and ignored to know what Bartleby's going through—and the boss offers him a place with him and offers help and food, but Bartleby refuses—and then because Bartleby refuses to leave the office, the *lawyer* moves his office to another building and *leaves* him there. Then when the owner of the building has Bartleby *removed* and taken to jail, *still* the lawyer's blinded by himself and offers Bartleby *what he needs*. What he needs! It's enough to make you scream with laughter it's so painful. He *kills* Bartleby because—here it is again!—he *can't go all the way*. Don't you *see*! The law has nearly killed *him*, the lawyer. He's let reason nearly kill him, yes. His impulses are almost frozen. Do you see? And what could be worse in this whole world than Bartleby's words when the lawyer visits him in prison the last time: '*I know you now*.' And he *does* know him. It's at that moment that the lawyer should understand Bartleby and know *himself*. Bartleby is standing for the first time in open space; he's no longer walled in. The lawyer begins to understand something's happening to him, but it hasn't happened yet. His conscience bothers him enough to impel him to tell us Bartleby's story, but his understanding of Bartleby's need is incomplete. *We* see that: *he* isn't complete because he didn't *go all the way* with Bartleby. Poor Bartleby!"

Such pity came into his voice and his eyes were so filled with some sight Cory could not see that he had the illusion, with his fleshier face, that Fatso was becoming someone else, that a Fatso he did not know was trying to break through the skin of the one he knew. Though it gave him joy to see what was happening to Fatso, the unformed image of a Fatso that was emerging made him apprehensive. What would the new Fatso do in this town? Where would he fulfill himself?

Fatso said in a heartrending high pitch, "Why didn't he go all the way, Cory?"

"I suppose because he's human like the rest of us."

"Selfish, you mean."

"Human, I mean, and therefore selfish, but not wholly selfish. Like most of us, he probably feared going all the way might be to die."

"Or live!"

"We can't be sure. We're comfortable with what we know from experience. We like to know where we're going before we act."

"Because we *think* too much! You see!"

"That's the human part. If he did what you expect, it would be what we call the divine part. If we all did it, this would be a utopia, heaven."

"Yes!"

"What good would the suffering and the irrational—you say it's everything—be then? Would we know what we had in this utopia?"

"You don't know the terrain till you walk on it, do you?"

"Touché."

"Our natures might be transformed then in a way we can't imagine now, so that we'd be perfectly adjusted to a new terrain. It's hard for us to imagine we won't always be what we are."

"You've got a point there. We're always evolving."

"Oh, we are?"

Fatso threw back his head, his great shock of black hair a splay against the ceiling light, stared grimly and then with Cory burst into laughter.

As abruptly Fatso gripped his shoulders, "You, Cory— To have you here! You can't know what it's like after all our letters and all the books. Sometimes—it's been so long since we came together—I don't believe you exist; you must have happened in my imagination. When I doubt I go to Tom's; then I know it's all real. Tom saves me."

"You startle me at how far you've gone, Fatso. When do you study with all the jobs you've got?"

"Who talks to me? I work alone most of the time, and always carry a book. I eat and read, or read between jobs. And—you'll laugh—when I'm digging holes in the graveyard, I talk to the dead. You know Emil. Somebody left at his back door some shoes he needed but they were filled with mould that infected his feet and laid him up—that's how I got the job. I used to laugh when he said he talked to the dead. Now while I'm digging, I talk out loud what I've been reading. I argue with the books. Talking keeps me from going crazy. If I didn't talk to them or Tom, I think I'd lose my voice. You don't think I'm crazy, do you?"

"Crazy! You're too logical for that, unless crazy means being obsessed. You're certainly that. I have to hand it to you; I've never known anybody waste less time. And you . . . you even look different."

Part was his keen scrutiny, rapid shifts and halts as if visualizing his thought point by point *out there*. Part was his face: the cheeks had filled out so that the thick upper lip was more rounded—sensual, almost beautiful—and the lower lip, far under, receded into his neck, full too, and softened the harshness slightly, though nothing could not remove the stigma of those teeth. The flesh and high cheekbones made his deep eyes look black.

"You see that, then?"

"Yes."

"I *feel* different."

"You're changing inside."

"I'm not who I was that day, am I?"

"Which day?"

"The day at Tom's—you remember—when you were reading the story of Joseph and his brothers from the Bible?"

"That's years ago . . . How could I forget? It's from that day we became friends."

"You can't know. Something was happening while I sat there. A thing inside me. The more you read and the more Tom and you talked, the more it moved. I thought I'd scream. It was like the thing *wanted to get out* and *couldn't*. I couldn't control it. You and Tom couldn't know. I had to hold my own hands to keep from pounding something. My ears were thundering. I almost couldn't hear what you were saying. When I began to ask questions, it stopped, like it was satisfied, it got its way. It let me alone a minute, but it didn't leave. From that day it hounded; it would come, like driving me. And you know what I think? There's a *thing*—call it some*body* so you can *imagine* him—trapped inside us. It wants to escape. It has to struggle against skin and bones it doesn't want. That's what I think."

Fatso stood over him, looking down, expectant—waiting for judgment? approval? agreement?—and with that sense of wonder on his face again as if the revelation had just occurred.

"You *have* found the man inside, Fatso. What are you going to do with him?"

"Do with him?"

"You could do other kinds of work. You don't have to clam and clean fish and dig graves all your life. You could leave this town."

"Leave Greenport! I'd die, Cory. Why . . . I love this place. I know every face and every house in town, the docks and boats; and I love the bay, all the water, the sand and wild roses and boulders. What would I do if I couldn't hear the gulls—they're like friends—or watch the kingfishers. I know every kind of insect and flower and tree that grows here, everything that lives in salt water, and in the fresh water, in the dump, and my god where would I find fiddler crabs and what would I do if I couldn't fish or crab or just stand in the water and look down straight through the sky and see what's going on in the silt and sea grass on the bottom? And *them*, my family—they're here."

"But you always wanted to get away from them."

"I am away. But if I went too far, I think I'd be afraid. If I didn't see them, I'd think they didn't exist. I *have* to see them, even if it's from far off and they don't see *me*, even if they hate me. They do hate me, Cory, they do. But I couldn't stand to be without them because if they hate me, they must love me too, or why would they be *at* me all the time. They *are*. Why don't they just let me alone?"

He threw his head back and gripped his hair and drew it back taut. The angle emphasized the ledge of his teeth. They gleamed with saliva.

"Simply because you're here, Fatso."

"I know, Cory. Nobody needs a reason." He cupped his hands around the raw bulb hanging from the kitchen ceiling. They darkened the room. His fingers cast bars. "I keep telling myself what's going on in me is going on in them too, and maybe they don't know it. *I* didn't till that Joseph story. It's hard to feel all that inside you that can't get out. When I stop to think, I feel for them. I want to help them, Cory, but I don't know how."

"What you give them helps, Fatso."

"All I give's money, and food."

"They're not ready for anything else; they may never be."

"But they must feel what's going on in me, I mean . . . if they're me."

His hands parted. The light was instantly too bright.

"Do you think such things, Cory?"

"Too often, Fatso. You could go crazy thinking about such things."

"Oh, I don't want to go crazy!" A laugh scraped. His hand gripped his throat. Standing, poised, balancing on parted feet, he swayed—ahead, back, ahead, back—silent for so long that Cory thought Fatso'd forgotten he was there.

"What I want . . ." Fatso went to the back window. Shelter Island was a black mound against the dark sky. He was staring through his image in the pane. "You ask why I don't go away. I gave you one reason. I'll tell you one more. The real one? Yes. The whole world's *here*.

Why should I go if the whole world's right here? What I *want—you* know what I've wanted from the first minute—is *to understand* what's here, what's in me, what I'm for. What *am* I for, Cory? Nothing? *No,* not nothing. Something's in me. What? I want to *know*."

He flattened his hands, spread his fingers, but the pane hindered.

"I know. You love Greenport, Fatso. It's your place. It always would be even if you did leave. Greenport's like family—it made you, you wouldn't be you without it."

"Yes. Do you feel that way about your place?"

His place. Bristol? No. He hated it. He loved *here*. You could hate. Your hate could be responsible for your love. One balanced the other. *Was* one the other? Or from both had he created an imaginary third place?

"This is my place. Bristol made me, but Greenport stirred my imagination so that my imagination transformed Bristol too. Now all I have to do is close my eyes and I'm back here. At moments even when I don't want to be here, the place fills my head—the Sound, sand, pines spread around me, and the apple tree, the shady maples, the house, all the land the family once had, and the widow's walk from my great-great-grandfather's house projecting through the trees blocks and blocks away. I see the potato fields and the cliffs of the Sound, I smell the fertilizer, the cauliflower in the fields . . ."

"Then how can you leave it?"

"I have to go where my work is."

"I don't care what work I do, I'm staying."

"The place never leaves me."

The dead were with him. On the Island he felt the weight of them. They were inside him. If they went anywhere, they died into you. You couldn't be what you were without them. The ghosts of his mother's people he felt close, but he could not summon up the others, his father's, though they were in him too. He could not find them. His father, a ghost too, was the most evasive; he was in depths inside him he could not delve.

"They go with me."

Fatso cocked his head. His eyes seemed to retreat into shells.

"Who?"

Fatso didn't move.

"My ghosts, my people I carry with me."

He heard Fatso's heavy breath.

"All of us?"

Cory smiled. "Yes." He lay his hand on Fatso's shoulder. "It's meant a lot to see you, Fatso. You've brought back—everything. Hard to believe anything's happened since, though we haven't said a word about the old days."

Fatso laughed. "We carry them with us."

"You're getting too clever, Fatso."

"Ha! I mean to! I *do.*" Fatso's hands gripped his, gripped. "When will I see you, Cory?"

"I don't know. I'll be going back to Wisconsin soon. I'm on the GI Bill. I'm trying to catch up on the war years, so I'm taking heavy loads."

"But you'll come back, won't you?"

"As long as my family's here, you don't have to worry about that. They've been here three hundred years, so that's a threat."

"I like threats. They keep me on my toes." Fatso's throat sounded husky.

When he was well up the road, Cory turned. Fatso was still there, a silhouette against the light in the open door. He waved—Fatso must have been waiting for that recognition—and went along the dark road, past the lone streetlight, where in the dank field, in the deep sea grass, an army of cattails stood vigilant in the vague light.

When he went back to Wisconsin, to the same room with the Koenigs on Bowen Court, he was already overwhelmed by an accumulation of letters from Fatso, long letters, energetic, in a style—style?—impetuous and passionate yet with a complex logic, with a structure of comments which bred questions, which in turn bred comments and questions, from which he would return to a previous question, ascending finally to his original question. The letters were obsessive, seemingly chaotic, but ordered. He assailed Cory as always: Is chaos *contained*? If it is, how can it be chaos? If the primal *stuff* is absolute, and the absolute is irrational, can there be anything else *but* the irrational? I mean: If *reason* is part of the primal *stuff,* then isn't reason a part of the irrational trying to gain supremacy over itself, the irrational, like the head over the body—like me, like you, Cory, like everybody? Isn't it struggling against itself to *be* something? Order must be its strongest obsession; reason must be the irrational's strongest element, but it must have to struggle every second to try to order its own part before it can order the whole.

He did not answer Fatso at once. He had a week before classes. In his delirium at the fall leaves, the lake laden with gliding sails green, blue, yellow, with rowboats and canoes; at the tremor in the air, the excitement of renewals, beginnings; in his delirum he wanted only escape, *escape* from thoughts of the Island, his mother and Reggie

Webb, from those questions he had spent too much of his time on already. *Fatso's speaking my own mind and I'm not up to that right now.*

Savannah! She was waiting in her place—with Dalton. How glad he was to see them! He kissed her. He gripped Dalton. They were all sunned Indian brown. He did not know how much he needed, them. "I could eat you both."

"Try me first. Dalton's tender!"

And he talked, talked out his Plum Island Eden, his passion for every tree, flower, house on the North Fork; his reading; Gramp and the cats and Pal, telling as much as he could of his mother and Reggie Webb, skirting Fatso—aware that Savannah was watching, sensing omissions. She would wait. Savannah *could.* It was, he kidded, her specialty, letting him talk, studying silences, where substance always lay awaiting her quick intuitions, intuitions never spoken but which he knew she had because she acted on them, she assumed and she was right. She never said, "You wouldn't have gone to the Island if you didn't love her," "You wouldn't feel guilty if you weren't selfish." "If you'd known your father . . ." Sometimes he yielded to her sympathy, to her hand, her lips on his neck, even her breast she held his head to and made him press his lips to, holding him, maternal.

"God, Cory," Savannah said, "you haven't lost your gift for talk. I could listen to you forever."

"She's right, Cory. It's a gift. You ought to make something of it."

"A million? *Now* I know you—you must be Dalton Ames!" He shoved Dalton's shoulder affectionately. "You're right. I may turn preacher like my grandfather; but I'm afraid I'd have to feel what I preached the way he does, but it wouldn't be religion."

"You'll end up quivering the flesh and bone of graduates and undergraduates, that's what." Head tilted, eyes saintly raised, tongue ahang, she mimicked his adorers.

"Saint and bitch combined—as it should be. You haven't changed a bit, Savannah Goshen."

"Haven't you heard? People don't change; they merely discover unrevealed aspects of themselves. *I* haven't—yet."

"But you two haven't *confessed* your summers. Let's get *with* it."

"We've seen each other. You can imagine the rest."

"I don't know about you two and your imaginations, but *I'd* like to live it up in style before classes start. How about the weekend at the Dells. We can take a cabin, tramp the cliffs, take the boat through the Dells—gorgeous this time of year, the leaves'll be perfect—booze it up Saturday night, and come back Sunday for the royal shakedown on Monday."

"*Die drei kamaraden?* You want me to make like Maureen O'Sullivan?" Savannah mimicked adoration.

What had changed in Savannah? All weekend—on the boat, swimming, in the cabin, picnicking—she was so self-contained, listening to him and Dalton now and again try to goad her into intellectual conversation, laughing in that throaty half-chortle, letting herself be seen, breasts a tease.

"You and your boobs, Savannah."

"You and your macho talk."

"Macho!"

Only Dalton was that. His lean, balanced body when he dove from the cliffs a fine knife slitting sky, splitting water. All weekend their only moments alone were when Dalton was "performing for me," she said. Was he? She chain-smoked nervously, her eyes alternate darts and rivets, her coughed laughter too frequent.

"You two estranged?"

"Ohhh." Her yawn did not conceal the abrupt glitter of her eyes, the sudden yielding to frustration, her lips bitten almost sore, so red, wet.

"Listen, Savannah, you're not going to make yourself sick, are you?"

"You care?" Instantly her hand leaped to his arm. "I'm sorry, Cory, sorry." She avoided his eyes, following the clean cutting strokes of Dalton's arms as he swam. "One, two. One, two. Just like that. That's our Dalton."

"What happened over the summer?"

"Dalton found an 'entertainment.' I don't know whether it's a real one—I think so—or pretended, to keep me *at* it. You'd think I'd know better, but I'm used to him, Cory. He's a habit. I'm—go ahead, laugh—a creature of rhythms. Jesus! My body, my fucking body, *demands* its rhythms. It drives me crazy. Without Dalton . . . But you'll be proud of me. I've been fighting it. I haven't capitulated once since I got back—it's a tug-of-war—but Jesus, Cory, I think I'll go crazy; I don't think about anything else but what we *do* when we're together. It isn't because it's Dalton; it's because I'm frustrated. My body's frustrated because my mind is. When I'm with Dalton it's the only time I don't think of my life, my mind, that cottage and a man, or you. I can't imagine my life without you. Bed with Dalton and talk with you make almost the perfect thing except for the ring and the house—and kids, yes. Did I fuck up because I put Dalton between you and me, sure it would turn you off but daring myself, or you, I don't know; or because I put you between me and Dalton and I should forget the mind, this place and what it does to me. I can't *not* think of those things. Dalton puts you between us. Did you know that? There are times he prefers you, he takes your side, he talks you up with me, or he leaves me to have a beer with you. He thinks he makes me jealous, and he does, I'm jealous as hell, only what he doesn't know is that it's not because of him but because of you. In my head you're mine, you belong to *me.* Dalton can't know that; he'd never understand. What makes it worse is that I know that for him *I'm* a habit too. His indifference and his almost *mechanical* expectation challenge me to the point of insane excitement, but he can't stay away from me too long—that girl just may be a thing of the summer; at least she's not on campus. And you know what that does for me? Gives me a certain power *I* can wield in turn. I don't want to think that way, I don't, I won't. But how do you stop, Cory?"

Her voice trembled, and her hand. She kept tapping the cigarette. She shivered.

She couldn't bear to lose Dalton. Lose *that.* She'd fall apart. Always, no matter her thought, she turned tender, kind, indulgent at the mere sight of Dalton.

"If you can't stop, Savannah . . . let it run its course. Hope something interrupts."

She tossed her head, and stared up at the sky. Sky glittered in her eyes. She lowered her head and stared at him. He saw himself reflected in her tears, dark against the lake. Her gaze would not free him.

"I can't much longer. I can't, Cory."

"Hey, you two, no conspiracies!" Dalton, his flesh gleaming with light, streaked up the slope. He sank beside Cory.

"See what I mean?" She reached over Cory. "Cigarette, Dalton?"

Dalton—whether from a sense of inviolate privacy, respect for Savannah, or the old gentleman's code where sex was concerned—had never broached Savannah with Cory, never mentioned sex, love, marriage. He was content as a kind of third, who had the privileges of the mate, knowing that Vanna veered magnetically toward Cory and could no more break out of her orbit than one of the planets. What both of them marveled at in Dalton was that the attraction did not affect him in the least, he seemed perfectly indifferent to their relationship. Maybe it was self-control, enviable. The certainty of his sexuality gave Dalton one kind of peace. Cory envied that too. For Dalton it was no curse.

All the way back to Madison, driving, Dalton talked—the new economics curriculum, the falloff in postwar industry, his best chances in business, the problem of postwar Germany, the interest in Von Braun and the German scientists—"his way of putting us lit people in our place," Savannah murmured. Implacable, Dalton laughed.

"Dump me on campus," Cory said. He knew Dalton would take her home. Unintentionally Dalton would torture her with insistence, precisely what she wanted, and Savannah torture herself, doubling her desire with resolute rejection. Tomorrow Savannah would relate in detail and frustration the conversation with Dalton. But she was weak. "He makes me *melt,* Cory. I'm afraid. I'm afraid of where it will lead." "I'm rooting for you, Savannah." "You are? Why? Because you don't want me to have what I need?" "I want—you know better than that—all of us to have what we need." "That's love, Cory. Don't you know it?" "Yes." "Then you love Dalton and me. There are ways you could show us; you could put us straight." He knew what she meant—he did love her, she knew that—and he was afraid, she knew that too: "Because you're afraid of sex, aren't you? Sex and love *can* be the same thing, but you're afraid they might not coincide, aren't you?" "I believe—" "Don't tell me that again. *I* know what you believe, you and your theory about only one real love, but how in hell are you going to know it if you don't dare sex? Or *is* there someone you love but haven't had sex with or have had sex with and not the chance for the other? I wouldn't believe any of that if you did tell me because if you wanted a thing you'd go after it till you got it. You're stubborn, you're a wall, and Savannah can't break it. Why? Because she's been touched by somebody else, is that it? You couldn't bear to fuck what's been already fucked and smirch your beautiful ideal, my Shakespeare kid with the high-flown language, his DeQuincy head in the clouds and his feet in the mud. You forget your lit, don't you? Oh, Cory, you know I'm just spouting off my frustrations. I love the Shakespeare and the rhetoric and you reading it; and regret every minute we're not together, every minute, yes, even with Dalton, *especially* with Dalton, if you want to know. When I'm in bed with Dalton, you know what? I'm thinking of—" "*No,* Savannah, please don't." She bowed her head, laid it against his shoulder, and he pressed her head hard against him, not removing his hand till her head was hot under it and the tears were hot on his shoulder. He knew he loved her in a way he couldn't express to her; he wanted to but he could find no words. He felt her hot scalp was his, the tears his, the heat. He wanted to say I understand, Savannah, because it's happening to me now, but he could not find the who, though he knew that who was in him, deep in him, that kept him from her. *There's some thing trapped inside* . . . Fatso! What loomed, harassing, was fear: Suppose the who is *not* inside me, but out there? If it is, why doesn't it come, why does it keep itself from me, or why do I keep it from myself?

Now, the thought was sudden as grit under his eyelid.

He halted at his corner. Beyond the house, in the clouds, low and shifting in the dying afternoon sun, he tried to read a face, *wanted* a face, yearned for a face, but thought *I'm afraid of it too, Savannah* because he felt the face close, struggling to reach the surface.

Nothing happened. The clouds moved.

In the hall, the landlord's daughter, Mary, appeared in the kitchen doorway.

She was wiping her hands, those large square hands the image of her father's with fingers made thick from farm work before the Koenigs had sold their country place and come to the city for Mrs. Koenig's health. On crutches, she went only from the house to Mass and back. Years before on their farm she'd fallen and broken her leg and dragged herself across a field to the house, and the incurable open sore on her leg kept running ever after; she had to dress it daily. Despite that, she was always pleasant, filled with the love of life and Jesus.

Mary said, "There's a surprise waiting for you upstairs."

"For me? Who'd send me a surprise?"

Mary was coy, barely repressing laughter. "I promised not to tell."

Mrs. Koenig hobbled up behind her, smiling too. "Better you go up and see."

He heard Mr. Koenig, unseen, chortle at the conspiracy.

But Cory was too late—above, his door opened, steps crossed the hall:

"Cory?"

Rod?

He clutched the newell post. At the top of the stairs, in the half-dark, it *was* Rod, long, lean, his flashing smile, the thick unkempt hair.

"I'm no ghost, Cory."

Mary and Mrs. Koenig broke into laughter.

"Come on, man!"

He took the steps by twos. Then he clutched Rod. "I didn't realize—" Until this instant he didn't realize how much he had always missed him.

"You're supposed to be starting classes at Kingston. What are you doing here?"

He went down the hall to his room. A suitcase was open on the bed and on the floor cartons were piled high.

"What's going on?"

"I'm unpacking. I brought everything with me."

"Nothing's happened? You haven't done anything?"

"No, worrywart, not a thing."

"Well then, what is all this?"

"I'm starting classes."

"You're what!"

"Tomorrow I'm registering for the semester with the rest of you."

"You've left Kingston?"

"I'm here."

"You didn't say a word to anyone."

"Why should I? I'm a free agent now. My summer project took every weekend; that's why I didn't get to the Island to see you. The transfer took some doing. I wanted to surprise you—and I did, didn't I, Cory?"

The plea in Rod's voice startled. He was solemn, too solemn for Rod.

Standing with his back to the windows overlooking the backyards almost lost in darkness now, he looked solemn, too solemn for Rod.

"Surprise? Shock is more like it. But why here?"

"Wisconsin's terrific for agronomy. What better reason?"

"That's what you said about Kingston."

"It's true. But you weren't there, Cory."

"I haven't been since the war."

"Don't you think I know that? That doesn't mean I got used to it. We never had the best years together. I had them with Ma after you enlisted. She was great. We did everything together. You don't know what fun, a real riot, she can be. Sometime I'll tell you about the fun we had with rationing. And Gramp too. I waited three years for my big brother to come home, and then he's gone, kaput. Now with her out there with Reggie Webb, and Pete alone . . . I want some family, Cory. I'm not like you—"

You're my father, Cory.

His mother had put him, not Pete, in his father's place.

My son Rod.

And what was *he*? He had never been a kid, never felt like one.

"You hold everything inside, Cory."

You had no choice but to buttress yourself against not having them, against distance, and to hold what was left however you could.

"The summer at home may have been the last time."

And you weren't there, Rod. He bit it back. All summer a figure had wandered in the shadows on Plum Island. All his youth he had felt the presence close, just out of sight, teasing his sensibilities, feeding his imagination, as if his beloved Indian, King Philip—moving through the Mount Hope woods behind the meadow across the street, vanishing behind tree after tree as he pursued—had become as he grew older other presences. In service he had felt the presence as inseparable as breath. Sometimes it had stood there in one of his buddies, in an officer, in one of the Land Army girls he'd dated in Hungerford or met at the Palais de Danse in Nottingham. He had thought he'd recognized it, but the illusion was as ephemeral as a veil turned dust. Finally he'd told himself it was his *self*, it was his nature, *he* was the shadow he'd insisted he'd been waiting for in someone else. He must stop imagining the other. But the shadow, serene and certain, kept insinuating.

"You're glad, aren't you, Cory?"

Seeing Rod shadowed in the pane, he felt as if a hand gripped his intestines, afraid. Of my brother. Why? As quickly a sudden joy impelled him to draw Rod to him and he laughed recklessly.

"You crazy you! Why wouldn't I be glad!"

"I banked on that."

"Who else have I got?"

"You've always got Ma."

"She's got Reggie Webb."

"You've still got Gramp."

"And he's got God or a reasonable facsimile."

Rod laughed. "Yes. He's lucky. Gramp loves us, but he doesn't need us. And Ma doesn't either, really."

"You'll stay with me for the time being. Right now, come on. We'll go for a beer to catch up on what you've been doing and then worry about where you'll live."

He and Rod had decided—cheapest, to share. He hated telling the Koenings he was leaving. Miraculously they found a third-story front apartment on Langdon, a hop from the Union.

The Koenigs watched them load the taxi. They stood in the doorway, a forlorn trinity, Mary clasping her big hands before her, her mother on her one crutch, her father with Mary's long hunting dog face contemplating him with eyes as dark and warm and vivacious as hers.

"That's some brother you got there, Rod," Mrs. Koenig said. "Take care of him. I never asked, but I was hoping he'd go down the street with me some morning." To Mass, she meant. "He'd make a good Catholic."

"I'll stop by to see you."

"You better." Though Mary laughed, her narrow eyes glittered nervously.

He had called Savannah about the move.

"Not see you? Will it take that long?"

"Other business. Tell you when I see you."

"I never liked puzzles, but what can I do? See you when."

When. Shades of dejá vu.

In the Rathskeller the next noon, in her original place, Savannah tilted her head coyly when she caught his eye.

"Ah, Eve after the Fall." He mocked playing the harp.

"You have to believe to have a fall."

"Oh, woman of little faith."

"No faith, no falls."

"Don't you believe that."

She slouched over the table toward him on one elbow, her cigarette atilt from her lip, one eye lazily asquint to shut out the smoke, too self-assured.

"Cory Moorehead—" She dramatized with a hiatus. "I can't believe this."

"Whatever it is, you wouldn't—*no faith, no falls*?"

"I—can—not—believe—this."

She sank back, rounded against the wall.

"Go ahead—play."

"You, my best friend, or something."

"Well, something is not nothing."

"Everything's point of view, and mine—" She straightened, threw her head back, shook her hair, and, with a bold smile, stared over his shoulder. "—is, at this moment, strangely interesting."

He turned to observe the strangely interesting.

"Rod!"

"Hello, Cory."

Savannah laughed.

"She said you'd be surprised, Cory."

"Oh, don't look so vacant, Cory. I saw you two leaving the gym at registration and decided to find out who my competition was. So—"

"We had a long talk."

"A long listen, you mean."

"Bastard!"

"It was great, Cory."

"I bet it was. She can do that."

"Can I?" She flowered warmly, ingenuous. "You never told me that."

"You never mentioned Vanna to me."

Vanna.

"Don't be offended, Rod. He didn't say a word about your coming either."

"To be fair, Cory doesn't talk much about himself. He never did. At home he was always the quiet one. I'm the extrovert, so they always said."

"I didn't know Rod was coming. You could have knocked me over when I saw him on the landing."

"Well, he knocked *me* over."

"She came straight to me and asked when I'd seen Cory Moorehead last."

"I know the game."

"All right, Cory. What else could I do? You were being evasive. I hadn't seen you in days, Dalton hadn't, so I called Bowen Court. The girl told me you'd moved, but they had no new address or phone number yet. She didn't mention a brother. He sure can tell a story," Savannah said.

"Rod?"

Rod laughed.

"If you've never heard him, you'd better start listening."

"Vanna's exaggerating—"

"I know a storyteller when I hear one."

"It's just that lots of things happened to me while Cory was in the Air Force. I worked the garage, a regular grease monkey; and the lumber company, driving a truck; and on a skimmer boat out of Greenport one summer. I wrote Cory that, but when he came home, there was no time to catch up on the three years. You have to be around somebody long enough. Then we both went off to the university."

"Then it's time we got to know each other, Rod."

Savannah raised her beer. "It's time we all did." She chug-a-lugged, rose, and took Rod's hand. "I'm going to give your brother a big sister's view of the campus, first the long range from the lake, then gradually zero in—"

Rod fell in with her like a shadow. Savannah had a gift for creating ease like settling an invisible warm cloud around you. Her flesh, her rounded hips and full breasts, when she was at her most natural ease, appealed in a maternal way. She would not have been insulted if he'd told her that; she would have taken it as homage. Rod succumbed.

But she had succumbed first. Then, to his surprise, Dalton succumbed. Cory began to see in Rod aspects of the boy his mother had written about during the war:

> Rod's a three-letter athlete this year. I knew he would be, but I'd never have believed he'd play in the senior operetta—Rod, who never sang a note in his life! You should have heard him. He was simply marvelous. He's started going with the music teacher's niece—she played the lead—you remember Mrs. Clayborne's niece Jan?—and of course he still drums with the band. Everybody loves Rod . . .

Everyone always had. Rod was natural, spontaneous. The moment he walked into a room, he caught everyone's eye and held it, he had such personality. An extrovert, pure extrovert, Cory had always said, and me the introvert, though sometimes, in a rare fit of anger, Rod would lash out, "Maybe I'm just a better actor, Cory. You didn't ever think of that?" "Why would *you* have to act?" "*You* know so much, Cory—you tell *me*."

Dalton, on the run between classes and work, would dash to their table in the Rathskeller, hunting Rod: he and Rod were going to work out in the gym, they were going to play football, they were going sailing. Savannah watched, silent, lost herself in studies beside Cory. Rod, when he wasn't with Dalton, would track her and Cory to their usual place in the library. Rod would drop in on them at the Campus Grill after eleven, when they cut off the 3.2 beer at the Union. He tagged along with them after. "*Die neuen drei kamaraden*," Savannah said—sadly, Cory noticed, because he and she and Dalton (Dalton unpredictable now, quietly withdrawn, playing whatever private game with Savannah) no longer regularly closed the Campus Grill, smelling of onions and grease, each so reluctant to abandon the other that all three walked from rooming house to rooming house and back till they'd walk the night away and go to the diner for breakfast before classes.

They were in the Grill one morning at two.

Savannah sank into a long stillness, lost, quietly rapt.

He said, "You look the way I feel after a lecture by Sánchez-Barbudo. Ask me what any other professor said in lecture and I'll tell you in a line, but ask what the great man said and if you've got fifty minutes I can repeat every word he said."

"I should learn Spanish then."

"It would be worth it just to hear him."

She closed her eyes.

"What's wrong, Savannah?"

"Frustrated, damn it. Just let me listen to your voice. It sound's even better with my eyes closed. You know what sounds do to me. Your voice . . . it's a hand, Cory. Some voices touch deep and rouse. Yours does."

"Come on, Savannah. You're perverted on the subject."

"Perverted, but not on that subject." She coughed her little laugh, deep.

"Does everything have to be sensual?"

"Everything is."

"You react to my voice because we're friends."

"Do I?" She shivered. "I love the sound of your voice." Her hands loved the book. "Read me some lines from *Macbeth*. Professor Eccles' lectures are brilliant, but his monotone murders the words. Poor Johnny-one-note!"

"You asked for it."

"Read the early scene where the king visits Macbeth's castle," she said. "It's the only peaceful moment in the play. Maybe remembering that one glimpse of beauty is what makes the king's murder and all the terrors of the play doubly horrible."

"You're turning into a regular critic. Careful! You'll end up doing theater reviews for the *New York Times*."

"That would shock you, wouldn't it? Prick!"

"Would you be surprised if I said No?"

He could see from the way she slumped into herself, readying for him to read, that she was savoring his praise.

He read:

This guest of summer,
The temple-haunting martlet, does approve
By his loved mansionery that the heaven's breath
Smells wooingly here. No jutty, frieze,
Buttress, nor coign of vantage, but this bird
Hath made his pendent bed and procreate cradle.
Where they most breed and haunt, I have observed
The air is delicate.

Her cigarette hung from her mouth, smoke coiled up the side of her face, over her eye, into her hair. She didn't close her eyes. She didn't move. When he ended, she was too still.

"You're doing it again," he said.

"Damn!" The cigarette almost burned her lip. "Doing what?"

"Going wherever you go when you sit right here and disappear."

"I was thinking Rod's stories and your voice would make the perfect match."

"You like him a lot."

"Why wouldn't I? It's all in the family, though you wouldn't know it, you're almost opposites."

"Almost."

"But there's something, some sympathy—I don't mean affection, but sympathy—between you."

"Jesus, Savannah, why make something esoteric of it? He's my brother and you're my friend. Are you using us as guinea pigs to figure yourself out?"

She closed the book and stared at her hands.

"That's not worthy of you, Cory."

"Don't try to give me the guilts, Savannah Goshen."

She bit her lip, her breasts rose and fell. She turned her head from him, too late. Her breath broke.

He could not help reaching over and laying his hand on hers.

"It's Dalton, isn't it?"

She lit another cigarette, blew, breathed deep.

"You going to tell me?"

"*You* told *me*." She gathered her books. "Let's go."

It was Lake Mendota that kept the Island so present. When the fall winds tore leaves flaming from the trees and sun blazed the forests and turned the ground red and yellow fires, the Island seemed to call. He and Rod grew restless and often wandered together in silent sympathy. The least move in the lake, a far dark figure in the woods, a man fishing, a face on the square downtown was enough to halt one of them: Remember the Cat Rock? Jimmie-the-whisper? the Polacks on Easy Street? innocent Connie the Pole who had to serve time for supposedly molesting the Matson's thirteen-year-old girl because he couldn't speak twenty words of English to defend himself ? Gramp's brother, uncle Gill, wasn't he a pistol! Rod seemed happy remembering, casting side glances, measuring, as if to say You're not bored? You follow me?, and interjecting spontaneous laughs.

It was Savannah who could draw Rod out: Jimmie-the-whisper, who's he? What's Preston's? How far's the lighthouse from your place? Why Easy Street? One Sunday afternoon—the mellowest Indian Summer, the air all warm embraces, the earth dizzying with yellow orange red brown leaves— Savannah packed a basket lunch and Dalton bought a case of beer and the four rowed over to Picnic Point for the day. They walked, swam, played ball. Toward sunset, flopped all four, Rod said, "Look, Cory— Reminds me of the Cat Rock." Far out, a man hunched in stillness in a motionless canoe did look like the round of a rock protruding from the water.

"Cat Rock? What's that?"

"It's a gigantic rock," Cory said, "one of the multitude the glacier dropped when it melted. Remember Professor Finch's lectures on end moraines? They're all over the north shore, eerie and beautiful, primitive, especially when there are no people around. The Cat Rock's in Greenport in deep water just below a sand cliff with wooden stairs to the beach, called the Sixty-Seven Steps.

"It's where we almost killed Sinic."

Rod was staring with a look of unmistakable pain.

"Sinic!"

"You mean *you* did?" Savannah's startled mouth opened; her teeth caught the light.

"You never told me, Rod."

"No. You were gone then. It's not something I like thinking about."

Cory understood that. Some memories you tried to repress—bodies, buddies, no one would ever see again. The *nothing* could not fill their spaces; the spaces were theirs, and forever.

"What happened, Rod?"

"Don't, Savannah," Cory said.

"Tell me, Rod."

"Savannah!"

She ignored. "Tell me."

With Rod she was insatiable. What did she want? Was it a lust in her to know everything about them both. But he wanted to know too. Dalton glanced from one to the other, always the discreet, silent observer.

Rod said, "I won't tell that one—it's too near a crucifixion—and I get the guilts. You remember Jimmie-the-whisper, Cory. The summer after high school—the summer the Krauts surrendered, then the Japs, and you came back to the States on points, Cory—I went on the skimmer boats, the *Annie B*, pretty much of a wreck, half the time in dry dock because of a sulky engine. Had a good skipper then—McCurdy his name was. I was green, too green, though I did know the water—always before that on small boats, yachts we took fishing parties on, the summer before on a ferry between Greenport and Shelter Island, and once on the old *Catskill* out of New London, and all my life—don't laugh—rowing in the crick for crabs and setting out lobster pots on the Sound."

When he started to tell it, the Island came back with all its thick heat, the heavy scent of pine and shell and acrid salt.

"That summer I worked on the *Annie B* with some Polacks I've known since I was a kid. It was my first trip, and the crew made fun of me because north off Block Island I got seasick despite all my years on the water. My soft hands bled from the work. Once I was nearly swept overboard. 'Too bad, no good riddance to bad rubbish,' they kidded, but they depended on me because I knew songs by the dozen, played the guitar, and told stories and jokes to keep up with the best of them.

"There was an old man, fifty-five maybe—Jimmie-the-whisper they called him from a throat ailment he'd had for years that made his voice come like a brush scrubbed over boards. He'd been with the *Annie B* since they christened it and he looked it, so gray that his bloodshot eyes wet and shining seemed to be bleeding openly. Half the time he'd not shave. 'Does the skin good not to,' he'd say. It gave him pleasure to rub it. At first he didn't take to me, but one night he stumbled on me, knocked a book out of my hand, picked it up. We stared at each other for an instant; then he dropped the book into my hands and left without a word.

"Jimmie didn't say anything until two days later, crossing me after he'd left night mess. 'That's the book's got the boy Tom's Alone, in London?' 'Yes, by Dickens,' I said. `And that died?' he said. 'Yes.' From that moment on Jimmie adopted me. One night on deck he said, 'Listen—I got a *new* system of reading. You just make like every bit of you's one naked eye—got it?' 'Yes.' 'Then one ear and then all nose—one thing at a time, see?—and then a hand. Now open your mouth and let it all come inside you—got it?' 'Yes,' I said. 'Boy, when you get that down pat, you get to be part of everything, your toes are seeing and your eyes feel and your hands can smell—got it?' 'Yes. You're trying to tell me I'm dead,' I said, instantly ashamed because Jimmie looked so trapped, his eyes glittering in the faint light, so close I could smell sweat and tobacco and rancid and something indefinable I'd never smelled before. I was about to apologize when Jimmie burst into such an overpowering laugh that it struck like a mute's who'd suddenly gained speech. Everybody looked. His eyes filled from such hard laughing. He shouted it, 'Dead! By Jesus, you're right, boy—you got it! *You* can read. Ha-ha-ha,' and dashed off, roaring. You could hear him all over the ship.

"For the first time the ship appeared strange to me. The men guarded silence for the rest of the night, breaking out more noisy than usual only in the morning when Jimmie was around them again.

"After that Jimmie developed an obsession for turning to me. He woke me early, prodded, led, initiated me, describing every facet of the ship, talking and teaching, fearful he'd never tell it all before the day was over and we bunked down. Sometimes waking, I could hear him muttering in the night; other nights his bunk was empty. Once I slipped out on deck and seeing Jimmie against the rail turned back, but Jimmie said, 'Come over here. You think I didn't mean what I said about the eye? You think that?' Jimmie sidled up against me. He looked angry, his wet eyes caught the moon, his cheeks hollowed to mere cavities, and the clothes hung as if his flesh were dissolving on his bones. Even in the thick fresh sea air I smelled the rancid breath and that indefinable odor of Jimmie's flesh; and staring at that narrow bony head and the loose sack of skin, I couldn't speak. 'Speak!' Jim clutched my wrist. 'Boy,' he said, his voice vibrating so that now I understood it was not anger, 'I taught you what I know, but I still want to tell you *me.* All that . . . My wife and I, we fought from the first day, she cheated on me. My mother went quick, I was three, and my father . . . Well, on Easy Street everybody drinks, they fight on Saturday night so bad the paddy wagon's always on call, the cops beat them, husbands come over to haul their wives out of somebody's bed. You don't show for work on Monday, you get laid off, live on somebody, and that's life—it stinks. You crawl in muck—you can't get clean, you can't even stop the smell, you can't see no end to crawling. Christ, you wish it'd end, but where's the guts to end it? The throat's dying—see? Only all of a sudden a corner inside you comes to life, it burns—yes, *burns.* You feel heat inside you, something's making *heat.* You know what? I took all my clothes off and looked at my body in the mirror. I felt my flesh, every inch. I looked at the fine blood in my eyes. I never *saw* it before, so red, moving, moving. I *heard* it moooove—like that! And I never really saw my wrinkles before either, every one clear—and after that saw them in everybody's face. A lady comes down the street in town now, I got to stop and look. I want to touch what she lived in those wrinkles, sex and sickness and dying, the kids torn out of her, all that life. Oh, you think I'm just an old man raving, but I'm not, I'm all alive now. One day I touched my throat. I said *I'm going to die, it's eating me, I'm disappearing.* Suddenly I felt the sound moving. I felt *me* in my throat, moving. And now I want to feel, I want to hear everything. I sit on the john and hear me and feel the heat. I'm glad it's eating me. I don't want it to stop.'

"His hand pulsed. I felt the blood. It drove into my own heart so painful I wanted to shout *What are you telling me for*? Quick too I thought, *He's trying to pour all this into me,* and I cried, 'Yes, *yes!*' then abruptly said, 'I'm going to be sick.' Jimmie let me loose. 'Yes, be sick,' he said. As I quickly turned, I caught a glimpse of Jimmie's face, thin and long and gray as leftover ashes, nothing but white fire in his eyes. I vomited over the side and hung on to the rail, relieved, drawing the air in deep, of a sudden so exultant that I laughed, feeling the impact of Jimmie's words and turned to say *Yes, I know,* but Jimmie was gone.

"For the next three days nobody, under orders, saw Jimmie but the first mate and the Captain. But they heard him off and on. Between snatches of sleep and passing out, he screamed in agony. On the third day the men wandered the deck, not seeking one another's company, staring at the water, only occasionally coming together and laughing and joking with more noise than they could usually stand—then silence. Jimmie and the sea were hatefully quiet and there was no wind to batter the silence away.

"We were headed home.

"When the crew heard the mate shout (it was almost dark, that minute when the sea and the sky and the ship began to be one dark thing), they thought something had happened to the mate because Steve heard him stumble and swear 'Goddamn it' and then 'Je-*sus*!' soft with shock and surprise, and go down on his knees, and then shout, 'Steve!'

"'Jimmie looked so sudden strong, you wouldn'a believed, and looked—he looked *well*—ya know?' Steve said.

"'He's dead,' the Captain said. The mate didn't move, though he knew it too. When he did move, he touched the head and the hand. The others came around.

"I couldn't believe the size of him, a shrunken pile of used rags and almost no flesh under, even the bones hard to see, just head and hands, dried things. 'It's not Jimmie, it's nothing,' I said. Instinctively my hand went out and Steve told me, 'Don't,' for no reason. I looked defiantly at him and slipped my hand into Jimmie's shirt to feel his chest where the heart is . . . Cold. How long had he been lying there? I pressed, I couldn't help it—it felt so hard and all bone. I tried to touch something solid but I couldn't, only could look at Jimmie's hand stretched out to the rail—reaching for what? And know what? I pulled my hand out and went to the rail myself and—I don't know why—stuck my own hand inside my shirt and rubbed it over my chest, I couldn't help it, and I felt my own heat so hot after Jimmie's cold chest that it shocked me. I said, 'It's me so alive,' and for a minute I wished I were dying, I *was* dying. I knew that was true too and I was suddenly giddy with a strange kind of joy, in some way glad Jimmie was dead. I seemed to burn with the fire in *his* blood, his disease, and I wanted to tell Jimmie. I went back, but Jimmie was gone. Steve and two others had carried him in. I went after them. I wanted to tell Jimmie I knew, even when I knew it was too late. I said 'Jimmie' and started to laugh. I almost fell down the steps. 'Jimmie, listen!' I cried and then the mate hit me."

Rod was staring at the water. Did he see Jimmie there? Nothing but the wind moved. Leaves fell. Rod caught at one. It crackled in his hand.

Savannah was silent, fixed on Rod's face. Cory knew her—voices caught her, carried her. She eased into a story and could hardly get out; she was long coming back. She gazed. It was hard for *him* not to stare at Rod. The moment was unfathomable. Rod was. And *it* was, this hold he had. From where? Cory thought, unable to quench the wonder. From his father? He couldn't know; he'd never known his father. From Gramp, the preacher in Gramp? From Gram? She could tell a story in such a soft voice, so near a whisper, that the vaguest rise and fall of her voice, the near threat of silence, the halts, held you spellbound. Cory was filled; he would spill. Savannah gazed, hung. Cory wanted to slap her out of it.

Dalton said, "I'd hate to have been in Jimmie's shoes. I couldn't have handled it." A fine leak of sun made Dalton's hair luminous.

"None of them could." The lament in Rod's voice galled Cory.

"You never told me, Rod."

"When'd I ever get the chance?"

"You could've written it."

"There are things you don't write. That's only one of them."

And the others?

"*I'd* hate to have to write that," Dalton said. "It'd be as bad as living it all over again. Not for me."

Savannah said. "What you do to me, Rod."

"Come off it, Savannah," Cory said. "You do it to yourself. One sight of the *Annie B* would cure you forever."

She was watching Rod.

"It's old, filthy, the chains and winch are rusted all over, and the crew's so dirty they stink. Nothing romantic about it."

"Whoa, Cory. *I* was part of that crew. They stay as clean as they can. *You* try to stay clean on a skimmer boat a week or two at sea sometime. At least, it's an honest stink from honest work. You can wash it off. That's more than you can say about people whose minds stink—you can't wash them. How'd you know the *Annie B*?"

"You forget—it's my town."

"Bristol's your town."

"No. Greenport is. I've made it mine."

Once he had hated it all but the sea and shore. Every object of his loathing was clear to him until the war, when Bristol and Greenport were suddenly places on the other side of the ocean, which only his imagination could cross. Then, because objects of shame become so specific, the objects he had expended his shame on crystalized so clearly that he could visualize them in the air, sure he could touch them: they were all he had; they made the world he'd left real. So he clung to the summers on the Island as the only real world he knew, clung to every object and every person. He needed them, he loved them, his love stirred his imagination, and his imagination made the town live in him.

Maybe his true town existed only inside him.

"I eat it up, digest every corner of it, if you want to know."

Then that summer there was the other island. Plum Island. Eden. His mother. And Reggie Webb.

But where was the father?

Now, in so short a time, Pete seemed to inhabit a life Cory had lived long ago. Study did that: it set earlier times far back; in the intensity of study they lost their own intensity. The loss seemed unjust. Study was too obsessive; like the stress of war, it was out of proportion to what was *out there*. Here, all your energy, usually dispersed, was concentrated on one thing at the cost of too many exclusions; and constant study made relationships too abnormal, frictive.

"You've got your secrets too, haven't you?" Rod said.

"We all have."

"I haven't." Savannah looked out toward the sky over the lake and smiled to herself, untouchable. The light made her eyes and lips bolder, and the sharp shadows between her teeth made them bold, base, enticing.

"Plain Savannah Goshen," Cory said. "What you see is what you get."

"Depends on how keen your eye is. You could miss a thing."

"If it's there."

"It's here, Cory." Her voice faltered. She rolled over on her stomach and, leaning on her elbows, gazed into the ground. Rod's eyes were on her breasts. Savannah turned her head.

Dalton caught Rod's stillness. "Shall we take the boat back?" He headed for the shore.

"You satisfied, Savannah?" Cory said. They were gathering their things.

"Why do you have to spoil it, Cory?" Rod said.

"Rod, don't," Savannah said.

Cory did not admit it, but at times something in him spilled and stained, smudged. He couldn't hold it back or withdraw it. He feared it. It was like a secret thing he had not been able to define. Sometimes he thought *It's family,* something handed down in blood which must run it. He imagined it as a curse on the Verity side—in Gramp's marrying that girl who hung herself when her parents had the marriage annulled; in the fire and all the drownings and Gram's divorce from Gramp because of his crippled hands, *I can't, Tom;* in Ma's living with Pete all those years till her lifelong passion flared at sight of Reggie Webb and, once released, broke all law when she ran off to live on Plum Island alone with him as if it were Eden instead of a welcomed refuge from the world. She had deep pride—not vanity, but pride that she was a woman, and *that* woman, proud to be the daughter of Tom Verity. That pride she buttressed against the world's pride in its conventions, knowing they would, and did, say You see what it comes to, pointing to her and Reggie Webb and to her abandoned sons and common-law husband and to that old man crippled in the fire at sea, whom she would always harbor with love, to whom she would remain loyal even in clashes between her and any of her husbands over her father: Pa's staying with me. Pa goes where I go. What'd Pa do if we sell the house? You're my husband and I love you, but he's my father. He's been a help to me all my life, Pa has, long before you ever came along, and I couldn't give him up, ever.

Was her father her curse?

Passion. How could one woman contain so much passion? Was there too much in all of them? Their prison. His.

His he fought down.

It did not blind his mother to what he and Rod and Pete and all their friends (she hadn't told even Agnes) would suffer after she had left to meet Reggie Webb.

That summer on Plum Island she'd said, "Cory, I'd never say anything mean or untrue about Pete. I tell you this simply to be fair. I don't tell it to clear my name with you. What I chose is my responsibility, but I know Pa and you and Rod have to bear it too. Pete's a good man. He was always good to you kids and me, but he'd got to drinking after hours and he'd got in with a crowd with plenty of money—you'd know some of them by name at least—and he'd come home at all hours of the morning, later and later. He'd begun to run around and I was afraid of what he might bring me, *you* know. You must have heard us arguing at all hours, though the door was always closed. Finally he started going out with a little Portuguese girl, Mary, from State Street—he thought I didn't know—and I think he was helping her out, giving her money, maybe buying a house though we were renting. He'd always remind me—I never meant to tell you and Rod—that we weren't married."

"You and Pete!" It pricked his heart.

"No, we weren't. . . . I'm sorry, Cory."

All the day stained.

"Better to hear it from me than from— Well, only three people know. I know how much understanding you have, though sometimes you fester about things. You still do, about my leaving, don't you?"

How she knew!

He smiled.

"Still."

She set her hand on his neck, fingered the hair.

"That's my boy. Nothing can change that, not a war, nothing."

"Didn't you want to marry Pete?"

"Pete wouldn't marry me. He'd never marry anybody. He won't marry that Portuguese girl either. Something Catholic maybe. I don't know why he didn't go into the church; maybe he just couldn't direct all his energy that way. . . . Pete's a good man. It was an accident we fell in together. It was after the divorce from your father. I was living with Pa. We were barely making it. I ran into Pete on a corner one night. I'd just gotten off the bus from Warren, and he was hanging on the lamppost. He'd got a job at the diner, just started, not a cent to his name. It was terribly cold. We started to talk. He had nowhere to go. He couldn't stay out in that cold. We could set up something in the kitchen . . . There was nothing between us. It went on that way for a while; he stayed to help me. That was before I got Rod. Since the divorce, Ma'd had him in Greenport. Before I could get custody, I had to prove to the judge that I had a place for Rod to live and could support him, and between Pa and Pete I could make it. But every time I got a job, sooner or later your father'd call and tell them I was divorced—they'd fire me. I had to lie. Nobody'd give a divorced woman a job. He was mean about it, he wanted me back. That was long before I got custody of you—that was the next step. Your father was going to put you in a home, and I didn't know it. He'd written to Ma, and Ma wrote to me or I'd never have known. Your father loved Ma and kept in touch with her for a while. Put you in a home!

It drove me near crazy. I had to get you before it happened. I went to a lawyer.

"Pete was all for taking you. He never questioned anything, but he never wanted to get married, never wanted to own a house, never wanted a baby, never wanted responsibility—I don't know why. Things happen inside us that we don't know are happening; sometimes we never find out what they are. I always wondered what had caused Pete to avoid a permanent attachment. I always felt single. . . . "

She'd confessed it all to him. At that instant she was abruptly too real, too woman, but he knew she was acknowledging him as an equal, the war veteran, the man Cory. They were becoming more than mother and son—friends, partners.

That day, after she'd told him, he'd wandered the beach. Drifting clouds cast dark shadows over the sea.

His father.

Pete.

Reggie Webb.

I don't know why I spoil things, Rod.

Stained.

"Poor Pete," Rod had said when he'd told him. "And she *married* Reggie Webb? That's bigamy, isn't it?"

"She's a common-law wife, and she's in another state. Who'd know? Who'd care?"

"Pete might."

"Not if what Ma told me about that Mary is right."

"Well, he's entitled—isn't he?—now, anyway. He can't sit home and brood. He'd go crazy. A man goes nuts without somebody around. I'd hate to be in his shoes. I'd hate to be alone. I'd want to be near the one I loved."

"Did you have someone special in mind?"

"You. We have to stick together."

"Like Ma and Reggie Webb."

"All right, yes, if you must know—like Ma and Reggie Webb. If you think about it, you can't blame Ma, can you? *I* did when it happened because I was thinking about what everybody'd say, but what good did that do? Do you think people care about *us*? No. We have to care about each other. We're all we've got."

"Are we?"

"Why do you pick at me like that, Cory? You're my brother. Do you think I'd let anybody stand in the way?"

"She didn't. You're like her, Rod. You'd go all the way."

Passion chose. You went where it carried you. Something in you succumbed to it; something made you aware that without it you were dead, made you think *this, now.*

Why don't they go all the way, Cory? Oh, Fatso!

Rod said, "Wouldn't you, Cory?"

Why don't they?

Ma had gone all the way. That, against his will, he grudgingly admired in her, her instinct not only to yield but to direct it her way, knowing what it would cost. She was willing to take what the world cast at her; that was the measure of her passion for Reggie Webb. She found in him what the world was blind to. Such passion could make life quicksand. Something in you had to die so you could live it.

"I don't know, Rod."

"You don't know?"

"*No*, I don't!"

"But I'm your brother."

"Well, you're here."

"That's not what I meant."

"Why should I have to *say* it? We'll know if ever a situation comes up, won't we?"

"It won't ever come up."

"How do you know that?"

"I won't let it."

"And how will you stop it?"

"I'll know that when the time comes."

"You're a mystery to me, Rod."

"To you of all people, I don't want to be."

He hated himself when he upset Rod or Savannah or Dalton—because Rod's coming had actually brought him a kind of peace: Rod was a lifeline to the Island, to Ma and Gramp and the past he'd felt cut off from in service and here at Wisconsin. In Rod he could see and touch and hear the past, it *was*, and the future was *now*. Then, Cory thought, the *father* is inside us, waiting to escape into the son and his and his; scapes again again againagainagainagain, always now and always ahead.

The thought maddened. A voice silently formulated that thought. The voice was familiar. Fatso's! Never had it occurred to him that the voice he had *heard, seen* so often in letters, was incredibly like his own.

Cory was disappointed in himself: Am I becoming dependent on Rod? He'd sworn he'd never be. *She* had made him, if not actual head like Pete, emotional and practical head of the family. The three war years in the ETO had reinforced his independence. Was Rod's presence making him let down barriers that had enclosed all his youth? He didn't want to be weak. He *would* not. Yet when Rod was not at dinner at the Union, not at the library or the Rathskeller or the Campus Grill, he found himself in a restrained turbulence. And if Savannah were there—poor Savannah!—she became the victim. Then he was ashamed. Why should he be? He grew furious with himself; and the fury made him ashamed of being ashamed. Why would he be? He would ask How did this all start? What's happening to you, Cory Moorehead? At other times he wished Rod would leave campus, study elsewhere, take a job, go, get out of the apartment, leave him alone as he'd been before Rod had imposed—he *had*. Hadn't he been freed of ties once? Rod was quicksand under this tower Cory Moorehead. He saw Pisa leaning, saw Babel falling.

I'm afraid.

Of my own brother.

He sought solitude. He abandoned his table in the library, virtually exiling himself from the cafeteria and the Rathskeller and the Campus Grill, and studied with more than his usual concentration. That isolation cost because he wanted Savannah and Dalton and Rod; he had never realized how much. However, as always, he resisted his desires. Why? Professor Mann in one of their long meandering talks had said, "Because there's something of the propensity of the saint in you, Cory. I don't mean you're a saint or even interested in the church except as history and psychology, but you have a strong sense of sacrifice, a self-restraint inordinate in one who's young (surely it isn't something you learned during the war; it's been typical of you since youth). Like most distinguishing characteristics, your control may be both your salvation and your destruction or, to put it more mildly, the source of your successes and your failures as well as your joys and your agonies. You stand in your own way, so the miseries are multiplied and the joys are few, but, when they come, intensified almost beyond endurance, so much so that one desires them and fears them because such exaltation not only becomes almost unbearable but because the aftermath, the emotional troughs, are devastating pits which one fears even more than the exaltations. You've read St. John of the Cross and St. Theresa, Fray Luis of Leon, Meister Eckhart, and Hildegard of Bingen with me. You didn't recognize any aspect of yourself in them?"

"*You're* a mystery, Cory," Rod said. "We sit, we wait—no Cory. You holding a grudge against one of us? If you are, spill it or you'll never get rid of it. You know you."

"I'm writing papers. You know what that does to me."

"We all have to write papers. That never affected you before."

He thought he was safely hidden in a corner carrel in the stacks when a shadow cut off his light.

"Dalton! I thought you never studied in the library. Or has the world of economics changed?"

"I've been looking for you. Can we talk somewhere?" Dalton was always serious, but there was softness in his voice, not Dalton the callous. "In my car? Or we can drive somewhere for a beer."

In the car, Dalton was reluctant to move, ran his fingers over the wheel, dropped his hands to his lap. His thighs were thicker, and his waist.

"Are you wanting to gain weight?"

"I'm eating a lot these days."

"Since when? You were always too spartan for that, Dalton."

"Yeah. Well, I'm not that complicated, Cory—Vanna always says so—and I guess I'm not."

"You know better than that. There's no such thing as a simple person. So?"

"But it's not me. Or it's me, yes. And it's Vanna."

"You and Savannah?"

"No. You and Vanna."

"Me!"

"Aren't you aware, Cory—you should be—that you hold all of us together, but Vanna most. I've seen her in ways you haven't. She's splintered inside. I've been with her after she's left you—she goes to pieces. Her thoughts, talk, everything shows it—as if she's having a breakdown. She can control it as long as you're around, a superhuman effort on her part—at least, *I* couldn't do it—but the minute we're alone—"

"She takes it out on you?"

"Absolutely not—ever. I take advantage of it. I always have."

"I can't believe that. How?"

"Sex."

"Sex!"

"It's the only thing that keeps her going. I won't lie. That's not why I take advantage of her. I did from the beginning because it wasn't long before I realized she was using me. I don't believe she was consciously using me. She took everything that was happening to her out on me. I mean she put everything into sex, to *escape*, I think, forget. Jesus, she can fuck, Cory, if you want it straight. It took me a while to realize that it wasn't because *I* was so good that she wanted me. That was a blow. For a while we stopped. When Rod came and she came after me, came to the house at all hours, rapped on the door, threw pebbles at the window. She had to have it, she didn't care where either. God, I swore I'd never tell this, but I have to. I don't know how much longer she'll hang on. You'd think we'd all know, you and Rod too, but oh she's sharp, that girl. She's an actress. It's pure will, all she can summon up, that keeps her from letting you and Rod see a thing. For a while she kept it from me too. I thought she wanted *me.* Of *course* she wants me. She wants to get married. She's afraid for some reason she never will be; and I'm *home* to her. Now, since we'd started something, she thinks nobody will ever have her. She wants me but not because she loves me; she thinks I can't stand to give it up it's so good. I'm too strong, or weak maybe, because I want what I want and I'm going to have it; and my plans—it's brutal—don't include Savannah. That makes me a machine, doesn't it? Well, I admit that, and the only thing that helps me justify myself is that I realize it's not me she's fucking. How do you like that, Cory? She's just fucking—she's using me to keep on being Vanna, to keep sane because she feels sure the real thing will never come along. The hell is, while we're fucking, she's so good I'm not myself. I don't think—I *believe* this, Cory—anybody else will ever be able to do that to me."

He believed Dalton meant it because he wasn't the familiar Dalton now. Was this the true Dalton? His hands struggled, his usually controlled voice tumbled words out, and his usually serene eyes flicked and darted, though nothing could change that cold blue, belying the soft goldish hair, too angelic for his lithe, lean, disciplined body and his too often rigid mind.

"I can't handle her anymore. She breaks. Nothing matters to her. I *know* it. She can't find her *mind,* Cory. Rod helps. Since he came, he at least staves off a kind of madness in her. He doesn't know that. In case you're thinking it, I'm not jealous of Rod. You see why I wouldn't be, because whatever she needs *I* can't finally give it to her. I'm a stopgap, and I care too much about her to go on this way, fucking just for the sake of fucking, the way we started off, the way *I* did anyway. I've hurt her, but I don't want to *harm* her, her mind I mean, just by hanging on for sex, though there's really more than that to us. She taught me that. She's selfless, Cory. She doesn't exist for Vanna; she exists for us. I realize it now. She can't stop giving. And who's going to be there to deserve it?"

Passion. It laid its head against the seat cover between him and Dalton. It lolled on its very white fleshy neck. Its mouth was open in an ambiguous half-smile. The wide separated teeth were wet; the eyes glittered with sun; and the hair, not thick, spread in savage Medusa strands. Vanna.

A miserable feeling came over him. He felt dirty, smirched by his lack of volition because he had had to wait for Dalton to come to him and tell him. He himself was so selfish in his indirect possession of Savannah and Rod and Dalton, each in a separate way, that he had lost the habit of putting himself in their places. He had been looking at them only from his self-centeredness, which was—wasn't it?—a kind of madness too. But Dalton! This confession was a measure of Dalton's love for her, a measure too of his own niggardly self-love, *mine.*

Dalton, as if reading his thoughts, pricked him:

"You can save her. You two are like a seesaw. Some tug of war goes on between the two of you all the time that can be hell or fun or brilliant or just comfortable, so enviable that I wish *I* were you, Cory. Does that surprise you? But I'm not capable of that kind of intimacy. Sex alone can't give that, but with sex it'd be almost perfect. There's an emotional chemistry going on beween you I don't know a thing about."

" You think we do?"

"I think deep down you could."

"I could force it? That's what you're telling me?"

"I'm telling you—because it's going to make all the difference for a while—I'm not having sex with Vanna anymore. I've already stopped."

"You know what that'll do to her."

"I told you, but if we keep on it will be ten times more destructive. She's half crazy now. She can't disguise that with me. It's a miracle she's been able to with you and Rod."

To remove all disguises would be the miracle. The simplest path was the most difficult. *Always take the hardest way. It costs, but it takes you farthest. You'll know yourself.*

"I didn't think you had this in you, Dalton."

"Now you know." His hand settled comfortably on Cory's leg. He said gently with an intonation that might have been Savannah's, "Don't go too far away from us, Cory."

"You're the one who's leaving. It's already begun. It's going to hurt, though it's for our own good."

Cory visualized the four figures at their oak table in the Rathskeller. Three. Two. One. A table and four empty chairs stood dark against the window and the lake beyond.

Nothing.

"Sometimes it's you who leaves, Cory. You seem to disappear right in front of us. You're not with us."

"You haven't missed a thing, have you?"

Dalton cuffed him. "Poor Dalton the Econ major!"

"Speaking of disguising things!"

"Vanna never said, but I think what hurts her most is you cutting us off in midair."

"The mind has its own rules."

"I know. It's easy to tell others what to do, but—" Dalton's voice bolted. "*Look* at me, Cory. You'll be there for Savannah, no matter what?"

Dalton's cold blue eyes exacted the promise.

"You will, won't you, Cory?"

"Why, Dalton, you're saying . . . you love her."

His head and shoulders went rigid, military, his gaze unflinching.

"I told you: I can't love her, and that's it. But you'll *be* there?"

"You don't have to ask me that, Dalton."

"But I do. I want to hear you say it, because if *you* say a thing, I believe you."

"Yes, then. You know I will."

Dalton released a slow, almost measured sigh.

In the fall there was a national long distance telephone strike. When the landlady left a note to call Operater 28 in Riverhead, New York, Cory was apprehensive.

"This is Cory Moorehead."

"I'm calling for your mother . . ."

"My mother!"

"First, she wants you to know she's all right." The operator's voice was cautious and kind. "Your stepfather and your uncle Ben were drowned in the Gut on Wednesday."

"Drowned!"

"Your mother saw it all and it left her in a state of shock. She couldn't talk for three days. She *particularly* said to tell you not to come."

"But the funeral—"

"The bodies and the rowboat haven't been found."

After a silence, she said, "Are you there?"

"Yes."

"Your mother says there's nothing anyone can do for her right now, you can't help her, nobody can. She wants you both to stay and take your exams."

"Yes."

"I'm very sorry," she said.

"Thank you."

He hung up and sat on the edge of the sofa. For a long time his eyes traced the pattern in the carpet. Hinkle, he thought, and Samms, Arlen, Pansa, dead in Normandy. All he had were the names because he could put no face, no body, into the space they had occupied. Was Ma staring at emptiness, trying to see, trying to *create* Reggie Webb and Ben, trying to defy her own sight and comprehend emptiness? She would never yield to *nothing*. She would work, work with more than her usual vitality, though he knew that sewing at her Singer, on the sun porch alone knitting, she wouldn't be able to keep from staring into vacancy. Ma! He was overwhelmed by a feeling of guilt—he wanted to confess to her—as if *he'd* been responsible for Reggie Webb's drowning because he had not wanted Reggie Webb with them. He had never liked Reggie Webb. Somehow he'd feared that dark hairy image of the uncouth he had too often seen that summer coming up the beach like a monster out of the sea, feared it as he had feared the face in that window in the house next door on Benefit Street. She had all her life loved Reggie Webb. She had dared to risk all, even him and Rod if they were obstacles to her love. Passion. How could she know it would bring her to Nothing? *Was* it? No. Now it came to him with such piercing revelation that his eyes filled, his throat pained: *she did not care*. She would take whatever came. Reggie Webb meant life to her. Her love gave all the rest meaning. *Why don't they, Cory?* He wanted to cry out *Some do, Fatso*. She did. She had been willing from the outset to face even nothing. He was ashamed; he had misjudged her. He knew her now. She could bear anything. He was certain she would do it again, even knowing how it would end.

"Enormous. She *is*," he whispered, flooded with ambiguous elation. He had never known how much he loved her.

He could not see the pattern in the carpet.

At the news of Ben, Rod broke down. Ben, whom he had lived with his first few years after the divorce, had been like a father to him, with Gram his Ma.

"I should have gone when you were on Plum Island with them, Cory. Ma won't be able to talk to me about him. She'll know he's a blank in my life."

"When you talk about the dead, you talk to yourself, Rod."

"That's the way you handle yours?"

"Mine?"

"Your war buddies."

"You can't hold the dead back." They came at will. You could never get them out of you. "She won't be able to."

"She won't want to. That's the only right thing about it. She'll have him forever, the way you have *them*."

"She may not have anything else."

"She won't need it. She'll hang on to that. That'll be enough for her."

"No. It's never enough. It won't be for her, she's too alive. You don't know what you'll need tomorrow."

"It'd be enough for me if I had the one I wanted. I could stand the rest. But I'm not like Ma. I'm afraid."

"Afraid! You were never afraid of anything in your life. You'd take on anybody or anything—"

"You're thinking athletics, Cory—that's different. What you do in a game may not change a thing in your life. When Ma left, she knew what the effect was going to be on all our lives. Suppose you loved somebody and wanted that person and nobody else, somebody you were afraid might not love you . . . That's no ball game, and that's worse than your war because it goes on all the years. I'd be afraid I'd be rejected. Then what? And I'd be afraid if I *didn't* act because I might have been accepted. So I'd do nothing, I'd be in limbo forever. Dead. I wouldn't have anybody inside me, I wouldn't be inside anybody. and I want to be, Cory."

"You'd be dead then too. She's inside Reggie Webb and he's dead. And Ben too. But that's only half. Reggie Webb and Ben are alive in her. What's important is what she has *here*, what she has of when he and Ben were alive."

"I wish I could talk to her. We had such good talks when you were in the ETO."

"When the telephone strike's over. Besides, she can't talk now. If she could, I don't believe she could concentrate enough to listen."

Rod was looking out across the lake, his hands gripping the window frame. The window went blank. It was starting to snow.

"You coming to the library?"

"No," Rod said. "I'm meeting Vanna to straighten her out on trig."

"She's no mind for trig."

"She took it as a challenge to prove to you she could handle it. Your wisecracks get to her, Cory. You should be careful what you say."

"She has more sense than to take my gibes seriously. They're signs of affection."

"Not if you don't let up. They bite."

When the phone strike was over, his mother called. "I wanted to tell you I'm getting along all right. Without Pa I don't know what I'd do. And Ma's staying with me. I can't tell you what help the coast-guardsmen have been. The Captain and the sailor who brought me home after Reggie and Ben were drowned drop in all the time. They can't bring me enough food. They make sure I'm not alone too much."

He heard her breath break.

"Ma?"

"They did everything, the paperwork, all the running around. But I'll tell you all that, and what happened to Reggie and Ben in the Gut, one day when you're here. If I tell it, I see it . . . I can't go near the water, Cory. I was afraid to cross the Gut on the boat. The water was rough. I couldn't stay on deck. I wanted to because I didn't want to be with anybody; but I had to go inside the cabin because if I looked into the water—I can't explain it—the waves moved and moved, and the water . . . I don't know . . . fascinated me, I wanted to go into it, I was afraid I would. The Captain must have known it would be like that because he made someone stay with me all the time. He had a young man bring me home. The coastguardsman didn't want to leave me. He's been back as often as he can. He's so good to Ma . . ."

"We'd give anything if we could be with you. Rod'll be sorry he missed you, but he'll call now that the strike's over. He misses you—he doesn't say much—but he loved the time with you when I was in service. You were his first war buddy."

She laughed.

"That's the first time I've laughed! Oh, Cory, it feels so good."

"It'll come. Just don't let anything stand in the way. Let yourself go."

Don't cling. He couldn't say that to her at such a moment. He'd wanted to bring his buddies back to life too. She'd been beside him at the Congregational Church when they'd had a memorial service for the dead and missing in the war. He'd heard her tell Pete that evening, "Cory was trembling. I dared not look at him. I didn't want to embarrass him."

"Remember—I'm all right. You can't do anything for me. It's enough to know you're there and putting all you have into your studies. I'm proud of you both."

"Tell Gram and Gramp hello."

From October on, off and on all winter, snow fell in silent veils or in furies of white riled by winds or in heavy straight falls. The white city was too beautiful to believe, quickly illusive, but almost at once defiled, darkened by pervasive slush. Damp went to the bone, but the cold fired life—skiing, skating and ice boating and ice fishing on the lake.

His mother's rare letters were sparse. He read them quickly, handed them to Rod, replied sporadically. In spring, feeling guilty one night, he called her—"Just to catch up on things."

"Out here?" She laughed. "There's just wind and water and sand. Thank God for spring. The tulips are beginning to break ground. The forsythia's like a fountain. You should see the swamp willow blaze when the sun comes up—it's almost golden then. The lawn's coming to life. My azaleas'll start coming soon. Ma's glad. She sits on the porch with me all the time. She loves color. Ma's the one who began all this gardening I have to keep up all summer long."

"You love it!" Her green thumb made anything burgeon.

Her talk burgeoned too, such a blue streak. She must have been too quiet too long; her voice took on increasing strength.

"It's so good to talk, Cory. I'm sorry you and Rod didn't call together. Next time . . . What, Ma?"

"Gram's there?"

"Yes."

"Let me talk to her."

"Just a minute . . . German, what's she saying?"

"Who's German?"

"The coastguardsman who brought me home from Plum Island. He keeps tabs on us both. Hold on, Cory."

There was a long hiatus.

"Cory?" Gram's whisper, that whisper so ghostly it had made him and Rod rivet eyes and ears whenever she'd tell them stories, was softer now, and so far off. He strained to hear.

"Gram! I thought you'd all run off on me."

"Oh, no I was resting in your mother's room. I had to put my robe on. How's my first grandson? And how's my baby?"

"Getting too big for his britches, but between me and our friends Dalton and Savannah we keep him straight for you. He's no great scholar, but he's holding his own. Don't you worry, Gram."

"Not with you there, Cory."

His mother interrupted. "Hon, we're thrilled you called, but this is costing you a fortune. Ma couldn't be happier. Tell Rod— Well, you know what to tell Rod. Ma and I always miss you both. Come when you can."

"Wait. You didn't tell me how Gramp is."

"Since Reggie and Ben, Pa can't do enough for us. He's in and out all the time. You'd think he lived here."

"That's a new twist." Independent Gramp! He'd come to the back door, stand there, ask for the loan of sugar, bread, an ice pick, and seldom come in. "Pa," his mother would say, "there's some leftover goulash and a slice of pork," and before he could leave, he'd always tell Cory, "She'd load me down with eats."

Ma, he thought after, sounded actually happy; surely she was compensating for her grief. Ma believed in keeping sufferings *at home*. Naturally she didn't want him and Rod to worry. And she had Gram and, she had said, *German*.

The next call, in May, was from her. He could hear only breath, broken. "Ma, what's wrong with your voice?"

"Ma died this morning."

"Gram! But she wasn't even sick!"

"I didn't want you both to worry. Ma had cancer. I thought she was getting well. All this time, six months, I never for a minute believed she'd die. I can't believe she's gone now—"

As she spoke, bits of Ma's earlier conversation surfaced: *Ma's staying with me. Pa's in and out all the time. Ma's tired. Ma couldn't be happier.* How could he have missed the signs! What's happening to you, Cory Moorehead?

"Ma got out of bed yesterday, she put on her robe and came to breakfast. She looked so good, her cheeks were actually pink. 'It's a miracle,' I thought. We had such a good morning together. Then this morning I went in to Ma and raised her. She said she was tired and laid her head on my breast, and I held her. Sara happened to come in from round the corner. She went out to the kitchen. I don't know how long it was after, but I was still holding Ma when suddenly Doctor Spurling was standing in the doorway. 'What are *you* doing here?' I said. He came over and lifted Ma out of my arms. 'Your mother's gone,' he said." Ma went silent a moment. "I said, 'She can't be, she was just talking to me, she's just sleeping.' Sara came back in. I looked up at her. Then I knew Sara must have seen Ma was dead in my arms. She'd called him."

Cory said, "We'll come right away, Ma."

"No." She was emphatic. "No, Cory, there's no time. We're burying her in the morning."

"Tomorrow!"

"I know that's fast, but after Reggie and Ben, it's too close. I don't want to go through that wait again. German's helped with everything. I don't know what I'd do without him."

German.

"You boys were always on her lips, Cory. She was so thrilled to talk to you on the phone. She clung to that. She'd tell everybody, 'Cory talked to me from Wisconsin. He sounded so good, my Cory.' Is Rod there?"

"He's in class."

"She was the first mother he remembered. It'll break his heart."

"I know."

"Be gentle with him, Cory."

"I will, Ma."

"You were always the one Rod turned to. . . ." Her breath faltered. "He had to. Pete was good to you boys, but he was no father. He couldn't help it. He didn't know how to be."

"I'll tell Rod, Ma."

When the library closed he spotted him coming out of the reserve room in the quonset hut behind the library and intercepted him crossing to the Union.

"I've got some notes for Vanna."

"Walk with me a minute, Rod."

Perplexed, Rod followed as he took the path around the geology building to the dark slope overlooking the lake and the far woods.

"What's the mystery? You all right?"

"All right. I wanted to tell you—"

"It's not Ma!"

"No, but Ma called."

"What, then?"

"Gram died this morning."

"Gram!" It was a loud call.

"She had cancer for a long time. Ma didn't want to upset us."

"Jesus!"

"We can't blame Ma, Rod. She really thought Gram was getting well."

"Gram." The books bound by the leather strap quivered.

"Rod—"

"I'm fine, fine. I'll see you at the house. I promised Vanna the notes." He struck out in a half run down past the Union and headed up Langdon.

Cory too blamed his mother for not telling them. Always she wanted to protect them from pain and grief. Wasn't that a kind of theft? Inadvertently she was stealing some life that was *his* from him, and in his selfishness he *let* them; so he was stealing from himself, he was evading emotion, he was hoarding it against his will.

Gramp. He wanted to be there with Gramp. He saw the man who had never ceased loving Gram, looking out at dark windows where her light would never come on again. She had been taken from him again: the fire had taken her first, and now death. She had gone farther this time.

Gramp had always been courteous to her second husband, Otis, but in his heart the man did not really exist. Mary was his. She would always be his. She would remain inviolate, untouched, sacred. Gramp's life was founded on that love; there could be no other. He had never said why he had built his own little house in the rear on the old family plot, but he had claimed he would never leave his house for long, he would die there and be buried where his people were. Surely the unspoken reason was Mary. Between sips of tea which he couldn't keep down and regurgitated into the bucket he kept by his table, Gramp catnapped on the daybed. He must have tired of staring at the ceiling. What did he see there: the jilted girl who hung herself when he married Mary? his ten children? his trips from town to town carrying the Word? his grocery gone bankrupt from doling out credit to his own family? his partnership in the barge? the fire, poverty, divorce? Did the place help him bear the dry nights of his life, the hairshirt days shared only with his cats and the mongrel Pal? Unwillingly divorced, he could not survive without being near her: there, he might glimpse her in a window or doorway, crossing to Stell's, walking down any street, passing downtown: Morning, Mary. *Morning.* Nice day. *Beautiful!* You're looking fine. *Thank you, Tom.*

Though Cory had always loved Gram, he could not free himself from a certain change he'd come to feel for her because once, in a moment of compassion for Gramp, Ma had confided, "I don't know how Ma could have left him after all those years. Ma told me that after the fire she couldn't stand it at night when he touched her body with those crippled hands. She said, 'I can't, Tom. I can't.' I never got over that."

Cory never had either because he took Gramp's part. He identified with him. Gramp had lived so much of his life with them or in such close vicinity that he'd seen him virtually every day. He had lived in Gramp's words, in the rich undulance, the variegated tones, and vibrant resonances of that preacher and storyteller voice. He was convinced that after Gramp's divorce all the passion he felt for Mary sang in those sermons in the pulpits of the North Fork of Eastern Long Island, the itinerant substitute preacher's sermons of such concentrated and controlled and channeled passion that his words rose to the height of hymns, sublimations of such love that they stirred that invisible motion in the congregation. You could feel it in the silence.

"You know why I married your grandmother, Cory? She was the only woman I couldn't touch." Gramp would break into a cackle, but that was man talk and he was certain Gramp was not being vain about his conquests and his legendary good looks, but about her virtue. He would mock himself, the handsomest of the Veritys, the town legend, in the words of the old ballad,

Oh, where have you been, Billy boy, Billy boy,
Oh, where have you been, charming Billy?

Gram hated housework. Summers she'd put on her cap and sneakers, take a couple of buckets, and Cory and she would go berrying in the woods along the Sound. Most days, strange and solitary, she'd walk for hours along the shore. In Cory's early years, before her second marriage, rumor had it she'd walk the beach to meet her lifelong friend Frank, her lover then. Afternoons, she'd visit ailing Mrs. Fenton in her house on Main, thinking—she'd tell him this—maybe Mrs. Fenton would leave her a dollar or two one day. Often at dusk she'd sit on the lawn or in the falling light in the front room and in that remarkably soft whisper begin to tell stories, at intervals raising her voice with such natural art that her sound trapped you motionless. At his graduation, after his valedictory address, quietly, as he was opening her gift, the pink-gold Gruen watch, she said with as much overt affection as he was ever to know from her, "You were my first grandson."

He knew by heart what Gram had told. But what *hadn't* she told? He longed for that now. He wanted what had been in her head, and *more*, everything Ma and Gramp and the family knew. Her memory had died with her, what only she in all the world knew. *That* struck. History. Mine. Rod's. Because it was theirs now. Our life. History was a great cheese with holes. What had the girl, the woman, the old lady experienced? Faces from photographs, faces he'd never actually known, rose before him. *She* had known them—and how much more? On the dark street he imagined a horde of faces, the bodies of those dead of old age, war, drowning, of scarlet fever, whooping cough, *black* diphtheria . . . In the wake of Reggie Webb's and Ben's drowning, had Gram seen their deaths as a herald of her own? Now, all that remained of time gone lived in Ma and longest in Gramp. He must know that time or it would be gone too because all the family's time and space stood only in his flesh and Rod's. Too much of the past was blank, a dark terrain he could not tread, darker because if he dared venture into it, he would not know what ground he was moving on. He felt the emptiness. His thoughts tangled in that emptiness. He wanted to be there at home, with *his*, to hear what they were saying, to hear what all the relatives would reveal that he could hoard against time going.

Hours after he had told Rod about Gram's death, Cory went up the three flights to their rooms. The door was unlocked. Rod's books lay on a chair in the living room.

His bedroom door was half open. The sight on his bed halted. He never left it unmade. The spread, blanket, sheets were hanging from the foot of the bed. What gives?

Jesus!

Rod was sitting on the edge of the bed facing the window.

Savannah was stretched on his bed, naked. She thrust her head into the pillow.

A smear glittered on her leg. He couldn't take his eyes off it.

"Jesus!"

Then he slammed the door. He went into Rod's room and slammed the door.

He heard their rustling. He heard one—her?—leave.

Below, the street door sounded. Then nothing.

Rod was waiting.

"I was going to make the bed up. She wanted to, but I didn't want her to touch it."

She.

"In my bed!"

"We couldn't help it. It just happened, Cory. It was a bad moment, Gram and all. *You* know that. She felt sorry. She touched me, then we were on the bed . . ."

"Mine."

"She went in and sat on it."

"Bitch."

"She's your best friend, Cory."

"Best friend you call that—with my brother, on my bed?"

"She didn't intend to."

"You don't know her."

"It's you who don't. She's the best thing you've got."

"*I* haven't got her."

"She's your friend, Cory, more than a friend. You could have had her anytime. Why haven't you, Cory? Did you ever think of that?"

"Obviously *I* don't have to. You've got her now. How does that make you feel?"

"You really want to know . . .?" He hesitated. He said very quietly. "Like a man, Cory."

"Well, you don't have to prove your manhood in my bed!"

"What difference does it make?"

"I trusted you—both."

"And you can't now? But I'm your *brother*." Rod's voice cracked. "Okay, so *I* did it. Don't blame Vanna. She was just trying to console me. I was weak. It was the right moment . . . Now leave me alone."

"I'll leave you alone all right. I want you *out*, Rod."

"Out?"

"I want you to get out, move—"

"What?"

"As soon as you can."

"You mean that?"

"*Yes*, I mean that."

"Over Vanna?"

"My best friend and my brother. In my bed."

"You're jealous of Vanna?"

"I'm *not* jealous of Savannah."

"Then what? *What*?"

"From now on I want to be alone, alone. Do you understand?"

"That's what you want?"

"Yes."

"What you really want, Cory?"

"Yes."

"Then that's what you'll have. I'll get out as soon as I find a place. That suit you?"

"Fine."

"You really think it does, don't you? You know what your trouble is? I'll tell you straight. You don't know shit from Shinola about love, and you know why? Because you're afraid, Cory. We're all afraid. I'm afraid. Vanna's afraid. Even Dalton's afraid. Because it's unknown territory. You have to take the chance, like Ma. You ought to know what some of us want and how far we'd go for what we want, hoping it wouldn't destroy, or even if it did. Destroy—that's what we're afraid of. Well, what you get may be worth the destruction. You've got to take chances, or you're nothing, Cory."

Nothing.

"Cut it. Sermons I don't need." Rod's intensity, his recklessness, its sudden release made him apprehensive.

"I want to live by myself." He shut his bedroom door. He was trembling. Afraid. I'm afraid of *me*. He was. He stood facing the door. Rod hadn't moved, but when he did, Cory heard the hall door open and close and Rod go down the flights of stairs.

After, he saw Rod dark, a shadow. It wouldn't go.

It has to struggle against skin and bones it doesn't want, Fatso had said.

In the mirror he saw the bed.

He tore the bedclothes off and jammed them into a pillowcase.

He would not flag. *Work, for the night is coming when no man can work.*

He took up *Paradise Lost* where he'd left off: Eve. She had just eaten the fruit of the forbidden tree. In her absence Adam had been weaving a garland of flowers, a token of love for her. On her return blithely she told Adam what she had done. And Adam

Soon as he heard
The fatal Trespass done by Eve, amaz'd,
Astonied stood and Blank, while horror chill
Ran through his veins, and all his joints relax'd;
From his slack hand the Garland wreath'd for Eve
Down dropp'd, and all the faded Roses shed:
Speechless he stood and pale . . .

When his eyes met the words *first to himself he inward silence broke,* his vision blurred.

Not now, Milton.

But he insisted. Work saved you.

Back to Adam.

Rod came back late that evening to tell him, "I hit it lucky. Your old room on Bowen Court was empty. I took it. The Koenigs were happy as family. Like having you back, they said."

His room. There was an instant of something akin to jealousy. Was Rod moving into his past?

"It's better this way—for the books, everything."

"Yes."

For Savannah too. With him she showed no change, did not speak of the move. When Rod was present, and Dalton, whatever constancy was developing between her and Rod, she never flagged in her attention to him.

One night at the Campus Grill she insisted he go over Schopenhauer with her.

"Donovan's so exacting. He makes you reason along with Schopenhauer; if you can't, then you haven't read it. The concept of the will drives me crazy."

"Schopenhauer says everything's one great will, Will, and every man has a will which is part of the great Will."

"Then man hasn't a will of his own. If he's governed by the great will, what *it* does he does. That's determinism, isn't it?" She rested her chin on her bent arm, her head tilted concentratedly, cigarette ahang and bobbing from her full lips, eyes asquint as the smoke drifted up into her hair.

"The Will's life, and it's irrational. To the degree that you accept its impulses, you live."

"But that's chaos."

"No, because reason, which is one part of chaos—or maybe I'm adding this?—is constantly struggling to realize itself by ordering chaos. It's like the head—the little will has to use the larger Will for its purpose or you can't function. Ironic as it seems, that's part of the action of the irrational—it *makes* reason realize itself; it challenges reason to channel impulses. Unfortunately reason can never rest because it may be so suddenly overcome by the very irrational it is trying to direct. Every outbreak of chaos is a reminder to reason, to go to work and reorder things."

She gazed into the wall behind him. "It's clear but too abstract for me. I have to see things, and touch."

"You don't usually see and feel your heart beating, do you?"

She laughed. "Not unless somebody takes my pulse."

"And then it's ordered, isn't it?"

"I see that. But you do feel your heart if some powerful emotion overcomes you, and that can blow your mind. Then where are you? It's hard to look at the world outside yourself and know what Schopenhauer's talking about. I mean reason it out. It seems to me you're dependent every minute on what *it,* the Will, is doing to you. You're born that way. You don't have any choice. If you're a victim, how can your little buck against such an enormous thing running through you and the entire universe?"

"Discipline. Reason. That depends. Schopenhauer says there are those, most of us, who are caught in the struggle for survival; those, like saints, who resist life to fulfill it in an afterlife; and those few tragic heroes, who *choose* to defy the great will and try to direct its power their own way for an instant, but by doing that they reveal the *very power* of that great will working through them. If Medea *must* be swept away in that great passion, she seizes the opportunity to use it for a moment *her own way."*

"But in tragic works most of the heroes die!"

"Yes, but *not,* as Schopenhauer and Nietzsche claim, resigned.

Neither really understood tragedy. After expounding so much about the Will, both of them failed to see that the true tragic hero *never* resigns his will to the greater will, no, but defies that mysterious universal will. The irony is that in defying it he *allies* himself with the great will, he's *loyal* to it, but he doesn't realize that the great will is acting through him—*he's* brought *that* about by his action—and that the cost of its revealing an alien justice incomprehensible to our human sense of justice is his own destruction. What's so awesome is not the extremity but the absolute *purity* of the hero's actions (what Christians would call unadulterated good or evil, like Macbeth's) *beyond good and evil.* If the greater will is *not* capable of an act of such purity, then the hero's action in the face of it diminishes the greater will in our eyes because in that moment *the hero* seems greater than *it.* He becomes more than himself. But in defying that will, he allies himself with it. He *reveals* it. The Will is terrible. It's too immense to name. No word can hold it all. Now, Savannah, *look* what you got me into. I've gotten away from Schopenhauer. His view is resignation to the force, and reconciliation. Now I'm just confusing you."

"No, no. It's so clear when *you* say it. God, Cory, I could listen to you all night, though I see your point—yours interests me more than Schopenhauer's. You make the effect of Macbeth's murders so clear. I mean, you don't like Macbeth but you pity his suffering; he's absolutely loyal to the impulse in him and you're left in awe at the unredeemed purity of his commitment to the original *stuffe* he is made of, his acceptance of that, and his responsibility to whatever it is for his crimes. If *Macbeth* were merely a Sunday School lesson with a moral, we wouldn't be reading it today.

"It fills you with wonder at the enormity of the thing in us that Macbeth directs against his world, us, and the mystery of what he directs himself against. Is that what you mean?"

"You're becoming quite a lecturer yourself."

She laughed. "A rub-off."

"But, yes. If it weren't for tragedy most of us would never visualize the extremes of what we contain. You question yourself, the world, and morality, but you cling to what you know of order because true chaos is too terrible to live for even an instant."

Six million Jews, he thought. Murderers reveal what's in us. Their crimes challenge our nature to define itself.

"Fair is foul, and foul is fair?"

He laughed. She knew his loves. No play teased his thought more than *Macbeth.*

"Here. Read me my passage."

She slouched forward on her elbow, her hand pressing her lip and cheek up distorted, and gazed, pendant.

She amazed; she was two worlds. How keenly she seemed to separate them. Rod was one thing. He was another. At this moment Rod didn't exist; he was all.

"How you explain things! You'd make a great prof. I may flunk philosophy, but it won't be your fault."

"I don't know. I identify too much with student weaknesses."

"That's precisely why you'd be so good—you feel. You don't fool me merely because you conceal so much behind that tranquil facade."

You're nothing, Cory.

"Oh, I let it out, though not enough. The war taught me a good bit about that."

Repressed, you might be led to turn your emotion against anything. With enough repressed people you could create a reasoned chaos. War. Again. Six million. Six million *what* next time?

He was spending more time with Savannah. She flowered under the double aegus. He clung even more to his and Savannah's preferred study table in the library; and when he left her, he had no desire to go back to his apartment. He came to dread the silence. He deliberately warded off his little expectancies—breaks in reading, comments, radio news. Sometimes dozing off in bed or asleep, a sound would wake him. "Rod?" So he kept Savannah as late as he could. He found himself seeking her. She had always hunted him out for beer, walk, movies, plays, talk; but when he considered how he was acting, his behavior gnawed. He didn't want to *depend*. Was he trying to keep Savannah from Rod or was he seeking Rod? When he was with her, Rod was a silent voice, a shadow.

She'd say with wonder, "Rod's stories!" Did that irk because "Rod's stories" had replaced "your voice"? He didn't like to admit that he too surrendered to the captivation of Rod's voice and missed, even desired, it. Rod's voice had worked like a lodestone drawing the four of them together.

Savannah was aware of that. As the time approached for Dalton to finish his degree, she said, "I dread the breakup." He would finish in December, two years ahead of them, and not return to receive his degree at June graduation.

When the night came to celebrate Dalton's leaving, they went to the Italian Village for beer. Dalton was nervous.

"Settle down." Savannah touched his leg, laughed. She was in her world, holding her three men in orbit. "Whaddd you shalll meees—," she mocked the physics professor, Professor Lumecki, "is de legg-chures on de construgshun of atomic bomb, not?"

"Not! What I'll miss is not having bombed this place to kingdom come. I'd do it too if you three weren't here."

"You'd do no such thing. The place has been your passion, despite pinching every penny you ever had. Your life was as empty as mine was before The Badger. Now confess it," she said.

Dalton winked.

"There! You see? Low key, silent, sententious Dalton smiled, a confession pure and simple. He loves Wisconsin, he loves us, he loves—"

"Better stop there," Cory said. "Commenting on a man's loves is a danger zone."

"Don't interrupt, Cory. I was savoring, salivating this scourge of alliteration. I was savoring my own sound for a change." She raised her glass. "A toast to all Dalton's loves, and to the true one." She met his eyes, her own glittering, and chug-a-lugged.

On her way, Cory thought.

Rod said, "We've never even seen your true one, Dalton. She must be really something to keep her in hiding the way you do. I have to hand it to you." He too chug-a-lugged.

"Now there's a man for you. *You*, Dalton, are *not* drinking." She filled her glass. "And *you're* not, Cory."

"Savoring my sips."

She laughed. "Bastard."

"*Sing no sad songs for me*." Dalton hissed alliteration.

"Why, Dalton, *something* has rubbed off," she said.

"It's what I'll miss."

"What you've loved?" she said.

"Yes. I'm too used to it. I have to keep imagining you three will be there when I arrive. I never thought such a thing could ever happen to me."

"Well, we *have*—and we're *irremediable.* You must tell her—" Savannah gulped a laugh. "No, no. *That way madness lies*." Gently she touched his leg. "I wish her well, Dalton."

"Oh, I leave it all behind."

"By mutual agreement," he added.

"You're good at that," Savannah said. "You're a machine, Dalton."

"Relentless," he said, "till the mechanism runs down."

"I hope you recognize it when it comes. I mean that," she said. "If not, you may end up engineering robots, artificial intelligence."

Rod raised his glass. "To a new beginning."

"After tonight," Dalton said.

"Two farewells, then?" Savannah said.

"I'm afraid so. She's waiting."

"Speaking of waiting, and things in hiding . . ." Rod peered through the golden glitter in his glass.

"Here," Savannah said, "it comes." In delight she slid into a comfortable slouch on the table and sank her chin into her palm. "Back—" Her throat throttled. "—on the *Annie B.*"

"You *know* it was the only ship in the harbor!" Rod's voice went soft. Shades of Gram! And his look went far. He was there. On deck, maybe. Cory knew the ship, dingy black and white, bigger than most of the boats docked in the harbor. You could pick it out a long way off, hellish against the edenic green of Shelter Island and the infinite sweep of sky and sea beyond. Against that vast space, the waterfront was a tiny refuge on low, flat land and, when sea rose in hurricane weather, vulnerable.

"Polanski his name was. I never told you his story? They had him off the *Ida K.* I worked with him on the *Annie B.* I never knew about the girl. It happened after I'd left, but I learned it from Jeff."

Savannah coughed up a laugh and smoke. "And when not a girl?"

"That Polanski! He *was* a troublemaker. He was inventive and full of tricks. He'd have drowned me a hundred times if I hadn't been alerted by the others. I thought at first he did it because I was a smartass kid, but it was simply because he was Polanski—you couldn't change him—only how'd *I* know what Polanski was? Just before the dredges were to be dropped, he'd tempt me—'Go ahead, step in that coil, put your foot in that rope.' If I had, I'd have gone to the bottom with them. 'Not if you're quick enough,' he'd say. 'How fast *are* you, kid?' 'Put your own foot in it!' I'd say. It was a game he played, a fierce game, one thing after the other. He'd loosen a rail chain in a storm, there'd be a space—when the ship rocked, you had to make for it so you wouldn't go flying into the water. He was a bastard. He'd *get* it from the skipper, but he could talk himself back into almost anybody's good graces. He was enormous. There's something about having a big guy on your side—so big almost nobody dared challenge him, though everyone *wanted* to. He made them want to, he'd taunt them, only *that* wasn't because of his size; he had to, there was something in him never rested. After a while you knew he had to let it out. Driving him it was. Maybe all those tricks and temptations cleaned him out until he started filling again. Who knows? One night—in *Helen's* bar it was—he secretly brought a girl aboard, Una

Morrell. The Morrells lived on Second Street, generations. The way Jeff told it—this isn't my story, it's his, he should be here telling his own words, he *can*—Polanski'd got tied up with her. She followed him around, sat on his doorstep nights, waited in the alley beside his father's house where he stayed when he was shacking up with the first thing he'd pick up, drunk, only he didn't get so drunk when Una was around. She'd be waiting on the dock when the boat came in. He'd make dirty cracks to her, call her *bitch, little whore, frigging cunt,* only he'd come to *expect* her, his eye'd be out for her; then he'd curse worse than ever, even go out into the street and shout at her to get out, stop whoring around, get her ass away from here, what'd she think he was and her a minor, a kid hadn't got her panties dirtied yet. He'd come back onto the ship and go on and on about her, he wouldn't stop. And one night she crawled through his bedroom window at his father's house, and—just what you'd expect—he told everybody, but it didn't make any difference to her, she was more determined. 'The bitch wants it!' He'd slander her everywhere. Still she followed him. 'What you think of that! The bitch wants to marry me. *Me* married!' She wouldn't go to school, she wouldn't work, she wouldn't stay at home when he was in town. 'Well, if she wants it, she'll get it. I'll shove it up into her till it comes out her mouth,' he said finally; and then he told the boys, 'You wait. If she likes it that much, she'll get plenty.' They didn't know when Polanski did it, but he'd got her aboard. The ship went out that morning at five, and nobody knew a thing, except he was strange, quick laughs, all day making jokes and laughing, working with nervous frenzy and quipping—they never heard a man laugh so much over nothing. By the time they got out to sea, she was up in the cabin, a feat, anybody'd know that, jammed in the way they were, and how and when he did it only God knows, but nobody knew it yet. He'd got her under the bottom bunk, loosened the side board and got her under it, and that poor kid lay there till almost two in the morning when they got through dredging, the last skimmers hauled in and the deck ready for first light. Then when they were in the cabin, dead, too tired and restless maybe to sleep, he brought her out. She was bare. He'd hid her clothes. He was more frenzied than ever, his dark eyes gleamed, he seemed to gloat over her. 'There she is, boys,' he said. She stood there, quiet, not looking at them, only at the floor, waiting, not even with shame, but a kind of submission, as if she knew it was the way to him, she would get to him. But he got to her: 'Fifty bucks a throw, gents!' he said. 'What say?' Her eyes fixed on him suddenly, wide, startled, unbelieving, and she never took them off his face. 'You wanted it,' he told her, 'now you'll get it. All that talk about love! This is your chance to prove it, baby. You can just fill Polanski's pockets with your love.' It was the same taunting he used with all of them, something running through him he couldn't even stop. 'A gang bang. Don't be shy, boys, the little lady's all get-up-and-go. Break it in for me.' He tempted them in a whisper, quiet—the Captain and the mate up in the pilot-house—but nobody moved. 'S-mattuh, you guys?' He tried to intimidate, he went at it boldly, trying to make cowards of them; and you could see Teddy and Rolfe and Mud couldn't take their eyes off her. *He* saw that, he played on it, especially with Mud. 'I thought you liked white stuff, all time bragging how you can keep them white girls happy, eh, man? We'll leave. How 'bout it? One at a time, no gawking, just slip it to her.' He put his hands all over her. She closed her eyes. It drove them crazy—even though they wanted to, Jeff wanted to, kill him—the sight of that girl with her eyes closed. 'Jesus, man, I can't take this shit,' Rolfe says. 'Fifty it is. Now get out.' Eddy and Jeff went to the door. It was then she said, 'No,' to Polanski, said it like just discovering she had a voice, 'no no no,' and he said, 'I thought you loved me, you told me you loved me,' and she said, 'Yes, yes,' her eyes filled. 'Then shut up and do like I tell you.' And he told Jeff and Eddy to get out. 'Go ahead, Rolfe.' Mud was already at the door. He couldn't take his eyes off the girl either. They went out. 'Keep it quiet out there, you bastards, not a word.' He said to Rolfe, 'You tap when you're through,' and closed the door. The boat hardly moved, the night quiet, the sea almost still. They waited so long Polanski went back in. 'What the fuck you doing?' he said. Rolfe was standing there. 'Nothing,' he said, 'I couldn't do nothing. She wouldn't.' 'You goddamn coward. I thought you was a man.' Polanski hissed and shoved him out, his eyes glittering in a still stare at her, her own never leaving his face. Then he said, 'Go ahead, Mud,' and Mud couldn't wait, but she said, 'No, don't touch me, don't you dare touch me.' Polanski let her have it, a bash in the face two three four times, with her not moving her eyes from him. Her eyes filled. Nobody dared say a thing to him. Mud was excited, the slaps had excited him, or her tears, and he said, 'For Chris' sake, man, get out of here before I'm off in my pants.' 'I *won't*,' she said, staring at Polanski, 'you can't make me.' Maybe it was what he was waiting for. That set him off, frenzied. He laughed a low intense laugh, his hands trembled, he grabbed her neck, 'You don't do it and you'll never have this one—get it?—never in this life.' He smacked her again. She groaned. He slapped and she bit her lip; it began to bleed. 'Jesus, man, let's go,' Mud said, but Polanski still had her by the throat, cutting off her air, she choked. 'You do as I say?' he said. 'Think you're too fucking good for a nigger? Who you think you are, girl? You better wiggle that ass of yours.' And he shook her, her eyes still riveted on him shaking her, 'Do it?,' shaking and shaking, 'Do it?' till she said finally, 'You want me to? You really want me to?' and he said, 'Betchyarass I do.' She nodded and dropped her head and he flung her against Mud till she near fell from choking for air and Mud already tearing at his clothes when Polanski closed the door. By then he was whispering, laughing in little hisses to himself, mumbling, 'She won't, won't she? I'll fix her little ass, bucking me like that. He'll give it to her.' Then in an instant, as if he could no longer restrain himself—to be sure? to see them in the act? to press her on?—who knew!—he opened the door: he tore Mud off the girl, pulled the girl out of the bunk and held her up with both hands as if in disbelief, accusing her, shouting now with no care for the Captain, 'You goddamn bitch, you said you loved me. You'd fuck anything with pants on, would you?' and clamped her against the wall with a terrible blow. Her eyes fluttered, her head slumped and rolled as if he'd broken her neck. He slammed her against the wall again and again with one arm, beating her, wild with blows, smashing her face with his fist so fast that by the time anyone could catch his breath and leap at him, her face was battered, broken, bleeding and by the time the four of us had him, the Captain was there, shouting, 'What's going on? Holy Jesus, Mary and Joseph!' as the girl fell to the floor, her face unrecognizable, smears and pours of blood from her broken flesh, and the wall smears and streaks, and the floor and bunks. The Captain said, 'She's dead.' Then as abruptly as he'd turned on her, Polanski went dead, his body went limp, it sagged so heavy it sank free of them. He crawled to her, seized her body and held it in his arms and began to cry. Great gasps of heaved air came from him, his body shook, he kissed that unrecognizable face. 'Una Una Una,' he said, choking, clutching her to him, burying his face in her bleeding body. Then he raised his head and with his hands cupped her battered head and clutched it to his chest, and stared, choking in great heaves. It was the Captain who had presence enough to move. He tore a metal spike off the wall and struck Polanski a blow on the back of the neck that made him go limp. The girl rolled onto the floor face down, her ass so white. 'I had to do that,' the Captain said. 'No telling what he'd do. Tie him up.' He went up and started the engine and headed back to Greenport full throttle."

"Jesus!" Dalton said. "Did he get life?"

"The book. Remember it, Cory?"

"Something. A rumor." He was gazing at Savannah. Abstracted, her cigarette motionless between her fingers, her eyes too still, she was tonguing her lips.

"True?" she said.

"It's one version." Rod's smile was cryptic, serious.

"You know others?"

"I could tell others."

"You'd have to know them all."

"I don't know the girl's."

"I do."

"How could you?" Dalton said.

"Empathy pure and simple. I know enough. She loved him."

"You can't know that," Dalton said.

"Oh, yes. She didn't have to say yes."

"She had no choice," Dalton said.

"But she did. When he insisted, she could've kept saying no. And she didn't."

"What good would saying no do?" Dalton said.

"It would prove something."

"Prove what?"

She laughed. "The opposite of what it did prove."

"What would that be?"

She chortled. "Ponder that. On your way home. My legacy to you."

Cory said, "It's one hell of a farewell story, Rod. Why'd you tell that one?" All through the telling something prickled like a splinter.

"That's my Cory! Always wanting to know why," Savannah said. "God, it was spellbinding, but I'm glad it happened to somebody else. There you are, Cory. That's why, to make you glad it happened to somebody else."

"She's telling me to shut up, you guys."

"The truth is," Dalton said, "she's telling *me* to watch out."

"*Before* you go to Massachusetts," she said.

"Last chance tonight. You're mean, Vanna," Rod said.

"My only meanness—Dalton knows it—is loving all three of you. *Die drei kamaraden*. But he's got to leave us, *nicht wahr*?" She rose. She kissed him.

"We'll walk you to the car," Cory said.

"No." Dalton pressed Cory back down. "No." His sudden sadness erupted with force. "You and Rod take care of her. I know she'll take care of you."

"Bastard." She forced a smile. "You go on, Dalton."

They watched him move quickly down the aisle. At the doorway he turned and threw up his arm and smiled, his hair a flare under the light.

"Look at that! You'd really think that devil was an angel." She wet her lips.

"There's no telling."

"There go my house and kids in Black River Falls." She chortled, but the sound bit, sad. "What made me ever think I'd tie him down?"

"He'll be a winner—in a big place. He'll make it. We'll be hearing about him," Cory said.

"I'll feel one-legged without him," Rod said.

"One third of me gone," she said.

On a summer night not long after, Cory had just come in from canoeing alone on Mendota when Rod showed, sudden. Since Cory had booted him out, Rod had come only when necessary, whether from a continued subliminal resentment or a delicate respect for his privacy or a fear of alienating him further. Each knew, in extremes, the other's latent violence: "You got your brains from me and your temper from your father," his mother would always say, laughing, aware that they would reverse it when joking with her.

"What's happened?"

It's Savannah! he thought.

"Ma got married."

"Ma!"

"To German. Ma phoned me at the Koenigs."

"German!"

"That coastguardsman who kept tabs on her when Reggie Webb drowned. She said he was so good to Gram when she was dying—sat with her, carried her from the bedroom to the living room and to the sun porch—"

"He must be big."

"Ma says he's over six feet, weighs 230 or more, says he looks German but he's not, he's French, blonde and blue eyes with a perfectly wonderful smile, beautiful teeth—"

"She was that exuberant?"

"Bowled me over, so close to Gram's dying."

"Maybe that's why."

"Lonesome, you mean."

"Caught her on the rebound, I mean."

"Any man who's that kind to a dying woman's bound to be good."

"I'm sure she believes that."

"And you don't?"

"No. I can't believe she knows. Right now I'd bet she can't think of him in any other way. Ma lives, she doesn't think about it. Living that way can be terrible, almost as terrible as not living but thinking all the time."

"You talking about yourself, Cory?"

"I'd rather not. I'm talking about passion."

Passion: *that blast the roots of trees.*

"You resent it."

"How can I resent it?"

"You always did in the rest of us. *You* think Ma's whorish, don't you?"

"No."

"Oh, yes you do. You're a purist, Cory. You think you're supposed to love only once. You think you have to go all your life without your one true love. Are you supposed to rot away? You think it's impossible to go on with anybody else and grow and live even if a second or a third love isn't as great as what you dreamed of."

"Rod—"

But Rod's voice pitched shrill, driven at him.

"Suppose you want somebody you can't have so bad you can't stand it, it might even kill you if you don't have that somebody, but you don't want to die—why?—because that person is alive and as long as that's true you can love from a distance—that. You can hope the person's happy, you can live for that, it keeps you going. You have that secret even if that love's impossible, so what's wrong with settling for somebody else who loves you and that you can love enough?"

Cory was struck dumb by the fire in Rod. His voice pitched shrill, driving at him.

How could Rod speak such pain without pain?

"You love somebody that much, Rod?"

Silent, Rod gazed long at him.

"You never told me. You're that miserable? Did Ma's getting married bring it on? You feel that strongly about it?"

"You don't have to go to war to know misery. There's plenty of it here at home. Besides, Ma doesn't have to live your ideas."

"Maybe I got them from her and Gramp. All her life she loved Reggie Webb. Everything before she ran off with him must have seemed a mistake, a necessity. Ma's sensual, and she couldn't betray love. She's like Gramp. His first marriage was a mistake, but his marriage to Gram was his passion. He couldn't help that. He can't control it, and Ma can't either."

Was passion something that tore through them all and lived on after them, outside themselves, and entered others, and went on forever and in everything?

"Maybe—it's the most devastating thought of all—her biggest mistake was loving Reggie Webb, and Gramp's biggest mistake was loving Gram . . . if we judge by what it brought them to."

"You're forgetting what they had, Cory."

No. He had thought about it too much, how passion besieged animal, man, family, nation, nations—too destructive.

"Why must the greatest thing be so destructive?"

Destruction meant Gramp. Always he saw Gramp's hands, the crippled claws. He saw Gramp in flames, streaking out of the galley, up the steps and into the open air which fed the fire; saw someone rush to throw the tarpaulin over him and smother the fire. He saw the body wrapped in bandages, lying a mummy in a hospital bed for months, only his eyes and nose and mouth visible. He saw the hands emerge from the bandages with the fingers drawn back from the protruding palms like perfect crouched spiders.

Cory knew the hands long before he knew the story. They were part of his everyday life. They were Gramp. The fire had happened years before he was born. Tell me the fire! Ma and Gram and relatives had told him the story, but his grandfather had never told. Each had told him a different version, till it was as grim and horrific and beautiful as a fairy tale which he could never hear enough; it had become part of his self. But he had to imagine the true version. Though the fire may have had nothing to do with Gram, he felt that if he could recreate the actual moment, if he could know what chance thought had so distracted Gramp in the galley that he blundered and seized the tin and poured oil or kerosene over the hot stove that threw fire back and turned him a sudden living flame, Cory would know that it had had something to do with Gramp's passion for Gram.

"We can't know why it's so destructive. It's what happens."

The maturity of Rod's acceptance of that simple fact startled him. What had Rod been through to bring him to such stoicism?

"It's happened to Ma again," Cory said.

"I'm glad. I want her to be happy. Don't you?"

"More than anything, after the hell she's had. But we don't have to worry about Ma sitting still and dying. She's too alive. She'll always look for somebody else, and she won't consider us. She hasn't. We're outside that. Whether she thinks it or not, she's got to live. so there'll always be someone else no matter what the consequences."

Passion made you obsessive, one-track-minded, undeviating.

"You forget Gramp," Cory said. "*She'd* never forget him. Maybe she'd have defied even Reggie Webb for him."

"Oh, don't worry about Gramp. He'll stay in his house. German'll take him for granted."

"Ma will see to that."

They both laughed. It was the first time they had laughed together since the night they'd separated.

You're nothing, Cory.

"She's carted Gramp around till you'd think he was the family Bible," Cory said.

"He is. The Bible in the flesh."

"But the Book says leave father and mother and *cleave* to the husband."

"You know Ma. She lives her own Bible."

"Yes. But you pay for that."

"Don't, Cory."

"I don't mean God punishes, silly. I mean people. *They* make you pay. She's paid."

"She was willing. She had what she wanted. Has. Ma's never complained. She won't either. She's strong."

"Because of Gramp. *He* knows, he's been there. And she with him."

"Because he's *in* her, Cory."

Rod took his very words. Did Rod know what they meant? Cory was afraid of what passion was in them. Once it seized them there was too much of it. It overran. They lived for it, brooded. Gram's ease in moving through life like an actress impervious to the audience did not seem to be in Ma or in him and Rod, as if Gramp alone had sired the entire family.

What presence had Gramp been to his father? to Pete? to Reggie Webb? What would he be to German?

German was an intrusion as sudden and bold as an exposed reef they would have to skirt. He changed the perspective, as Reggie Webb had, and he and Rod had had no time to adapt to *him* before he'd drowned. Cory could not imagine even the semblance of *father.* German was barely older than he was. German had been in the war too, one of his unknown buddies. He could be his buddy or his brother. It would be as if Ma had three sons. The thought violated.

Cory could not let his mother go—to German or Reggie Webb, even to Pete. She had fostered this attitude. *Ask Cory. Ask Pa.* Gramp's presence was palpable because she wouldn't let him go. To Cory he stood as monumental as Stonehenge or Aku-Aku. In him was embodied the whole sweep of time, barbarians, Greeks, Romans, and the Old Testament and the New, which he had preached in pulpits over the entire North Fork.

Since Gramp had been born on a ship in Bristol harbor, Cory always visualized him rising from the sea as fully grown as Venus in a scallop shell and standing as tranquil as Jesus on the waters. He'd kid Gramp: "Served up like an oyster on the half-shell!" Cory loved scallop shells most. "You know, Gramp, medieval Christians wore the scallop shell on their headwear or breasts as a sign that they were on a pilgrimage to Rome or Jerusalem or one of the other saints' shrines." "You don't say." "They'd stop at hostels with a scallop shell over the doorway as a sign the innkeeper was friendly to pilgrims." "You don't say." Gramp would go on puffing a hand-rolled cigarette, squinting, half from the smoke, half from his quivering eyes with their tinge of albino pink, Pal close by, and the perennial stray cats that had moved in on him. Cory would get out the metal cigarette roller he'd bought to make it easier for Gramp—Rod usually rolled them—but he'd say, "My hand-rolled ones taste better—it's the spit, dampens the tobacco a bit—but thanks, Cory."

Now Rod said, "You thinking of Gramp?"

"How'd you know that?"

"You're my brother, remember?"

Wasn't it Rod who had forgotten? Cory turned back to the desk. "We won't be able to meet German till the end of summer session."

"You going out to the Island then?"

"That's a long time off. I haven't thought that far ahead."

"It would be better if we went together, wouldn't it?"

"Would it?"

"Why should we upset Ma?"

"I don't know that going separately would upset her so much."

"Oh, come on, Cory. You know how perceptive she is; even her skin seems to catch signals. She's already suspicious something's wrong. She can tell by my voice."

"Your voice!"

"Yes."

"What've you been telling her?"

"That's just it. Ma reacts to what I *haven't* said. Anyway she kept saying, 'You're sure nothing's wrong?' And said, 'Why doesn't Cory call? You call. Why can't he? I know it's money, *but*—' It's the way Ma says that *but*."

"She's nervous. After all, she doesn't know how we're taking the news about German."

"You should know better, Rod. Ma's no dummy. The *fact* that you've been calling her is enough to make her suspicious. Why have you? You've got somebody to talk to. Savannah's not enough?"

"You're a prick, Cory."

"See! Even her language is rubbing off on you."

"If you want to know, there are some things I can't discuss with Vanna."

"I don't know why. She's understanding enough."

"She wouldn't be about everything."

"Such as?"

Rod was silent.

"Why not try her—in everything."

"Prick."

"You said. Well, thanks for coming by. I'm glad Ma's married again. It's hell to be alone."

"How would *you* know, Cory?"

You're nothing, Cory.

Cory went back to his desk. For a long instant Rod didn't move; then his fast furious steps sounded across the bare bedroom and den; then the furious slam of the door, the clip of his steps down two flights and the thud of the front door.

"You're too hard on Rod," Savannah said when she ran into him in the corridor of Bascom Hall.

"*Now* what's he been telling you?"

"That's just it—nothing."

"Rod not say anything?"

"He's too sullen, Cory. You know Rod's never sullen."

But Rod could smolder. Still, he spoke, endlessly sometimes, and he told tales masterfully. Maybe the telling concealed the smoldering. His loquacity was a veneer. Was that it?

"Maybe my mother's marrying again has just got to him."

The corridor was hot, the day a swelter.

Close, the carillon reverberated, note after note, for a moment drowned the voices in the corridor.

The class bell broke the harmony.

"Damn! If I keep worrying about Rod, going to class won't do much good."

"Rod can take care of himself."

"Why'd he come here in the first place then? He was doing better at Kingston."

"The last thing he needed was to come here."

"You know better than that! He came because you were here. He needed you. That makes you responsible. Oh, you don't want to be but you are. You can't help it. If I knew what's in you, I'd dig my nails into you and tear out whatever it is so I wouldn't be plagued by it."

"You think *I'm* not?"

He closed his eyes. When again he looked, he saw she was nonplussed.

"I never thought—"

"We don't."

"I should have. I'm so close to you."

"We live too much in our own skins."

"But shouldn't."

"Hard not to, isn't it?"

"Not so hard. That's what *I'm* for, Cory, and Rod and Dalton and God knows how many others."

"Perhaps."

"No. There're always some who can break through."

"Perhaps."

"Unless you ward them off."

"You think I do?"

"You don't exactly rope us in."

He laughed. Her hand chafed his.

She said, "You ward me off and Rod and Dalton—and who else before? And who'll they be after?"

"We can't help who we are. With some of us who we are's the burden."

"Tell me about it!"

"Don't be a fool, Savannah. You have beauties all your own."

"Why, Cory . . ." Her voice sank, her eyes quick glazed over, and as quickly she shook her hair and laughed, throaty. "Enumerate, if you please." Yet she didn't wait. The corridor was empty. "I'm late. See you." She turned back—"But, Cory, don't forget Rod, please?"—then ran buoyant on her toes despite the rounds of her hips and thighs, her balance and daintiness a constant surprise to him. At the lecture hall she glanced back, then ducked in.

Somebody who can break through.

Perhaps.

Once somebody—he flushed at the memory—had almost broken through his reserve, a perilous moment. As he descended the hill, he envisioned over the roof of the library below the finely chiseled, very masculine head of his quiz instructor in English literature, Mr. Randall, Jeremy Randall. He saw the lean body of that young Southerner with the precise but easeful voice, who would lecture sitting behind the desk or leaning casually against the blackboard or standing by the window, his head with its soft-looking hair drawing light tilted in unconscious almost feminine pose, his deep brown eyes gazing beyond the carillon, over the trees and the women's dorms toward the lake and the far woods, his eyes surely envisioning with sheer empathy whatever it was he was describing to the class.

Obsessed with the class, at the slightest drop of a writer's name—Kafka, Hesse—Cory went out and spent even his restricted food money for the mentioned books, isolated himself, ate, yes, digested the words. He followed Randall's thinking, nearly memorizing Randall's comment, repeating them in solitude, mulling. Though he had read since childhood obsessively if indiscriminately (How did his mother cater to his desire for books, filling his every available shelf?) and during the service devoured the cheap editions of classics made especially for the troops overseas, he had never realized a story was a body, its organs functioned, it lived and breathed and moved in you. Randall took him on that journey under the flesh, exposed the skeleton of poems, stories, novels. Above all, he lived the *experience* of moving through patterns that lured him deep into the labyrinth of passion or led him into the excitement of the most subtle twists and turns in the labyrinth of reason. Randall *was* his eyes. But Randall tore open his vision. Randall widened it breathtakingly. "It's like seeing the truth and the way!" he thought. "It *is*," Randall said. Suddenly one day he felt let go, a colt stumbling on new legs, straightening, confident, certain. His eyes were his own.

But when he read, Randall was beside him. Released, he now saw Randall apart, outside himself. Alone, he carried on dialogues with Randall. Randall was his companion, but that was not enough: he could not really *invent* Randall's discursive mind; they were his *own* discussions. Randall recognized the quality of his mind. It was obvious to Randall and to the class, mostly to the veterans like himself, that he transcended the thinking of the others. Randall had helped him *break through* and now he spilled; now he had to have someone like Randall, Randall himself, to talk to. He could not wait for class days to come. He lived the literature, dwelled on it; and he thought about Randall, wanted to discuss the developments he traced through the fictions. He prepared himself, wrote them down for class discussion once a week. Once a week! It became an agony of waiting—and then there was *no time*; the class frittered it away on trivia while he chafed, wanting to keep Randall focused on what was significant, probing into what affirmed life.

He had to talk to Randall, alone. He had thought about it for a long time, but Randall was an instructor, a Ph.D. candidate, and he was his student. Since the service, he himself had a hatred of hierarchy; shed now, hierarchy still intimidated—each world had its own. But he yearned to talk to Randall, he could not ward off his presence—he didn't want to—and in the Union, cafeteria, anywhere on campus, in downtown Madison, startled at his own persistency, he found himself looking for Randall. One night he was reading Dostoevsky, Raskolnikov's dream: the man was beating the horse, beating. Cory was *there*, he felt the blows on his own flesh, the blows infuriated. His thoughts struck out in all directions—he *saw* thoughts, snakes he couldn't *get out of his head.* If only Randall . . . Randall. He must talk to him. He would understand this, he would know. His small room—he was living at the Koenigs' then—was suddenly tiny. He felt enclosed. He felt suffocated. He must get out, yes, and talk, he must talk—and to Randall. He couldn't to Savannah or any of his casual classmates—Dunphy, Reese Bailey, Alcott—with any penetration about *that* experience: the Dostoevsky was too complex and intertwined; *he* could not untangle those complex threads. But he must. He was miserable. He could not explain his misery. Randall!

Randall lived just a few minutes away in an old Victorian house converted to apartments. He passed it every day on his way home from campus. He had seen Randall enter a couple of doors beyond the girls' rooming house which people joked about because it was called The Doxy House. He would call Randall. Surely he would be home, preparing lectures, correcting papers. It was Sunday night. He went quietly down the stairs. Why was he being so stealthy? He would not call from the house, so went out and around the block to the corner phone. And if Randall weren't in the directory? He dreaded to think. He had to see him. He'd go to the house, knock, ask for him—

The address was there! The day was cold, but he was sweating, his armpits gluey. He put his dime in, dialed, waited—

That voice answered! Its resonance ran through him. He closed his eyes. Thank God!

"Mr. Randall, this is Cory Moorehead—"

He expected some response, but here was a hiatus.

"Mr. Moorehead?"

"I was wondering . . . I was reading Dostoevsky. I need to see you. Could I come by?"

"I usually don't see students at home."

"I wish you would."

"I'm afraid it's a little unusual."

"I have to see you, Mr. Randall. You can't know what it means to me to talk to you. . . ."

He held the cord taut.

He could hear Randall's breath.

Please.

Randall said finally, "You know where I live?"

"Yes."

"If you'll come in about fifteen minutes . . . I'm on the first floor, apartment A. There's a side entrance."

"I'll find it."

"I'll expect you, then."

He rested his head against the cold phone box. Fifteen minutes!

He walked quickly. It was cold. The banks were patchy with dirty snow, the air raw damp. Hands in his pocket—he had rushed out without his gloves—he walked to the corner before that house he had thought so ugly, gloriously trajpnsformed at this moment because *he* lived there, then went around the block twice, constantly checking the time.

At the door his throat was palpitating.

He almost turned back, but his feet would not move.

He rapped the knocker. Before his hand dropped, the door opened.

"Come in, Mr. Moorehead." Randall smiled generously and stared straight into him. That confounded. He was so used to distance, to Randall's gazing off and talking as if he were being overheard. It was almost a style with him.

He stepped into a small anteroom and Randall closed the door behind him. Black drapes over the side walls swayed. He glimpsed crowded shelves of books behind. Without a jacket Randall was startlingly thin, and loose black trousers and a loose chamois shirt made him long but small-boned and delicate. He followed Randall, his eyes on his back, through the inner door. He was in a small room with no windows and immensely deep walls, almost dark, with only two dim lights, a corner upright and a table lamp on a small mahogany desk in an alcove opposite the window seat. The walls were papered in mauve brocade, the carpet purplish. Between bookcases was a window seat with a purple cushion, all against dark woodwork. Two dark-stained doors led elsewhere—bedroom, kitchen, living room?

"Be comfortable." Randall indicated one of the two small upholstered chairs. He himself sat on the window seat, his face in shadow. "This is my talk room, where I do most of my thinking. It's silent and restful. Nothing distracts me here."

Cory watched. He wanted to absorb everything, hoard it. Randall set an ashtray on his knee, was long lighting a cigarette, and waited. In the shadows his eyes seemed pitch. The desk lamp made tiny distant glows in them. Cory's eyes ate. His throat contracted. There must be some mercy—

"You were reading *Crime and Punishment*?"

"Yes! I got to the beating of the horse in Raskolnikov's dream and—" Before Randall he felt shy as a boy. Almost, he dared not tell him. A spasm ran down him. He clutched his hands between his thighs. "I felt *I* was being beaten. *I* was the horse. The man was beating something out of me, something hot, blood maybe. I was afraid I'd spill—"

Randall was so still the cigarette almost burned his finger. He jerked and crushed it out.

"What was so terrible was . . . suddenly *you* were the horse, I was that cabbie, I was *beating* you, I *wanted* to beat you, I didn't want to stop, I couldn't stop—"

Randall averted his gaze. He stared at the small lamp.

"I closed the book, but it kept on in my head. I *saw* the beating. I felt I'd burst. I had to see you. *You'd* know—"

There was a long silence. He watched Randall, and waited, an agony. Then Randall turned his head and gazed at him a long time. Randall seemed to be seeing into him. And he clung to that gaze. At that instant he *loved* Randall. If Randall moved—

He bent forward.

They were so close— If he reached out he could touch Randall.

He waited. Everything depended.

He raised one hand slightly toward Randall, vacillated, and let it fall.

"Mr. Randall—"

Randall broke the gaze. He reached for another cigarette and lit it. He said, "You're an exceptionally sympathetic reader."

"Because of you."

"No. You've got the gift. You're very sensitive."

"But you brought it out in me."

"Many people might have done that for you."

"But *you* did."

"That doesn't make your achievement mine."

But you're responsible.

"It's as much yours as mine when we've shared—"

"Yes, we've shared, and we'll go on sharing. However, I'm just— To be trite, I'm just the vessel the experience pours through. Literature's my passion, it's my love, it's what I dedicate my life to; but don't confuse what you're experiencing with the one who leads you to it. That's easy to do. It's natural, especially for somebody who lives the experience so intensely that it becomes his. Obviously you do."

"I had you on my mind."

"That's not so unnatural. After all, your passion seems to be literature, and to you *I'm* literature or you wouldn't have come. I understand that"

"But it's more than that. You were in the dream."

"*You* read me into it."

This time Randall did not, as in class, address some far invisible face. Randall did not move his eyes—they commanded.

"Didn't you?"

Randall raised his head, turned sideways, and blew a cloud of smoke. Cory followed the fine line of his face, and down his neck, and over the thin but nicely broad frame of the shoulders, down the loose shirt, to the crossed knee, where the long thin hand with the cigarette rested, relaxed, and down to the loose loafer that hung from his toes. For a moment Randall seemed to have withdrawn into a painting, posed, as if deliberately emphasizing the effete in this purple Pre-Raphaelite enclosure.

He nodded. But he felt an edge to Randall's intention. Abruptly Randall had retreated a long distance off.

"You can't judge a man by what he is in class, Moorehead."

Moorehead.

Don't, Randall.

"What you see there is only part of the man."

"Perhaps that's enough for me."

"No. You can't judge that way. What you've made of me is an illusion."

"You did that to me."

"No. You did. We read things the way we want to. *You* have."

"You have to have illusion. Nothing's worth it without illusions. How would we stand war, death, passion?"

"Illusion has to be grounded. You know that. Your work shows that. You're a veteran. If I've unfortunately blinded you to what I am . . . I'm not what you think I am."

"You don't know what I think you are."

"You're very much mistaken. I believe you really know that, though you won't admit it to yourself."

As Randall said it, he realized something of the truth of it.

"You don't want to give up your illusion."

The words were cold, and the voice.

"Do you?" It chiseled. "Moorehead?"

He felt a threat in Randall's insistence, a perversity. Was Randall intentionally opening up a new kind of hope for him by pressing him to reveal a weakness? Did he expect him to cry out *Yes* and fall before him and see himself for what Randall insisted he was? Or was it Randall who was now revealing a weakness and behind the subtle cool facade reducing himself to an implied confession, subtly insisting he break through that illusion to the reality Randall was offering him?

He did not blame Randall; he could not. *He* had called, *he* had come, *he* had led him.

But he wanted to preserve the other Randall. He wanted the illusion which Randall claimed—rightly, he saw now—that he had projected from somewhere inside him. From where? And why?

"Nobody wants to give up his illusions," Cory finally said.

Randall, leaning back, looked frail in the loose shirt and, with the loose slipper suspended from his toe, rather flip.

"It's because we have so few illusions," he added. "We depend on them."

With that Randall's head cocked. He seemed newly interested. "Yes," he barely whispered. He sounded—and looked—vulnerable.

"The war took most of mine."

Randall stilled his foot, waiting.

"What's left I guard jealously. You weren't in the war, were you?"

"No. I was a student." Randall's glance, as in class, went to a far place. "I missed it all."

"You missed a great deal." Cory rose. "As terrible as it was, some of us needed the experience. I wonder, too often, why the worst things in life are necessary. *I* believe they *are* necessary, absolutely. Without them, do you suppose we'd ever be challenged to become the complete things we dream of being? Or maybe after suffering, since we can't understand why, we make meaning of it."

Randall seemed to ponder that. "I think I understand now your affinity with Dostoevsky."

"Do you?"

"He was drawn—against his will, he claimed—to the edge of the abyss. He was attracted, irresistibly, to irrational types, criminals and saints. There was too much of the irrational in himself. He was afraid of it, but wanted it and pursued it. Remember his gambling years."

"Yes. The thing is *he* didn't waste his madness, he used it."

"What do you mean?"

"No matter how deep in he went, he was aware, he always knew his actions aroused his conscience, and then his mind made use of his passion. That's his triumph—he made use of his weakness. His weakness *was* his strength. He gave it shape and meaning for the rest of us. Think what his life would've been! Without succumbing to passion he wouldn't have known his own will, or *the* will. Who wouldn't envy him that?"

"And you haven't?"

"Haven't?"

"Succumbed to passion?"

"In that hallucination—"

"Triggered by your reading—"

"It happened to me. It released something. I came here, didn't I? I shouldn't have."

"Why not? You too had to pursue it to see where it would lead."

"I had to because . . . I'm afraid of passion and . . . fear attracts me. A great man taught me the only way to live is to turn on what you're afraid of, walk smack into the middle of it and face it. I'd like to be able to say I was consciously doing that when I called you. I wasn't. I called in a frenzy. I'm afraid because I want passion too much. It attracts me and repels me. I know it can be the most wonderful thing and the most terrible. In my family there's too much . . . but I didn't come here to confess for my family."

Randall stood. "Then since you know why you came, you're satisfied . . .?"He had never been so close to Randall. Randall looked so parched and tired. He was frail, bony, and looked underfed. And in this room of dim light and shadows and mauve walls and tapestry he was half unreal, spectral, not the physical creature his hallucination had embodied. For a moment he was tempted toward pity for Randall, but that intensity in Randall's gaze defied pity. It was too enviable. That was what had first fascinated, then captivated him, what he knew would forever bind him to the memory of Randall. In Randall's gaze now was that intensity of longing, of abandon or escape which he so conveyed in class when, though always with them, he seemed to connect with a far-off but real elsewhere founded on this concrete world, one which he made live, close and now, as if he were speaking from immediate experience as it was happening.

"I came. I'm glad I did."

"I'm glad too. You've challenged me—"

"How?"

"Not to step across lines for the wrong reasons because you were vulnerable, you are."

"And are you?"

"Yes, though in some way over the years I've walled myself in. I've had to. To simplify—you don't need one more of my lectures, *but*—I believe the world is composed of two kinds of people, those who always look down and worry about the children and the car and the bread and butter, and those who always look up and ponder how everything fits together. The world needs both types, they depend on each other. You look up. You won't be satisfied, ever. In some ways most people aren't, but your kind, ours, is never satisfied."

"I can't believe that."

"Because you're hungry."

"Hungry?"

"For something invisible."

"*No.* You're wrong. Or yes, invisible, but if I can't touch what it's in, I don't want it, I can't believe in it, I can't accept it. I won't. The agony's in everything, and the joy. I don't care whether it's the agony of growing into your own body or some strange agony of a stone forming or the leaf or the butterfly out of the chrysalis. The motion's in them, invisible, yes, but you can feel it. You can touch it even if you can't know what you're touching; otherwise it's not worth having. And it *is* worth having. I know because I experience it, but not enough, not all; and I want that. Some of it's in you. I've seen it when you talk and move in class. It's physical, but something moves the physical, and that's what I'm drawn to in you. That's what I experienced in that hallucination. The hallucination was as real as you are. What's in you is real to me. I wanted to touch it. I know that now. That's why I called you. That's why I came—"

"But you didn't touch me."

"No. If you'd laid a finger on me, brushed against me, I *would* have because I was so excited when I came, too excited to think. I was too under the spell of that fascination. All I knew was I had to see and hear and touch you. I couldn't get here fast enough. And I was afraid."

"You don't want to touch me now?"

"I touched you, but not the way I wanted to. I *did* want to put my hands on you, and I wanted yours—and I *saw* that. I saw it happening all the while I was walking around the block before I knocked on your door."

"You worked the passion out of you."

"No. I was seething with it when I knocked. The slightest thing would have made me clutch and hold and cling to you. I wanted you to know I'd never hurt you as I had in the dream, and say I knew you wouldn't hurt me; but I had to know the Dostoevsky hallucination wasn't true, I wanted to prove it."

"Did you?"

"But it *was* true."

"You mean because it happened?"

"No. I mean the passion was, but . . . *you* weren't."

"I wasn't?"

"The one I was beating."

Randall's eyes narrowed, mystified.

"You were the one who was beating me . . ." He hesitated, feeling muddled. "I'm sorry, but I have to be clear. I'm trying to. It's confusing. It was you, but . . . *not* you."

Randall did not move, his gaze did not flag, and he said, with no skepticism, softly, "How did you come to realize that?"

"The instant you sat down, when you lit your cigarette . . ." He did not say, I saw how thin, bony, fragile you were, though he thought it, how you relaxed into an almost effete nonchalance. "Then I realized . . . a difference. I can't say what it was . . . or what made me think it was you except, of course, that I had you on my mind. I do have, often. You're important to me, or why *would* I have thought of you and called and invaded your sanctuary. I think of it as that because I feel a kind of love for you. I know that now. I can't deny it. You'll say it's the literature, but it's you too. You bring some magic to it, a fascination I don't see in anybody else except Professor Sánchez-Barbudo. A touch of genius, that's what it is. The instant he begins to talk about literature his whole face changes, something inside him transforms him. *That's* what I mean about the invisible in the visible. It *is* there, I've seen it, I've seen it in you. So why wouldn't I come see you?"

"Why not Professor Sánchez-Barbudo?"

"It was your face in the dream."

"Then it *was* physical?"

"What I *saw* was. You say I'm a sensitive reader, and I *am*, but why would the reading *release* that connection in me! After all, I read all the time."

"Maybe you had your satisfaction in the hallucination without being aware of it. Maybe that *was* your sex. Maybe you had it through me, had me without having me. Maybe I was just the image your mind or desires were hiding it behind, veiling them."

"If I were satisfied, why come to you?"

"Possibly you wanted to turn the violence into something else, tenderness, or love—turn it back on itself."

"Give it the lie, you mean?"

"No. Make it into something positive."

"With you?"

"With me."

"Suppose it wasn't me."

"That would've been destructive!"

"How?"

"Because this wouldn't have happened. I'd have kept feeling it was really you I wanted."

"Then you came to confess."

"Confess!"

"Yes. You've been confessing. Isn't that what you're doing now?"

"But what for?"

"Guilt . . .?"

"Guilt! But I'd know why."

"Something's trying to handle your guilt, or shame. But *you* must know that."

Cory broke into an ironic laugh. "I know it when it happens to somebody else."

Randall laughed. "Don't we all!"

It banished their seriousness, and Cory said, "You've been awfully patient with me, Mr. Randall. In your place, *I'd* have—"

"Never say. You don't know."

"This has been like being in class with you. No, better. Talking to you like this, I feel I'm inside your head. You're—and that goes for the war too—one of the most extraordinary experiences I've ever had."

" But *not* so violent?" Randall's head cocked, smiling.

"Too violent. I hope it's put my whip away for good."

"Don't count on that. If your mind has sidestepped it, it's still there and it won't go away. I hate to leave it on that note, but let's be realistic. You wouldn't want to console yourself with a lie."

"No. That's the last thing I'd want."

"Then it will come, if ever—when *it's* ready—and you won't have a thing to say about it."

At the door he turned to Randall, gazed at him, feeling an eruption of admiration, and awe. "How'd you ever get to know so much?"

Randall's lips parted, his eyes quick on him, startled. "What I know is so little. In a lifetime perhaps . . ." He had saddened Randall, not intending to.

For an instant Cory contemplated the image of this man about whom he knew nothing but his world of the classroom and this interlude with him, this single man rich with his gift, cultivating with the dedication of a saint willingly secluded in his dark cave, who would spend his life reading and teaching, humbly transmitting what passed through him illuminated by his particular genius, for he *had* that, reaching out and tasting life when he could, or letting it enter when he dared . . . *No, not for me that, never.* He felt such a stirring in him that he felt his eyes burn with the threat of tears. He said, "If I could know one day what you know now," and Randall said, "You will, and so much more." Cory turned and took the three steps down in a run. "See you in class." But he halted within safe distance, and turned. Randall was still in the doorway. "Thanks. You'll never know—" Then he sprinted down the block, his vision clear, feeling for Randall a confusion of love and pity.

Now the image halted him on the walk down Bascomb Hill. Over the library at the foot of the hill, where wind was roiling the treetops like shifting sunlit foam, it came to him; it rose clearly from that green sea: Randall's face in the doorway to that dark vault. He saw again that head with its strong masculine bones, the thick hair which when long gave his face a soft almost feminine look, and the far but intense gaze. The head, divorced from its body like that, he had seen a thousand times and not *really* seen it: Rod. Its lineaments were Rod's, its far gaze Rod's, but *without the body.* He remembered the moment in Randall's room, his awareness of Randall's bony frailty, his almost feline moulding to the furniture, the moment he realized he might have made a mistake. He closed his eyes: Randall's head. Rod's body. Yes. He felt as if a hand had reached up into him and gripped his guts. He wanted to cry out. But he stood still. The sky was so clear, serene. On the walk were a few stragglers rushing to class. Only the wind sounded. The trees moved. If only Savannah hadn't gone to class. *She* had evoked it in the way she'd halted at the classroom door, turned, and waved. Savannah might have been himself turning to say goodbye to Randall that night, and he Randall watching her go.

My brother.

He felt the hand inside him. It gripped his guts. He belched gall. His eyes smarted—the day was too bright, the edges of things too sharp.

My brother.

He went down the hill. He wouldn't go to the Union, or home. He didn't want to run into anybody. He skirted the science building and descended the slope and took the lake path below the girls' dorms. He headed for Picnic Point, where he could be alone. *The only way to get rid of a problem is to walk straight into the middle of it.* Get rid of it? His problem was as invisible as air, and ambiguous. He was afraid. He wanted to walk and walk. He would go deep into the woods. He wanted dark. But you couldn't escape yourself. He'd learned that from the service. He'd volunteered and gladly, but one day more and he'd have hated it. You lived situations between men that might never have happened otherwise, which forced you to discover ambiguities. Like it or not you understood more about them, and yourself.

Dannie Marouski he remembered from his squadron.

This: in the front bedroom of that little Parisian hotel on the Rue des Capucines, Dannie Marouski took an empty whiskey bottle and broke it right there on the bidet at two o'clock in the morning and scraped the fine edge over his forearm, not even flinching from his own drunkenness or the sight of sudden blood. "There!" He held his arm out. Blood crawled straight down and dripped hot on Cory's skin, scaring the living hell out of him. He was eighteen. He wondered what strange thing Marouski could be at such an instant, what he was doing to let his blood drip on him like that, even if he *had* known him for all of six fast months. The blood caught in the hair on his arm and dried. (He would be awake half the night, touching to see if it was there, hard and crusted. Now and again a clot would crumble into dust under his fingers.)

"That's me right there—Dannie Marouski. Un'stan? I never been this close to nobody, see?" He was too drunk. He was always friendly when he was drunk, but never this friendly before. "If we get in trouble, you'll fight for me, hey?"

"You know it," Cory said.

Marouski didn't know he was sick, but he couldn't hold it back.

He had all he could do to drag Marouski to bed, undress him, finally giving up with half his clothes on and rolling him onto the bed. But the spot of blood on his arm still felt so much like a burn that he had to turn the light on every once in a while to look at it, then at him, at his face all greasy in the light, dark and homely with thick nostrils, hairy at that, the same hair thick as shag on his brows and his straight animal lashes that had no fine shape to them. The worst thing was the faint little ribbing at the corners of his mouth where the blood had dried after he'd sucked his arm, and the long stab-streaks dried on the pillow by his face that lay in the crook of his arm, in sleep.

When he woke up the next day and saw those streaks, then the broken bottle, Marouski said he didn't remember any of last night.

How close so long ago seemed!

Now came the worst of the Wisconsin summer, burdening heat and incredibly regular build-up of creeping dark clouds that broke in afternoon showers till the weeks were one long humid swelter. In class, sweat poured off his forehead onto the paper, his hand smeared the ink, bare wet flesh made a sucking sound when he raised his writing arm from the desk, the clothes felt glued to his skin. But the weather was a challenge—to ignore it as an act of supreme discipline, to insist on performing as if he were physically and mentally impervious to it, to *being* impervious. He studied with discipline as always, a pattern of repetition, apportioned a time to each of his seven subjects every day, though classes met three times a week—if no mystic, not for nothing his study of the saints.

He neither avoided nor pursued Savannah and Rod. While with them he practiced being absent. He was not silent, but he had developed a mask. He went on living the outer social moment on campus, over 3.2 beer in the Rathskeller, at the Campus Grill, the Spaghetti House, at plays, movies, dances, art exhibits in the Union—and concealing the private emotion he feared might poison the social moment.

One day in the Union art gallery he had seen a painting entitled "The Young Man Who Read St. Thomas Aquinas." At times he found the face easing into his thoughts, and then with a peculiar insistence appearing on the page of a book, in a tree, reflected in the lake. He kept returning to the gallery and going straight to the painting. It was a head and shoulder portrait. The eyes in that innocent face were fixed on Heaven, impervious to this world; what they saw must be the Everything. His first impression of the face had been admiration for the perfectly captured innocence of a novice. That hardly explained his captivation since he had little sympathy with that secluded life. With repeated visits he noted that those uplifted eyes were blank. Ironically they reflected nothing but blue sky. Finely etched shadows gave a weary aspect to his face. The boy's hair, at first sight as fine and thin as a recently born baby's, was an old man's last hairs, as if the baby had emerged from the womb old. The skin was parchment, surely from seclusion. The young man had chosen perpetual innocence. He was a corpse. His body was dead.

I'm cut off, Cory thought. Dalton was gone, he had made Rod move, and he had changed tenor with Savannah. He had made himself an island. Wasn't that isolation death? He felt locked in, but he couldn't change it. He dared not.

Rod, my brother.

He gazed at the portrait. He felt deceived, but he knew he had deceived himself. Fascinated, he had let himself, had wanted to, be lured more and more deeply into an awareness of the visceral which each detail of the careful surface of the portrait ironically pointed to by emphasizing its absence. He had penetrated the surface. What he saw was himself. He disliked what he saw.

"Looking for a model?"

"Savannah!" She was standing some feet behind him, one arm supporting the elbow neatly poised with her perpetual cigarette, one eye squinted against the drift of smoke.

"You must like that piece? You've looked at it enough."

"I'm a slow learner. You following me?"

"Of course. The black widow keeps tabs on her mate. She doesn't want you to stray too far."

"I couldn't with St. Thomas as my model."

"Is he?"

"Only for his discipline."

"Good! For a moment you scared me. You'd do better to stick to St. Augustine. He at least had experience—of the body. Lust, it's called. Remember, it took old Augie a lot of years before he got rid of his concubine. Smart of him to name his illegitimate son Adeodatus, gift to God. *I* should give God such a son! I'd say he'd had a very good life before he went holy. At least it gave him a solid basis—if touch is anything?—for his judgments on human nature. That's more than you can say for a lot of the saints."

"It's not like you to track down saints, Savannah Goshen."

"Don't be deceived, young man who read St. Thomas Aquinas. Nothing teases a woman like the purity of a good man. It challenges the devil in her. And nobody's ever managed to purge me of *him*."

"Not even—"

"No, not him either, Cory."

"Well, you'll have that temptation removed. I'm leaving."

"Leaving!"

"For Long Island, to see my mother and finally meet the new stepfather."

"And escape me."

"Could I ever? You've gotten about as close to me as anybody could."

"Not quite."

"You scare me, Savannah."

"I mean to." Her fingers touched his."You don't mean for long?"

"A couple of weeks, the last of summer, and back for the fall semester—the last."

"Last. Oh, don't, Cory."

"That."

"You're going without Rod?"

"We haven't really decided."

"He has—mentioned he should go, I mean. It's time, he said. He's a little ashamed that you haven't gone after all this time, both of you."

"He can do something about that."

"Go without you?"

"Why not? I'm not his keeper."

"You're not being very subtle. Sometimes I think you're actually jealous, Cory."

"Jealous?" He turned back to the painting. His hand rose to within touch of that concentrated face and fell.

Jealous.

"Is that so impossible?"

"Useless. Jealousy usually is."

"But possible."

"Savannah, why do you go at me all the time!"

"Because I'm a woman, and I want."

"You've got what you want. Haven't you done enough already?"

"I didn't *do* anything. What happened, happened, Cory. A woman needs. *I* need something concrete to go on."

"Rod looks pretty solid to me."

"Not Rod. Between you and me, Cory."

"You don't go for the . . . spiritual between us?"

"Not unless you can touch it. If there's anything important you've ever said to me, at least that I've agreed with, it's that: if the real's not *in* what you can touch, it's nothing. I want to touch it, Cory."

In her seriousness her brown eyes seemed to grow larger and encompass him. He touched her cheek.

"So do I, Savannah." He nodded at the portrait. "So did he, and look what's happened to him. I wish it were as easy as just deciding."

"Maybe you're too cerebral about it."

She ran her hand down his arm, fingered his thumb. Then she smiled up at him—painfully, he saw—and nodded, and left. Sadly he watched her go. He would have given anything if he could be to her what she hoped, but he would live no dubious desire, no half-truth, no lie. He ached to understand all that was in him. He wanted to be released; he yearned for fulfillment. He took one more lingering look at the young man. Only the empty rich blue of the sky reflected in those eyes was alive, yes.

By August, after finals, they were all exhausted.

"Well, Churchill was right," Rod said. "It takes blood, sweat, and tears to get us through."

Rod's was not exactly a victory. Despite a surface bravado about his classes, his quick comprehension and his ability to expound on his subjects, "I flubbed the exams," he said. He had not made a good showing the fall-winter semester either. He did not complain. He seldom mentioned his classes. Savannah worried not about his performance alone, but the cause. She couldn't get to that. "He rubs shoulders with the best—I mean you, not me." She let out her scraping chortle. "Seriously, from us he's picked up the best habits—he's always at the library, he reads, he never misses his homework or a test. If I bring it up, I can't get a thing out of him. Couldn't you?"

"Rod's one-track minded. We've got that in common, though we don't pursue the same things. He has to be fired by something, and I don't think that's happened since high school sports. He's floundering."

"Or brooding?"

"Does he—with you?"

"Never. He jokes about it."

"That's when he's apt to be most serious."

"Rod wouldn't be secretive, would he?"

"He doesn't contrive, if that's what you mean. Rod's too open and ingenuous for that. But he could be brooding. He does hold things in, yet he's considerate. He'd never let you know a thing if it would hurt you: there's that. Under that master storyteller and extrovert, there's a sensitive boy."

"Maybe he has reasons, though I don't think he's as complex as you make him out to be. You're not protecting yourself? He's no threat to you in some way?"

"Threat! We're brothers, Savannah. He loves me."

"That's a subjective way to put it. Why not 'I love him'? You certainly haven't acted much as if you do."

"Perhaps that's when I do most. Perhaps it's even what I do best. *Love and be silent*, it says somewhere."

"You're being evasive, Cory."

"Why don't you let up on it, Savannah."

"I don't like to see Rod looking so haggard. Have you stopped to look at him lately? He's lost weight, he's tired, his eyes are dark, he's distracted. You don't know the times I've caught him staring off into space. He goes walking alone. When I mention the change, he laughs it off. It's no false front. When he's with company, he's gregarious, and for the time being seems to forget what's bothering him. If the change is driving me crazy, it's because I care about him. We'd better do something. You'd better."

"Maybe he needs home. We'll be going soon."

"Together?"

"I told you once. Rod and I haven't decided."

"O*kay*. I guess I've gone too far, but please, Cory . . . if you've got a grudge, hold it against me, not Rod. It was me. You know it was . . . Anyway, exactly when are you leaving?"

"The early evening train Friday."

"I'll be here before train time."

"Come early."

She left him in an emotional sink, made him feel he was the cause, and again he didn't like himself. He felt sorry for Rod. He never thought of Rod as feeling so deeply, brooding alone. For what? He had always been the callous athlete. What had Rod ever done that he should brood? The last thing in the world he wanted was to hurt Rod. He was ashamed of his fury, for making Rod move out, for sulking, for being so silently possessive of each of them, apart. Savannah was his, and Dalton, and wasn't Rod? And it was as much their intruding into his life with his brother. But what right had he, Cory, to dictate relationships in order to preserve his own? Rod had suffered that trait in him silently. Like the good loser (as he was not), Rod had always endured him.

Looking back on the days when they were kids in The Block, it shamed him when he thought how he'd fought with Rod. He'd get him down on the kitchen floor, sit on him and pin his arms down with his knees so Rod couldn't move. He'd take Rod's head in both hands and beat it against the floor, 'Take that take that take that,' till Rod's face contorted in pain, he cried, and gave up. Now, whenever he mistreated him, Rod's contorted face always came back to shame him. If he could undo those moments! Rod had always said, not with resentment but pride, "I'm the athlete, but my brother's got the body." Growing up, Rod had been scrawny, with a metabolism which so burnt up his food that the day he was to try out for the football team he'd stuffed himself with bananas just before weighing in and barely made the minimum weight. But he, Cory, was no athlete: a loner, an ace swimmer, a high-bar performer. Shorter than Rod, slim, it tickled him when Ma said, "Cory's got the shoulders."

But he could not bring himself to go to Rod. Intuition told him Rod would come to him. He waited, testing intuition; and at the last minute, early Friday afternoon, as he was packing his suitcase, Rod did come.

"Hello, Cory."

Savannah was right. The sight stunned Cory. Rod did look haggard. Haunted. He was too still, as if the least movement would cause him to spill. How could what was eating at him change him so quickly?

"You look like death warmed over, Rod. You need the Island." He heard his own anguish.

"I see you're ready."

"I'm taking the afternoon train to Chicago."

"You're not going without me?"

"I didn't know your plans."

"My plan's the same as yours. What would Ma think, and Gramp?"

"When'd they ever expect us together? Just because we're together here doesn't mean we'll always be."

"But we are now, and there's no reason, there isn't, Cory, why we can't travel home together—at least that. We may never be together again. When we get to Greenport, you can do what you want. But why upset them?"

Cory finished packing and went into the bathroom for his shaving things.

"Cory?"

There was a tremor in Rod's voice. Cory dared not look at him. He said, "I'll meet you at the station just before train time."

He heard the suck in Rod's throat.

"I'll be there."

A few minutes later the familiar footsteps sounded on the stairs.

"Savannah?"

"I ran into Rod. I'm so glad you're going on the same train. I told him I'd be at the station."

Outside was a miracle of light in the trees, Lake Mendota like white steel, the woods endless darks beyond.

"No train for hours yet." His palms were wet. He had told her *early* deliberately.

At the end of next semester, would Rod take her wherever he went or would Rod send for her?

"I suppose you'll go with Rod when he graduates?" He felt the needles in his own voice.

"Cory?"

"Well, will you? Will you, Savannah?"

Something was coming over him. Since Rod had left, he had wanted something to come over him, and it had. His mind had not articulated what it was, but his body, yes.

He trembled. Needles seemed to prick his flesh. For a second there was a pleasant swirl, he was giddy.

"Well, will you?"

"*I* don't know."

"He hasn't said ?"

"No. We've talked—"

"You've *talked*."

"—around it."

"What does *that* mean—?"

"I've still got two semesters to go—remember?"

"You can do better than that, Savannah."

"You want me to shove myself at him, insist, weep—all the romantic slush—is that it? You *know* Rod better than that."

"You know *me* better than that."

"Then what's the push? Why are you edgy, and so picky? *Look*, Cory, it's our last day for a while—"

"Our last hour. And Rod's?"

"Of *course* Rod's. He'll be at the station waiting. Listen, Cory—because he's your brother, we're even closer. You know that. Rod knows it."

"Does he?"

"*I* don't know what goes on in his head, but I suppose so."

"He's told you that?"

"Of course not."

"Well then!"

"Christ, Cory, you can't always go crawling into people's heads the way you want to—"

"The way I want to!"

"Always. You do. For God's sake, Cory, let's don't—not now, at the last minute."

"Why not? As good a way to end things as any, isn't it?"

"It won't end a thing. I won't let you go this way. You're just upset and nervous and maybe even a little sick."

"Sick!"

"You don't look well, you haven't been. I've been watching you, weeks now."

"Just like you, Savannah, sitting in the Rathskeller and watching: Big Momma collecting data. I'm fine, if you want to know—fine."

He threw his arms up, gripped the window frame. From down Langdon came the cries of other students. He closed his eyes. Savannah. Rod. Island. He felt it coming—a surge, a fierce power.

"You just think you're fine," she said.

"All right, I think I'm fine."

"It's because the apartment's emptied of Rod's stuff. It's too naked, I felt miserable when I came in. *You* must."

He trembled. His armpits were damp. There was the sultry stick of his clothes. He could feel it all come together. He bit his teeth hard.

"Cory?"

He didn't want to turn and face her on his bed, but he did. He crossed to her.

"Cory?"

"I'll be all right." She knew his hyper moments—before exams; after; reading his favorite passages; discovering unfamiliar species of algae on the lake. "I'm fine." The edge of his voice said *not.*

"I haven't been seeing," he said.

"What?"

"I've been in a daze."

He was staring into her part, but she raised her head.

"Y ou still are. I can tell the look. Cory . . ." Her head nuzzled his thigh, her hands gripped his pockets and drew him close. He set his hands on her ears now, fondling, and closed his eyes.

"Rod wants you?"

"I think so," she said, "but I don't know why. I never did."

"You sound like me. You want reasons that can't be given."

"Or maybe I knew, but Rod didn't. I could never say what Rod himself might not know."

Now he knew it was happening. She could feel what was happening. He could feel she didn't want it to happen. She could feel his flesh growing. There would be the triumph she had failed at before; there would be the disbelief in her voice, and the wonder. For a moment it would have nothing to do with Rod; it would be their own love he would nurture it on. When he pressed her face against his thigh, when she touched, he burned, he felt her hot breath, felt she could not move, her mouth a damp breath through the wool.

"God, yes, Savannah."

Her eyes were closed. The lids were wet.

"I know what you're thinking," he said.

"Yes, you do. I can never have you. You don't even know that I can never have you."

He did not say, Why *Rod*? She would say, Because Rod is the nearest thing to you.

He said, "These years," knowing she wanted love that *was* love but not *this* that he was giving. From early morning this had been coming into his head, where it had all happened early. Almost, he could not bear her breath. Still, he kept his eyes on the part and kept his hands moving and drawing her breath to his growing flesh.

"It's been terrible," she said.

It would always be.

"It needn't be."

"No. But I could never have you."

"No," he said.

He knew her futility now. He knew Rod now. He knew himself now. He sank his hands over her soft cotton, gripped and drew it up, and she cried out, "Cory, I could never have you. Never." She knew him too well. She knew through the years of study with him.

He unbuckled, unzipped, when she was round and white again, stretched out again. "My God, Cory."

Her resistance was fraught with confusion, doubt and desire.

Rod.

In a minute she would know Cory. There would be no Rod. For a long minute there would not be Rod.

For Chris'sake, Rod, will you get out of here?

He feared *Rod* from her mouth, but then it came, "Cory, Cory . . ."

She began to cry but did not stop. He must watch. He could not let himself and her not be watched: he became Cory. His mouth was in her hair, his face in her wet hair. "You don't know why you're doing this," she cried in the agony, "Cory, you don't know why," not stopping, maddening, drawing him so in that he almost forgot *Cory, not Rod, Cory,* and then said, "Yes, you can, Savannah," meaning You can have me; and she said, "No, no, because you don't know why," crying, lying thrown back on the bed now, arms over her face smeared with strands of wet hair, "because I don't know why either, but I can't, I can't, Cory."

He said nothing. What had come over him had gone. He was detached now. Everything isolated—her body, the window, the far trees . . .

"You, Cory!" Her voice, her face, suspended between fury, love. "What you did to me."

"What you did to me," he said.

She was dressing, furious.

"What I did," he said.

"Yes!" She was crying.

"The hell is you don't even know why."

"And you do."

"No, I don't."

He sat on the edge of the bed, exhausted. Rod had sat on the edge of the bed.

This time the glitter had fallen on her breast, a tear.

He heard her brushings, the shoes sucked on, her coat. "Did you have to do that?"

He clutched his head.

"Stop that!" she said. "I'm as much to blame as you, but what did it prove?"

He could think only *Dogs.* Dogs pissed on trees to oust dogs, to lay claim, take possession. But what had that to do with it?

"You want to get rid of me for good, don't you? Don't you?"

"I don't know what I want."

"To destroy."

"I don't know."

"To begin clean. Begin what? Nobody can begin clean. We're not slates you wipe clean, Cory. It'll always be there."

"I didn't say I wouldn't take it with me. How could I avoid that?"

"Why take it with you *this* way? You have to, don't you? Do you know why, Cory?"

"You tell me, Savannah."

"You're cruel, Cory."

"Yes, cruel."

She had called him cruel before when the three were arguing evil at the Campus Grill: "You're cruel, Cory, because you lash out at people out of deepest feelings, which brings you worse evil—an excess of good, would Aristotle say?—because evil in itself is nothing but an excess of good, which can only be parasitic to the very good God has created, an abuse of good which leads to misproportion and imbalance in the human being." "God!" Rod had said. "God is a voracious old man who eats his own, trying to consume his own good but cannot."

"You didn't want me," she said, "did you?"

"If you know that, why do you ask?"

"I want you to say it, Cory. I want you to say *No, I didn't want you, Savannah.*"

"No, I didn't want you, Savannah."

"You son-of-a-bitch." She was crying again.

"You wanted me to say it."

"I knew it, but didn't want you to say it. You couldn't even leave me that last one holy dignity between us?"

"Not even that."

"Not for Rod?"

"For Rod?"

"Not to make what I have with Rod corroded, putrid, absolutely wrong?"

"Only you and Rod know what you have."

"And *you*, Cory, because you know your Savannah, your friend, your close ineradicable, inescapable friend you'll carry with you all your life, *my college pal and inseparable Savannah*."

"Does Rod really know what goes on between the two of you, and why?"

"You think I took him to be near you or get you to capitulate. That's partly true, but Rod's Rod. If he's got something of *you* in him which made me burn for him in the first place, yes, if you want to know, a soft spot. His tenderness spills out, mostly he can't conceal it, but when yours spills, you cut it off, you with your the sea and sand made me, you escape like one of your damned crabs doing a sidestep."

"And Gramp," he said.

"Gramp what?" she said.

"Sea and sand and Gramp."

"I've heard all about him. What's he got to do with this?"

Everything, he thought. Nothing. He said, "Because he's there; he's always been there."

"Sometimes there's madness in you, Cory. I really believe that. It's why you're great and terrible at the same time. It made me love you and it makes me hate you."

"A man's defect, like a writer's, a genius's, is the source of his greatness as well as the source of his failure. Take, for example, Faulkner's style—"

"Stop making fun of me, Cory!"

"Not fun, not fun, Savannah."

"Destroy, Cory. You're trying to."

"We've been that route."

"We keep coming back to truth. That's the thing about truth, you know—it attracts."

"All right! If you've spoken truth, truth it is. Cut it!"

"Well! Big brother can be gotten to—on *some* ground."

"Some."

"There's the wedge!"

"Leave it, Savannah. Truth is a bitch, like you."

"Right, a scorpion. It bites at both ends as you've so—unpleasantly?—just found out."

He did not speak.

"Or as *I* have so unpleasantly found out."

Still he said no word.

"Well, what is it we've found out, then? What are we going off with, a permanent rift? Well, if that's what you want . . . Cory?"

"Nothing."

"Cory?"

"I said *nothing*."

"Remember. You can't undo things."

"I can't undo *nothing*."

"Then that's what you get if you're so goddamned stinking about it: nothing."

"Ditto."

She was at the door.

"Don't let me go this way, Cory."

"Go what way?"

"All right, persist, damn you! In no time you'll be gone—"

"On the next train for Chicago."

"Without Rod."

"What makes you think I don't know that?"

She slammed the door. Her shoes echoed. He waited for the creaks halfway down, for her to stop, the door to sigh shut, her faint sound slow down the porch steps. So many hundreds of times. The next would be his—when he decided to go.

He was not finished.

He sat on the bed. He saw how Rod had sat on the bed. Savannah was white and round and a diamond drop glittered. He saw her face, the dark hair darker against pillow and sheet.

He sat where Rod had sat, facing the window blank against the next door clapboards.

He was waiting. He would wait until Rod. He would miss the train. Rod would miss the train, or would not. If Rod missed the train, they would come back, both of them, Savannah and Rod, or maybe Rod would come back alone. He would sit and wait until then.

Light began to go. Dark came up the vault between the houses. Next door lights splayed up the clapboards, dim, and made dirty windows hazy. In the room the furniture sank away, the edges tinged by the vague light. Dark took the room. Dark sent time away and made was in his head.

"What, then, am I doing here?" he asked aloud.

Sounds came—sighs in the walls, creaks, faucets, clumping on stairs; but here, inside, nothing. Still, he had decided to sit him, or them, out. He did not care how long. He did not look at time. *I'm just here.* He waited. He had started it: something was not over yet. He had not reached *what* yet. He was aware that, even sitting still, he was rushing toward some end he had started moving himself toward, unaware of what might be at the end. He had to wait. He did not question the dark, only waited.

He wanted footsteps which he knew, years of up and down steps which he had waited for.

Then—how had he missed hearing steps?—the door was flung open and the light switched on. In the pane the raw bulb made everything dingy.

"You, Cory!"

So Savannah *had* told. Or Rod had seen her face and got it out of her. She wasn't actress enough to hide losses. Rod knew her.

He dared not move.

"Your train!" It escaped Savannah, low.

There were always trains. That's what the world was about, trains.

"What in hell do you think you're doing, Cory?"

Rod's mouth was fury.

"Waiting for a train." He felt all abrupt acid.

"You'd better haul ass then," Rod said. "You know where the station is."

"Everybody knows where the station is," he said.

"I ought to kill you," Rod said.

"Yes," Cory said.

"I ought to!" You could hear a cry in his voice—for which of them? "It wouldn't be hard, goddamn you."

"Rod," Savannah said.

Cory could hear her repentant. Oh, he knew. He could hear what she'd say, *I hated to tell but Rod made me, I couldn't lie to him, Cory, I couldn't go on with him after a lie, you know that.*

She couldn't either. He knew Savannah. Coldly, at this minute he knew Savannah.

But not coldly Rod.

Somewhere he was trembling: in his center a quivering was beginning and he stood up.

Rod said, "Get your goddamn suitcases out of here."

"This is my place."

"You heard me."

The quivering reached his lungs. It began to catch at his breathing. He was afraid. If he had to speak, he could not bite his words.

He stood by the bed. He remembered Savannah white and round in the bed and her hair so dark on the pillow.

Actually she was standing by the window, looking toward the lake, against the stark white lace the light from the house made in the branches of the trees. Her head tilted, and her hair edged dark. Her hands clung to the sill.

When he moved his eyes, the image of the diamond glint moved with them.

"You're filthy," Rod said.

He heard Savannah's breath catch.

"Rod, no," she whimpered.

The one thing he would not do was look into Rod's face. He would spare himself that. He knew what it would be. He did not need that image to carry down the stairs, out past the light and the leaves into the night sky, into the street interrupted by the lights of passing cars.

"You filthy Judas. We waited at the station. She cried. She wouldn't tell, but I *knew*, and she couldn't deny it."

"Well, then, you know." That would stop Savannah. She wouldn't, couldn't, say anything more then.

He heard her breath break.

Rod had turned at that slight sound. He saw quickly Rod's back and Savannah reflected dark in the window, black against that lacy light outside, as if standing in the branches. She covered her face with her hands. They were all so still. He was sure, far out in the growing dark, there was a lone sailboat with one dark figure, streaking across the lake. The carillon tower struck on Bascomb Hill. He counted: four, five, six . .

"My own brother," Rod said.

The quivering had reached Cory's throat.

"Unclean," Rod said.

His eyes hurt. He could hardly move, but heard his breath moving.

"Get out," Rod said. "Out—damn you!"

Cory didn't move.

"You heard me?"

"Rod, please." Savannah's voice was so tender it startled.

Rod came over to him. Rod's eyes were wet. He knew Rod would not touch him.

"You're nothing, Cory."

His heart beat so hard he would fall.

He turned around quick, seized his two grips, and went down the stairs, hard, slow. The steps creaked loud. The suitcase kept hitting the shaky railing.

At the bottom he stopped, his breath near gone. All his skin beat.

He held the door and slid a suitcase out, then the other. The warm air flooded.

* * *

Rod had the oars, locks.

Cory followed.

German was at the crick, waiting.

The crick was four houses away, past the Polacks' place, the Dombroskis,' and old Catalina Hannibal's. Katrinka his mother called her with some affection (she'd planted the maple in their front yard "for your brother who drowny," Mrs. Hannibal had said) but with some reserve too because her Puerto Rican skin was weathered dark (black, his mother thought) and because she'd married the half-Indian half-black Geebo and had the son Dannie, very black too.

She came now, that frail little Puerto Rican woman in skirts to the ground, long sleeves, bandana, tiny against the lot of withering corn stalks that ran hard against the rise of Al Dickson's green, green lawn studded with his dozens of sunning cats. She stood on the edge of her property. She seldom crossed, knowing the distrust of *dark*, knowing *nigger*. She laughed. She showed all her false teeth, white joy, her long hands praising in the sun.

The tiny thing touched Cory and kissed both his cheeks.

"Oh boy oh boy oh boy, my boy." Mrs. Hannibal soared into laughter, high.

"You come home. Good! And broder come too."

She waved to Rod, who kept a distance.

She said to Rod, "Speaky good Spany, you broder. Usted no habla Spany?" and laughed. "One day you come. Still gotty good tomatoes—for tu madre."

They waved. She stood watching, thin, her skirts fragile feathers in the wind.

At the corner, they crossed the street to the crick.

A row of houses ran along this side of the crick. Behind them, the bank dropped steep, so the sight of the crick came sudden, that narrow jaw of water between the houses on this side and the wide sweep of sea grass on the other. The jaw's lip pressed almost up to the road beyond. Its open end widened into Stirling Basin, the bay, and finally the ocean. Though he couldn't see it, he knew too well the road beyond the sea grass, where it ran between Stirling Cemetery and St. Agnes' Cemetery, past fallow fields and through a dark ridge of trees to the shallow beach at Gull Pond.

On a jut behind St. Agnes' was his uncle Gill's place—Gramp's brother with the loud raspy voice and permanent squint, albino pink worse than Gramp's, behind glasses that made you stare through tunnels at a quivering sliver of blue family eyes. Across from Gill's was Sandy Point, a prong into the bay.

The tide was out. Most of the boats too. Labor Day. The rotting piers were bared, the broken planks thin and dark as insect legs clinging to the bank.

Raynor's old dock shimmied under his and Rod's weight. With the missing planks you could be standing on water.

Moored alone there, German's rowboat was too bright, virgin. It shamed the crick, all that flotsam floating in this backwater—bits of wood, Dixie cups, rotting rope ahang from cork, a beer can—scarcely moved in the rise and fall of normal tides.

German loosed the mooring and hugged the boat against the dock.

Rod stepped in, set the locks in, and oars.

"Try it, Cory." German held the rope taut.

"She's sure buoyant," Rod said.

"Has to be to hold me, and move." German dwarfed both of them. Though his father and Daddy Pete were small, his mother preferred big men.

Cory slid down into stern, German tossed the rope in and shoved them.

"Wait!" Cory cried.

Rod gripped the oars—

"Rod! You tricked me, both of you."

Rod laughed.

German echoed his laugh. "Give it a good workout."

"Where in hell are we going?"

"You've been hankering to row out to the Orient light. Well, that's where we're going."

"The Point's miles!"

"Easy by water. We've got all the time in the world."

Skillful, Rod cut between isolated piling stubs split and rot-brown as teeth in an old mouth.

He was a master rower. The oars and boat, he made his body, his limbs under perfect control, the control of an athlete, or ascetic. Since he had been in service during Rod's high school years, he had missed Rod's talents. This close, Rod's mastery awed.

Rod was facing him and the land. Cory faced sea. On the right the familiar houses and Pell's Fish Market glided into a postcard view, and on the left the sea grass was a golden field of shimmering sun.

Rod's oars sliced the water clean, no drips. In the water the pull of the oars coiled serpents of blue green red yellow oil, and where the prow cut the oil, serpents wriggled on each side in perfect balance.

Ahead, hospital sat on its ledge of land like a great brooding creature, its myriad windows made blank eyes by morning light.

"You put German up to this?"

He thought Rod always too ingenuous for collusion.

Cory touched the oily snakes. They shot from his hand, split and multiplied.

"German. Maybe Ma and German."

"What does that mean?"

On the lawn of the Townsend Manor Inn people clustered under colorful striped umbrellas. Kids' cries broke from the pool. From far the autos in the crowded parking lot looked like rows of shiny June bugs.

"Don't underestimate them. They know we're strange with each other, Cory. Why else wouldn't we come home together? Well, if you must know, I only had to drop the hint . . ."

"Roped me into this, you mean?"

The Booth House, freshly white, seemed to stare into itself in the water.

And far on the left appeared the long narrow bar of Sandy Beach, its single file of wooden houses looking vulnerable between two waters.

Rod was veering from town and harbor. At Young's Point he rounded the breakwater, headed through Peconic Bay toward open sea.

He succumbed to Rod's rhythm, his natural meticulous urging of the boat forward, maintaining an almost motionless balance, the boat responding to his least shift. The water seemed to breathe now, as if awakened, pressing in a slow heaving at the boat's bottom.

The beach at Gull Pond—a clean arc of yellow sand between Young's Point and Cleave's Point—was already dotted with the Labor Day crowd.

Inland, a narrow body of water lay between the beach and the mainland. A wooden bridge the width of the road ran over that inlet. There was the Girls' Hole on one side of the bridge, the Boys' on the other.

Behind, the same high wall of trees you saw from the crick, deep and dark, now cut off the crick and town and all the west. Cory was watching for life moving along the dirt road, where the few cottages caught the morning sun.

Rod broke the silence.

"There's Fatso's place—"

In a square lawn of startling green, its kitchen windows facing the bay, the white house was purity itself, the two windows and the pane in the door as blind white as the hospital's.

"He sure keeps the place up. Have you seen him yet?"

"No."

"He works day and night, that Fatso. And reads. A regular Jew with his time. *I* can't even get him to fish anymore. Used to be we'd spend hours in a boat or off the breakwater."

Fast the house shrank, and the trees.

As they approached open sea, the village of East Marion and farther off Orient seemed perched bright and white over the water.

Tiny rags of cloud, motionless, hung.

"He won't talk."

"Who?"

"Fatso, Cory! He just stares all the time. He's thinking. You just know he's churning away. His eyes look dead."

A wind was raking the waves.

Along its harbor the village of Orient gleamed, the houses a row mostly white in the fading fall green. Between, sails streaked colored fires like signals.

"Fatso never talks. His house is full of books."

As they approached the Long Beach sandbar, the lighthouse, like growing out of the water, rose to full size. Past it, sea spread. Behind Rod, all was sky, nothing. Alone against that space, moving with steady ease, he looked monumental.

"They're your books, Cory."

"Some."

"Your name's in them."

"Some."

"You sent them from Wisconsin?"

He nodded.

Over the water, low, a furious buzzing came from off Ram Island. Far right, motorboats were streaking, no doubt warming up for the Labor Day race.

"And some during the war, and before—from Bristol. Years I've been sending them . . . almost since we were kids. Since Gramp's. *You* know, a chapter a day in the Bible."

Rod laughed.

"Do I!"

In the dark corner of Gramp's kitchen, Fatso's dark eyes had glittered. They stared out of the depths like an unknown animal's. Roused, they darted as if they yearned to break through. Fatso himself wanted to break the mystery: God had chosen Joseph, but why?

And with justice—but what was that trial for? Why did God abuse what He made? Or did He? But Fatso had since gone far from any view of that God.

"Gramp was more than school."

Rod was still somewhat paralleling the sandbar that was the stretch of Orient State Park. The Labor Day multitude of cars glinted in the parking lot and people speckled the beach. Here and there breaths of smoke from the kookout pits dissipated into dark webs and dissolved.

"Yes, because he sees."

Abruptly Cory laughed.

"Just think," he said, "Gramp *sees.* The old man with quivering eyes sees the connections between things when half the teachers I've had with perfect eyes are blind to them."

"Well, I'm glad *somebody* gets a reaction out of you."

He rested the oars and let the boat drift and give way to the slow suck and sway in wider troughs and crests that almost imperceptibly weaned it from the shore.

"You want me to take over?"

"I'm not tired. Let's just enjoy. Today's my day."

Rod sank into the bottom, stretched his arms and let his hands rest loosely over the sides. The loose flexibility of his body was a gift; he assumed the shape of things, became wood, water, sand, never alien, while Cory, stark still, projected, "lived into" them.

"Gramp was our Bible, and you're Fatso's. Yes, you are—don't deny it. He got onto you."

"Fatso's just a good listener."

"Something in you made him listen."

"In Gramp. He's the magic."

"Him too, because Fatso had Gramp before he had you. Gramp's shack was his refuge when he couldn't go anywhere else. When his family kicked him out, Gramp'd always give him a corner. But you inspired Fatso."

"You're just imagining it."

"You can't brush it off that easily. It's not because I'm your brother. *I* didn't want to believe it either. Things seemed too easy for you."

"Easy! But it's you who attracted everybody. You were, always have been, the popular one. You're no loner like me. No group sports for me."

"Oh, yeah—me the big athlete, popular, yeah; hail fellow well met, yeah; everybody loves a champ, yeah; But me*s* come and go—I'm not talking about that, no. I'm talking about something you can't help. It's just there, Cory. You affect people, even against their will, yes—that—even against their will."

"Rod, I never intended to do anything."

"Against their will, Cory!"

"And not against mine?"

"And you must know it. You couldn't help but know."

"You think that's something I want?"

"There, you admit it! You couldn't cut it out of you even if you knew what it was. But it's there, and you're responsible even if you don't want to be. Maybe it's not even part of you. Maybe it's indifferent, indifferent to you too. Anyway, you've hooked us—me, Vanna, Dalton, your teachers, Sánchez-Barbudo and Henry Mann."

"You're describing Gramp—"

"*Yes*, I'm describing Gramp, and that makes you happy. Doesn't it, Cory?"

"You don't know how happy it makes me."

"Because you love him more than anybody else."

"Yes."

"And *he* was just *there*, wasn't he?"

"Always. There's so much in him that speaks—"

"*What*? Tell me what."

What spoke was the quiver of blue sky and moving white fire on the water, like the quiver in Gramp's eyes.

"See! You can't describe it anymore than I could. Look what you did to Fatso. Fatso's not the same—he's silent, he stares. I hate to say it, but he scares me, Cory, he's so quiet; and embarrasses me too, because—*you* know I'm no scholar—the subjects he brings up are too philosophical, justice and the absolute and the irrational and the metaphysical. You name it."

Cory remembered the fire burning dark in Fatso's eyes; either they flashed it off as if it could not enter, or it burned from within.

"Years ago he worshipped you, Cory."

"Don't be silly, Rod."

"He did. I think he wants to *be* you."

"Be me!"

"Yes. Of course he couldn't, and knows that now."

Drifting, the boat was turning. The swells, more frequent now, shorter, rode under. The boat rose and fell in that steady pulse of sea.

Cory looked back. The Long Beach bar lighthouse was far behind. Greenport was gone, and East Marion. Only a fine white bar of sand glistened, and a line of green edge.

And Fatso's house?

Oblivion.

We live at the end of the world. Ma loved it because family dead and alive were here—in their blood; in these houses; in Stirling Cemetery, which you could see from the upstairs window; in the maples and swamp willow and birches and lilacs they had planted in the yard; in the sea that possessed the bodies of some of their drowned.

I'll never leave the Island again, Gramp had said.

Never, Ma had echoed for herself.

Sometimes Ma and Gramp were one. They were so rooted, they grew here. Their eyes were some days fog or sea or sand. They could stand and dissolve into a swamp willow or rambler or blackberry bush or fog or sand or fine black potato dirt. They were made of that. After centuries of family here, they *were* the Island.

German hated the Island. He said sand sucked blood, sea bloated, damp air stifled. "Give me Detroit." "You say that," his mother said, "but you can't stand traffic or crowds, and children playing drive you crazy."

There were days Cory would gladly have become a blackberry bush or silver maple or Gramp to keep from leaving the Island. So he understand Fatso's love for it. Rod did not. "Fatso." He seemed to be facing Fatso and did not see how seaward the rowboat was headed. Too directly east.

"Rod, we're getting too off course."

Rod laughed. "What course? Today's a first. We're pioneers."

The sun was high, too stark down. It made the surface an undulating mirror. The reflection stymied sight, and would burn.

Rod took an oar and turned them parallel to the sandbar again, to the spread of State Park beach, then resumed with both oars in steady rhythm now.

Rod didn't take his eyes off his face.

Despite wind, skin was turning sweat. Rod's shirt was sucked dark to his skin. Cory did not know that body.

Headed northeast, now the boat rode its own shadow. It eased Cory's vision. Left, the beach materialized, a long rib almost white that blended with the mainland and narrowed to a fine arrow, its tip aimed straight at the Orient Point lighthouse and the Gut, which cut between the Point and Plum Island.

Cory sent his hand underwater. Too cold! Despite the heat reflected off the surface, he shivered with the heralded winter.

Rod's face was dark, half sun, and darkly serious.

"He makes me afraid, Cory."

"He?"

"*Fatso*, Cory!"

"You—afraid of Fatso?"

"Yes. Not physically, and not for me. For you."

"Me? But Fatso's gentle. He wouldn't harm anything, least of all me."

In Fatso's domain, the dump, there was not a corner, not a moving thing Fatso did not survey with affection.

"Least of all's the worst. You're wrong, Cory. I said he couldn't be you. He can't. So he vies with you. Everything shows that. Since he can't, I think he hates you, Cory."

"Not Fatso."

"Yes, Fatso."

"What makes you believe that?"

"Only hate could be that still. Sometimes it's as if all the motion in him stops so still you'd think he was dead. But he *isn't*."

"Rod—"

"*Lis*ten to me, Cory. I feel it. You won't credit me with that sensibility? If you never paid any attention to me, do it now."

The oars hung high. Far, behind Rod's head, gulls swooped and rose, and rode on the wind, still, as he was.

"Please, Cory." His voice held such pain.

Rod was new to him. He feared this new, though in it he suspected something familiar but not articulated. He felt humbled—Rod might have been kneeling—because he knew what it cost when Rod had had nothing but fury.

You're nothing, Cory.

Cory nodded.

He waited.

Rod said nothing. He closed his eyes. His head fell, almost prayerful. Then he rowed, rowed, relentless.

For a long time each was alone, concentrated. They cut across low waves. The ridges battered. The boat replied with quick hollow utterances.

The sun burned. Heat was raising a fine haze. In spots it thinned to wisps coiled between waves and burned off.

The end of the island narrowed and thinned to the dead end of Highway 25 at the Point. On the far side of the road the long white facade of the Orient Point Inn burned white, the long white gingerbread porch and its upstairs veranda cresting the rise opposite the Long Island Ferry dock.

"Look! There she comes."

The ferry was just emerging from Plum Gut, turning to make the arc to the landing.

Deep, just out from shore, two great pilings marked the narrow dredged docking area.

"Jesus!" The sight shocked Rod. "It's an LCT."

"Since the war," Cory said.

The ferry was a low war-gray beast thrusting its flat blank whale front through the waters, its advance sending long waves like white whiskers off its sides.

It was bearing down. As if Normandy. Only with other machines in its belly now.

"It's not the *Shinnecock* or the *Catskill*."

The sight startled reverie. In an instant you traveled from pre-bomb childhood to post-bomb technology.

Both gazed.

They were drifting again.

"Remember the first time we made the trip alone, Cory?"

In early years Ma took them back and forth summers between Rhode Island and Long Island.

"Were we ever such little tykes?"

Tots, really. Seven and five. "You boys're old enough to go to Gram's alone now." Ma rode with them on the bus from Bristol to Providence and at the depot put them on the New York train. "Stay on till you get to New London. When you get off, cross the train tracks—you be *very* careful there—to the ferry dock. Pop Converse, the purser—you know Pop—will meet you at the boat. He's expecting you. And your grandmother or one of your aunts or uncles will be waiting for you when you get to Orient. Behave yourselves on the train. Your egg salad sandwiches with onions the way you like them are in the bag, Cory, in a damp towel. Tell Gram to save the towel. Here's money for milk on the train and a nickel apiece for a Dixie cup. I've talked to the conductor. He'll find you a seat and see that you get off at New London. Now give Ma a kiss and a big hug. I'll see you in a few weeks at your Gram's. Now you do what you're told out there, both of you."

At New London they descended, all pins and needles. They crossed the tracks to the ferry dock and spotted pudgy Pop Converse in his dress uniform with gold buttons about to pop free and his white cap, a very Christmas-red face. From the upper deck they watched the cars fill the boat's belly, the people down there waving and crying out good-byes and messages. They were twitchy almost to peeing till Pop Converse said as always, "Here's a nickel each for a Dixie cup in the lounge," knowing he knew they had one, but not saying a word. They would sneak up and down the three decks, scurry past lifeboats, in and out of the waiting rooms and ballroom, but mostly with other passengers toss scraps to the gulls that rose and fell in the ship's wake and in wide high rings drifted off, back, both he and Rod all the time eagle-eyed to spot leaping porpoises till they saw the Island like a monstrous whale humped out of the sea

The ship told when they were almost to Orient because as it went through the Gut between Plum Island and the Point, the tides churned and thrummed, the water boiled whitecaps, all the ship vibrated and shuddered. The passengers always became wary when the ship's sounds were muffled dead, till the ship emerged from the Gut with a sudden sigh that seemed like silence itself. The *Shinnecock* swung sharp right—"*To starboard*, Cory!" smarty said—and made the arc to the Orient dock, hooted its arrival so loud it threatened to burst ears and skin. He and Rod from the top deck scoured the shore to be the first to telescope and scream "Gram!"

Had there ever really been a *Shinnecock* or a *Catskill*?

Now only that great gray metal whale the LCT slowly lowered an ugly Hapsburg jaw; slowly it oozed clusters of passengers, a string of cars, from here tiny as a thread of glistening fish eggs. In the lot behind, a long thread of cars waited to refill the ship's emptied gut.

Distant, they passed the flat stern of the LCT. It was heaving in slow undulation with the turning of the tide. Voices and cries came quite clear over the water.

The Point lay like the half-submerged tail of a sunning beast studded with dark knobs—a stretch of great rocks mottled with reddish brown seaweed and gray-white barnacles. Toward the reef and the lighthouse rocks trailed off underwater.

By now the water was roused from lethargy. With quick laps it ran up over the dirty edge and withdrew, and lapped.

It sucked at the rowboat, thrust, sucked. The current pulled meanly at the oars.

"Kids! Those happy days." Rod was live with memory now, laughing to himself. He rested the oars to wipe his forehead with his arm and slide his trousers off his green swim trunks.

"You'll burn tonight."

"I'm already burnt. I can feel it on my shoulders. On Labor Day yet!"

Labor Day could be a treachery. Some years hurricane winds heaved sea over the sandbar, cutting Orient off from the rest of the Island.

Rod's body shone wet. Responding to the sea, gauging its rhythm, he was joyful. The waves flicked chaos, but there was a confident exactitude in the balance with which Rod moved the boat in a straight line, in an awesome, willed order. Rod's body was part of the motion of water and wind and grass and sky, carrying him, Cory, for the first time into that motion, into a terrain he had never shared before. Rod smiled to himself. You could see it made him feel good. He seemed to be listening to what only he could hear.

Where was he?

Despite watching Rod become part of the sun, move light as air, fuse with the rhythm of the waves, Cory felt separated.

They eased parallel to the shore. The land's end was going under. In insistent strikes and swirls, the tide was isolating the boulders. Only the tops emerged like protuberant monstrous eyes.

The end of the world.

Rod turned almost giddy. His eyes darted, swept. He could not take in enough.

"There's your lighthouse, Cory." Rod crooked his neck. Over his right shoulder it began to grow. Rooted deep in a circle of boulders, its base was black metal with a narrow rimmed walkway halfway up, the tapered top white, its head the light itself.

"You can see the reef near it."

You could see sucks and swirls and white lashings around the dark shadow of that underwater reef.

Cory also saw the far white light on the Plum Island cliff and the stone house where the keeper and the two coastguardsmen, Bobbie and Ed, lived and kept vigil over the light. Were they still there? Below, to the right, rose the government dock and the jungle of trees and shrubs autumn brown and green behind it. Deeper in was the house in the officers' quarters where he had spent last summer with his mother and Reggie Webb.

Passion.

Where the tides met, even sunstruck, the Gut made a dark path between the islands, slate now between dark green waters.

"You wanted the light. Well, there it is." Rod's voice was a triumphant shout. He threw his head back and laughed. But the wind broke his laughter. Then he bent forward, abruptly too intense:

"Are you happy now?"

Cory felt a heave at his blood.

"*Are* you, Cory?" Low this time, Rod's voice was tender.

What startled was that he was. Immersed and unaware, he *had* been.

"I am."

"Because I want you to be. *I* am. I knew you would be if I could get you out alone. I wanted it. I planned it, Cory—to be out here, just the two of us, with nobody in the world around."

"You planned this?"

"You can't know how long I've wanted this. It's the only way I could be sure to have you to myself and to talk to you, make you listen."

All motion seemed to halt.

Rod, the lighthouse, Plum Island stood too sharp.

"You brought me out here for this?"

"Because you wouldn't speak—"

"No, Rod, you wouldn't. You were so furious I thought you hated me."

"Hated!" Rod threw his head back, his chest filled, his breath burst into a stunned laugh. "Christ, Cory!"

"All the time you lived with me—"

"All the time, all the time, all the time, oh godhelpus, Cory, all the time, if you could know what I suffered—yes, suffered—but not just then, oh no, long before: ever since you left me."

"When did I ever leave you?"

"Oh, you couldn't have known, but you left me when you enlisted. *I* didn't even know till then. I was just coming to know, but that told me; because when you left, I *felt* you then, you were everywhere, you touched me, the house was full of you, so full I had to keep busy every minute. Ma couldn't believe what I could *do.* I was so busy at school and at the lumber company and weekends at the gas station, and with sports and the senior operetta, and with my crowd so I wouldn't think of you, but *did—Jesus,* Cory— night, day, in our room, yes, in *our* room. You didn't know —I took your bed. Ma didn't care. Next to the window, for the air, I said. But it was you, I was with you, my brother, the brain. At first after you'd left, the teachers were always comparing me to 'the brain' and I resented it; but you were my secret pride because you were my brother and in a way I was sharing your brain, looks, dignity—you were a natural—and your body too. I thought How could Cory be built that way and never exercised, just *had* it, born with it, and me skinny and working all the time building my body up to make the scales. What Ma didn't know all the time was I had to work out and take jobs to keep from getting sick and, sure, to try to keep up the valedictorian's reputation *in my own way*, and add to it because I was more than your brother. I was Cory

Moorehead while you were gone. I stood for you. That's why I wore your things. I never told you when you got mad because I wore out your mosquito boots you got in Recife, Brazil on the way to the ETO, and your machete you sent home, because while I was using them I felt like you. I felt some of you was with me. You don't know how I was waiting for you, Cory."

He was nearly shouting because the wind, low, insisted over the surface, and the jags of waves, irregular, in unyielding tumult, in raps against the bottom.

"And when you came home and I was in Kingston, I was sick. I was, Cory. I wanted my grades to satisfy you, you to be proud—you'd *see* me then, look at *me* and maybe know what . . . was here . . ."

The rowboat was turning slowly away from the Point. Cory went down on his knees to change places.

"Rod, we're moving out. Let me—"

"No." Rod gripped the oars. "Why'd you think I suddenly showed up at Wisconsin? I couldn't stay away. I couldn't stand it another day without you."

Far, the ferry gave three deep hoots. Rod's head jerked back sharply.

Now Rod was facing the Gut, Cory staring back at the ferry. Distant, Shelter Island was a mere hump. All else was Gardiners Bay, and the ocean, endless sky, nothing.

Except for the last night on campus at Wisconsin, he had never seen Rod so intense. He was sweating sun. It seemed to burn out of him. Naked, there was nothing he could hide. The boat, bucking waves, rode high, thrust Rod enormous against sky, then down against dark waves; jutted the island and the ferry into abrupt view, then angled them out of sight.

"Didn't you know, Cory?"

He saw now how the thinness of Rod's face made his mouth thick, his nose finer, and made the dark eyes imperative. *Fragile your face, Rod.* When Rod came home the first weekend from Kingston, he said, "Sometimes I think I'll go crazy studying." Ma had touched the cheekbones, fingered the narrow chin, the lips, worried. Cory had shivered. "I'd rather have you quit the university and become a taxidriver than go crazy. You too, Cory."

"Didn't you, Cory? Tell me!"

"Something. When you came . . ., you made me afraid."

Whenever he'd looked into the mirror, something had emerged from the depths. When Rod was not in the room, he was always somewhere behind in the no man's land of the mirror.

"I saw you were afraid of me. You *needed* to be."

"Afraid, yes—like swimming down too far underwater, where it's dark, and you can't see but you feel something's close to you."

"Yes!"

The LCT was bearing down rapidly, relentlessly driving a great white lip of foam before its square jaw.

"You didn't have to face it, Cory, but *I* did or I wouldn't have gone to Madison. I had to know, but you ran away from me at Koenigs'; and in the apartment, when we moved, after a while you were never there. It was so easy for you. At first I had nobody, but you had Vanna."

Both went silent, staring. Savannah might have risen from the sea. Neither had spoken her name since the return.

The LCT seemed to be headed straight toward them. The insect heads were growing human as it approached.

"You never had to be alone. You could always go to Vanna."

"But I knew Savannah. We were friends before you came. At first she was everything."

"Everything! How do you think I felt? That made me nothing."

"Dalton and Savannah took you in right away. They love you."

"You didn't! You ran away from me, Cory. You ran to Vanna, always Vanna. She was always between us."

You could hear the shuddering of the ferry engine. Over the surface, the sound magnified.

Cory shouted above the grinding. "I never had Savannah."

"Only because you didn't want her."

"She had Dalton."

"No. You're lying to yourself, and you know it. She *let* Dalton because she had to have you, and couldn't. She was, is, afraid she'll end up with nobody."

"She *said*."

Because you had to love something truly, a cat, dog, person, first or you could love nothing, the rest would *be* nothing—beggary, crumbs.

Cries came at them from the ferry. Along the deck heads made irregular beads, arms made bright colorful lashes, waving and waving, as the LCT turned away from them into Midway Shoals, fringing the churning of the Gut.

"You wouldn't have her, Cory. I'd like to know why, Cory. I'd like to *believe* why. I want to. I'd give anything to."

"*You* had her."

"Yes! I fell into it. When Gram died she tried to console me. I knew—you hear *me?—knew* that was my moment. I took advantage of her, Cory. I did it because it was the closest I could get to *you*."

Cory felt the sea churning inside him.

Why do you think you didn't touch her, Cory?

He could not bear the silent thunder.

"Rod—"

"She was the only thing I knew you really cared about—you did, you do—and how else could I get that close to you."

"Please, Rod—"

"Let me *say* it, Cory! I'll never have this chance again. And I was afraid."

"Of what?"

"Afraid you'd give in and sleep with her—and love her—and I couldn't stand that. So *I* did it. I had to do it to keep you from doing it. It was insane, I knew it was insane, but there was no other way for me. It was as much *you* as I could have."

The waves thrust by the passing ferry heaved the boat, but it rode motionless as the crests and troughs moved under it.

"Sometimes I think something in me made me do it so you *would* throw me out because having you so close I was afraid, because you were the only thing I wanted. Why do you think I took the room at Koenigs'?"

"Take the oars, Rod."

"No."

He pinioned them back like gulls' wings.

"But we're nearing the Gut."

They drifted.

The surface was turning irregular, spat and lashed.

Far out on Gardiners Bay, fishing boats looked tiny and still as gulls riding the swells.

"When I was in bed with Vanna . . ."

Rod closed his legs, gripped his knees, and stared—long. Naked sky filled his eyes.

There came the other sounds now, clear over the surface, the churn and thrash of the Gut.

"Vanna was you, Cory."

Rod closed his eyes. When he opened them, he seemed strangely rested, peaceful, but too motionless in the mull and clash of water.

"I thought . . ." Rod's eyes held the miracle. "I'd never be able to get the words out."

Cory's vision blurred: Rod rose, magnified, till the bright glare made him fall, smaller, clearer.

For an instant Cory envied him the stillness which followed confession. He himself yearned for that peace.

"Cory . . . It's not your fault. It's how I am."

"*We . . .*"

Though the wind battered his quiet word, he saw Rod understood.

My brother.

Cory was stunned. What was in him. What he could hold but not touch.

"Don't hate me, Cory."

"Impossible—"

"I can't be without you, Cory. No. Can't live—"

Rod threw his head back, breathed deep, breathed, breathed. Some new life seemed to come into him. He laughed. He bent forward. He had a giddy look. His lips quivered, nervous, and he laughed tense quick laughs.

"Listen, Cory—"

Cory could barely hear him above the churn now.

"I wanted you to know. If you knew, that would be all, everything to me—"

Behind Rod, he saw the edge of the Gut churning up a chaos of low dark leaps and lashes that the wind blew into quick white foam and constant spray.

The chaos threatened their hearing.

Rod's mouth laughed. It shouted, "We'll go to Plum Island, to the lighthouse." His arm flung it up—there, to the keeper's house and the towering light. His mouth laughed.

Behind Rod the Gut was a dark band, a chaotic dance of whitecaps. Beyond that, the water along the Plum Island shore was lighter, greenish, not turbulent.

Toward the lighthouse the LCT was cutting relentlessly along the shoal edge of the Gut.

"Rod!"

They were entering that irregular edge. Waves butted the bottom with a hollow *puk puk puk,* and thrummed, thrummed.

"We'll spend the night," Rod shouted. "You know the boys and the lighthouse keeper. They'll put us up. It'll be paradise."

He was laughing.

"We can't get across that Gut, Rod!"

"Before it's really bad, we can, yeah."

He was quick to the oars. Straight across he headed the boat, straight into the Gut.

"Rod, you're tired."

"Who's tired!"

"You can't row through that."

"I'll show you *can't*."

The repetition pricked.

"Turn back, Rod!"

Rod laughed.

Stubborn, intent, with masterful regularity he rowed.

The boat heaved through bumps of water, hollow *puk puk puks*, maddening. The whipped spray smat Cory's eyes, blinding, and the salt burning.

In the distance the scattered fishing boats, surely pursuing the last fall run of bass around the Point, dipped and straightened as if all Gardiners Bay were a chaos.

"Then move over. Let me have an oar. Two's better."

Cory moved.

"No." Rod elbowed.

Intent, flexing, Rod was caught up in a ritual rhythm. All his muscles defied that disordered surface which lashed, spat.

Rod was staring straight ahead, rapt.

What was he seeing?

"You'll wear yourself out."

Rod wouldn't hear. He was fixed, indifferent, imperious.

"Rod—"

Cory made his face cut off whatever Rod was seeing.

"What?"

"Move over."

As if suddenly fathoming, his eyes set, Rod ceased rowing.

When Cory went to clutch the left oar to take his place beside him, Rod whipped his own arm back, high, along the oar, sending Cory's hand sliding off with it. The oar was sucked back, down, through the lock into the water. For an instant the oar stood straight as an arm reaching out to them, then went under so fast that Cory's grapple for it missed. "Jesus!" Hard after, Rod's arm lunged over the side for it, the boat dipped, his other arm grappled air. The remaining oar struck Cory. He caught at it and held—

Suddenly he was on his back, clutching the oar, and thrashing.

The sky was empty.

He was alone.

Rod.

"Rod!"

He was shouting and shouting.

He scrambled up after Rod.

Nothing.

Then he was in the water, a cauldron, and his head a cauldron. Pain jabbed.

He saw the arm, white. White streaked.

The boat was veering and turning, and his head.

He was under dark. He was under the boat. He was hanging to the tow rope. His eyes filled with surface light, the only white, no white arm.

Rod!

His head was shouting and shouting. He was calling to Rod against the current. His head, his one arm, his legs struggled to keep him from the tearing. The current sucked his clothes, pulling. He could not hold.

No white.

Nothing.

The boat was bucking and veering. It would tear his arm loose. He caught the tow rope about his arm, latched it. The chop battered.

The Gut would swallow him.

Why do you think you didn't touch her, Cory?

Rod.

No Rod.

No!

He needed all the strength in his arm—he could hardly feel his left—to pull himself up the rope.

The boat struck his shoulder. He cried out. Sea filled his mouth. He sank back, choking, heavier, but hung, held till his mouth could suck air. Breath broke. He cried sounds and sucked sucked sucked.

The current tugged. The waves would tear him from the prow.

He got the arm up, and hung, and breathed—

He held against the thrum and churn until he felt, with a last frenzy of tredding, he could thrust himself high enough out of the water to latch his arm over the side—

He held. He brought up his half-dead arm, gripped, and hung, *mybrotherohmybro*, not no never believing.

He pulled himself over the side and drew a leg over, and hung long, then drew the other in and fell. His head struck the seat. Pain ran burning in his arm. Against his ear the water striking bottom made that hollow *puk puk puk.* Then all he could hear was the sound louder than *puk puk puk,* waves, wind, that sound that filled the boat, racked his ears. He didn't know what it was. Then it was his voice making sounds he had never heard before.

Savannah,

It was German who came through, made all the funeral arrangements. The whole town—you wouldn't believe—turned out. It was for Ma, more for Gramp. You don't know *loved* or *respected* till such times. I kept Gramp by me—he leaned, yes. German held my mother all the time; but what she'd already been through has made her stronger than any of us knows.

She and German took good care of me. He's a big man, but in this crisis he's been as gentle as a woman. He's a good nurse.

Cory could talk to Savannah on the page. He couldn't give her his voice yet or hear hers, her pain, which would be his too. That would have to wait till he went back to the campus. He couldn't help feel now an intimacy with distance and with a certain shame he couldn't overcome. Remotely he felt like some of his friends who were intimate on paper, loyal, attentive, compromised, but coming to town would prefer to stay at a hotel, that intimacy with distance, a habit which he never fathomed but now found himself resorting to. For the same reason, fearing *immediate* intimacy, he could not go back to her, to talk to, to bear the burden with. He saw her now as that first day, his girl in white. He would go at the last minute, arrive the day before classes, not before, no, he could not.

He knew now the privacy of what had happened to his mother. When her brother Ben and Reggie Webb . . . In the Gut too. A rowboat too.

You have to forgive this disorder, Savannah.

It is *time*. Something's happened to time, as if I've stepped out of it, see isolated things and from a great distance, can't account for the missing continuity. I *know* it, but can't act. Even a nightmare has continuity. The drowning is a hiatus. Rod's not being here is now a continuity, and I can't connect the continuity from before with the continuity of now. I see a long cord and then a piece cut out and then a long cord. The piece cut out is the accident.

I keep hearing Rod's voice.

Was he trying to ask for help? Was it suicide? Did he want to take me with him?

I can't talk to *them* about this, Savannah. They wouldn't believe. They'd think I'd gone mad. To them it was an accident. To me it's the same as—I have to dare to write it, I've said it to myself a thousand times, I have to see the word—*killed*. There are so many ways to kill. The war was killing, the worst kind and the least because it was all so mental and contrived and cruel, impersonal, unless you imagined—mostly you *couldn't—them*, each, Germans and Japs as individuals, flesh, dead. Mostly you imagined numbers, heaps, platoons, squadrons, and after it was all over even *cities* of them, Hiroshima, Nagasaki. Yes, so many other ways of killing. You know them, I know them, most of us do; but we don't think of them as *killing* because it's happening so slowly, this killing. I was cutting Rod off. He wanted, all that time wanted—it didn't matter what, Savannah—a look, a word, me to touch him, yes, me, my hands—I see now—my body, my mouth. I was starving him. *You* know what it is to want. Yes, Savannah, of course you do. I see that clearly now too. We all want. He waited, my brother waited all during the war for me, hoping for a word to hold, wanting to be held. Loved. But I lashed out sometimes. All my lashing was needles, daggers, and must have been fire to him, invisible fire. His insides must have been more burned scarred incurable than poor Gramp's flesh. And burned by his own desire, Savannah, passion. Passion's everything. Not to follow it is immoral. But the *truly* moral thing? Rod knew: love where it's your nature to love, and succumb, yes, to the only flood fire death that gives you life. A man kills because he's not moral enough to do the immoral thing. What I did not do, Savannah. What I did was worse, the worst, the most vile—*neglected.* Turned my back. Refused to see what my blood knew. Refused to *be.* I cut his life off as clean as with a knife his windpipe. He couldn't breathe. I cut his air.

I never *talked* to him. I never let myself, or dared. Silence can be—*sin*, Gramp calls it. Unless you can hold silence in your arms, in somebody's blood. You can touch blood, and hear. Then silence is salvation. Of the body. Gramp knows. He's been there. He heard it in her, his Mary. After all the years, divorced, he still hears it. When he's still. When memory . . . It's a still fire that moves with such lightning speed you don't even know *moving*, but know *it*; and it burns till you're burned away, till you *are* your love; you're *Mary and Tom* and you're more than one could be alone; and you want it forever because you know forever now: you were in it, you had it, or it had you.

Fire.

Except that fire destroys. Does it create? Something escapes?

Gramp says it's waiting in everything, fire; moving inside—in insects, animals, air, cloud, water; in still things too, trees, stone. And it's the same fire, all the fire, and the other side of the fire. It's inside you. It's out there.

Sometimes you release that fire.

It lives in Gramp's eyes. Sometimes I see the fire that near burned him to death blazing in his eyes. His eyes quiver like fire itself. He never told the fire. The family did, every version different. *He* kept the true. It was too terrible to speak. The terror was in the silence.

In the hospital he looked like a mummy, Ma said, right out of the Egyptian tombs, all but nose mouth eyes bandaged. My mother (she was thirteen when he was burned) said, "I know what kept him alive. I tended his body. Ma wouldn't. She couldn't, Pa said. But Pa loved her, lived for her That kept him alive."

The moving, still fire.

Gramp said, It's just one fire, the same all of it, but you have to recognize which side or you'll miss it. If you do, you're doomed.

Doomed. Gramp was. But *not*: that fire near destroyed him physically, but, he says, that other fire, Mary, saved him, saves him still, though she's dead: because he can walk the same earth, her path, see his own house he'd built for her which they'd lived in, the house next door now, where even after the divorce he could see her every day, saved—by memory of what he had, by what he has.

And me? A fisherman from Jersey saved me. Alfred McCready, German says.

The ferry passengers, a drove of them, the Coast Guard said, rushed to the Captain of the LCT. But *he*'d already seen and called in to the Coast Guard. Even faster, one of the fishermen in Gardiners Bay, that McCready, picked it up on his short wave. Close. He came right to the Gut. Came right to me. He said I was on my knees in the boat, holding the sides, trying to balance because the Gut rocked and pitched the boat forward and back, side to side, so violently it could have been a gigantic hand under the boat trying to toss me out—it *felt* like that. Some sensations I remember now, but they're vague. All I could do was hold on, near blind from staring into the water, trying to spot Rod, no trace, and the sun high and that madness of chopping water flashing and blinding like mirrors throwing too many suns at me.

I couldn't do a thing with one oar. It was a miracle it was even there. I think I tried to scull—impossible—and pulled the oar in.

McCready tied German's rowboat to his. They said I screamed and shouted at them. They said I wouldn't leave till they found Rod.

They had to get out of the Gut. The Gut's a killer, it boils, it can swallow almost anything but big ships.

McCready told German the fishermen had to get me on his boat by force. McCready said I got quiet then.

German said they hauled his rowboat to Greenport.

I don't remember. I just remember saying "Let me" to Rod and getting up to row and him saying "No" and standing and losing the oar and lunging for it and going over so easy, as if he'd dived in. *Did he*? That. I try to understand that. In my head it begins with "Let me" and goes on, I see it, and when it's over it repeats and repeats . . .

Then I was in Greenport, and I saw Ma. One look at me and she covered her mouth. She knew, she sank down, she didn't touch me, she sat in the chair. I knew she was seeing *them* too, Ben and Reggie Webb, only with Rod's face now, and maybe with the faces of all the others drowned before she was even born and didn't know except from photos and family talk, tales, our history, the sea we can't get away from.

Because your grandfather was born on it, Ma said, though that had nothing to do with any of it, as if we all hadn't been born from it. Three hundred years of sea, here on the Island. You'd think this family would have sense enough to go so far inland the sea couldn't touch us. Never, I said, never too far to keep us from being attracted. How could you stop hearing the sea in your blood? *Or the dead,* she said, though I know she was thinking *Or the drowned they'd never found,* who will never fill the empty lots waiting for them in Stirling Cemetery.

Is death the only true order we will ever know?

I as much as killed my brother.

What's in me that drove him to it?

What was in him that made him do it?

Are they the same thing?

It goes round and round in me. I don't trust my head, Savannah. I can't go back to the campus right now. I have to graduate. I'll get there at the last minute, I promise.

Savannah, I do know that in some different way you'll feel it more than any of us because, whatever Rod really felt for you (surely a special kind of love), what you felt for him may even have been more (I can't really know that) because you loved both of us in him, and surely will go on loving him in me as I will him in you.

You kept him alive in Madison. I know that now. You didn't know that because you couldn't, as I couldn't, have known how close to death he always was.

I kept myself from him. That was his real death. It's my death too, part.

I don't know when his shoes and trousers disappeared, but the Gut took them. The only thing left in the rowboat was his shirt.

German has been very kind, quiet—he never talks much anyway—detached, courteous. Whatever roughness he may have, he respects the sacrosanct. Besides, he has ground for sympathy. Accident and death are familiar to him. In the war he himself nearly drowned when a Jap sub torpedoed his ship. He can't go in the water without feeling he's turning upside down and strangling. I can believe how good he was to Gram when she was dying.

Ma has kept active. She hasn't isolated herself in her room. She wants to *see* me. She wants to be sure *I'm* still here, I think. And though she's always been very attentive to Gramp, she's in and out of his house more, her excuse taking him something she's whipped up for him or going out to borrow or rummage around in his kitchen for a thing she doesn't need at all, to *make sure* of him too, to *verify* there's no vacuum there. I believe, like me, she has such an overactive imagination that she must contradict her imagination by seeing and hearing and touching what's real, to be sure she's not imagining.

There are moments I can believe, with Rod gone, that Wisconsin has never existed, or you haven't, and that I'm emerging from my own imagination and don't know at what point I'm continuing the life outside it, which I did *not* imagine, especially with German here, who didn't figure in the old life I *didn't* imagine. I'm set down in the middle of something half-recognizable.

I can't talk to you over the phone, Savannah. I want to, but can't. I can't hear your voice. I don't want to. Yet. But since Rod, I'm with you, I've never been so much with you, as if he left me you and you me, two islands, we *are*, as if he cut out a middle thing, himself, so we'd be one. I don't think he *wanted* to be between us. *I* didn't want him to be, and *you* didn't. It was what he *made* happen. This minute I think that anyway, though he said *then* that it was a weak moment, Gram's death, I believe that was the circumstantial excuse, that's all. He wanted me to console him. He wanted *that* to be the minute his Cory would break down too (but Gram was his Ma not mine. *I* had no mother with me when I was with my father, who did not want me, who wanted Louise and who took her son, Anthony, instead of me). Rod wanted his Cory to break down and take him in his arms; then Rod would be what he'd dreamed of being. He would be mine if I touched him in a way I never had before, and I his.

If I *had* touched him, he would be alive now, Savannah.

I keep thinking that. And thinking it, I know it's true—I wanted to touch him, possess him—as if this admission would correct something, bring him back, start us. I wonder if I'm telling myself this because now I know he wanted me, because this love was always just beneath the surface, the source of all my antagonism with him. Whatever, his death has made it *true*. Rod's body is always with me. I yearn to touch him, to *prove* him. I'd give that to have him back. *My* body, my *self*. is incomplete. What's worse, now I know it was incomplete, always has been, and may never be fulfilled. He stands in the way. It's as if I missed my chance to be whole, the one experience required to be me, Savannah. There's something in me that gives myself to people up to a point. I have to learn to pass that point. I'd like to blame something (God, say, It), tell It, You put fulfillment and happiness so close to me it blinded me, I missed it. You dared me to break all the taboos and take my brother, and I didn't. I was too weak and afraid; the coward in me held back. I cut Rod off, so cut myself off, a death to each of us.

Ma told Gramp about Rod. She wouldn't let anybody else. She went out back to his place. She said he was doing some corking in the outer entry. "Pa," she said, "come sit." He said, "I can't interrupt the job. Just you wait here." She reheated his water and poured it over the SALADA dregs in his teapot, then poured some tea in his bowl and added half evaporated milk, his way. When he finished, she said, "You're sweating," and wiped his forehead with her handkerchief. "It's honest sweat. Plenty more where that came from." He laughed, and sat, and sipped, his face in the steam. Shasta leaped into his lap. "Good girl," he said. Ma said suddenly it was too silent. From behind, she lay her head against his shoulder and bent close to his ear so he'd hear good because she didn't think she could repeat it, and said, "Pa, Rod's gone. He was drowned in the Gut this noon." She thought he hadn't heard, he was so still. Maybe he didn't believe—or too fast believed, because it had happened before to Ben. Or maybe he could have been thinking she'd made a mistake. Then she sat with him. He wasn't squinting, she said. He was looking straight and quivery across the kitchen through the curtains blowing and the screen into the Raynors' yard and past the car and boat and doghouse to where just blue sky went on forever. She knew what he must be seeing. She'd seen it. Finally he said, "Rod, you say?" His hands must have hurt the cat because she let out a cry and leaped from him. He never said another word till after the funeral. At the cemetery Ma kept watching him. She'd told German, "Keep Pa between you and Cory." She feared he'd buckle again—because of Gram, his Mary; and they did have to hold him up when they threw in handfuls of dirt. He said, "Mary," too loud. Then they turned him away. I saw Fatso lingering beyond. Fatso would wait until we all had gone so we wouldn't hear the sound of the shovel as he covered the casket.

Ever since Rod, people have come to visit, a tribe of them. Ma's held up fine, and Gramp. It's easy to say he's protected, he's so *deef,* but no—he's locked in, alone, cut off. He presses his hard hand behind his ear and bends to, and his quivering eyes fix on the face, trying not to miss a word, but losing a lot; and then Ma repeats, and then he says, "What're you shouting for?" because she's one of the few who have just the right pitch for him to hear.

Old Mrs. Doyle, who's known Gramp and Gram all her life, came with the permanent appendage, the daughter, Carole, hipping along, her short leg swinging her deep-soled shoe. It's not the mother but the daughter who has the old-woman face, grim-lipped, narrow-eyed, with a tongue that bites words quick and hard, a fury of old maid celibate hate in her face. She and her daughter sat in a corner. They sat hours. Mrs. Doyle never said anything but "How old are you, Tom?" He'd tell her, and she'd say, "I'm eighty-five!" and cackle. After a while she'd ask him again. In silence Gramp chain-smoked his hand-rolled cigarettes he kept in an old Marvel pack.

Even then Ma didn't miss her Wednesday morning in the Dobbins' trailer. Every week she spends two hours taking her turn to exercise the Dobbin boy's legs and arms. That gives the wife a chance to drive off in her car, do what she likes, or relax. The boy's been lyingthere growing twenty-seven years; he's grown six feet and never moved or said a word, but the Dobbins keep hoping. "And beautiful," Ma says, "you should see his face, an angel's." I kid her, "Now how'd you know an angel?" She says, "Oh, I know a few, though they're not pretty like him."

Not a person who knows Ma or Gramp or who knew anybody in the family stayed away—the mayor, aldermen, owners and all the workers of Preston's and Wash White's Hardware and the Arcade and Helen's and Meier's and The Diner and Paradise Sweets and the two hotels and Katz's Dry Goods. They hadn't even known Rod, most of them, but knew Tom Verity and all the Veritys and so Ma. Before a week was out they'd gone over the entire family history a hundred times, and theirs, and the town's, as much as they knew from fact and from hearsay. The mayor's wife came, so "big with child" she was embarrassed for them all to see her—fearful, she seemed, even to speak Rod's name without resting her hands on her big belly. The next day she was rushed to the hospital; a false alarm it was, a hysterical pregnancy, that belly big with blood—it just poured out of her—and after showers that reaped a houseful of baby things she'll have to give back now. She can't face anybody, Ma says, she's so disappointed, ashamed, and grieving so, at her age the last chance for a baby.

And all the Polacks came—not just the farm owners, but the ones we, Rod and I, but especially Rod because of his first years here, have known since we were kids. You have to know that between our house and the crick there's a small block with three houses on one side of the street, one on the other. The three houses are back to back with Al Dickson's house and an enormous empty lot my bedroom looks out on. Al was Ma's first sweetheart—at least, *he* loved *her*. They used to meet in the cemetery, the only place at the time they could be alone, till Gramp caught them said he'd horsewhip her to within an inch of her life, and Al too, if he caught them again. Al never married, came to be a fixed sight riding his bicycle to and from the oyster factory like clockwork; but he loves her and Gramp. For Gramp he'd do anything. Strange how time makes you love what you once feared. Al's always been good to the Polacks behind him, the Dombroskis, and to the old Puerto Rican woman in the next house, Catalina Hannibal—the *puertorriqueña*, I call her at home, and Ma calls her Catrinka. Mrs. Hannibal loves Ma. Ma *thought* she was black until she came home one day and said, "Cory! I've been to Catrinka's, and she showed me a medal of the Virgin she wears, and you know, Cory, I was never so surprised in my life. Under the high collar and all those layers of clothes she wears, her skin is as white as milk. It's the sun, the sun's got her, her face is so dark below that bandana she always wears, but her skin's white above." "You thought she was black because she married black Geebo," I said. "I guess," she said. But most people here think of the Puerto Ricans as black or the next thing to it. Ma can't quite shake that conviction. Geebo's been dead years now. He was black as the ace of spades, but he was only half black, half Indian, son of a Narragansett chief. And his son, Danny, was as black as his father, the image too, a lineman for the New York Telephone Company who married a girl from New York, a pretty Latin thing. She didn't last here, hated it, wanted Brooklyn, so left. Danny went back and forth; but she didn't want Danny either, it was clear, only his money. She came and went regularly only to collect that, though maybe she couldn't stand the confinement after the city, the wood fire even in summer, the jam-packed *portorriqueña's* house, the dirt, the smell, in the icebox the food mouldy that the *puertorriqueña's* cataract eyes couldn't see. They didn't work out. Danny went his father's way, booze, and they think he fell to his death from a Brooklyn window, drunk. Some think suicide.

The *puertorriqueña* won't go near the Polacks or let them cross her property line; she has walled their yard off with a high hedge. She blames Geebo's drinking and Danny's, and both their deaths because of it, on the Polacks. She hates, she's always hated, drink, because the Polacks' life for decades here has been carousing. Emil's is on the other side. He's half a mentality. I can't remember when he wasn't an old bachelor, all his life dependent on his Momma, "My Momma" every other word. *My Momma* was a German frau so fat she couldn't get out of her chair once she got down in it on the lawn in summer, under an apple tree, where she was a perennial sight, and Emil at all hours sitting out beside her and playing his accordion, zipping along. You could hear his laughter, his little gurgles and cries of joy the wind carried. "You like dot, Momma?" "*Ya, gut, sehr gut.*" And the Polack boys knew how he loved a beer, so they'd offer him his own paid-for beer till he tied one on. Emil loved a crowd so, tripping his fingers over the accordion keys, sipping his beer till he'd wave and call out to every passerby and laugh and say, "Momma," who loved it too, but furious at the Polacks cheating her Emil, she herself loving beer and music and her boy and the feel of the breeze and the sun shining down on her, motionless—till Emil was drunk and Momma asleep. Then the Polacks would eat the house clean, steal what they could get their hands on from the house and the several sheds, and sometimes even when Momma Hinkelman was sitting still, humming, singing, with Emil and the Polacks all over the lawn, drinking—yes, in and out of the house to the icebox, and stealing, without caring about the ruckus Emil would make the next day when sober or about Momma Hinkelman muttering, mumbling, sometimes shouting and always swearing. But tomorrow or next week and always on the next whoever's birthday or anniversary or wedding and any holiday excuse, they'll repeat it, draw the human flies, litter the lawn with human refuse, as some of the neighbors call them, those from the surrounding blocks and all within hearing distance of the music that goes on into such long hours that when the cops called they're prepared for a bloody clash and sure to haul off one or two or more of the boys, the best fighters those Dombroskis in that house between Emil's and the *puertorriqueña's*. They'd all end up with such cuts and bruises and broken teeth and cracked bones or skulls or maimed limbs as to justify the name of the place because nobody calls it Bridge Street anymore and not because the bridge has long since been removed and the land filled in. Town dubbed it—and the name stuck—Easy Street, and not merely for the live-it-up Saturday-night-after-Saturday night, month-after-month, year-to-year eternal music and drink, but because on Saturday nights too under the corner streetlight across from Emil's place the *boys* gathered, men, to throw dice, gamble all night long, or on the corner opposite that, on the stoop of Stankus' grocery store. They all kneeled and hunched in circles by the great phallic-looking rock, a monolith from the Sound shore which the Stankuses must have had hauled there maybe to keep the hellions in cars from rounding the corner so close or at such speeds they'd clip the side railing of the store porch because there was no curb. When we were kids, Saturday nights all summer long Rod and I could watch them through the side half-window of our upstairs bedroom. In daytime Stankus' monolithic stone was a perfect perching place to watch the whole neighborhood from.

Those Polacks came to Rod's wake too. It was heart. They felt. But when you know those Dombroskis are feeling, you're in trouble. If it means sloppy sentiment, it means booze, any kind. They're here to drink you dry. Ma knew. Her law was no drink. "Not in my house. Not on my land." Final. It kept them courteous, but it didn't keep them long. She'd counted on that. "You got a beer, Stella?" "Nothing." Polite but curt, with that one word she cut them off without sending them away. They sat, great lumps, heaps of flesh, held together in unaccustomed clothes, and clean, which the sister Mirta kept them in. Mirta was the toughest—she bossed them. "You bastards ain't settin one goddamn foot in Stell's house filthy and stinkin-a fish and piss. You get your ass outa them clothes." That's Mirta, mother to the gang of brothers that were left to her years before. That Mirta, she was there to avoid a free-for-all at Rod's funeral, though the boys stayed longer despite no booze, the two youngest, Henry and Iggy, because they'd grown up with Rod the years he'd lived with Gram before Ma could take him to live with her and Daddy Pete and me.

You don't run with Polacks, Gram taught her own boys—and us. It did no good. Rod ran with Henry and Iggy, and my uncles with their buddies, Polacks their own age, handsome in their youth, big, impressive, who would quick become all pudge growing round, sinking all traces of form or looks, leaving only *big* and tall, and bellies. Even though Gram preached No Polacks, turning her head but seeing, as everybody who passed turned heads and saw, old man Dombroski drunk on his lawn the whole weekend, his parts exposed—he'd shake them at any female—and pissing on the lawn, sinking down, konked out to sleep there just as easily as the family slept inside on straw on all the floors, pissing out the back door or in a bucket in the kitchen, where they'd play cards all day and all night long too. Their big Ma Dombroski would outsit all of them, eyes on them and tongue lashing out keen, and hands too. She was a cheat and thief, who would end up with all the money the boys didn't give her when they came home from two or three weeks out on the skimmer boats. "You give money. You, Dolfo. You, Jozef. You—" Down the boys she'd go—money. With hands like a man's, she could clobber. Money. What she didn't win from them, she'd steal. It all ended up in her coffers, a bulge under her breasts. She stashed. No, Gram said, no Polacks. But when the woman had one of her babies in the field during potato season, she left it in a small washtub in the field and went right back to digging potatoes. Gram came on it lying there, all dried blood. "You can't leave that child there, Wanda, it'll die." "You take, Mary," she said. Gram took it and washed and wrapped it and kept it till day's end. But *No Polacks.* Ma's good with Emil, but she won't have the Polacks who live in his shacks cross the sidewalk into her yard if she can help it, and not a bottle in the yard, but likes Mirta, who can be mean as a snake with her brothers but really absolutely devoted to them, in and out of the bed, they say, with one of them, can't resist him, pets him, "My baby, my love, my boy, I'm saving that ham for my baby, don't you touch it," raging they don't give her money, but cooking for them and cleaning that house in legal succession they've been fighting over ever since Ma Dombroski died, which none of them will sign to divide, so they live in it rotting around them. Mirta comes to visit Ma. She will, like her mother, steal you blind. She walked off with Ma's watch one day, right under Ma's eye, no doubt to chuck it into her collection of hundreds of watches she brags about stashed away in a room locked off in that Polack house though the boys break into her room now and then, rousing Mirta to beat hell out of them, and she can. Maybe she has at last even cured them of breaking locks. Ma always says now "*Uh*-oh," in unconscious imitation of Gramp's *Uh*-oh, "here comes Mirta," and rushes to get a sheet of plastic to lay under a laprug on the chair Mirta sits in because she's at the stage of loose sphincter muscles and piddles before she knows it. Mirta tells Ma all the dirt, "diarrhea at the mouth," nobody free from her tongue, not the Episcopal minister, not the priests, not the ones on welfare, not the rich she works for. Mona Stock says, "You can't beat Mirta for a worker, but I had to let her go, she was stealing the pictures right off the wall," no surprise since she has a roomful of frames. Still, you can't help liking Mirta. There's a good heart under her bellowing and lying and stealing that even those who ward her off can't help admire. She's too blunt to believe. You have to laugh almost for self-protection. An hour with her and the laughter will make your muscles ache. Ma says they take to her because they know what she is, she can't fool anybody. What do you expect, a liar to tell the truth? Since they can't avoid Mirta, best to settle in with her and keep just out of striking distance the way you would with any snake you know has a poison tongue. Her tongue's her protection, people are afraid of her tongue, town's too small to keep her tongue out of houses, and there's too much to hide here. You get entertainment, gossip, and a moral lesson all in one. Ma says, "Without the Mirtas of this world, how'd the rest of us know what we are?"

Jana, Mirta's daughter came too, always standing out of the way, sinking into backgrounds as always, her hand clutching her husband's. Jana's the mystery. How can she be Mirta's daughter when she's really her sister? The comment's usually made to bring up the story: how Mirta *swelled* and disappeared to Connecticut on a visit, the way problem girls did then, and came back with the child, but the culprit was in the same house with her, in the next room: Mirta's father and lover and Jana's father and grandfather were all in the house together and nobody said, could ever say, did ever say—in front of them—a word. For sure the father did not, or Mirta would have killed him because she loves her Jana madly. Yes, she would have. She can wield anything from a scallop knife to a butcher knife. Nobody—but everybody—knows. Nobody says a word.

Fatso

Fatso García grew up between the town and the dump. His first memory was of green. He crawled in green, under green, tall green jungle. Through the green came glitter. When wind parted the green, when sun, came flashes and sparks, glitter. The brightnesses sent quick blind spots before his eyes. When winter, when cold, green died. The green wall died. Stark and dark came the tree trunks and branches and bushes.

Far was blue and gray.

Then glitter shot from dark piles, mounds littered with colors. The mounds burned. Fires everywhere sent up thick black. Streams and streaks of dark rose and broke and spread in webs and thinned and disappeared. Sometimes myriad thin dark lines of smoke all over the dump ascended all together into leafless trees still but moving. The earth burned. It was fire and smoke, and dark and glitter.

And smells.

All the far backyard down to the dump was the smell of sweet, all tiny yellow and white flowers he would suck.

"It won't kill him, it's just honeysuckle," his Ma would say.

When wind, came the other smell—sweet too, but foul sweet, rancid, sometimes a stark sharp smell that halted you.

"Just smell that goddamn dump," his Ma would say.

He felt the smells in the wind. He could taste smells. Sometimes he ate honeysuckle. Sometimes he ate what he didn't know.

"Don't eat that shit!"

His mother or one of his sisters or brothers would tear it out of his hand.

So sweet and shit were sounds too, soft and loud, sweet and shit in their voices. All the voices were different, but soft and loud were the same. So he lived in many softs and louds.

He knew white. His mother where she pressed him was white. White was warm skin, he sucked warm, he tasted white, her warm went into him, and flowed, and warmed.

After, he cried for her white warm skin. He was torn from it, every time torn from it.

"Jesus, he'll wear my tits out, that one."

He was handed around to faces and arms, hauled, dragged, set down—till he knew from sizes and faces and feels—gentle or tugging—and smells and sounds María, Renata, Sol, Agnes, Dot, and sometimes the boys, Mike and Tony and Manny.

Because he crawled, he met wood, metal, burn, cold; but once they set him down on black, outside, and he crawled after every crawling thing, and put any moving thing into his mouth, and ate dirt.

"Christ, watch the kid, can'tchya!"

His mother would smack screams out of them.

"Your fault, you little son-of-a-bitch."

They shoved him; they hugged and kissed; they slapped his ass, face, arms; they pinched, till he knew which sister or brother to reach for, run to, scream at, crawl from.

But it was black dirt, outside, he screamed for. When he stood, and walked, then the green jungle drew him, and the far glitter, and when the leaves fell the dump filled his eyes, the fires, the dark mounds, the trucks and cars coming and going. He would follow the smoke that made still pillars in the sky, or that the wind blew into dark webs till he stumbled down into the thorny blackberry and raspberry bushes, his flesh torn bloody. He would rage at the streaks of red, scream.

But he would go back every time.

The day he was old enough not to be followed every minute and walked to the dump and explored fresh piles of refuse, and ash heaps, and islands of bushes, he found that the dump, like the yard, had its confines. Trucks and cars entered it from a road three houses away from his. Two great telephone poles black as tar tilted inward, with a crossbar, made a gigantic gate over the entrance. On the pole nearest the house, a kingfisher had built a great round nest. Hours he watched for the birds, the flap, and the fire off their wings.

A cemetery ran along the far side of the road. Some days he would crawl over stones and climb and trace the designs and words cut into the stones.

But on two sides the dump sloped down to a dead pond. Beyond was a short stretch of land and then the Sound. At its edge here and there were bushes, wild white and pink beach roses, blue and yellow and pink weeds, buttercups, wild poppies.

The surface of the pond was near covered with scud, with growths of green and brown, great leaves that flowered in white lilies, and brown thick muck that floated. Dragonflies and beetles and bluebottles and myriad insects flew over and hummed and buzzed and settled. Close, he watched the movement of their tiny legs and wings.

And he heard invisible moves, crawlings, the movement of scud and water. He came to see how different the leaves and tendrils and flowers were and the glidings and crawlings of insects and even the multiple sounds of their wings.

He saw his first rat there, a fat round gray thing with a long tail and eyes with a glitter of glass; and later, in dark, he would see rats ascend, carrying fire in their eyes as they moved over the mounds.

And he heard the dirt move, the tiny breaks as insects emerged, as trapdoor spiders, bees.

He could spot far off a toad from the ground it resembled and knew the sound of its stillness, and the frogs' as they beat; and sometimes he was filled with joy when on some days all the dump—frogs and toads and insects and the birds, swallows and starlings and gulls and jays, myriads—were all humming and singing and vibrating at once and all the perfume of the flowers filled the wind and overrode even the stench of rot and the burning and ashes so that the scents themselves seemed to touch his skin.

The first snake he watched spellbound, how it wriggled and was always the same, how it moved yet seemed still, its head probing, the eyes glittering with day, its little forked tongue red when it shot forth. He came to hear the almost silent slither, and not to disturb he would go still and let it pass unharmed, one of the garter snakes or black snakes that flourished in the dump and the cemetery, and sometimes overturning a stone or a board, a whole nest of tiny snakes would squirm in the light and he would replace it.

At home was always a clutter of bodies. In bed he knew his mother's heat and smell and the soft warm nest between breasts, though soon he was jammed between bodies, always buried in flesh, hot and sweaty all summer or winter, at first almost suffocated between the girls. When he grew and came to know dick and cunt, he was stuffed in any bed with the boys.

They smelled of fish. He did not know the smell he smelled was of fish.

His father was a fisherman. Every morning before light his father went out on the boats. So his father was mostly gone. His father was for nights. He was the figure who came late and who mostly ate alone at the table with his mother. But Fatso had many fathers—three besides the man, because Mike and Tony and Manny were older, they bossed him, *Fatso* and *Fatso* and *Fatso*! till he was not sure who was boss.

Father was a name, then the figure at the table he knew from the smell of fish.

Before he knew fish, he knew the smell. His father's clothes and hands and face and beard and mouth smelled of fish. And the bags and baskets and buckets he brought home smelled of fish. He came to know clams and scallops and skimmers, shrimp and crabs and lobsters, and fish of all sizes and shapes and colors. So then whenever he smelled his father, he saw fish, the fish heads his mother would cut off, the flat gleaming dead eyes. When he saw his father he felt the sticky scales, he felt the shiny slippery stink.

The fish smell was the same damp smell of their dicks and cunts and asses, their feet, and their bellybuttons, and their mouths sometimes.

The rot the rats went after in the dump smelled of fish, and sometimes a rat itself when he came across a dead one.

Fish.

A time came when he would examine the fish mouths for teeth. His fingers got sticky feeling for teeth like his own.

"Jesus, whatta ya doin' in them fish?"

"Nothin'"

Ma'd grab his hands and dip them into the soft soapy water in the tub she'd be washing clothes in.

He did not tell her *Teeth*.

He liked to run his knuckles down and down the washboard; the sound excited him.

He never knew his look till the mirror.

He never knew his look till the grown-ups. Their eyes were mirrors—they would drop their eyes or turn them from him, or turn their whole heads at times. And their voices were mirrors—because their sound dropped, so he knew *pity, shame* but no word for them.

And then school. When his brothers and sisters talked teeth, it was to look and touch, but at school the kids pointed and laughed and cried, "Lemme see!"

Couldn't they see? He couldn't hide his teeth.

When he grew up, his teeth would be like his brothers' and sisters', wouldn't they?

After school, the kids chased him from their games, or made him watch from the sidelines. And if he caught a ball or headed for a slide, they shooed him off.

"Well, I'll be goddamned." His mother let them have it. "Seven of yas and you can't protect a kid? Ya better shake your asses and take care-a him or *I'll* do the whackin."

At least there was only one school and his brothers and sisters ganged up—they made a circle around him against all the other kids.

"Now come on, ya bastids." Tony headed the ring, and some of the kids did come, there were fights at recess and after school, and the principal came out and the teachers and had them all in the office, till his brothers and sisters tired of the whole thing, and he was glad—he was too ashamed they were protecting him, and told them.

"Let *me*. I'll fight'm."

He couldn't—there were too many—but he learned to put on a face, to stare with hard eyes straight at them and not move no matter how close they came, right up against him even, breath to breath, till they were afraid he'd move, sudden; they couldn't gauge. But all his insides quivered, he was going to throw up, he was afraid to hit, but he stared without blinking. His ruse worked. Or they grew tired of him, accepted his presence if not his company, except when they could find nothing else to keep them interested, out of boredom they abused him.

Besides, he sprang up fast—not tall, but already rugged with a taut build, a good chest and arms and a bold sway. It was the large head that made him look big, even top-heavy, partly because his forehead was low; from his widow's peak the black hair seemed to spring thick and coarse—it riled, he couldn't control it.

So, early, and for some years, he was bigger than most of his class.

He was a thumb.

He never looked at the teachers. Only Miss Kellogg could make him look up because once after a big ruckus in the schoolyard, so bad his mother came to give a piece of her mind to the principal and all the teachers whose offices she could stick her nose into. Miss Kellogg, with that soft voice that made them all listen like hawks so not to miss a word and maybe flunk, asked his mother to sit down and talk about his work. The soft voice worked like a command because his mother sat; and before she could say a word, Miss Kellogg was talking about when Carlos and Martha were students. She was calling Pa Carlos and Ma Martha because Miss Kellogg was that old, gray. Her hand was so abruptly set on his head he could feel the heat right through his hair, and she turned his head up and said to his mother, "He's intelligent, you don't know how intelligent," so his mother gazed at him, smiled in a way he had never felt from her before, and Miss Kellogg added, "And he has the most beautiful dark eyes I ever saw, they're like black velvet, and set deep like that they look enigmatic."

"Enig—"

"Mysterious."

"Oh—"

Miss Kellogg lightly touched his forehead and brows and lashes and all through him went little vibrations.

Some afternoons—when spring, when meandering, when sudden music—he'd sit on Miss Kellogg's front steps in the big old house on Front Street and rest against the balustrade and listen to her play the piano. Her hands were making the music he had heard when she'd touched him. He saw her music move the wind and the curtains; the wind poured it over his skin and it made his blood music.

Did she know he was here?

Ma would scold because he was late.

"Donchya know you got chores to do?"

He hadn't tried to escape his chores. Ma kept all the kids busy when, if, they came home (they'd grown wise to her), but he couldn't tell her *the music*. It went singing through his hands while he scaled fish, cut the heads off, and slit the bodies open, and filleted them, or opened scallops. His father made him a special strong short opening knife and showed him the weak spot to penetrate the shell, split it open, and flick out the scallop muscle and toss it into a bucket and flick the rest into the garbage all with one fast easy motion.

"The kid's good. He's a real worker," Pa said.

The work was tougher with clams and skimmers. He never had to bother with the now and again crabs and lobsters, "the good stuff, fancy, for the city people," his mother said, because they never saw any of that stuff on the table. It went to Pell's Market or the restaurants or on the train early mornings to New York City. And he learned from Ma and Pa's talk they got money for his work. He never saw any, but it made him proud.

"How much, Ma?"

"Ask Pa."

Pa would never say.

He told the dumpkeeper, "Pa made me a scallop knife, Huey."

"You doing any good with it?"

"I opened a bushel today."

"Wow! You'll be rich before you know it. What'll you do with all that cash?"

"Ma keeps it."

A cold wind swept up the slope from the Sound, but they sat on the bench against the shack Huey kept his rakes and hoes and tools in, catching the last bit of sun. He loved Huey's shack. Every minute there was no school or Ma or Pa wasn't after him he was here, but not to sit. From early, he had cried, "Let me rake. Can I? Can I, Huey?"

So Huey had let him rake refuse into mounds with him, then go through newly dumped trash for junk to salvage and sell—bottles or metal or silver foil or rags.

"You sure come to be an expert in no time, Fatso."

Fatso swelled, laughed, toed the ground, proud.

He loved the dump. It was his. Huey didn't know that. When Huey went home, Fatso would return: he would sit at Huey's shack on the height of the slope, where he could survey the whole dump, all his terrain from the left edge that touched town and along the bank of the still pond that fringed the dump to the cemetery and the road on his right.

Mine.

He would wander over the mounds, down the slopes to the pond's edge and listen for a move, watch bugs, beetles, the tiniest insects shifting on the scud that grew in great patches, brown and green and yellow that sometimes undulated and even shifted places when wind tore them in storm. So he came to know them and it was no revelation when he found their pictures and names in books. The pond was fresh water, and still, not like the sea visible over the fields and crest and road just beyond. He would watch sun turn the pond and the shrubs gold and pink and crimson, then make the shrubs myriad black arms and fingers reaching out of the ground. And when dark rose, the many little fires grew alive, as if the ground fed them, and burned bright and held back the dark. Then the rats came, their eyes carrying fire.

He was never afraid. He knew them. It was his world.

One day after school he counted out $2.38 on the kitchen table.

"Jees, where'd you get that money?" It scared his mother. "I won't have no stealin."

"Sol Golden. He buys bottles and rags and silver foil."

"Well, I'll be damned. You musta done a lota huntin."

"Yeah."

"Your Pa said you was a worker."

"I take after you, Ma."

For a second she put her hand on his head and stared into his eyes. He could tell she was thinking.

Her hand was hot and good.

He was waiting for the music.

"Well, give it here. A couple a bucks'll do *some* feeding!"

He handed it over.

"I'll get more, Ma. You wait."

From that day, before and after school, his Ma's eager beaver expanded his terrain, he was all over town, collecting: he wandered yards and beach and docks and behind The Diner and Mitchell's and Claudio's restaurants and Preston's dock and into the metal barrels by the train depot and the Shelter Island ferry and behind the Wyandank Hotel and the Stirlington Hotel and Helen's Bar and Meier's and Grant's and the A&P and Bohack's and the whiskey store, sometimes dragging his burlap bag it was so full.

Nights he balled foil, packed rags tight, and arranged bottles tight in boxes. Nobody could get to his booty. In Huey's shed he made a place. Under the roof was a hollow. Where a small window had been, he fashioned a board he could easily lift free, but no one would suspect. He stored his goods in this secret place till he accumulated enough to sell to Sol Golden.

So he was in business. He was steady. He was making money now. He gave it all to Ma.

"How much this week?" Her eye lingered on him. "That all of it?"

"Yeah, Ma."

"You ain't lyin' to me?"

"I wouldn't lie, Ma."

"I'll have your ass if you do. I ain't raisin' a buncha liars."

She was about to raise her tenth. She was swollen and sweaty but still scrubbed clothes (now she did laundry for others), cooked, picked up things—she never had time for a real clean, and the girls were useless, always "off somewhere," despite, maybe because of, Ma's tongue. To tell the truth, Ma was glad, hoping to be rid of the other four the way she now was of María, married as soon as she'd graduated.

"Twenty years of kids. Thirty-eight, and me caught in the tide again. Nine years since Fatso. I'm through with it this time."

He thought it was a lie Ma was young—her hair was gray, taut in a bun, and she heavy and shapeless, and standing with her stomach out as if she'd lose her balance. She'd had nine "with not much time between." The boys kept out—afraid of work, always running around, "headed down the wrong street if they ain't careful," she said.

"You keep your nose clean, Fatso," Pa'd say.

From Pa's mouth his name always pricked like a little crucifixion. The word sounded alien, a judgment, condemnation—by a stranger—because he hardly knew the man. Days, two three weeks at a time, his father was out on the skimmer boats with Wilkes and the Polacks. From the beginning, his father had been a mystery, the stranger from the sea, far. His father was still the strong smell of fish. At first, whenever his father came home, he had to give up his bed with his mother—she stuck him in with the girls, then, older, with the boys. All he knew of his father were the night sounds when his father took his, Fatso's, bed—the stranger's deep voice, the talk, laughs, the jingling old springs, Ma's little pig grunts and bird cries. On those nights Agnes and Sol kept squirming and turning in their bed with him and whispering. "They're at it again."

Ma was an animal. He knew that the day he came in the yard from the dump and heard her cries. She'd fallen on the floor. She was lying there, the floor bloody, the bloody head half out of her.

"Grab that heavy string. Get a knife."

He was all eyes, and fast. He knew animals. He'd seen.

"Cut this thing. Yeah. Tie it."

She had the little animal by the legs. She smacked. *Whaaaa*! *Whaaaa*! It kept up.

"You want Doc Kaplan?" The women loved Dr. Kaplan though he was brutal with them. "You're going to have this baby if I have to slap hell out of you." He'd knock the fear out of the nervous ones, smack them to get it out of them, but women never gave him up.

"Shit, it's too late for that. This one sure was in a hurry. Took me by surprise! Get Annie Buckle. She knows what to do. She's done it enough. And you stay out a while."

In baby trouble everybody called Annie.

He ran down the street to the nigger house. He hated to. Most of Third Street over to Fifth was nigger. Their church was almost across the street from his house, so there were always tribes of them, and in high spirits, laughs and cries, except when a death, and then those long lamentations like waves over the earth that shivered him and carried him. All down his side of the street to the little park with the bandstand was nigger and on the opposite side to the two blocks closest to downtown. The niggers made no bones about his jaw. "If your dick's as long as your jaw, you're going places, Fatso." They pretended to pull out their own, but sprang switchblades and lashed out at him if he went anywhere near. And in front of girls too. They threw things at him, swore, spat, made signs, held their hands up in crosses against the monster, evil spirit, taboo, death he might bring, and—worst—laughed and imitated, *ugh-ughing*, malforming their jaws.

This day was hot July with wind, so the niggers were everywhere on porches and hanging out windows and kicking balls and running and screaming in the dust because the street was dirt with no sidewalks and ran right up to the front doors.

Somebody started. "Hey, there's Fatso!" interrupted their ballgame. They drew their lower jaws in and made Frankenstein arms and shoulders and sounds, and started for him. One of them, bold, had his knife out, and slashed, closer and closer, tempting Fatso to fight, finally slashed at his balls—too close.

"Hey you guys, cut that out!"

They stopped as if they were playing statues.

He was white, thin, taller than Fatso. He'd been playing ball with the niggers.

"What's with you, Rod?"

You could hear *respect*, he was their side, he was the gang. Now *not*. How come? That unexpected challenge stilled them long enough.

"Never mind what's with me—just leave him alone. Put the knife away, Dink."

"You fucking up a party, you know that?"

"Put the knife away."

He was smaller than half of them, but his taut body spoke; and he had a sound in his voice. It *meant*. It threw up a wall you had to throw down. *That* Fatso heard. The hiatus got him to Annie's door. She was already at the screen.

"Ma needs you."

Annie hustled across.

Before the niggers had time to catch on and gang up against them both, the boy, his voice casual and his arm fast, with no explanation to the niggers, said, "It's about time you showed. I was wondering when we were going fishing," slipped his arm around his shoulder and, pressing him away from them, said softly, "Walk slow. Just don't look back or they'll think we're scared and go for us."

We're.

Nobody'd ever said.

They walked straight up to the end of Third and turned and followed the cemetery wall. Rod did not let go of his shoulder till they reached the Episcopal Church.

"You got a pole?"

"Pole?"

"You can't fish without a pole."

"Fish!" Fatso laughed.

"You don't want to?"

And him about to piss his pants with *want*!

"Where'd *I* get a fishing pole?"

"Make yourself one, that's where. But my gramp's got a bunch. Come on. Jees, you never go fishing?"

"Never have time. I work."

"Who'd give kids our age work?"

"I got the dump with Huey, I cut fish and open scallops, I got a bunch of jobs—for money. You don't?"

"I help my uncle Ben and my uncle Rich sometimes with their cars. They always used to say, Stick Rod under the hood, he's half a mechanic already and he's small; but I'm getting tall as they are now. They taught me plenty and I'm a regular grease monkey."

When they reached Sterling Place, Fatso said, "You live on this street?"

On the corner was Hinkelman's. The Polacks would be out, ready.

"My gramp does. Why?"

"Nothing."

"And my gram lives next door."

"How come they don't live in one house?"

"Don't want to, I guess."

He crossed his heart and hoped to die. Not a tough Polack in sight. Only Connie sat in his open doorway, staring at ground. He crushed something with his foot.

When he crossed the lawn to the cottage in the rear, Fatso halted.

"That's Mr. Verity's place."

"Yeah. He's my gramp."

"Tom? Everybody knows him."

You could see him in town any day pulling his cart.

When they entered Mr. Verity's, there was a scattering of cats; but the dog came straight to them, wagging and chafing their legs and his wet tongue panting.

Mr. Verity was at his kitchen table with his bowl of tea, and the raw bulb on in day.

"That you, Rod?"

He raised his head, the unkempt hair sandy with some gray at the temples, his eyes wide—the bulb made them strange white suns.

"And a friend. We need fishing poles, Gramp."

"I better get you some then."

He stood and stared head on at Fatso. For a moment the man's eyes squinted closed to his face.

"You one of the García kids?"

"Yes."

"I thought so."

Fatso watched the old man's hand rise and touch his arm. It was hard as bone, and heavy. He had never seen the hands close. The nails were tiny mounds dark as dirty yellow wax.

Mr. Verity led them outside and into his shop.

The sight halted. Fatso quivered. He was standing in a jungle. The shop was a dump: everywhichway were bicycles, scooters, wagons, mowers; snow shovels, spades, hoes were stacked against the walls; the shelves were set like crooked ladders crowded with jars of nails, screws, boxes and cartons, tiles, remnant rolls of wallpaper, cloth, leather, color after color; hundreds of tools new and rusty hung in notches and from nails; and from the rafters dangled web after web of ropes, wires, hoses, tubing as if great spiders had been at work for years.

Rod's grandfather knew every inch of the way through his chaos. He wove straight through to the rods.

"There you go, boys."

Two professional rod and reels, as perfect as if newly bought.

In a few minutes they reached Gull Pond, walked the breakwater, and settled in with their bucket and bait and rods.

Strong the air smelled, thick with salt and fish.

"Was he born that way?"

"Who?"

"Your grandfather."

"What way?"

"What happened to his hands?"

"He was in a fire—on a barge."

Fatso's eyes filled with fire.

The line jerked him from the flames.

"A porgy!"

"Me too—no, a swellbelly. Darn!"

"You can eat swellbellies. My Ma cooks them."

"Keep it then."

He tickled its belly, making it puff, round and firm as a miniature basketball. Fatso laughed. Despite its spiny belly, they tossed the swellbelly awhile.

He was disarmed by Rod. He was not used to people other than his teachers looking him straight in the eye. Rod didn't even see his mouth. Rod's was perfect. Rod's was so perfect and he laughed so hard with Fatso that Rod made him feel his own teeth had vanished. The thought made him laugh; and when he laughed at the thought, the teeth reappeared, more prominent. He tried to imagine his teeth on Rod, but he couldn't.

They caught a mess of porgies.

"This'll make a whole meal."

It was darking. Shelter Island was tipped with sun, but the shore dark, and all the water shadow. High, the clouds were pearl, an edge of pink moving up over them.

At the house Rod said, "Take the bucket. You can bring it back next time we go fishing."

Fatso's temples beat.

Next time.

He never. Never.

"There ain't much time. I work."

"Work! You're too young."

"I'm not! Been working since the dump—"

He told him the dump and Huey.

"Huey? You mean Huey that lives right there, by Stankus' store?" Under the corner light where the Polacks played craps and drank beer almost all night long, or till a fight broke out and the cops came.

"Him."

Fatso told him Huey and the dump and his junk business and all his jobs, how he had to hustle to get them done and make money.

"Wow! You're something," Rod said. "But you can go fishing with me *some*time."

Fatso never had a plea before.

"Just tell me when!"

He would make up the work. He would buck Ma. He would stay late at the dump, and work more hours cleaning fish.

I don't care, I *don't.*

A friend. He never had.

So it was Saturday then, every Saturday, when he would sneak away—silently vanish from the house, sure Ma was with little Joey, thinking he was out scrounging for junk.

First, the dump. Then little Joey. And now Rod.

Sometimes at the dump, thinking it, he could die happy.

He loved animals. Little Joey was his animal. Though Joey was Dot's chore, as Fatso had been Agnes's, it was Fatso who came straight home to feed and clean and cart Joey between trips hunting junk. After he once heard Ma say to Pa, "Be careful you don't suffocate the kids, Carlos," nights Fatso took Joey from Ma into his bed.

"Fatso's his Ma and Pa," Ma said to Pa.

"Behaving like a goddamn woman," Pa said.

"It helps me some. *You* ain't had to bring up ten," Ma said.

"I haven't, hey?"

Fatso loved school, but that year he missed so many days that the truant officer plagued his mother, appearing almost regularly mornings.

"Haul him off. Go ahead." She was bitter with work and Joey, Renata and Sol gone now, married, and the rest in school, and—so used to Fatso's bringing in a few bucks—she complained, "Fatso, you got to do better'n that."

The truth was Pa was not only out to sea longer, but with more crew and a smaller cut of the take when the skimmers were sold.

"I brought more this week, Ma. Count it."

His Joey grew faster than the weeds along the dump. Joey's skin was light, but his eyes the blackest brown ones in the family, his hair already going dark—a pretty face.

Fatso studied that face, fingered the mouth, watched, waited.

For the teeth.

When Joey started to cry, cry, cry, and the tiny thing broke gums, Fatso's fingers soothed; and when he saw they were growing nice and straight and beginning to make a neat semi-circle, the jaws perfectly matched, he was so happy he scared Joey, crying and squeezing him till he screamed. Fatso's nightmares stopped. He no longer dreamed two Fatsos walking along the streets with two bags, heads bent, eyes on the ground, passing every house, up and down all the streets, going by the the bars and restaurants and docks, expecting the sounds of neighbors or drunks or familiars or the kids from school or the men off the boats or the blacksmith or clerks in the stores when they spoke to him or spoke about him within hearing distance, sounds which meant pity or scorn or affection or indifference or repulsion or sometimes compassion.

Because teeth. Jaw.

By the time Joey was five, Fatso knew love. The girls and Mike and Tony were married now, and Manny was in the Marines. Perhaps, though he had never formulated the thought consciously, it was then that something in him decided he would be Joey's father.

Fatso was fifteen now, his mother pressing him for money, the teachers pressing him to do his homework and appealing to his mother not to let him miss a day: "Santiago's so bright, Mrs. García." "He's quick and perceptive." "He never forgets a thing once he's read or heard it." "I never saw such concentration." "He's got the most alert eyes I've ever seen."

All over town he was known as a real worker, going lickety-split from one job to the next, torso bent forward as if heading into a snow storm, eyes on the ground, his hands never empty. There was nothing he wouldn't do.

At six every morning he cleaned fish for the market on First Street, and after school for Pell's. Twice a week he opened clams or scallops or skimmers or oysters for pay by the bushel. When in a pinch, the gravedigger, old Emil, hired Fatso to help keep up Stirling Cemetery and dig because he did such fast, precise work. Fatso knew what it meant: kicked out by their sister, the Polacks next door to Emil on Easy Street had not only rented for six dollars a month two of the three little outhouses on Emil's lot—six bucks each he'd never collect, if you'd ask anybody in town—but soon had taken advantage of Emil's good nature and also of his fear of their violence when they were drunk. Whenever he challenged the two other Polacks (Connie the Pole always paid) for his money or his own food and sometimes his own bed, with no kind of conscience they'd beat him up and leave him for dead till some neighbor, seeing him lying still and bloody in the yard, would call the ambulance and he'd be laid up in the hospital. They took over Emil's house three-quarters of the time, eating up his victuals, getting him to buy the beer and charge the food at the delicatessen on the corner, so that by the time Emil did stagger down the long block from his house to Stirling Cemetery, smiling, laughing, waving at anybody who passed, singing his German songs, he was too drunk himself to dig. So more and more it was Fatso who helped dig the graves.

The oldest Polack brother, Dolfo, called out, "What're you digging them with, your fucking teeth, Fatso?"

"Can it, Dolfo," his brother Jozef said.

But, drunk, Emil shrieked, "You got pick on people. You goddamn Polacks can't leave nobody alone, by Jesus. Dot kid work, ya, dot kid work like none of you goddamn Polacks ever done work, I'm telling you, by Jesus."

"Shit, Fatso don't care what we say. He's used to it, ain't you, Fatso?"

It happened that Rod's grandfather was passing, even he heard, and turned to those boys and said, "Here, here! There's no need for dirty talk."

Nobody contradicted Tom.

"Boy, you get over here."

Fatso followed old Tom into his shed—the shop, his daughter Stella called it.

"Rod says you're looking for a lawn mower. There's one in the corner if you can get to it. I got it running fine. It's sharpened and ready to go."

He squinted out of his right eye, against the smoke from the cigarette hanging from his mouth.

Everybody said Tom had anything.

"I got no money."

"We'll worry about that when the time comes, boy."

"I'll bring it straight back every time, Mr. Verity."

"No need. It's yours."

"I got no place to keep it. They'll steal it first thing on Third Street."

"You can park it here when you're not using it.

Unfortunately, going home from the cemetery, Fatso had to pass within a block of the house and from Emil's yard the Dombroski boys had a clear view of the intersection. Still Fatso always went a block out of his way, hoping none of them would spot him, though he had long since trained himself to an instantaneous cutoff at the least sound of hostility in people's voices.

Sometimes Joey wanted to tag along. He went into tantrums when separated from Fatso, and Fatso did not like to leave him. A day came when he said, "Why not?" It relieved Ma, and nobody minded the boy romping and playing while Fatso worked; he was quiet and always minded Fatso. The pair soon became such a common sight that on days when he left Joey home people would call out, "What'd you do with Joey, Fatso?"

Fifth Street across the railroad tracks was forbidden territory. No Joey. Mrs. Redburn's husband had died; she had given Fatso the upkeep of the yard. Hers was the first decent house on the south side of Fifth, with a wide spread of lawn and a high, deep hedge which cut off the cluster of four shacks beside the small cottage confined to the narrowest strip of sand by the tracks.

Though he had never seen, Fatso knew—everybody knew—what was on the other side of the hedge, so on the days he left to cut Mrs. Redburn's lawn or trim the hedge, no matter how Joey carried on, Fatso abandoned him.

Now he was used to glimpses through the hedge of the small one-room shacks, weathered gray and decaying, looking abandoned in day, but not abandoned. Pieces of drying clothes, always women's and usually undies, fluttered on a flimsy line nailed to the corners of two of the houses, the trash barrels were full of empty whiskey and beer bottles. Around the shacks were sand and tall field grass and weeds, and no lawn, a wasteland.

Well into September, when the season waned and days were shorter, lights went on earlier in the shacks, cars began to arrive earlier, and men on foot. Sometimes Fatso saw the occasional man or group of cronies with a bottle outside one of the shacks, in shadow, drinking, laughing, living it up, till one of the doors opened and sent a solid block of light over the ground for an instant before a man's shadow darkened it leaving and another darkened it entering, and then total dark, far voices, sometimes laughter.

On rare occasions, as she was getting in or out of a car or standing in her doorway an instant as she dismissed a man after some business, he saw the woman, Madam Pam, the *high yellow* men talked about when their women weren't around, who had the separate *place of business,* no doubt where the women sometimes congregated and ate and received their *remuneration* for the week's *activity.* Hers was the big house in which, the men said, she did not *receive* (guffaws, winks, pokes). Persistent listener that he was, Fatso was adept at knowing what the sounds in men's voices meant. She was dressed as the men said, *fit to kill,* long skirts that in the instant of light in the doorway flashed bright rich streaks of red green blue yellow, and blouses with mazes of lace and coils and dangles of gems and gold aglitter on her neck and breast, and a queen's head piled high with yellow hair too and always her white teeth in a smile, and sometimes a pleasant deepish voice and throaty laugh that made Fatso quiver to the marrow.

At such moments, fear ran through his marrow too. Already asweat from work, he felt a second wave of damp break out, coat him, as if trapped under the first, stifling. He turned away, almost frenziedly piled the raked grass, and hustled his mower noisily up Fifth, not daring to look back.

Those nights his sleeping was spasmodic. He heard laughter. When he woke, it did not go. In the dark he saw nothing. But the laughter had hands. He heard hands moving closer and closer. He gripped the sheets. He was sweating.

Some nights he didn't want to go to bed. In bed he was afraid to sleep. Sleep conjured hands.

It was when he cut Mrs. Redburn's lawn the last time for the season that he saw the woman—or girl, because she was too small, too thin and bony and almost flat-chested (undernourished she looked) to be a full-blown woman like Ma or that Madam Pam or Rod's mother, even Mrs. Kellogg, or any woman he knew.

Cleaning under the hedge, he had caught his rake; he could only free it from the other side.

When he loosed the rake and turned, she was standing a few yards away, a white piece, something she must have taken off the line, a bra, dangling almost to the ground from her left hand.

He wanted to run, but he was stone.

She might have sprung from the sand. With his sharp ears, how come he hadn't heard?

She was staring.

He wanted to hide his teeth, but couldn't move.

Then he saw she was not looking at his teeth. Her eyes, too still, were on his. Besides, he was afraid to move—she might shift her gaze to his teeth.

So they stood, silent. How long? He didn't know. The ground was trembling, then throbbed. It pulsed up so fast his chest swelled so tight he nearly cried out.

She was still not looking at his mouth when she moved.

But he *couldn't.*

Something in him waited, curious, expectant, frightened too.

She crossed the few yards to him. For a sec he thought she wasn't really seeing him because she didn't stop until she was so close their clothes chafed. The touch made his blood surge. It ached his head.

Now he saw how short she was. He was looking down into light green eyes. She was so close that without trying to he saw down inside her flimsy wrap the white slightly rounded mounds and the nipples, dark and large, the flat stomach between hipbones too bold, and an edge of dark hair at the thin thighs. She smelled of soap, some flower. He wanted to breathe and breathe. The smell dizzied.

Her free hand rose. It was long and thin and very white. It touched his forehead and hair and left ear so lightly that he closed his eyes and an instant he was her hand her heat moving.

"They're the darkest I've ever seen," she said.

Her voice was slow and low with a vague rasp. The rasp made him see *rust.*

"Open them. Look at me."

He opened them.

He would fall into those green eyes.

His grip threatened to break the rake in two.

Abruptly her gaze released him. Fast her glance over and down took him all in.

She said, slow again, with that edge of rasp, "You are quite a boy." *Bow-oy* it came from her mouth.

Then fast she was gone. All he saw was the loose wraparound fluttering; she might have disappeared behind it.

She went into the second cabin. A light went on, but he couldn't see even a shadow through the oily-looking yellow shade over the window.

The ground was trembling violently.

The whistle shrieked and a great white eye loomed, making quick white fires of the tracks. The six o'clock train to New York thundered the ground and streaked past like a monstrous blacksnake gliding into the gathering dark.

In bed it was that vague *rasp* he heard, *green* he saw, and *hands soft* and *white* he felt. They would not stop, and he could not stop his own from touching her touching, could not stop his own moving and moving over his forehead, hair, and down, *down*, ohjesusgod. He had to get up—because Joey. The house suffocated. He went outside and gulped air, sucked, and touched, touched—he could not bear.

A night in October in dark he went back. He stood behind a tree, hiding, petrified someone would hear because at the least move of his feet the dry leaves crackled. Between long silences from one shack or the other came laughs, a man's, woman's, sometimes both, and clunking sounds, doors opening and voices. He watched the second shack so long his muscles ached. He saw Henry Wallace go in and come out, and then Clive Bates, and after him the short fat wop everybody called Tony Baloney. He stood through the time of the three men, wanting to go close, wanting to hear her sound, see her *green*, see *white*, feel *soft*, that hand.

When a car drove up and strangers got out, five laughing drunks, he slunk behind the shrubs and followed the tracks back to the depot at the foot of his own street and sat on the edge of the railroad dock. The harbor made a half-circle of tiny white fires moving in the water. Opposite, Shelter Island stood black against the sea beyond. The ferry with its strings of lights was crossing from the island to the railroad dock. It seemed to ride its own reflection in the water.

He stared down into his own body darker than night, undulating in the water below.

What was in her hand that could make his heart choke his chest and almost take his breath and split his skin?

At the thought of her touch he could die.

Die.

All night he lay awake.

Die. What did that mean?

After that night he never went back to the shacks.

And he spent less time at home. He didn't want *them*, he didn't want the stale air in the house, he didn't want to defile the flower scent he'd smelled on *her*; so he was out mornings long before his mother was up and he stayed out till he thought they'd be in bed, and all that week he spent more time than ever at the dump.

Then it was all over town that Huey had won the lottery, for Huey a grand sum. Everybody kidded him about giving up the dump. Even Huey joked. "You might end up with the dump all to yourself, Fatso." He was all talk about what he'd buy his wife and kids, what he'd pay off. Wednesday morning Huey went early to collect his winnings.

Fatso did not get to the dump till dusk that afternoon after school. The dying sun turned the pond a still crimson fire. The clouds burned. The sight smote. He had never seen the dump more beautiful. He watched the sun sink. The pond turned dark, the horizon vanished, the sky faded gray as the dark rose.

Then it struck: *all* the dump was dark, not one mound burning!

The shed door was open. Huey always locked it! In the dim light the tools hanging on the wall glinted.

"Huey?"

He stuck his head inside the shed.

"Huey!" he called out over the dump, but nothing. Silence.

He listened. Too much silence.

He went behind, between the shack and the thick wall of shrubs and trees concealing the dump from the town's eyes. When he turned to survey the dump, he saw Huey. Why hadn't he seen at once? He knew every single shape, the least change each day—

Huey was lying on a heap, his body assuming almost the contour of it.

"Huey!" He fell upon him.

The rats scattered, but reluctantly. They had already begun their work.

"Huey!"

He clutched Huey's face. It was cold.

He tried to shake him, but he was too heavy and stiff.

He could see Huey's head was too dark. He touched where it was dark—blood, matted, cold, crumbly.

From the shed he jerked the tarpaulin he kept to move trash from place to place, threw it over Huey, it'd maybe hold off some rats. Then he ran—

It was the supper hour, not many people on the streets, and in no time he reached the little white office on Main with the blue neon, POLICE. He saw Cash the cop. He told him quick, "Huey's dead at the dump. I found him," Cash was quick to the phone calling an ambulance, then out the door, and shoving him into the car, "Get hold now, Fatso," because his chest was heaving, his breath gulping and wheezing almost like an asthmatic's. Huey! Poor Huey! They were back so fast it was as if he hadn't left yet. Yes, real, it was, Huey under the tarpaulin, only it was night now, and at once he got a long stick—in dark the rats were bold—and whacked. He told Cash again and again how he'd come and found Huey, told till he couldn't stop even when Cash said, "Okay, Fatso, that's enough. I got it. I'll write it up. You'll have to sign a statement. You're *sure* you seen nobody?" "Who? Who'd hurt Huey?" "There's always somebody." Huey didn't even think *money,* and Cash did not mention *lottery* yet.

Fast as they were, the ambulance closed in with an almost unbearable piercing, then cut off with a silence so unbearable it thundered, the ambulance's red light casting mad circles over Huey and the dump. People were racing now up Third and Webb to find out what's what.

Then all the talk was *murder* and *lottery.*

All over town, first, was *Fatso.* Who else had the perfect chance?

If Fatso was shocked, it was at the inevitability of what he had learned to expect from men who did not have his teeth.

Nonetheless you walked past them as every day, with your burlap bag, eyes aloof, and a motion of indifference, though seething.

Too easily it was demonstrated—marks on the ground, footsteps and movements, tools (Huey had been struck with a shovel), the condition of the shed, the open door—that two men had assaulted Huey. And the autopsy showed that the body had been dead since about eleven Wednesday morning. Fatso, of course, had been in school at that hour.

He knew from their words and looks how he had failed his accusers.

But it was Ma who crucified.

"Fatso, if *you* took that money—!"

Ma! You too?

He could not meet her eyes. His hands trembled with the invisible money. She shamed the air. He had to leave her. He rose. He felt he could hardly stand. The words were lashing and lashing at his back, all his body. They cut his insides. He could not bear the invisible blood.

All day her words did not stop.

A hundred times that day he halted, thinking *her* hand could stop the lashing. If he closed his eyes, that hand soft white long might touch his forehead, his hair. This time it would calm him.

But he was afraid to go near the shack.

Now he returned home late nights, hoping Ma would be in bed. He did not want her; he was too hurt. And most of the time she was in bed. And Pa too when he was home from the boat. He would get "That you, Fatso?" and crawl in with Joey.

Joey was getting too big to hug and hold, and now Joey accused, "How come you don't take me with you no more?" and Fatso would console him with promises—"Saturday, Sunday we'll do something," because Joey was started in school now.

Not long after Huey's murder Fatso turned sixteen. But for his mother's accusation he might not have had the courage to go to the Town to see Lyle Talbot.

He was stone when he thought somebody else might have the dump. He knew then how much a part of his life it had become, more with home not *home* anymore.

"What is it, Fatso?"

"It's Huey's job at the dump, Mr. Talbot. Nobody knows the dump like me. You know that."

"I'll let you know, Fatso."

He went through nine days nearly sick with apprehension, clinging more than ever to the dump, fearing that if they did not find him when they wanted him, they might give it to somebody else on the spot.

When he crept quietly into the house the night of the ninth day, his mother said, "I hear you, Fatso. You had a visitor. That Mr. Talbot come and give you the job at the dump." He was so relieved he had to duck out into the yard and heave. The ground was white with moon. He stood long, staring at the dump through the leafless web of bleached branches. The moon moulded the dump a mystery of irregular dark shadows. Only he knew the key. He laughed. Mine. *Mine.* He embraced the air. And laughed.

"*Now* what the hell is it?" his mother said when he went in, but he didn't answer.

So now he had something. In reality he possessed two things, the dump and Joey, so associated in his head that one became the cause for the other, for entrenched now was the idea that he needed the dump to support Joey because his mother gave Joey nothing, hand-me-downs found in old drawers and closets, but never for himself a new thing, a loose nickel his, a plaything, clay or pencils or colored sheets bought and abruptly left for Joey because he needed or wanted them. Fatso didn't understand. With the others gone Ma had grown greedy? After years of scrubbing and ironing for her own and others, years of Pa's irregular share of the take, years of Fatso's handovers, had she decided to clutch and hoard. Because she went to work in Mitchell's kitchen now; still she took every cent of Pa's and his. Even Pa complained, "Jesus, woman, you always *could* stand on a dime, but now you're so tight you squeak. Where's my beer?"

More than ever now, time ruled his life. He moved with a rhythm as regular as the motion of the sun and moon and stars. He was all discipline. He sacrificed none of his regular jobs. Six days a week, except for school hours, he worked from six in the morning, when he began cleaning fish, till long after dark, when he stopped work at the dump. That left all Sunday for the dump and preparing and packing the week's collection of foil, rags, and bottles to sell.

Already he was setting aside money from what he gave Ma. He had cut and hollowed out a section of two-by-four which he fit in place of oneof the roof supports in the cubbyhole of Huey's shed. It looked permanent. Only he knew how to remove it. In the hollow he kept his dollar bills. When he accumulated too many small bills for the hollow, he exchanged them for larger ones. He did not open a savings account because in town nothing was secret; one visit and the news would reach Ma even before he could leave the bank, and then she *would* come down on him. He had never kept any money for himself and he felt guilty, until he thought *For Joey.* And he was vigilant—he removed the beam only with no one in sight and only in full day; and on each return always he observed for the least sign of pilfering. The police had no concrete evidence to prove who had killed Huey and taken his money, though there was no shortage of speculation or even outright supposition.

By design he went home so late that he seldom saw his mother now. That was grief to him because he wanted to see her, but his grief at the thought of her betrayal was greater, doubly so, because it somewhat cut him off from Joey. Though he had hated the fact that all twelve grades were housed in one school, now he was glad because he could go to and from school with Joey and see him between classes and at lunch. That meant he didn't have to cut back so much on the time he gave to his several jobs.

He did no homework now. If anything, he was a superlative listener, and most of the work was easy for him. His classmates showed a reluctant admiration for his agile mind. He knew from the consistent mouthing of his name, *Fatso'll know, Ask Fatso, What else would*

Fatso do but study? from the pronounced emphases, the refusal to look into his eyes, a certain irritation from their perfect mouths. He was not flattered by their notice. No. It was no compensation. He'd already been denigrated enough for a lifetime, but he was flattered by their denigration. You could be. You could live among them through denigration. Though his looks agonized him no less, he accepted their tribute to his ugliness; he accepted their inadvertent confessions of certain inferiorities. He saw words could be *invisible* teeth that disguised and revealed. Their words sharpened his perceptions of himself and them. If his teeth were the obstacle to his relationships with them, they concealed a prominence of another kind. His deformity had made him see and hear *under* things. If the others could not, it was because they were blind and deaf except to faces like their own. He could pity *them.* He felt his superior knowledge. There was a pleasant feeling of power in its secrecy. He thought this way because of his teeth. At moments he took a perverse pride in them. Still, he wouldn't wish them on his classmates, on anybody, no, never.

If there were people in town who respected him for working all the time, and him young to boot, he knew the ones who went further and pitied him—and in his own way he let them know with a nod, a wave, a "Hey!"—but didn't they also pity dogs, *poor things,* the same way, and cats, homeless things, bums, the good-natured local drunks, *poor things.* To him they were only one step above the Polacks from Easy Street, who worked, yes, who were good workers, but who worked to blow it on booze and gamble and get slopping drunk and sleep in the yard and piss on the lawn and dangle their dicks at whatever girl passed.

But there were those few who didn't show *pity,* didn't *shame,* didn't seem even to notice his teeth or maybe saw something more than a face or simply took the teeth for natural in him: he wouldn't be Fatso without them. Some, thinking about it or not thinking about it at all, must have seen themselves in him.

Like Tom. Since the summer day years ago when he and Rod had gone for the fishing poles, Tom had taken him in—the instant that bone hand had touched him—as if he were Rod, just as the day Joey was born Rod had defended him against the niggers as if he were Fatso.

With the brother, Cory, he'd had no truck, though summers on the rare morning when he could stop by for Rod to go fishing, Cory would call out, "He'll be right out, Fatso." The brother's voice was a sound warm and resonant, and he looked straight at him with familiarity. Other times the mother would open the back door—because Fatso never went straight to the back door but lingered on the lawn—and invite him in. "Rod will be ready in a minute." She was small, slim, too pretty and young looking to be Rod's mother. "She sure is pretty, your mother." "Yeah. It makes me mad," Rod said. "The kids at school always make wisecracks and whistle and ask if she's my sister. So when I see her coming, I cross the street so the guys won't see me with her."

"Your brother don't fish?"

"Naw, hates it. He's a bookworm. The brain in the family. Swims a lot. At school he's great on the high bar and the hobbyhorse. He's a loner."

"Oh."

Fatso was hearing the brother's voice. The sound stirred, as physical as a worm in him.

He would give anything if it were summer and Rod and Cory were here, but it would be long from November to June.

When school closed for Thanksgiving, snow and snow covered the town. All the earth between the harbor and the Sound lay white, the last tree and shrub. Even the horizon vanished. The dump lay under a disguise so pure he hated to mar it with his steps. He hovered, entranced by the soft white that molded the mounds and slopes, softening and rounding the edges into one unboken form now like the flesh of an enormous body, the wind coming like breath down over him. When sun emerged, the white glistened. Wind blew the dry snow up and made the air itself glitter. Then sun and cold turned the snow hard, so he could do little to sort and pile and burn debris at the dump. If the blow bit and cut, he sat inside the shed with the door open and gazed out, exhilarated by all that beauty.

But the air warmed. The melt came. Patches dark as wounds opened snow and spread, chaotic. They gave the dump a scabby look.

One late afternoon, towards dusk, he was leveling a mound. Halting, he heard the sound, *light, moving.*

Not rats, no—

"Hey!"

The *rasp* went electric through him.

She was standing almost against him.

"You can't see to work in this here dark, now can you?"

He was trembling.

He could not make his mouth go.

"Well, *don't* answer then. At least, I know you're breathing." She laughed. "Well, I got enough words for a bunch. No stopping my mouth, my momma always said. She was something, my momma." Again she laughed openly, higher now. The laugh sent hands all over him. He quivered.

"Here, give me that." She took the hoe. "We'll put it where it belongs. A man can't work all the time, now can he?"

She was quick. Already she was in the shack. He heard the metal strike the floor and the handle hit the wall.

Then she was outside again.

"I know—you're thinking how'd I find you. Easy. Everything's easy in a town this size—mine was small, I tell you, but this place, it's no bigger'n a pinhead—easy, sure, everything but getting out. *We* don't. She don't like us *seen*. No talk—you know. And cooped up, you go nuts, you know that? Oh, we're busy. She makes sure of that, makes sure we keep them coming back too, or out we go. She don't keep any of us long, she tells you that the day she takes you on. 'Now don't get too attached to any man or this town either,' she says, 'cause I keep changing girls. Men like variety, and if they get a little itchy about one too long I'm in trouble; so I'm telling it to you plain right now, don't count on a long stay.' Wasn't a thing here or no place else could keep me, I told her, or why'd I be here in the first place?"

Wudn't, she said.

Silently he said it. *Wudn't*. He hoarded all her sounds.

"Yes, easy," she said, "'cause another thing about small towns, you can't hide, everybody knows you, any fool'd know that."

Even in cold and dark his face flushed quick hot.

She leaned against the shed, darker against dark, barely visible even that close, but her smell made him see honeysuckle, her voice soft and *white* touched his hair, his forehead.

In a minute he would not bear—

"You still there?" She laughed.

"Yes." After hers, his sound was harsh as cussing.

"I *knew* you had a tongue! Cat gave it back, did he?"

This time her throat held the laugh. It vibrated deep in his.

He felt the fire in his face.

If she had ever seen him before the mirror!

He would stare at his tongue. You could always *see* it; his tongue always wanted to overlap his jaw. He couldn't hide it, he couldn't close his mouth. *Even dogs can*. He tried to hide the tongue. He practiced trying to close his mouth, but the lower jaw was so small and recessive that it was lost under his tongue; and his upper teeth hung a long ledge like over the entry to a cave. A man can do anything if he wants to badly enough, they always taught at school; he can overcome the worst odds, they said; any man can be president, they said. He was sure his teachers were not lying. Simply they did not know or they were right, but he hadn't yet discovered the way, not because he didn't want to badly enough. Sometimes he felt he thought about nothing else but his teeth *without knowing it,* perhaps because either he wasn't ready for other thoughts or he depended on something outside himself he did not yet know.

He had practiced exercises before the mirror, trying to elongate his jaw, manipulate his tongue, make it retreat in its dark cave like an obedient creature, jam his protruding upper mandible back and press and pull his jaw forward. Hour after hour he struggled till tears, agonies, furies made him strike walls, break glass, broomsticks, anything. He cried out *against.* He cursed. He raised his arms and shook them against, against—but against what?

Against.

Years—sporadic, in secret—he had practiced.

Even dogs . . .

And he still believed.

But when the class began to make cracks about him—his mind, his study—he ceased practicing, convinced: I'm off the track, there must be a different way, but a way, yes.

She said, "But I didn't have to ask because I saw you—"

"Saw me! Where?"

"Yes, I told her, Alice—you know, Madam Pam they call her here—there were some things I wanted at the drugstore; so when she sent the nigger for groceries, I'd go. She looked funny, but didn't ask was I up to something. I can't blame her—she knows her girls, I'll say that. I didn't have to look far. When I went out the back door to the parking lot, there you were, going through boxes like some old coon dog."

He shrank ashamed in his clothes. Never before, no.

"Hunting junk. It's my job."

She laughed.

"Oh, don't you be offended now. It's just a way of talk I got. It's work, ain't it—and honest, and not to be ashamed of ? Don't think I wouldn't've stopped and said a thing, but not with the nigger never out of sight, oh no, I'm not that dumb. I didn't even ask the boy with the groceries, but he told anyway. That's Fatso what keeps the dump, he said. So, like I said, *easy*. I didn't even have to go out, only ask one of the men where they took them booze bottles and stuff. Up Third a few blocks, he said. And me on Fifth. No walk a-tall. Easy. So here I am."

All the time she spoke she was leaning against the wall of Huey's shack, her hands behind her, touching the wall no doubt, because she moved and moved, forward and back, as if riding the backs of her hands.

Now he saw them because her movement stopped and for an instant she blew on them. *Soft* came to him, and *white,* and so sudden that he threw his gloves down and fast cupped her hands in his to hold and warm.

"Mmmm, hot your hands."

Almost he didn't hear in the surging, surging, his blood.

His hands drew her till she was against. He trembled worse than from any cold.

She was even smaller in the mackinaw. The top of her head came level with his nose. When she raised her face to him, to the night, her eyes were dark glitters, and her teeth, and her lips even in this cold a wet dark shine.

Everything was moving. He couldn't stop the moving. Nothing would stay.

When she slid her hands free, he let out a sound. As quickly her hands were on his neck. "Shhhh, shhhh," she said, her breath or lips or tongue on his neck too, and her hands moving down over his, insinuating his arms under the open mackinaw till he was holding her with such fear to hurt and such yearning to warm her and be *soft, white,* warm, be her.

She said, "Tender. You are. I knew, yes, I did, when I watched you through the hedge—you didn't know—more than once. I said—it was like something told me—*him.* I knew it was just time, when. And it would have to be me to start it, yes, because you would never, not dare. Would you?"

"I almost—"

He could not confess the spying.

"You didn't need to, no. *I* needed to. Once a thing hits me it has to happen. I have to make it."

This time she groaned. Her hands were chafing his thighs, and she was moving, her hips and hands somehow became all of her, a rhythm moving and moving over him so his own thighs stomach chest chin rode and rode. His legs trembled. Almost he could not stand. He was sure he would faint, fall, die. "Easy, easy, yes," she whispered, "easy," with such a long slow move up his body that his blood swelled, his head reeled—"easy," his temples nothing but a *pound-pound*—"easy," and his ears— "easy," and under her hard close grip, at the very instant her mouth at last found his lower lip, bit, sucked.

He shuddered, he would burst, he heard his own moan. She laughed with a sound of triumph, joy. Their sounds must have gone over the dump, anybody could have heard, he didn't care. He kept clutching and clutched, clutched because she was whispering, "Yes, yes," at the hot, the wet in his pants, "because I knew, I did." She didn't let go and he wouldn't. "You never did, did you? No girl—woman, I mean. I was right." She was talking into his mouth, her breath was hot on his tongue. He never before felt *inside* a mouth, lip, never a *tongue*. He could taste. Nobody had ever. "No," he said and his tongue caught her neck; his tongue lapped where his teeth lay hard against her neck, he could eat. "You haven't yet," she said, "but you just wait!"

She released him then.

"I got to go."

He felt broken off, an island in dark.

She buttoned her jacket and adjusted her knit cap and pressed the long hair into place. Now her face was a thin thing barely visible in the dark.

"Listen, I got no time. She makes sure we don't have. But at the end of the day, just before she lets them in for the night, she likes us to get together an hour or so, a very late breakfast she calls it, with her girls, but it's to keep her eye on what's happening to us. She can spot a change better than any dog, get the town news. She knows her territory inside out and backwards."

He was hoarding her sound. He had to touch where she'd roused the madness.

"But there's the waking-up time, and dressing. Four o'clock, five. These days it's dark by then. I can sneak off. It ain't far. You here then?"

"Yes." He said it again loud to make sure. "Yes."

She laughed.

"You're going to be something. You already are. You just don't know."

Then she was gone. Her steps were quick, light, an almost soundless brush.

He stared where she went seeking the dark of the street and avoiding the streetlights till she rounded the corner.

He leaned against the building where she'd been, pressed his body against it, pressed his palms, pressed, then struck his head hard against it, struck and struck. "OhgodjesusFatso, holyfuckingjesusgodFatso," he muttered over and over.

He wanted a name—to know, hoard, whisper. He *saw* what he had seen the other side of the hedge, the narrow face so white, the eyes green sights of sea, the fullest thing the lips he knew now, and a neck long for such a little thing, and that too thin body. How could a tiny thing make such madness? He remembered the body as almost mist vanishing in the wind-blown wraparound; but now he knew its shape, heat, power; knew that the glitter of eyes, mouth, teeth in dark came from a creature burning with invisible fire.

But he had to name.

He knew her on his hands, skin, all his body. But he wanted to hold her in his mouth. He wanted to swallow, hoard her in his heart. He wanted to be able morning noon night to call up his secret part, her. In his mouth she would be his. Alone, his hand sought her. He tried not, but she was on him. He left himself wet, exhausted, exhilarated, yearning, unfulfilled.

Next time, she said, "Name's Diane," with that faint rasp, which every time was new, fresh, startling with the promise of some novelty. " And yours? You got one?" And laughed, throaty.

Not Fatso, not to her.

He would claim himself.

"Santiago."

"Santiago." She was silent a second, then said, "Sounds so strange . . . like far . . . exotic . . . mysterious."

He swelled with the mystery of his sudden self.

And laughed happily.

And let his head rest against hers.

"Santi. I'll call you that?"

"Yes."

"Santi. Yes, I like that."

"Santi," he savored, and her sound saying it.

She was coming to the shed with some regularity now, though he could never be sure on which day, so he hustled, sure to arrive early, and even on days of inactivity, when rain or snow, he hovered till she did come or it grew much too late to expect her. She came always in the same mackinaw, red, with the knit cap, red too but not the red of the mackinaw, drawn down over her ears. "I'll never get over being Southern." "Because you got sun inside you," he said. "Why, Santi!" She kissed his closed eyes. "You're turning into something else!"

The winter was fierce, unyielding. No sooner at the dump, she drew him into the shed and shut the door. "For sure nobody'll come this time of day." He had arranged some comfort. His tools and equipment he had set aside and ordered to make room along the rear of the shed for a bench on which he could spread a discarded sleeping bag and old blankets. She was never in a hurry. She was magic. She made it seem they had all the time in the world together though they had only the hour, slightly more sometimes; but she had to allow for the time it took to walk from the shacks and back. She seemed quick because she was so efficient in that short time with him.

Once inside, the moment they touched, she had no fear of the cold; if anything, she met its challenge. She insisted on nakedness. "Everything else is a lie." She was teaching him his body. With each visit he was startled at the agonizing pleasure she could bring forth. She could ease out of him or tease to gradual intensities of sensation or make erupt only to make him climb beyond to undreamed of silent shrieks his sex could make, leaving him moaning as she moaned, moaned. There came a day when he realized: she's learning her own body too; maybe that's what keeps her coming to me. Even in this cold she liked to lie and talk. Still, her talk was fast, she had so little time, and she never talked when she loved him, when she took him, as she did, carrying him where she would each day. He could not believe it had happened before, and when it seemed she began sometimes to repeat, even then she moved with novelty, touching where a stroke at the certain rising motion could agonize with a new ecstasy, a fingertip grazing his under arm, edging the round of his buttock, whisking the hair of his groin till he had to end, end.

She was a good talker, a rambler. Her breath was hot against his neck. But when she spoke into his mouth, it was the most intimate sensation he knew. She would cross to the shack, talking. Her faint rasp stirred his blood to life. She made him begin to know what *dead* was.

She was from a place "somebody must've spit on the side of the road" in Alabama, Lickskillet, near Huntsville, a metropolis compared to her town till she realized *it* was too small, oh maybe ten thousand people half of them "all time singing out of the side of their face how they love The Man Upstairs, some even believing it but most sure don't act it." It wasn't her momma or poppa who drove her out of Lickskillet to Huntsville, no, it was the country. "Don't let me kid you. I loved just the sight of fields and smell of country, but it's no place to go nights. It's night after night of boys wanting to walk you somewhere or got cars and thinking you're one more animal on one more farm got to go at it all the time; and me, I never would, not with nobody. I was going to keep it, see, and I wasn't even thinking to keep it for a special one yet, just keep it."

Wudn't.

He laughed.

"You making fun of me?"

He laughed. "I wudn't."

"You sure got an odd sense of humor."

"Yes."

"You sure don't look it."

Now she got *her* laugh, but he knew she'd accepted the teeth before she'd even spoken to him by Mrs. Redburn's hedge. He was sure now it was the teeth that made her take notice.

That instant the teeth were a gift. What church people said, a gift of God. But why? With her he never thought *teeth, gift, God.*

He thought of the singing-out-of-the-side-of-their-face people. You didn't know what *they* knew was inside them that you couldn't see. They must *want* too. Everything wasn't obvious like his teeth. When he was with her, he could believe even in his teeth.

"And me thinking Huntsville'd be the dream place—"

He loved her sound. He mouthed it, *Hunsvull.*

"And me honest, but what's for a country girl in Huntsville, me half the time out of school because somebody's sick, Bubba and my daddy all time working on a old car always broke down. You can't live in the country with no car. Waiting on tables, that's what. And working them clubs, private, go-gos and not, and no niggers. Clubs are all that town had, more'n a body could count. I didn't like what I seen and heard. My daddy, he wouldn't stand for talk like that. Me, I took to housecleaning then. It's what made me want to get out. You listen good and it's a hell you learn. You don't want to know it it's that bad, the town so rotten it'd send you running to New Hope or Owens Crossroad only it'd be the back door of the same house. You learn rot you don't want. Just to hear shames you for them and you too, but most it makes you afraid of your own self. I thought Momma had it bad, suffering work every minute she's living, but she'd choose to work and suffer every time if she saw one minute the kind of women had to live with their men's doings and some even lying they're proud to. No wonder it's a heap of bottles you wouldn't believe goes through some women's guts just to make them stand living with the little bunch of men runs things, most of them drunks half the time off to Nashville to get soaked and whore around, the mayor with his crowd, the police and car dealers and businessmen so dirty it's scary. You got to *get* if you're smart. It's too much power too close to you. A little power makes you stink, but good. Wipe you out slow, not fast like they wiped out so many, and not the twick of a eye. I seen. They'd kill me for just knowing what I heard. No difference stepping on a stink bug or me. One I worked for, I let her know I'd sure like to move—I mean I said I wonder what it'd be like in Maryland or some place—and she said *Go.* She said Go far when you do go. Oh, she was a fine lady, still a beauty but frazzled, just before tacky, that rot got to her. You could tell love, she loved him but what good, nothing changes. I don't know why she told me Go. She must've known better because you can't go to a place where there's no people and you can't make people over either. There's some white trash in everybody. A body sure got to struggle to keep it down."

It was as if she had hoarded talk, had never talked to anyone before and was fighting time, as if she had saved it all for him, had to get it all out before her chance went. He listened, avid. He was tracking and retracking her journey. He rode her voice place to place, and her sounds revealed, every intonation telling him her feelings about every person inside her she'd never be able to get out, and each city, St. Louis, Detroit, Chicago. He listened, hoarding too. He was learning her. He was waiting for what drove her to Greenport. He wanted every second of her life right up to the minute she'd seen him.

Now he worked in frenzy, to be sure he was at the dump at the consecrated hour. It cost. He sacrificed Joey, though he tried whenever he could to take Joey with him, though the most difficult moments were when Joey wanted to accompany him to the dump. He didn't want to lie, he gave excuses, but his excuses were really lies. What helped with Joey was that Renata and Sol had come home, divorced, Renata with Susan, two, and Sol with the ten-month-old Marcia. So they did not miss, suspect, him, though whenever he did return, always his mother was waiting, and hounded. "You think they're living on air, Fatso? What's with you?" Not to rock the boat, he was quick to appease.

Because *Diane.*

He could not risk.

She was a light in dark he went straight to. He felt himself being hurled with wonderful terrible velocity straight toward that light. Each time he was consumed by flame. He wanted to be.

Then it came clear she was learning him too.

"It took some doing to loosen up that tongue of yours. You sure talk good, you know that? I mean you got a good voice and you sure got a handle on words."

His hoarded gold threatened to spill.

"Things stick."

But it was not Pa, Ma, the brothers and sisters, Third Street, town, fishing, history she wanted to know. It was something in him. She touched, listened. She seemed to want to know only what was inside his skin. Still, she didn't seem to *want* anything; yet each change, reaction, in him gave her delight. He became aware of a peculiar admiration in her voice, peculiar because—who had ever overtly admired him?

"Your head's so quick, you don't miss a thing, you don't forget, and you only—"

"I told you—sixteen."

"I don't want to believe it. But a man, yes. I'd've believed that from your body, that day by the hedge."

"It's the work does it. Since a kid . . . I almost can't remember . . . except the first sight of this dump, following Huey, just big enough to drag a hoe. He let me."

"You sure don't need to grow. You're man enough for any woman now. And built."

Sometimes he was frightened, because the fright would come sudden to her: "With you your age I could be sent up—you know that?"

The thought turned him icy as the air.

Because he depended now. Nights, days, his body longed, his head filled. When streetlights came on with that sickish afternoon blue, he felt his body go pale, tremorous, sensitive as eyes alerted by the least scrape, any sweet waft or far flick of shadow or unexpected touch of twig or wind or a snowflake or two. She could not tell or promise which moment. So he hovered, hung, till the later it grew, the more tense, edgy, irritated, the more it occurred to him to dare to go meet her, look for her, even approach the shack. When it was unquestionably too late for her to come, stubbornly he stayed. He raked and hoed till he was asweat. He sorted. He made fires, piling trash on till they flamed high. He exulted, thinking she might see them from her shack. When they burned down he felt bereft, wandered the streets, the docks on Front Street, roamed the Sound beach or sat in a sulk at Gull Pond.

When for days she did not come, he swore he would go to her shack, he would knock on the door, he would go just before morning came over the sky. Her night work would surely be over by then, she would be alone, he would take her in her own bed.

(He was not jealous of the other men. He did not even think of them because he knew she did not think of them as people with names, emotions, identities. Besides, he knew that, to her, what she gave him, no matter what impulse had at first impelled her, was now vital, inescapable, necessary.)

He did not have to.

At seven one Monday morning in March—they had been meeting

now since November—after cleaning fish for an hour, he went to the dump.

"Hey!"

She appeared from behind the shed, stark against the open sky over the Sound beyond.

All the dump quivered.

He was too thrilled to object It's early, somebody'll see. Why'd you come. Only *You* ran through his head, *You*!

Since the moment at Mrs. Redburn's hedge, he had never seen her in bright day. She looked so small, too thin. There was a beaten look in her that roused him. Her face was naked, clean, no makeup. She was almost twice his age—she had never lied—and she looked thirty now, more, fine lines and plenty around her eyes, ribbing her thin cheeks. In her eyes were fine webs of blood.

"You don't eat."

She shook her head, and smiled, obviously moved by his tenderness.

"Or sleep?"

Boldly he took her face between his hands. Anybody could see them through the bare trees, but he didn't care.

A little choke escaped her. She closed her eyes.

"Yes. Oh, yes," she murmured, and turned her head to kiss his hands to madness. "Now, yes, now."

He pressed her quickly toward the shed, unlocked it.

In a moment they were heaving and heaving, wordless. And lay wordless after, briefly, knowing day had eyes, ears.

Only when she was back in the mackinaw, drawing the red knit cap down, staring past the tarred beams marking the entrance to the dump, did she break the silence.

"They'll all be sleeping. Maybe she'll be. If not, to hell with her."

So it started that morning.

Now she came at odd times—afternoons when he left school, the first thing mornings, before dark, after. He never knew when to expect her, and she would not hazard a promise now. It was as if she were intentionally trying to confuse, excite, frighten; as if she feared she had run out of ways to intrigue him and so taxed her imagination to invent or deceive, whether herself or him. For a while it was an implicit game in which he could not anticipate or outguess her.

Then he knew it was not merely a game because now she materialized across the street from school. Standing to sharpen a pencil or asking permission to go to the john, he would see her standing under a tree the far side of the road, and he would break out into sweat from confusion, excitement, fear. Clearly, she saw him. She knew his homeroom.

She knew his house on Third. The house directly faced Center. You could stand on the porch and stare across Third down Center Street and see straight through town and in winter catch even a glimpse of Stirling Creek. She would appear, if rarely, standing against a tree a block away on Center Street, or on Third she might be seen nonchalantly eyeing the house; but she was not so nonchalantly eyed by the neighbors for she was a foreign object in town and therefore of consuming interest and thus made familiar. And surely, since in him she had chosen a familiar fixed object made more familiar and more foreign by his infamous teeth, she stepped into the town's annals because, although Fatso had already been a character for legend, until she came to Madam Pam's there had been no character to evoke the legend.

He knew something was happening to her.

He was sure because she talked less now, talked in spurts as sudden and rapid as if she were a timed geyser cut off too as suddenly, in mid-sentence sometimes, as if the source of her words had dried up or she were helpless to name with what allotted speech remained to her, so groped silently. At those times she would stare, too still, shrunken, like a creatue helplessly fascinated into immobility by the eyes of a snake. And he was helpless because he could not know what invisible thing she saw. Perhaps she did not see. Perhaps that was the horror, because clearly it was terrible for her; if anything, he knew the vacant eyes of despair.

Because *she* depended now.

(It must have been unfathomable to her. She must never have planned, expected, imagined. And it was as unfathomable to him how naturally it had come about. There came moments when she would actually fall into his arms and they would simply stand clutching each other in silence, long, hard, still, with some fear of anything outside their touching and some joy, heightened by that fear but tainted by it too.)

At the dump one cold night of late March snow, hearing steps, he went to meet her—

But it was his mother. She had trudged the snow straight to the dump.

"Why aint'chya showed at the house? What kinda trick you pullin'? You think we ain't seen that whore you been runnin' around with, her showin' her ass all over the place like the filthy hussy she is . . ."

She raged, but by now he had learned from Diane to hear but not listen, a part of him turned off to emotion. He watched and waited, for Ma depended too. In a minute it would be need, money, and it was; but he didn't fault her now, merely endured her tirade: ". . . a houseful again, the boats aslump, and you spendin' every cent on that slut and her flauntin' it all over the place—think I ain't seen her hangin' around on Center?—and us not able to make ends meet. Yeah, it's so bad the girls had to go on welfare or where'd the hell we be—and you cuttin' us off for *that* thing."

In the silence she raised her voice, but it fell, impotent, over the mounds, the pond, the fields beyond, and the sea.

And on him.

"I can send her off to jail, you know that?"

"Then you'd never get any money, would you, Ma?"

"You smart-assed little bastid you, Fatso."

He did not, would never, tell her that he had long since taken the bus to Riverhead and opened a savings account at the Riverhead Bank. His plan was not complete yet, but he was doing it for Joey, who was never far from his mind. It was the first impotence he had discovered between him and Diane. Joey evoked something more steadfast than her obsession and his desire.

"You listen to me, Fatso," his mother said. "From now on you hand over every cent or—no bed. That clear? F-you don't slap it into this hand every week faithful, you just getchya-rass out."

He would not have that now.

I owe Diane that, her. If she can live in hell, independent, so can I. It's no great thing. Who'd care but me anyway?

"I already left, Ma."

"You what?"

"Yes. I'm not going back to the house."

"And where the hell you think you're goin'? Who's gonna take you in, that crowd at St. Agnes?"

"I don't need them either."

"Well, ain't you the independent one!"

"I'll get by."

"You just try it then and see if you don't come crawlin' with your tail between your legs. You wait."

Then she was gone, a noisy trudge over the snow, a dark shadow, double, on the bright snow.

Diane had stopped coming to him in dark. She sought him only in day now. She wanted him always in light. She knew his work, his rhythm. At some moment she must have started going to the other places where he did work, collecting the sites so that when he mentioned them she'd know them and when alone she could imagine them, because she spoke of Pell's, the fish plant, the oyster factory, Art White's Bait Shop with familiarity and timed his arrivals and departures perfectly. In that shack at Madam Pam's he must have been all her preoccupation when she was not with the men who paid her or perhaps even when she was. In her mind she must have been following him from place to place in his rounds, the itinerary of her passion.

Yes, *she* depended. Perhaps for too long she didn't know she depended on him. Especially early mornings, she could find him more easily now because since the night his mother had come, he'd been holing up in Huey's shack. Perhaps he knew from her talk long before she knew because it had gradually shifted—perhaps she didn't know that either—from talking about herself to talking about him.

"I *say—listen* to this—I say to myself What're you doing here in this town? Oh, I know why I'm in Greenport, but I mean why'm I waiting for the hour, the minute even, to get to see him, you, Santi, me saying your name SantiSantiSantiSantiago till I'm eating you. Oh, don't misunderstand. Don't be afraid. I'm not asking a thing only what you give me, what I got, no, but listen—I'm trying to understand *me* because—listen— Something's backfiring on me, maybe *me* backfiring on me. I mean from the start at home and in Huntsville, I thought *no man*, no. I'm not going to be Momma. Oh, I love my daddy, he's a good man, but it'd have to be some man to make me be Momma or one of them rich women in Huntsville putting up with old Mr. Big, letting him shove his whole rotten life right up into her anytime he takes a notion to. So it's from the start a man I'm running away from, but no man I *knew*, no, just *a* man, like somebody I didn't know was behind me and I couldn't turn and look at or I'd die on the spot but had to wait till *he* said *Now* look. Like that, only not—because I'd already decided *None, no man*. And it came a day, with men, so many, always after me, and me tired, and me tired of rooms all alike and jobs alike cleaning up other people's shit, and people, and any city, or any town, if you want to know. So don't you ever leave this town, don't do it, Santi. Yes, it came a day it struck me so hard a body'd think *She got Jesus*, but it was the Bible where it says Cain *knew* his wife. What'd he know? Her body. It's right then I said Your body's all you got, Diane, whatever gave it to you, and it dying. I said Diane, you're no fool, or the stupidest, lying into your own mouth, you'll choke to death on your own lies, you'll never be a girl again, don't you know that? and thinking it's sin not to use what you got, *sin*, like I committed it all along not using it, *sin*. It was like deciding to punish myself for *not* using it all this time, something in me pushing me right into it, like I was all the time *wanting* to be stomped on, *watching* myself like I was somebody else to make sure I couldn't get away once I made my mind up, because I did. I was coldblooded with myself. *You* know I'm not cold-blooded—you *do*, don't you, Santi?—because with you— Well, never mind. I said It's where I'll go, I'll go to one of those houses. I had to ask men where to go. The whores wouldn't tell me. I already seen what would happen, I *believed* it would, because it was like looking for Jesus in all the men that'd pass through. Why'd they go there, all those men? Oh, sure, sex, sex, but something in their life was empty as mine and them thinking like me sex is the way but maybe don't know yet what *to* any more'n I would till it come to me. But I was going to find him. I was going to be better than anything just good, learn it, do it perfect. One day from all the men, the kind who come there—I didn't care married, lonely, unsatisfied, strange, desperate, crazy even, but all needing, and looking too but maybe not even knowing *looking—I* was sure one of them'd be hit so hard it'd take his breath. He'd *have* to come back because he was a man thinking it was a good fuck he was looking for but got something he didn't bargain for. He got a look at *him*, his own self he never knew before, like he was tore open and his eyes clear and he seen his own heart beating for the first time, like it's some kind of miracle because it brought us back to life, we weren't dead no more, we'd stop being nobody, because it'd happen to me too at the same time like my hand was right on his heart and his on mine and you couldn't tell which was which, but *knew*. So he wouldn't leave without taking me, he wouldn't want to be without me or me without him, so it would be more than fucking, it would be . . ."

She would go vacant sometimes, her eyes would dart over the horizon going dark, over the forever moving sea, over the sky always so low and close over the flat land, over the roofs of the houses—

"I ain't got the words!" she would cry and raise her hands ready to pummel his chest, but they halted in mid-air, suspended, like the paws of Tom's dog, so pathetic he would take them into his hands and kiss them wherever they were, startling her not merely because they were "out in the open" where there were always eyes, but because *he* had come to be the lover.

She knew now *she* depended.

"Listen," he said, catching her smile because he had listened so long, so closely, to *her* sound from *his* mouth. "I don't care, just so you be what you are."

"But I *got* to—I got to work it out, what it is, because something's happening to me—"

"What's happening is—now don't get mad—you're wrecking it all if you don't stop coming out where they can see you. *She'll* find out—"

"She knows—been knowing all along. She's watching me. Well, let her! I don't give a damn."

"But there's still time. She'll give you another chance."

"Who wants it!"

"We do."

"No. I had my chance. I flubbed it. I can't go back to that now. It's not I know she won't keep me. It's I can't stay now. I won't stay in *that* either, no more, because I can't trump it up like that with men, I can't fake it anymore. Or maybe could, my head might could cut off what my body's doing, just from habit; but my body can't, it can't fake it, it's a lie. I faked it way back in Atlanta, not the sex, never, because every man was maybe the one, but faked it to myself the day I said Do it, get your ass in a real pro place, the place to find the man."

He saw she was too decent to name men. Well, the town wasn't, and would name them. *Fatso and his tootie. The one called Diane.* Hadn't they always? *Fatso.*

"Well, I flubbed it. It was the wrong place. He never came. Then I knew he never would. Every day in that shack when I looked out the tiny window at the harbor, I thought And where in hell *would* a man come from—out there? on one of them boats? from the ocean? out of nowhere, nothing? It got to be a laugh, my big joke on me, stupid Diane."

Her look would go hard, the green eyes almost cruel in her self-judgment, as she looked straight through whatever she was staring at, maybe seeing the ocean, empty. Then she would look up at him. She would whisper, "You, you, you," her face abruptly tender, and tears fill her eyes, her hands tight as knots raised as if to strike his chest. And stop. In an instant she would be so close, so insistent he was sure she was trying to go blank, the way you did when you wanted to forget, to wipe out whatever it was that had stopped her words. It would not matter where now; she did not care who saw them. She liked the sound, the sand, the damp salt air, the open space of potato fields among last season's dead twigs. She liked the bare springs of the unused bed in Gill's shack. She liked behind Grant's. She liked the tiny cemetery on Moore's Lane. She pulled him against any tree, against any rock on the shore; she would straddle; she would turn, turn over; she would chafe, tease, till he ended. She would deny him.

She would madden with her hand, her mouth. There was nothing she knew that he did not know now.

Then the moment came when the words did stop, at first he thought Because Madam Pam gave her the boot.

"She told me yesterday. She was decent about it. Gave me a day or two—more'n I deserved, I knew it was coming because—well, you know why, and because I wasn't putting nothing into it, not since you; I let them, that's all, and they weren't asking for me anymore. Said she'd call a contact she got in Brooklyn. Said I knew her girls had to stay out of town. Said men like secrets, mysteries, it ruins things to see us girls in day. But not that, no— Said I'm lost, what happened to me?, and really wants to know, sure she does. I can't fault her there, because she knows women and wants to be sure she knows every little twist that's different, see? And she's right, lost—I *am.*"

But he was wrong. Madam Pam was not the reason.

At once she took a room over Helen's bar. There were outside back stairs. Others, locals too long a part of the town's history not to be accepted, lived there, no secret about that, a busy place upstairs but quiet, private.

That's when she told it. She took him there at high noon, so many coming and going in the parking lot behind Helen's and Meier's bars that nobody or everybody saw them. It went through his head: *Yeah, the tootie herself leading Fatso up Helen's back steps by the hand, right in front of everybody. Imagine.* But he didn't care. He was an island. If he was not free of them, he was isolated. *He* had not isolated himself; teeth had, town had, and what had clinched it was Diane; but what had done it was his. What had done it had brought the experience with her. He had wanted that, and it was not over yet. They went down the narrow corridor, dull linoleum, to the one window, its pane and curtain dingy as fog. She unlocked the door and let him into the tiny room under the roof, so low it seemed improvised only to sleep in, painted a dull blue, the floor the same linoleum, foggy too, the thin mattress with two sinks impressed by the many bodies that had lain there, the discolored chenille bedspread blue too, and a tiny bureau, a narrow mirror hung beside it, dark and scabious where the silvering had peeled.

She was voracious now. Already she was unbottoning him, and already talking, going over it as if she'd never told him before, or forgotten she had, repeating what seemed verbatim, practiced to perfection, maybe first to convince herself it had really happened or to explain it aloud to herself with absolute clarity, discovering, with each additional word and every nuance, more nearly absolutely *what* had happened, so she could make him understand exactly and know her fully?

That was imperative, that he *understand* absolutely.

And she could not know that, striving as she spoke. Her very desperation brought him sensations to which he responded with such subtleties that in fear she struck him away, then in desire gripped him closer. "No, you *can't, can't*—you're not a man, just a boy—it's not possible; but, yes, a man."

His body followed the rhythms of her verbatim speech so closely that he delayed his ecstasy till his body could silently cry out with the cry of her unfailing last phrase, "He never came . . ."

But this time she did not stop, she held him to, she wouldn't let him slip free as if she wanted him to *feel* her words flowing into his body and feel them returning to her, given back.

Now she did find words. Miraculously they came, or she had had them but refused to give them until she knew she could no longer do without them because there would be no other time, she could not miss her last opportunity.

"*You* were the man I could never have."

Her palms gripped his head. They were hot, sweaty. She made him look straight into her.

"No, not the man I was looking for, not him. I mean *the man I could never have.*"

He would have turned from her tears, but she held him.

"I should never have watched you through the hedge. I should have turned around and gone into the shack the minute I took my bra off the line."

She closed her eyes, a long stillness, then shook her head.

"I don't know what happened to me, but something. I didn't even know what I'd done till I was back in the shack. I *had* to go to you, *I* couldn't help it, but I *knew* I couldn't have you—never. It wasn't because you'd never in a million years come into that shack; it wasn't that, though I knew the minute I seen you what a fool I was. That other, *he*'d never come anyway; I'd been lying to myself for years. No, *couldn't have you* and didn't even know what that meant, not just sex, and maybe didn't even believe it, but had to go for you, to find out. It was me watching myself go straight to you dumb as a moth beating at a bulb and can't have the light, never in this world, but wanted to touch *something*, I had to, because the times I seen you cutting the lawn, it turned over, my heart, and a thing went right out of me all the time I was watching you."

Pity, he could not help think, *dogs.*

"That never happened with anybody before. It sent me crazy when I was alone. I kept seeing you. I couldn't get you out of my head. I didn't want a thing from you—no, *I didn't.* I said to myself I want to give him something— And then *that day.* That day! JesusGod, it come like a miracle. I was in a spell. I mean I wasn't me, or maybe I *was* because when I got back in the shack I was afraid—of *me,* not you, because I was never so alive as when *my hand*— Then it come over me I wanted to give you something—"

You *did.*

Never would he forget the tenderness, terrible, of that first hand over his forehead, hair.

But he had never said.

Remembering, he closed his eyes.

Then he started. It was her hands again. She was running her fingers over his teeth—

She had *never.*

Horses, he thought, seeing tails and galloping.

"Santi, you're trembling."

Her fingers kept moving softly over his lips, tracing them, then up under his lips, sliding, slowly caressing the soft underflesh, back and forth, running slowly over his gums—

"I want to know, I want to remember . . ."

He could not bear. His head fell, his forehead met hers, he shivered and lay trembling against her.

" . . . everything."

Her tongue was sudden under his lip, silkish, moving, maddening. He moaned. She was holding his head. She didn't let go of his mouth till he gripped her hands, kissed and kissed his own wet on her fingers, then thrust her arms up over her head against the bed, roused again. He was panting, *dogs* thinking, *horses,* as she whispered, "Yes, oh yes, yes," submitting, whispering, whispering. He didn't listen.

"Lost," she said when he sank away from her, apparently not forgetting for one instant that she must *say.* "You got a madness in your body. I must've known that. It's like I answered it. You were so still in the yard. No insect I ever seen was that still. It's the stillness, that. Nobody'd know what's in you. And you're smart, quick, you learn fast. You learned so fast you're teaching *me* now and don't even know it because you don't know what you got, but *I* know it now. You practiced it on me and didn't know you were doing it, did you? There's madness in your body, but you got it *so controlled.* Where'd you learn that? I'd like to know. You make it like it never was before, I never had anything like you, it's perfect, but the worst thing ever happened to me. And you know why? Because you don't care about me. Maybe you don't even know that. Maybe you're too young to care, but I could put up with that, it come to be normal with me—and you know why?—because you're not even there, *not*, you're alone, you're sure not with me. I want to think you don't even know you're using me. Oh, that's all right with me, you can't do a thing about it. Besides if a person *wants* to be used then it's not being used, is it? And I wanted to be. I wanted to give you something, but I can't no more. Don't you see even that, you!"

She rolled against him, and he did hold her, and close, but as always, wordless, waiting.

He smelled the odor now. It came up from him, her, persistent, strong. *Fish*, he thought, *fish*.

"I can't no more—or I'll be crazy thinking it every time I look at you or you touch me, *the man I can never have*, he's there, but I can never get to him or him me. And I can't stand it no more. I can't live with that. Better I go back and live with what I had, nothing but a thought, a kind of dream, phony even if I *didn't* know it, but a dream. With you it's worse than nothing because I got nothing to give you, only my body."

"No—"

His forehead tingled with the memory, and his hairline. He could not tell her the tenderness of her hand.

What he could not give her.

She had not pitied, no. For that his heart thanked.

But more and more as she talked, lost in her obsession, he began to pity.

She was empty now, emptied. Only he could fill her for a moment with that madness she knew in his body, but he did not deceive himself anymore than she did: her eyes were as blank as they had been by the clothesline, her gestures as futile, her body returned to its lassitude. Nothing had changed. Nothing had happened to her, or to him. It might not even have happened because he had given her nothing, a madness yes; and she was right, he could do anything he wanted with her. He knew his control. He felt his distance even when he himself could cry out with her at the pleasure which he, not she, was giving his body.

He felt her despair.

All he had to give her now was his body, and he had learned to withhold; the discipline gave her more exquisite pleasure, which increased his own sensation; but he did not know yet—and he was aware of that—what was in him to give. He had not discovered it.

"It's done now. We can't help it, can we, Fatso?"

Fatso!

He slapped her mouth hard. He wanted to drive the word back. It had bolted a hidden monster up. *Fatso*. She had never. All these months he had been Santiago, Santi. No. In a breath Fatso was back.

She said nothing. Her face remained indifferent. Sometime she must have been used to it.

But his hand! He could have *burned* it. He didn't know what to do. He stared at the hand, still raised. He wanted her to strike it, smash it. But *her* hand. He quivered with memory. His forehead and hair prickled. . . . His eyes of a sudden burned.

She was standing against the dingy curtain, the pane that fogged the ice cream parlor sign *Paradise Sweets* and the bit of sky, her hand run half through her long hair and suspended, and still. When she turned, her hand still suspended, the long dark strands quivered an instant, then still too, her eyes not even on his face but staring with the same blankness that negated even the images of whatever was reflected in them. Even as he left and she said, "Later," still without removing her hand, he was not sure she saw him.

He did not know it was the last time. He remembered "Later," and he waited. He would not go to her. Long since, he had assumed she would always find him, and she had; but when three days went by and he had begun to make the rounds of the places she liked to appear and surprise him, it occurred to him suddenly that "Later" was her farewell. He realized, but his body did not believe; it was too well trained to her now: desire battered like an animal caged in him. At times he would almost cry out. At the dump he *would*, he would call her name, he would send it aloud over the pond, "Diane, Diane," and listen. He talked to himself, releasing all the words he had never said to her. Still, all the time he did not really want *her*. He knew he did not care. It was his body crying out. It was habit. He had been alone too long and he had fallen into the habit of her. It was his body crying out for his habit. At first he imagined her as he ejaculated, stilling himself, and then refused even to imagine her. He stilled his body with habit. Once more he filled every interval with work. He worked, worked.

Then he quit school, not formally; he simply did not go back. Sixteen. He was free now.

Mr. Walsh, the superintendent, sent for him, but he ignored the notice. To the teachers who ran into him he listened with half-muted ears, as he had with Diane.

Only Miss Kellogg, inviting him up onto the porch on Front Street one surprisingly warm afternoon in late March, where she was sitting in a wicker chair with a book, seemed in her natural way to understand.

"Why, Santiago— Come join me."

He hesitated, realizing how filthy his clothes were, and his shoes. He was used to himself, but from the kids' cracks and signs at school he knew he smelled. Them he didn't care about, but before her he felt *shame,* and he was startled that she did not—not from his clothes, but from the other, the talk, *Fatso and his tootie.* He could scrub face and hands wherever he worked, but the other he couldn't wash off.

"I'll mess up the chair, Miss Kellogg."

"Oh, you can't hurt that chair."

The gingerbread porch was high above the fence and the street and he might have felt his discomfort more if he was not so impressed by how full the view was—you saw all up and down Front Street from Main to St. Agnes' church, a view of the harbor through the wide parking lot of Mitchell's Restaurant, and the ferry dock and the train depot and part of Shelter Island.

Though she would have him back in school, she said, "Of course, there are years ahead for you to take your degree when you're moved to, and I think you will be because you're so bright, Santiago, and your mind will want all it can hold, but let that come in good time."

He was looking at her, listening—but it was not her words he was hearing, or the soothe of her voice so soft you could feel it wrap warm around you, but the timbre thin as a thread drawn threw him, moving and moving, going on even after her words stopped. Under his lids he *saw* the thread of invisible white fire.

"Santiago . . .?"

"What?"

She laughed in that same timbre, but higher.

"Well, why *wouldn't* your mind be wandering on a beautiful day like this?"

He leaped up, because she rose, dismissing him to the street below.

Afternoons, after school, as often all through his affair with Diane, he waited for Joey at the shortcut back of school. With Pa always out on the skimmer boat, he was Pa, he felt the pride of *father* when Joey came running to meet him. The boy sprang, agile, athletic already; and at the sight alone of that streak of thick dark hair, he felt his heart pulse as if Joey were really his own. But the boy's face was white, too pale. They kept him in too much, ignored him. They didn't fool Fatso. It fretted him. Fatso gave him what pads, pencils, supplies, change he needed; bought tidbits, sometimes candy and cupcakes. But their excursions made Joey happiest since at home he had to submit to Renata and Sol; alone, he had all Fatso's attention. Joey was most absorbed when they followed the tracks, climbed the train, sat at the end of the railroad dock or walked the cliffs overlooking the Sound. They watched the oil tankers headed for the ocean. Fatso pointed out landmarks along the far Connecticut shore. Fatso showed him how easy it was to lower a net over the hole of a swallow's nest in the cliffs and capture one. "Here— Hold the bird, but don't squeeze or you'll hurt it. Now let it go." After, though his mother surely knew Joey was with him, but not to flag her anger, he left Joey at Fourth and watched him walk home.

At the dump one day Renata balked him and Joey.

"I didn't mean to come, but Ma won't give me any peace, and no sense to talking to her about you, she cuts me and Sol off. She wants the kid home right after school."

"I want Fatso."

"You're going home to Ma, Joey," Renata said.

"Let me go. You let me go."

"Let him, Renata—one more time."

"Okay, this one time, but I'll get it from Ma. You know she's hell to live with. From now on—"

Reluctant, she kept looking back.

At the house next day it was Ma, a bald stare at him, then her back; and when he said, "Hey, Ma," not a word, not even "Don't you *Hey Ma* me"; and he talked *Joey* like never before. So from her silence he knew her fury. No, not fury, he thought. *Jealousy*. Ma's jealous. He knew now it was not of Joey. *Of me*, my independence. Because she can't do a thing. Or she would. *Vengeance*. If she could. And when Joey came running straight to him, she stepped between, bold, whipped out an arm, still without a word, and hauled Joey after, screaming as he was, "Let me go, Ma! I want Fatso," one arm grappling toward him, "Fatso!"

Sacrifice Joey he would not, no. Not to be defeated, he still met Joey for a few minutes at lunch time, and Joey, stealing up the street when he could, tailed Fatso and helped.

"Take me to live with you, Fatso."

"I got no place, Joey. You can't stay here at the dump."

"You do."

"Not much longer. I got to do something."

Joey pouted. His lips were Pa's, only his white skin made them look wet and soft and redder.

Invariably, Ma sent one of his sisters trotting straight after him. He noticed Joey no longer cried or resisted, but wouldn't let them touch him. He went, but did not yield. Fatso saw the invisible wall beginning. He knew that wall. A time came when the wall was too deep—few could penetrate, fewer wanted to. (After a time you didn't want them to. If they got through, it was despite you.) He wanted no walls around Joey. He wanted him free. Joey's handsome face gave him a certain freedom. He wanted him to stay free. He had to find the way for Joey, but he had not found it for himself.

"Pull that skillet out of the trash."

"That rusty old thing!" Joey's tone said *crazy*.

"Tom's big on skillets."

Tom would say, "One man's garbage is another man's grace." Tom was a regular, pouring over the dump to rescue what he could. Fatso liked to save whatever he knew Tom was after.

"You want to take this to Tom before anybody comes for you, Joey?"

"Right now!"

"Whoa! Whoa! Never waste a minute. You carry this bag in case we see anything we can use."

"I'll put the skillet in it?"

"Now you're cooking with gas, Joey."

It was the mongrel that greeted them, no bark but his long tongue languid, eyes asheen, and his wide open jaw looking nothing but happy. All his body shivered with the force of his wagging tail.

With pride Joey handed Tom the iron skillet.

"Well, I'll be! That's a beaut." Tom had half an eye on Joey. "Must be your brother—got your forehead, and who could miss those dark eyes?"

Fatso swelled, laughed. With his squint, how could Tom see? "See what I want to," Tom'd say to any doubting Thomas.

Pal nosed under Joey's chin, pressed up under his hands and nudged till Joey's hands ran over him. Joey sat on the kitchen floor and Pal sank beside him, his head flat on the linoleum, between his paws, his eyes not missing a move, giving off contented little sighs.

"Must be a good boy. That dog knows."

Tom busied himself. You had to go some to catch Tom still, except when he took a catnap or drank his tea out of that bowl with the little Jap figures on it. He kept a kettle on the old black oil burner all the time, half the time so forgetful it went dry.

Whenever he came, Fatso liked to fill the oil bottle for the stove; it was heavy and with those hands Tom had to carry it in his arms.

Hands.

For an instant *Diane.*

With a knife and wire brush and heavy sandpaper Tom went scraping the rust off the skillet onto a newspaper.

"What good's that old rusty thing?" Joey went down on his knees. Pal's head rose, his gaze mystified, then settled back, resigned. Joey's eyes were level with the tabletop and watched every movement, his eyes wide.

"Where's your fingers?"

Fatso poked.

Tom laughed. He tapped Joey on the head with his palm.

"It's hard."

"Bone." Tom took a walnut and smashed it with his palm. "There you go. Eat it."

"Wow! Wish I could do that."

"Wish in one hand and spit in the other." Tom pressed his own face almost up to the skillet bottom, squinting.

Fatso shoved his foot under Joey's butt, but Joey was spellbound. He touched Tom's hands.

Fatso prodded.

"Stop it, Fatso."

Tom stopped to let him look.

The fingers lay like closed crab claws.

"Can't you move them?"

"The ones on this hand." The right. He propped with the left.

"Nobody's hands are like that."

"I hope not."

"God make you that way?"

Tom halted, the brush suspended, and his eyes opened wide and stared blankly across the room through the upper window at the sky over the Sound. His blue eyes quivered with sky, and pinkish flecks.

"No. I did."

"You made them!"

Tom didn't contradict.

"Wow! Ma says God made us, and you ain't—"

"Shut, Joey!"

Not long and Tom had the skillet cleaned of rust and crusty black down to the iron. He set it on the stove with a little grease in it and when it was hot poured off the grease and wiped it inside and out with newspaper.

"You do that half a dozen times and it'll be so seasoned you never have to grease it to cook in. Never wash it, just wipe it out good every time you use it. No frying pan in the world can match an old iron skillet."

He hung it on a hook behind the stove.

"Wait'll Stell sees that." He chortled.

"Tom can do anything."

"Not so much."

Those hands could do miracles. Rod had told him. They had built this house.

"How'd you learn so much?"

"Had to. But it's all piddling."

Rod said he was a preacher. He could knock you down with words.

"I tell my grandsons the more trades they can master the better they can defend themselves in this world. Rod can do anything, especially mechanical. Cory's more concentrated—he's going to take the long chance. He'll be a professional. He studies day and night, always did."

Fatso didn't mention having dropped out of school, but it sounded as though Tom knew. Maybe he knew about Diane too, but Tom never prodded and never abused people in talk.

Fatso came back one day and told him, though his true reason was to talk about Ma keeping Joey from him. Tom was the only one he could talk to.

"A man's got to live for himself, not depend—you said that, Tom—and I can't give Ma all the money. I love Ma, but I see now how she is. If she had her way I'd be giving her everything till the day she died, and maybe would but for Joey. If I don't do something, she'll bleed him too because he's the last. She won't let him go, and Pa's away working; and, worse, Pa'll be old and can't make money. She can't help it, Tom, I know that, but I got to stand up against her—for Joey."

A long time Tom mulled. His jaw moved slightly back and forth, and the chafe of his false teeth sounded.

"It's hard to down a mother, saying no's hard, but if she's not out in the cold . . ." Tom was gazing at him, his quivering eyes almost still an instant. "If a man gives his mother his life with no need to, then where is he? Or gives his brother his life with no need to, then where is he?"

Tom could stake you like that.

"You mean I have to choose."

"You already did. You couldn't help do it."

"But I got nothing—not Ma, not Joey either."

"That's the risk. What you bank on is hoping they'll come, one or the other, maybe both, maybe none. When you bolted, you gave them the chance, if the time ever comes, to turn to you."

"Or I'll have nothing."

"No, not nothing. Never nothing."

"And me alone."

"One way or another a body's always alone. Even with Joey you'll be alone. Besides, he'll go one day. You'll want him to. You won't want to hold him back. You're not doing it to keep Joey with you forever. Isn't that why you're complaining about your mother?"

"What'll I have then?"

"Experience."

"What good's that?"

"It's everything."

"Everybody says love is."

"It's all in experience. You can't take it back. There's no changing it. You can love too little or you can love too much. You can't help which. You think you can. Experience is what tells you, after it's over, you couldn't help most of it. You have to live with what's done."

"I got to help Joey, Tom."

"Then you help yourself first, or you won't be any good to Joey or anybody else."

"I'm trying, Tom, I *am*. You don't know how I work, Tom."

"I don't? I may be deef, but I don't miss everything."

You wouldn't think so to see Tom's face pressed almost against the newspaper or his Bible, squinting, as he mouthed the words in a whisper, or his hand behind his left ear, the better one, pressing it almost against the bellowing radio to catch the news, Father Coughlin, Bishop Sheen, any Sunday religious service.

"Before you go, you take a shower if you want to."

He knew he stank, but you got used to it, you didn't care, you forgot till you saw somebody's face or somebody made a crack, and even then your smell made them see you. But not Tom. Tom was different.

"Or maybe you'd better take a shower and take the cot in that back room for tonight and in the morning pick out some fresh clothes. There's plenty there. That suit you?"

"You mean it, Tom?"

"Wouldn't say so if I didn't."

Fatso sank to a kneel beside Pal and gripped the dog's head. He had to hold, or reel. He rubbed his cheek against Pal's head, grateful when the dog nudged, and lapped.

"That's enough, Pal." Fatso threw his head back to escape the slop, laughing.

"What'd your daughter say if she came?"

"She's got no say here. It's my place, I built it. Well, till you get set up somewhere, whenever you need a wash, you come by."

"Spring's coming in. The shed's not so bad now."

"You can't stay at the dump forever."

The dump was the first thing, green, and home. He loved that dump. Tom couldn't know.

That week, every minute he had between jobs he traipsed town for a room—tough anytime, he knew, because almost every family owned, and some had for centuries. You knew the houses by their family names. Poor old, half-senile Emil had one of the biggest hearts in town. He'd take him in, yes, but the filth in the house—since his momma died Emil couldn't bear to touch a thing—was worse than any dump; and even if one of the outhouses came empty for six dollars a month, his pride, dump or no dump, wouldn't let him live with those Polack outcasts, not because he cared about the judgment of the whole town, but because he wouldn't be subjected to their drink and fights and abuses, imprisoned like that.

At the dump he was free.

Much he thought about Tom's talk. He understood Tom: if you did not submit, you could not go further. *Diane.* She alone had experienced his capacity for submission, for silence and discipline; but even she knew he had reached a limit in her. She had never said *teeth.* He hated them, but knew now they had bred silence in him and discipline, and these were gifts, and secret. He would use them.

For a moment Albert Dickson vacillated and almost rented him a room, a shock because Albert hardly ever talked to anyone. His house on the crest looked down the slope to the Verity place, Rod's, and Tom's behind. Nights there was always a light in the upstairs bedroom facing Albert's. Albert was a true guardian over Tom. It was because Tom was Tom. You couldn't turn from him, he drew you. No, it was not *hands* or pity. The hands awed. The hands were a sign. Once you saw them, you couldn't forget; but what you remembered were not the hands, but Tom. The hands made you look. Then you saw.

Albert didn't let him have a room. Perhaps Al couldn't share his cats. Fatso was relieved. All those cats! Dump smell was nothing to cat smell!

Maybe Al was afraid somebody'd see him with his cap off. Nobody had in years. Nobody knew if he had hair under it anymore.

On a sunny day in April a familiar clatter made Fatso look up: there was Tom pulling his cart over the dump's rough terrain.

"You know Mrs. Fenton on Main? She might let you have the back spare room—the door's off the porch, you wouldn't bother her—for a little work and a few dollars a month."

"Rich old Mrs. Fenton? She don't need money."

"Well, it won't hurt to have a body around for protection."

"Who needs protection in this town?"

"That old, you need somebody in the house in case anything happens and for errands. Anyway, you talk to her if you care about it. Oh, I brought you a load of bottles."

In bending to unload them beside Huey's shack, Tom halted, squinting. "Why—" His hand went out to a bush of burning yellow. "—it's forsythia."

Fatso laughed. "You didn't expect that here, did you? Well, you just look—"

Tom followed. Everywhere dandelions were yellow sparks in the black dirt. The wall of trees was turning the first yellow green, and all the shrubs. Fatso stopped at a sudden slope and drew aside.

"Look—"

The slope was alive with swaying daffodils.

Tom stared long.

All through the swamp and over the pond life was returning in fringes of green, and the rolling fields to the back road and the Sound were great swirls and streams of green and gold among last year's brown dead stubble.

"Just wait till it really gets going, Tom."

Fatso couldn't wait. Though Tom hunted useful castoffs somewhat regularly, one June day Fatso pleaded with Tom to go see the dump with him.

"Look, Tom—"

No longer bursts of early gold against the black earth, the dump was burgeoning in a rage of random blue green yellow reds. Honeysuckle covered the cemetery wall with their tiny white and yellow lilies, morning glories pink white sky blue purple climbed shrubs and trees. There were stretches of mustard weed, patches of wild poppies, and bluebells opening, islands of stray fuzzy blue bachelor buttons, tiny yellow-eyed wild daisies and black-eyed Susans, here and there tall sunflowers opening, wild phlox red purple and white. The swamp was purple with giant iris. Along the edge of the pond beach roses were beginning to bloom pink and white. Great lily pads floated in the pond, their buds just beginning to show white. On mounds, around Huey's shack, over the bare ground where nothing else grew, persistent little colonies of pink and columbine bobbing cheerful red had sprung up. Everywhere vines encroached, wild grass spread. A creeping of green shrank the dump and transformed it.

"You ever see anything like it, Tom?"

Tom was spellbound, or meditative.

"Now tell me there are no miracles, Fatso."

Fatso quivered with pride.

"Thought you couldn't see."

"I can smell. Never smelled anything so sweet, I tell you. Besides, I can see what I want to. I told you that. You getting forgetful?"

Alone, Tom went down to the pond edge and peered over the bright shimmering fields beyond toward the Sound. He could be standing alone in the world, he could be surveying his domain, he could be waiting for something to come. He was still so long that Fatso went down beside him. You'd swear Tom's squinted eyes were closed.

"You hear it?" Tom said.

What Fatso heard was the finest hum of wings—of bluebottles and dragonflies or a fly, wasp, or the glide of water striders over the surface, or a far bird. He heard bubbles move and break, and the sound soft as a sigh made by the long underwater tangles of plants, and the whisper of water.

"Thought you were deaf."

"A deef man can hear strange things."

Fatso knew Tom couldn't. What made him wonder was what Tom meant by *strange things.*

"You can't beat nature, it takes over, it always wins, it never rests. Even in winter it's working; it's waiting, stubborn. We forget. It's in us too. We don't listen anymore, so we don't hear it."

"Hear what?"

Tom stared, silent.

Maybe even he didn't have enough words.

Tom was right. It was as if nature—quick, powerful, everywhere moving—had decided abruptly to ignore them and repossess the earth.

"Look here—"

Fatso scooped up a new garter snake.

"He never stops either." He held it close for Tom to see. Its tiny red tongue forked out futilely. "A beauty." He set the snake down and watched it wriggle into the deep grass.

"Watch your step, Tom." He held him back a moment.

"Now what?" Tom squinted all around.

"Just a few toads."

Dozens, tiny as fingernails, hopped in all directions from Tom's feet.

"Now you can move."

"This is getting to be a dangerous place. Where's my cart? Got to *git*. The boys are coming on the five o'clock ferry."

"Who?"

"My grandsons—from Rhode Island."

"Rod?"

"And Cory. You know Cory."

"Some."

He would pass the Verity place deliberately at night, late, for the days were long now, feeling like a spy—worse, self-conscious of his footsteps because in the dead quiet of night every sound carried over this flat land and the water. The house would be lit up, and Tom's behind. He would glimpse their heads round the table, at times Tom's daughter playing cards with friends, sometimes Cory's head illuminated by the reading lamp, at others both the boys moving about in their rooms upstairs or Rod's or both boys' heads moving about in Tom's living room or kitchen.

He felt shut out. They cut him off from Tom, or he cut himself off, because as much as he treasured the summers with Rod, he avoided the encounter. Rod, coming out of The Diner, caught him off guard. "Fatso! I've been thinking about you." He hung onto the car meter and talked a blue streak, reminding him, "And you and me and Iggy played Mussolini and Hitler and Haile Selassie, but who'd think it'd go this far. I'd hate to be in London when the siren sounds and the buzz bombs hit. Some think if we don't get into it, England's done for." Though Fatso felt flattered before all the familiar passing faces aware of the attention of this laughing, talkative, handsome athlete, he felt detached as Rod spoke, felt increasingly distant, as if Rod were speaking to him across a ravine. Something in him cut him off from Rod, alienated. What was it? He grew impatient, bored by Rod's rambling, his clear confidence, his casual stance, his surety, his washed look—skin, teeth, eyes, hair almost too bright clean. He was relieved when at last—after telling Rod (ashamed—was it that?) he had long since quit school, was working the same jobs, no, not living at home but rooming at Mrs. Fenton's on Main—Rod said, "Guess fishing's out this year. My uncle got me on the *Annie B* for the summer. You know it, don't you?" Then, as he watched Rod stride off, it was the walk, something of an attitude in the boyish swagger that made him realize the distance between them, and abruptly it came, what it was.

He's just a boy. He's not a man yet.

Diane.

Experience, Tom had said.

Tom had said you can be the puniest thing and be a man if you accept your responsibility to other men.

So maybe *he* wasn't a man yet either. Would Tom say a man wouldn't quit school to work? But he was working for Joey, wasn't he? Except for the few dollars rent he gave Mrs. Fenton and what niggardly amount he spent eating, he hoarded and banked every cent.

He was cleaner now, his body, and aware of his own smells, so that the clothes had to be clean too. He scrubbed and hung them out himself. If he was pleased at Mrs. Fenton's smile when she said, "Fastidious you are," the word enticed. Festered, he wanted to ask the meaning, but no, not even of Tom. Proud (he could hear Tom say, "'Pride goeth before a fall'"), he went to First. He stood across the street gazing at the library as if he had never seen it before, though from the hundred passings he could have painted it in detail: it was very small, stone gray and brownish and white, surrounded by a low stone wall, with a cement walk up to the wooden double door, over it FLOYD MEMORIAL LIBRARY in letters too large for the building. It startled now that he had never gone inside. For a long time he stood there. Why didn't he move? His palms were wet. He was afraid. But as always his awareness of his fear impelled—he crossed the street to the low wall, again hestitant, then as determined as an invader bolted up to the wooden door, opened it, ascended the foyer steps to the inner door, entered, and stopped, stunned by the shelves and shelves of books, racks of magazines, tables spread with pamphlets and open books. His hands wanted to grip. What was in them all? Who could know all that? He was afraid again. Something struggled in his throat. *I can't, no.* He felt he was going to cry. The silence overwhelmed. He had not expected here the same silence that sometimes settled over the dump, submerging him so deeply in the stillness that he began to hear moves and whispers. If he listened long enough would he hear words? But at a table an old man's head rose. A chair scraped. Fatso moved. By the door straight ahead was a stand exactly like the one in Miss Kellogg's homeroom, with the gigantic open dictionary always waiting. Fatso hunted *fastidious*:

Exacting.

He mouthed his prey, *exacting,* and would have turned to leave, but the rows caught him. He could not resist the rows, so many shelves, and entered a stack and touched and touched the backs and titles, and turned down another stack, and touched, reading title and title and title till *Dentistry*. Teeth. He couldn't resist. He was flicking pages. He recognized illustrations like those from Cory's cheap edition of Darwin's *The Descent of Man*, only not just Pithecanthropus and Cro-Magnon and extinct and extant heads but head after head with teeth. He couldn't stop; then did stop, gasped—Was he mislocated in time?—because *he*. His head. There *he* was, those, his *teeth—his*, but *not* his: because his jaw protruded much farther, there was no sketch of such a long protrusion.

And then the lower jaw. Brachygnathia. But nowhere near as short as his.

Macromaxilla.

Micromaxilla.

Micrognathia.

He read words and words.

Words.

Describing *me.*

Mine.

Macrognathia.

Opisthognathia. An undershot jaw.

Prognathia. An overshot jaw.

He had a name, names. He was identified there. Me. Santiago García. Yet no picture matched the extremities of his jaw. One. Unique.

Brachygnathia-prognathia.

Named.

Santiago Prognathia García.

He swelled. He could burst with knowing.

He turned and left before he was caught.

But he *was*. He was mystified at how now and then the library room intact would rise from the ground, palpable, enticing, menacing, and vanish as quickly.

That night he couldn't sleep. He was in torment. The joy agony of the library caused it, but it was Tom and Cory too, comfortable together in that kitchen and talking like cronies about Joseph and Abraham, with the Bible some kind of bond, a friend. And Cory. He couldn't clear his head of the sight of Cory on the porch day after day filling his head with books, and in that voice talking language so easily. He could see how Cory's mind was moving and connecting and arranging. He could hear all the rich changes in rhythm, and Cory just a couple of years older and with that voice, filled with words that poured from him so easily, and ideas, and—

Fatso tried to imagine how he looked in Cory's eyes, how his voice sounded—tortured with struggling, bungling, to *say*? because last night he *felt,* he wanted to *say.* Never before had he felt so completely the torture of not being able to *say* and *then and there.* He felt words in his guts. They ached to tear free but were stuck deep in his guts and *could not.* And in day his torment did not let up.

Thoughts, those thoughts about punishment and justice, had entered him from outside, from Tom and Cory and the Bible and from all the other books Cory had read, kept reading. Thoughts evoked by Joseph's and Abraham's dilemmas went round in his head till he was sure thoughts were living things. He *felt* them move, and they multiplied. He wanted to know what they would turn into, how they were connected. He wanted to string them together in continuous talk like Tom and Cory's in which even during the little breaks, silences, the thoughts were going on, growing, connecting, because in a minute Tom and Cory would resume where they had left off, so that he knew the thread had never really been broken at all but had merely gone under till it could work its way into words.

He was afraid of that thinking. Abruptly he understood his instant of fear in the library as he stared at all the shelves of books, and why he'd wanted to cry. How could he *hold* all that?

Still, with more and more frequency he found himself almost unconsciously passing the library, drawn, tempted by what must remain secret till he penetrated the page. But he didn't enter. He went to his room at Mrs. Fenton's. He brooded hours, working he brooded, and brooded doubly because he had to work a bit more to make up for the rent he was paying Mrs. Fenton, little as it was. He was going to help educate Joey because Pa'd never be able to, and Ma wouldn't; though he had quit school, he knew she was not even educated enough to *think* education. Cory and Tom had started him thinking, and it pained; he would like to tell *somebody* how it pained, thinking. You couldn't stop, you had no choice, you were a slave to it. How many things did you have to be a slave to anyway?

Now when he passed Connie the Pole, who sat day after day in good weather in the open doorway of his shed at Emil's place, staring at the ground, now and again raising a foot to crush an ant, for the first time he wondered what Connie thought about. Or Mrs. Fenton, sick and alone except for Mary Verity's afternoon visit for tea and talk. Or Tom trudging along pulling his cart with those hands or sitting alone in that kitchen with a raft of cats, living on tea, or working in that shop of his, repairing anything he could for somebody's use. Or Ma. Or Pa on that skimmer boat. Or anybody when he stopped what he was doing, the way he himself did at Pell's or the fish factory and stared at the lopped fish head in his hands, at the flat eye. *So it's not just me.* It was everybody, no matter what he was or looked like or had. Nobody was free of it. Nobody could stop it.

Fatso *saw* thoughts. They went through your head like uncountable invisible threads, sometimes separate and sometimes touching and then the mind went quick, electric, connecting. If it happened to everybody, then what was different about Cory? Nobody had affected him like Cory. Was it because Cory thought more? Was that why Fatso had felt *dragged down under* at Tom's when they'd talked about Joseph and his brothers and God and words, because he'd never thought such things? Or was it because Cory had different thoughts about things? But many people must have different thoughts. Maybe Cory could cut out other thoughts to concentrate on one, obsessed till he found his way, and then concentrate on the next. If Cory could, then *he* could. Fatso saw threads running through people's heads. Maybe sooner or later, no matter how different the thoughts were, they kept moving from head to head and all the thoughts kept on, alive, making a vast web, electric, even when the heads they went through were gone, dead. Would all the thoughts come together one day? The very idea, the thinking of it, excited him. Such joy leaped up in him that he had to tell somebody, had to. He had to know where to go from here, how. He would go to Cory. Hadn't he graduated? Wasn't he the valedictorian? Cory was *headed* somewhere. He would understand. Cory would tell him.

Since the rainy night of the Bible and the Joseph story long ago, Cory had been sending him books. He had written Cory, but he was still shy of Cory because he saw him only summers. These nights Cory read on the sun porch. Fatso finished work late. He fussed—shower, clothes, hair. He approached the house—he heard steps inside—and stood on the walk. At the break in those steps, he saw Cory look up. Fatso remained till it was obvious he was waiting. Cory rose, looked out the screen, and opened the door.

"Fatso! Is Gramp out?"

"No. You, I came to see you." His hands clutched his agony steady. "I told you. I want to know what you know, and Tom."

"I don't know anything more than what I've sent you—to read, I mean. I'm just beginning."

"All you read. I want to know that."

"Oh, it's a hodgepodge. There's no order to it."

"No no no. I don't believe that."

He had caught Cory's curiosity.

"A thing starts you. Maybe a thing attracts one *thing—you* know, a magnet—and it another, and each one brings all the others it's attracted. We don't know that, do we?"

Fatso startled himself—he was *talking*. Cory did that to him with those books he'd sent.

Cory gazed at him, but unseeing. Mulling?

"*Do* we?"

"No, but we might someday."

"Yes! I thought— You want to hear?" With no hesitation he plunged into his thoughts about thought, those threads . . . When he halted and Cory made no reply, he said, "You think I'm crazy?"

"You're not crazy. You're metaphysical."

"What's that?"

"It means you sense a connection between what's here in us and what's out there that may exist above and apart from us."

"No no no, not there— *Here*." He struck his chest, his head. "In me. I feel—I'm trying to—I'm talking about— See? *See*? I don't know. I can't say it."

"We have to say it as we learn it, and we're always learning. We're in that together."

"Yes, together."

Before Cory could reply, footsteps interrupted and she was in the doorway, Tom's daughter, so young-looking she could be Cory's sister.

"I thought I heard voices. I'm glad you came. With Rod on the skimmer boat, it's quiet here. Cory doesn't have many friends in Greenport. He's always reading. Has Cory offered you something?

Before her, Fatso went mute.

"How about it?" Cory said.

"I can't— No."

He was instantly ashamed, because he *wanted*.

"Well, tell your mother Estelle Verity said hello. She was a couple of grades behind me when they sent me to Bristol to live."

She left the air perfumed with some flower he'd never smelled before.

He had never imagined being inside. It was so quiet, neat, clean, comfortable. If he closed his eyes and listened, he would hear, smell, imagine what Cory did. When he opened them he would be sitting in Cory's place, see what Cory saw. Fatso would be *there*. Cory would be *here*. He would be Cory. He would reach for a book.

But he was Fatso. He would have to be Fatso.

And he was ashamed. He had Ma. He loved Ma anyway. And he had Joey. Pa was his, and the brothers and sisters, and he had the dump.

Cory had none of them.

Still, there was whatever Cory did have. He could not say, but it drew him. He could not stop *wanting.*

Did he get it all from books?

He bolted up.

"Wait!" Cory cried.

Fatso's quick animosity was not against Cory, but against—how could *he* know what it was against?—because Cory was nothing if not gentle, generous.

"You have to swear to yourself to be faithful, or it's not worth it, Fatso. Discussion takes time. We don't want to waste it."

"Have we yet? Oh, don't worry. I'm disciplined." *There's madness in your body, yes, but you got it so* controlled—*and where'd you learn that*? "But I don't know much, Cory." *My body, but not my mind. I don't know my mind.*

"You don't seem to believe me, but I don't either. We could make a quick review of what we've done the last couple of years and you can read what I'm reading now and I'll send you my books from Wisconsin—"

"You'd do that?"

For me.

"We'll do that."

"Yes." He stood. He saw the Floyd Memorial again, all the books jammed inside lining his head. He couldn't hold. He would be dizzy.

He laughed. "Cory." He laughed again, giddy. He wanted to grip Cory's hand and hold steady. It *was* true?

He clutched the knob.

"Wait— We might as well start now. I've just finished this. It's not hard."

"I *want* hard." His voice was—adamant, and made Cory turn. "I'm serious."

Cory smiled. "You asked for it, then. Try the first chapter of this. I'll see you Sunday in Gramp's. I'll fill in what you missed as we go? Okay?"

He nodded. The room quivered.

He took the treasure.

"Oh, before you start the Darwin—"

Cory seized a pad and quickly explained that there was an order—you could classify all life—and explained *species*. I'll tell you the thing that's helped me most. The secret is to ponder what you read after you close the book. That's learning. One of my teachers taught me that."

Anxious, he walked fast. When he got to his room at Mrs. Fenton's, his arm ached from holding the books so tight. He lay them on the bed and stared at them. *Physics for College Students. The Origin of Species.* He was stunned by them. Why? He had had books before; he had had to study, but he could not wait now. What was it? Cory could take him somewhere; he would let Cory take his mind as far as he could. And then? He *saw* his mind, narrow as the crick, open into harbor, widen to include Peconic Bay and Gardiner's Bay, the Sound, and at last it would contain the ocean, all the oceans, sky, stars, planets, everything out there, all. It was as if he now raised his eyes for the first time and looked—and it was flat and too wide and endless with nothing in sight. He trembled with excitement, and fear.

He sat at his table and opened the physics book and read the first chapter slowly, and read it again, and pondered.

He was too fired to sleep so he opened the other. *Species.* He wanted to write the classification Cory had outlined, but he didn't have a pencil. Tomorrow, pencil and pads. He remembered: species was lowest.

He went into the book. It was slow, hard. He crawled over the words. He crawled back in time. He didn't know *time*. He could not conceive. He shrank as time grew; it stretched too far back, his head could not *see* so far. He saw earth, sea, sky. They changed. Something changed them; he couldn't *see* it, but it was changing them. So *it* moved, it had to be moving invisibly, and it changed things. And it brought what hadn't existed before. Where did they come from? Nothing? But how? Nothing could come from nothing. He read. He read. Growing thoughts clogged his head. He could not bear. He closed the book. The ideas frightened, and excited.

All night his head was filled with vines moving and tangling, threatening to suffocate. He couldn't get through them. He bolted out of sleep, sweating, relieved, only to sink back under the dark tangles, saved at last when dawn called him back to the world and work.

Now it was a new rhythm. His reading—all day thinking about it, concentrating—made him move faster, more efficient with the knife opening scallops, skimmers, oysters, cutting fish; collecting; mowing and trimming lawns and bushes, so that his night hours for reading were assured and unimpeded. He was relentless. He read, stymied; and reread, stymied; and read until he was no longer stymied; then moved on, stymied again—that too part of his rhythm now, advances and halts, with frustrations but such pulsing joy when his stumbling mind grasped, connected, leaped ahead.

Cory was startled and thrilled with how fast he had gone through the books and with their first session. It was a madness of questions, his questions, Cory's, and he saw at once that Cory's way was to question both him and himself. He saw too that he was for Cory both a student and a guinea pig, Cory probing for answers through him. Cory decided twice a week, and as the summer went, *More nights?* Fatso appealed; so theirs became a three-a-week rhythm.

He was coming to know Cory's mind. It was remarkable not just for what the boy—he *was—knew*. It startled that Cory was only two years older because he always felt the *man* in Cory, something wise and authoritative and secure. Fatso didn't understand how the father in him had come so early, where from. How could Cory's presence both stimulate and comfort? When he listened to Tom and Cory, he felt in the presence of two men who were wise, as if Tom were talking to his own younger self in Cory, who, Tom said, had more knowledge than Tom had had at that age. Fatso saw evolution close then, the other—cultural—evolution. He and Cory went on with Darwin because he had become obsessed with that moving of time in evolution, seeing old Tom and all things that lived in space as the activity of time.

He was imitating their talk, their words. He had to learn their words. He had to talk like them and get rid of Ma's and the shitty street talk from Third.

"You know what, Cory? Listen! The world's changed. I mean I see it different—differently—now. I never knew before. Listen! I'm opening oysters the other day and it hit me: the oysters are part of all that, they're *me* too. I almost screamed it out right there in the factory, and I wanted so bad to tell Rich and the others, but I know them, they'd say Fatso's nuts. Listen— It's like everything's me now. I'm everything."

"We try to live with that idea because it's beautiful, and hopefully true."

"If it's all me, why do I have to keep killing *myself* and eating *me?*"

"It's the law of life."

"Who made it?"

"Whatever started the whole thing."

"Then, if it's evolving, maybe we'll go past that and someday we won't have to eat each other?"

"If science ever could find something so basic to feed everything on . . . It's ironic—life's already feeding on itself. And men are the worst because we're the only creatures that can destroy others by eating up their minds. . . . Imagine how it might be if one day we come to be virtually all mind, if evolution ever gets to that. . . . You have to have a good imagination for that."

"*You* do."

"You're own isn't so bad. I don't know anybody who pictures things the way you do. I never could, not in a million years."

Before going to Cory's, he scrubbed and changed. He washed his own clothes in the tub at Mrs. Fenton's and hung them out. She was pleased at his habits and readily said yes when he asked to use the ironing board. He could not go unkempt to Cory and Tom and the mother. And now he went clean to the dump, where he kept work clothes. He looked different and smelled different, but above all he felt different—clean inside, and not just physical cleanliness, because he knew now *pride*, knew *vanity*—they were not the same thing. Tom taught the difference—from his Book he would always go back to for stories and poetry. Nobody could make the words resound like Tom. Sometimes—more and more—after his session with Cory, he stayed to listen as Cory read a chapter to Tom and they all discussed it. That first night—about Joseph—he'd been too petrified to speak, holding back till he felt he would piss his pants if he didn't have his say and broke in; and they had gone on as if he'd been expected to interrupt and discuss, and all evening long the three of them let go and he went home soaring, the talk rushing in his head.

Tom was a preacher too, Cory said. He called Tom an itinerant preacher because he was known all along the North Fork. He would go on a moment's notice. Congregations called him whenever a minister was sick because, Cory said, "he's experienced and wise, above all a good man, and knows the Bible and he's got—you've heard him—a spellbinding voice. It can do anything from whisper to sing and you *have* to listen. You feel the words flow right through him from God if anything ever did."

"Pride has two faces, like so many things," Tom would say. "When the face turns inward and is selfish and cuts itself off from others, then pride is negative—that's vanity; when the face turns outward and accepts its responsibility and uses its gifts for others, then pride is positive—that's not vanity." And Tom would *tell*: "There was a man who had two sons." Tom called the boys Rod and Cory. Rod was the prodigal.

By the end of summer his mind was constantly teeming, his body and mind attuned to his new balance of work and study. He hoarded his knowledge; he saw it as bits, stretches, little wells. He liked to hear it. Alone, he recited to himself. And he was vigilant over his speech. He imitated *them*. He wanted to, he would, talk like them. It seemed that his hours with Cory had just started. His mind had just managed to lay out stray threads of algebra, grammar, physics, history, lit, science—when Cory said, "I'm leaving for Bristol."

"Then it's over!"

"Over? Why should it be? I'll send you my reading lists and notes and exams, and my books when the semester's over. We can write our ideas back and forth. And you'll still have Gramp."

"You'll really write?"

"How else can we get our ideas clear? Miss Sisson in Problems of Democracy said you don't know what your thoughts are till you write them down. She'd say, 'This is what you *thought* you meant,' and make us rewrite it until it said what we really did mean. Her point was that once you've struggled to clarify your thoughts precisely in writing, you could speak them clearly without stumbling. She was great, Miss Sisson. Something had happened to her face—a fire, maybe—that made her lips thin and taut and her skin red and shiny; but, you know, I bet that's why she was so great, it made *her* concentrate on what she knew and on us."

Fatso looked out the window. Miss Sisson. In the dark he saw her face. He understood *scarred*. He could be inside her.

"I won't know what to do without you, Cory."

"What you're doing now, only more. It takes work, but it's not like any old job, because knowledge depends on knowledge, it builds and builds. You can't stop or you lose the habit. Once it gets you, you can't stop anyway."

Fatso struck the table, threw his head back, laughed. "No chance of that. I'm all habit." It was his first consolation.

He was not consoled for long. Fatso received long letters in October and November and some books sent apart. In December the Japanese bombed Pearl Harbor and Roosevelt declared war. For an instant, everywhere, the world stopped; then, everywhere, it was teeming. Town moved like a body abruptly awakened from half-sleep. Then the following November Cory too was gone, enlisted in the Army Air Force. Fatso hoarded every letter from Fort Devens and Chanute Field and Fort Wayne and Louisville and the ETO—England and southern France and Tarquinia and Civitavecchia in Italy—as if each would be the last.

Your letters are my salvation, Fatso, because they make me write out thoughts which go beyond the war and keep my mind on studying. Besides, you're my nemesis since every time I write a possible answer and end with a question, your scepticism makes you answer with a question. Fortunately ours is going to be a permanent intellectual frenzy.

Nemesis?

Fatso reached for his dictionary.

By then the town seemed to shrink, men's faces began to disappear, and the women's were seen less; for many who had never worked took jobs for the war effort. Kids acted out the war in planes and buzz bombs and mortars. Cars and buses, fewer now, were jammed coming and going. And the Island went dark—shades drawn, outside lights forbidden; the streetlights became dim blue islands, and the town seemed to sink into the sea.

Fatso went into the fish factory full-time. The war had boomed the pay, time and a half for overtime. There was a shortage of men. The place was a hive of women. He was glad because they were kinder than the men. They took to him, maybe because so many men were gone; but they did tease, even chide, "Sticking your nose in a book every break when there's plenty to look at right under your nose," the boldest flopping a tit half out or shaking her ass so they all laughed, and Fatso too.

He became the gravedigger at Stirling Cemetery. Somebody had given Emil a slightly used pair of shoes stuffed with newspaper and moth crystals. Both feet became badly infected from mould and he went to the hospital. It would be a long time before he could walk properly, so the doctor urged him to retire. Home, drunk, Emil cried. He insisted he'd work, but when he tried, he could not make it to the cemetery two blocks away. People passing his house could hear him whining, moaning, mournfully playing his accordion and calling for his dead Momma, the Polacks that invaded his house were all drafted now, only Connie the old Pole who could not speak English still occupying his little shack in Emil's yard for six dollars a month. So Fatso, who had filled in for Emil before, dug graves and in spring and summer mowed and trimmed.

Junk sold high. He'd trained Joey to keep his nose to the grindstone, to be fast, not to waste time, to pick up anything he saw, to sort, pack, sell. When Ma found Joey brought some money in as Fatso once had, though still distant, she softened a bit. She put up with his seeing Joey now and then, though, despite her own work at

Mitchell's, she must have been aware of the rushed time they spent together when he hustled from job to job.

Throughout the war, like everyone else, he slept little—less than most, perhaps, because he kept up his dialogue with Cory, who actually had more time in the ETO than ever. *So much of war is waiting. That's why these months seem an eternity.* But Fatso had his own war—with his mind. *I have to train it as rigidly as they're training your body* because he had grown up in that madness of Ma and the kids with no Cory and Tom and no world at home like Rod's and Cory's to guide him.

Because Cory could not send books, Fatso had conquered the citadel, acquired a library card, at home among the books and the mostly old men and women and summer people who took them out. He devoured them, but he had learned to digest *slowly, meticulously, repetitively.* Hours he spent rewriting his letters to Cory, *and be sure to correct everything, Cory,* meticulous too in trying not to repeat an error Cory had pointed out. He read Cory's letters and much of his reading aloud. Always the sound was Cory's, the intonation Cory's, because who else? With Tom, Joey, and during rare moments with Ma or Pa and the girls, and when he had to talk to anyone at the fish factory or on the street, he spoke with deliberation now. He seemed to see the words forming, building, as they came out; and when anyone looked at him with that quiet startle of those whose habitual expectations are violated, he felt the authority of words, voice, and a little thrill of power ran through his body like a music. He repeated radio voices too, hundreds of times repeated unknown words that leaped from others' lips, words that fell leaden to him—*facetious, epitome, rehabilitation*—till he too could send those words flying.

He wasted nothing he had learned. With Joey he never ceased insinuating. He talked, recited, read, sang even, till Joey, unconsciously repeating, mimicking, became a half-echo. Fatso discovered he had a natural talent for teaching by suggestion, making it a game that not only enriched the moment but also bound them. At the same time that he could teach Joey how to fish, he could explain the structure, food, locale, habits of fish, till Joey made a parade of questions as he had with Cory. So they worked, constantly talking, cronies.

His one luxury now was cleanliness. He loved his tub at Mrs. Fenton's, and a rubber hand spray he'd bought. He luxuriated in the water and the slide of soap, but mostly in the rich scent that each night rid him of the fish stink that permeated his flesh, especially his hands, and his work clothes. Instantly removed, he hung his clothes outside. He cleaned his fingernails obsessively.

Only white convinced him that he was clean—he had to *see* his cleanliness—and though he dreaded spending money, when his clothes grew threadbare he bought cheap white pants at Grant's and white shirts for work, a sweater, and an off-white wool mackinaw for after work. On the way to a quick errand, he'd throw his clothes into a machine at the new washateria downtown on Main and stop off again to leave them whirling in a dryer.

He met Mrs. Kellogg carting a box to the Legion hall "for the boys over there."

"May I take them for you?"

"Why, Santiago, you've become quite a gentlemen."

His cheeks went hot.

"You've also become something of a town legend, I understand, like a white phantom streaking through the dark under these eternal blue streetlights like Ichabod Crane only with your head in the right place."

He swelled with his sudden fame.

"Do you think this war will ever end?"

He had not felt at all self-conscious when he had turned eighteen and been called up and rejected. He had no feeling for the war. He didn't want to go. It would have ruined his plans for Joey. He smiled when the "leftover" men kidded Fatso the 4-F reject for "raking in the money," "hand over fist making the long green."

To him the war was money and Cory. The war helped him—more money brought his aims closer; made quickly, money gave him time. He was hoarding money and time.

His sisters, no longer dependent on the town, were working in the fish factory too, and Ma was satisfied they were bringing home support. Because she had enough now, she was superior, almost scornful, with him. He knew it was a pose, as always; knew in some way he had hurt her and she would not get over it, not let herself, just as he for different reasons had been hurt by her rejection, cutting him off from Joey, he who had done most and loved her, still loved her most, who would always feel her betrayal, the one invisible wound that would not heal, perhaps never heal for her either: because now he realized Ma had depended, not on Pa or any of the others, but on him; depended on his always being there, her mainstay. So he had unknowingly betrayed Ma too, though to her it must have seemed intentional. She did not forgive him. Perhaps she never would.

Tom merely by being there consoled. Tom was his rock. All through the war he felt Cory's presence at Tom's and in his letters to Tom, and in Cory's mother too. In some measure—he could not gauge it—he was sure his presence consoled Tom and her when she visited the Island.

They're my family now. I'm their Rod and Cory.

In the last year of the war his opportunity came. Old Francis, the last of the Beckers, had died. Not long after, a FOR SALE sign appeared in front of the green cottage with the white trim at Gull Pond. The house was set deep under an enclosure of thick trees, darkish, near the wooden bridge that ran over Gull Pond and connected the long sandbar, the beach, with the mainland. The house faced a dirt road and the deep cluster of trees that nearly concealed the half dozen other houses and the crick; its rear looked out over the beach and Peconic Bay to Shelter Island and the ocean beyond.

At the fish factory the next morning he asked for an hour's time off, and he was waiting at the door to Front Street Realty when Joel Ravin himself opened up, obviously caught off guard. Fatso's voice would not falter, or his eye.

"Well, Fatso!"

"I want to buy Becker's place."

"You want—" Joel stared and tilted his head—to study, or recover.

"Just tell me how much."

"You may have some trouble getting—"

"I've already made arrangements. I've got the money."

"You've—"

"Yes." He was already on his feet. "If you will draw up the papers, I'll pay the earnest money right now. I have to go back to work."

"You're aware there will be fees, and you'll have to get a lawyer."

"Weems."

"Fine. The deal will take the usual three months for closing. Besides, there may be some delays, minor of course, since the heir lives in the City and has appointed a lawyer from up-island and we will have to arrange meeting times for signing."

"I can put up with all that."

"Then come back when you get off. We'll start the ball rolling."

"I'll be back after my shift. At three-fifteen?"

"Fine."

He strode out and did not look back, but turning the corner let his breath burst in a stifled cry of triumph, beat his hands together like chalk-filled erasers, and breathed deep, breathed—and laughed. He wanted to touch sky. He had commanded—himself, and him. He had made Joel Ravin *recognize.*

At the foreclosing he signed before W.P. Fenster and his Lawyer

Weems. He watched the lawyer's eyes linger over his signature exactly as Ravin's had, as if he had in some way become created in their eyes for the first time.

Santiago García.

So he became a landowner and between jobs and studies worked on the house. Even *he* wondered where miraculously he found the time—to clean, repair, paint, restore the grounds, cut and prune, nurse grass. After leaving the fish factory, he picked over furniture throwaways at the dump to take to his empty house to refinish.

By then he was a startle to the town with the piece of land he—Fatso García! Imagine!—had bought, and the cottage he—Fatso García! Imagine!—had painted himself and bit by bit furnished, where the lights seemed to be going all night long. (He impressed the librarians at the Floyd Memorial with his constancy. "You'll have the whole library mastered," Minna Royal said. "I intend to," he said.) The place stood like a beacon if anyone looked across from Sandy Beach or from the houses bordering the crick or Stirling Creek or from the hospital on its knob of land.

"High and mighty now," Ma said. He had to ignore, or suffer. And he *would* not—no more, no. He would cut himself off, had to, though he coveted news of Ma, which Joey brought. Joey was almost ten, hard to track down; and while Ma thought Joey was fishing or swimming or playing ball at school, he was stripping and sanding furniture, working at the cemetery or the dump or opening scallops, skimmers, oysters with him, a tireless little worker.

A wholesaler from the city said, "That's some helper you got there!"

"My brother."

"You don't say!"

He heard the disbelief. Because *teeth.*

What if he dared to say, *He's mine, and he'll have sons and they will be mine, and theirs, and theirs too?* Because there were moments when Joey, bent over his work, suddenly turned his head up to talk to him, and Fatso saw the image of his own pride: he saw the son he was creating.

In the fourth year the war died, in the spring in Europe and in the fall in Japan. In town there was a V-J Day madness. People in the hot August streets cried, shouted, laughed, clutched family and friends and strangers, danced and sang, and thrust fingers up in the Churchill V for victory. All day and night the radio broadcast recapitulations and the happy-sad hysteria. Then came the windup; the discharged vets came home—the sons and fathers and brothers and the women, WACS and WAVES; then came the extensive optimism, then the exhaustion which follows unstinted work, and then relief.

Nobody forgot the bombs. Spread over all the newspapers were photos of mushrooms of unimaginable size penetrating the sky. He read the accounts, but the atomic bombs were too big for the words. Death was in the mushroom. Much of the two cities dissolved in the mushroom. There was no time to slow rot and die like in the dump. Where did the bodies go? He went to the library to read *Life*. Though he understood every word, he could not comprehend. He could not imagine a mountain of all the lopped fish heads he had ever seen, all the wide eyes staring at him from the conveyer belt, *suddenly dissolved*. Joey begged, "Let's go to the pictures. I want to see the bomb." Everybody in town was talking about the Pathe News on the nuclear bomb. "You won't believe it till you see it, and then you won't want to believe it." He hadn't been to the moving pictures since he was a kid, and he never spent money he did not have to, but he had a hunger to know the bomb. Sitting in the dark, he and Joey watched the planes. They saw bombs fall. They saw the ground, then the blinding white flash, beautiful; then a column rose straight as a hard dick from the earth and penetrated sky; its enormous head spilled like come and turned cloudy and cleared. It took people, buildings, trees, everything. The cloud was heat, energy, motion; then *they* were. They were gone a zillion times faster than six million Jews burned, gassed, made soap.

Then the screen was empty. He was looking at nothing. Then it was sky.

Death was in the theater. Nobody said a word.

The bomb was in him. He would never get the bomb out of his head. It was in Joey. They were history. He had seen the war from a great distance, but now it was in him. He and Cory and Joey were bound to the Japs Italians English French Germans Russians. But what did it *mean*? He and Joey found fossils, found Algonquin arrowheads and artifacts. He read history. Men made sense of it. They put things together and recreated worlds that fascinated. They explained, but after he read and when he looked around him, all he saw was that things just kept happening, things happened not only to men but to animals and insects and fish over and over and over. Maybe something in them they could never change made them do the same things in all the times and places he'd read of. *I'm in something that doesn't make sense.* If men were extinct, would history mean anything to anything? He would like to look out of the eyes of a praying mantis or shark, blacksnake, chickadee, rat, or be a weed, rose, tree, moss. Maybe history was as dead as Joey's bat when he wasn't using it.

Cory did not come to the Island right after the war.

Fatso was alone now because Tom had been in Bristol off and on during much of the war and this last time for many months. On the way home to Gull Pond, whenever Fatso passed the three Verity houses, Cory's mother's and Tom's and Tom's divorced wife's, two were empty and dark on the early winter nights, darker for the snow, darker when the neon lights of Warner's grocery on one corner and Stankus' on the other went out. He could hear nothing but the crunch under his own steps and the wind off the crick chafing the tall stiff sea grass, cutting over the snow. His house was an island under the trees, a lonely light, because the few neighbors there and along Sandy beach were mostly summer people who had seldom come during the war and who were gone for the winter. So he read more, and more he depended on Cory's letters. When they came, not so frequently as before the war had ended, but long, they excited him so much that he filled his answers with questions. Terrible questions they came to be, which haunted him.

Between times, as if to ward off all thought of mail, he sought Joey. The boy became of necessity sneaky, spending more time with him, meeting him after his hours at the fish factory, helping him at the house or at the graveyard. Fatso was glad he had succeeded in making the boy enjoy work because he could fish and scallop and he was a good opener. Fatso had made him a special, short, very sharp little knife, a perfect fit like his own, for opening shells efficiently.

Joey was as tall as he was now, and smart, all A's. He was a good listener, in fact listened so intently, with such empathy, that Fatso was sure Joey heard or saw nothing outside the moment. Fatso, so obsessed was he with the books Cory kept sending, would seem to wake in the middle of his explanation with Joey, realizing that, instead of escaping all thought of mail, he was actually sharing the last letter with Joey, sharing what he was learning—he couldn't help it—and laughed, somewhat with awe, then with admiration, when Joey, who had somehow followed where he was going, asked, "But suppose it wasn't true?" He said, "It was," and Joey said, "But suppose it *wasn't*!" with frustration when he couldn't answer because his mind abruptly reached a ledge, a ravine, dark, endless, invisible, more terrifying than any rock wall.

They were approaching the Verity place. "Look, the front house is all lit up," Joey said. Passing, they could see through the living room into the kitchen, where Tom's daughter was busy. The daughter rarely came to the Island alone, and rarely stayed. She didn't stay long this time, but she didn't go back to Rhode Island either. For a time she was gone during the week and returned weekends; and then one day at Preston's dock, he saw the government boat from Plum Island dock long enough to let her off. She waved and called thanks to the sailors, and the boat pulled out, and she walked straight up Main toward her place.

Then one night after Christmas Tom was back. Fatso knew—because Pal leaped, lapped. As always before leaving Tom had said, "Al'll take care of my dog and feed my cats, "and I've asked the Clipp boy to hand out the Christmas stuff to the kids. Al's got the key to the shop. You take care."

He noticed Tom was always settled when she was in town, eased. Tom could always be humorous, but now the devil would twinkle in his eyes. He'd even make one of his stale "clean dirty jokes"—"Now don't forget, boys: wash down as far as possible, then up as far as possible, then wash possible"—and break into a cackle. They would roar at him enjoying his joke more than anyone else. Little dishes covered with napkins appeared on his kitchen table; though he'd not touch them, he'd say, "Stell was here." As he sank into a ponder his jaw would involuntarily move from side to side.

Sometimes arriving when she was there, Fatso would hear her: "Why, Pa, you haven't touched the stew or the muffins." "I took a mouthful or two." "A mouthful! You've got to eat, Pa." She scowled. Fine lines came into her forehead. Her gray eyes lingered. "How long can you go on this way?" Tom was all bone. Even his head, when he'd get her to cut his hair close, was suddenly skull, surprisingly small when the rage of blonde hair with the silver fluffs at his temples was shorn. "Well, leave the muffins. I'll have them with my tea." "I'll leave it all. Maybe *you* can get him to take a bite, Fatso." But Fatso couldn't. Tom would sip his tea, but he never ate with anyone around. Then one night Fatso realized it was out of delicacy for others that Tom dunked and ate only when he was alone because when Fatso opened the door, Tom hustled his bucket aside. Tom couldn't keep anything down but straight tea; he vomited everything else he ate into that bucket he tried to keep out of sight. No wonder he was a skeleton.

Now gossip followed Tom's daughter home. Fatso caught bits, what town said when the boat docked, when she walked to the house, when her father passed with his cart. She had run off with an Army soldier to Plum Island and left the husband and sons high and dry in Rhode Island. She was getting her house ready for when the soldier was discharged. If she herself heard, she seemed impervious.

He watched with awe, admiring the way she moved. Though small and thin, she seemed tall—it was her straight walk, her raised head, a confident resonant voice, always pleasant with a cheerful pitch, and a quiet dignity like Tom's, especially when her shining gray eyes rested so still and candid on you.

The gossip infuriated Fatso, because people *would,* they had to violate, they couldn't *not* touch, they had to stain—

Teeth.

Eyes.

Hands.

What most infuriated was that his *sacred* was tarnished, and she couldn't change it, she couldn't reject it. He didn't know *her* or how or why it had come about; but he knew Cory's mother was tainted. Even if she had blighted herself, their mouths would taint her before everybody, everywhere words, and Tom and Rod and Cory with her: their *clean* was smudged.

On a bright day, after snow, he saw the cause. The GI in ODs was very tall, so tall he seemed not quite with Cory's mother, skin very darkly leathered and rich hair burgeoning from his cap and his collar, and eyes sunken, dark too with deep glitters; but what held him to the face was the immobility of a cigar store Indian's, the abstracted stare, *vacant—demonic,* Fatso wanted to think because the gossip tarnished. The man seemed not to see anything before him, though when she spoke and took his hand, he smiled down with obvious pride in her. Fatso felt a twinge—he didn't want to misjudge. Still, he smiled at the Mutt and Jeff incongruity in their heights as they walked up the street from the dock.

Though he hurt for Cory's mother, he was furious with her too because she had changed things. Torn between pity and fury, he could cry.

He wished he were a schoolboy again and could go and sit on Miss Kellogg's steps and listen to her play as he used to. He took to listening to classical music on the radio. He remembered clearly pieces Miss Kellogg played. Long segments ran through his head, anonymous to him but familiar. He reveled in hearing familiar passages identified with the anguish of scenes with his mother or Diane or Joey or others, which had driven him for consolation to Miss Kellogg's porch, where he had heard those passages for the first time.

He met her walking in the little park by the bandstand on Third late one April afternoon—and ventured: "What stuns you is how many musics there are?"

"How many different pieces, you mean?"

"No, no. I mean how many musics. The score's a music—you hear it the instant you see all the notes, but it's silent. And what you play is one music, but not the same one; and even the one we hear's different to different listeners, isn't it?"

"Well, that's a problem of how you play it, the interpretation the musician gives it, the listener's attention."

"And there must be a music the composer took his from."

"It's what he feels. It comes out of him."

"How did it get inside him?"

"Oh, there's so much in us, Santiago."

"Where'd it come from?"

"Why, from living, I suppose. Experience creates strange pressures and makes each of us different. An artist . . . A work is a kind of crystalizing of a significant experience to the composer."

"But he hears it—"

"He must."

Her gaze escaped for an instant to the harbor beyond.

"Then maybe it's outside him? Maybe he hears just bits of it? Maybe he has to shape them because he can't hear all of it? Is it too big?"

"I'm afraid you'll have to go to the artist to find out. I'm just a pianist. . . ."

He had unsettled some silt in her.

"A pianist's an artist."

"Some. The great interpreters. But they're not the source."

"Source?"

"The composer. He's the one who hears."

"Can't the rest of us hear it?"

Under little pouches sagging over her eyes, her gaze was unblinking. He had never thought till now *old*. She was beginning to look like Tom.

"Not what he hears. What we hear comes through him."

"Then what do *we* hear?"

Blunted, she raised a hand. It stood motionless. He watched as if it would speak. Then fleetingly it rested on his arm.

"Perhaps all we hear, Santiago, is the sound of ourselves struggling . . ."

He did not answer. Of *course*: she did not know. He must go to somebody. He must go to something. He would have to keep going from person to person, book to book. How long could it go on? His life was this street. He would go from one telephone pole to the next and the street would go on and on. Was it endless?

"I didn't realize you were so sensitive to music, Santiago."

"I don't know anything about music except what it does to me."

He did not confess his afternoons on her porch steps, trespassing and stealing sounds.

"I'd say that's enough, but actually the more you know the more there is to experience. You liked math, and music has the precision of mathematics and its beauty of form. It's seeing the relation among things that finally counts most, isn't it? For me music is the richest of all pleasures. I never get enough of my piano."

"Even with the lessons?"

She laughed. "Even with the lessons. You'd be surprised how sometimes a student, at a certain stage of preparation, startles with what he brings out of the music."

"You mean when he releases himself to it?"

"Why, yes . . ." He heard the wonder. "You can do that after you've acquired control and technique has become second nature."

"Discipline's my middle name. It got me through the GED and even some correspondence courses from Wisconsin."

"Santiago! You don't mean it! Why didn't you tell us?"

The ground would heave and buckle. He laughed.

"It takes all my time to *do* it."

"I've wondered what brought about the change in you. Did you think nobody had noticed?"

He didn't say he didn't care about *them*, but he did not.

"And how come Wisconsin?"

"Because Cory Moorehead started me on his books. I didn't study those for credit."

"Cory! Estelle Verity's son? Why, her mother, Mary Ward, and I were in grade school together. I remember when Mary sent your mother off to her aunt Jane, the couturier, in Rhode Island to avoid diphtheria, and she stayed for good." Her voice cast no stone. "How long have you been doing this with Cory?"

"All through the war, and since he went to Wisconsin—"

"You're working for a degree, then?"

"I never thought that. I just want to know how to think, and know what others know, and—"

"Why, you could get a degree in some field. There's no telling what you could do or where you could go."

"I don't want a degree. I don't want a profession. I'll never leave Greenport."

Poor Miss Kellogg! Bewildered by his blunt barrage.

"Then—?"

"I just want to know. It's my greatest pleasure."

"To learn." Her nostrils dilated as if scenting a flower.

Learn?

To *know*.

A few days later he received a long disquisition from Cory in reply to his negation of a meaning to history, ending, as usual, with questions: "We want to mean, don't we? History gives order to life. As long as there is order, or the illusion of order, there is meaning or the illusion of meaning. If you reject images or historical order—evolutionary or futile straight-line theories, or cycles that are futile, or repetitive and ascending with beneficial change—you reject the very means of coping with order, because history includes all aspects of religious, scientific, and cultural life. If you reject them, what would you have?"

There was a P.S. in the lower left corner, "Spending summer with mother on Plum Island. See you then."

All spring he was in an anguish of anticipation; he could barely wait for Cory.

One Friday in July Cory did come, and they did talk. They talked Melville and Schopenhauer, Raymond Lull, love, desire, madness. He realized when Cory was gone, it was not enough. They had left so much untouched and what they had touched on they had not gone into enough, though Cory had promised he'd try to return before summer was over.

So Fatso's mind raced: Can't you order what has no meaning? Does everything ordered have a meaning?

Partly he still wanted to talk and talk, discuss years of pent-up thoughts, because in letters they could only write crucial questions and the peaks of thought. From Cory's letters he had imagined Cory's world—the girl, Savannah, important he figured from the casual but repeated mention; the other students, important some of them too; and then suddenly Rod. Visualizing them around The Rathskeller table with books and beer, he *heard* them; and he felt frenzied, jealous, not of them, but of the talk. He wanted to *talk* to Cory in person. He wanted, at least for the moment, to oust *them,* to prove to Cory what his mind could do now with the least guidance; and, more, he wanted to perform for Cory, parade, prance a little, be his own Barnum and Bailey, he who had never in his life dared but who now had some reason to be proud, hadn't he?

Cory did not come. After waiting for him the rest of the summer, Fatso felt betrayed. Only once did he allow himself to speak of his disappointment—to Tom, "Cory didn't come. He *could* have." His thoughts, all those he had stored up and all those Cory's very presence had bred the day of his visit, riled like trapped snakes striking to escape. Fatso festered. He resented *her* now, Cory's mother, and that new husband he had seen only once, and Plum Island itself for interfering. When he mulled, he realized Cory too had his work, summer was not all vacation for a student, and Cory was exceptionally dedicated. Still . . .

Only later, when at last a letter came from Wisconsin, did he subside somewhat. But in frenzied moments he wrote and wrote, accumulating pages for some days, and then mailed them to Cory. Between letters, sometimes catching himself racing past Stirling Cemetery and down Manhasset Avenue to the house for mail, he said, "You fool, you! What are you doing to yourself?" But he kept it up day after day.

Yet his indignation smoldered again whenever he saw Cory's mother; he could not disconnect the summer from her. His resentment, easily aroused, persisted; though afterwards he would be ashamed.

He understood Ma's jealousy of Joey now; Joey was the last thing *hers.* Besides, he was her pearl, taller than any of them now, kid-slim still, with that perfect boy-girl grace when he moved, and smart—that mind was what Fatso seized on; its action was his joy: *Joey's mind will be his way. It will take him far. All I have to do is watch and lead, and he'll do the rest.* The thought sometimes made him as giddy as his own race down the labyrinths he plunged into with a kind of delirium.

"She won't let me move, Fatso. She's at the door, she's always calling me. All I get's Where you been? Where you going? What you been doing? Who with? And she'll never let me stay with you. She *won't.*"

"That's Ma. You just have to put up with it. She can't help it, she loves you. When you're older, you can choose what you want—that's the time. And someday you might want to live in my house, you might have to."

"I want to now."

Fatso wanted Joey but didn't want to take him from Ma, yet he did want Joey to be all he could, and Ma didn't realize she could be the one thing that stood in the way of that.

"Don't you hurt Ma, Joey."

"Why does she hurt me if she loves me?"

"She doesn't mean to. It's because she loves you."

"Then I'll never love anybody."

Fatso laughed. "Yes, you will. You won't be able to help it."

"I'll try. I don't want to hurt anybody."

You won't be able to help that either, or being hurt.

Fatso would no longer touch him—Joey was no kid, too old for that—no more trace the perfect full lips, jaw, chin; no more smooth his sandy hair back; no more put his arm around his shoulder. Only his eye was free to roam that perfection, his and not his. Talk was touch now, thought, as intimate as love, as deep, tangled, inescapable.

He had the room always waiting for Joey. Ma knew. All the months, the years he had the house, every week, especially summers, Joey pleaded, argued with Ma till she had now and again to let him spend the night to avoid "hell to pay." Maybe she knew she'd lose him; he'd run off, hide, never come back. She inched out permissions. Whenever Fatso stopped by, she smoldered. No, she did *not* want him in the house, but he knew deep down she depended on his being in town because Joey was near, because Fatso bound Joey and Ma and, know it or not, like it or not, Joey bound him and Ma. "You come to see Pa, I s'pose. Well, he ain't here. Where the hell'd you think he'd be? He's out to sea." Inevitably she'd talk the long green. She must have been secretly grateful for the money Joey was still bringing in from the dump, but she'd chide, gripe, whine. "You'd think the girls' husbands'd come across with some cash, but nothin' doin'. Behavin' like niggers and Polacks, that's what. I'd have their asses hauled straight to the Riverhead jail. I wouldn't put up with no shit, not me." The girls came across with some. But Fatso wouldn't yield. *Money* he didn't hear. All his was for Joey's education. Someday Ma might know better and be glad, though knowing Ma he doubted that.

"Ma's mind closes like a clam," he told Tom.

That day his mother had sent Joey to spend some days with his sister María in Stonybrook—to keep Joey from him, Fatso was convinced.

"No such thing, Fatso." Tom clutched his bowl with both hands and sipped tea. "Your brother will have a little change, and your mother some rest. We get too used to seeing the world just from our own eyes, and we could be wrong."

"I know Ma can be good, Tom, but she sure can be mean."

"It's easy to make good intentions mean."

"Not when you're the one she's foul to, Tom."

"Well, maybe it'll turn out for the best. She can't know, and you can't. Nobody can. You want some tea?"

"No." He sank into the chair beside Tom, brooding. Pal nosed between his knees as if conscious he needed consoling.

Through the back kitchen window he was watching the blow tear leaves from Tom's maples and poplars and streak them in a multitude of dark shadows over the falling October light. On Pauline's back fence one of Tom's cats lashed out to catch them. He laughed.

"Your cat's having a time."

But a knocking distracted him, and he rose.

"What is it?"

But Tom heard the second knock, louder.

Fatso opened the door.

It was a Coast Guard officer, too big for the low frame.

Tom squinted. "You got the right house? My daughter lives out front."

"Mr. Verity?"

Tom waited. The officer, with a glance at Fatso, hesitated.

"I have something personal—"

"There's nothing you can't tell me in front of the boy. What is it? Sit down. Get him a chair, Fatso."

"No. I won't be . . . I have some news I'd rather not have to bring you, Mr. Verity."

Tom's eyes were suddenly still.

"Is it Stell?"

"Your daughter's going to be all right."

"What do you mean going to be? Is she or not?"

"I'm sorry to tell you your daughter's husband and your son, Ben, were drowned this morning, Mr. Verity, and your daughter—"

"Where's Stell?"

"She's resting, she has good care, there's a nurse with her. Actually, she's in a state of shock. She's lost her voice. The doctor says it's temporary. In a day or two she should regain it, but she made it known right away that you should know, and her sons. There's a national telephone strike but an operator has got through to them. She wants you to know she'll come as soon as—"

"Drowned, you say?"

"The keeper and the two boys at the lighthouse told what they knew, but we won't know all the details until your daughter can tell us. Reggie Webb and Ben were trying out the rowboat they'd built—in the Gut—in the change of tide and—"

"I know the Gut."

"—they haven't found them yet. It may be some time, but as long as the light holds they'll be searching . . ."

Tom's eyes quivered.

"Are you all right, Mr. Verity?"

"Fatso, give the officer some tea."

"Thank you, but I've got a car waiting and I've got to get back to the island to check on what's happening. If there's anything we can do for you, Mr. Verity, anything you need, the men will see to it right away. They've known Reggie for some time, and your daughter is a great favorite of the men. They admire how she's standing up to . . . all this."

Tom nodded.

"Well . . ." The officer held out his hand. He showed no reaction to Tom's.

Then he left, the car drove off, there was only the sound of the wind and the spasmodic strike of leaves against a pane.

"What's that?"

"The wind, Tom."

"I hear something."

"It's just the leaves."

"Oh."

The cats shifted. The dog scratched for entry.

"That Pal?"

"Yes."

"Let him in."

The dog bolted through the entry and jammed between Tom's legs and lapped, and finally settled beside him.

Tom's hands rested on the table. He gazed across the room, at the kitchen window. The sky was graying. On his back fence the dead morning glory tangles made a fine black web in last light. The birdbath, and the boat on its trailer in Pauline's yard, and the garage, gradually disappeared, and the fence and clothesline in the Raynor yard beyond, and all the shorn trees. Night filled Tom's kitchen window.

Fatso stirred himself.

"I'll pour you some tea, Tom."

"That'll be fine."

Fatso shivered, thinking *graves*. He shuddered. But he would let no one else dig these.

He did not have to. The bodies were never found.

It was strange to pass the front house, where Tom's daughter lived alone now, and her mother's next door, for she too lived alone, and Tom's out back, where he lived alone—three islands, if together. Sometimes at Tom's, or sometimes through a window or in the yard, he saw Cory's mother, as still as Tom's flagpole, staring. He felt ashamed he had ever resented.

But the three were not islands long, for the young coastguardsman was there more and more frequently; and Cory's grandmother next door, whose captain husband was at sea most of the time, spent nights, and then more and more days, with Cory's mother. As the months passed he occasionally caught a glimpse of the coastguardsman carrying the mother in his arms out to an old Ford that was parked out front most of the time, or see the three driving past the cemetery toward the Sound or the ferry at Orient Point or see them from his kitchen window parked at Gull Pond, enjoying ice cream or a snack or the sun.

So it was clear the grandmother was sick then. She no longer appeared in public and the sailor and Cory's mother were confined more and more to the house. Dr. Spurling made regular visits, and the Methodist minister, Reverend Parker, and Tom went in every day "to see Mary" and stayed long. It became clear to everybody but the daughter that Mary Verity was dying.

She died in May, and they buried her at once—Rod and Cory didn't show—and this time Fatso did dig the grave. At the graveside he was all eyes for Tom, vigilant, though in front of him his daughter whispered to the sailor, "Put Pa between you and Al, German. Watch Pa," a smart move because when they lowered the casket, Tom uttered the quietest agony Fatso'd ever heard, "Mary," and his legs gave, but quick as that word German's and Al's arms were under Tom's, holding him up where he sagged. Then Tom wanted some dirt—and Sara from up Tom's block reached down and gave him some—to throw in and touch that casket, that wife. Fatso's insides were trembling because *Tom* . . . he felt he'd choke if the burial didn't end soon, but it did right then as the hard sod plopped hollow against the lid.

When they had all driven away, Fatso fast covered the grave, rounded it neat, and put his tools in the shed and locked it. He did not stop at her place, where the cars were lined all up the street, but halted a moment at sight of the crowd in the windows. In the cold stillness he could hear the busy voices, rounds of laughs, a sudden bold voice from inside.

The day was hard for Fatso because *Tom*— He couldn't bear Tom's stillness. Although usually quiet when he sat at the table with his tea, now Tom was too still, one death stilling him, and one more killing layer by layer, diminishing him. About that day he couldn't write to Cory.

That night, worked up, he went to Ma, had to. He said, "Joey's spending this night with me, Ma, and I won't take no, and that's final. Come on, Joey."

His rare belligerence must have disarmed Ma. Only after they were out the door, Ma came out of her stun. They heard her tearing into JesusMaryandJoseph.

From that night he dated his exercises in imitation of writers from the old days, *Santiago, His Book,* in which he would try to master his thoughts, definitions, relationships. *I want to* place *myself, Cory. Know what I am. Where I belong in all this. What is it? I want to be able to define precisely and clearly.* With Cory's letters, arranged chronologically, he kept his exercise book in a three-drawer metal filing cabinet Irving Price & Sons Insurance had dumped. In it he worked on his questions and answers to Cory, writing and rewriting so that he could arrive at a clear condensation in his letters. There were loose pages too, a multitude of moments, apart from reactions to his reading and Cory's letters, which had *caused* his thoughts: the sight of the white moths of summer bursting into life one hot night in July and filling the air like snow, so thick that the trees palpitated like white hearts in the moonlight; the sight the next morning of the thousands and thousands of dead moths that did not get through, washed up in a thick fringe along the Sound shore; watching horseshoe crabs mate; the damaged waterfront and the eaten sand cliffs after hurricane winds; certain sensations from passages which Miss Kellogg played; the sudden rank whiff of beer, cigarette, grease as he passed Helen's and Meier's bars on Front Street; the winter fields of dead potato twigs; the lopped heads of fish, eyes and eyes, the fish bodies moving along the conveyor belt at the fish factory . . .

Some days he could not believe in time. Routine gave the illusion of staying time.

Every day he saw Jimmie-the-Whisper float in and out of Barth's, half shot, with the white handkerchief ahang from his chin or loose about his cancer-eaten throat. Every day at Emil's he passed Connie sitting in the doorway of his shack, in warm weather crushing ants, in the worst cold inside staring out the one small window. Every day from somewhere in Emil's house came the sound of the accordion or Emil's bachelor talk: "My momma, she wouldn't stand for nodding, my momma. She'd have you goddamn Polacks outa here." And at precisely the same instant each morning he would pass the workers from the docks and Claudio's and Mitchell's restaurants and Paradise Sweets and the Coronet, the drugstores, Katz's clothing, the barbershop, Grant's and the Arcade; the Stirlington and the Wyandank, and the raft of people coming from or going to Shelter Island on the ferry, and the ticket clerk and the railroadmen on the six o'clock train to the City, and the men dropping off bundles of papers at the tobacco shop, where in no time the men would be drifting in to place their illegal bets for Ed to phone in to the bookie.

All year round fishing boats would dock and haul anchor; and in season there would appear on the same day and almost at the same hour the excursion boats, the fishing boats for hire, and boats of every size, yacht to rowboat, of familiar vacationers who owned summer houses or rented the same house or visited relatives for the season, so that he knew from repeated years of them the names of the boats—*Ida K, Annie B, Dora, Arethusa*—and the recurring faces, even the specific dates when he as a casual onlooker could expect the famous seeking anonymity or the nobodies seeking fun and relaxation.

Summers, especially on weekends or the Fourth of July or Labor Day, he stood on the Sound cliff looking down the long beach at the hundreds of invading vacationers in and out of the water. From a distance they looked much like the scattered clusters of white maggots he might come upon breeding in the dump or in somebody's garbage pail, and it was not any *body* he saw but all that *moving,* and the waves moving unceasingly, the drift of clouds and their shadows. The people were as anonymous as gulls soaring or as still as their shadows on sand and sea. It was that motion, its anonymity, that intrigued, teased, maddened. What it was. Where it came from. Where it went. Whenever in a crowd—at the annual art show on the docks or at a carnival or Barnum and Bailey's circus on the old polo grounds—with too many bodies and faces too close to single out any one for long, carried along with them like one thing moving, he felt he was helpless. He felt they were. He *felt* that motion. He was as afraid of that anonymity as he was of the undertow in the Sound that tugged and threatened to suck him under. Yet he was torn: he was attracted, but afraid; he wanted to know, but he feared knowing.

Cory, I'm afraid. Suddenly I'm not me. It's as if in a crowd something in every one of us recognizes itself and comes together and negates each one of us. But then I think, It couldn't do that without us, so it must need us. It must need me. It's in me. If it's in me, it's me. If it needs me, then it needs the house and the bay and trees and every single thing, or it couldn't be it.

Now all his thought was to make the town his as he had made the dump his. He could walk his familiar streets, paths, shortcuts blind. Now, systematically, he traced shore and covered ground he had seldom or never trod till at last he could close his eyes and instantly visualize his chosen terrain. He had cut a quadrangle out of Long Island and made it his own island. His town was no more than two miles of sand and black topsoil between Long Island Sound and Greenport harbor, and it ran four miles between Southold and East Marion. *His* was bounded on the east by Manhasset Avenue, running past the Protestant and Catholic cemeteries to where his house sat on the edge of Gull Pond, facing Peconic Bay and Shelter Island; and on the west by Chapel Lane, which cut across the Island almost from Pipes Cove to the Sound.

His.

When he gazed out his kitchen window at the bay at the same instant each morning, he was sure he could tell the hour and the time of year by the color the water took on from the angle of light. Sometimes he felt the seasons as close as another's skin that merely moved around his own in an unceasing circle in which nothing seemed really to change except within him.

Cory, I'm afraid when the church bells ring. On Sunday and every night at supper time the Episcopal Church bells play that same hymn. The sound dissolves everything. For a moment everything dies. I die. Only the sound lives and moves. Suddenly the sound stops. It breaks. Everything's where it was, separate, as if the fragments are trapped inside each thing and everything's itself again, the same as after a storm. I think we want to be all one thing together. It's a music they dream and teach and preach to us, but nobody wants to give up his own bit of it. When the moment comes nobody can give up his own body, mouth, sex. No matter what charity they preach, when there's just enough money or food or water for one baby or one wife or one husband or one friend or himself alone, a manll kill the other for it. He can't help it. He wants to live because he wants the sound, the motion. It's his as long as he can keep it inside him. He won't let anybody take it. He has to keep it. It makes him him, and he's afraid not to be him. He wants to be more but he's afraid to be. He doesn't dare. He's afraid he might be nothing.

The boss called him into the office after work one Thursday.

"There's not a job you haven't done, Fatso. You know the factory inside out. You've never missed a day. You keep your distance from everybody, and in my book on any job that's one in an employee's favor. Starting Monday, you're the assistant manager, twenty a week boost in pay. You keep things moving, keep everybody in place, and don't miss deadlines, and we'll get along. Think it over. Tomorrow you tell me."

He nodded and left.

He couldn't believe. Since the war, money came hand over fist.

"Bully for you," Ma said when she found out. "Pa should have your luck."

Pa was laid up with a leg infection. "Caught it in a defective metal rope and tore hell out of it." Pa, always quietly factual, was smoking tranquilly in a chair in the kitchen, his leg raised.

"There goes his pay." Ma was already at it.

Gangrene set in and four days later he died in the hospital.

Fatso did not miss him. He had never known him. He had been a stranger. He had been, was, the memory of the smell of fish.

It was not too long after that Ma started again. "Without his pay, what?" Ma couldn't let up.

Alone with Ma, Fatso said, "I'll give you the twenty raise every week, *but* only on condition Joey stays with me if he wants to."

"If he wants to! You're a sneak, Fatso. But if that's all Joey's worth . . ."

"Well, take it or leave it, Ma."

"You ain't bribin' me, Fatso García! Keep your money."

But Friday—Ma couldn't resist money, he had her there—Joey showed up at the house:

"Just for weekends, Ma says, because it's too far to walk to school from here."

Ma had cheated him, but he said nothing. Be silent. Wait. Bit by bit all would come. Time. Joey he gave freedom. Because he didn't know anything else but work and study, he Fatso could be Joey's silent model at least in discipline and order. For all else the way to discovery was open to Joey. With Joey Fatso found himself talking. He had been so accustomed to talking in his head while walking, working, writing his words that he never thought how few people he actually spoke to, even at the fish factory, where day after day he was bent over fish—heads, bodies, eyes, miles of eyes. He startled himself—more, because Joey listened, obviously fascinated whenever Fatso got started on starfish or the Pilgrims or the Algonquin Indians. An anthill was enough to start him on order, or a dead leaf on plants breathing or threat of snow on how to keep bushes from freezing. All the time his hands were busy. He would have Joey sanding the bottom of the rowboat with him or repairing lobster pots they'd then set out in the Sound and flag so they could spot them quickly when they returned to collect the trapped lobsters.

"Jeez, I wish you was—"

"Were—"

"—were at school. Those teachers are so dumb."

"Not if you listen. You'll be amazed at how they make you think. But you have to listen. That's the secret."

He was thankful Joey was all eyes, proud that Joey had something of his own meditative stillness; proud too that, though Joey liked being with him and was intensely curious, he almost instinctively balanced his time between him or Ma and the house and kids his own age. Joey at the drop of a hat could choose his company. All the world was attracted to his looks and good nature. That thrilled. Fatso marveled. Yet for all his sympathy, he could not overcome mirrors. He could not conceive being Joey. Imagination failed.

"He's a fine boy, Santiago, and smart," Joey's homeroom teacher told Fatso one afternoon on his way to Miss Kellogg's classroom. "I bet you're proud of him."

"I hope to be."

Since the day he'd quit, he hadn't been inside the school. *Prison* everybody called it because the enormous building looked like Sing Sing.

"Why, Santiago, what a pleasant surprise!" At her desk, Miss Kellogg looked almost ephemeral in the flood of almost blinding late afternoon sun. It edged her hair and dress with still fire. "Here, let me—" She rose and closed the louvers. "There! Now we can see—"

Of all the women teachers, Miss Kellogg alone was always charming. She bore something of long ago, a feeling, busy as she was, of serenity. Everything around her seemed to fall into its ordered place, the world timeless, with no rush, always time for everything.

"You never change, Miss Kellogg."

Though a girl somewhere in her laughed lightly, the teacher waited.

"It's about piano lessons—"

"With all your interest and questions about music, I was sure you'd come round to taking lessons."

"Not me. Joey."

"Joey. Of course! But . . . I had no idea he was caught up in music."

"It's my idea. He's so good at everything."

"Though it's you who seem to be quite sensitive to music."

"It's sound. I'm very sensitive to sounds, not just music, voices too. Some sounds make me quiver. But I don't think I could ever play. It's one thing I don't think I could control. I lose myself. But Joey, he's so talented at everything. *He* could. He says he's always fiddling with the piano here at school."

If she was listening, she was watching his restless fingers.

"You're very devoted to him, aren't you?"

He stilled his hands on his knees.

"He's my brother."

She said, "But you've no piano for him to practice on. It requires hours."

"There's the one in the old music room, isn't there?"

She considered a moment, then smiled, and stood.

Standing himself, he felt her presence, small as she was, fill the room.

"You send Joey in, and he and I will have a talk. Maybe we'll come round to something. And you?"

"Oh, I go on working. And thinking." He laughed, nervously excited about Joey's lessons. "I didn't know what a riddle it all is, life. Sometimes, thinking takes you under."

"Under?"

"Down under, deep. The farther in you go, the deeper it gets, bigger. It's like the Sound, you could drown in it. The trouble is once you go at it, you can't stop."

"Everything has its two sides. What's worthwhile costs."

"I couldn't go back. I wouldn't be dumb again for anything. I *wouldn't*, Miss Kellogg—honest."

He saw from her softening glance, the parted mouth, that he had revealed.

"You were never dumb, Santiago! On the contrary—"

"Joey's smart, he'll work, you'll never be sorry, Miss Kellogg."

He was in the corridor, lunging. He was hot in his clothes, sweating. He had to get breath. Outside, he gulped for air. The cool wind touched his face.

By the weekend the winds had turned into a heavy blow. A storm was on its way. The hurricane season began. The fish factory closed early, and a team boarded the windows up. Fatso hurried. Joey would be there, if he were, alone. By the time he reached Gull Pond the blow was battering. The wind howled and whined, horrendous. He could hardly walk against it.

Joey was on the front stoop.

"What're you doing out here?"

"It's great. I want to watch."

"You get inside. Something could hit you any minute."

Inside he went from window to window.

"*Look* at that water! You think it'll reach the house, Fatso?"

"If it does, you may end up under the eaves. I'll bolt the cellar door down. Now don't you leave this room."

Fatso went out into the sudden dark. The air was deep with rain. Shelter Island was cut off by the rain and the wind that thrashed the bay into chaotic waves that crashed water up over the beach, filling Gull Pond and overflowing into his yard and the woods beyond.

Back inside, he locked his storm blinds in the house and cellar, hoping the hurricane would not hit heavily.

Joey's excitement was nerves, so Fatso talked while they played monopoly.

"People thought nothing could be as bad as the famous hurricane of '38, Joey. Nobody knew it was coming. They didn't even know what a hurricane was like it had been so long since one had hit here. After that, hurricanes never stopped coming, one after the other every fall. But here '44 was worse. The hurricane carried away half the waterfront, just about drowned Front Street. Next day the yards were filled with boats, boards from docks and buildings, whole window frames, glass, fallen trees; and half the electric and telephone wires in town were down."

The eye of the storm came abruptly blue and calm as if there were no motion, then went, and the tail of it came and petered out in rash cold rain, and sun broke clear for the second time that day, the sky cloudless. The tumult had riled the bay into a dirty brown. Water had seeped into the cellar, and a leak had developed in the corner of Joey's room, where a few pieces of roofing had blown off.

"As soon as everything's dry, I'll take care of the roof."

To be prepared, he and Joey were setting the ladder and spare shingles out when a car drove up and halted. The door shot open.

"It's Ma, with nigger Annie! Ma! Ma!"

Ma threw the door open, heaved her legs out, and bolted straight toward them; but Joey halted her, gripped, kissed, gripped. She threw her big arms around him. Legs parted, staunch against the ground, she held and rocked, rocked. Ma's teeth dug into her lower lip, her eyes closed, and her wet lids glittered. For a long instant she rocked. And Joey did not let up his hold. Ma's eyes opened. She released him but clutched Joey's face between her hands and looked and looked.

The sight blunted. Fatso had never seen Ma *hold*. Or break. Ma had been scared! Joey too. Fatso had not realized how scared. But the sight of Ma's love smote. Joey. Her baby. Fatso had never seen it, no, not with Ma. Never.

Then, caught self-conscious, Ma thrust Joey aside.

"What in hell'd you think *you* was doin', Fatso, tryin' ta kill the kid? You know what coulda happened to him? *Do* you? And you think you're so damned smart. Well, you're just plain stupid! That's the last night the kid'll ever spend with *you*—ya understand?—the last. And don't you dare come shaking the long green in my face neither. Keep your fuckin' twenty bucks! Hear me? Get in the car, Joey." Ma's tone left no alternative. Joey moved. "Let's go, Annie."

Ma slammed the car door. She did not look back.

He stood, staring at the ground. The long pink bodies of drowned earthworms lay in all the puddles.

He felt lopped. How many times lopped? Was *lopped* his permanent state? Was that it? Well, lopped, he would not waste. He mounted the ladder to replace the missing shingles.

He did see Joey. He sometimes went inside the old music room to listen while Joey practiced and sometimes when Miss Kellogg gave him lessons in the big white house with the green trim which he had come to love like the embodiment of that sound, of everything he remembered too about Miss Kellogg from the years at school and since. Listening to Joey play, he felt the sound flow into him as naturally as breath; felt it flow through his blood and through his skin and carry him till a noise from the street broke the flow and he was startled to be back in his own body.

Apart from those stolen and treasured moments, more and more he kept to himself, read Cory's textbooks all fall and winter and into spring, plagued, he wrote Cory, by the philosophers, first by Spinoza, then Hegel, Nietzsche, Schopenhauer. *Thank God (or Cory?) for your notes. I'd be doomed without them. Philosophy's my destruction. It will turn me to stone if I keep staring at* things, *trying to make the abstractions concrete. Philosophy, except for ordering things, doesn't make sense to me. It has to be real or I can't live it or live with the idea of it. If everything's* really *an Idea, then my senses have to live the idea or metaphor. My body has to know it, or no idea, nothing, is real.* If the invisible were real, then he *knew* his body would feel it just as his body heard motion and felt sound whenever he swam underwater in the Sound deeps, or what was the invisible for? Or was it only his own body he heard? If it *were* only his own body he heard, was there an invisible?

Swimming underwater was the nearest sensation to music. Hunting furniture when he had bought the house, Fatso had done some work for the heirs of the imposing stone mansion, Brecknock Hall, on the back road. Andy Sykes from Fourth Street was dismantling to sell.

"Something here you want instead of cash?" Fatso said, "How about the phonograph?" The RCA Victor, complete with horn, though it didn't play, was actually a beauty. Sykes threw in the raft of 78 records of classical music "if you cart them." Fatso had taken the phonograph to Tom, pointing out the dog listening to "his master's voice."

"He's as attentive as your Pal."

"Leave it, and I'll see if I can't get as much noise out of it as his master makes!"

"You never talk that much," Fatso said.

"Just to myself when nobody's listening." Tom chortled. It was the family prize story on Tom: how, because he was hard of hearing, he would pick up the receiver and say, "Nobody's home."

Whenever he entered the house, Fatso did usually hear Tom muttering inside.

Tom fiddled with the player for a long time but got it to play.

"You can do anything, Tom."

"I do what everybody does, Fatso, keep muddling along."

Fatso had set it in the corner of his study room and, except when he had to reread chapters that bewildered, he listened when reading or when sitting or lying in bed, exhausted, or when working inside or in the yard with the windows open: Liszt or Brahms, Schumann, Borodin, Tchaikovsky, Bach, Chopin, Beethoven. Played over and over, they never failed him. He knew the compositions, though he knew nothing technical about music; but what he could not fathom was his own surrender to the music, to each composer in a different way. Sometimes he *consciously* listened to try to detect the instant, the passage, the very note which carried him as lightly as a feather on the water. Music was stronger than sea, its tide irresistible. His mind could not swim against such feeling, and after whatever serene or turbulent journey, when he had been delivered, when he was back at last and the silt settled, he plagued himself with questions. He was convinced that each composer *sensed* something about men, about him. Each had found a *way* into them, to make what was in men respond. What was in the composers? How did they sense it? Where did it come from? Why to them?

One early evening in late July, coming in from hosing the back lawn, he heard a ferocious pounding on his front door.

"Hey, Fatso."

German!

His hulk, dark against the sun, filled the doorway.

Fatso waited, mute.

German smiled winningly.

"Going to ask me in for a beer?"

"I don't drink, but come in."

They sat in Fatso's study room.

"Just kidding, Fatso. I came to see if you had time for a job. Say, you've sure got a pile of books. You running a college or something?"

"Something like that. Call it a one-man college. What'd you want me to do, German?"

"My wife's sons are coming home."

"Cory and Rod! When?"

"The end of August. Estelle says you know the boys. Rod loves to fish and scallop, and the rowboat needs a good going over and a paint job, and I'm worked day and night, bushed. Give you good pay. What do you say?"

"Sure will, if you haul it in a hurry and leave it out back. With my other work, that doesn't give me much time."

"Great! Everybody says 'You can depend on Fatso.'"

The boat was ready long before the boys arrived. Fatso and German dragged it over the bank into the shallow Girls' Hole; and German tested it by rowing into the bay, around the breakwater and back through Stirling Creek to the crick, where he kept it moored at old Pooptail Raynor's dock, close to the Verity house.

Fatso was primed for Cory's visit. Only now did he realize how hard he had studied, how long, how alone. He dared not look back down that road, fearing he could not face the longer one ahead. How long did you go on alone? When did you reach *knowing*? But *Don't! Remember Joey*, he reminded himself. Now he would impress Cory not merely as the good student, but also as a worthy antagonist, a fellow mind, an intellectual brother, and (despite his menial tasks) a presence, as he knew the town, obviously mystified by his "intellectual" dedication, was grudgingly aware.

On a Monday evening from the yard he saw a man walking slowly down the road past the boatyard toward his place. In a moment, from the big body, the slow rock, the eternal straw hat, the care he took to plant his feet down—he was favoring his once-infected foot—he recognized Emil. From constantly tippled beer, Emil's body and his mind were molasses.

"You going for a swim, Emil?"

Emil's cheeks were wet, his blue eyes red. Nothing new. The older he got, the more beer, the more easily he cried—about his dead momma and poppa, the Polacks abusing him, something left at his door, the kids stealing his green apples. He'd whine it all out long on his accordion.

Emil sat on the bench behind the house, facing Gull Pond.

Tears sloped down his long nose.

"The boys steal from you again, or beat you up, Emil?"

Emil shook his head.

"You got dig grave." His voice was more nasal than ever. His big hands kept floundering.

"Who died?"

Emil's chest heaved. He wiped his eyes.

"Stella's boy, he got drowned in Gut."

Fatso waited, stone.

"Dot younger one."

"Rod?" Fatso would break.

"Him. Ya. Them fellers fishing got him. Spotted body and dragged him in. Called Coast Guard. Stella, she can't keep nobody, nodding, poor Stella."

And *Tom*.

"But Rod could swim!"

"Not in Gut. Nobody swim out of Gut."

"How could such a thing happen?"

"Cory, he told it."

"Cory! He was with Rod?"

"In rowboat. Cory, he's out of head. Said Rod fell. He jumped in Gut for Rod, but find nodding. Doctor Spurling, he came to house 'cause Cory was every minute calling *Rod*. Gave Cory shot. Cory slept. Now sits in window like dead. Don't say nodding."

"I'll get right to it, Emil."

"Ya, you do dot. Poor Stella."

In dark the next morning before work, he went to Stirling Cemetery to dig. He had hardly slept, thinking of Rod. All night they were boys again. He went down the years with Rod: they swam in the Boys' Hole, trapped swallows on the Sound cliffs, netted crabs in the crick, fished, scalloped at Pete Neck with Rod's uncle Ben, romped through Barnum and Bailey and carnivals on the polo grounds, dived from the railroad dock . . .

Now broke in. It kept suddenly being *now*.

Digging, he was trembling. He knew the two plots, the Verity plot with a place for Tom and his son Ben never found, and beside it a place for his daughter and the husband never found, maybe for the new husband now, and two places for the boys. He talked into the grave. "I never dug a hole for anybody I knew well." He worked steadily to finish the job, but he did not want to *see* the empty grave. It was waiting for Rod. He could not believe. Part of his own life would go in the hole with Rod. He shivered. When the earth was piled high, he leaped out, glad to leave the cemetery, glad to be going to the fish factory, where there were so many people. But he was not relieved.

At Horton's parlor Cory and his mother and German were waiting. He was suddenly gripping Cory's hand. "Cory!" Cory closed his eyes for the briefest instant when he said, "Fatso," apparently all he could utter, and, releasing his hand, turned him to face Rod.

He did not know that stillness.

Not Rod.

He was startled to feel nothing for that still form. *Not.* But as he turned away his stomach pullulated, and his chest swelled so he pressed his hands against it. Tom, seated by himself with his legs crossed, raised his head at that motion. He squinted. "Fatso," he said. He sat in silent sympathy with Tom only an instant and then went out into the dark.

At the burial, he stood behind the gathered cortege. As he gazed at their backs, at the dark clothes, at the minister facing the family around the grave—apart from it, as always, waiting to cover the casket with earth—he was staring at what he had seen dozens of times, a format that never changed, only the body different. Watching, listening, he thought *They're looking down at mine. Reverend Parker is talking about me, Santiago García.* Then they were gone. He was left alone with it.

"Rod?"

His voice spoke only to himself in that field of stone.

No, not Rod. No part of me, that. *He's inside me now. Not only memory, but what was in him.*

He had never hesitated before. Rapidly, he covered and shaped the grave.

Not till long after did Cory come to his house—one night of wind and rain. He shook his raincoat out the door.

"I couldn't sit still another second. My feet were itching to move." He smiled. "Sometimes you have to do what your body tells you to. I'm sorry I haven't been before."

"Why would you? I knew. And I knew you'd come. There's some fresh chowder."

"Chowder! When have I had any Long Island chowder."

"I dug the clams myself."

"I always expect the real article from you."

"You'd better hold off judgment till you taste it."

"It smells of sea. . . ."

"Don't, Cory . . . Will you be going back to Wisconsin to finish? Work—you said so, and Tom swears by it—solves problems."

"They need me."

"You can't do anything for Tom or your mother. You couldn't before. Nobody can, nothing, not God. You handle it alone. After, a time comes when you let them in, you have to. *You* know. You didn't come at first because I couldn't do anything for you. You had to. It wasn't the rain. It was your legs, remember?"

They both laughed.

"You do me good, Fatso."

"Oh, I could do you bad, like bacteria and insects and hurricanes and tornadoes and earthquakes and . . . mostly other people."

"Okay, okay. I know they rouse something in you that makes you stand up against things, as if you weren't *you* till then. Suddenly you're unfamiliar, but it's you."

"You mean we're subjected to whims. Whose? Don't tell me a god's of any kind. Don't tell me about divine justice and human justice. Where's the divine justice in clobbering Tom time after time? That's madness."

"Maybe madness makes sense, or we have to make sense of madness. Maybe that's what it's for."

"There you go! You mean *we* have to rationalize it as if we were responsible for it. It's up to men to make sense of madness. Maybe men conceived of Him out there to challenge themselves to be worthy of their own creation."

"Something like that, or we wouldn't be men, we'd be animals."

"We *are* animals, only we forget that because we don't want to be animals. Why's that, when the best things come from our animal selves—sensations, yes. Even the art you love, all of it starts in our senses."

"You forget, Fatso—something has to order those sensations."

"I don't forget, and I don't forget that it's men and nothing else who have to make sense of it to live with it; but that sense is meaningless for any other purpose, and men are still as irrational as they ever were."

"Irrational, but maybe that's the very thing that was given us to rouse the mind to order it. There may be method in that madness."

"You!" Fatso laughed at the verbal play, but was roused, almost angry. "Why do you *insist* on things being *given.* You can't get away from your religion, can you? Tom really got to you—didn't he?—though I think Tom, for all the preaching he's done, has a broader view than yours."

"You think ordering the whole thing's narrow?"

"Using one head—a Him, His head—to order it, yes."

"Everything's a metaphor, Fatso."

"*No.* Art's a metaphor, but a metaphor's to understand what's real, and what's real is *not* a metaphor 'by extension,' as you say in your letters and as so many of your texts say. You can wear out the idea of things being the shadow of a shadow of a shadow till the shadow itself means nothing."

"Well, let's at least consider a metaphor a way of explaining the real, then. That'll let me give you a metaphor for chaos!" Smiling, he rested his hand on Fatso's knee. Fatso shrugged impatiently, but his eyes never left Cory's face.

"In every myth I know, the universe is ordered out of chaos. In the Greek view all was Chaos and Old Night till enough of that irrational *stuff* was used to make the universe. So: picture a circle that we call the universe *holding back the chaos all around it.* And then picture a circle in the center of that, the earth. And then a third circle in that, a man, or a man's head. And all three of them made of the same basic substance. I'm sure you've seen the image of those three circles in plenty of Christian books and art."

Fatso reached for a pad and drew. "Yes." He glued his eyes to the circles, listening.

"So what is ordered is chaos, the irrational. And the rational is *part* of the irrational, a small part. That's evident when you look at man: one small part, his poor head, is always struggling to order his body because his emotions are always threatening to break order."

"I don't see how you relate the three circles."

"Each is like a wall holding back destruction in all the chaos around them."

"Like the dike in the story?"

"Exactly! The boy sticks his finger in the hole to hold back disaster till men can restore the wall. There's always something inside and outside us that attracts us to break order. If we yield, we're in collusion with it. Something in us consciously or unconsciously *wants* to break the order."

"I don't see how that relates the three circles."

"Everything that disturbs one, disturbs the others."

"Nature smacks us with hurricanes and droughts and what not—I see that—and I can see what men have done to the earth, and that may have some tiny effect in the universe; but how can *one man* disturb the earth, or the universe?"

"Look at it this way. Remember the wall, our body, skin. Each time we're weak and give way to something destructive and act, it's as if we open up a chink in the wall of our body, like the dike's, and let chaos in. At that instant we're in collusion with it, it disorders, it imbalances. Something, no matter how infinitesimal, is set in motion, and once it is its effects reverberate and can't be stopped until it has run its course. That's what tragedy is all about."

"Because life is tragic. What good is tragedy if it doesn't explain life?"

"Nothing explains life."

"Something *will. Someday*, Cory. It has to! Questions can't go on forever."

"Why not? So far, questions have kept us struggling for a meaning. Maybe questions are the only worthwhile things."

"Look at Tom— Tell me what your grandfather ever did to deserve those hands?"

"Now who's talking justice? Why do you say *deserve*? That means a *Something's* judging him when he'd be the first one to admit he caused the fire. I don't believe even he can remember now where his mind was—why he was upset, stupid, careless—at the moment he mistakenly poured the can of grease or kerosene over the stove."

"Even though he did it himself, some impulse might have caused it. You said he doesn't remember what happened before that, and there had to be a cause; there must have been one leading up to that."

"Maybe. But at that moment he *let it in*—that's what I mean by an unconscious collusion with chaos—and it nearly killed him, he nearly burned to death, and it didn't stop there—"

"You keep saying *it*. You make *it* sound *conscious*."

"That motion, then. The effects, then. It's a tide—it goes, it comes, you can't stop it, it's inevitable."

"But everything depends on how you react. You can control it."

"Not other people's actions. Because of his hands—I shouldn't tell it—my grandmother divorced him. He never got over it. She's dead, but he still loves her."

Fatso remembered: at her graveside, they had to hold Tom to keep him from falling. When she was alive, Tom never mentioned his divorced wife; but Fatso would see him gaze out at that house and linger a little before returning to his tea. Tom lived on tea.

"My grandfather couldn't do every kind of work."

"But Tom can do anything. He wouldn't depend on anybody."

"Not unless his condition forced him to. He took state welfare—he was entitled to it—before he'd impose on anybody. My mother was thirteen when the fire . . . In the hospital and from the first day home, she nursed him. My grandmother wouldn't; she couldn't face his hands. My mother was—is—always there. He lost practically everything, but he has her. She'd never leave him for long. The fire changed her life too, and my father's, and her other husbands' after him. But I can't tell all that. It's hers, and I can't know it all; but if she hadn't had Gramp, she might not have bought Gram's house. Oh, she bought it for herself and us, but I'm sure she had him most in mind because it was his father's and the land his family's for generations. She wanted him back on it . . ."

"Don't, Cory."

"Don't stop me. I haven't really talked since . . ."

"You don't have to go into that."

"But I do. If I don't say it, it'll rot inside me. It *will.* Fatso. Maybe I'm already rotten. Maybe that's the trouble."

"You're not rotten, Cory. You're too good. That's the trouble."

"No, it's Gramp. He's too good to everybody and look what it got him."

"I never heard him complain."

"He never would. You'd think he was an Old Testament Jew. Obey and be silent. Even Job complained."

"Yes. And Job got back more than he gave, but it wasn't what he lost, Cory. He couldn't get that back. That's strange, isn't it? Even his God couldn't give him what he lost. But Tom got back nothing."

"*I* know that, Fatso. God, don't you think I know that? And what would be the point if He *did*?"

"He'd prove himself."

"Then the experience wouldn't mean anything."

"That's right. If Job's experience shows anything, it's that you have to accept what happens and go on to the next thing, better or worse. You don't need God to know that."

"That doesn't keep you from feeling guilty."

"Why *should* you feel guilty?"

"Because of what you do, and who you are."

"Or what *they* make you feel before you've even had a chance to do anything or become anybody? What about that?"

"What you do makes you what you are."

"And not the other way around? Does what Tom is make him do what he does?" He smiled at the riddle. "The dog chasing his tail. The chicken and the egg."

"Maybe you can overcome what you are."

"Unless you know what you are, you can't, and how would you

know till you did something? You may have deceived yourself all along."

"Yes, that."

"Maybe they deceived you, made you think you are what you seem . . . till you find out you're not. I believe you learn who you are despite them. They may keep you from it, they may make it almost impossible for you, they may be the biggest obstacle, but you can free yourself from them."

"Unless . . ." Cory bent his head. He opened his palms. He appeared to be studying the lines in his hands. ". . . you don't want to be free of them because you're who they are, and want to be. If I could be anybody in any other body just for a short time, I'd be my grandfather. I'd know then what went on in him, how he felt and thought. Though he can preach a sermon and tell a story or a joke, or ramble, he's silent, as if silence is some kind of retribution for whatever he's silent about."

"You don't think Tom's guilty of anything . . . serious?"

"Oh, I don't mean of a crime, but guilty, yes. I think Gramp feels that. I think some people are guilty just because of what they are; and if you have some kind of faith—he has—then you feel you're punished because you've betrayed something *in* you that you discover only the instant you betrayed it or the instant you feel you're punished and discover what made you do it."

"His hands?"

"Hands, yes. They're his hell—he'll always see them. Hell might be the visible invisible, like Macbeth's dagger. Maybe that's what hell is, that even knowing you're being punished or punishing yourself, you'd be loyal to what's inside you no matter what it led you to, what you didn't want or wouldn't have chosen for yourself, because it's made you *you*."

"But how it's Tom's hell isn't clear to me."

"It's not clear to me except that I know my mother feels it too. She's as silent as he is. They even get the same distant absorbed look when I mention some things—Gram, his divorce, and Ma's, and Reggie Webb and Ben and . . ."

Cory's voice scraped, he turned his head, but met sea, and turned away.

" . . . Rod," he said.

Fatso would not interrupt that invisible sight.

Cory, glimpsing some blue yarn probed by knitting needles jammed over the books on a shelf, said, "I didn't know you knitted."

"Lap rugs. For servicemen. Lots of men in town knitted for the

Red Cross. I dropped that one on V-J Day; it's been collecting dust ever since. It would have been a coincidence if you'd gotten one of my rugs over there!"

"Might have, too, if I'd been wounded . . ."

"Lucky you weren't."

"Sometimes it's saved for later. You wonder—you can't help it—what you did . . ."

"You didn't do anything, Cory."

"If it weren't for me, Rod would be here now."

"You don't know that."

"But I do."

"You mean you could have avoided it?"

"No, that's just what I don't mean. It's just what my mother and Gramp wouldn't mean. They feel guilty too because something in them they *know* caused it. They'll never get over it because they can't undo what they themselves did. They can see farther back than I can; they've lived it, they know time. Sometimes the effects come about slowly through generations."

"Everybody would be guilty then, and everybody doesn't feel such guilt for what he does."

"That doesn't mean they're not."

"Do you want to be guilty, the three of you?"

"It's not want. We can't help it. It's what we are. Ma and Gramp are responsible, Fatso. It's that—they accept their responsibility, the guilt; that's made them better. That's why, when it goes on, when Gramp sees it happen to her, and they both see it happen to me, it seems to be piling up on them. I don't know how they bear it all when I . . . Sometimes I think it would be easier if I'd gone down with *him* than living it over and over."

Cory's voice was thin. His breath clutched. He said no more. Now Cory raised his head and did gaze unflinching toward the bay. The electric light cut off any vision of out there. Fatso stared at Cory. He wanted to comfort, but that would be weak. Let Cory bear. It would make him strong. Didn't they all have to bear?

Cory's visit was the year's highlight. He came to measure time by the weeks, then months since Cory's visit. He looked on Cory, young as he was, as his master, almost his cause. He loved Cory as Cory, but it was a conscious love, he told himself, objective now, and so was no longer a real love because it was tinged with the superiority of the pupil who had begun to outgrow his master. The detachment had led to a certain depreciation; he could not say scorn because he respected Cory for his deep feeling, but was sometimes appalled at how far he himself had grown away from such feeling—more because he associated it with his feeling for Joey than because he shared Cory's and because he knew he could not share with Cory that feeling for anybody else except Tom. He felt nothing for the others in town. Each year, living out of town, like that kingfisher nested on its piling at the edge of the dump, he grew more distant. He knew more about them. He observed, listened, and recorded, hoarding every detail of their lives simply because it was *now, his, this*. Since the first green and the first hopping toad he'd ever touched, he'd had an obsession with how each thing moved, what moved it, how everything moved together. He did not like people, and he did not actively dislike them, but looked on them with distance—interested but no longer involved, wanting to know what they did, why. When one of them no longer appeared on the streets, he—who moved about the town on foot, regular, relentless—was the first to notice that some change, imbalance, had occurred in his world.

He hunted for details about each event, and listened. His head hoarded, but not as history. He did not believe in history; it told him nothing about the instantaneous happening. He no longer spotted Jimmie-the-Whisper's white handkerchief downtown—Jimmie had died. The youngest Sprague girl had fallen drunk off Claudio's dock. The oldest Warren brother, Johnny, had somehow hit his head while scalloping and drowned. His mother's neighbors moved to Riverhead because of *the niggers*: "Yeah," Rosie Blanchard said, "we got to move—you imagine that?—because my girl's twelve now and tall and pretty, and developed, and they're after her, and we're afraid she'll get caught by some nigger because already two of the nigger girls beat her up because she wouldn't date the nigger they fixed her up with, nor no nigger." The circumstances of each death, change, disappearance, move, he tracked down, traced. Greeks began to rent and move in colonies from the city. The barracks for the Puerto Ricans imported as cheap labor to pick potatoes were torn down. Two new motels went up on the Sound shore. New houses changed the landscape of Sandy Beach, and he noted each new resident. On Front Street a fire burned out Mitchell's Restaurant, leaving a gap opening on the harbor as prominent as a missing front tooth in anybody's mouth. He missed the frequent train whistles—the Long Island Railroad cut its services, and the train now halted on the railroad dock extended over the harbor, reflected like a dark snake shimmering in the water below. They tore down the Wyandank Hotel and remodeled the Stirlington next door to it.

Town.

For him town moved, breathed, a body, as his breathed and moved within it, with it; though he could not say what organ he was, how he functioned in it. He pondered that, sitting sometimes at the edge of Gull Pond, between the bay and his cottage, as he used to sit at the edge of the pond between the dump and the stretch of sand to the Sound. Mine, he thought. But *what* was his? He did not yet know, but he waited, watched. He was sure he would know. Or what was this all about?

Two or three nights that summer he was tempted by the July evening lecture series at the Methodist.

The sign read

What On EARTH Is God Doing?

Find out here every Thursday. 7:30 PM

He told Tom with something of a guffaw, and Tom said, "It won't do to put down God, Fatso."

Winter was always so still and silent here, death, except for chickadees sudden on the snow and the cry of gulls soaring, and waves so constant that, whether heaving or only a hush hush, the rhythm negated their sound until sometimes when he sat long, his whole body absorbed in listening, he was moving with it. He felt he was walking into the silence, an infinite terrain he had not known existed, his feet probing cautiously, daring to inch into that unknown dark that was *filled*. He could hear, sense, presences. He desired to *see*, but he was afraid. Foot would not move, yet blood went, urging his foot forward. Mesmerized he moved, wanting to move, yet blind, all his body blind to what was as close as skin, breath, hands, eyes, till a ship hooting in the harbor or the town whistle shrieking the hour startled him out of his spell. Jarred, he was furious. Displaced, he wanted to return, wanted to see what his feet and fingers would touch, where they would lead him.

> *Cory, I begin to understand something of the murderer Macbeth. He walks an invisible terrain* no man ever walked before. *Every murderer enters the invisible* for the first time. *If a dagger materializes, what things* within touch *fill the air, waiting to appear? With each step what unknown ground does each step touch—quicksand, burning stone, mud, swamp? He enters the invisible country. Desire leads him in, but once inside there's no turning back. Desire turns to fear, but despite fear* he must *know.*

Music helped him imagine the invisible. It lured, led to new terrains, roused feeling which evoked visible worlds.

Miss Kellogg had retired and though Joey still practiced at school, "because he's progressing by leaps and bounds, I've been giving him more time here at home."

At first, when Fatso's free time occasionally coincided with Joey's lesson and he stopped by for him, Miss Kellogg would invite him in for a few minutes; and on rare occasions, when he listened to her brief discussions of technique with Joey, she would illustrate passages, repeating, having Joey try, repeat, repeat, repeat. She would sometimes go on afterwards, play, rapt; and as if she couldn't stop, as if it were sacrilege to leave the piece in the middle, she would play to the end. Always a moment of silence would follow. Nobody moved, sensing she "must return"; and then, depending on the mood of the piece, she would stare or raise her brows cryptically or smile or even throw her head back and laugh girlishly, her hand gracefully touching her throat. "I can tell by your face you were with me this time," she now and then said to Fatso, leaving him wordless; but quick warm prickles ran over his flesh and sometimes tiny white dots shot across his vision like blown milkweed.

At home he dared the mirror.

He marveled at what could not be discovered in a face.

Fatso told Tom, "You wouldn't believe how fast Joey's learning. Miss Kellogg says he'll really do something if he keeps it up."

"If he's got some of your get-up-and-go, that'd be no surprise to me."

"He may end up a name pianist, but he'll have to go off to some fine school like Juilliard or find some great teacher to train him. We could do that."

"You could?"

"There's time yet, Tom."

"It's no easy row to hoe, music. Nothing is, if you want to be the best."

The best.

"What's the best, Tom?"

Tom squinted. Silent, he lit a Marvel and puffed. It was early in the month so he was not rolling his own cigarettes in the little metal contraption Rod had given him. He ran his bony hand down Pal's back.

"He's the best."

"Pal!"

"You surprised? Why would you be? Pal gives deep feelings nobody's ever really explained the source of. He's so near it, he is it. The men who reveal that must come closest."

"The Beethovens and Leonardos."

"Well, whoever comes closest to stirring the deepest feelings, because they can't be said. Even Jesus couldn't say them, and—" Tom smiled. "—he wasn't so bad."

Fatso chortled.

"He had to speak in parables. But his death was the thing that truly spoke. The nearer you get to the thing they're all trying to say, the nearer you get to the best. I'll take Pal. Some people are born with something more than the rest of us have. Jesus wasn't the only one."

"More what?"

"*There* you go! You can't say it. People of all kinds have tried. Think of how many are willing to give even their lives before sacrificing what's in the works of the world's great men. They know such men and women had more."

"More what?"

"There you are! You want to say it too. Just try."

"But there are millions of men—and dogs!" Fatso laughed. "Do they all have what Pal has?"

Tom laughed too. "Maybe more dogs do than people, but just because they're not known, don't think they don't have it. We don't like to think greatness is ordinary, but it is."

"Joey's special."

"Maybe. But don't wish too much on him. We don't know where it will lead."

"But if it's good?"

"Depends on what he does with it. Just keep your fingers crossed. If Joey's got enough of it . . . A man might become a little Schweitzer or a little Hitler. Who knows?"

Who knows?

"You have what you have, Fatso. Don't question it. Use it."

What you have.

At home Fatso dared the mirror again. You shaved, washed everyday, yes, but did not look, study, ponder. Now he stared. Mine. My life. He didn't think now *Something gave me this* or *Why me?* He thought merely *Mine*. What it concealed? He was responsible because it was his. Nothing made him responsible. He simply existed. His mouth was. His teeth were. His weakness. A weakness to *them*. But *not* to him. Not now, no. His strength, yes. You made your weakness your strength, whether they knew or not. You did something of worth with it because it was what distinguished you from them. *Yes*, he was marked. For what? *They* couldn't know, but he would use his mark and they would see his mark, see *it*, whatever it was, in Joey. It would be through him, because of *teeth*, that it would come. His teeth would be no source of marvel to them, never, only to him alone; yet what came through his efforts because of his very teeth *would* be of wonder to them, yes. So he could exult in secret, without their knowing or caring, and enjoy the fruit of his efforts. Yes, his defect was his strength.

Don't talk to me of divine justice, Cory, or of human justice with its law and the spirit of the law, or of moral justice. Let me be personal. The genes are a chaotic jungle—in this sense: who knows in which of a predicted number of us the combination will be fluky, which not? So my combination falls on one side, Joey's on the other—within the prediction, each is an accident—one might have been the other. I might have been Joey, and Joey me. But I'm me, and I accepted what I look like. What choice do I have? Sometimes I take a pride in my uniqueness. My uniqueness has made me accept what I am, what's in *me. I've sworn to be loyal to what's in me. It's the only thing I can fully know. So there's a justice that's born of the self, and that's the justice of being loyal to the purest thing in you, and the way is to use what's in you to make something meaningful for the world and you won't be wasted.* I won't *be wasted. That's a justice of the self. For the first time I understand—do you?—why you said that if Macbeth were just the object of a Sunday school lesson in Christian morality, we wouldn't be interested in him at all. And you're right. What's sublime—yes, sublime—about Macbeth is the incredible* purity *of his loyalty to what's in him. It's awesome, It's staggering. It has finally nothing to do with good or evil, but the very composition of everything. As much as he violated men's values, and though he lamented the loss of what men set such sacred value on, he would not demean that ultimate purity.*

If he didn't succeed with Joey—he broke into sweat at the thought—then what was his life for?

Still, wouldn't he have converted—he was already converting—his anguish, fury, hate, his defect, *prognathia,* into a sense of justice? What good was a sense of justice if it produced nothing of worth? If he didn't, wouldn't he have failed?

One Friday afternoon when the days had just begun to turn warm, after work, when he rounded the house to the yard, *she* was sitting on the back stoop.

"Hey!"

Diane!

That throaty chafe! His legs trembled. He couldn't force them still. Her voice threw up memory, nights of memory of the only body he had ever known. She was small, fragile still. There was the familiar long girlish fall of hair. Her elbows rested on knees delicately pressed together. Her chin rested casually on her hands.

"Cat got your throat as usual?"

He nodded. He couldn't figure, but he had to.

"Just out for the night. We got us a room, me and a girlfriend. She wants to get away from Jersey City. Can't stand the niggers, to tell the truth, though she's retarded finding it out. So I was thinking maybe Pam—"

"She's gone. They all have. Everything torn down."

"So I found out. That old eyesore. Well, I see you got yourself all set up. Wasn't hard to find you. It's still easy to find things here—that's a change from out Jersey way. You sure have changed into a man. In a way you always were—" She laughed, throaty; all his flesh quivered with it. "—only now you really look like one."

She stood, so thin that she looked tall and fragile with the wind pressing soft against her till the thin white cloth was a skin.

"You need a housekeeper?"

His blood bolted.

"Or maybe a fly-by-night or . . . day?"

Suddenly she embodied all that time during which he had never known another woman, never dared know. She was nights and days, years, of masturbating with his eyes closed and her filling them. If she knew . . . He felt so weak the wind would sway him.

She walked over to him and scrutinized, long.

"Yes, different. Still cold-looking but ready to . . . explode. You always were. That drives a woman mad, you know that?"

Close, he saw the years in her face, more so because she had coated it so heavily.

He saw her sordid now.

But his memory was afraid of her hands.

Her gaze was creating a familiar, fearful scene. His shed might have been her shack.

"You could invite me in."

Her hands moved and moved, restless. If she touched—

He swung away, took his keys out and unlocked the shed, and took out his edger to neaten the lawn.

"You won't?"

He faced her across the lawn, wondering if she too were thinking it could have been that shed at the dump.

"I've got responsibilities."

With feigned concentration he began to trim the lawn.

After a long silence she said, "So I see."

She did not ask what responsibilities.

"My girlfriend will be wondering," she said.

He worked vigorously, his mind fogged with fear of what she could say, what he could do.

She did not approach, but turned. He saw the white flutter cross the back lawn to the side of the house near the road back to town and halt.

"I'm really glad to know you're . . ." She smiled sadly and turned away before she finished.

Her words wrenched. He felt sorry for her. He had a moment of regret. He felt weak. But what really weakened him was relief, the relief of her going; and in the wake of that relief, for some fifteen minutes or so he worked frenziedly, halting abruptly, feeling a surge that was almost dizzying because he thought *You don't know how suddenly an obstacle can come. You could kill to get rid of it. You could. You could kill and not even know you were doing it.* With all his energy he jabbed the edger into the ground, resisting *her*; but once inside, before time for bed, he could no longer, no longer. He lay down and closed his eyes and touched her till his hand made him moan.

A disease invaded the scallop beds. All along the North Fork the fishermen, the women and children who opened scallops, and even vacationers who dug for a basketful, were disgruntled. Everywhere—crick, docks, waterfront, bars, the Legion—the men bitched: next would be skimmers, oysters, mussels, then fish. Pollution. Wasn't there already a ban on swordfish because of radioactivity? There had been several outbreaks of botulism and certain national brands of frozen fish had to be withdrawn from the markets, so the fish factory clamped down doubly on regulations and precision in inspections. Prices on bay scallops went soaring. Scallopers had no alternative but to turn to fishing.

The disease cut out a small but steady income for Fatso. Though he could not know whether Joey would pursue the piano as a career, he had worried about Joey's hands. Opening shellfish endangered them, and the disease, as undesired as it was, at least freed him from worry about Joey's fingers. He also worried about his playing sports; however, he had learned from Ma, whose lashing tongue wrecked her relationships, to hold his tongue rather than alienate Joey and, whenever he could, to veer him into another interest. He would never try to cut him off from sports because he was an ace; the teams counted on him. More, he was liked by young and old, popular.

It would never be *Joey's brother Fatso*, no.

It was *Fatso's brother Joey*.

Fatso exulted.

When, after two years of intensive practice, Miss Kellogg told Fatso, "I want Joey to take part in my students' annual recital. He's made exceptional advancement. The recital's grown too big for my parlor, so I've moved it to the school, and this year for the first time I've opened it to more than parents and friends. Though I tell you because you pay for his lessons, I'll want his mother's permission. I'll reserve rows for special guests. Is there anyone you want on the invitation list?"

There was a pummeling in his head.

"Santiago?"

Tom. Though he could hardly see, and said he was *deef*, he'd hear music and revel in Joey.

Cory. Though he was at Wisconsin.

"Mr. Verity," he said.

For the presentation night Miss Kellogg had mimeographed programs, and it startled Fatso to read José María García. For the first time his brother was an entity apart, *out there*. From that moment, all evening, though he stayed in the hall and did not enter and sit in the last row until Marcie Renwood finished her piece, he saw his brother at some distance, as if through a window, framed. He felt strangely divorced. The thought frightened: Would it *remain* that way? When José María García began to play, he watched the hands and fingers, detached, but with fascination, more fascinated because he was so *aware* that he was watching those fingers so intently that he could not listen, did not hear, could not succumb to any sound because his nervous blood with its own music of fear and pride was *competing* as he watched the image of his own body seated there, his own fingers producing an interminable throbbing note by note—

Applause abruptly interrupted the sound of his blood-beat. He rose with Joey. Though he was behind the audience, he felt *pinned* to the wall in front of them, felt they were all staring at him; yet at the same time such a confusion of pride and self-consciousness came over him, *Joey-me*, that he bolted up and hurried outside. He was sweating. Feeling the fresh air, he laughed, laughed loud. Afterward he thought, *I didn't hear a note, nothing. What will I tell Joey?*

So persistently was Joey on his mind that one afternoon when he was standing on the sidewalk outside Lawyer Price's on Front Street, he looked up and saw himself in the pane; saw the buildings across the street and bits of the docks and harbor and Shelter Island and high clouds and the sky; *saw* them but was gazing through them; and something ghostly and evanescent and temporary in the reflection made him decide to go in on the spot.

"I want to make my will."

Old Price smiled.

"You're pretty young. Are you planning on dying anytime soon?"

"Right now I'm not planning on anything but my will."

He saw Mr. Price did not miss the innuendo.

"I want to leave everything to my youngest brother."

"Joey?"

"Yes. José María García."

"All?"

"Yes. My house is all. He's already beneficiary to my savings account in the Riverhead Bank."

"Since he's so young, you'll have to have an executor, in case you die before Joseph comes of age."

"Yes. That will be Cory Moorehead."

"Estelle Verity's boy? Which—?"

"There's only one now."

"Ah, of course. The other—"

"Drowned in the Gut. Rod. Rodney."

"The Veritys have had more than their share of bad luck."

"Yes."

"Do you want to make any provision for your brothers and sisters?"

"No."

"Your mother?

"If it's to keep it from . . . No. She wouldn't know what to do with it."

He felt the scrutiny.

"If that's your wish, fine."

Fatso jotted down his and his brother's full names and his address.

"Drop by the first of next week, and we'll have it ready for you to sign."

Now night after night spring pulsed and broke earth. Green-gold leaves burst through bark, stems, twigs. The tiny modest blue and white and yellow crocuses inched up everywhere. The soft lavender myrtle spread in the dark green beds in the cemetery. Forsythia leaped in still yellow fountains. Daffodils blazed their silent cries and gave way to deep purple iris, which filled the swamps. And in the yards peonies began to burgeon in great balls ready to break open. Honeysuckle and morning glories climbed. Spring. It called blood. Always the dump called. He never forgot. He never resisted, never could. He would not go up Third past Ma's. From Main he turned right on Webb and went straight to the dump entrance at the dead end. The sight of the familiar black arch over its entrance roused such nostalgia that it brought quick tears to his eyes. Home. It had been that, more home than Ma's. It was where he had learned. It was, it would always be, his private physical and spiritual terrain.

The dump was a wild now; the new keeper did only his duty. Fatso made his way through deeps of weeds, shrubs, bushes, and young saplings that cut off a sight of the pond and the Sound. Huey's shack was still there, weathered more foggy gray than ever, its windows broken, holes battered into the sides, the door lying loose beside it. The woods beyond had grown so thick they walled off Third Street. The warm dry air was thick with new perfume. He stood in growth waist high, listening. Soon the familiar sounds came—the near rustles, the fine whir of a hummingbird's wings, falls of dirt, rats . . . He moved through the shrubs down to the edge of the pond. The lilies were opening and everywhere the wild roses were laden with buds. . . . He heard flies then, and bluebottles, the finest hum and vibration of insect wings, little breaks of bubbles from underwater, the suck of lily pads when the surface scud moved, and tiny water bugs exploring the leaves. Frogs plopped, only their bulging eyes staring up out of the water, and along the dry edge the toads poised still as clumps of earth. Near him a garter snake raised its slick little head. . . . Untended, primitive, the dump was an infinitely beautiful body with the wind off the sea moving the tall grasses along the edge in long slow sways, whisking a great breath from it.

That hand. That body.

He did not fool himself. *She.* Diane too had driven him to the dump. He suspected she had not gone. He was afraid of her. He had to be sure she was not *here*, waiting. He was afraid of what was in her, and in him. Because passion was always there. What was it? It waited. It grew. One thing listening had taught him: silence had sound, stillness moved. He had heard the sound. He could hear it moving. He knew nothing was still, ever. He was sure that the black still silent Nothing before the universe could *not* have been still, *not* silent. Something had been moving, seething with its own chaotic sound till it *burst* into forms. He thought how everything grows and bursts like that—sex, fury, a birth, flower, fruit, a thought. Something in Diane could rouse his body, and something in Cory his mind—the same seething but in such different directions. Insistent, it could overcome. He was afraid of that motion, but *more* he wanted to *know* it; and he never wanted to know it more than when he went out to the end of the breakwater just beyond his house. He would sit on those rocks between Gull Pond and the harbor, feeling wind, listening to waves and wind and gulls' cries till nothing existed but the cry itself, the same cries he had heard all his life, a sound moving through millions of years. Gulls died but nothing could kill the cries that tore through them all.

No, Diane was not at the dump, and not in town, though he caught glimpses—hair, skirt, arm. Hers? He had to resist. He had a strong will, didn't he? He had to have, for Joey.

But desire kept imagining.

One Saturday afternoon in June he was headed up Moore's Lane to the back road to secure a mowing job. The carnival brought to the old polo grounds for the annual firemen's benefit looked like a great shapeless creature which people were exploring. He was going past the trailers, set along the road, where the troupe lived; and through a line of hanging laundry he saw her legs, saw the frail thing saunter up the three steps and into the trailer, saw her raise her hands and flick her hair and throw her head back and laugh, talking to someone he could not see. His temples were throbbing, but he dared to step between the sheets to spy. Someone inside must have seen him and said something because at once she turned and looked directly at him—*not* Diane—and he saw the woman's horrified look. Her hands clamped her mouth, fortunately stifling a cry. He retreated fast, scurrying to the woods behind, ducking in and following the path cut by auto tires toward the road back to town.

The experience jolted him. He was so used to his virtual hermit's existence after work hours, reading and listening to music; and it had been so long since he had directly confronted a stranger that he had forgotten how used to him town had grown, indifferent.

Reliving that moment, *I was too startled*, he thought, *I'm not sure it wasn't Diane.*

After, he left the house only when he had to.

But the terror excited, made him masturbate.

He saw Tom, but he did not complain to Tom that Cory had dropped him. For some time the books had stopped coming. At first he was disappointed since copies of the syllabuses from Cory's courses no longer came. Besides, his supply of books, almost all not available from the town library, diminished; and he thought of nights without books of substance, without the guidance of Cory's courses, long nights, nights which were images of the dark gaps in his own mind which he should fill with knowledge. His mind, hungry, raced. As he considered the few books he had not yet touched—Ortega's *The Dehumanization of Art* and *The Rebellion of the Masses;* a collection of essays on evolution; Newman's autobiography; and the Kierkegaard—he became irritated with Cory. He festered, resented. It was not right of Cory to abandon what he had long ago begun. He needed him. *He* was not ready yet. But then, of *course* he didn't need him, he *was* ready, soon he could work on his own courses by mail, he could go on to . . .

Where was he going?

He would strike the desk, wall, sink—

Damn you, Cory Moorehead!

Though Cory seldom, almost never answered now, he wrote—had to—to Cory. As long as he was writing Cory, he was maintaining the dialogue; he was keeping Cory *alive* for himself. If he didn't, who would hear him?

Who would know he existed?

Tom he could count on for moral support—he was the impervious rock—and on Miss Kellogg for an intuited understanding. From the moment years before when she perceived his surrender to music and saw he was as careful with things as he was with Joey, she lent him records. Sometimes when he returned them she asked his reactions, but his humility before something in her restrained him from elaborating; yet he would go directly home and answer her questions in a clear reply in letters to Cory as if the writing were still necessary before refining his opinions in conversation. During the last year she had introduced him to all she had of Bach. She talked of the Bach he returned, sometimes almost as if he were not there. Was she still teaching an invisible class? She talked about the so-called almost mathematic precision with which, critics said, Bach pursued perfection in sound, in forms structured with relentless *reason.*

> *And Bach. Of the composers I know he was nearest to madness. Admirers talk about his supreme control, his reason, his perfect structures. Control! Reason! He must have been near mad with emotion; otherwise, how could he have had such a passion for reason? Obsessive reason can lead to insanity. Bach's reason had to work against itself* every instant of his life *to channel his passion into perfect forms or he would have* become that raw emotion. *By transforming his excesses into beauty he saved himself from insanity.*

Form contains the madness within and holds back the madness without. Form gives shape to madness because; as long as it has form it is not madness.

Summer weekends, to make up for what he lost because of the diseased scallop beds, up before dawn, he went crabbing—good money, with softshells always at a premium—or hauled up and emptied lobster pots for old Holt; sometimes went out with local bass fishermen, but never with strangers. He had never gone out on skimmer boats like the *Ida K* or the *Annie B*—the Polacks from Easy Street were permanent crew, for one reason—but he doubled up on his three-week vacation pay by taking up a challenge from Ferris, the ace college football player who still found his reputation in a bottle, a good worker when anybody gave him work. "I'll go if you go, Fatso." Big Ted the Polack guffawed. "Shit, Fatso couldn't do nothin'. He ain't used to real work." Fatso wanted the money, but Ted's challenge furied him. Real work! "I'm ready when you are, Ferris." And he was—on time, fast, efficient. "The kid's all eyes and moves faster than his eyes see," the Captain said. Ferris, master worker himself, was philosophic: "Shit! Just wait a few days!" But Fatso wouldn't flag, though when they dredged, hauled up the skimmers, working on the metal side panels with no rails and the ship heaving in the sea with full nets, it took all his strength, fortified by will and pride, to maintain himself just above the breaking point though he knew he could not have if they weren't so well-trained, experts all of them. As a good worker he admired that in them, despite a certain scorn mixed with pity because they not only insisted on not thinking but on cultivating, and with pride, the animal. So, long before it was over, he knew he wouldn't go to sea again. What awed him was how they *enjoyed*, and what: "a good catnap," "a short snooze," "a mouthful of grub," "nothing like a good healthy shit unless it's some good pussy," "a piss over the side," "you can't beat this air." The world ended there. He understood that, but had he lost the capacity to enjoy it all? Would he have lost it if he had stayed in the dump all his life. Or if no Cory? He thought, *My father*. Day after day, years, his father had lived this. The son was doing what the stranger who came to Third Street between hauls had done. He could be his father. He was sitting here in his father's form. *In my father's house* echoed. *Tom*. But this skin was *not* his father's house, no. This skin stifled. Something in him wanted to break out of this straightjacket. He couldn't contain himself. At work it was only Ferris who, if he couldn't perceive the pity Fatso felt for their limited lives, sensed a certain fellow disdain in him for the others and baited him: "You ever read any psychology, Fatso?" or "You know, I did this experiment at the U with a bunch of students on timed eye movements to measure differences in emotional reactions. You know about that, don't you, Fatso?" But Fatso didn't have to respond. Ferris preened with trite factual tidbits. "Timed eye movements, sure," Ted knocked. But Ferris was speaking to Fatso. He was speaking with growing resentment, louder, groping for his lost pride, his one far-off moment of victory gone sour and rationalized. "Can it, Ferris," Ted said. "So who's talking to you, Ted!" Fatso silently accepted the unconscious tribute Ferris made him by singling him out *intellectually*. "Shit, you never went to college, Ferris. What do you know?" Ted said, eyeing Fatso with a subdued smirk. Under attack, Ferris bent closer to Fatso's face. He spat words. "You got to read, you got to know, Ted. Ain't that right, Fatso? Fatso reads. Don't you, Fatso?" Fatso stood, brushed himself off, and said, "Say, Ted, we were going to scrape the rust off that old chain." "That old chain, that old chain," Ferris said. "You want to work on that old chain, do you, Fatso?" Silent, Fatso headed for the heavy chains coiled on the stern deck, crossed some nets which the crew had untangled and laid out on deck, when suddenly the ship seemed to leave him, he was floundering in air in a strange sweep off the deck, over the water. His arms jerked to his sides; he struck the water and sank. He thrust his arms out; they met rope—net!—and again and again he tried to kick, tread water, but his arms and legs met rope, heavy, too heavy; it weighed, pulled him down, down— Suddenly with a violent jolt it evened out. He was suspended underwater. He struggled furiously, but the wet rope was too heavy, his clothes heavy; he tore at the rope, at his clothes till he was almost without breath. *Be still, be still,* he told himself—and he did *not* move. He lay cradled in rope, hanging from the ship, holding his breath, not to burst. He could see the light and the black hull. He was sure he could touch it. *I can't hold my breath any longer*. His body beat. A sound battered like hands in his chest, head, stomach—

He could hold his breath no longer. His mouth would break.

Then his body moved. He was hauled up. Water broke, light blinded, his lungs made a great cry and he gulped air, sucked, gulped.

He was swung over the deck and lowered.

"Jeez, where'd you think you was going, Fatso?" Mick said.

He lay a long time coming back after Mick and Ferris and Rolfe freed him from the net.

"How many times you been told you never step into a net, man?" Ferris shook his head.

"It was hanging from the winch," Fatso said.

"You never know about those winches," Ted said.

"I could have drowned," Fatso said.

"You could have." Ted stared, unperturbed.

In his bunk, deep in night, Fatso felt himself sink, sinking. He couldn't move. He couldn't cry out, but his blood drove like fingers violent against his flesh, split his flesh, broke through his stomach, chest, groin, reaching— He woke. He was wet with sweat. Now his fall over the side, underwater, came to mind, and the battering in him. Was he trying to get out of his own body?

Then Ted's stare came to him. It lingered, that deliberate stare. He had carried it down into sleep, yes. Ted kill him? No. Ted was mean, but wouldn't kill—in a fight maybe, but not that way. He was no coward. Besides, Ted hadn't done it against him, Fatso. No. Ted's constant antagonism with Ferris made him use him, Fatso, to put Ferris in his place yet at the same time side with Ferris against him. Fatso knew. Ferris and Ted needed each other, but they didn't know that.

He wouldn't go out on the *Ida K* again. The experience confirmed that he was a landlubber, town and the near waters were his terrain; the closer he clung the more deeply he loved this place. Yet he couldn't shake the experience. Perversely, he was grateful to Big Ted for his treachery because the net had taken him down to the very edge of breath. In that moment when his body was still and silent as death he *felt* the sound struggling like an alien thing trying to escape his body, and he could not forget the sensation.

"Like hearing a voice when you can't make out the words," he told Tom.

Tom squinted. "You're not hearing voices?"

"Only when they're really there, like Abraham's."

Tom scrutinized his bowl. There were always dregs because he'd add tea to tea till daughter had a fit and washed his bowl.

"Abraham. You know Abraham?"

"We read it together, Tom!"

Fatso had little else on his mind. He had just read in *Fear and Trembling* Kierkegaard's version of how God appeared to Abraham and told him to kill his son, Isaac. It had shaken him. It had left him not only filled with fear of himself, and trembling, but elated—with the same excitement the *sound* had stimulated in him.

"So we did. I forget."

"You don't believe God really spoke to him and told him to kill his son, Isaac, as a sacrifice to Him?"

"You're hard, Fatso, hard as God in the story! Well, Abraham believed it was God speaking, didn't he? I for one don't doubt that in his head he did hear God, and some impulse, maybe to prove his own faith, to test how far he could go, to find out if there *was* anything, must have made him command himself to kill Isaac, so when the ram appeared—it maybe wandered in from the hills—in his frame of mind he read it as a sign and took it for the answer to his faith, maybe even thought it was his son. So he slaughtered the ram instead. And who knows if that wasn't the answer? His faith answered him, didn't it?"

"No."

Tom cocked his head.

"How come?"

"Abraham should have killed his son."

This time Tom stared, his eyes wide. They did not quiver.

"You mean that?"

"*Then* he'd have known."

"Known what?"

"What's in him."

"*In* him?"

"Yes."

"But what?"

"He'll never know. He turned his back on the terrible moment. He betrayed his true impulse to find out."

"You're on dangerous ground, boy. Some days the mind's the worst enemy. A man needs little things to occupy him or he's in trouble. Work's the thing. And some pleasure so's your mind won't dwell on such thoughts too long."

"There's always you to keep me from falling, Tom."

"Not with these hands I couldn't."

"It's your heart'll hold me back, Tom."

"Humpf!" Tom grunted. "Not this one. Not this old brain either. Depend on your own."

Fatso was on dangerous ground. He was trembling with it. Something was always wrestling with you—in silence, in secret, sometimes in open struggle. *Underwater*. It haunted.

Kierkegaard thrilled him because like him Kierkegaard couldn't understand why Abraham would obey God. Kierkegaard could go only so far with Abraham, and Kierkegaard was afraid. Like him, Kierkegaard wrote to try to understand. Like him, Kierkegaard began again and again, each time getting closer to saying what he meant. But Kierkegaard could only do it by pretending he was someone else, pretending he was someone named John speaking out of the silence—to keep his distance, maybe to keep himself from going mad.

Who would kill because God said to?

If Abraham told his people that God had commanded him to kill his son, they would say he was crazy, they would say he was a murderer.

So Abraham could not speak. He was alone with the silence.

Underwater Fatso had *heard.*

"Tom, *you* don't think Abraham was crazy, do you?"

"Heavens, no! He was listening to the voice. A man hears his voices but wants to obey the right one. You don't want to make a mistake. Sometimes you confuse voices and don't know that till it's too late."

"Did you ever hear them, Tom?"

Tom clamped his knees together, to keep the cat, the Persian, from sinking, and ran a hand down her back. She tilted her head back, eyes closed, expectant.

Tom was still a long time before he said, "I expect so. I suppose when most people hear voices . . . memory's talking to them, or conscience is."

"Did they confuse you?"

Fatso was thinking *hands.*

"When you have your mind on the most important thing in the world to you, you don't think you're confused, and you may not be. Who can say what the most important thing can blind you to? It may cost you—forever."

Cory had said *a fire at sea*, but Tom had never talked about the accident. What was Tom listening to when it happened? Fatso couldn't ask.

Tom said, "Nobody in the world knows what you hear. Abraham heard God. Even if nobody believed it, *he* knew he heard Him. He was the only one in his world who heard Him."

The only one in his world.

That stunned.

"Why would Abraham be the only one in the world who heard Him?"

Tom said, "He believed that. Lots of people claim they hear Him, but He doesn't command them to kill their sons. That's the difference."

"Why Abraham, then?"

Tom chortled. "You'll have to ask God, Fatso."

Fatso broke—he could not stop laughing.

Tom, startled a bit, said, "It may have been to prove what true good is, how pure faith is, a model good that can't be turned bad. Even if we never knew an Abraham, we'd want to believe there was a man filled with such faith, no matter what god we believed in, wouldn't we?"

"Unless you don't believe in any god?"

"Most men believe in something even if they can't name it. If a man spends his life searching, that's believing."

Am I a believer, then?

"Suppose he finds nothing."

"There's no such thing," Tom said.

No such thing.

Fatso's torment did not let up. Abraham. And that God. He felt an agony for Abraham—because why would God test Abraham by demanding he sacrifice his son to God? Why torment him, even if Abraham didn't take God's demand as torment? Was He testing *Himself*? Did He *need* that? He must have, because Abraham did *not*, no, he didn't. Why would anybody think up such a demand? Don't we have to take enough as it is? And who was God anyway? Did men conceive of him out there so they'd be challenged to be more worthy than their own conception? He felt a fury. He thought of Tom's hands. And Tom's no: *I did it to myself.*

Abraham, he wrote Cory, *fascinated Kierkegaard because he didn't have enough faith to be Abraham. He said he didn't understand Abraham, but Kierkegaard's miracle was that, without knowing it, he revealed how tragic man's situation is. Cory, you remember drawing man as a circle, earth as a circle, and the universe as a circle? I can't forget that picture. You remember you said when a man commits a crime, say, he makes a hole in his dike—he makes a hole, an imbalance, in the wall of the universe—he lets chaos in? Well, Abraham was about to kill his son, but he didn't kill his son because God provided a ram or it happened by. But Kierkegaard, without even realizing it, shows how Abraham's faith kept Abraham from knowing what was beyond his God's walls. He took the ram on faith. His faith did not let him make a hole in the wall. If he had killed his son, he would have opened the wall, chaos would have poured in. He'd have had to face the chaos he released in himself and the world and the universe; but his God keeps him from knowing that chaos.*

Kierkegaard says that Abraham heard God but could not speak to anyone in the world about what God commanded because what God commanded him to do wasn't ethical and men would not accept murder, they would say he was insane. Kierkegaard says Abraham had an absolute relation with the absolute. *And Abraham did have such a relation when he had the impulse to kill his son, but what Kierkegaard did not say was that the absolute is not God, the absolute is beyond the limits of God, God is man's way of protecting himself from the conception of the wonderful/terrible absolute.*

An absolute relation with the absolute.

Before that thought Fatso was like a victim hypnotized by a snake.

To stand alone with the absolute. To be silent because nobody would believe or understand or accept.

Few men dared *choose* the absolute. To know what it was cost everything, maybe life itself. He thought of Macbeth, Medea, Oedipus, Lord Jim. *They* dared to confront it, but they could not tell us what they saw. What was it? To show us, Shakespeare himself would have had to confront it; he could do it only through his characters—and even then he couldn't give us words for what it is. But he could take us to the edge.

It was in the silence. But it was there.

The silence had its own voices.

"Mostly mine—I guess they were voices—moved me to speak. Preach," Tom said. "That wasn't my work. I wasn't trained to preach. It came. I couldn't resist the call; it was too powerful. Words have always been too powerful. I was short on grammar, but the words came. They weren't perfect, but they came. It was what was behind them. Seems it runs in the family, wrestling with words to give what you've got. Cory's got it, quiet. It was a power in Rod, a personality people couldn't resist. Well, you know, of course."

Fatso remembered how fast Rod had once stood up against his own friends the niggers to defend him, his friend too, because Rod knew *fair.* The impulse was as natural to Rod as to Tom and Cory. That impulse seemed stronger in some than in others. Suppose Rod had fought that day—and killed. Conscious or unconscious, impulse could lead to good or bad. What was the thing inside him? He wanted to know, but he was afraid of it.

Diana's hands, her mouth, heat, sex had riled till a thing trapped inside him strived to escape.

Cory's words riled him till his trapped thoughts battered to break through.

What was in him subsided, but it waited.

It.

Now more and more he listened to Joey practice the piano. He halted at Miss Kellogg's, sat on the porch steps listening to her play. Easily now he surrendered to sound, sounds, because at times the movement was the ocean, waves—at the breakwater, on the Sound cliffs; at times the radio in his living room; at times the machines at the fish factory, regular, automatic, driven, and the conveyor belt moving, moving. He was certain that he heard in the rhythm of the music, the water, the machines, or pulsing crickets or wind the same sound moving.

Sometimes he would stand and watch the lopped fish heads fall one and one and one and one till each wet glittering vacant eye was the same eye, all one eye one vision. He would stand mesmerized by the constancy, the repetition, the rhythm: he might *see* the motion itself leave the lopped body, thinking *because vision must go on when it leaves the eye, because motion must go on when it leaves the body. Nothing can stop it. It's ours but not, because it's ahead of us even before it leaves us,* till the foreman broke the spell—

"Hey, Fatso, what gives?"

In his sleep now, eyes—a flow, endless.

Sometimes in day he couldn't stop the eyes.

More and more he stared at people's eyes, startled when one of the niggers wisecracked, only half kidding, "Shake your ass, man" or "Get with it!" or the boss came down the line and stood, hands on his hips, scrutinizing him.

Off the job he was making his old rounds. He was going over town, naming, naming as if he wanted to be sure he had not forgotten a street, block, house, family, person; back to the dump no more his charge, sitting in the deep grass, isolated from his old view of the whole dump, listening; back to the school not to listen to Joey's playing now, but to see floors and stairways, auditorium, corridors, classrooms, johns. He went down the docks, traipsed the harbor, the line of shore to East Marion and back along the Sound side and down Chapel Lane and back, encompassing the town.

He went back home more. He saw it actually *shook* his mother because he would sit in the kitchen with her, sit in almost absolute silence staring at her, listening to her talk because she *did* talk, not because she had always had an endless spew of words but because she was nervous with him. It was nervous talk as if she were trying to fathom this unfamiliar conduct. She was not used to such frequent and purposeless visits, not used to his sitting and staring at her. Yet she did not hurl words, swear, rage as she would have years ago, but talked almost to exhaustion, then offered him coffee and some fresh bread she'd made, strawberry jam she remembered he'd always liked. Her patience startled. For the first time he was aware that all the time he had been becoming himself she too had been changing. He saw she stole glances at him, evaded his, but gazed straight into him when he did speak—expectant, she seemed—and her hands could not rest. But patient she was. He was grateful, because he couldn't *say* why he had come. He was just here, his feet had brought him here, it was that simple. But each time he entered it was to the memory the sight of Ma on the floor with the baby and umbilical cord bloody and the floor bloody and Ma bloody, her hands. Only, his head was not fifteen now. He was seeing her from this time and with these older eyes. All his time here Ma made talk of his brothers and sisters and their kids and sometimes Pa and sometimes neighbors and gossip from town, which he heard and registered. Every word of that virtual monologue would come back to him when he went back to his house at Gull Pond. He would examine it for some clue to his unconscious reason for going home to Ma just as he examined his meanderings over town and the dump: because nothing of *then* returned, nothing of then told him, nothing of then revealed.

Is everything *now*?

He stared at the floor, where blood, where Ma's legs, the umbilical, where Ma's bloody hands . . .

Joey. His. His and Ma's.

He had cut Joey loose and tied the cord.

Something had escaped Ma—into Joey.

Is what's inside us always *ahead* of us, then?

Were we always on the edge of its coming and going?

He saw crabs and lobsters clawing in the bucket, struggling as if to hold onto *it;* saw the piles of shells, thousands and thousands, which Al and the gang at the skimmer factory had to open against the stubborn muscle, to flick the meat out; saw the oysters dredged from their habitats and hanging in the dredges before the life would be cut out of them; saw the wriggling fish, the lopped heads of fish and fish, eyes, eyes. He could lose himself for hours staring into a fresh water pond at the myriad movements of insects, plants, flowers, fish; gazing into the bay and the Sound, where the longer he looked the more rife the number of creatures moving, a razor clam opening, a horseshoe crab inching ahead, a swellbelly easing past, minnows, green and brown seaweed far under, and tiny colonies of bugs drifting on the surface . . . And when he passed the cemetery, when he dug a grave, he halted long, thinking of the ones he'd buried, *I knew them but only as long as* it was in them. He did not know *them* now because *it* was not in them.

It maddened that there was something in him he did not know.

That spring his manager gave two weeks notice.

Beside Fatso, Sears said, "You're the favorite, Fatso." All down the line and in packing and shipping, the word was Fatso. If some few begrudged the *freak*, some blacks *white*, even the diehards bore respect for his hard work, efficiency, maximum output, promptness (never a day's absence, never a minute late). With his hopes fed, Fatso began to believe he would be called into the office.

Max Robbins—no bad worker, a likable black, presentable—was called in and promoted.

Fatso didn't resent Robbins, who was friendly without condescension toward him.

He resented himself.

At home he tried to avoid the mirror, but the more he thought—it peeved—he went to it. This face. He scrutinized. For years now nothing had made him contemplate it with such scrutiny, as if all his dedication to thought—reading, digesting, writing, and writing to Cory—had made him unconscious of his teeth, had made him at times even forget them.

He could pass through that facade now. He knew there was a man under whom others did not know, had no inkling of, and would—Max's promotion showed—never know: because they saw only this face. He tried to forgive them that, he wanted to, he was sure he could. How could he blame anybody, even himself, for not knowing the man who lived behind any face?

Yet as the days went by, thought festered. The more he thought, especially when inadvertently glimpsing himself in a mirror, the more he festered. Then he resented the other workers. Why didn't they see his qualifications? Why didn't they know? It stands to reason that— But if he resented that they couldn't know a Fatso he knew, whom he now wanted them to know, more he resented not knowing the something that was *in* him. He resented the very desire to know because that desire was a worm eating into his brain, leaving hollows, slowly, relentlessly carrying his motion with it, breeding on his own life.

He was not promoted.

Teeth.

Frenzied, in the terrible hot damp, he worked in the yard. His hands tore at green. His fingers felt green move. It burgeoned strong. He wrenched at the power of weeds, clipped shrubs, hacked at stubborn volunteer mimosa and willows, yet all the time exulting at how his blood burgeoned too with each opening flower—orange, gold and red marigolds, a rage of peach and white gladiolas, bachelor buttons so blue. He worked till he near dropped, almost could not stand, too exhausted even to take a shower so fell on the bed. Next day, first thing in the morning, waking before sun, a quick bite and he was back out, hacking, hacking. This went on the entire weekend, into Monday morning before the fish factory, into afternoon after punching out—this rage to shape the yard, to control that raging green. When finally he lay down, he was momentarily content that that quiet violence, that lust of green and rainbow, was for a moment shaped *his* way, under his hands *held*, if only apparently still.

But he knew it wasn't still. It was never still. Even in winter it waited. It could tear. It could break. It gave no peace.

Only music gave peace. He filled the intervals with music, filled the house. His blood moved with music, became sound. He could lose himself, disappear in sound.

Did death come that way?

By the third day no music gave peace; nothing did but work. When he stopped, his blood bolted; his blood wanted to keep working; or thought rushed. He thought *promotion*, thought of the money *for Joey*, and thought *teeth*, thought *Who is this I am*? and *What do they see*? and thought *Diane*. She loomed ahead on the grass, in the kitchen, living room, bedroom, standing by the deep sea grass on the road to town! Thinking her, he could feel the *pum*-pum *pum*-pum drive of his excited blood as if it were turning directly against the regular regular easeful unheard rhythm of the flow his blood should be making. No talk could slow it. *Fatso, you just better calm down, sit still till it settles.* His *head* he couldn't keep from racing and *wanting.* All he wanted came, rose, crowded—Joey, Miss Kellogg, Tom, Cory, Ma, his brothers and sisters, Pa too, and Diane, and town, all town. He *wanted* to see, confirm, verify them; wanted them all; wanted in some way he had never known to *know* them and all at once. He couldn't. He could not contain them, not contain even the *idea* of them.

His blood wanted. His head.

He quit after dark, exhausted.

Exhausted, he lay down.

Words hung. He saw. They burned in the air:

An absolute relation with the absolute.

What way?

His heart thudded. He could not control his thunder. Could not bear.

What was struggling with him?

He put a record on, the first he touched. It began easy. He lay back. He didn't want to think, willed *not* to; but thought *What have you done to yourself*? thought *You, Cory*! But a few notes told Polovtsian Dances. Borodin. Danced. And danced. The Polovtsian maddened.

No more. Stop.

He flipped the needle back, seized the record and smashed it against the edge of the table—and broke the halves, and broke and broke—

He had to get out—to air, space—move.

He flung the door open, left, and walked fast. . . .

Only after did he visualize where he'd gone, like a *map* stark dark as nerves against the clear sky: up the road past the fallow fields and swamp of deep sea grass, past the boatyard and St. Agnes Cemetery and where the crick flowed under the wooden bridge over the road; and at the entrance to Stirling Cemetery turned left up past the crick and Al Dickson's and the Fosters' and turned left again at Warner's Delicatessen to the Long Island Hospital and right to Main and then left at the Episcopal Church and straight downtown till he turned right at Front Street and halted at that two-story white house with the green gingerbread trim, the porch with its wicker chairs and in the windows the curtains he ever imagined fluttering against the screens in clear, dry weather, as they were now.

Stood there.

What was he . . .

Joey? *Joey* came whole in his sight. He walked up a step, but *that* Joey didn't move. If he moved ahead he would walk right into Joey, become Joey. He would go to the door. Miss Kellogg would invite him in for a lesson, or simply to play, and he-Joey would enter and sit at the piano and play, or maybe with Miss Kellogg beside him playing together with him-Joey.

"Santiago—?"

He must have stood so long she wondered.

Miss Kellogg said, "You've come for Joey. He couldn't come this afternoon or this evening. He told me at the last lesson he had a conflict. Just between us, I think this time it's a special girl."

It couldn't be. Nothing would interrupt Joey's lessons, would it?

Would it?

Or only *nothing*.

He thought, And what does *that* mean, Fatso?

Miss Kellogg looked strange—direct. Miss Kellogg always knew too much.

He shifted. His eyes went beyond her. He concentrated hard.

He heard ". . . all right?" Thunder was in his head. His skin felt taut, no room for a thought to move.

"Won't you come in, Santiago?"

He heard her through water.

She was holding the door, waiting.

"You don't have time?"

Time?

What he had.

What did he?

"Yes, time."

But it was thunder impelled him up the stairs. Borodin. Madly in his head. Through the dance her words—some—separate—stood black on the walls, carpet, the open score on the piano:

". . . first-rate . . . Joey . . . a few years more . . . mustn't yield to . . . Joey . . . could win . . . Jiulliard . . . Joey . . . a university . . ."

Joey. Yes, all.

"Sit down, Santiago—there. You like that chair. And I'll bring—you could use it?—some hot coffee."

Chair. Habit made him. This one.

Before, the room was three—Joey, Miss Kellogg, himself—and music. Now, during the wait, the room—he blinked it off, but it came and came—was colors. They splashed nervously. He heard the soft green flowers. They climbed the walls— He blinked at dark green pillows, and rust, and islands of throw rugs bright as fires, and white antimacassars bold on the sofa and chairs. He had never seen. The room was new, strange. It filled with glitter, glass green and blue and rose, vases, candy dishes, a paperweight, a big cat clear crystal with a ball under one paw. All the wood floor streaked with light. The light shouted from the enormous mirror where the other dark piano gleamed. Miss Kellogg walked dark into the glass. The other Miss Kellogg set the tray with cups steaming down on the table beside his chair and said, "There you are—black, the way you like it. Drink it while it's hot, Santiago." Her hand held the cup out, her fragile hand that he had seen moving and moving over the keys. So thin and long, delicate, her hand, so white.

He had to hold the steam and glitter with both hands.

He saw her eyes still on his an instant and bowed his head. He stared into the steam and glitter.

"You're just in time to hear me play a bit. Lucky!" Her light laugh was girlish.

He knew—he watched her—for him she was to play, special: to

. . . console? calm? caress? He felt a laugh quiver his throat because now the question she must have spoken registered *Are you all right, Santiago?* or had she actually spoken all the words?

Delicately, with one hand she swept her skirt smooth under her and sat on the piano bench poised as the center of a flower in that greeny frock. Why did she sit so long still? He waited, waited. His hands were beating with the dances. But he wanted to beat against the dances, strike. Time. Time was the activity of space, Cory had said. Time. Between him and her, him and the piano, was space. He listened for activity. Why didn't her hands—? Time was Borodin beating in him. Then she straightened, then relaxed, then her hands—touched. At the first notes almost he groaned as—it was the Schumann *Reverie*—the sound flowed against the Borodin, flowed soft as a slow gathering mist rising to meet, muffle the beat of Borodin— He quivered, feeling the sounds meet. He shuddered as the sounds fused, struggling. A spasm ran through him. He closed his eyes, clasped his hands—to control—and strained. He strained to listen, hear Schumann, and drive back, back, Borodin, the dances, that pulsing, Polovtsian pulsing.

He opened his eyes. Miss Kellogg playing. She was swaying ever so slightly, and with the light fall of her hands lilted, frail as a flower. She was near. His chair was near. He liked this chair. She said he liked this chair. It was set just to her right, close. He could see her hands, the fingers rise, fall, spread; her feet, one press and release, press, the other; her thin small form, so little flesh, too much bone in her greeny dress; the head, a beautiful shape, firmly held, proud, with a profile to envy; the fine hair now shiny silver, simply combed, loose, with the slightest fanning at the neck, but pressed back at the temple.

He was staring at her temple.

His own was throbbing. Hers must be. He stared. He watched the blue straining vein throb—

But her hands distracted. Her hands. The fingers for no second stopped. The hands moving rose and fell—wind, water could be moving them—and him too now with that motion, with— The motion of the hands lured, he heard the motion: in it he rose, fell, ran, flowed. The moment came that lifted, persuaded over a rise: he felt himself lifted, lifted; and then that passage vibrant, *quick*, before a sudden fall, easy. His eyes closed—and he let go, sank, adrift, that dance Polovtsian throb *far* now, far, a vague far *blood*-blood diminishing, not so much driven back as distanced from. Still, the *pul*sing *soun*ded, *strugg*ed against Schumann; but *not* Schumann, *not* her hands, could override, drive back, kill that throb, *far*-far, *far*-far, Polovtsian. He opened his eyes to her hands: butterflies blown in a field they could be, rising and falling in the same space, fluttering against wind, but still and by the wind carried. Her hands were moving against the white curtain the wind sucked against the screen the other side of her, against the wall of the house next door steeped in dark. Her hands were dark and long and fragile against the lowering light. Her hands seemed to be making light, holding the light against that dark coming; but the light throbbed too with that *throb* in him that was *not* driven back because now in that sound of light she was making he saw throbs black as notes, every throb of that dance made a black hole in the light. The sound struggled against the Schumann; but it was inside the Schumann now, all a single music, note against note, sound struggling against sound, against itself.

Against himself. Inside. He heard. He felt note against note strike, every sound strike, but held in, surrounded, fall. All the music.

Me the music.

He watched her hands.

He watched.

Music was passing through her hands.

How could her fragile hands contain the music?

It was too big, that river.

He stared at her face: her eyes closed, opened, closed. Her head nodded like a flower in a slight wind, all her body still but moving with the music passing though her, him, going—

Where?

What was it carrying?

If she stopped, what would happen?

Stop?

But music never stopped.

It went on in the silence.

The silence was not silent.

Nothing was.

Schumann poured. Under, it pulsed. Polovtsian.

Let go.

He stared at her hands till his hands moved. They were hers. He was nodding, swaying. He was Miss Kellogg. He felt the madness of sound passing through. He was giving it form. His hands were controlling the madness. Control. He closed his eyes. *Let it come.* And he gave way. *Let it carry.* He was passing through Miss Kellogg. He sank into it, a current, down, down, drifted, carried, lifted up, up, hurled up—

He opened his eyes—

His eyes were on her neck—it was throbbing. He stared where her neck was throbbing. He heard the throb Polovtsian battering against the Schumann—the throb was striking at her neck, it was trying to escape. He *saw* the sound. He would touch the sound. His tongue wanted to touch her neck. It would hear the music in her blood, in his. They would be music. One. He *wanted*—

He bolted up.

At his movement she stopped playing. Schumann ceased.

No!

The room came back solid, each *thing*—piano, lamp, painting, vase, carpet, glass cat, sofa, chair . . .

Miss Kellogg was a frozen thing with her eyes on his raised hands—

He looked at his hands. He heard Santiago cry "Noooo!" to them because the pulsing Polovtsian did *not* stop. It was coming again, pulsing louder in his blood Polovtsian. He felt its leaps in his heart. He was afraid. He was afraid because it had gone out of her neck her hands. He must not miss. He had to follow Polovtsian, touch, go with—

He jerked his hands back, thrust them behind him, backed away—

He did not turn from her till he struck the screen door.

"Santiago?" she whispered.

He dashed down the porch steps.

"Santiago . . .?

He heard steps cross the wood floor.

He ran, her voice *Santiago*? *Santiago*? pursuing him.

Fast he went—he *must*, the music was *ahead*—along Front Street to Second and Third, only a minute, and two, three, to Ma's, home.

It was almost night. The faint high sky made the streetlights dingy. He ran west, straight toward the narrow edge of scarlet; the buildings and trees were dark against it. Last red fell as he ran. He thought nothing, felt nothing, only heard the thud of his step striking at first hard against the cement sidewalk and then soft when he hit the unpaved ground of upper Third, but he could not tell the thudding of his steps from the thudding of his heart.

The house was dark but for the one kitchen window this side and a half moon of light that touched the dirt and near tree trunks out back. He cut across Rolands' lot straight to his yard. He halted, rasping, to catch his breath, and stood just below the two wood steps to the back door, peering through the screen; halted too by his mother's startled face—she must have heard his running. She was sitting at the kitchen table, her right hand on the spread newspaper, the other raised, suspended, as if interrupted while scratching her head. She was staring at the door, her eyes wide, fearful; her face full, fat; a little obese the thick neck, the breasts; her buttocks ahang over the edge of the armless wood chair; her thick legs aspread. It was only an instant's hesitation. Then the screen door slammed behind him. He was in the light, inside the walls.

Right of the blocked fireplace was the door.

Santiago said, The hall goes straight through the house to the front door.

He said, On that side's your Ma's and Pa's bedroom, on the other side the two small bedrooms.

Santiago said, The kitchen stairs go up to two tiny bedrooms under the eaves. Yours is up there.

"Fatso!" He heard her breath break.

But he stood silent. He couldn't stop listening.

He was still, but the running went on.

Why wouldn't it stop?

"Jesus, you scared the shit out of me!"

Home, Ma. Home Ma. HomeMa HomeMaHomeMaHomeMa.

This is the kitchen, Santiago said to him.

Fatso could barely hear the voice against the thunder in him. He was staring at the throbbing floor.

Fatso?

Ma said, "Fatso?"

The floor was wet. The puddle was shiny. It was spreading slow.

The green linoleum was so worn he could barely see the yellow flowers. Wet spread, red; it glittered, and moved slow. It looked sticky.

Fatso? Santiago said.

"Jesus Christ, Fatso, don't just stand there!" Ma cried. "What's *with* you?" The voice was far behind the throbbing, but he saw her mouth move.

Ma was lying on the floor. Her gut was bloody, and her legs. He couldn't fathom all the blood. The baby was all blood moving. The red cord moved.

Fatso couldn't take his eyes off the baby.

Me.

He was looking at the mouth.

"Where's Joey?" Ma said.

Fatso didn't move.

Santiago said, Your brother.

Fatso was gazing at the little struggling flesh.

Son, Fatso said.

Brother, Santiago said.

Mine, Fatso said.

"Mine!" he cried.

"Yes, your brother," Ma cried. "Where the hell is he?"

Fatso saw her parted thighs, dark, bloody. She smelled of fish. The red cord was beating. He saw where it was coming from.

He heard it coming through her.

"Joey's been off all day with some girl," Ma said.

Diana, Fatso said. He smelled fish. His mouth tasted fish. *It* stank.

"I can't get him to do nothin'," Ma said.

Your brother, Santiago said.

Son, Fatso said.

"If your father was here, that kid'd shake a leg."

My father?

Me.

My son. Me my son was on the floor, bloody. He heard the blood. He could not stop the blood battering—it was trying to get out. It came out of Ma.

The music.

Your brother, Santiago said.

Me, Fatso said.

My son my *son* my *son* my*son*my*son*. He couldn't stop the *son* the *son* the*son* the*son*.

Brother, Santiago said.

Son, Fatso said. Mine. Me.

He could hear *it* in *the son brother him her me.*

He wanted to *know*. He *would.*

An absolute relation with the absolute, Santiago said.

Fatso wanted to touch the blood. The music was palpitating on the floor, in the baby, in the cord, in Ma. He saw where it was coming from—

The music's always ahead of us, Santiago said. It's in us but trying to get out; it wants to get to itself because it's always out there, ahead of us, Santiago said.

Ma said, "If Pa was alive—"

Fatso's head jerked.

"Pa."

Ma was sitting at the table.

"Yeah, he'd let Joey have it. Pa wasn't home much, but all he'd have to do was take one *look* at Joey and—Jesus!—don't you think that kid wouldn't snap to!"

There was no blood, cord, son. *Where*?

He stared at her.

"Sometimes when you look at me like that, it's like you're him, Fatso—'cause you got his eyes."

Her eyes glittered, green.

"Him." A hand went to her mouth. She half laughed and bowed her head.

"Him?" He almost shouted. His blood was so loud it ached, his body beat hot, the beat battered his head. He couldn't contain.

"Damn, Fatso, I ain't deaf."

She was glancing at the newspaper. He gazed at her head, his eyes too beating, *rapid*-rapid, tracing the hairline, forehead, nose, the mouth, lips, teeth, the—his eyes halted by that enormous vein on her temple—throbbing. How it throbbed and throbbed. The temple. Not Miss Kellogg, Santiago said. Your mother, Santiago said. Fatso would touch the temple. His tongue wanted the blood. The music was beating and beating at her temple. His tongue wanted. His hands.

To be.

He *could*.

He would know who he was. What.

If he could touch it. Go into. Be it.

Santiago was saying words to him, words and words and words, so fast he couldn't understand because they all made one word.

Beating.

He had the word in his hands.

"Fatso!" Ma cried, but his hands cut the shrill. Her head jerked up, her eyes cocked straight at him, but he had her neck, he lifted her right out of the chair, his teeth groped at her forehead, her hair was in his mouth, his eyes were close to hers, her eyes bulged, a light burned in them, they were wet, he pressed his tongue against her temple. "Agggggg" she cried. His tongue heard, it trembled his body, *an absolute relation with.* He screamed her scream, "Agggggg." The blood burned through his hands. He was blind with fire, everything was beating. *The absolute* Santiago said. He was inside fire. He was moving with the light. He would know the music who he was. He would see. *Abso* Santiago cried out, giddy, lifting her half off the chair, feeling the music hot in her he would never let it go. He gripped the neck, gripped. He pressed his tongue against her temple, struggling against the struggling head, the body struggling; pressed his tongue against her temple—his tongue touched the music, his hands touched the sounds in her throat.

He held, held—

He saw his face in her bulged eyes. His teeth glittered.

My face, give me my

He raised her almost to a standing position.

son.

Suddenly her throat went dead. Her head went loose. Her body slumped.

She was too heavy to hold. His fingers gave. She sank back onto the edge of the chair and sagged sideways away from him onto the floor almost silently, careening the chair across the room, nudging the table leg—the table moved—and she settled in a heap, arms under her, her right cheek pressed against the linoleum. A sheet of newspaper slid off the table and fluttered across the floor.

She was still. The room was dead.

The air was palpitating.

His muscles twitched.

He stood staring down at her till a sound made his head jerk, startled that the chokes came from his own throat. *Ma.* He tried to cry out words but his voice broke in mutilated cries and grunts. Again he tried, but his throat was so full it strained, it hurt.

Then he knew it would do no good, she wouldn't hear.

His body was still seething.

The curtain moved. It caught his eye. He became conscious of the breeze from behind. He backed into it, toward the door, staring at her body, his hands feeling behind him till he met the screen.

He turned and ran. The clatter of the door echoed sharply in him. And he ran faster—through the yard and down the slope, right, cutting his way through thick shrubs and bushes, waist deep, past Huey's shed, a mere black skeleton of itself in the dark, across the vast stretch which once he had kept bared, neat, with mounds of burning trash.

In the middle of the dump he slowed, then halted, and waited till his eyes adjusted to this dark night.

The dump settled in his vision. Far right, the edge of land cut dark under the sky and went into sea. Left, the trees made a far ridge, and the dark houses of town stood solid. Placed. Home. He could have mastered it blind in dark. Then he moved through the thick of it down to the edge of the pond. Water made dark glitters. Her *eyes.* They glittered.

Fatso said, "Ma."

He stood there, listening. Gradually the sounds came. He waited. His blood was slowing. Calm came—from the wind, the chafe of grass, a touching of the water. Far, the waves sounded.

He said, *I always knew . . .*

He said, "I always knew it wasn't my face. Nobody else knew it wasn't mine, not even you, Ma."

He went down on his knees by the water. He settled back on his haunches to watch his pond and listen.

German

"Up with the birds again, German?"

She had the best ears. Not a rustle escaped Estelle.

"Not another nightmare?"

Always with Pearl Harbor Day the nightmares came.

"I'm going up to the Sound awhile."

"It's not too cold?"

"Nippy. You go back to sleep. I'll be back in plenty of time for the parade."

"I'll remind Pa. He wouldn't miss a parade."

Pa.

First thing in the morning *Pa.*

Nothing but a Jesus-bitten itinerant preacher from Greenport, Long Island, with the fear of God in him and the doctrine of no work on Sunday, not lift a finger, not to cook even. "You can eat cold victuals," he says. And his ear glued to the radio all day Sunday and it turned up so loud the whole neighborhood has no choice but to listen to the Word. "They could do a damned sight worse," he says. Even a police complaint wouldn't stop him. "It's my right under the Constitution, ain't it?" he says, "or you throwing that out too?" But the neighbors had long since been used to him. "It's Tom," they say. "It's Sunday," they say.

German kept his lip buttoned.

"Your uniform's ready," Estelle called as he went out the back door. "Now don't be late, German."

He was out earlier than Rush next door, who drove downtown to

The Diner at six for his coffee so Edie could sleep. His Olds was still in the driveway, its gray back wet with morning.

The Volvo hummed. Proud, he kept it in perfect shape, though he regretted the buy, and *she* did. He blistered when it broke down. He had to get somebody to take him up-island, bring him back; had to leave the car a week; again had to get somebody— "You mean you have to run halfway up the Island for one little part?" "That's where the nearest dealer is." "You and your foreign cars! What's wrong with an American car?" "It broke down because it's a *used* car." "There you go again, German, always wanting a new car. How many cars have you had in three years?" "Yes, and every one *used* !" *That's* what really blistered—he'd never had a new car; it was his dream, to have a new car. "But that's childish, German. You buy what you can afford. A car's a car." "A new one is." "Well, when you can afford one and can keep it up, you can buy one and not before. All you do is spend money on that Volvo." "Because it's *used*." Couldn't she get that through her head? When he'd married her, he hadn't complained because he'd come to her with no divorce, owing money to his ex, and with plenty of bills of his own. She'd paid them unhesitatingly, he had to admit.

"Well, why shouldn't she?" he said aloud as he turned off the highway onto the dirt road which years of use had formed through the deep brush to Clark's Beach. After all, she had money, didn't she? Had it stashed—savings, inheritance, insurances. Rich hinted that often enough when he dropped in on him and Therese in Patchogue. Sitting pretty, her brother'd said.

Well, if she was, he'd find it yet.

Holes and humps in the dirt road made the Volvo dip and climb clumsy as a turtle. His head sometimes grazed the roof, his major gripe. He was too tall for it. He needed—he'd get it too one of these days—a classy car the size of a limo.

He parked the Volvo, virtually hidden, between two gigantic boulders, retrieved oars and locks, and took a bucket and burlap bag out of the trunk. He came up onto the cliff edged with dead shrubs sparse as an old man's hairs, and the sudden sea. The abrupt sight always struck him with joy, hate the Island as he did. The water looked so pure and untouched it made you feel you could start again. Serenely, four gulls circled wide. The cliff fell away in a graceful slope to sand, then pure white stones now at high tide spread like a mat under the greeny water. A dark brown fringe of seaweed marked the beginning of the ebb.

Across the Sound, Connecticut was clear, the petroleum tanks gleaming silver. Far out, a freighter headed east toward Orient Point. A lone cloud drifting made a curious white pupil shimmering with sun. *There's a defect in the family eyes from marrying first cousins, they say. You see how Pa's quiver. And his sister Penny's and his sister Martha's do. I was afraid it might show up in Rod and Cory.* The gigantic boulders, like scattered malformed eggs, cast long morning shadows . . . *evidence of glaciation, monolithic granite boulders deposited as the glacier receded . . .* He laughed aloud. Estelle's aunt Bertie thrived on the Island. You'd think she'd been an eyewitness. But the layers *were* there in just the order the glacier deposited them: the great rocks, then smaller ones, then the strip of white stones worn smooth, then this massive island of sand shaped so like a whale on the map, with a topsoil of *the finest black potato and corn dirt in the world.* Bertie had it down pat. He always listened to her—and her husband, Cliff, the ex-lawyer.

"Bertie's all *right*," he'd said to Estelle.

"Because she always takes your part."

Against the boys, she'd meant?

"Maybe she sees clearly and logically, not warped by love."

"Warped! That's lawyer talk. This is family."

"I'm family too." He'd balked, shaming her.

"Of course you are, German." Close, he could see her scattered gray. Her hair was always fragrant.

"Well, then?"

"You *don't* let go, do you, German?" She'd moved off to herself. Her shoulders rose to reinforce her resentment, her little citadel.

Her sons!

Son. One now. Poor Rod. If he hadn't helped Rod get Cory into the boat . . .? He and Rod had hit it off like cronies, the boating and the fishing, and Rod's experience on the *Annie B.* He'd had enough of the skimmer boats himself, some hard winters.

The stones ground noisily underfoot; then his feet struck the wet edge of sand, firm, easier to tread. He followed the shore straight to the large pond—Cory's pond she called it—hidden from the shore by a sand ridge grown over with wild roses, shrubs, and sea grass and hemmed in by woods beyond. Coming upon it startled. Sky lay in it, a great blue eye staring out of the earth. Swan were there, seven.

Once he had gone close. Cory was lying flat on the bank. At the crunch of sand, Cory turned, piqued, then smiled. "Oh, it's you."

"What're you doing?"

"Listening."

"What to?"

"You listen. Get down close. Low's best."

"I don't hear a thing."

"Takes a while. I've been listening years. Everything has its own sound—bluebottle wings, fiddler crabs, a razor clam burrowing . . ."

His dark eyes brought the deeps up with him, but darting with restless agility over the pond, they belied that calm. There was something soft in that darkness that discomfited German, a filled look, quiet and deep, that he couldn't fathom. Yet his face was candid with wonder.

Now, the swan were still there!

The beach was clear. Above the pond the Hammill house, the only one on the point, fading redwood, capped the bluff, blending with it.

The judge's rowboat was drawn up beyond the high tide line. "Help yourself anytime, German." The judge had taken to him while bass fishing, when to pick up a few dollars between jobs he'd work as crew on one of Wiggins' yachts for fishing parties. It was always to him the judge turned: *German. Ask German.* He was flattered. "Don't overdo it with Judge Hammill," Estelle'd said. But her tone meant don't turn—why didn't she say it?—lackey.

Always *against*, she was.

He set locks and oars in, shoved the boat, leaped in and heaved, heaved. Deep, the water was slate. The rowboat cut hard, bucked through low waves with a series of whacks. He headed where old Hulse set out his lobster pots; the spider-thin stakes and cork markers made a web just under the water. Free. Release came as he braced his feet, his muscles alive as he pulled the oars, pulled over this serene sea. The Island fell away, and Cory, Pa, Estelle, the family, the whole shebang, and with it his discontent. If he hated the Island and his life here, he loved sea, space, sky. On the water he was free. He was himself, German. He admired the sprayless flick of his oars slicing the water. He was proud of that mastery. Not Jozef or Ferris or even Big Ted, not one of the boys on the skimmer boats could row better, or fish or crab better for that matter. Mastery had cost, but he had gone at it day after day.

"Are you spending too much time on the water, German?"

"I have to live on this Island, don't I?"

"Have to! Why must you throw it up to me all the time as if you had no will of your own. You chose it."

"Did I?"

She looked tired, looked her fourteen years older than he was, when she turned to him, filled but wordless.

"We wouldn't be here if it weren't for your father."

"I'm not leaving Pa. You knew I'd never leave Pa when you married me."

"You could at least make me feel I belong."

"What do you want life to be? If you had the house, land, all, you'd sell it—you would, wouldn't you?—sell it right out from under us, to go back to—where? Carbondale? Detroit?—and where would we be then, the boys and—"

"Your boys are old enough to take care of themselves."

"That's not the point."

"Exactly what is then?"

"They have to have a place even if they don't come back to it, simply to know it's there, theirs to come back to, to have the right to choose to."

"As I have?"

"No. Different. Better. We always want what's better for our children. You'll feel that way when we have a child. Wait and see."

"They have expensive tastes. They'd sell it the minute you're gone."

"That'll be their right. But I think they'll keep it, or Cory will. They've known this place all their lives. The feeling goes too far back for logic to explain."

"That's sentimentality."

"It may be to you, but it's more than that to us."

She fingered her mother's glass bud vase, lavendered from decades of sun. *My dearest treasure. Imagine! Ma bought it when she was eleven with the first quarter she ever earned.*

"And when the time comes what'll I have to show?"

"You'll have me, German, and I'll have you."

You.

He gripped the oars taut and ceased rowing. The boat turned sideways, cradled in the troughs. An instant he allowed it to sway, tilting sky and sea. *And you'll have me.* It ate, maddened. Was she insuring her life with this hold, making his failure her lease on him?

Well, he'd have something to show yet. The cash was in that house somewhere. Her brother Rich had said so. He'd find it yet. That house! He had the northeast corner leak to look after, some shingles torn in a blow, the toilet drain to the cesspool, three light fixtures needing parts. He had seen a bargain on copper tubing at Wash White's Hardware. She was always after him about finishing off the walls of the cellar, where water seeped in during hurricane weather. "What'll the boys think, you a healthy man always around the house and obvious things not done. Will it take their coming to get you moving?"

That cellar! Oh, he was tending to the digging all right!

He glided between old Hulse's markings. A pull at his arm: the oar was caught. Goddamn, if Hulse *hasn't* got his pots out, the greedy bastard! The boat flanked against floating stakes. His muscle sprang with a little ache. Once in a while early morning he'd find a large lobster clawing around in his own rowboat at the crick. He knew it was from Hulse. "Tom says Stella always did love a live broil." *Tom. Tom.* Well, he'd beat Hulse to his catch. *He* was here now. How 'bout that? She'd have her live broil—on Hulse. He hauled up a pot—yes, trapped—and released the lobster, and went on till he had four, good two-pounders, crawling in the bottom of the boat. He plowed straight to shore and at the first scrape of the bottom against the sand leaped out and pulled the boat up and fastened it to the iron hook in the rock by the long wooden steps down the cliff from the judge's house.

He looked up. Was it the judge's white shirt in the morning light in the window? And him helping himself to—what would the judge call the lobsters?—"alien property." Just in case, he waved at that vague whiteness. He tore at some seaweed and covered the lobsters and trudged the sand back.

Sand! Three years of sand.

How'd he ever get into this?

Why had *his* ship been called to pick up Reggie Webb's widow on Plum Island and take her to Greenport?

That accident had sent him straight to her.

All the coastguardsmen in New London had known the two boys and the old man stationed at the Plum Island light and the only Army private, who lived in one of the abandoned officers' quarters and tended the secret underground machinery of defense at the far end of the island. And his wife. They'd known about the woman's husband and her brother drowned in the Gut, caught in the change of tide while testing a rowboat they'd built.

She'd been standing on deck despite the rough weather. He went up behind her. He felt his own awkwardness.

"You'd be warmer inside, it's such a blow."

Her chestnut-dark hair was already growing matted with the heavy damp.

She didn't seem to hear.

He touched her shoulder. Her head stirred slightly, rose as if it existed apart from her body. Then she turned to him. He saw first her gray eyes, still and unspeakably full. Then she gazed beyond, not into the water which had caused her tragedy, but out into the slate sky, which made such a dark flood.

"You'll be warmer inside," he said louder.

Slowly she nodded, without the faintest flick of her lashes, as if nothing could close out what she must have been seeing for days; and before he could take her arm, she moved away, opened the door herself, and went into the cabin and sat on a tarnished brown leather window seat with her back to the porthole.

That was all. He stood in the doorway an instant, feeling his size—twice hers he felt—because sitting there, she was actually so small. Standing—perhaps because of her slimness and that immobility from grief, the pallid stoneness of her face—she had seemed tall. Again he wanted to touch her. It bothered him that he was so moved by her. Her stillness stirred him. He was not—he was very aware—particularly sensual; most of the time he preferred cards and dice and hours of small talk with the men on board to nights in town, though he'd had them too—nights of barhopping, drinks, hotels, and cheap women to kill time till he got back shipside to the familiar enclosed man's world where he too had his tales, tall tales sometimes, that spotted the nights of pinochle or poker, gin rummy, or craps.

He'd said nothing about her to his buddies. He did not realize how she had invaded his mind until the one crack, some weeks later, made by one of the sailors back with the tale of the drowned man's wife daring to cross Greenport to arrange for the moving of furniture and goods and private papers left behind in that house in the officers' section:

"She's got a mean pair of knockers."

"Knock that!" He found himself sweating, from no tussle but a shove which had intimidated Wick.

"Christ, can't make a crack? What's she to *you*?"

Wick's question pricked.

Something had happened to him. He had to find out what.

December then too. And rain. He'd been doing duty for Emery at the Plum Island light when the government ferry was heading in toward the Plum Island dock below the lighthouse.

Walt said, "Today we go to Greenport for supplies we can't get from the commissary. *You* know—" He snaked his tongue out. He was missing four teeth, uppers, from a brawl in New London.

"Don't mind him," the old man said. "He's really a non-alcoholic virgin."

German said, "I've never been there."

"To Greenport? You may never go back neither," Emery said, "once you seen it."

From here he could see past the Orient Point light the land, so low and flat that it might any minute be swallowed by sea.

"I'll try it one time." A nerve quivered under his left eye.

In the rain the Island rose gray out of the dark sea, gray the leafless trees splayed out in queer nerves into sky.

At the dock he said, "I got a thing to do. Just tell me where the P.O. is."

"You're practically at it. Most everything in town's sitting on the docks."

The post office was a few buildings away on Front Street.

"Estelle?" the clerk said. "Oh, Stella."

"Yes."

"We're not allowed to give out people's addresses, but if you were to go to Warner's Delicatessen at the corner of Sterling and Champlain and ask . . . everybody knows the Veritys."

Verity.

"Verity," he said, and "Thanks," shaking his yellow oilskin.

In the dark noon the blue and red neon made the delicatessen window like a sore eye. Inside, the rugged, puffy-faced woman pointed to the opposite corner. "You're looking at it."

It was a two-storey house, old, with a one-storey cottage on the back lot.

He went under the maples and around to the back door.

She opened it.

"It's you," she said, warm, intimate even, as if expecting him. "I saw the bright yellow go by—like a great butterfly. *Look* at you, poor you. Don't stand there. You'll get double pneumonia in no time if you don't get out of those shoes." She was speaking almost in a whisper.

Still he hovered an instant, staring. She was thinner, her face so white. Tired all her body looked; even her hair had a tired look. He wanted to touch it.

Sensing, her head turned evasive. Her own hand rose but checked itself in midair.

He said, "You don't even know my name."

Her smile made him feel terribly innocent.

"You're German, German Beaufort, and you can't stand there all day." He shook the oilskin violently outside and ducked in and shut the door, evidently too hard for a hand went to her lips and at the same time a voice far off, fragile and tired and faintly impatient, said, "Stell, don't bang. And don't walk so hard, the noise hurts."

When Estelle said "Excuse me," he realized the air was heavy with putrefaction.

As she moved lightly off, too thin, she said in that voice of abrupt and comfortable familiarity, "In there—take off your clothes. There's a brown woolen man's robe. Put it on and sit by the stove. I'll make you some hot lunch."

Undressing, he heard her soothing whispers from the bedroom ell, "Yes, Ma. Is that better? Now try . . . try," and the energyless grunt, her mother's hard breath, a quiet piddle against metal, stillness, a flushing from the bathroom beyond.

"She'll sleep awhile," she said. Now he noticed she was in blue, light blue wool, and he recognized the gray eyes he had carried in him since the day he'd spoken to her on the cutter.

"I'm glad the robe's such a perfect fit. We'll talk while I get some lunch. Will that be all right?"

At her candidness, his hands rose. She laughed.

"It's strange—I think it's because I'm so busy tending Ma—but already I'm not used to a man in the house. I think you're almost too big for this kitchen, bigger than he was."

At once the other man was a presence. He'd known Reggie Webb only by sight, a man dark, hairy. He welcomed talk of him because talk would rid the house of his presence.

"I can talk about him now. For a while I couldn't." He remembered she hadn't said a word on the cutter.

"They told me you'd lost your voice for a few days."

She set the food out. "Some roast beef I had, a little gravy. Potatoes hot enough? Coffee in a minute."

Perhaps it was the woman in the bedroom she did not wish to dwell on because she kept talking, and with that soft insistence.

"How is it you came today?"

He dared touch her arm briefly. There was a sudden caught breath.

"That's the second time. I haven't forgotten," she murmured, her eyes far as if seeing that sea again, and set her hand fleetingly on his before turning to remove the whistling kettle.

"My talk leaps. I'm sorry. I'm so used to listening for Ma. The slightest sound alerts me. I didn't realize how conditioned I'd become."

A moment she was gone and returned with his trousers on a rack, the rest draped over her arm, and hung them over the heat vents.

"They won't be long drying."

He marveled, watching her small body, her hummingbird motion, at how the house seemed to take on her size, dainty and delicate. He would be almost afraid to move about among her fine pieces of porcelain, the meticulously placed furniture with the doilies and antimacassars starched and pinned with such an air of cleanliness; yet there *was* space, a feel of openness, and plenty of light. He had never really been inside a house with quite this feel of time.

"Is it old, this house?"

"The kitchen. We've built on till you can't identify the original. Once, centuries now, all the land to that house with the widow's walk—see it?—" She pointed out the back window over the sink. "—belonged to my father's people." Over the trees he could barely see the window and the wrought-iron grating like a crown on the concealed house. "Grandpa ended with *his* piece of land and the carriage house. He moved it here—you're sitting in it—and built onto it, pantry and parlor, those stairs along the wall and two upstairs bedrooms, and then the ell when Bertie, Pa's sister, came along."

That house!

Now he hated it.

She'd made him no stranger to the house, yet things, family, even the Island, sand itself, had made him come to feel alien, a coalminer's son turned factory worker for a quick few months after the war because his brother was a big shot in Detroit. He had tried to reckon with the life he'd found in this house, but some indefinable presence in each object turned him away, a mole blinded by light.

But then, when he'd seen himself fill her soft gray eyes, already he'd felt it verified—something was happening. No, something had happened. He was lost, doomed, to her.

And by the house doomed too.

Perhaps that day, that very moment when he had touched her the second time, he had actually thought It's mine. There's nothing more to do if I can have her, keep hold. From her body it would pass into his.

Oh, he didn't think that at sight of her, no; he was moved by her, her dilemma. He was drawn to her, her kind of beauty, an inner spontaneity, an energy. He wanted to touch her, hold her. He was proud to be with her, beside her, not only for her looks—a girl's face and figure though she was fourteen years older—but for a quiet dignity, a pride that was no vanity. He felt good standing beside her, walking with her, entering a room with her.

More, he knew now what it meant to hear devotion, what the security of love that could reside in such a delicate body as hers could mean. Sitting in her kitchen in her husband's robe, listening as she'd related the drowning, he'd envied her husband and her brother as much as he'd envied her mother lying in her sickroom and being tended by those hands. He knew she couldn't get the drowning off her mind, she was still too close to it, she needed to tell and tell—to believe the incredible, to relive it, to place it if she could:

"They'd built a rowboat, Reggie and my brother Ben. They were trying it out in the Gut not far from the lighthouse. I went down to the small harbor—you know it—where the government boat docks with the supplies, where they kept the boat moored. I wanted them to wait—it was a darkish day—but they insisted. The water was rough, no blow yet, but dark clouds were coming. Reggie got in, Ben pushed it out and leaped in after. Reggie was rowing. They were going toward the Gut, fast too. I could hear them talking and laughing. You know how clear voices are over water. The boat seemed to do fine; it was moving fast. I could see the dark strip of the Gut where the tides meet and churn—it never quite stops—and the whitecaps behind them. I turned and walked along the beach. It was—it seemed like—only a few minutes when I heard a shout—Reggie's—and when I looked, the boat wasn't there. I could see Ben's head, and then suddenly Reggie came up. They started swimming in but something happened. Reggie went under. I shouted. Ben turned and went down after him, they came up together, I saw their heads close, they went under again, and then one head came up—I couldn't tell whose—it bobbed up and went down so fast— I saw a hand reach up, straight out, fast, and stand there for a second, and then it was gone. They didn't come up again. I ran up to the lighthouse. The Jeep was there but I can't drive. The boys were in New London; the old man was there alone. 'Ben and Reggie turned over, they'll drown,' I shouted. 'Get the boat out.' The old man said, 'I can't row in that rough water. I'll call the Coast Guard.' 'Can't!' I shouted. 'I'm a woman and *I* can.' The wind *was* up, the sky'd gotten so fast dark, and the Gut was boiling. In such a short time! I didn't wait. I ran down the rocks to his boat. I pushed it. It wouldn't budge. I screamed to him. He came down. A cutter was just coming around the point. . . .

"They still haven't found the bodies."

Her eyes were as empty as the sea.

"I don't go near water. If I look down, something in me's drawn—I can't explain it—I feeling I'm going down, I want to— I can't stop seeing that hand, the arm reach up—in all that space—then sucked down into the waves."

At once he wanted to fill her eyes. It lay in his power. He had never felt so able.

It seemed the shortest moment of his life. Nothing had ever filled him like the urgency of her voice. When she stopped speaking, such silence—palpable—descended that he could hear that woman's breathing in the far room louder, closer, till he seemed to be drawing her air breath for breath.

Then Estelle rose.

"Excuse me. She may need something."

In a moment she was back.

"She wants to see you." *She.* He was struck by the incongruity of a nearly nude stranger walking into her mother's bedroom in a robe belonging to her drowned son-in-law. "Like this?" "Like that." She took his hand and drew him after like a child until he was standing steeped in the fused odor of decay and disinfectant and scent. "Ma, this is German, the young man who was so kind to me on the boat." He felt her mother's hand rest light and dry as a twig on his. She turned her small, already diminishing body slightly, leaning into him, and said softly, "She's so alone. You're good to come. She's a good girl. You must be a very good person." At the very instant Mary Verity spoke from the body that seemed a thin wrinkle of blanket, from that pallid face which took on a child's innocence because the eyes in illness were so large and wide and wet with a shine of palest light from the lamp on the bureau beside her bed, he knew—marriage. It was that. Beyond any other known intention, unsuspected, that was why he had come. But she shamed him, not because of the robe but because he was not particularly good and because Gloria loomed. He was still married to Gloria. He hadn't really known her; he had never lived with her except on furlough. He had married during the war in a moment of fear that he might never have someone waiting, no mail to tell him yes somebody was there *for the duration,* anchoring him in a familiar place so that he could say *My wife* and *Home* and *Gloria* to himself and to the buddies he'd spend his time with. It didn't work. No letters arrived. She collected his allotment and whored around, but despite his sense of family, loyalty, possession, it wasn't the whoring that shocked, but that she had married him for the monthly check, the trivial money, his own commodity, the thing he liked to deal with in the thousand nights of card-playing; that she had tricked him in the name of love on his own ground, for what *he* lusted after but could never make or hold, money.

"You'll come often, I hope," Estelle's mother said, letting her hand slip away as her lids sank; and he said, "Every day of leave I can."

Later, dressed in his dry trousers, he said to Estelle, "You mind my coming? Am I interrupting—?"

"The idea! Such a thankful interruption!"

He was sure she too knew now that something was happening. There was no changing it; it remained to find the right course.

"Besides, it's very quiet here, too quiet these days."

"Because you're alone."

"Yes. Without my sons."

Sons.

"Sons?"

"Both the boys are in Wisconsin, at the university. I didn't want them to come. I couldn't talk. They couldn't help me. They couldn't do anything."

He took both her hands in his, but he said nothing.

"I don't know what I'd do without my father."

"He's here?"

"Oh, we'd never be without Pa. He lives in the house in the rear."

At that moment there was no room for any other thought but the possibility of a life with Estelle; it loomed as vast and overwhelming as that gray down-pouring sky.

After, at the New London Coast Guard Station, playing poker, rapping the table for two cards, he would count the hours until he could escape awhile from the world of men which had been the one satisfactory home in his twenty-seven years. Before that he counted his life—he was big, a *man* at fifteen—as a constant escape from Carbondale to Scranton (he could not name the rooms, apartments, women he had known in that time); and he gambled, *my besetting sin.*

He'd gambled on *her*: to get into the range of that voice which somehow had made him for the first time in his life feel secure in the presence of a woman other than his mother.

But it was *her* mother who'd given him security.

"Is it German? Has he come?"

She would say, "Open the window," and watch the curtains flutter and close her eyes and smell deep, so deep that Estelle would say, "When she does that, the smell comes into me too. *I* smell wild roses and pine." He would carry her in his arms. "Come, Ma," he would say, and feel her shiver with delight, and set her in her chair in the living room, or set her in the rocker out on the lawn in the sun of her final spring.

Ma bought him a used Ford—Estelle didn't drive—to take her out on afternoon drives, she said; but he knew better: he lived in her mother's eyes. She did care for him, for himself. He was sure of that. She wanted him in the house, but ultimately she wanted him for Estelle. Afternoons he carried her to the car and settled her in, on her best days cradled her in his arms and descended to the beach, where she sat and at times with the delight of a child let sand and water run through her fingers, at times gazed at the sea and the endless sky.

Now he ascended the cliff to the car. This high, the wind smat, cold, almost belligerent. He lay the oars in the back and set the lobster bucket in the trunk.

What always peeved him on the drive back was the sight of her family's "big house" ahead, that widow's walk, then the two stone columns bearing the name VERITY at each end of the semicircular driveway, then the sudden break in the bushes revealing the house on a spacious lot framed by thick trees cutting off town behind. He tried to avoid it by staring straight at the road, but he found himself giving way. The house lured. The life she'd come from held a fascination for him. Even, he had a certain fear of it. It alienated him. *They*—she and her father and her sons—spoke of the past. Visibly they stepped into a world which closed him out, a time before his remembering. "It's natural," she said, "just nostalgia. Besides, you've heard our stories so many times you know them all by heart," as if by now he knew the actual people. Didn't she realize they would always be mere names to him?

From the trunk came the sudden metallic sound of the lobsters clawing for life. The bastards weren't alone.

Far ahead, on the opposite side of the road, something pink was fluttering wildly, somebody lurching head-on into the wind.

Bertie!

Past her now, he braked and went back. Some yards ahead, he got out to intercept her.

She had on pajamas, pink, under her pink cotton robe, and pink slippers with fleshy pompons.

"Bertie?"

She halted, her arms frozen in midair like a clumsy ballerina's. Plainly she didn't know him—she might in an instant. As he'd walked into *her* time, it was up to him to adjust.

"Going somewhere?"

"I'm going to Tom's for breakfast."

"Well, then, let's go to Tom's."

Except for Tom's quivering albino eyes, which squinted to see, they looked alike, both so thin you couldn't tell whether a man or a woman's body. Her eyes were deep, the strawberry blond streaks were his, but her face was freckled over in bitty cancerous outbreaks.

She stood back, skeptical.

"Who're you?"

"I'm a friend of Tom's."

"He's sure got 'm, plenty."

She tilted her head into the breeze. Wind seized her hair and threatened to draw her after. She gripped his arm.

"What a wonderful car!"

"You ride with me? I live near Al Dickson."

"Albert's!" She knew authenticity. From Tom's you could see Al's place.

He opened the door.

She laughed, coyly catching her long hair and wrapping it around her arm.

"Hot damn! I always did love a good he-man." She belted laughter, sat, preened, despite coffee stains down her front, grease, and bits of hardened food her bad eyes couldn't spot. Grand she sat.

"A whale of a ride!" Her laugh ripped and popped. She'd drive you crazy with her whale-of-a-this-or-that cracks. Obviously she was young now. Sometimes you could bring Bertie back to the present in a hurry; but lately she'd travel farther back, get younger—get ready for grade school, ransack for her bonnet, ask about the horse and sulky, want to dress in her father's duster.

Nearing the big house, she cried, "Back!" Her fierce grip belied her old bones. "Tom's *back*." Her hand shot the direction. "Turn at the blinker at Main and take the second left to Sterling Place. It's the corner house, near the crick."

But opposite the big house he turned onto her plot with its little green cottage and the three small summer rental cottages she made her living by.

"Here we are, German!"

German! Just like that—so fast it dizzied—she was back to today.

Being on her terrain must have done it. Verity land! He'd grown damned weary of Estelle's family tale—how when her great-great-grandfather, the richest mason on Long Island, had died, the money and property were divvied up among his ten, and then the great-grandfather divvied it up among his own ten. By her father's time each of the family carted off an outhouse and built onto it, adding rooms as each piled up kids. Her grandfather'd moved the carriage house to his lot. Once the whole area was Veritys; now Estelle's block was a cemetery of Verity houses.

Bertie's husband's easygoing nature had got him into trouble in his law practice. He had taken—unavoidably—the rap for a bunch in New York City as powerful as the Mafia. Bertie had moved the cottages she'd inherited across the road from the decaying mansion. After his prison term, she and Cliff had scraped and painted, remodeled and installed, until a quaint ramble of guest cottages caught the run-off from the nearby motels along the Sound shore.

"Come on." She had his wrist tight.

He balked, knowing what he was in for. Genealogy. She was a bug on it. She'd swim but drown others in the family river.

"A drink?" She tugged.

"It's a little early, and there's the parade later."

"Scotch, German."

"Scotch?"

"Oh, I know my men." She laughed, tugging him out back toward the kitchen. "Come *on*."

In a minute she had the bottle, poured his glass, and coy— he saw how she had him then—she drew him into the parlor. The sight always startled. Her parlor was a museum—an antiquarian's, or kid's, paradise. She'd covered every chair, table, the desk, almost every inch of the floor with mementoes, photographs, clippings. Here and there were little piles—you tiptoed through channels—and miniatures littered the shelves, the whatnot, end tables; and family portraits crowded the walls.

"You interested in genealogy?" her loud Verity voice belted out. You could always hear a Verity. "Did you know we're 36th cousins to FDR."

He laughed. "Everybody's 36th cousins, Bertie."

"Someday I want the pictures Tom promised me—for the complete collection. That's Tom's Gladys when she was thirteen." The girl, beautiful, stared from the ornate cardboard oval of her day.

"Tom never got over Gladys. In the great diphtheria epidemic Tom sent Gladys over to sister Jane's in Rhode Island to escape it. I took her and Stell—Tom trusted me. Woe's the day. Tom'd sent Gladys straight into the heart of the sickness. Caught the black diphtheria and died, Gladys did."

For an instant he feared Bertie might be gone back into that time.

"And they wouldn't let a soul out of Jane's house. They embalmed Gladys on the kitchen table. Tom couldn't stand Mary's eyes after that. Her look said *You sent Gladys away, Gladys would be here if you hadn't.* After that everything was 'Where's Stell?' He wasn't having anything happen to Stell too. Part, he'd sent her to Rhode Island with Gladys to get her away from Al. And her just a child! 'She running to the cemetery with Albert Dickson?' Tom, he'd surprise Stell, his tongue flailing the wrath of God at her. He clung to Stell so. I think it made life hard between Mary and Stell. And when the fire happened, the burden of Tom all fell on Stell. Say, you tell me: What's it all about?"

"About?"

"You think there's a reason why Stell's singled out?"

"Singled out by her father?"

She squinted and her finger zeroed in. "Singled out. How do I know what by! Like father like daughter. She *saw* things. It's why Stell bought the old family place, you know that? She *said* for a summer place, or maybe for the day she'd ever be alone, but Stell wasn't fooling *me. I* knew she bought the house for Tom, yes, because Mary divorced him and his children abandoned him and scattered to kingdom come." She let out a harsh laugh, cryptic and hard. "Because of his hands! Could *Tom* help his hands? He did what he had to do for his kids, *them*, what they are. Those hands. Tom himself was the first to say 'They were the beginning of something and the end.' Claimed it was bad enough the family sin came out in his albino eyes. Papa and Mama were first cousins. 'But I didn't have to go and add insult to injury, did I?' he'd say. I don't know what he meant.

"Look at that picture!" She singled out a great oval photograph on the wall, Tom's eyes hand-tinted blue and cheeks and lips pink. "He had beautiful hands then. That damned fire! You know about the fire?"

He nodded. A hundred times that story.

"Tom's a family legend."

"Because of the fire?"

"The fire! Long before that. Because of Alice Wilson maybe. It was scandal in those days. He never told you?"

"He wouldn't."

"Tom jilted Alice. In those days that was bad enough, but then Alice hung herself the day Tom married Mary. Nobody ever said the reason. The families went on speaking. But Tom knew—and Mary. Could be the thing drove him to preaching, to keep Alice in his head and put him on the straight and narrow. I'm thinking people maybe get a place in your head and stay there till the time comes to step right up and make you see them so stark you've got to face them."

"That would be enough to drive a man crazy."

"Truth is, Tom did go crazy—but not then. He went crazy years and years later, when Mary divorced him. He'd go off and talk to himself by the hour, then be so still it'd scare me. That's when he went to Rhode Island to Stell. Lucky for her 'cause she was pregnant. Oh, how the family'd pick on Stell 'cause she had everything and 'cause Tom took her part as she did his. They claimed Tom brought her two boys up, not Stell. Damn their hides."

"Why'd he keep coming back here?"

"Why'd Tom keep coming back *here*?" She attacked with a hard eye. "You know what? Every time he came it was a sign." She was talking like Tom; and she wasn't here with him, German, now; she was talking to herself. "We should've watched out. He was a walking lightning rod, that Tom. Every time he was near, a dark thing came. Still, *I* couldn't live without seeing Tom. My Cliff sometimes got a little jealous when I wanted Tom and Tom wanted me, and Cliff'd mock me: 'Where's Tom!' 'I'll give you *Where's Tom?*' But Cliff didn't mean a thing by it. I was all he had after the world turned on him and we scooted back here to start from scratch with the sheds Papa left me. How come we all kept running back to this place?

"Drink up," she said. "There's plenty more."

He laughed, turning and staring through the deep amber in the glass.

"Come back from the fire, Tom did. Come back to bury all of us but me. Come back when Stell run off from her Pete, and when Stell's new man and Ben were drowned in the Gut after the war. You remember that."

Remember? How could he forget the beginning of his love, and his hate for the house.

"Yes, Tom come back here when Stell bought her mother's old house 'cause when Mary'd divorced Tom, Mary'd got the houses, Tom's father's and *hers*, the one he'd built special for her next door. Stell couldn't know she'd end up buying the old house from her mother and making a home for Tom in his own house. Oh, maybe she *did*. Maybe selling it to Stell was Mary's way of admitting what wrong she'd done Tom or how sorry she was she'd divorced him and stolen the kids' affection from him—'cause the kids sided with her. Maybe they felt betrayed 'cause he singled out Stell, always Stell. Who knows? But I know one thing—when Stell got the house, she got everything goes with it."

"Everything." His breath stilled, and his hand. The whiskey leaped in the still glass. "What everything?"

"All that happened in that house, and all of *us*."

Shit. He drained the glass.

"And you're one now. Oh, yes, you're in the clan. You're a Verity. You think you're up to it, German?" She laughed. "It takes some doing."

The whiskey made gall burning down.

"Who knows what a Verity is?"

But she was quick and hard: "You better find out."

For an instant her eyes were still and deep with mystery.

"You believe in signs? Oh, I know—nobody does these days. But wasn't it a sign Stell moving back here, and bringing Tom here, and him and Mary living next door to each other? You think Stell could've guessed what she'd finally have to do? When her mother was dying next door, Stell took her in. It was like Stell was a girl again and got them both back, her mother in the house sick and her father out back in that house he built with those hands."

Those hands!

"That's where you came in, wasn't it, German?"

German. She was still lucid.

"When Estelle's mother was sick, yes."

"The only blight was Stell had Mary's new husband on her hands too, times when he was home from sea—Captain Leeds, Otis Leeds. Married him for his pay, Mary did. He'd sit in his rocker, smoke his pipe and never speak, rock and rock. Drove Stell crazy."

Yes, he remembered. Her father would come to the door, say "Stell?" softly, because every sound was a needle to Mary Verity's ailing flesh. He would not enter until Estelle invited him in to see her mother. If the Captain were there, he would nod, "Evening, Otis," and go past him into the sickroom.

German swigged the last whiskey and let his tongue savor it.

"Well, Bertie, I've got to go get into my uniform."

"What for?"

"It's Pearl Harbor Day. You know, the day the Japs bombed us and got us into the war."

She sized him up. "Uniform!" She turned flirty. "I always *did* love a man in uniform."

He laughed. She hibble-hobbled out to the car with him. Going down the road, he saw her in the rearview mirror as if trying to keep up with her long morning shadow. Sometimes he'd come upon her, dressed in her brother Tom's clothes, headed toward her brother Gill's long abandoned place a block before Fatso García's. Gill's was on a jut into the Widow's Hole. A shipyard had invaded and almost cut off sight of the house, but you could find Gill's dirt driveway meandering through thick reeds taller than any man. German would go in after her. "Well, Bertie! You here?" Caught in the stalks, her sight blank as time, filled with too much space, she'd squint and scrutinize, her face wary. "I know you?" He'd never know *when* she was—in which year, moment—and since Gill was long since dead, he'd lure her from the abandoned old caretaker's house, a shack now. "I'm headed for Tom's." "You *are*? Tom's my brother." "And he's my father-in-law. I'm Estelle's husband." "You don't say! That makes us related. Say, you interested in genealogy, German?" *German*! Just like that—so fast it dizzied—she'd be back. She'd be now, today, this moment.

Pearl Harbor Day.

But he didn't want to think *war, water*. He could fish and boat but not go *into* water, never. He'd relived his moment. Dizzy he'd go under, panic. He couldn't control that. Though he loved parades, he dreaded December 7th, dreaded *them,* the dead buddies: they were too present. They were the thing he was sentimental about. He'd never say so, but it hadn't escaped Estelle. She knew. He'd heard her: "You should see German, Cory. He goes silent. I don't know what he's seeing. I don't want to. It's *his*, the memory's private . . . and sacred. You can't get a word out of him then."

It bit that she'd confided that to Cory. She was always handing Cory weapons; he felt Cory judged him.

In the trunk the lobsters set up a clatter, clawing at the bucket.

Marge.

Alone, he dared utter it aloud, "Marge," and laughed.

He took the devious way home, past the crick, hoping to duck into the Club for a quickie. After all, it was *his* day. Gary's truck was there but the shades were drawn, so he rounded the block to the house.

Even in winter the house had charm. Always a little pride it gave him whenever somebody said, "A pretty place you have there." She kept it up, vines, flowers, trees; and her father did his part. That *you* bit. *In my name it should be.*

Morning fired the patches of gold-brown winter mums. He smiled, thinking Bertie: *Richest black dirt on Long Island.* He had no luck with the soil; he'd had a time keeping up with the names of her flowers. Estelle had tried: "The special ones are spider mums . . ." They spilled outward in fountains of spider legs. ". . . and the forever ones are marigolds, those are zinnias, and those dahlias, those asters." In spring the poppies were sudden bursts, and along the house came her rows of iris, the peonies, bleeding heart, coxcomb. Suddenly all morning long the trellis fronting her father's—*shop*, she called it—was a wall of morning glories, trumpets of pink and blue and white blazes; and all summer roses and some to the edge of winter. He remembered the mimosa because he was struck the first time he saw its blooming pink canopy. "Damn, if that's not beautiful!" "A mimosa. They *take* anywhere. You can't get rid of them. The roots are a menace." But though she'd call flowers and shrubs out like names of children, he confused them. She'd laugh. "Stick to your fishing, hon." But with pride she'd tell visitors, "German caught and filleted the fish. Nobody can fillet fish like my German. He has a special knife, so sharp it scares me."

With only winter mums in bloom, the house stood hard and bleak as the ground; but with the stripped lilacs and shade maples, the straight silver birches making a neat supple line on the south side, the house looked defiant. *It's seen a thing or two, Pa says.* Beyond, the leafless maples arched protectively over her father's house and along the right lilac bushes, ugly in winter, and her father's *shop* ugly without the morning glory cover. *He'd* like to tear the old eyesore down, but she'd let nobody touch what was Pa's, oh no.

When he slammed the car door, there was a quick leap behind the big maple.

That nigger kid!

Emmy.

She peered out and ducked back.

What in hell was she doing here so early in the morning?

He could see her hind end as she sat. The day might be warm for December, but too cold for sitting on the ground.

"You!"

She turned and charged down Sterling Place—nothing more than a green sweater against the cold, pigtails with pink ribbons flying—rounded the corner, and disappeared.

Jesus! Night and day you had to put up with her, a little black ghost. Uncanny how she popped up everywhere. Estelle's fault! She went out to every stray, couldn't resist. She herself said she'd never learn, so ashamed years now for leaving those shoes, practically new, for Emil on his back stoop only to find out that mildew had infected his feet. Still, she fed the kid, invited her in, let her roam the house—she'd be sorry when something was missing, you just wait—and carted her about, played games with her, dressed her. He'd come in—day, night—and catch the two of them laughing like kids together.

"Hasn't she got a home?"

"Now, German—"

He wished they'd never seen the kid, never given her the doll.

"Give the niggers one thing and they keep coming back for more."

"German! You've worked with enough of them, and you love children, especially little girls."

He did. He'd wanted a little girl of his own. They'd almost had one, but she'd lost it, and she'd had the hysterectomy. He didn't like to mention it. She never did. Emmy *was* cute. But he didn't want her underfoot every minute or skulking in the shadows secret as a little spy.

"Well, it's our fault," she'd said.

"Yours. You gave her the doll."

"But you won it."

He claimed to hate the Catholic Church, which he'd stopped going to "when I found out what the priests were," but never replying when she'd say, "And what were they?" He'd speak nothing against the Church, but if *she* suggested anything negative, out came his loyalty. When the Kapsteins went bankrupt and almost the next day opened their jewelry shop, set up by the flock of Jews, he pissed and moaned, not against the Jews, but against hypocrite Protestants who'd bitch against the Jews but not help their own. Je-*sus*! Besides, he'd defended the kikes whenever talk against kikes was unjust. "There's a soft spot somewhere in that heart of yours you don't like to show, and I think it shows most with little girls."

On a Saturday evening last August he'd asked, "You want to stop by the St. Agnes' charity bazaar?"

"Oh, yes—" She loved to go—anywhere, always ready in a jiffy. She came down youthful, a white dress light as air.

In the church lot strung lights blazing like day pressed the dark back. All town was there, the merry-go-round piping, kids screaming, the hot dog and drink stands jammed. Barkers cried out: "That's it, put your money down, little lady. Here goes the wheel. Round and round she goes, where she stops nobody knows . . ." "Toss your quarter inside the square and choose your prize . . ." "Get the hoop over the chosen object and it's yours." "Throw the baseball in the hole and anything in the house is yours." "Step right up . . ."

"Try it, German. You've got a good eye."

"Yeah, go at it, German," Jack Beatty said, and the other boys from the construction gang chimed in.

German swelled at the friendly goading. The jam made a semi-circle. Several were lined up waiting. When his turn came, Jim handed him three balls.

"You want a go at it first, Estelle?" German said,

"What?"

She was staring at a little black girl in a yellow dress, sitting cross-legged on the ground, her elbows on her knees and her head resting cocked in her hands. The big dark eyes fixed fascinated on Estelle.

She had a thin face. The bright lights gleamed in the clean sharp line where her hair was divided and drawn down into two pigtails.

"Who's the kid?"

"What?"

"Skip it. You want to throw?"

"Oh no. You do it."

German threw—three times failed. "Three more, Jim."

"Close, German!"

"Three more."

"Wowee!" This time he saved face; he struck home—three times!

"Pick what you want," Jim said.

"What'll you have, Estelle?"

Her eyes were on the girl. "What would *you* take?"

Wary, the girl did not even blink.

"A doll I bet. That one."

She herself had picked up at rummages and auctions and yard sales a collection of dolls because she made clothes to dress them up new for Pa to give to needy kids at Christmas.

"Isn't she lovely." Estelle laughed, turning it over, examining. "It's beautifully made."

The little girl stood up and brushed off her dress, but without once taking her eyes off Estelle.

Estelle was fascinated too. She was gazing at the child. For a moment German felt something was happening that he was shut out of.

"Let's try the wheel of fortune. Maybe I'll win myself a bottle of wine."

"German, wait."

"What's with the kid?"

In an instant she pressed the doll into the girl's hands.

Emmy gripped it, clutched it close to her cheek, but did not glance at the doll once. Her eyes were on Estelle. German thought she was about to cry, she was so still, but she didn't.

"It has dark hair like mine. Call it Estelle. That's my name. I love my two boys, but I always wanted a little girl. Now she's your baby."

The girl nodded.

"*Now* what?" German called back.

"I know you," Estelle said. "What's your name?"

The child stared straight into Estelle's eyes.

"Emmy."

"Emmy. That's lovely."

"Emmy Lou."

"And that's music." Estelle laughed. "Now I know. You're one of the Bascombs."

There was a raft of them. On Third Street.

"Emmy Lou Bascomb," Estelle said.

The girl gave a quick nod. She was looking hard into her eyes. Suddenly she laughed.

"What?" Estelle said.

"I see two *mes* and two Estelles in your eyes," Emmy said. She laughed again.

Estelle drew her close. Emmy pressed her head into her waist.

"Let's shake a leg," German called.

"You're always in such a hurry, German."

When he looked back, Emmy was still in the same place, clutching the doll and watching them.

The next day he was startled to walk into the bedroom and see the doll on the bed.

"What in hell *is* this? I thought you gave that to the nigger kid."

"German, don't—"

"Well, the kid then."

"She brought it here to protect it. Yesterday she hid it under their porch, but she had to fight to keep Estelle hers. She said they grabbed and smacked it the way they do her—imagine, German!—so she asked if we'd take care of Estelle and if she could come see her sometime. Of *course*, I said. Why shouldn't she?"

"Why? Je*sus*!"

After that, everywhere he looked the kid appeared—in the yard, in the house, downtown—miraculously knowing wherever Estelle was, a dark shadow as insistent as a disease he couldn't get Estelle to cut out of her life.

"What in hell do you want with that kid around all the time?"

"German! Emmy's bright, she learns fast, she has promise. In a big family like hers she's apt to get lost in the shuffle."

"You can't save the world."

She laughed. "Not the world, just Emmy. Besides, she's all sparkle, and good company."

"Not with me!"

Now, bucket in hand, he went into the house. The kitchen was brilliant with morning.

"Had your exercise?" Morning was in her too, her movements charged. For a moment her glow shamed him.

This day. I can't do this to her.

"Lobsters! You've been to the docks this early?"

He wouldn't mention old Hulse's pots. And she hated a lie. He turned to the sink to wash his hands.

Marge.

He said, "Your girl's hanging around out there."

"Emmy?"

"I scared her off."

"You didn't!"

"Not intentionally. She ran. She'll be around somewhere. You can count on that."

Something moved him—the girl in her, lithe in the way she set out the barely flipped eggs, the slightly browned sausages, the toasted English muffin, intuiting his moment of arrival perfectly though refusing to admit her habit of it. Her hair was pressed back off her face in neat waves. At the mirror she'd said, "Cory says he likes it drawn back." It had changed her face slightly by slackening the emphasis of its fine heart shape, less pointed her chin now with its faintest thickening. He felt cheated, the morning sight of her denied, for there was a perverse pleasure in seeing her hair loose mornings, trying to find in her the woman he had married: Since, her body had begun a slight gathering of soft flesh. Her clothes had grown snug, the size the same; they thrust up her breasts, a gradually perceptible voluptuosness about her which he couldn't associate with that other woman in her with whom he'd first sat in this kitchen—thin, ravaged by Reggie Webb and Ben's death, and Rod's, and her mother's after the long illness. He found himself searching for the other woman in her, pardoning in his delusion his running off to the Club, his escapes to knock about with the men on the docks, his drop-ins at the Legion, the fishing parties with Judge Hammill, and driving past the—he hesitated even to think the name—Verity place.

Estelle hated the Club. "Because you know I won't go near the water, you're safe from me there." He'd keep silent. He couldn't argue with her; she had an uncanny way of chafing truth without the least intent. Until he heard her say it, it would never have occurred to him he'd had a motive.

Now she said, "What is it, German?" Her hand rose to her hair, she half-turned, drawing the dress taut over the loose flesh of her waist. "Why are you staring?"

"I was simply calculating my needs from Wash White's Hardware—for the bedroom windows, the cesspool, tubing for the boiler."

She'd picked: "I've asked you forty-eleven times to fix the bedroom window in Cory's room. Now it's winter and you're inside so much you've time. And Cory's coming home from Brown for Christmas. Before you go buying anything, check to see what Pa's got. He hangs on to everything."

He hated her father's *shack*. The makeshift shop her father had built on for odds and ends was loaded now—rolls of tarpaper by the door, damaged bicycles, broken toys galore, boxes and crates, a mound of parts, rags. German had ordered his own tools on one wall so he could reach up blind and grab a screwdriver, saw blade, whatever. Why in hell didn't the old man tidy up *his* part?

The windows of his house were smeared but despite bright sun he could see the naked bulb and her father at the kitchen table huddled over his eternal tea. He knocked hard and pushed the door wide.

The heat! Must be over a hundred. It buffeted, suffocating, with the smell of cat, tea, cigarette. A cat—he always had one in his lap—scooted into the bedroom.

So closed up. He wondered if the old miser was hoarding.

Her father turned his head up. Sun quivered in his wet eyes.

"Ah, it's you, German. Come, Shasta, don't be scared. She never sees anybody. Come in, come in."

He had built the door frame too low for a man German's size. He ducked in.

The oilcloth on the table was streaked greasy and stained from tea. The stove was laden—his kettle and several dirty pans—and in the pantry beyond, the sink was full.

"Have some tea, German?"

"No, thanks."

"Well . . ." He sipped meditatively. The bowl fit perfectly between his cupped hands.

Sometimes when German balked, she'd accuse. "What do you mean you can't do it? My father can. He built that house with those hands and no help."

Those hands! The mere sight discomfited German. He was always relieved to escape.

"Stell all right?" The old head cocked, the thin blue eyes squinting.

Why did his eyes always make him feel condemned?

"Fine."

The old boy nodded, rose, opened the door to release the cats—the sudden cold air was salvation—and halted in the doorway.

Across the street old Mrs. Doyle in her black coat and hat and slippers, her white hair like a tight close cloud around her face, was wending inch by inch along the sidewalk on her daily trip to Warner's delicatessen on the corner.

"Hey, Mrs. Doyle!"

She stopped. Her whole body turned. She peered across.

"Hey, Tom!" She cried out her age and waved, then inched along.

"She hardly hears and barely sees, but's been stopping on her way to Warner's every morning since I can remember."

"It's Pearl Harbor Day, Pa."

"I know what day it is."

"You going to the parade?"

"Never have missed a parade." He stared into the oilcloth.

His son Dave, of course, and Ben.

"I'm going downtown early for the line-up. You could ride with me."

"Not as long as I can go on shanks' mare." He laughed.

"Suit yourself."

"You're not going this early? Where you headed?"

"Wash White's got a sale on. Thought I'd slip in before the parade. I've got some repairs to make on the windows and some plumbing to tend to."

"In bad shape, are they?" His eyes flickered up curiously. "They're made good. Grandpa Verity put them together so they'd stay for a hundred years. I got anything you can use? Plenty here." He rapped the shack wall. German winced. Apparently the hand felt nothing. Pure bone it looked.

"I don't think so, thanks."

"How'd you know? You didn't look."

"See you."

Across the street old Emil was rapping on one of the outhouses behind his place. Eyesores! German hated the sight of the two shacks facing his place and the third set between the apple and pear trees beside Emil's vegetable patch, dead twigs now. At least the handful of Rhode Island Reds were gone since Emil's old momma had died.

"You dere, Connie?" Emil's fluty pitch always carried. "Connie?"

The door opened and Connie's prison-clipped head appeared. Poor bastard. A crying shame he'd been put away for years because of an eleven-year-old kid. The Matson girl would sit on his knee and beg for nickels in plain day, and then one day when he had no change told her mother he'd *done things* to her. Connie didn't know enough English to defend himself, trapped by his own ignorance. He wore cast-off clothes given to Emil or the two Polack brothers from next door, who'd invaded Emil's house after his mother had died, playing on his sympathy: "Where'll we go if you don't take us in. My sister Mirta, she'd give ya shit 'f ya asked for anything." Truth was, Mirta was the only one who'd work. She cleaned houses. The brothers sponged.

"Hey, Choiman," Emil called, "how's t'ings? Never seen you lately. Stell okay? Connie here's going to crick. Got job with Hulse fella."

In a minute Emil was whining, "Them boys they're stealing my beer, Choiman."

German cut him off. "People steal more than beer, Emil." But they don't get everything. German will see to that, he thought, because somewhere in her house or on that land was something. Where there's smoke there's fire. Something he'd counted on, but had he counted on it when he'd met Estelle?

When her mother was very ill, Estelle had wheedled a visit from her one remaining brother. "Why can't you come, Rich? Your mother's sick, you *should*. I don't see how you can stay away." Her anguish curdled the words. "You may not see her again." Rich *had* come, but stood at the door of his mother's bedroom door, reluctant to breathe the cancerous odor Estelle had been steeped in all those months, and talked across the void to his mother. Cloistered in the kitchen with Estelle and him later, her brother had said, "You'd better get Ma to make a will." "Will!" Estelle slumped as if his words weighed. "You *think* I can go in there at a time like this and make her think she's dying! What do you think I am?" "You want your share, don't you?" he said. "I don't want anything, only for Ma to get *well*." Haggard, Estelle was. She'd aged ten years during the months of lugging and washing, nursing around the clock, sleeping upstairs, jerked into waking by a cat's cry, footsteps, the distant whine of a car on this flat land, the wind moan, the willow branch tapping at the west bedroom (he'd finally cut it off). Thin, worried, vigilant, Estelle had become a citadel guarding her mother. She *knew* her mother would get well. Fearful for her, German tried to prepare her. "You mustn't be too optimistic. It's a fact that in cases like this, just before the end—" Her abrupt scowl, the hurt gray eyes, halted him. "You don't *want*—," she cried, but clutched him. She would not admit the enemy to her mother, though she knew it stood waiting. So there could be no talk of will. She would *not* have it, she told her brother, whose vindictive retort, "*You* don't need it!" alerted German. "Estelle?" came from the sickroom. "Shhhh," Estelle said. "Don't raise your voice. The least sound makes her bones ache. I'm coming, Ma." Rich leaned close to German, his breath blighted by rotting teeth. "Don't let her kid you. She has to have it somewhere—from her first husband—a pile. And insurances. Two hundred thousand, maybe. Money doesn't dry up and blow away." "Estelle?" "Sure, Stell," her brother said. Rich was so like her—the thin nose almost too long, the fine cheekbones, the lips almost thin, the fine dark hair, all but her beautiful gray eyes, his a cold blue—that the similarity disoriented him an instant. In the brief quiet came her mother's faint voice, "I'm cold." "Here's aunt Marilda's afghan, Ma."

Was he *blighted* by that moment with Rich? Mary Verity had come to love him: he had replaced her sons. He could hear her soft voice, "Is German here? Estelle, I want German. Has his boat docked?" Actually he'd spent more hours with her than with Estelle before they'd married. In their moments together upstairs, stolen from her vigil over her mother, the presence of death in an insidious way worked to make her passionate, fierce, and fearful, because they were always hurried, tense, violent, as if they were children experiencing the immediate joy of stealing. He'd hear her mother's voice insist softly "Marry German," and with the same clear love and concern for Estelle she'd promised in a whisper, "I'll see German has it all. He'll never be sorry. He'll be good to you, Estelle. He will. Don't you see that?" trying too to soothe her into forgetfulness of the husband and brother drowned, drive the gray sky and the sea she feared out of her eyes. "I'll think about it, Ma. Now you rest." Long afterwards, remembering that, somewhat ashamed of his own wandering desire, he accused, "You married me because your mother said so, and for no other reason. You're too loyal to the dead." His argument fed that other desire already latent when his buddies at the base kidded him with *a widow, rich, not so old, with her own house, money,* a desire which smoldered when Dick's *two hundred thousand* fed it and when Mary Verity died shortly after Rich's visit.

Did all that veil the woman he married?

He wasn't sure. He could never fully untangle his views of her from his own desires. When the old woman died, his memory of her went with the swiftness of transience, maybe because her place in the emptiness of the house was filled with two Estelles. Or was it two Germans? He *was* two—wasn't he?—the German who saw the Estelle who summoned up property and Rich's cryptic two hundred thousand and the German who envisioned the gray-eyed woman standing stoic and delicate and vulnerable against the sea on board that Coast Guard cutter in the Gut.

Her mother had left no will.

Her other children fought, vultures descending to carry off in dark night through broken windows objects, furs, silver, even—so covetous was her youngest sister, Lila—a nine-by-twelve Persian rug through the smashed back door pane, brazenly attesting to her right to her mother's possessions. So German urged Estelle to sue. She refused to—"Oh, I *couldn't*, German"—but he pressed; and she did, reaping a niggardly few hundred "to cover the cost of what she'd spent for medicine." "Jesus!" he cried, declaring it "an insult if there ever was one" after her tireless devotion at a cost and a visible wear and tear to her life which she was forever silent about.

She became a third Estelle too, the mother of two sons, of the "family you married into," who she claimed rightly deserved the land and the house. "German, they've come here all the summers of their lives since I got custody of Cory, and Rod before that. It's home to them. They'll always have a place to come to." Sure. *And* surely the two hundred thousand for which he'd like to have a hazel divining rod. Somewhere in the house—attic, walls, cellar—or on this land it lay hidden as securely as it was in her when he so much as hinted at "what you must have lived on, hon, with all the luxuries you gave the boys," meaning while living with an Army private without a pot to piss in. She was quick in their defense: "My boys have *always* worked. They've earned what they have. They started young. Cory waxed the kitchen floor every Saturday morning for his allowance, twenty-five cents, and in high school cut lawns and weeded gardens; and Rod delivered papers when he was a kid so small he could barely carry them and worked at a gas station after school and all day Saturday at the lumber company. They're both ambitious." He could bite his tongue, for she'd judged him if indirectly, innocently. Could she suspect what he had his mind on?

Her sons!

Well, he'd satisfied her mother's last wish before she'd died, he'd married her. He hadn't yet met Cory and Rod then and had seldom seen the old man, though without knowing it they were already his stepsons and his father-in-law. But he was struck the low blow almost at once: *no will*, leaving him with nothing but that old Ford her mother'd bought in his name. Even then, for a time after, he'd been the stranger coming "home" on passes till he'd served out his time and Uncle Sam had given him his discharge and Estelle and her father'd so decisively installed themselves here on his father's father's father's site that it would entrench him, German, in this town for as long as the bonds of matrimony—or whatever might come over years to be claimed in its name—trapped him.

Four o'clock.

Long.

Marge. He must *not* think.

But *Four o'clock.*

Long.

Thank God for the parade! Time it would kill.

He gripped the wheel. The road quivered.

He hated the road. It led to the pier the government boat had docked at from Plum Island on the day he'd sought Reggie Webb's widow. That road began at Orient Point and the ferry to New London and the mainland he felt cut off from. Downtown, the road led almost to the railroad dock and that train he saw as some peculiar engine of fate that left at 6 a.m. and arrived at 9 p.m. daily but never with him on it, leaving him here in this asshole of the world. He hated the railroad station and that train which linked his two particular hells, *her* house and the hole on the east side of the City, where he'd left that whore—what else could he call her?—who'd married him surely for his size and his looks and the niggardly allotment the government had mailed her every month so she could live it up with other men while he sat the war out on a Coast Guard ship.

Yes, he loathed the road with the familiar loathing of love. Though he thrived on bitching about the town, whenever he didn't see the familiar faces of the Polacks across the street or Judge Hammill or the hangers-on downtown or the men at the dock, Bertie mad old thing, the neighbors, Pauline in her garden, Edie running down to the Arcade, their absence created an emptiness which sometimes caused him even to go roaming in the car. He was startled when suddenly it occurred to him that he hadn't seen Jimmie-the-Whisper on the street, or Fatso García, or Zac in the doorway to Katz's. . . .

He hated to admit the town possessed him. Witchery could do no worse. He loathed the very asphalt. Hell. Yet he must know everything about it. Estelle would laugh. "Why, German! You're worse than any woman. You know more about us than anybody who's ever lived here. Good thing you don't talk. Men are the worst gossips."

It was true. The figures in town assumed for him, as for everybody else, the tightness of a chess game. Their movements were transmitted in an instant. Before a man entering a house could leave, his motion was made over a dozen phones even before it was a completed fact.

And his own movements?

Marge.

He'd been very careful.

Until Estelle reminded, he was not aware of how much he had absorbed the town. No longer was town a few faces tagged with names; they'd become expectations: Minna Scanlon riding her bike to work at the hospital twice a day at precisely the same hour, Al riding his to the skimmer shop, Warner in front of his delicatessen on the corner, Hans and his Irish wife at the Seven Seas. . . . He knew he didn't make friends easily. They were a world seen through a window, screened off from him, though now, filled with the details of their lives, he felt he knew them better than she did. "No, Carrie's *grand* father left that house to her, *not* her father," he'd say. Scowling, she sifted over the past. "You're right—it was James, not Edward." With gusto he absorbed, came to possess knowledge of the town, keen in ferreting out each history, with a quiet feel of displacement of one Verity after another, so that he'd even argue with Bertie: "No, they're not blood cousins. Jeff Landry married into the family. His mother was no Verity. . . . Marriage doesn't make you part, and bearing the name doesn't either, not until you have children and the blood's mixed . . ." Who knew that better than he did? He'd send Bertie searching through the mounds of loose papers that littered desk, chairs, night stands, for facts which *he'd* take home, satisfied with his little triumph only to ask himself when it was over, *What am I trying to prove*?

But he knew. *Someday, somehow, the house will be mine, I'll work it out yet.* Then he'd be a true part of the town.

Nothing irked more than her talk about the house; it had been the source of his first blow-up with her. Downtown, they'd run into Judge Hammill. "Stop by my place anytime, Judge Hammill," she'd said. He had contained himself till they were in the Volvo. "Why'd you have to say *my* place? What'll the judge think?" "Think! Why, Judge Hammill's known us all our lives. He knows it's my place. He's always known the Verity place." "There you go *again! My* house, *my* flowers, *my* yard, *my my my.* Jesus! I'm your husband. How long do I have to live in the house before you say *our* house, just *one* time *ours*?"

Her and her house and her boys!

Boy. Cory now. Cory, the smart one. He lamented Rod. Sometimes he had the guilts. If he hadn't helped Rod trick Cory into his rowboat . . .

It was too late for kids now. He'd tried, hadn't he? He'd wanted one before it was too late.

How thrilled when she'd become pregnant! Oh, she'd wanted a girl so!

"German, there's something wrong in my womb or intestines. It hurts when you bear down on me. I get shooting pains—"

"There's a growth there," Dr. Spurling said.

"But the baby?"

"We'll have to operate. I'm afraid you're going to have to lose it."

She heard German's breath break. Poor German. Her hand went to his lips, her eyes filled, she laid her head on his chest. "German . . ."

The doctor removed a fibroid that looked like a many-fingered rubber glove that had crawled like a creature up into her. The hysterectomy—a partial, she'd after defend, though that changed nothing. Forty-three was too dangerous an age. Too late now.

"It would have been a girl, Dr. Spurling said."

My one chance. He felt sick.

She lay in the hospital, sad, doubly sad for him.

When she was released, he carried her lovingly, carried her out into the yard, set her into a chair, watched over her, waited on her. He wouldn't let her move without him, he was that worried about losing her.

"*I* can do it, hon."

She hadn't told Cory before the operation. He was at Brown. "Oh, I can't interrupt his studies, there's no need, he's brilliant." "And if something happened to you on the operating table?" "Nothing's going to happen to me, German. Don't even think that way, darling."

She'd protected the boys when Ben and Reggie Webb were drowned and when their grandmother'd died, and she'd gone on protecting Cory the brilliant. He was her double treasure since Rod's drowning.

So Estelle was left empty, and he without a promise.

Nothing.

Four years now. And what'd he have? A Volvo, a wall of tools, his clothes, and what he carried in his pockets.

A little he had stashed away. He deserved that, didn't he?

He rounded the corner into Easy Street past Emil's place, the Polacks', Mrs. Hannibal's, and followed the crick to the hospital blazing in the morning sun, then up Monsell Place to the Episcopal Church—the sun made its brown shingles look warm—and turned right as always. Day and day and day this route, his only direct way to town, his life now. In the center of the tiny park at the fork dividing Main from First, the World War I soldier, green with age, charged at you with his bayonet. Beyond, above the trees the spires of Presbyterian and Baptist and Methodist blazed white with morning.

He surprised himself: without thinking, he turned right onto Webb and passed the old cemetery and, just before the arch black as doom over the dump entrance, turned down Third by the three run-down trailers looking like cathouses, passed the nigger church on the left and on the right the García place, where Fatso had killed his mother. Farther down, left, was the small house the black kid lived in with a raft of niggers, but he turned behind the old schoolhouse straight into nigger territory. The street was strangely sparse of niggers. The spic farmers imported from Puerto Rico to pick potatoes were gone for the winter. No treacherous small dark men who swamped into town, who parted when you passed and clobbered you from behind. *He* knew. "How could a big man like you be clubbed unconscious by such shrimps?" Estelle had said.

Rounding the Pelham hedge came Denny the mailman, sacked down, looking, with his bulged eyes and long pointed face under a black cap and black earmuffs, like a poodle.

Denny waved. Passed.

He flinched. What am I *do*ing! *Damn*. He was headed straight to Marge's. His skin felt as if a hot breath ran over it. That feel was as unpredictable as Estelle's hot flashes, when her face turned quick pink and her hairline went damp. She'd press her forehead and draw the skin tight and say, "It's nothing. I'm all right," and laugh.

After her hysterectomy he'd spent day and night with her; she looked shrunken in that bed, a bit of a thing, delicate and ghostly. "You ought to eat something, German. Go out and get yourself a good supper, please." When he'd left, scared and lost—*Estelle, don't leave me*—he drove around town. He drove to Gull Pond, to the Sound beach, seeing her face always ahead in trees, sand, water, sky, defenceless as a little girl. And he felt—he never *had* before—fatherly. In the hospital he'd wanted to take her in his arms, his little girl *not lost*, and take her home and care for her, nurse her back. *Estelle*. Driving in the dark, he felt empty. Only wind, the vigor of the blow, roused him. He wanted *movement*, wanted to *embrace*.

Aimless, he'd found himself at the Elbow Inn.

The place was a pit, dim. The world was suddenly too close. Instantly he was steeped in *human* smells, grease, beer, tobacco; *human* sounds, crowd talk and laughter. The juke vibrated the floor and sent shafts of green blue orange yellow light over the ceiling and glitter over bottles and glasses.

Relieved, he closed his eyes an instant, and opened them to the deeps of the mirror behind the bar. The waitress said, "What for you?" "A Bud." In the mirror he saw her face over his shoulder. *Bergman*, he thought at the healthy glow, high cheekbones, full lips. *Healthy. Young*. When she leaned over him from behind to wipe the counter, her arm and breasts chafed his back; her warmth spilled through, a flush to his bones. In the mirror her mouth, teeth, skin looked fresh. He trembled. "Hey, Marge—" "Margie." "Marge." All evening he watched. Marge knew he watched too. And he played up to her—she knew it—and he stayed, another Bud, no food, a Bud, a Bud—and sat finally in the corner, where he too could call "Marge?" to make her come to him. Late, near closing, she could sit at last, talk, though he told her—what'd he tell her?—yeah, he was from Michigan, on construction, oh yeah lived in Greenport now, skipping the wife bit. Crowd's gone. We could dance a little. He held her, aching for it, his hands, skin, day's growth against her neck, cheek. Play the game, play ever so serious. He liked what he was holding, liked. So time came to close, she locked up. They went out to their cars. "Well?" "You follow me," Marge said. He remembered he laughed a lot, played, teased, wanted and *went at it,* whispered insistent, kind *of lining her up for* permanence, some *escape.* In the morning he felt guilt when he thought *Estelle,* recalling her face, too white, the delicate thing left to him.

He was half ashamed thinking it *now.*

But *Marge Beck.*

With the car running, he parked across the street from the last row in Cardboard City.

Had she spotted him? But she didn't know the Volvo! Last time he'd still had the old Dodge.

He turned back to downtown. At the end of Front Street the two enormous Washateria windows seemed to be staring straight up the 110 or so miles of road to New York City. Downtown. Two blocks on the harbor. You had to pass the inevitable theater, the inevitable Bohacks, the inevitable Diner looking like a great silver bullet aimed right at the inevitable cigar store on the alley to the inevitable village blacksmith; you had to pass the inevitable post office deep in the tiny mall across the street; and you had to take the inevitable turn on Front to Main that led inevitably back to the house.

My house. He could hear her now.

He hated this tightness. Town was a square mile with water on three sides—south the harbor, east the bay, north the Sound—and all the rest of Long Island to New York City on the west. A square. A box. The box he moved in every day. He hated it most when dark clouds came down like a close lid over this flat land and sea.

He stopped for coffee. Inside The Diner, Win Laughton, Rex, and Barnie were on break from the A&P. Time he had to get to Wash White's and to dress for the parade. He stopped for coffee. The three were at the newspaper.

"Hey, German!"

"What is this? Only one of you guys can read? Jesus!" He laughed.

"Here ya go, Germ." Angelo slid him a mug.
"You haven't seen the paper yet?"
"I'm missing something?"
"García got life."
"Fatso?"
"Yeah."
"Life!"
Cory. He'd be frantic to know. And her father. Estelle said the murder had pierced the old man, said he'd muttered and muttered to himself "Fatso?"
"I'd sure hate to spend *my* life in Sing Sing." Rex said.
German would see Fatso go in and out of her father's. He'd stay long. Sometimes German saw the boy in the corner he always chose, the dark eyes glittering, and the teeth.
"A guy should lay off his mother-in-law." Barnie slapped German's back.
They all laughed.
"I can't figure it," Ben said. "Why'd he kill his own mother?"
"Wasn't for money. And not a thing touched in the house."
"Life's all she had, and a hell of a life at that." Win was an old-timer. He'd remember.
She was familiar, a fat woman, straggly, meandering through the stores, standing on a corner staring, as if waiting for somebody to talk to, a real talker—maybe because her kids were grown, gone, except for the youngest boy, and Fatso in town.
"Crazy's all," Rex said.
"You figure it out, German? I can't."
Fatso had worked in the fish factory. They said he'd do anything. Dug graves—fifteen bucks a throw. Worked like a beaver. Ambitious. Had a house on Gull Pond. His *own*. And him only a kid, twenty-some. Living alone. Looking at the empty bay.
Had Fatso struck out against all the emptiness?
"Sometimes you just have to *do* something," German said.
"If that's the case, we'd all be killers," Win said.
Maybe we are.
"Christ, there's better things to do than killing," Ben said. "Christ, *I* got kids."
"I told you—crazy's all," Rex said. "Back to work, gents. See you, German."
"At the parade."
"You marching?"
"It's my war."

Killing. This day to commemorate.

He could hear Cory: *Just the thought of killing is enough to double your lust for life. The threatened life becomes so intense you almost can't bear it. Do you think that, German?* Was Cory being serious with him, or ironic? He was never sure with Cory.

The murder had devastated Cory. He came right home. He had had to see Fatso. *Fatso needs somebody.* But when German took Cory to the jail, they wouldn't allow him to see Fatso, not before the trial. He'd told Cory that. And upstate, Fatso'd refused to see him. Cory said hardly a word, but his silence told.

Blighted, the morning. The sky cracked. Against the post office the wind flung ragged ends of newspaper in a mad dance.

Time pealed out downwind from the Episcopal Church bells. Church! Always something imposed on you. Talk about freedom! He'd fought for that. So had all those boys with him, enlisted mostly.

He touched his temple. His pressure must be up.

The bay flicked gold with morning. After the war he wouldn't go in the water—one reason he'd taken his brother up on a job in Detroit—and he still wouldn't. "I'm okay on a boat." "At least the boys were spared that," she'd said. But not him spared. She would massage his head, sometimes his back and chest. Sometimes he had a peculiar sudden clutch at his heart—"a constricted artery" the doc called it. At times he expected it, as if any minute somebody he dreaded might come up the road.

She knew his looks when lack of circulation cut him off, his uncontrollable retreat. He couldn't hide it, after. The old man saw too. His eyes hooked up, quivering. "You all right?" He cared?

"Remember: Pa lost a son drowned after coming home safe from three years of running into battle as a medic unarmed and carrying out wounded, and lost my brother Dave in the war. . . . Someday you should read Dave's letters."

German was proud he was a vet. He'd been glad to go, but it amazed him how soon people forgot. Only the vets remembered, and the families of the dead. Estelle flew the flag holidays. One thing about the old man, he flew his every day.

"Missed the first World War," her father'd said, "but my boys, two, were in the next, and Cory. And you at sea, German? Spent part of my life at sea too, cook for a while on a private yacht, then set up a grocery store at home, did some mason work in between—hoped to make money enough to buy the old family house back. Seen it, German?"

When *didn't* he see it! No matter where you were in the village, you could see that widow's walk, and nobody in the family'd let you forget it.

He parked between the Washateria and Wash White's. At the mouth of Main, the Socony pump, the few boats tied at Preston's and Claudio's docks and the great houses on Shelter Island stood stark with morning.

Whit, on duty, was just pulling past in his *red wasp*.

"Guess you heard, German."

He nodded. "A goddamn shame."

After the glare, the hardware store was a sunless cave where stock glinted on counters and heaped in bins like small treasures a man liked to run his hand through. Back, was a maze from fishing rods to roofing. Henry's enormous head and torso were dark against the window, where he like to read his paper by daylight. His great bulged eyes turned up, a fish face out of the depths if ever there was one.

"Well, German, we're not so bad off when we read stuff like that. People're always wanting something they'll do a crazy thing for."

Across, Whit had stopped the car to talk to Nita Landowski. Tits like an upended cow's. Horny he felt.

Marge.

"I don't know." He tilted his head, to view.

"Got some flea powder if you're feeling that itchy." Henry laughed. "That's been milked, plenty."

"Is that the voice of experience?"

Henry rose, elephantine, his round womanish arms fins moving in dark waters.

"My Minna'd like to get ahold of dirt like that. *Been* waiting fifty years for it. Might be worth shocking her at my age. What'll it be, German? You making hay while the sun shines up at the house?"

"At it all the time. Got to be or it'd blow into the Sound?"

"What can I do for you?"

The list, crushed, he flattened out and handed to Henry.

"Houses come and go like us, German, unless we keep them up. The hand-me-downs are the real hell. Look at this place. Three generations. Ever think how many people came in that door? Wear out the building looking at it, you'd think. But if we weren't here, we'd be someplace else looking at another wall."

"You can always step outside and see the water."

"Oh, water's something else! Got a will of its own. It'll come right up the street and drive you out. In the hurricane of '38 she didn't even ask in, just took over the store. Same in '44. Nobody ever saw the town in such shambles. About the time you think dullness sets in, she's acting up again. Like everybody, once in a while she's after something we got on land and doing her damnedest to get it. You know how much of this town those hurricane Annies and Bellas and Claras have carried off. Even when she's quiet, she's waiting. I've seen bodies float right up against the pilings like she's sent them back after sucking the souls out like she's trying to tell us something, I don't know what. Takes a man down a notch or two. Last one they found was Rhetta Webster under Claudio's dock. You remember? No foul play, maybe just fell in. Who knows what? Three kids left behind and not enough insurance to feed a fly."

Insurance!

"There you go." Henry handed him the change.

"See you at the parade, Henry?"

"You bet. I'll be out on the steps when you go by."

Estelle doled out exact cash. "For our own good. I know you from the service days," she'd half kid. But the mention ground like bits of glass into his skin: debts incurred by the whore who'd married a GI allotment delivered with godlike regularity by Uncle Sam, who had her man safely tucked away in a nest of card-playing, gambling males; debts paid by Estelle to allow him to sever ties and come free and clear, *clean*, to *her* bed, *her* house, *her* Pa, *her* boys. And him in this box of a town, treated no better than a cat or dog or, worse, a stinking goat like the one Gill had kept on a chain behind his unpainted caretaker's shack on the jut across the crick from the hospital. The poor nannygoat would wind round and round the stake it was tied to till it nearly choked. The old man's brother Gill, lusty as any goat ever was, brought women home for himself and his friends, women of all ages from town or the City or New London for a night or afternoon's lay or a week's layover. Deaf, with the loud Verity voice to begin with, he'd boom, "Got a case of Jack Daniel's and three broads hotter than firecrackers," his cap accenting the Verity ears, his head atremor as he squinted to focus his vision. For a while German had caught Estelle's fear for his own baby's eyes, but her hysterectomy had taken care of that. Barren. Nothing to fear now. Good-natured Gill had never cared: "Stay as long as you like, girls. Plenty to eat and drink." There'd be booze and dancing and screwing till they flopped. And what'd old mister preacher brother Tom think of that?

She'd said, "Why, Gill's his brother. Pa'd never say a word about his shenanigans. Why would he? He loves a good joke himself."

But a barren life, Gill's—always left with a houseful of bottles, the unmade beds, empty rooms not his.

Barren too, this day, despite sun.

Whit's police car was gone.

German went down to the dead end at the harbor. Almost no pleasure boats were docked, so no traffic. Claudio's closed for the winter. The skimmer boats were in—the *Annie B, Ida K, Martha*—inactive and silent. The ferry, white, was cutting a white spray. Gulls, with quick forlorn cries, were streaking shadows against the morning sky.

At that moment from the *Ida K* came the Polacks from Easy Street—Dolfo and Big Ted and Jozef. No man liked to tangle with them when they were back in town and on a spree. Whit and the others never welcomed them; they meant a Saturday night drunk, fights, a free-for-all.

"If it ain't old German!" Dolfo cried.

Behind them came the Swede, a sleepy-eyed giant with a sister in Jersey who kept his little daughter for him. Under his drooped lids his eyes seemed to be gazing a long way off and he always had to be poked into attention. The Brooklyn wop, Mannie, was a butterball beside his giant shipmate, as comic as Mutt trailing Jeff.

"Oh, oh, the town'd better watch out tonight." German laughed, genuinely glad to see them. Their sailor swagger, as if the ground rode up like a deck to meet their weight, evoked uniforms and Coast Guard and U-boats and icy water. His hand rose to his head but fell as he gave way to his nostalgia for the old camaraderie. For an instant the time since his discharge fell away. But he wasn't deceived by the boys' invite. You had to be a GI to know what a gut pal was. The boys could be treacherous—narrow and mean, all self. Nothing was sacred.

They'd come in loaded, four or five hundred apiece after every trip. In no time it would be gone on booze and women.

"They're just laying for you guys at Helen's and Meier's."

"Yeah, well they'll be laid too before we're through." Big Ted slapped his chest. The bills were like a hard growth there. Evidently the Captain had just doled out.

Beyond, elderly and slim, the Captain was just emerging from Preston's shipyard.

"Hey, Zack-o!" Dolfo cried. Anticipation seemed to make him already a merry drunk, who did a good bit of business with him.

The Jew was standing in the doorway to his clothing store, watching the Captain.

"Look at me, cooped up. I should be a sailor." The boys' freedom Zac envied. He'd tell you the years he'd spent staring out the store windows to sea. He was thin as death. Zac's old mother worried she'd die before Zac married. In public she'd cry, "What! No girl's good enough?"

"What's new, German?" Dolfo hadn't interrupted his stride. German fell in. They were headed for Helen's and before they were through they'd do Meier's and Frank's and the Stirlington and end up closing the bar at the Wyandank.

"Fatso was sentenced to life yesterday."

"Life! Jesus!"

"*I* ain't surprised," Jozef said. "The kid's cracked is all."

"A cracked kid doesn't build himself a house and pay it off and keep it up with a steady job," German said.

"You oughta know. Hey, guys— German, he knows everything," Dolfo said.

German braced against the onslaught of Dolfo's tongue, which respected no man, but Dolfo said, "He's a good guy, this German."

Mannie edged his great tortoise-shell stomach close. "What'd Fatso git out of it?"

"Maybe he was looking for something."

Cory. After the murder Cory'd said, "Fatso was looking for something. He wasn't completely to blame. I know he wasn't." "You mean he had an accomplice?" German asked. Cory's gaze went far. He went silent, and after a while he said, "Everybody has an accomplice, German." "Then who's Fatso's?" he asked. Cory never answered. He still didn't know what Cory meant, yet Cory was miserable. How could Cory suffer like that for somebody else? What German did understand was the feeling for a buddy; but Cory lived here only summers, and not every summer at that, so how could he have known Fatso that well?

"*What* somethin'? His old lady didn't have nothin'. Up poverty row. You shittin' us, Joiman?"

He laughed. "I wouldn't do that to you, Mannie. You guys going to paint the town red."

"Don't you know it!" Dolfo said.

In German's *hard season* the winter after he'd married Estelle, he'd gone on the *Ida K.* With his usual luck the ship's engine had broken down off Brooklyn. They'd had to spend a few days in repairs. He had no money so he called Estelle, realizing he was being cajoling, lovey, arch in the face of her factual response, "What do you need money for? You're on the ship, aren't you?" Stymied, he sulked. A few minutes away from the City, stranded on a hack ship, his first trip out, broke, he wouldn't accompany his shipmates. "The war's over, German," she said, cruelly he felt. "Men on ships stay boys too long, irresponsible, carousing, while their women at home— Do you know how hard it is for them?" "I'm not talking to them but to you." She had money, didn't she? and plenty? and what was hers was his too, wasn't it? "I don't believe in waste, German. I can't help it. We're from centuries of puritan blood. You don't shake long family habits overnight. Maybe you were brought up differently, but—" "Why do you always try to find reasons for not spending." "There are reasons we're the way we are. Aren't there, German?" Her voice—pained almost—suggested it was more than a question, a plea. "You live once. That's all I know," he said. "Yes, but maybe we live by something in our blood so old that . . ." She flagged. German said, "I didn't know you thought such things." "No, you didn't." "And where . . ." Where did she *get* such thoughts? "Where what?" But too baffled and exasperated, he asked, *"Will* you send the money?" "Yes, since that's what you want." That addition cankered, but when he hung up he felt no guilt, but wondered: Was she insinuating that she knew about his casual inquiries about money and his forays to probe cellar, attic, chimney . . .? Once on his way to Brooklyn, he dismissed his fears. Today was all that mattered, wasn't it?

"'Bout a drink, German? Get *in* here," Dolfo said.

"Yeah, c'monnn." Big Ted mauled with friendly paws.

Who'd he ever see but *her* people, *her* friends, *her* town? Pearl Harbor Day was *his* day, wasn't it? And he still had time before the parade.

Already he heard her *self-respect . . . the kind of people who go there . . . for the good of your name in this town.* He'd shocked her one day: "I have no name." But she came back with "You won't if you keep that up." His shame made him goad further, "I'll have *yours*. It's all I have now."

Annoyed thinking it, anticipating a release to a comfortable lassitude where money flowed, he felt for his wallet.

"Keep your fuckin' hand outa ya pocket," Dolfo said.

German let himself be towed in.

"What say, Pat? Bring us a round," Big Ted said. "What you drinkin', German?

"Scotch."

"Bring him a double."

"Dolfo!" Bea Blye flagged from the juke box. Bea had a sixth sense for timing their landings. She lived on the likes of them. Before the day was over she'd traipse one or two of them to one of the tiny bedrooms upstairs. "Gimme a quarter." She rose, all show, an eyeful of roundness against the juke lights. "Atta baby." Dolfo ran a hand over her thigh. "Buy me a drink," she said. "Hey, Pat, give Bea what she wants." Dolfo guffawed. A few guys laughed. "You son of a bitch," she said, but turned all smiles when he put his hands around her waist and sacheted her around.

Before the song was over Tommie the cook called from the back door, "Hey, Dolfo, your sister says she gotta talk to you."

"Mirta? Ah, for Chris' sake! I no more'n put my foot on the dock 'n she's here—"

She was already inside.

"You comin' or not?" She was short, solid, as belligerent as Dolfo.

"Yeah, I'm comin." As if to show her, he ambled, slow as you please.

The two could be heard in the rear, Mirta's "I'm takin' care-a my kid. You got a decent roof and plenty food, ain'tchya?" Mirta was single, had to fight for her rights with the three brothers. If she didn't get the cash when they docked, it would be gone in a night and they'd be griping there wasn't food or drink in that house and them supporting her kid, a lie—she supported herself and the girl, cleaning houses.

"Je-*sus*," Dolfo said, returning, "women'll bleed you every time."

"What's wrong with women?" Bea massaged his neck.

"'f-I had a year, I'd tell ya."

"And before a day's over I'd cut the heart out of you, you bastard." She laughed and settled in beside him.

"So you got to go around killin' to get what you want?" Big Ted said. "I beat up a few in my time but I ain't killed nobody."

German cornered him: "How'd you know when you started beating them up you wouldn't end up killing?"

"Yeah." Jozef poked a supportive elbow into Big Ted's arm.

"Cause I wouldn't kill nobody, that's why."

"Fatso wouldn't have either, but he did."

"Say, you tryin' to make out I'm the same as Fatso?"

"Well, how're you so different?"

Big Ted cowered an instant. His eyes made quick flights from face to face. Then he reared back. "He did it and I didn't," he cried, triumphant in their round of laughter, though his own laugh turned quickly self-conscious when he saw German hadn't lost his serious tone. "So," he made his pitch, "Fatso's guilty and I ain't!"

"Could be Fatso killed her but is not guilty."

"*Hey*! What you talk!" Mannie's head raised over his mammoth stomach. "*You* the crazy one, Joiman."

"Say, gimme a quarter, Dolfo." With a handful this time, Bea sidled up to the juke again.

"Anybody could kill."

"Don't you know it. I been there myself." Jozef stared into his beer.

German was thinking not *war*, not *police*, not *deliberated crime*, not *electrocution*, not *accident*, but . . . what'd Cory call it? . . . he didn't know . . . but *the other*. What happened *inside*. He was annoyed he couldn't name it, couldn't find a word, a reason; worse, annoyed because *Cory*, four years younger, could *name*. It hooked, how involved Cory was, how devastated by the killing; and Cory's sense of involvement confused him. *She* didn't understand it either. When German mentioned it, she met him with silence. Faith it was. She knew her Cory, and the old man did too. *He* was devastated. Why wouldn't he be, with Fatso running in and out all the time. German hated to say it, even think it, but *what a pair*! because instantly he visualized the two, Fatso's teeth and the old man's hands, a pair, yeah. But Cory—*Collusion*, he'd said.

"Collusion," German muttered.

"Je-*sus*!" Jozef said. "What's *with* you, German?

Dolfo laughed. "The Scotch got him."

"Shut up, you guys, and *listen* to the boid."

"I'd like to know what really happened to Fatso."

"Shit, nobody'll ever know."

"*I'd* sure like to."

"Say, Joiman, you ever been in jail?"

"No."

"Well, I'm tellin' ya, ya'll never know what happened even if you *was*."

"*I* know," Jozef said. "My ex has my ass hauled in every winter for child support. You think that bitch I was married to's gettin' my cash? Let'm give me a roof and grub. I'm turnin' myself in tomorra before she gets to whinin."

"What's all the hogwash they're talking?" Bea leaned heavily against Dolfo and slipped her hand into his shirt and fingered the hair. "You sure are wasting a lot of time."

The Swede leaned toward German. "You t'ink only people in jail suffer."

"You sufferin', Swede-o?" Big Ted said.

"Ev'ybody suffer."

"Shit!"

"Dot sufferin', it makes you reach out."

"Here, Bea baby, reach out and grab this." She slapped Dolfo resoundingly, but pressed her boobs against his head and he turned and nuzzled between, grunting.

"Atta go, Dolfo!" Laughing, Jozef slapped the table. The beer bottles leaped. "You want we should cry about Fatso, Joiman?"

"Nobody's cryin' for nobody around here," Big Ted said. "It's too shittin' bad about Fatso, but he done it. Let'm pay for it like everybody else. *I* do. Why shouldn't he?"

"*You* t'ink somebody save Fatso?" The Swede spoke into the shadows.

A voice said, "Nobody can save Fatso."

It was the Captain. Bent forward, his face caught the juke lights. His bony sockets were dark as Lazarus eyes. What startled was that he almost never spoke. Only the eyes in that skeletal face seemed to speak. The men respected him but were uncomfortable with him because his silence was so enigmatic. That would have been reason enough not to hire on with him, but he paid better than any ship in the harbor. Besides, though he ran a strict ship, there wasn't a situation he hadn't lived through; he had a reputation for being fairly untouchable.

"Why you say dot?"

"Because the law is relentless." The Captain's deep, hollow voice reverberated clear above the juke.

"Can change law."

"Men change laws, but the true law is relentless."

The Captain sank back into the shadow.

"Un'stan' nodding," the Swede said.

The Captain's presence had laid a pall. Nobody had seen him come in. It was his ritual to sit alone over a drink, then disappear. He was aloof even in the most intimate situations, though he worked his influence on them. His authority held something hard and final. But you could brand him as the skipper; he bore something of the ship's tackiness.

"Say, Swede, you wanna know a thing or two about the law, just ask German. He'll give ya what-for."

"Aw, shut up, Dolfo," Joe said.

"What ya mean Shut up! I got's much right's *you*— Ain't that right, German? Ole German, he'll give you the straight dope on the law, eh, German?"

The bastard! They all knew he and Judge Hammill were fishing friends. And, fool that he was, he'd mouthed about his school ambition to be connected with law. He was thinking *cop, law, big*. "The law's not for the likes of you." His father'd hit it right. He'd fallen in love with the idea of quick bucks. He loved playing around, and he'd lived it up—years. At fifteen he was so big women thought he was full-grown. He was worn out before he got started, he'd finally told Estelle. His passion came in spurts, and seldom. Or age—hers?—had ceased to arouse, discouraging him. But when the spirit did move . . .

Marge.

Same day, same time, same place, she'd said. *It's my day off.*

"Hey, Swede, want another drink?" Big Ted said.

"No drink." He hadn't touched the first one.

"Suh-matta with ya?" Dolfo bellowed. "Je*sus*, what's goin' on around here? First thing you're talkin' Fatso, and pretty soon the whole fuckin' place is a funeral parlor. Say, Bea, how 'bout shakin' a leg?" He clutched Bea and strutted her across the floor in a half-drunk show.

Jozef struck German's shoulder. "Captain, German's no water rat like me, nosiree, he builds things."

German had seen the Captain now and then, but they had never spoken. The Captain gave a hard grip. His hand was cold.

"Dolfo gets that way when he drinks," the Captain said. "He's sick—been sick anyway. Last year I thought he was going to die. We laid over two weeks in Bridgeport, but had to leave him. Dolfo claimed it was just another binge, but he was near dying—yes, dying. Now I keep my eye on him. I don't want to lose him. I always go back for my men."

Dancing, Dolfo saw them watching him. He thrust Bea aside and lumbered over. He gaped first at the Captain, then at German.

"What the hell's goin' on here?" He edged close to the Captain. "Goddamn you! Leave me alone, whyn't you?" As if to tear his authority from him, he seized the Captain's cap and slapped it onto German, suddenly bellowing his triumph.

German threw the cap down on the table. He was trembling with anger. He would have headed out the back door if the Captain hadn't halted him with a light graze of his arm. "Oh, don't let Dolfo bother you. He doesn't mean anything by it." Retrieving his cap, the Captain himself rose. "Have the boys bring you aboard sometime." He gripped again with that cold hand.

"Dolfo didn't mean nothin' by it, German," Jozef said.

"Well, Dolfo's lucky in one thing—seems he's got a good Captain."

"A little coldhearted's all. But a captain's a captain. Dolfo don' complain. They say the Cap's got a family somewhere, but nobody ever seen 'm and you'd never believe it the way he hangs onto his men, sticks to the ship, 'most never comes off. Some say his family 'as killed in the war."

"Where, Germany?"

"Don' know. Could be from anywhere. Cap himself looks a little-a everythin'. One thing, he got fat on the war, but he sure's a ghost now. Maybe Mannie's not feedin' him right, hey?"

"Well, you're all in good hands."

"God's—who else's?"

"The Captain's."

"Yeah. Like a father. When he's afraid Dolfo and the rest of us won't make ship, he sends a taxi or comes himself. We're all his, us men. He don't let go. He keeps his men till the end. Surprised me he talked. Never talks, just sits and watches. Quietest man *I* ever seen."

From the floor Dolfo cried to German, "Hey, Captain, where's your cap?" and guffawed.

"Shut up, Dolfo," Big Ted said.

"I got my rights," Dolfo said. "Ain't that right, German. Yeah, he'll give you the straight dope on the law, German will."

"I said shut up, Dolfo!"

"Now *look*, Ted—'f-ya keep smartin' off, I'll wipe the room up with ya-rass."

"Christ!" German said.

"Hey, German! Where the hell ya goin'!" Dolfo cried, but German lunged out the back door. He felt cold to the bone.

Already he could hear Estelle: *You know what fools they make of everybody, those Easy Street bums. What on earth ever made you go in there in the first place? You haven't done that in a long time.*

Grim, he thought, When you left the bars, you almost tumbled into the police station, the perfect location for business. He turned onto Main and crossed to Wash's for the Volvo.

Law. It would have done him some good. Nothing made him look back on his life with such bitterness as being broke. Cash was the wall against *them*. People admire you and admiration is envy. We've got a royalty of our own in this country, power that doesn't have to say a word. In this town it's the long green that commands. "The world's your oyster," his father'd say, then spit. "*That's* the only oyster *I* ever had." "And you can clean up your own oyster too," his mother'd say. German laughed then, but now the sight scarred the morning sky.

He'd got out of muck. He hated home, the memory of home, with a hate born of pity for what he couldn't escape; he could never free himself from the sight of his unshaved old man. Old! Pa had always seemed old, from his first memory old. Ma too, tall, frail Ma forever in her homemade straight flour-sack kitchen dresses. They were really young, but Pa was tired, and Ma too. They dragged. He could hear Ma's feet along the wood floors. He could see Pa and the other miners hauling their bodies up the steep paths to their houses. That wooden two-storey house with its narrow rooms clung to the almost vertical slope. Sitting on the narrow porch with the treacherous steps down paths to the street, the only pleasure in good weather, you looked down onto the spread of Carbondale, the air always blighted with dark smoke and coal dust from the mine stacks. In winter the snow quickly turned dark and when it turned slush the exposed earth looked like dirty scars.

Nothing made him see Carbondale so clearly as Long Island with its stretches of sand and clean-smelling pine woods and glittering sea under a vast low sky. It was as if something had razed the mountains that had once made his vision vertical, razed the town and all his boyhood, and he had fallen into endless space. Space tricked his mind so that he sometimes doubted that his other world had ever existed. He doubted memory and it left him floundering as if *he* did not exist either, did not know who he was. Then he had to retreat to imagination, only to find that his imagination held that town and Ma and Pa and those years which the Island made him ashamed of yet yearn for whenever he rebelled against his life here. Then for a moment his imagination reduced this town and Estelle and her father and Cory to an illusion, but in an instant they returned. Imagination tricked him here too. For them, the place was blood, it was inside them, they took it for granted, their families had settled it, they had given to the land and they had taken from it, they *were* this place on Long Island, they had been for three hundred years.

It set him outside. And because he was outside, he yearned. Despite everything, he wanted this place. Despite the war and his head, he loved the water. The town knew him. The natives had an eye; in a sec they could spot anybody who had not *grown* from the soil here, as he himself had been able to spot people in Carbondale. The cruds and the cream gave you the illusion of friendship—or collusion?—but took you for what you were and could turn on you treacherously. Even Dolfo, the dirty Polack, had him pegged, insulting him buddy-buddy fashion, the rest of them laughing. They knew.

Gunning, he slammed the Volvo door, turned around at the dead-end circle in front of Claudio's retaurant, and headed out Main for home. Sun made the naked trees gray and bleak. He passed the bronze soldier with his bayonet poised to charge.

His buddies loomed.

Dolfo, that bastard! A vet too. The waste! But Dolpho had fought. He'd earned his rights, hadn't he? Rights!

Ole German, he'll give you the straight dope on the law, eh, German?

And *his* rights? To be her lackey, and her sons' and the old man's. And broke to boot.

A vigorous toot-toot-toot from ahead fixed him on old Judge Hammill, sporting in his antique Packard, not out for show—the Judge was too down-to-earth for that—but he loved the weight of his auto and took pride in the upkeep. German flagged an equally vigorous three toots. The judge slowed, pulled to a halt and German braked. "How are things, German?" In the old gent's gentle pink face the eyes were warm. "Haven't seen you around. Vinnie and I have been on the lookout for you. Work cramping you?" "Since that spell of Indian Summer I've been working on the side to keep the place from going to pot. Take a look in the rear and you'll see what I mean. Just about bought out Wash this morning." "You come by. I've got some Scotch that goes down like velvet. Even Vinnie condescends to ask for it." " I'll do that, Judge." "Oh, if Cory's coming for the holidays, bring him along to our open house. He's an impressive young man. He'll go places. Vinnie'd make the eggnog, I think, even if we did away with open house, she's that traditional. On a day like this I miss our fishing, German. Don't forget—you come by." He sank back with his usual serene dignity. His hand went up in farewell.

In the rear view mirror German watched that serene dignity resting on a pile—family's; and he'd made plenty too, and young. For nearly thirty-five years he'd been Judge to the county. Time and laurels with ease. Packard. Wife with a Rolls.

German's imagination scintillated. Overhead, for an instant blue joy arrowed down the avenue of trees, the sun rising gold. There was Whit, parked. Twenty-five zone. He was speeding again. Careful! He nearly brushed Al Dickson peddling past, not his hour, taking time off from the oyster factory for the parade maybe. Al looked straight ahead, never spoke. Bertie'd said Al had been Estelle's childhood sweetheart and never got over her marrying the boys' father in Rhode Island, one more ghost of her life German had to live with. Over the years she was weaning him away from his own past and absorbing him into hers.

By whizzed Curt Elliott, old Ted Wright, Dinnie Young, Walsh Graham—all in uniform. Hands shot up automatically.

Limping, out for her morning stint, went Carole Doyle, led on her mother's arm. Which the more senile, mother or daughter? At the Trinity Episcopal Reverend Rolfe was instructing Clarence in his chores. Attention to the church grounds made the manse next door, with its somewhat wandering fence line, glumly mangy.

Whit came up close behind. No flashing light, but a couple of quick toots.

He pulled over. "What say. Whit?"

But Whit wasn't particularly festive.

"Now, German, you know this zone."

Like the catechism. Twenty-five miles. The front of the sign just behind.

"You nearly skinned Al Dickson back there though he'd be the last to say so."

"I guess I *was* wandering a little. You know how it is, get to thinking."

Whit squinted. "Better be thinking about the road, then. If it weren't Pearl Harbor Day . . ." He nodded, all business. "See you."

Not if I see you first.

As he turned down Monsell Place toward the hospital, from the polo grounds at the other end of town came the first strains of the bands tuning up for the parade, isolated notes, abrupt trials of instruments, sudden passages.

Home, he parked—in the wrong direction as usual.

Now let Whit— The bastard!

He carried his buys out to the old man's shop and set them in *your corner, German*. His. A gift. He went into the house.

Jesus H. Christ. That nigger kid again!

"You're just in time, German, to see Emmy's new coat. I made it from one of Ma's old ones. Turn around, Emmy. Perfect, isn't it?"

The kid *was* a pretty thing, white features, not black black, with glistening eyes, secretive and beautiful. He'd never looked at her so close.

"It's a beaut," he had to admit.

On the chair beside her was the doll. Emmy kept it with her every minute she was here. "The doll *lives* here." She kept it propped against a pillow in the front bedroom upstairs, Cory's room.

The *doll's* room!

First thing they'd have the whole black tribe in.

"Finish your fruit, Emmy. Your uniform's on the bed, German."

He followed her into the bedroom.

"Shouldn't she be in school?"

"She was feeling peaked. She usually comes after school."

"Seems it's always after school."

"*Ger*man, she'll hear. She loves it here, and she's doing no harm."

"We don't have much privacy."

"Why, German, you're never home. And what's a sensitive child like Emmy, lost in a big family, to do —"

"No telling what she tells those niggers on Third she sees here. They'll be stealing us dumb and blind."

"Stealing what!"

"I suppose you'd like to replace your jewelry and crystal and god-knows-what?"

"Who'd run off with such stuff in this town? Why, not long since we never even locked the doors. Besides, we're insured."

"Open your eyes. The town's changing, the whole country. We've made life easy for all kinds of crooks. They can steal or walk off with your stuff, get hurt on your property, sue *you*, and who cares? Not the law. Jesus, the law *helps* them. *I* should be a crook."

"You're getting jaded, German. If we have to believe that about human nature—"

"Not believing doesn't change the facts: most people stink. Know that and you can live with it, but keep your eyes open just the same. *I* do or we'd have nothing with so many spics and niggers in this town. Only thing worse is a Polack."

"It's a good thing *you're* not a cop."

"Damn right. If I got my hands on them, I tell you, they wouldn't be pussyfooting around with dainty sentences because the whole damned democratic country has gone soft and the big shots from top echelons grown so petrified of the underdogs they'll concede anything, fearful as hell they'll be accused of tenderness and thrust out of office. I'd give them some kind of hell, I tell you. They'd dare not do anything but smile. Most people in this country are sheep scared shitless."

"*German*, please, that's no language—"

"No wonder the world's looking to Australia and South America now that we've got Germany and Japan and Italy out of the running. It'll be Africa next; then we'll be in double trouble."

"With your attitude, German, maybe that'll be the best thing."

"Well, your feminine logic won't work with politics."

"Not logic—experience," she said. "Besides, until *we* change the system we're at their mercy, aren't we? In your condition you're not about to help change the system."

"My condition!"

"Well, it's perfectly obvious where you've been at this hour of the morning."

"Jesus! Don't *you* start."

"What do you mean *you*?"

"That goddamn cop—"

"Not Whit again."

"He's always *at* me."

"*Please*, German, don't make a fool of yourself in front of—" She nodded toward the kitchen. *Emmy*. Next, that kid would be running his life.

"Now, listen—"

But she said, "You'll be late for the parade. Oh, German, your hair. You never let your hair go."

"I'll have my cap on."

She reached up and pressed it flat.

"So beautifully curly." She smiled. "Oh, I'll need some change."

She always asked for it. He drew out Wash's bill, $87.21.

"You don't have any?"

"Now where would I get any. Every penny goes on this house."

"German, now don't start on the house."

"Well, at least you didn't say *my*."

He laughed. He was beginning to feel good. There was the band, far. He felt easy. He was proud of the uniform, the men. He'd sure like to see his buddies again, the ones still left.

"Don't throw *my* up to me today," she said. "Don't mention the house. I'm sick of *house*. Sometimes when you talk this way , I wish somebody loved me enough to burn the place down."

He bent down submissively to kiss her cheek. She turned her face away but not before he saw her eyes fill.

For a moment she pressed Emmy's face to her breast. The child's eyes were fixed boldly on him. Then Estelle kneeled. "Now, Emmy, you run along. Your people will be expecting you to watch the parade with them. German's leaving, and on the way down I may stop off to see Maude Willis' mother. She's bedridden. Say good-bye to German."

Emmy clutched her doll and stared in silence.

"Tell German good-bye."

Emmy drew the doll taut under her chin.

He got Estelle's message: talk is over. I'm not leaving till you do. He was used to her little tantrums. But tonight she'd have supper ready, and be cheerful.

Tonight.

"Wasn't there any change?"

"I owed a few bucks to the station for servicing the car."

For twelve measly goddamned dollars and seventy-nine cents. But it *was* cash.

He half laughed.

The bucket gave him the excuse to go down cellar.

"We'll have a live broil tonight," she said.

In his zeal he struck his head—this goddamned house was made for little people—and ducked left where he'd finished the cinder-blocking, moved one, and took out his Prince Albert tin. Ingenious, how he'd melded blocks and cement, like a pro mason. He moved the block. Tipping the home till. Over the years he'd pocketed coins and ones and twos and fives from his bits of shopping, what he'd scraped from his allowance. *She* paid his gas bill. $12,330 plus 12. $12,342. From wheedling, lying, concealing, hoarding, plain going without, *apologized* for. And why? The money was his, earned, but she kept track. "I've had to all my life. The men in my family were all poor managers, even Pa. Bankrupt his store was during the war. He let everybody have things on credit; he didn't ever record what his family took. He gave Gramma Verity all she wanted free, he adored his mother. She and the family ruined him." "You'll sure never take after him." "One bankrupt's enough in any family," she said. "Pa hoped we'd learn from his failures." He envisioned his own skinny Ma—gall that sight—and the old man with his suspenders clutched, pants loose around his sagged belly balled as if his little nourishment and his few possessions were hoarded there. He'd gaze with a bewildered look, not blinking, as if he were trying to penetrate the grayed air, the shadowy veil of constant coal dust. Except for periods after rain, they breathed that insistent darkness, coughed it up, spat it on the ground or into rags.

He fondled the pittance, $12.79. He calculated again: $12,342. Niggardly. The fourth year! Giddy it made him. He'd like to see her expression. In her own house, under her very feet as she moved about in the kitchen, money her sons would never have, or her father. He uttered a thin laugh.

"German, you down there?"

"Just putting the bucket away."

But it should be more—five, ten times more—and would be. "It'll come." His voice sounded like his father's. That presence followed him out of the cellar and rounded the house with him. He breathed deep. The nippy day smelled clean. The paint on the house shone white and pure.

He lowered the cellar door.

Something dark as a post against the yard beyond, just short of the fence, wedged into his vision.

That kid.

She was standing with her hands behind her, watching him. She'd put on the green knit hat and the green coat Estelle had made for her.

She startled him. What'd she see? What was she up to? How many times had she watched him? She backed off, never moving her eyes from his face, and then dashed, not looking back, and disappeared around the corner of the Verity house next door.

Since Rod's death Estelle stayed away from the house more, on the least pretext spent double time in her father's. "I was just out to Pa's . . ." "I was storing some linens I never use." "I'll never get the shop in decent order." "Pa's kitchen needed cleaning. He can't see the dirt."

It pained him, it *did*, to come upon her distracted, to see her fade before him into a far place or time. Since Rod, he felt helpless—he seldom had before—because at those times she would lapse into age. Her face—at moments when unilluminated by energy and her passion for people and things—seemed to lose form under the wear of her long months fighting her mother's cancer, and the burden of Reggie Webb and Ben's drowning and Rod's, and surely through all the years the burden (despite the joy) of her father, and then of her partial hysterectomy, and (she didn't fool him) of the lost baby she grieved for and, he knew, the grief for him too, who so badly wanted one of his own. The baby would have changed his life, theirs, everything. If at such moments he was moved by the sight of her, he was also moved away from her. He looked at her with distance as somebody he didn't now quite know because of the gradual change in her, the—decay? And her ways of thinking, he realized, had come about from a lifetime of events he hadn't lived through, so he couldn't fully feel the weight of them. Their time together was short, but he did feel a loss he couldn't define, and regretted it, even floundered at times, feeling helpless that he could do nothing to recover the tenderness he'd felt for the widow on the cutter.

As she stood in the kitchen doorway gazing after Emmy—"sweet little thing," she murmured—she looked as alien as he felt. You *could* be alien in the heart of your own town. He bent and kissed her on the head, drawing in the clean scent he always associated with her (remembering his own words to the boys, "Your mother's the cleanest person I've ever known"), his feeling clouded with shame even as he thought *Marge*.

"See you at the parade."

"Oh, I'll be lost in the crowd, German, but I'll see *you* anyway." She caressed his cheek. "And, German—"

He didn't wait, but said, "I'll see you tonight." For surely it was the holiday she feared, the Club, the beer and Scotch.

As he did. Not because of Scotch with beer chasers—he loved them—but because of the times they brought back. He had *that* in common with her: he liked *them*. He lived Coast Guard, buddies, nights of gambling and jokes and laughter; and because he and she had lived through *that* together, losses, he felt for her there. *His* brother had had his legs all shot up in the war, patched and patched, re-boned and re-boned; but the legs became his brother's challenge. His mind went to work in a way German envied. Rudy rose to be a big shot in Detroit, GM. If his brother had learned to climb with shattered legs, what was wrong with him with two good legs? After the war, he had gone to Detroit to live with Rudy. Rudy'd started him at the bottom. "Stick to it. Learn every operation. It will take years, but there's no place to go but up." He wouldn't embarrass Rudy. Keep the job. Quick was for him. In no time reenlistment solved his problem.

Now he sometimes thought *I should go back to Detroit. Rudy'd treat me right,* yet something . . . He had to be sure. He felt close. *Surely* he was. He couldn't give up. Money. House.

To avoid going through town, he took the back road, the sun bright through the deeps of naked trees that cut off the Sound.

Music, a band struck up full force, brought him to. Damn. Daydreaming, he'd passed Moore's Lane. He rounded now past the old manse with the barracks built for the Puerto Ricans field hands. Abandoned till summer, the barracks remained an eyesore. Morning sun poured into emptiness; you could see straight through the dead eyes of the barracks to the main road into town.

Just beyond them, he turned down Chapel Lane past the little relic cemetery with its few stones—some of her forbears buried there—and the abandoned little chapel where her old man said he'd started spouting the Bible when he was young. The chapel was a ruin too. A pretty little building it must have been, half the roof gone now, windows missing. Set against the flats and tall sea grass and Mill Creek beyond, it made a painting.

Good crabbing there. Crabbing had been his breakthrough with Rod in his short time here. Cory'd hated crabbing. The time Cory had accompanied them, something bothered in the way he watched hawklike the reflections of the sea grass and the gulls drifting in a blue sky, and in the queer fascination and pain with which he watched the crabs caught struggling in the net, crawling over each other in the bucket, settling, then clawing again. "They want to get out." "You would too," German said. "Look how they try—" "Oh, don't make so much of it, Cory," Rod said, "a crab's a crab." Cory's silence chafed like a splinter. After, back in the yard, Rod was sorry. "Come on, Cory, I didn't mean anything." Cory's smile brought a flash of joy into Rod's face. He laughed suddenly and when he went off Rod followed. They came back wet and muddy, with a raft of cattails their mother could decorate with. Even at their age she said, "Look at you! There'll be mud all over the place. Out *there*—dress out there." Her finger wagged at the back hall. After, "Come here," she said, brushed Cory's hair from his eyes, a smudge from his cheek, and picked some granules from his lid. "They're not kids, Estelle." "You're all boys." She smiled—"You!"—to break his huff. At supper it would be "Jenny-wren's back in the basket by the back door. Gramp says she returns with the first leaves . . ." Gramp says! After supper they'd go out to the old man. Sometimes that was better than having them—no, Cory—hang around, sit there and disappear as if *he* weren't even there. He saw her father in Cory then, that peculiar concentration which defied him. Those eyes saw something he did not; they made a flight beyond where his vision stopped, to some knowledge he did not grasp, which Cory held *inside* him and did not share. *Couldn't* he? Rod shared. Actually German was ashamed when he'd been quick with Cory, but the boy (boy!) made him want to break things.

German recalled strange nights in the service after the war when he'd watched other eyes in hideaway bars or in the known wilds of the Astoria bar and other places in the City, when he'd found in the eyes of those sensitive boys he'd picked up for a night's throw messages he couldn't fathom, feeling on the edge of revelations which they could not carry him to but somehow tried to communicate silently, which even he might unknowingly have helped them discover. After, always, he felt he'd been used.

Used.

Was that his fate, always to be used?

Now came drums, tuba, trumpets, clarinets. The congregation of bands from all the North Fork were assembling. Instruments glittered. The Shriners' red caps and gold tassels dazzled, bright clean the whites and navy caps and ODs and flags of the yacht club and country club and insignias. Everywhere Old Glory flapped in the wind.

He parked far behind the waterworks and then crossed to the polo grounds, feeling the transformation. His blood surged; he felt *in* again, meaningful. That moment loomed: *The Japanese have bombed Pearl Harbor.* He imagined sudden flames, sirens, cries, ships careening, sinking as if his body itself burst burned listed sank; remembered FDR's voice broadcasting the declaration of war to the nation.

He swaggered. "Smart white cap you got there," Ken Williams

called. "Tall as you are they'll see you a mile away, German." German laughed, waved, seeking out where the other Navy and Coast Guard caps were bobbing like poppies. And there *were* poppies. Ralph Edwards' widow, Lily, was selling them to vets and to people hanging around to watch the formation. "You're a few months off with the poppies, aren't you, Lil?" "The fund can use every penny." "That's for sure." Any fund! But none of that. He plucked a paper poppy and pushed the wire through his uniform, bright blood. For them he'd wear it, for them, blown up, burned, drowned, shot, maimed, MIA. He had the metal plate in his head to remember one German torpedo by. He'd wear the poppy for Estelle's dead too, drowned; and for those Polack bastards drinking up their skimmer haul. He searched over heads, through the crowd. The bums must have made it home to get their uniforms. They'd be here. They talked nothing else but the war when they got started, pissed to the gills usually, Army all of them. That was when he liked them most, pitied them most too. So he hadn't gone far, but there was always an uneducated bastard who'd never get this far. One thing they *were* good at when they went at it, work. Such big bastards. He himself was so big that, except when he was foreman, in construction they'd put him on the heaviest jobs. Let German do it. They didn't know how his toothpick legs gave out, or his head—he'd pass out sometimes. At home sitting or talking to her he'd be a sudden *blank,* or so Estelle said. "You all right, hon?" "Me?" "You were staring so—" He didn't know he'd gone off, didn't believe it, because whatever had happened had been lightning quick. He remembered nothing.

A machine-gun burst of firecrackers startled. The crowd cried out, laughed nervously, relieved. A quick veil of smoke vanished. Group leaders were crying out for formation. Red Wilson called, "Over here, German." The outfits spread over the polo grounds in a great semi-circle, a glorious glitter and flash of sun off the metal, Army, Navy, Coast Guard, Marines, National Guard, each separated by boys wielding banners. Old Ed Walsh, Grand Master, checked the files and the line-up of vets from previous wars. Alone, old Mr. Thornton from the Spanish-American War could have walked right out of an old Griffith moving picture. German shook his hand. "German Beaufort. You don't know me, Mr. Thornton, but I know you." Flattered, the old man chortled. Shouts came down the line. The Southold band struck up the Army Air Force song, *Off we go into the wild blue yonder,* stirring them, setting the pace. They bobbed clumsily out of step, slowly falling into rhythm.

A car streaked across the lot, a door flew open, and out piled the

Polack brothers, slapping on their Army caps and breaking into a run for the formation. Made it! He saw why. Their sister was in the front seat with a strange driver. Mirta didn't drive, but didn't trust the boys with cash for a taxi; they drank up every cent she didn't get out of them. German knew Mirta. She'd hurl the uniforms at them. "Get your fucking asses in them uniforms, youse guys. It was your war. And don't give me no shit." She was a winner, Mirta.

Now music called the town. Stragglers appeared from the prefabs across the road. Out came the florists. The nuns and students from St. Agnes' flocked to the curb.

There were waves and cries and shouts from the sidelines—"Atta go, Dennie." "Good for you, boys!"—and sparse clappings here and there for old Mr. Thornton passing, even quips to the spectators from some of the boys; but most of it was quickly drowned out as the Greenport band struck in when Southold ended. German felt the joy of the moving waves of heads and the glitter going down Front Street, felt too a wave of nostalgia as memory fast threw up faces—Vermeer Falugo Randolph Bridges Dietrich Ranier White—and fast images of the war: photos of ships burning at Pearl Harbor, *The only thing we have to fear is fear itself,* the White Cliffs of Dover *I have loved deeply,* the President dead, that strong little man from Hannibal in glasses taking over from the aristocrat, firm with his bomb Hiroshima Nagasaki Rita Hayworth, all the dead, Eisenhower, and suddenly D-day, and finally V-E Day, then V-J Day. Though *he* German had not been in the ETO, but at home guarding the east coast with its subdued blue bulbs at night, a German sub had got them. The operation on his head meant no further sea duty, languishing till V-E Day and V-J Day and ending up in New London, never suspecting that the men drowning in the Gut off Plum Island would lead to escorting the widow on the cutter to Greenport, the sight of that woman his heart went out to.

That woman.

He craned, strained. *Marge.* Surely she'd be. He scoured the crowd—

But no face. No flame of blonde hair in the sun.

Maybe farther along.

By Kaplan's Market on Fifth, by Third, the niggers collected as the parade had a halt. The Matticuck band readied to play. They quipped and laughed. "How's it going, German?" One of the Blydenburghs. The neighborhood kids too young for school flagged him.

On the curb he spotted the green coat. He caught her stare—hard on him, not blinking. *Don't tell* me *kids are born good. The little bitch's got something against me.* Hexed he felt. But his eyes were tempted back several times.

If only Marge would eye with such attention.

Somewhere.

Surely she wouldn't miss.

Where was Estelle?

Smack downtown people gathered in a thin crust along Front, clerks from the P.O., the tiny mall, waterfront crews. Clerks he saw glued to the A&P windows, at Katz's a doorful chitchatting waved, some of the town council on the sidelines shook hands with the marchers, the Washateria and Corwin's Drugs doorways were clotted with the curious.

This day. My war. Yesterday forgotten. And tomorrow.

On Main the barbershop blinds were down—Rick was a vet. There by the bank, his hand raised to him, was Judge Hammill with Vinnie. The judge winked, Vinnie nodded with pleasure. He straightened, missing no step, swelling.

They passed the Kaplan block, where the housewives watched from the long cement stoop; passed the old theater, Goldin's now, furniture like monuments in the display window, Goldin himself standing out front; passed mostly people on porches; passed near empty sidewalks before the Methodist and Baptist and halted just before the Presbyterian.

The mayor stepped out of line to receive the wreath and place it at the foot of the Revolutionary War obelisk. The Riverhead band struck up lively, and the procession moved haltingly ahead to that bronze soldier.

An old legionnaire he didn't know, from out of town maybe, accompanied by one soldier and one sailor and one marine supporting a great wreath, initiated a ceremony of words to war heroes. ". . . sacrifice . . . an occasion . . . actions never to be forgotten . . . history will remember . . . new world . . . freedom . . . the dead and the living. . ."

Are we worth the dead? German thought.

Am I?

This stillness stirred.

Marge.

Estelle.

What had *she* ever done to him except marry him? Even that was her mother's doing. While she was alive she came through, helped him, slipped him a few bucks, knowing a sailor was too poor for what she hoped he would do, what he did do. Truth was, he had been smitten by that fragile widow with such staunch bearing, proud to be near her, roused because she was delicate and slim and soft and full-breasted and because she was tender with her mother and her father and, he found out, the boys. The least mention of them brought smiles. In nobody he'd ever known could the love of life leap into such flashes of pure joy. To preserve that was worth fighting for, but she was rare in a world that wasted too much, that sponged, *got* without lifting a finger if it could.

Where was *he* in all that? He worked construction, never flagged, did his job, his duty. *She* always gave him credit for that: "You can't beat German working." On the first day he'd ever come home before quitting time, he didn't want to tell her he'd fainted on the job. "It's because you're so big. They think you can do more than the others, and *you* think so. You don't want to let them down, but your circulation won't make it." She knew. He'd simply go down, out for a few minutes, till his blood got right again. "Go at a slower pace. Don't pay any attention to what the men think. One of these days . . . I hate to think about it." Once he got started, he never could slow down. He was his own downfall. Whenever they "went west" to the City, "Have you got your pills?" she'd ask. He'd deliberately challenge fate and leave them at home. "*German*, haven't you had enough problems? Sometimes I think you want to die, want to." In the car her face would go bleak, turn to the fields, the Sound, the passing town.

Abruptly now he heard the command "Ready, aim—"

A single burst of six simultaneously cracked. Silence, profound and startling, reigned briefly.

The Greenport band broke it.

Slowly, sloppily, they straggled around the triangle point back toward town.

In no time he was marching west on Center Street, headed straight toward that house that looked like a misplaced sharecropper's. The Garcías'. Fatso's. For sure that's what people would call it for as long as anybody remembered the murder, though if today was any indication of how long people remembered a war that wouldn't be long. And for most things that would be fine because today's today, you have to live now, *but* comes a time you have to thank the buddies who killed and died so you could go on living and having what you had. Not only that. The day stopped you long enough to sort out the men from the pricks who got out of it, who hid under fear and rhetoric about principles, some who dared to praise the others *to the skies* only so they could make the bucks as fast as they could on our blood.

Blood.

Empty the house looked. No chance of that with the raft of brothers and sisters Fatso'd had. But none of the whites standing in the dirt—when would the town get around to sidewalks here?—had teeth anywhere near like Fatso's monstrous uppers. *Big enough to eat you with, my dear.* He laughed aloud at the grotesque sight he conjured up—Fatso the wolf, the mother's head, and that mouth chomping.

Sing Sing for life.

Poor bastard. His mother dead. And Fatso harmless all those years. Estelle said you have to think of the living, and not just Fatso but the rest of them. What did it cost the State, us, to maintain all those stuck away for doing next to nothing, who could be put to use if judges and lawyers, and the public too, had any real foresight? But did they care? Shit! Damned few. If they really believed in men and justice, they'd be the first to go for an overhaul of the legal system, but who'd wreck his own monopoly?

On Third the little park with the bandstand was the only crowded place on the entire march. The nigger neighborhood turned out, plenty, talking up a storm and whooping, calling out friendly gibes, flagging.

The files crossed the main drag again between the theater and the two hotels, a few men outside the Stirlington bar and on the Wyandank steps watching them turn right just before the train depot at the dead end, where cheers and wild honking greeted them from cars on the ferry just pulling in.

On the last lap—maybe to pick up the pace home—a band struck up *Row, row, row your boat.* Now what bugged him—he glanced down toward the railroad crossing where Madam Pam's shacks used to be—was *nowhere Marge.*

She could have been, and seen him in uniform. She never had.

Time. It was only going for one o'clock. Three hours till—

Jesus!

At the polo grounds the parade broke up with cries, shouts, horns. Sweeps of dust rose as cars shot off.

"Say, German—" It was Dolfo. "Drop us off at the Legion? You think Mirta the bitch'd come pick us up? Not on your life."

The three stood abject.

"Sure, hop in."

Dolfo offered him a swig from a pint of JW. "Your brand, German."

No, he thought, *Marge.* It wouldn't do, he might not get it up, but then *Hours yet* so gulped a throatful.

"What every parade needs." He laughed.

In a moment they were at the Legion Hall.

"You come in for a game, German?"

"Maybe later. I have a thing to do."

"You'll be sorry. Might have been your lucky day, Germ."

"I don't have many of those."

"Then you got one coming."

"You got that right."

The Scotch renewed the slight glow he'd felt before the parade, the sun everywhere a promise, the sky almost too clear, the air crisp, the day so comfortable.

He passed that soldier charging with his bayonet. Forever. Quick he heard the torpedo hit, felt the ship bolt, the sky suddenly a wall of water; it struck him cold, then—nothing. The rest he never saw. He woke on a stretcher. On another ship. Wars forever, yes. Not a bad thing, come to think of it. If war was a crying shame, it somehow straightened things out, reminded you what you all were, not much when you came right down to it, if you could understand yourself. *He* couldn't anyway. At heart many men wanted war. It came out every day. You wanted to hit something. Better to have it organized, get the pressure off, clean up populations. Something has to. Maybe that's what diseases were for. But he'd given up his *Hail Marys* and *penances* and *the sisters* and the raft of *priests, those Jesuits,* long ago. Too many real things were worth bowing to than painted statues. You could make a statue represent anything. Keep the saints. That soldier would do for *him.*

He parked in his drive, in stillness staring at that thousand times stared at house. Empty. Gone for a while, she'd said. Well, then.

He went in and shed his uniform.

Time now.

He went down cellar.

He hated the place. "The first winter," Bertie'd said, "grandpa'd dug a hole under the kitchen for potatoes, onions and apples, the meal barrel, jars of put-up food. Little by little my father dug under, then the boys. Tom did his part when he had the house, before the fire at sea crippled his hands. But Tom's boys wouldn't do a thing."

German was shocked the first time he'd gone down. Why hadn't she paid to have it finished right? "The damned walls will collapse one of these days," he told her. He couldn't stand up in it. In the dark he could hardly find the one light or the gas and electric meters, and the fuse box was set in an obscure place behind the chimney. He stumbled over mounds of earth and god-damned sand. From working ducked so long, he emerged sweating, itching, arms smeared with grit, clothes filthy. "Why didn't you put on work clothes?" She brushed him. "Stay out in the hall. I'll bring you a robe and you can take a shower." "I wouldn't need work clothes in a decent cellar." "It's a perfectly good cellar, not finished is all, but you're getting there." "With the history of masons in your family, it's a damned shame they couldn't have finished their own house. Why didn't *you*? You had plenty of money." He watched. She didn't bat an eyelash. "Pa was always going to do it, but he'd a hundred other things, and *did* them." He didn't miss *that*. Still, she could have afforded to have the cellar finished off and put new sewage pipes in for the washing machine was hell. "All you complain about is how cockeyed Pa's makeshift work is, and done cheap. Well, here's your chance to show Pa what you can do."

He had settled for cinder blocks and several enormous jacks to screw the floor up even. "That'll do till something better comes along," she said. "We can afford better than that," he said, eyeing her. "I don't see how." At first she'd oversee his work. "Don't you trust me?" "It's because I'm used to Pa's bad eyes. I don't want him hitting a raw wire or falling and breaking a bone. Besides, I like to know where things are." But she'd finally given him his way. "I don't really care anymore what you do with the cellar."

Having gone over the house upstairs and down with a fine comb—room to room, closets, attic, walls, mopboards. His fixation on the cellar grew: walls, the old cesspool drain, the channel to the street closed off after the town sewage and drainage were connected. Her brother Rich's whisper resounded. He could never escape his suspicion. Somewhere money had to be. All that dirt. You fool, you! He'd started systematically, left of the cellar door, and worked around, on days when she went to the City, weekends if she crossed the Sound to her niece Marie in New London.

Bertie'd told him the cellar door had been shifted three times in its history. Under the bedroom ell there had once been a cellar, partially filled when they'd shifted the door from the ell to the side of the kitchen. He had dug out three quarters or more of that to get under the ell. The floor of the main bedroom, the ell, was separated from the ground by a foot, some three feet in. He had to crawl under. There he used to keep a lard tin under a piece of plywood. He'd keep change till it mounted, convert it always to fives to hoard; when he had enough fives, to fifties. then to hundreds.

Now he kneeled an instant, peering at the finest filtering of sun in the dark, a single golden spot on the back of his right hand. His position, the act, the very fact, struck him suddenly as ridiculous. What in hell am I *doing* here! In my own house, hiding money away, my own money, as if I were stealing it! He struck his head. Grit fell over his hair and neck. He slid out and came up—crack—against the floorboards. I've a right, more than a right. If it weren't for that son of hers! He hated her saying *German this* and *German that* before her educated son, for making him driver and delivery boy, handyman, any necessary appendage that occurred to her. Oh, Cory'd do anything he asked, and gladly. But it was Estelle, a regular quarterback for Cory: "German will do it." Well, German has his limit. A day will come. German deserves his killing. When he finds. Angry, he felt like a drink. He'd never had enough money to be sociable, even with her boys, when Rod was alive. Surely the town knew, even the cruds on the dock, German's wife held the purse strings. The fishermen and the Polacks had it better. If I had enough cash, I'd go tonight— His hand he thrust into the sand—it chafed, but felt good, cool, but not cold like outside. The cellar was actually warm, with an earth scent, pungent; but, more, he liked the familiarity of it. He turned to where he had last dug.What did keep him back? This? *This?* It was not the digging, no, it was the house—he knew every inch of upstairs, every foot under, the screwjacks, the very skeleton it rested on; and in a way that made it *his*, didn't it? He'd do them all out of it yet. He'd find a way—his justice.

This time he could dig with a shovel, hard right, behind the furnace—not sand. "Rich black dirt, famous potato fields," he muttered, grunting. In no time he had a black mound, topped with rusty brown as he dug farther down. The damp smell was good. He had to kneel as it deepened. Then he dug with a trowel. When his hand began to ache, both hands used it like an ice pick. Clods shot against him; the run-off caked about his knees. He was sweating and, thinking of her *Why do you go so hard at it?*, he stabbed more rapidly. He struck hard clinks. At each clink his blood surged. *Suppose*! He couldn't imagine, yet he couldn't imagine anything else. He dropped the trowel, dug his hands into the earth, pulled fistful after fistful. Dirt dribbled into his sleeves, but he couldn't stop. He imagined *it*. He'd find it—he *had* to—*this day*. If only—!

This house—and Marge.

If one time in his life he could get out from under. Sick to death of it. First his old man and his old lady, then school, then the war, then a measly factory job. Only *after* the war and Detroit, reenlisting, had he had a reprieve—if only he'd had the sense to realize—until he met Estelle and Pa and her boys and the whole goddamned history of this family and this barren sand, town, Long Island, one tomb after another he couldn't crawl out of. Maybe *today* was his lucky day, Pearl Harbor Day.

He wiped the sweat away. Mud dribbled down. His eyes burned. He blinked. He couldn't see clearly; but he dug, raged at the fucking dirt, thrusting it down in fury—*them*, and him *wanting*, wanting. He'd go away as far as he could get, buy a nice quiet place, never see this town or spics and niggers and Polacks, New York yids, or a Verity as long as he lived. She *could* encourage him—couldn't she?—share, give him what should be his. Then he'd be different with her, but, no, she couldn't *let* him be himself with *ours*. She held him down. She—

He struck and struck.

A door slammed.

"Shhh." He started at his own voice.

He listened.

The back door opened and closed, then the kitchen door. She crossed, set something down—

"German?"

She was moving about in the other rooms.

He quickly rubbed his hands against his jacket—futile!—backed away from the hole, and stood. His head struck. This goddamned cellar. Sweat ran hot down his face, down his neck, his arms itchy.

"German?"

He ducked, crossed the cellar, and went up just as she came out the door.

"Oh, I saw the cellar door open— German, *look* at you!"

He squinted in the sun. The yard rose in a blur. Sweat smarted.

"Your hands— It's blood!"

He stared at his hands, his discomfort suspended but for a second.

"What in hell did you *think* it was?" He strode past.

"Why are you so furious? I only said— You'd better bathe."

At once he undressed. He heard her stack dishes, slam the refrigerator door. He eased under the shower, soaping down, rubbing. His hands burned.

When he went into the bedroom, changed, she said, "Let me see your hands."

"They're all *right*. Just some scratches. I was wrestling with a piece of that old piping to the water heater, nearly broke the wrench twisting the rusty thing. The way the whole shooting works are put together down there . . ." But his mind was on the loose dirt down cellar. Damned good thing she almost never went down these days.

"Now, hon, don't start—not today. Please. Did you see Pa?"

"Yes."

She was staring across the fields. The sky made a blue sea in her. "You didn't tell Pa about Fatso's sentence?"

"I didn't know it when I talked to him."

"Thank heaven. Let *me* tell him. I still, after all this time, can't believe it. Fatso never raised a finger to anyone, went his way on that bike, just like Albert Dickson."

"Who knows what's in anybody's head?"

"I dread telling Cory."

"It'll be no news to him. You just have to wait so long for a trial in this country, but surely Cory knew what the sentence would be. Murder. And a mother. What jury would forgive that? It's what he deserves."

"Who knows what he deserves?"

"Murder speaks for itself."

"Speaks for itself? If *we* knew what happened. It's perfectly possible that . . . Well, why make up tales?"

"The tale's pretty clear. Fatso confessed it."

"You say it with such certainty."

Why *did* he when he felt for the poor bastard?

"Fact is fact, Estelle."

"It's terrible to say but the fact is his mother's *dead*, German, and Fatso's alive and young. We have to think of the living; the dead are gone."

Bleak, her gray eyes grayed the day.

"Now, Estelle . . ." He placed his hand in the small of her back and rubbed gently; she always went limp with pleasure when he did that, moaned.

She nodded away whatever sight had darkened the day.

"Hon, you've been drinking . . . so early. It's not two yet."

"I ran into Dolfo and the boys off the boats."

"Them. If you must have a drink—"

"I don't *have* to."

"—the first thing in the morning—"

"As a matter of fact I took a swig on the polo grounds. After all, it's *my* day."

"Well, drinking doesn't strike me as a very respectful way of celebrating the dead."

"Cory was in the war. You can just bet Cory'd—"

"No, not Cory."

"I wish you'd stop treating him like the living Jesus. You always paired your boys off like those Mormon kids plaguing at the door with their Jesus."

"Well, if you had children . . ." Blunted by her own words, she was clearly ashamed. Still, he couldn't help his look of accusation: *I* didn't have the miscarriage, *I* didn't have the hysterectomy. He bit it back, swerved with determination out the kitchen door to the Volvo.

"Where are you going?" She followed half across the yard. "German?"

Just as he backed out she cried "German!" again, this time a near scream. Another scream followed. He braked. In the mirror he saw Emmy dash behind the car and pick up something. That doll! Jesus! She screamed and clutched it to her breast, too still. How'd it get *there*? He turned off the ignition and got out.

"Why don't you *look!*"

The doll's head was crushed. The long blond curls hung from the broken skull.

"Emmy was behind the car."

"What was she doing there?"

"German, you might have killed her."

Could she dare think—? He may hate kids' noise, but he'd never go that far.

"German couldn't help it, Emmy."

Emmy was staring at him, not uttering a sound. Her eyes filled, but she seemed stubbornly to hold the tears back. That hard look again. She must hate him. From the first moment he'd seen that face close to at St. Agnes' bazaar, from the moment he'd veered Estelle away from that tent to other amusements, those eyes had seemed to accuse, that gaze had followed them. When he'd looked back, those dark eyes were fixed on him.

She bowed her head over the doll and broke into hard chokes.

He felt ashamed. But why should he? It *was* his fault, and *wasn't.*

Ole German, he'll give you the straight dope on the law.

"She's dead." Emmy's voice shocked. He couldn't remember ever having heard it. "She's dead." The voice was tiny.

He couldn't get away fast enough before the kid turned on him and said it direct. "Estelle's dead." With his complaints about her, the kid'd never believe in a million years it was an accident.

He backed out with fury and shame, seeing the three for an instant frozen in his mirror, Emmy embracing that doll, Estelle embracing Emmy.

Just what he needed this day!

At the corner he'd have turned left to the Club for a drink, but he'd fool her, he'd take the roundabout way.

Right, straight ahead, he glimpsed the widow's walk—*always;* you couldn't avoid the fucking thing, especially in winter through the naked trees. *Fools.* All her family were worse than chicks separated from the hen they longed for. Why couldn't they cut ties? He drove the three corners to the traffic circle. Bertie wormed into his head. *The oldest house on Long Island's not too many miles. John Holmes wrote "Home Sweet Home" there.* Home! Plagues of earwigs, silverfish, sand fleas, field mice, termites, salt water and salt air rotting the pipes out from under you, damp rot, hurricanes all fall long, his tools rusting, even the undercoating of the car going. For this you got out from under soot, the cave and holes and props they called homes in Carbondale, and struggled halfway through high school, went through a war.

He cut across the road at high speed. He could see Cory's window. No, no Estelle standing there. The house shot out of sight.

Safe!

He seldom went upstairs, hated the narrow stairway from the kitchen up to the two bedrooms, half the time forgot to duck and hit his head against the dropped ceiling at the upper end. But he'd had his day up there. *The Day of the Deed.* Oh, no money, but the deed to the house he'd found, and her Last Will and Testament. Was it bait? No. The last thing she'd believe was that he'd be sneaking around for cash.

In his early searches he'd removed the panel in the rear bedroom wall and crawled through the cubbyhole over the ell, a tight squeeze. Too big he was. He'd never be able to slip out in a hurry if she'd come in while he was up there rummaging around. Plenty of stuff. He'd taken his time, gone up again and again, gone with a fine comb over boxes of clothes, old papers, photos Bertie'd love to get her hands on; felt between old RCA Victor 78s, behind family portraits in frames, inside a Philco radio cabinet; felt along every inch of wall—in these old houses they'd line and stuff the walls for warmth with whatever came to hand. But *nothing.* He emerged sweating, blinking away darkness and cobwebs, sneezing, his nostrils clotted with dust.

The day he'd discovered the will he was standing by the old trunk, *my special linens.* Elizabethan, Estelle had called the trunk. Said Bertie wanted it. Not a chance! *J. Dampler 1599* was carved under the keyhole, the key gone centuries since. "That's Everyman carved into it with his pack on his back, setting out to make his way in the world, like the first Daniel Verity and Amanda and their son, whose bed it was for a long time after they got to the New World. Pa claimed *he* was brought up in that trunk too, but I think he'd heard the story so many times he actually believed he was Daniel all over again. You know Pa."

Pa!

He was too far gone, raging with failure, couldn't stop: the trunk *was* filled with linens. He lifted them, smearing them with dust. The bottom was laden with envelopes—insurances, deeds, will, each stamped and signed Donald J. Weems, Attorney-at-law. What a fool she was to leave them unprotected. He couldn't believe her stupidity—or his for being blind to the obvious.

And the will. It *was* her will.

His finger traced down . . . *All.* It left all *to my beloved sons, Rodney Llewellyn Moorehead and Cory Verity Moorehead.* So with Rod dead, all to Cory. Scrawled in hand was DO NOT RECORD. Do not record! Why had she held back? So it wouldn't be in the newspapers? So *he* wouldn't know? And . . . *when*? The date! A good year after their marriage! To hold the property over his head . . .? But *share*?

He thrust the papers into their envelopes, slid them back under the bottom linens, and restored the top layer. He slammed the lid and went downstairs, his stomach twitching ulcerously, and went off to the Club, his fury feeding a tumor in him; it festered real and growing, all he'd been hoarding in him. He'd sure like to make her feel what she was creating between them.

Months after the day of the will, when he'd gone home from the Club, she was reading in the front room, took off her glasses, smiled. "Hungry, darling?" From across the room in the mirror he saw his face caught in the lamplight, his eyes raw red and sunken. *Why* did she say nothing? She'd sulked at that look often enough. "Hon, do you suppose someone came in, some kid? My trunk's been opened. Oh, nothing's missing. Donnie roots around once in a while." But the mongoloid Matthiessen kid from the next block, another one of her lame ducks, would come and usually do no more than sit in the kitchen and stare at her as she worked. "You wouldn't want anything in there, and we never lock things." He said nothing. He was sure she knew. She was too calm this time, though she knew the bloodshot eyes, the reek, his steeping in it. She couldn't *bear* his escapes, could she? He sensed the warning. He waited for her to say "At the club again" before the tirade. Worse—she said nothing. She picked up her glasses and went on reading.

Now the Volvo hobbled down the eroded humps and ditches of the slope. He parked close to the water, low, out of sight. Bridge

Street dead-ended between two houses at the crick; otherwise, the street would have led straight to the Protestant cemetery on the other side. If you weren't familiar with the slope, you might drive straight into the water. Club members with one too many had had their accidents. The houses on the bank hid the Club from town. Only from the bay could you see it. Tucked away as if unwanted, half on pilings at the crick edge, neither on land or water, it seemed to huddle in shame.

He'd show her who was boss, not some old man with crippled hands burned in a fire at sea. "You should've seen him in the hospital, German. Like one of those Egyptian mummies he looked, one solid white bandage, only his eyes and nose and mouth free. I couldn't believe it was my father." "That's no reason to let him run your life." "Run! I've always *wanted* him with me." "You talk as if he was a weak old man? The weak run the world, don't you know that?" "You're bitter, German." "I don't have cause?" "If you do, you make it. Oh, everybody has cause to be bitter sometimes, but what would happen if we all gave in? Pa didn't. Lost his home, lost children, went bankrupt, near burned to death, crippled for life, abandoned by his children, lived for a woman who divorced him and married someone else, and *she's* dead now, and a son drowned; but he lives out there, independent, straight, doing for himself. Without us he'd get along. Don't you think he wouldn't. Now, *you* tell me— Is that weak?"

In a hundred insidious ways she confronted him with *Pa this, Pa that.* All *he* saw was a skinny old man forever puffing on a cigarette and staring into space as if *they* didn't exist, half-shaved— "He cut his face again." "He can't *see,* German—" "He can *feel—*" *"You* try feeling with his crippled hands."

Don't tell me those quivering eyes don't see things!

Something in her gray eyes, something which he could neither define nor deny, unsullied and as durable as steel, made him wince; and he remembered the woman he had come upon on deck of the cutter, four years now, and his old admiration returned. "Hon . . .?" he said. Her face fell against his raised hand. "I know," she said, "I know."

"Hola, Choiman." Dark in the bright sun was the Hannibal woman. *Je*-sus! He always feared he wouldn't understand Mrs. Hannibal's babble of English and Puerto Rican. Wisps of wiry black and gray hair fringed her bandana. She was carrying fish.

"How are you, Mrs. Hannibal?"

"Purty good, Choiman. You good too? Gottee fish. I go see Mrs. Pell, she gottee so much fish, no can eat in a million years. Ha ha ha.

Once givee me for my Dannie when he work on telephone poles. Good boy my Dannie was. He went Brooklyn. Gottee wife, my Dannie. She no like live here—after he fix house good for her. Died my Danny. Puttee new techo, roof. You see dere?" Her bony hand streaked a shine up. She laughed, her eyes twinkling dark. "Estella okay?"

"Yeah, yeah, good."

Any minute now Estelle might—

"No see fo' long time, she comin' when she can, have tea y cookie."

The thought sickened. The woman's eyes were bad, a heavy odor emanated from her clothes, she saw none of the dirt on her clothes and dishes. Her house was jammed with clutter; everywhere hung something, not an inch of wall or tables or furniture free. Heated by a black wood stove she kept going all year round, the house was suffocating, and the icebox half the time mouldy. "She'll poison you with that stuff," he'd say. "I'd never insult her by refusing." "It's your funeral then." "She's more dignity than half the people in this town. Oh, I know. They think she's black because she married Geebo Hannibal, but the Hannibals were fine Negroes. Geebo was good to her, and Dannie was one of the best boys in this town, a great athlete, and everybody loved him." "But wouldn't associate with them." "She's a good woman with a great soul. She's from a decent Puerto Rican family." Why should *she* be so hurt about it? "You don't believe that, do you?" "It's a fact. Ask Cory. When he comes he talks by the hour with her in Spanish. It's a revelation, I tell you. She adores Cory."

There came Ansel. A lifesaver!

"What say, Anse?"

Mrs. Hannibal said, "When come?"

"Who?"

"Cuando viene el muchacho? Cory. Cory come Christmas for see you y madre?"

"He'll be here."

She whooped. She clapped her hand against the packet of fish. "If he come, tellee come see Catalina. Goo'bye, Choiman. Say hello Estella."

She went up Easy Street, thin as a stick, the light breeze pressing at her long skirt.

"No Florida this winter, Anse?"

With the cold, businesses closed and the owners went South. Front Street was half deserted.

"Too many repairs. Sea eats up everything. No taming her."

The Club—with its dark paneling, low ceiling, the little bar in the side nook by the entrance, the enormous window framing a view of the crick—was cozy and consoling.

Gary humped over the bar.

"What say, Anse? German?"

A card game was going. Intent, the men merely raised their eyes and nodded—Floyd Eustis and his poker crew; and old Randall, the ex-court clerk, a regular presence since his wife had died; and Al Commerford; lifelong friends who had their rounds most afternoons.

"Darts, German?"

"I'll do you in, Anse. Scotch on the rocks, Gary."

Anse removed his jacket and rolled up his sleeves.

German's eye measured. The darts arrowed straight, struck hard.

"Got to go some, have I?"

"You've got to go it twice more," Anse said, chalking up the first game.

German did.

The poker game over, all gathered around to watch.

German won the third.

"Give us another round, Gary. Okay, Anse, let's go for two up, then I'll skunk you."

Laughter.

Rolfe Williams, who'd worked years under Anse, drew his finger across his throat. "Think so?"

"Jesus, don't *do* that. Gives me the willies, that empty house." Gary lived in the house next to Fatso García.

House.

German let fly a dart, too low. "Je-*sus!*" But ahead still. "Now, come onnnn, Anse."

"Fatso won't be seeing that house again."

House.

"Don't worry, Gary. Nobody'll go for your throat. You're not old."

"Yeah, who's got sympathy for the old these days?" Floyd laughed.

"Fatso's mother wasn't exactly old," Randall said.

Straight across the crick, under the leafless trees, the cottage was visible. Sun made a blinding sheen over the water.

"You, German."

Turning, German blinked. The dart board was darker.

Missed!

"I'll have you yet, German."

"Try." German prodded him forward.

Anse said, "When you get the impulse, old or young doesn't matter. I've seen men—"

"You better see the dart board," German said.

"—from the boats commit the worst atrocities."

"Yeah." Al Commerford, his pin of a head and wiry figure, almost freakishly thin, hunched on his knee. "And fed them to the fishes."

"I was court clerk a good many years and learned a lot about people."

"Well," Gary said, "you going to keep it all to yourself?"

"—but there's a lot more I'd like to know before I die—"

"You thinking of leaving us?"

Once on a track, you couldn't stop Randall. "—but I suspect there's little chance of that because I'd never kill anybody. I say that. I guess I'd never be in that situation, but I'd like to know what you go through. Oh, we all get mad, even say *I could kill you* to somebody—" Was he thinking of Addie, dead some years now? "—and even for a second mean it, but we stop there. *They* don't. Fatso didn't."

"Randall's right." Al went to the window, skinny as a crane standing over the water below. "You get tongue-tied and throw things."

"Maybe you wouldn't if you could find words," Randall said, "but most of them can't."

Words.

Cory. *There's something inside you you're responsible for.* But responsible to what? Cory never could say. *There are things you do you can't explain, you carry them inside you, and they tear at you. If you could get rid of them, you wouldn't have to keep facing them.* How did Cory know? What'd he ever do? He could see Cory's brooding eyes. There was a black fire in Cory.

Sometimes he hated Cory, Cory's education. Cory's questions clung thicker than burrs. Cory's prodded till *he* did nothing but dredge up questions. Why couldn't Cory let silt be.

"You're what your head makes you." German threw his dart.

"Unless somebody or something else does," Randall said.

"Now what in hell's that mean?"

Anse intervened. "Gary, bring us a couple more, Scotch and water, a double. German owes me, but I'll share one with him."

"You won 'm, you drink 'm." German laughed. "It's win or lose, no in between."

"Randall's been in the law. He should know. They try to make you make something of your life," Al said.

"They, they, they. Who's *they*?"

"Us, German."

"I'd have to think about that, Al."

"Well, there's no denying you've got to live with others even when they're gone." Was Randall still thinking of his wife? "You live with family, friends, even enemies, when you're alone."

"You got Fatso too much on your mind?" German said.

"I guess after this morning's paper everybody has. After all, Fatso was part of the place."

"Sitting up in Sing Sing for the rest of his life. I'd sure hate to be the poor bastard."

"I don't know." Randall gazed across at that house by the Girls' Hole.

"You don't know! Try changing places with him."

"Well, to tell the truth—sounds crazy—I *would* like to be in Fatso's shoes—"

"Je-sus!"

"—just long enough to know what went on in that boy. Oh, it's not the first time I've wondered. I've seen thousands come and go in court, and every face was different and most of the crimes were different in some way; but after a while—it's strange—I felt I wasn't seeing faces or listening to crimes. What I kept seeing appear in court was something in them, the same thing in all of them over and over, something that never changed, something that can't be put down, that nothing will ever be able to put down."

Law itself is a tribute to the unceasing power of the irrational, Judge Hammill always said.

"Like the sea," Al said.

"You make it sound like some people don't have a chance against it," Rolfe said.

"Like the sea," Al insisted.

"Maybe some don't."

"Shit, they've got heads on their shoulders, haven't they?" German flung the dart. Bullseye! "Take that, Anse."

"Not so fast, German. You haven't topped my score yet. I suppose you did that with your head?"

"A head's no good against it, Anse, some heads anyway. Passion's too strong. I can't figure it. I've been a long time trying."

"Judge Hammill says a man shouldn't hand himself over to—'dubious energies,' he calls them," German said.

"Well, I don't mean to speak against Judge Hammill, and I don't mean to say I really know what it is I'm talking about—I'm just talking—but if he really believes you can always choose to hand yourself over to dubious energies, then all his years on the bench he's been missing something most people know from blood instinct even if they never stop to think about it—and that's what most people standing in front of him waiting for judgment handed themselves over to."

"Well, they made the choice," German said.

"It's just what they didn't do."

"They got no head, then they're animals," Gary said.

"Aren't we all? That's our trouble these days: we forget—or deny—we're animals. The word's dirty. Most of our best pleasures are animal."

"And the worst," Al said.

"Maybe the worst is what we need most."

"Je-sus, Randall, you *want* us to be animals?" German plucked the darts. "Your eye's improving, Anse."

Anse kept a cool face, nodding.

"A man's an animal first."

"I'll stick to being a man myself."

"Maybe *they*'re the men at last."

"Those jailbirds? Come onnnn, Randall."

"They're responsible then, and that's when they become men."

"*Look*, Randall," German said, "use your head, can't you? A guy stands against all of us. Let's face it, he's committing suicide. Suicide!" He flung the dart. Almost! "I've got you, Anse."

"When the results're posted, I'll give in." Anse swept his arm toward the sheets posted by the bar.

"Being alone in that cell," German said, "you don't call that suicide?"

"Maybe it's nightmare, maybe peace," Randall said. "I'd hate to have Fatso's nightmares *or* his peace, but I'd like to know."

"You could ask Fatso himself."

Randall crossed and stood before the window, dark against the shimmering crick.

"He wouldn't know, I'm convinced. He confessed is all. I don't think what he'd tell was what happened. You can describe facts but facts aren't what really happen, there's more. Oh, you talk, sure. You talk to try to find out yourself. Maybe there are no words for it."

Nobody said a thing. Randall had drawn their eyes toward that house at the edge of the bay.

The light offended German's eyes.

The move drew German's attention to the figure of the Captain sitting at the window's edge watching, silent. He was so dark against the light German couldn't see his face. Why didn't he ever take his hat off?

"I wouldn't want to commit murder, but I'd like the experience without doing it." Randall laughed.

"A good trick if you could pull it off," Floyd said.

"My trouble is I'm short on imagination. I suppose that's why I was just the court clerk all those years."

"If you weren't so good at it, you wouldn't have lasted so long, Randall."

"Now I know you're getting drunk, Floyd Eustis," Randall said, but softly, pleased.

"Je-sus. We going on with this game or not?" German turned back to the board, but the Captain's voice interrupted. So rare, and so near a whisper, like thinking aloud, it startled them all.

"Maybe if we let criminals alone, they'd do themselves in."

He expected no answer because he sat again, facing the crick, a dark blot against the bright water.

But Randall said, "I've thought it many a time. Let them alone long enough and they turn against their kind."

"Yeah, but before they do, they sure take a lot of other people down with them, You wouldn't want that?" Al had turned to the Captain, but the Captain kept a void.

"It'd clean the jails out!" German said.

"The Captain has something there," Randall said. "Maybe they shouldn't be in the jails. They wouldn't be if we *dared* to know them. We might someday. The human race is still in its infancy; maybe we'll grow up. We're afraid of them. We're afraid because what's in them is in us, and what's in us scares us. When we put them away, we're running away from ourselves. If we weren't made to hold back our animal impulses every minute . . ."

"Sure. A blood bath," Al said.

"No, but what does happen?" Randall said. "Fatso lived straight across there. We saw him every day. If we didn't, we wondered where he was simply because he's part of what happens. Then he does a terrible thing. So he's not part of us anymore? Suddenly we're afraid of him. We hide him because—"

"You're an idealist, Randall," the Captain said. "I had something realistic in mind—"

"You'd better bring us down to earth then."

"—a network of killing grounds, land set aside where men could go to let out their impulses and settle their differences. Most men would never come out."

"We'll have to lock you up, Captain, or we never will finish this game," German said.

All this talk! *Talk.* He didn't like the Club talky. It stifled. Words. Bad as Cory. *He* was all words. *There are things in us, but how to get to them?* He dreaded Christmas. He didn't understand Cory. Cory lost him. He had—the newspapers said it about Fatso—a "deranged sensibility contrary to reason or common sense."

Deranged sensibility.

That phrase pleased. He tried it out on the Captain. "You and your deranged sensibility."

"Right on target, German." The Captain smiled to himself.

What was he trying to pull?

But German laughed.

He'd rather Rod were alive. Things were easier with Rod. When Cory got into one of his moods—most of the time that was—he couldn't help absorbing others into it. Rod had told him, *It's like Cory goes through a wall you don't even know is there and he's talking from the other side. It's unnerving, but you have to listen to him.*

"Two more, Gary," German said.

He flubbed his first arrow.

Rolfe said, "Aw, come on, Germ, you ain't shot like that all afternoon. Get smart. Stand at attention. See what you can do."

Do.

He shot.

Not much!

Randall laughed. "That's suicide, German."

"Atta go! *Said* you'd got it made, Anse." Al gave Anse a bear shove.

That crack goaded.

She would: *Darts! Couldn't you compete at something better?*

Champ.

Her criticism could scatter war memories like yellowed photographs spilled off a shelf: the men at mess, on docks, at open sea, in the hold, in parades. *This day.* Each expendable body *not* expendable. Floyd, Randall, Rolfe, Gary, Al—each had his own war. The Captain knew: Hadn't he gotten a crew of the Merchant Marine through. They were all champs, all. *He* knew. But he couldn't throw that at her for he knew she didn't forget her own, the brother killed in the war and Ben and Reggie Webb an Army vet his whole life before drowning. No, he couldn't fault her there. Many a night since they'd been married, and before—when Mary Verity was downstairs in that bedroom ell, dying of cancer—hadn't Estelle rubbed his scars with cocoanut oil? "In time it'll make them almost invisible, hon." And she soothed his head whenever he became aware of pressure on his metal plate. Sometimes, too, worry come over her face when he pressed his hand over his heart; he'd close his eyes at the quick pain, "pressure, the valve can't handle the flow of blood, circulation is cut off." What she didn't see was the sky at a sudden impossible angle. Water was choking him, his arms struggled underwater, he couldn't turn rightside up. Was he paralyzed? Then all fell into place, but it was *not* the hold or deck or gray sky, but the hospital, white, the end of the war for him. It was buddies, cards, craps, talk—in what others would consider prison. Not him. Married and held in a town he hated, working construction, with suddenly two son-brothers he wanted to appreciate, whose lives he was willing to enter; but no, you were separate, in a prison *outside* them because he couldn't survive the life they had lived together.

How in hell did he get into this life?

"There're all kinds of suicides, Randall," German said.

"Suicide?" In Rolfe's beer glass, held high, an eye of gold light glinted. "Oh, Fatso." He set the glass down and concentrated on his aim. "There!"

"Wow!" Al said. "If it were Wednesday night! A few more like that and we'd have a new champ."

German stared at the dingy cork eye so many times pierced. "Two more, Gary." His head throbbed a bit.

You ought to know better. Once it begins . . . Her eyes always pained at sight of his pain. *Me a son to her.*

Son.

Not Marge. No son to *her*, no. He laughed to himself.

Three o'clock.

Light was creeping up the trees, arrows of sun pierced the deep sea grass, the water was pale.

Sour he felt.

He rubbed his forehead with the back of his hand. The dart board throbbed a bit too.

He threw—wild.

"Whoa, German. Them Scotches're traveling." Rolfe again.

He threw, not so wild, but askew.

"Not a chance now. Better back down, Germ. Say, Floyd, how `bout a follow-up?"

A faint nausea pressed at the walls of his stomach. He blinked. The boats were swaying slightly. The sea gray blurred. *You know what happens when you take that extra one. Your nerves. You're too tense,*

German. When he got this way, slightly dizzy, he dreaded even the sight of water, he reeled. He'd sworn on discharge he'd move inland. *I* know *land. I want land under my feet.* He loved the sea, though he claimed he hated it. No, it was this town he hated so. Whenever he broached moving, it was always "Oh, I couldn't leave Pa. He's getting old. Who'd look after him?"

Pa!

"Who's challenging the champ?" Floyd said.

"I'll get *you* Wednesday."

German emptied his glass, for an instant seeing the dark trees rise distorted through the ice. The sky was paling.

Marge.

An ache insisted over his left eye. His stomach throbbed. He straightened, breathed deeply, and went to the john. "What goes in . . ." He laughed, but was relieved to shut the door behind and, when relieved, relieved too to let his head rest against the mirror over the sink. Cool. "Him," he muttered, "him him him, goddamn him," not knowing what to do with his raised fist, but his head ached with such abrupt intensity that he closed his eyes to shut it out. *A dried-up little stick of a man like that running my life. I took my discharge for her. I came over on the ferry to this fucking town and walked into that house of hers. I regret the day I ever saw her, I'll be a son-of-a-bitch if I don't.*

They were talking suicide again, but the ache and throb distracted and he lost their line.

"There're all kinds of suicides, Cap," he repeated, raising his arm. "S-long, fellas." Relieved, he struck out into the December nip, breathing rapidly, powerfully drawing into his lungs cold fresh air.

He half expected to see Estelle in his car, though she had never come to the Club after him. She knew better. He'd never forgive her the shame. Strictly *verboten*, that.

He slammed the Volvo door, backed, squealing his wheels. Through the skeletal trees came a few hard lights. The branches made black webs overhead. The houses were dark hulks.

His day!

He'd show *her*.

He'd drive straight past the house.

The house was dark.

She'd know he'd been there. She always knew. Knew everything.

Well, all but one thing. Marge.

Going on four. Jesus!

And him smelling like the place.

He'd give himself the once-over, a quickie.

The house was all deep shadows. He stood a moment, *expecting* the usuals. At least today there'd be no "German, you've been at the Club," triggering "Yes, yes," already forlorn, fast irritated at the time after time repetition, he and she colliding. "Why do you keep me out?" And his "I had a few with the boys." And her softening it, "Oh, German, today of all days." She could always drum up a special *today of all days.* "They're my friends." "Friends! Nobody makes friends in such places. Why would you want to?" Her hurt look she'd turn to whatever she was working at—the oven, from which she drew the cookie sheet, a deep pie, pumpkin or mincemeat, the sweet air already churning his hungry stomach; but not to be taken advantage of, he'd rebuff, "I can't have a minute to myself without your plaguing." *Plague, plague, plague.* "You'd think you didn't like your home." "I'd rather live alone than have you going at me like this." "Alone." Then would come that unbearable look of hers, worse than a buck toppled in the Montauk woods. "Maybe you're not the type for marriage," she murmured as if to herself. "You're too much alone. A person needs—" "Some of us can't be too much alone." "—to have someone around. You'd think you couldn't stand me sometimes." And once, drinking—he couldn't forget it, surely *she* hadn't— what'd come over him?—he'd dared to say the truth, some truth, part truth. Jesus! How'd he know with all the bickering? But it was *in* him or it wouldn't have come out like that: "Sometimes, if you want to know, I can't stand the sight of you." The words gave instant relief as if the roof had burst open, the walls fallen away, and he had spilled out into space. "German!" she'd asked, "do you mean that?" He stared at her, pain jabbing his head with increasing insistence, "You do, don't you? It's *not* just the alcohol talking, it's—" He raised his hand quickly, touched his head. Her face went quick to sympathy. He saw fear in her face. Now *she* seemed ashamed. At once her tone softened. "Your head. You've gone and done it again. Oh, you *will* let yourself forget. How many times—" He was waiting: *It serves you right. If you don't take care of yourself, suffer then.* It did not come. Instead she was rapidly beside him. "Sit comfortable, and let me rub your forehead with coconut oil." At her touch, he bolted from his chair. "There's *nothing* wrong with my head!" "Nothing! Well, if you won't learn to live with it, then you'll have to—" "It's *my* suffering, if that's the case." He turned swiftly and slammed the door, sluggish his mind, eyes blinking, pain making his sight sullen and overcast, but carrying the image of her holding the blue dish towel, her lingering eyes, the slightest fall of her breasts as she said, "Is it, German?" Then he felt empty, as if he *had* burst and everything had spilled, leaving him with nothing, nothing.

A sickish feeling.

Not now. Jesus!

He put on no lights until he reached the bathroom. He relieved himself, then scrubbed his face red, washed his teeth and rinsed his mouth. From his "little arsenal against aging," she called it, he spilled Mennen's in his hands and doused his face, then smeared Wildroot through his hair and combed it, pleased with the bright blonde sheen of little waves and curls, and examined his teeth, made a smile, then put out the light.

Ready.

No. A handkerchief he might need.

In half-dark he went into the bedroom and pulled open the first drawer of the bureau—there came her soft scent of Coty's —and reached around inside, groped, missed, groped, and pulled up—shit!—the brown paper she lined the drawers with.

He put on the bureau light—

He tried to slide the brown paper back under the carefully laid out hankies and underclothes. What stopped him was a white envelope tucked under the brown paper.

Something she was hiding from him?

A letter. Addressed to her.

He'd have tucked it back, but: Marge.

Marge? Crazy, I must be.

But it was: *Marge Beck.* And her address.

She didn't know Estelle.

And postmarked—days ago!

What in hell was coming off here?

Everything suddenly ran together: her vanity dish bottles doilies scissors nail files his hand fingers the letter.

> Dear Mrs. Beaufort:
>
> You don't know me but I want to warn you what kind of husband you got. I am not interested in German. I got nothing against him, only I want to be fair to you. I can show you in writing he can't wait to get the house and move some woman in—not this one, I'm telling you, but like I said I got it in writing he told me we'd have it together, he's just waiting. I wouldn't want no man like that, I tell you. Besides, he's not much good where it counts, and the cheapest thing I know. I don't know what made him think I'd want him for life, maybe because he

knows he's a good-looker. He is. But to be fair, I thought you should know. I didn't know he was married, but just found it out and who to. I know who you are by your single name Verity from before. I see you downtown. I don't want things belong to somebody else. I got my own little bit. You always was good with everybody and don't deserve his treatment.

Marge Beck

That bitch!

His hands trembled. Not *Marge.* He couldn't believe. Jesus H. Christ, what'd he get into!

Well, he'd fix that fucker.

But first: fold the letter, perfect, put it back under the brown paper, perfect, and arrange the stuff neat. Close the drawer. Perfect.

His head was thunder. The room was throbbing. He heard his blood. He dared not move yet. *Hiding the letter. Saving it for the time when, was she?* Bitch. Two! Never trust a bitch. He turned out the bureau lamp, but tiny stars shot through the dark. Jesus! He blinked, leaning on the bureau. Then his eyes filled—from fury, from pain—and the room, his dark self in the mirror, the bed, windows, the other bureau, careened.

He tried to steady.

She knew everything. She knew him. He couldn't escape that.

He listened.

The house was strange. Breathing.

Fool!

He put out the light and went through the house in shadow, out the back door, let it slam, thinking he heard her call *German;* didn't lock it—fuck it—and got into the car and started it but did not move yet, resting his hands on the wheel to ease the hard jabs in him: the blood was beating with such force he could hardly keep from nodding *beat, beat.* His hands gripped so hard they hurt.

Je-sus! That letter. He couldn't believe, but knew—Marge. He'd fix *her.*

A nightmare. He had plenty. No wonder his head acted up more and more. Not bad enough it was that house, sons, *son* Cory, her father, this town. Now—Jesus!—this day. Marge.

Nightmares.

He clamped his lids shut.

He was struggling underwater.

He opened his eyes, but it went on—too clear. He had dreamed it too many times. All week as December 7 had come closer, the more he thought the more he dreamed. The last three nights he feared sleep. This morning he woke right out of sea, gripped light *thank God*, too early but *Jesus* glad to wake up, escape.

The motor was running.

His hands were taut on the wheel.

He knew that sound. Suddenly the sky blazed like morning. The explosion stunned him. Voices screamed so close they seemed inside him. The water glittered black with oil. He tried to swim. A voice called. Two hands reached for him. The body went under. He went down, down. *Not my nightmare.* But he couldn't get out of it. The figure was floating over him. The arms hung. He knew the hands. *This is not in my nightmare.* He came up under the body. He clutched the head, *my face.* Darts pierced the eyes, cheeks, mouth, chin—

It was over in a second. His hands were still gripping the wheel. *Cold.*

"Christ!" he cried.

What was happening to his head?

That fucking letter!

He jabbed. The Volvo lurched. He'd go straight to Marge's, he'd have it out with her, he'd talk her into things. He had his own touch. He wasn't the worst-looking man in the world, far from it. A little soft-soaping and she'd come round. He'd find some way around this thing, satisfy himself and her and Estelle too. He' d satisfy Marge, he *could* too, and she *knew* it, the bitch.

He'd go straight through the village, straight to the house, no roundabout back way this time, oh no. He'd ferret Marge out.

Dark was fast. Lights were coming on everywhere. He went west on Webb, past the old cemetery. The neglected tombstones looked like giant teeth scattered over the lot. The dump entrance loomed like a temple relic. Jesus, he'd like to drive through it and keep going—anywhere. Sometimes, hate Carbondale as he did, he wished he were a boy back with *them*—Ma so skinny the sun could almost shine through her bones; and his old man, not so old but worn, wrecked, trapped in that place by The Depression. You could be born at the wrong time. His father always said *everybody* was. Maybe Ma and Pa were better off now; during the war people piled up cash.

The war—

Hang *in* there, his buddies always said.

A man should hang on, his father always said.

He saw a dark thing coming. It was moving down his side of the road.

Jesus! Not again! But it was no nightmare.

He passed. That kid! Emmy. Something she was carrying glittered quick—a bottle?

He quick slowed and watched her in the rearview mirror: she looked back.

Jesus! The damn kid couldn't stay away from the house. She drove him crazy. Well, let her waste her time; she'll be shafted when she finds nobody home. Serve her right. Teach her to stay with the niggers. Estelle's fault. She should have left the kid on Third, where she belonged. If it weren't for that damned doll! *He* won it at St. Agnes', but *she* gave it to the kid, and that did it, tied the kid to her for good.

He saw the crushed head hanging, the dangling blonde curls.

His fault. Always *his* fucking fault! What was the doll doing behind his car? If that kid put it there—! He wouldn't put it past her. She didn't like him. She couldn't the way he bitched to Estelle about her. Kids know, you can't hide feelings from kids. *He* knew. He remembered. He was always too big too young. At fifteen he looked like a man so his mother and father treated him like a man. To them he never was a kid, but he *was* inside.

Emmy crossed the road to the First Trinity and turned the corner—

Gone.

He swept left onto Third—*Marge*!—past the Garcías' and farther down past Emmy's, not even braking for the stop sign, and shot straight across Front and just before the dead end at the train depot made a wide sweep right, straight to *Marge Beck,* Cardboard City, Greenport, Long Island, New York, U.S. of A.

Cunt!

Suddenly the area was desolate, no trees, no shrubs in Cardboard City, two-family prefabs clustered low to the ground as cowered animals. They *needed* hiding. War relics. Thrown up overnight. In day the buildings were gray and smutty. Inside, you froze your balls off in winter, burned up in summer. Scars right smack under your eyes as you came into town. A crying shame.

Marge's was in the rear, the last row, the end building nearest the road. The second door. The big 5. He pulled straight up before the two wood steps to the door.

Dark!

And no car.

In 6 a head was moving in the kitchen.

He didn't believe she wasn't there.

Leave? Fool *him* would she! Not on your life. He wouldn't give her an easy out.

He threw the car door open, and stood. Reeling.

Je-*sus.*

He leaned to still the throbbing in his head, feeling like vomiting, hearing *her: You know you can't drink on an empty stomach.*

Shit! He let go and stomped up the steps and knocked, and waited, listening. Not a sound. He knocked again, a series of raps, saying *Marge*? in his head, anxious, yearning now, not willing to believe she wasn't there, not willing either to believe the letter he'd seen; whispering in his head Marge? Please, Marge, pressing his head against the door, the cool, *please*; not knowing what to do because she wasn't there. He wanted her. Where was she? He wanted her to explain. Maybe she hadn't written that letter . . .

Where was she?

He rapped. "Marge?"

He pounded. "You, Marge! *Marge*!"

He listened.

Something, quick, seemed to come from inside—like a whine, beginning low and rising, rising to a high pitch.

"That you, Marge?"

The sound ceased abruptly.

Then it was a whistle. It hooted: one, two.

A fire!

The door to six opened. A woman—he knew the face, but no name—appeared. She stood in the doorway listening. She called back into the house, "District two."

After an interval the hooting was repeated: one—two.

"Yes, two," she said.

She nodded to him, "Hello."

Cowed, he nodded.

"I haven't heard her all afternoon," she said and closed the door.

He stood staring at the dark pane in the door. Nothing. Nobody.

So maybe she *did* cut out on him. The bitch planned it, beat it off so she wouldn't have to face him. Used him. Screwed. Every time.

But still he didn't believe, didn't want to. Not the letter. Not Marge.

Something was pressing down on his head.

"Well, don't just stand here," he muttered. "Move it." But stood. Throbbing.

Then the air shrieked. A siren. Another.

Fire engines.

The sirens faded, but he could hear them steady in the distance.

A fire.

It registered then: *two*. His district.

He swerved down the two steps in a stagger to the car, sat on the edge of the seat a sec, then slid his legs in, and sat, groping in his pocket for the keys. He found the ignition, but had to lay his head against the wheel an instant.

Feeling heaped, he closed his eyes, but—swimming, Jesus!—he quick opened them, trying to down the nausea.

The street lights shone clean. Lit windows made bright holes in the dark.

Go.

Where? Where in the dark could he go?

Home. *Home.*

For a second he remembered the soft dark of his room with the thin wood walls he could hear every sound through in that house against the steep slope in Carbondale.

He could let go he was so sick fed up furious frustrated desperate.

Now came a gathering rush of traffic, then the far drone tapering off.

He backed off to the road. On Front Street, clear through the naked branches, the streetlights made a perfect straight way ahead.

A car passed and tooted. Waller, was it? And at Fifth another, loaded, shot across Front without stopping. Kids!

"Bastards!"

Where was Marge?

Tricked him. She could have had the decency to have it out with him instead of blowing the lid off.

He followed the string of cars up Main. What was happening? The trees wavered. He blinked. Je-*sus.* He blinked, blinked. The trees were moving. No. *Sky.* The sky was moving, bright over the crick. Clouds broke the light, dark and folding and spreading.

Je-*sus.*

Two.

Ahead, the Presbyterian steeple stood dark against the burning sky. Branches made stark nets against the flames, then were swallowed in dark smoke, then reappeared. He sped past the bronze soldier and swerved around the Trinity Episcopal corner. When he turned left onto his street, cars he saw lined both sides. The Club? Pell's Market? His head beat, beat. He felt dizzy. Not *now.* He heard the engines, shouts and cries before the block fell into place. The neon delicatessen signs shone straight through the engines' red lights and the whirling blue police lights.

Oholyjesusmy

The house!

The police had the block cut off.

He braked in the middle of the street, threw the door open, and got out. The car was running.

He stumbled to the sidewalk.

The house gave off terrible bright heat. Everything around it was leaping with light—the yard, Pa's house, trees. The fire engines were on the far side of the house, where the hydrant was. The great hoses lay crossed. Water battered the house. He reached the edge of the yard. "Hold it, Mac." someone said, "you can't cross there." "It's my house, I've got to—" Then a man said, "German." He blinked. Everything was etched sharp but he felt sick, he was reeling, blood seemed to swell inside his head. "It's my house!" he said. "Come on, German," somebody said. Then German saw the old man. He was slumped. They were holding him up. Pa's eyes were filled with fire. His shoulders were heaving. "You got to lay down, Mr. Verity," Lloyd Wilson said. "Carry him, boys. Easy." "I'll take him," German said. "Let *me*." Pa looked at him. His mouth was going. He was trying to tell him something. It scared German. "Pa?" German said. Pa's head was quivering. "Stell," he said. *Estelle*. An instant German's feet went dead, his arms. "Estelle!" he cried, thrusting Pa into the others' arms. He was crying out, but men were holding him back, he was jerking free, trying to. "She's in there. My wife's in there!" He was besieged by her face staring at him in that wind blowing her hair, stirring him so, his heart nearly breaking for that sad face, those gray eyes. The men grappled with him. He was fighting to get to the back door. "*She's* in there. Christ, my wife's in there. I've got to get my wife." They were gripping him, they were groping at his arms and legs, others were coming at him. "You can't go in there. Come on, German. There's nothing you can do. Hold him, boys." They felled him. His head would explode, his chest. Everything reeled. He was lying on the ground. "Bring a stretcher, boys." He struggled to get up. He got to his knees. There were so many faces. Faces were rising and falling. The sky was making waves of fire and dark. *My wife's in there, please let me—*, he said, but no words came. He was choking, he sucked for air. He was staring straight into a black face shiny from the fire. The mouth was screaming. That dark thing. Emmy. Walking along Webb. What was she carrying? *You*. He said, *In there, I've got to*, but nothing. His vision went. He was sinking. Hands caught him. His guts beat. He retched over the ground.

Cory

"More eggs?" Gramp had insisted on making Cory's breakfast. "Give me that pleasure. I don't have many visitors."

"You outdid yourself. I see where Ma got her talent."

"Taught her all the cooking I know."

He wiped out his black skillet. *Never wash a skillet.* Cooking had been his joy and pride. He'd cooked on yachts at sea. He liked to brag of Commodore Vanderbilt's yacht and the royal meals he'd fed the guests, but there would come moments when his gaze focused far as if he were staring at that other side of the fire which fed on him, and Cory would swear he saw that fire in his grandfather's eyes.

"I must have got my talent from both of you, then." Cory said.

"You come by it honestly." Gramp squinted. "Pretty dead out there, ain't it?"

Cory nodded. "Last night when the bus stopped at the corner, I could see just the chimney. I was sure I was at the wrong place. For a minute I'd almost forgotten. Would you believe that?"

"Sometimes I forget—till I look up. And I keep thinking I hear your mother at the door." He scooped the breakfast remains in a cat dish. "Want that, Jezebel?"

The cat purred, chafed his leg, then nosed into it.

With Gramp's penchant for giving his succession of cats the same names, biblical, Cory was never quite sure whether the cats were the same. But the five were enormous now, old. And the dog old. Pal. Albert's gift to Gramp.

"Sleep good?"

"The bed's great, Gramp." He had the rear corner room facing Gram's house next door. A cousin, Bertie's daughter, had bought the house, so it stayed in the family. There was that comfort—Gramp could look out on the place his parents had built. That sight made him feel close to Gram. Gramp would never leave this spot if he could help it.

"How does it feel to be an old man?" Cory laughed.

"Be pushing eighty years young any year now."

"If you get out of the kitchen this morning, I'll bake you a cake."

"You wouldn't!"

"Oh, yes. What'd you think I picked up a few groceries for? It'll take me no time."

"If you're that good a cook, then you're a chip off the family block."

"We're going to have a little get-together."

"Don't know who you'd drum up."

"You leave that to me."

"Humpf." But he crossed his arms and puffed his Marvel contentedly.

"Did anyone ever find what did it, Gramp?"

He hated the ineradicable black. The chimney made a public monument of the event.

Gramp's eyes quivered. "Kerosene or gasoline, they thought, if the Coke bottle meant anything."

"Coke bottle?"

"They found it in the kitchen, where the fire must have started."

"You mean . . . somebody . . ." Cory closed his eyes. "I can't begin to imagine—"

"Don't. If somebody did . . . Nobody could have known your mother was in there, for sure."

"What'd they *say*, Gramp?"

"Oh, there was a lot of talk. They brought it to me. You know *I* don't get around much."

"What talk?"

"Cheap talk. There always is. What you don't listen to. Mostly it was German they pointed the finger at. Talk of some woman in it all, there always is, but who'd begin to think he'd do that? You know German, he was stuffed with anger. Complaining's his nature but it couldn't hide some soft spot in him that'd keep him from doing a thing that desperate. Anybody with any sense'd see that. Besides, he got nothing out of it. Talk dies down soon enough when that happens."

"Is he gone?"

"Where'd he go?"

"He hated Greenport!"

"He said."

"You don't believe he did?"

"A man has to have a thing to pick at to let off steam. You remember when you were a kid and your mother always told you when you asked for things *Now don't go getting the gimmes.* German had the *gimmes.* I think he was disappointed things didn't turn out the way he'd hoped."

"What'd he want?"

"You'd have to ask him that. Whatever, I think he liked Greenport and the fishing and the water and the men on the boats—he hit it off fine with them—and the quiet. He never liked noise. Even the noise of kids playing drove him crazy. I don't think he'd ever go for city life."

"Then he's still here." It was almost a year since the fire.

"I said."

"But where?"

"He's rooming at the Manaton House on First. He's with one of the lumber companies now. Fleet, maybe."

"You've seen him?"

"A time or two."

"He's come here?"

"A time or two."

That laconic reply told him he'd reached the edge. Gramp wouldn't hazard falsity when he simply couldn't be sure what was in German's head.

But Cory would see him, he wanted to. German was part of their life, his mother's life. *She* would be there with them. He wanted as much of her presence as he could have while he was here. After the house had burned down, he'd wanted to see her once more, but the coffin was closed; so he felt she was not dead because he had not seen her that last time. There was a vacancy in the air here that could not be filled. He had spent little time with German, perhaps had even been unfair to him because they were so close in age, near brothers. Brothers. Rod, German, Fatso. Maybe being too close to his age had separated him and German, and his education too because the habit of education, once engrained, trains you to the habit of education. He knew German in no way understood that. German couldn't help it; he didn't know education. He wanted a package deal which would open up the world of new cars, yachts, the right people, fancy houses. He thought education was a gift some people had and he was not one of the gifted, but he, Cory, was. That mystified German:

"Christ, if I had your brains, I'd be making piles."

Maybe it was that town in Pennsylvania German couldn't get out of himself, as he couldn't get Greenport out of himself; though maybe German wanted to, where Cory could not have borne losing it. Some inkling of German's early life Cory had when his mother was recuperating from her hysterectomy.

He was at Brown. They were all proud of that—he too—because it was on home ground, in his own state, near his birthplace: and he had been awarded the graduate scholarship. At spring break he crossed the Sound from New London on one of the new ferries, an LCT from the war, that made him so nostalgic for the old gingerbread excursion ferries like "his" *Shinnecock*, which ran from Port Jefferson to Bridgeport now.

He had written he'd be there. He never wrote *home* because to them his home had been Bristol, but to him Greenport was his true home, was *family, time, bones, blood, this*. He felt *all* there.

He hadn't told them when he'd arrive. When the bus from Orient Point had let him off and he rounded Champlain Place and came upon the yard, "Cory!" she cried, "Oh, Cory!" She held her arms out to him but labored to stand. He was so startled that he dropped his suitcase and cried, "Ma? Ma! What's wrong with you?" At the same time he was startled because she was so much thinner, so *young*, her dark hair long like a girl's, her oval face prettier. She advanced, *inching*, and he ran to her. "What's happened to your legs?" She fell against him, and he clutched, closing his eyes an instant, drawing in that single scent of Coty's and sweet hair. She released him, laughing. "I'm fine. I've just had a partial. It'll take time before I can run." She caressed his face. "Oh, I'm so glad you're home, Cory. But you look so tired. What do they do to you at Brown?" He laughed now. "Beat at your brains." "*Beat*. You!" "Well, the professors never let up." She took his hand then. "Ma," she said to the woman, "this is my Cory." *Ma*. German's mother. She took his hand. "I might have guessed, just looking at you. They both talk about you all the time." Both? So German—? "Your ma and your grandfather." He laughed. "My ears don't ring." "That's because it's good talk," she said, smiling. It was her smile—nicely made teeth, but bad—and her voice, soft, suave, and her warm talk that belied the hard, thin, lined, even stony face. "German couldn't stay home from work—he took a couple of days off for the operation—so he wired Ma. She's been a lifesaver. You *have*, Ma." "But why didn't you tell me? You didn't call or write." "Oh,

I'd never bother your studies. They come first." The truth abruptly besieged: "But you might have died on the operating table, and then . . . I'd never have forgiven you, or myself." She smiled, her eyes brimming, and said, "You can't kill a Verity?" so that he had to laugh. "You sit down," he said. "Oh, I'm all right."

It was that woman who made the difference, a worker she was, who cleaned and tended, though it was the cooking that revealed—beans and beans, doughboys, the blackest coffee—for she seemed not to know how to prepare, to have had no experience with decent food. German never said a word, German the meat-and-potato man, who could never get enough steak, who complained so. He was completely submissive. He became the boy again, the *Yes, Ma* and *No, Ma* obedient son, who cheated mornings, afternoons, evenings, stealing Ma away to a bar downtown or to the Club for a beer. Beer was her weakness. When he could not, between-times they were cronies sitting out under the shady maples in the yard and sipping and talking and laughing. Cory knew his mother did not like drink or the loud drink talk and laughter that carried over the neighborhood when they were at their sloppiest. She was discreet and held her tongue, not to offend either.

The two women were not so distant in age. His mother must have felt some shift in balance, her place as German's wife subtly threatened. The situation made her a contemporary of his mother—two older women, two mothers—with the confusion also of the one mothering them both. Wasn't German's mother tending her and tending German? Wasn't she doing the chores for her two children? She was kind and easygoing and German was content, too content. Cory was aware that his mother didn't like to see German's unconscious submission to his mother's authority, to a certain power German had never reckoned with or *placed*, showing a weakness in German's self-determination, making her share that submission, making her more a sister to German, a daughter to Ma, making her feel the repressed daughter-in-law unrecognized by both of them.

Despite his mother's lament over the bad food and bad habits, she was delighted to see German's mother gain weight. It was strange to see her bones take on shape. She sat, dreamy. She loved the sea. "I never smelled such good air," she said. "It's the pines and wild roses, and the sea blow keeps the air fresh," his mother said. "It's so clean. In Carbondale every time you blow your nose the rag turns black." "German, look how pretty Ma's face is getting," his mother said. "Stay here long enough, Ma, and you'll be looking like a girl again." German's mother laughed like a girl.

When Cory visited at the end of summer, his mother was walking well, though she still leaned with both hands on the table to support herself when she stood up. German's mother said, "The old man's bitching I'm not there. I better shake my tail."

With her gone, German fell into his habitual silence, and Cory and his mother were alone again, and could talk.

Now Gramp said, "When you went back to Brown two days after the funeral, they had to cart German to the Vet's Hospital."

"Hospital!"

"There's that plate in his head, and that constriction. He couldn't stand the pressure. He kept passing out. The funeral really got to him."

"You didn't write me that."

"Wouldn't have much to talk about when you came home if I did."

When he did write, he always wrote in pencil. He squinted and pressed those quivering eyes almost flush with the paper, the pencil clamped between two crimped fingers, whispering words and letters as he made his way over the small lined pad.

"German thought it was his fault. He kept saying, 'I couldn't help it.' Nobody knew what he meant. The nurse told Judge Hammill. The judge went up several times, you know."

"No, I didn't."

"I see. Hmmm."

His smile wasn't wasted on Gramp.

"Judge Hammill's the one told me. He was worried. Loyal, the judge."

Judge Hammill had granted Mary Verity the divorce.

"What would German blame himself for?"

"It's pretty natural. After a person's gone, you think of all the things you could've done. Makes you feel bleak."

"But he wasn't home at the time."

"So much the worse."

"And he couldn't have known Ma was in the house. Nobody could have."

"I'd have been the one to know. It was a special day. She said she was going downstreet. She went. The car was gone. I was here that afternoon. I never saw her come back. She usually stopped in . . ."

Gramp was facing that space. That house would be in his eyes forever, and the fire. A year gone now.

Fires.

"Gramp, don't *you*."

"We all do that—get the guilts, you say?"

"Don't. There's enough to live with."

Rod.

"You know that, do you?"

"Besides, its too easy to feed on it."

"So it seems."

"German had something on his mind . . ."

Gramp stared through the blown smoke.

"She always complained he wasn't one to talk."

"Women always do. It gives them an excuse to talk and get every bit of their day in. But they'd complain if a man talked a blue streak and stole their talk time." He laughed. "What would we do without them?"

"You did. Do."

"Well . . . your mother was always in and out." He shifted his gaze to that other family house.

"If German did have something on his mind," Cory said, "we'll never know. He keeps things shut in."

"Well, German never did like to talk about people or like people to talk about others in front of him. I don't know where he got that habit from, but it's a good one."

"Smacks of gentility?"

Gramp laughed. "As good as the landed gentry's."

That was their little joke: With plenty of land and no money, the Veritys were proud they'd been landed gentry, if *property poor.*

"*Swamp yankees* is more like it," Cory said.

Gramp laughed till he coughed.

"It's those Marvels you smoke."

"Might be. Every man has to have a vice, don't he?" Gleeful, Gramp puffed like a little locomotive.

"Why would he stay here, Gramp?"

"Who?"

"German. I thought he hated the place. He always wanted Ma to sell and move upstate or someplace. But she wouldn't."

"Because of me. It was always because of me she stayed. Anywhere."

"Now, now."

"Well."

"We weren't going to get the guilts, remember. It's German we're talking about. You say he came."

"A time or two."

"And?"

"And what?"

"Well, he didn't just sit and stare at you."

"You don't paint a very pretty picture."

"Don't turn me aside, Mr. Verity."

"Said he was staying in town. Said he had his reasons. Said where would he go in his present condition. He wasn't happy. Why would he be? His wife gone. And some talk about him pounding on some woman's door the very afternoon it happened. Plenty of people around to make a lot of that. Pure coincidence for sure."

Gramp puffed in silence, squinting through the smoke.

"German chafed at the bit, years, Gramp. Things. Things he wanted."

For an instant Gramp's eyes ceased quivering.

"He was silent. And secretive, Gramp."

"Nothing wrong with secrets."

"Except when they fester and turn you against people. German's did. He wasn't happy. You could see that. *You* could, Gramp."

"No sense to bringing up what can't do any good, Cory."

"Unless it's still there and turns on you."

"Oh, I don't think German's that bad."

"You wouldn't."

"You telling me I haven't got the . . . fortitude to look a thing straight in the eye?"

"If anybody has you have, but fortitude can be worn down. You're not so young."

"Old, you mean. So I have to use my head. It's what we have, the old. They say we don't get so hot about things. I'm not so sure. But that's the key, keeping our wits about us—finally."

"You're sure of that?"

"No. But I put my faith in it."

"And in work. You always did." After the funeral Gramp had insisted, "Go back to Brown, Cory. Work saves. Don't you go worrying about me now. I'll be here."

They had lowered her into the ground, they had come back to the ruins, they had felt herded and locked in, there was nowhere to go.

"German never could stand me, truth is." Gramp clutched the bowl of tea between his palms and sipped, the tiny Japanese figures peering between his fingers. "He couldn't help it. I was always around, in the way. A man can't hide his feelings for too long. I have to say he tried, though—for her."

"He had . . . fortitude."

Gramp guffawed, spilling his tea. "Now look what you made me do." He set the bowl down.

His mother had bought the bowl in the 5&10 in Bristol for a quarter. *Look, Pa.* He remembered his mother turning it and Gramp squinting at the little figures. *Hmmmm.* It was the one thing Gramp had carted to all the places he'd lived in, the one thing his own when he'd left Pete to live on the Island. She'd wash the stains out clean. "There, Pa." Drinking tea was his ritual. Anytime of day or night, tea. It always seemed natural to see him bent over the kitchen table with that bowl cupped between his hands.

"There, you." He threw Gramp a rag. "You get out of my way and I'll bake that cake—from scratch."

"Oh, you needn't worry. I got a shopful of work waiting."

"I noticed. Only a spider could get through all that."

"That's me."

"A spider's ordered."

"Don't you worry. I got my own order. Know exactly what's next in line."

"And you'll do it too *if* the junk doesn't cave in on you."

"It'll be *my* doing if it does. You sound like your mother."

Cory liked the pantry ell. Gramp had built it so it caught light. On the left were upper and lower cabinets and a counter, on the right low cabinets and a counter under a full window overlooking the yard and the big house. Between was the sink with a window looking through the lavender lilacs Gramp had planted and over the side yard and across Edie's wide lawn to the deli on the corner and to the north end of Sterling Place and now with the leaves gone to a glimpse of Porky's Restaurant and the cliff giving onto the sea beyond. Facing north, afternoons it caught angles of western light.

Cory drew the flour tin from the lower cabinet. When he stood, he saw a thing dark and frail under the front maple.

"What'd you do, lose your ambition?"

Gramp turned his head.

"Why, it's a child," Cory said. It was her stillness that startled.

Gramp went close to the pane. He squinted. His head tremored slightly.

"It's Emmy."

"So that's Emmy."

So straight and still, the child might have been a sapling.

"She's just standing there. She doesn't move."

"No. Comes all the time. Comes. Stands. Looks a long time."

"What's she looking at?"

"That house. Same as you and me."

"But why?"

"Misses your mother. Used to come every day, but they put a stop to that, her people did."

"What for?"

"Wouldn't go to school, they said. Instead, she'd come here, spend hours waiting, like she was waiting for your mother, like she didn't believe. . . . Her family said at home she cried all the time. And mooned. Cried out under that tree too. I've seen her wet face. For a while they kept sending one of her sisters or brothers, her Ma came, but that didn't keep her away, so they gave up. They asked me would I please send her home. I said I'd do what I could, but she's a right to come. She spent enough time in that house. Your mother was crazy about her, you could say she adopted her, sort of."

Cory set the flour tin down.

"But she's still as a statue."

"She'll move when she gets ready."

"The poor kid. You've talked to her?"

"Huh! You don't get near that girl. Looks at you. Measures the distance. You get just so close, she turns tail and scoots like a strange dog that won't let you get to it but still hangs around. Pretty soon she's there again. She's sure sprung up in a year."

Cory went out but stopped just outside the door to the front yard.

The girl gazed across at him.

She was warmly dressed, a short wooly coat and a bright red knitted cap. Pigtails made her face very thin, long, beautiful. Because her eyes were so dark and so white, their purity stunned. But the defiant stillness gave her head a mature look terrible in such a frail face.

"Hi," he called out.

She stayed, stone.

"I'm Mr. Verity's grandson."

He saw now a doll in her left arm, stiffly clutched against her. It half hung, the torso, the fallen arms. From here it looked deformed, raggy , soiled. Great dead eyes stared from the upside-down head.

He took a couple of steps closer.

She did not so much as blink.

"I'm her son."

He heard Gramp moving behind him.

"Estelle's."

She must have gripped: the doll's arms rose a bit, and stilled.

"Hey," Gramp said. "It's Emmy, is it?"

"Emmy what?" Cory said. "I never knew your last name."

Her eyes shifted. She was watching Gramp.

Cory heard him go into the shop. There was a clank of metal objects, a drag and shifting, then the perennial half-mutters to himself.

Her stare was on him again, all vigilance.

"It's not dark yet, a little early for trick or treat." Moving, Cory laughed. "But you know Gramp, he's always got candy and surprises."

He stopped halfway across the lawn.

"You'd better come in and get some."

Close, he felt sorry for her because she was such a small birdy thing, all eyes and bones, and he began to feel guilty because she looked cornered as if fearful in a minute he'd cast his net—

"Ohhh," he said, for now he saw her doll's hanging head was split and wrapped and tied in something like gauze. "What happened to her?"

This time she moved quick. She clamped the doll to her chest with both hands.

"The poor thing!" he said.

Wary, she backed off a bit. No fool she!

"She's hurt. My grandfather could fix her up."

Her eyes flicked toward the shop.

"He'd make her just like she was. Honest."

For the briefest instant her eyes dropped to the doll's head.

"She looks pretty bad. Won't you let me see it?"

She swung sideways, protecting the doll from his view.

She kept a hard gaze, untrusting.

"I won't hurt her," he said, holding out his hands.

She swerved and dashed some dozen steps, halted, and turned, that clear hard gaze insistent.

"Well, if that isn't the damnedest thing," he said.

"What is it?" Gramp was holding a music box with tiny figures of Noah and his ark in the flood.

"She ran."

"You look up after a while and she'll be back where she was—I told you—just like a dog afraid but wanting you to touch him. No sense pushing her. She'll take her own sweet time. Let her. You'd better get to that cake or I'll put you to work on the toys."

"I work better with gas."

Now and then, until the cake was finished, set on a rack to cool, he did glance out, thinking of his mother. What was it in her even now drew that child to the chimney standing like a dark lighthouse charred, prominent, grim? He thought Emmy had gone, but twice he caught sight of her, once at the corner of Gramp's shop, once standing at the fence by Edie's rose of Sharon bush as if she were viewing the ruins from different perspectives.

But why? What made her skip school or sneak away from home and family and friends?

By the time he had finished and iced the cake, Emmy was nowhere in sight.

"You can come out now, Gramp. She's gone."

Gramp snorted. "She'll come round one day. Can't hold out forever. Must be all heart, that child. Give me a hand. That bike's got to come out. . . . Thanks. I found this old wheel with spikes that'll fit that back one. Rigging it up'll take a little doing."

He left, but before driving off watched a moment as Gramp bent over the bike, wrench in hand, and worked the rear wheel off. He remembered with a quick flush a day years before when he had been standing in a window of the "big house" watching him at the curb for the first time in many years get on a bike, a girl's bike because at his age it was difficult to swing his leg up. He had no sooner left the curb when, pedaling badly, the front wheel gave way, the bike flipped, and he fell on his side. Cory felt the blow himself. "Gramp!" he cried. He wanted to run out, but he wouldn't humiliate him: he was getting up, he was slow, and he stood there a minute, then brushed himself off and wheeled the bike back across the lawn to his house. Cory was ashamed. And whenever he remembered it, he was ashamed of his vacillation and inaction.

He had left Gramp before, many times; but this day, he knew, was a day of reckoning with this terrain of his life, with their lives. Oh, he would always come back; he could never leave him for long; he would always have his ties with the place itself. It was his place. There were always final things, but a time came when decisions divided like shears; and he felt now, without knowing what it was, an order imposing itself on his days. Without being able to define it, he *saw* that order as clearly as a row of properly arranged dominos and that decision as clearly as the motion of a finger whose touch would send them all rhythmically down, causing space for a new order.

To him, now, that motion seemed to have begun with Fatso, perhaps the day he had the news that Fatso had murdered his mother, perhaps before, as Fatso himself had insisted. Whichever, he had chosen that moment arbitrarily; and now he chose, he must choose, to reckon with himself.

In the spring following his winter graduation, when he was well into the semester at Brown, he had come to Greenport to try to see Fatso in the Riverhead jail, where they had been holding him after the murder. That night he wrote Savannah, *Fatso refused to see me.* Though he was forbidden to see Fatso by law, Fatso had given word he would not see him. *Savannah, I'm haunted by the image of Fatso. Since the murder, I see him everywhere. Even when I don't actually see him I feel he's there ready to appear. And he does. I can't tell you what it's like to look up and suddenly see Fatso standing right in front of me—on the grass, in the trees, in my room. I could touch him. It's strange. I have no control over it. Oh, memory has its own logic, I know that. I know the least sensuous association can make the past the present. Sometimes I think I'm in prison. I am. And I think Fatso's out here. He is.*

At the end of June Lawyer Weems wrote asking when he'd be on the Island again. Cory took a long Fourth and went to Lawyer Weems's office.

"I called you on behalf of Santiago—"

Santiago.

"García. He's had me draw up a power-of-attorney in your name to manage his affairs permanently, if, of course, you agree. He's certain you will. Evidently he trusts you completely. He's imposing a great responsibility on you and he knows it. He said this letter will explain."

> Cory,
>
> I ask you to be responsible for my brother. You have free license to do with my property what is best for his future. I know he has one. I leave the way to it to you. Weems has drawn up a full power-of-attorney signed and witnessed. You and my brother and Tom were all I really had in the world. My brothers and sisters did not count. Now I'm not in the world, but you are. You owe me this, Cory. You're responsible too. I wanted to know, and you gave me the way. It led me here. Don't come. I won't see you. Right now I'm too filled with pride and fury and hate and I'm frustrated by being cut off from our search.
>
> Santiago

Our search.

Our.

Cory had written *All these years I've been leading Santi, Santiago García—Fatso we call him—by directing his reading, sharing so he could have some kind of university education. And he's been amazing, embarrassingly intelligent at times, challenging me with ideas he is possessed by, ideas he has probed till he sometimes has intimidated me by turning my words back on me till I can't tell whose ideas are whose. He could be my own mouth talking to me, my own voice. He wanted to know, he wanted to know so badly, I've never been sure what he wanted to know. It's that 'what' that drove him to kill his mother. Who knows the reason? He makes me somehow responsible. And in some way I am. You don't know when you meddle with somebody's life, even when you don't intend to meddle, where it will lead. Fatso's right. In his eyes, I was there, I was an influence. He's carried me with him. It's a nightmare to think he might never have done it without my influence, but think of what a nightmare it must have been for Fatso. It began that night in Gramp's when I read the Joseph story from the Bible, but I've told you that before. Fatso's reminded me more than once he's guarded it as the seminal moment in his life.*

What have I done, Savannah?

He had turned to writing Savannah after Rod was drowned, over two years now. Since he had graduated and left her for good, as she put it, he had not turned to writing her again until Santi refused to see him last year. He wrote himself out to Savannah, though apart from one note of farewell, she had *never* answered. But he knew he was writing for himself, trying to clarify himself as he wrote, impelled—confessing. *Confessing!* But he became aware only as he wrote that it was not confessing in the usual sense because underlying the voluntary act of writing to Savannah was the pursuit of an involuntary impetus that bound him to her and now to Fatso.

I went to see Miss Kellogg about Santi, he'd written Savannah. *In town Miss Kellogg has become a legend because of Santi. She was the last person to see him before he murdered his mother.*

That *day—two days after I left you at Wisconsin in our—my—rooms, Savannah, after graduation and our miserable good-bye—* he had walked to town.

He had reached Miss Kellogg's in a kind of delirium because he had been to the Riverhead jail, he had gone the day before. The warden had said, "Moorehead? García said he wouldn't see you anyway." Fatso said that? *That. The words bludgeoned, Savannah. I'd swear Fatso was standing invisible facing me, swear Fatso struck me.* All evening, *Why?* he'd asked himself. Why wouldn't he see me? Once he'd inadvertently said it aloud, "Why wouldn't he see me?" Gramp, squinting through his cigarette smoke, said, "Don't hurry him, son." All day he'd moved, turgid. Fatso's words had dulled his senses, submerged him in a heavy drift. Whenever he'd tried to think of something else, he was drawn back down; he could not will against thinking about Fatso and *me, Cory.*

Miss Kellogg's house. He had never failed to stop and admire it, a balance and grace that seemed translated from Georgian brick to wood, with a wooden fence and gate, all suggesting both social attachment and serene detachment in a beautifully reasoned harmony.

But even thinking that, he stood with his hand on the gate, thinking too, *Here, Fatso's hand, so many times.* Then he opened it and went up onto the porch and knocked. It was a long wait. Then, through the sheers over the door pane, he saw her come down the long stairwell on the right. She was moving very slowly.

"Why . . . Cory Moorehead."

She was taken unawares—he caught her fleeting scrutiny—but her usual charm banished any startle.

"Yes, Miss Kellogg."

"What a pleasure. Do come in, Cory."

But at sight of her he wanted to back down, ashamed at abusing her privacy.

Poor woman! Savannah, she was bone, all eyes and teeth. Her hair is the thinnest down over her head, but such a staunch head, and she walked with determined steps, firm. But her voice! It was strong, and beautiful, resonant, as if her long life of music were distilled into a voice. Her hands—how they moved!—made the rhythm of that voice visible. Her hands are a kind of magic. Maybe they can't stop making music. The murder has blighted her life. It has brought her the notoriety publicity brings. There are people who would love that, but not Miss Kellogg. She's much too sensitive. She'll never get over that night. The publicity weighs heavily, but she bears it with dignity.

"I should have called. I shouldn't have intruded this way."

"Don't think twice about it, Cory. For a change, it's good to see someone who isn't . . . a vulture."

"Have they driven you crazy?"

"Let's say they haven't been very discreet. You know newspapers and gossipmongers and, of course, lawyers. But that was in the wake of that night, and after all it's still very close to us, though the visits have tapered off to almost nothing. I *am* grateful for that, but it's a delight to see you. Tell me about Brown."

"Ah, you knew that!"

"Oh, Santiago kept me informed, indirectly. He'd almost inadvertently drop a mention of you now and then. At first he never did talk much and then in a rare moment. He listened. But tell me."

"I'm winding up my M.A. I've got a splendid opportunity as an instructor. I've been very lucky. The job's a lure on the part of my best professors toward the Ph.D."

"Then you must have performed extraordinarily."

"Well, I did my best. I love it. They want me to teach. *I* think I want to. They're convinced it's right for me and don't want the profession to lose me. It's pretty flattering. But I'm mad to write, and I have my doubts about managing the two worlds together. The offer came at a good time. For the moment it will solve any number of pretty crucial problems."

"It's no wonder Santi admired you so."

"But he won't see me, Miss Kellogg. He can't now, of course. Still, he's refused to."

"Ah, I know it upset you, but don't let it. He must be in such turbulence. If he weren't, if he would see anybody, it would be you, Cory. You're perhaps the only person in the world he fully trusts."

Who else to trust but your destroyer?

"You must be nearly the same age, I gather from the few things he's said about you, though he was rather laconic—"

"Laconic! But he could talk a flood."

"Seldom here, though he sometimes loosened up. He listened. He came to listen to music. But being so laconic was indication enough when he did speak. I gather you've been more than a friend, a kind of father to him."

Father.

"—a true father. Otherwise, you wouldn't be here now, would you?"

"To be truthful, I don't know why I came. I didn't intend to come. I've been thinking of nothing else but Fatso. I'm trying to understand what he did and why. I stopped outside and stood there. Intuition, I don't know . . . I simply pushed the gate open."

Miss Kellogg was gazing at the door. In almost a whisper she said, "I miss him." There was a long stillness before she raised her eyes to the door. Her hands rose and fell in a futile gesture. "It is strange how someone in many ways so removed from you, a casual presence—he *was* a presence—becomes a habit . . ." She was looking out at the harbor. ". . . and a habit a need."

Need? He knew nothing of Miss Kellogg's life but that it was long, and dedicated.

"At first he would come sit on the porch simply to listen, and then to listen to his brother practice, and then—oh, he knew nothing about music, he'd be the first to say, but he was sensitive, superlatively sensitive, and when someone is that sensitive you cannot deny him, no—I would invite him in to listen. He would never *ask.* He was too humble, or perhaps proud; at moments they're the same thing.

The music moved him, he felt deeply. It's strange how the musician feels the listener's emotion. Gradually a kind of bond grows, and everything else falls away but the motion of the music you both surrender completely to. Once, in my young years, I spent well over a year working on a piece. One day my mother left me with two visitors, older women they were, and one asked me to play. I saw the chance to try that work, so I played it, and as I played I could feel their emotion in the profound stillness because there is a stillness beyond the music. . . . They were behind me and when I finished and turned to them, they were absolutely still, their eyes filled, and I knew I had practiced so long just for that moment. Their emotion was the measure of the worth of all my hours of practice, and I was elated. I tell you this because Santi felt. I could feel his emotion. And his presence—I'd never have believed it—made my playing better."

It was a strange kind of gratitude, Savannah. She's a woman rich in possibilities few people will ever know. I wonder if someone once did.

"I remember—" She smiled. Her arched head, her far tired gaze, gave a longing to her look. "—the first time I saw that boy sitting on my front steps: I could see only his head there in the tilt of the mirror. I didn't know he had stopped to listen, till after. He came time after time, and *boldly*—" She laughed. "—as if he had the right, laid claim to his orchestra seat as someone would his church pew.

"It was for his brother he actually came to the door. I think nothing else would have brought him here because he was, as I said, as I afterward observed, too humble or too proud or both. And surprisingly contained. He was certain his brother was special in some way, and when Joey became obsessed—he did—with the piano at school, well, it was all Santi needed. He kept coming. It was a pleasure to see *him*, Santi, bloom as—what else can I call him?—the boy's father. He was. Is. I mustn't think of him as if he were dead. . . . Santi said he didn't care how much it cost, *he'd* pay for Joey's lessons, he'd work and work—and pay he did, never failed.

"Now and again Santi would come for him. Evidently Santi's relationship with the family had changed, so he saw Joey here—but I wouldn't have interruptions. At first he went on sitting out there; then I told him he could slip in, he needn't knock, and listen till the end.

"It was that, and perhaps his sympathy—I mean his genuine desire to know Joey, what he was going through—which must have released a passion for music. How strangely one thing leads to another. Oh, he only said a word or two now and then, but when I did stop to talk to him, he could talk a sudden blue streak and with extraordinary penetration. His insights could startle. He was caught up in music, steeped, pursuing. He was relentless." She smiled. "One day after a rather strident outburst, he even apologized. He said, 'I don't mean to bowl you over.' He could. I knew he was sensitive but his ability to talk, expound, was a revelation; yet it struck me with a kind of horror. *Who was there to listen to him?* I had plenty of time to observe him when Joey was playing. He went through, I can't tell you, such transformations; it's amazing how expressive his face can be. Finally I'd invite him in to listen at times when I practiced. Of course, it was selfish on my part—*I* wanted to hear *him*—because almost invariably we'd talk afterward. . . ."

She looked straight into Cory. She went silent, long. She was too still, and he dared not interrupt where she was.

When she came round, she said, "He left his voice here. Since that night . . . sometimes I hear it. People do leave things behind."

Rod.

"They can't know what," he said.

"No."

He too heard. "Santi's was a voice to remember."

"For those who really heard it. He talked to so few."

"Yes."

"But—it sounds strange—he was talking all the time, wasn't he? His head was always going, wasn't it? You must know. I don't know what there was between you, but I know that above all things it was . . . vital. Santi was always thinking, and his body seemed to be always thinking—by that I mean feeling. He *was* vital. I could see it when he was listening. He could be so still, *too* still, transfixed; yet in his stillness I could feel his emotion as if the music were *in* his body and he was afraid the least movement would let it out."

"Something did." Cory's hands opened. "And that quickly."

"Yes."

"If they'd let me talk to him—"

"You think you'd find out?"

"Fatso'd tell me, yes."

"Under such powerful emotion he may have no recollection of his actual feelings. He may never be able to remember step by step what he did. In a way I hope he can't. I hope . . . It was too horrible. If he does, it may be in no way as it actually was. Emotion tricks the mind."

Or, he'd written Savannah, *Fatso may never escape seeing it as it happened, even if he can never bring himself to describe it. What Miss Kellogg remembers is bad enough. She has to live with memories of that night too, poor woman, and they're heavy on her.*

"Poor Santi!"

But she said it to me, looked straight at me, Savannah. Maybe she saw Santi sitting here. Then she looked down at her hands in her lap. I didn't interrupt.

"He . . . That night he had a look, a look he'd never had before. I saw right away he was agitated. No. Worse. Overwrought. He could hardly contain himself. Of course I thought *music,* music's usually the answer: people respond, it calms them, they relax. My playing had always worked with Santi. But not this time, no. Oh, no. Santi! I could have saved him. I *could* have—"

She was wrong to feel guilty because she couldn't know what was going on inside Fatso. She was looking back, and looking back it seemed clear to her; but, as she herself had said, emotion tricks the mind. Besides, when she was telling me all this, the murder had already happened, but that night with Fatso she didn't know, couldn't have known, what would happen.

"But I was *afraid.* I didn't realize until after, when he'd run out of the house, *how* afraid I'd been. I'd never once been afraid with Santi. It startled me afterwards that I could have been, though afterwards I knew, yes, there *was* reason to be: because he had come right in, he didn't wait. He sat. He didn't even—I'm *sure* he didn't—see me. It was his look that alerted me—beyond me, through me, I don't know—and that stillness, because he sat so still, stiff. Everything about his posture was so stiff, even his eyes; yes, his eyes looked *stiff.* I don't really know anything about madness, but I saw madness in that look. There's a stillness that's so still you know it's moving. It was like the stillness of those two women I played to, only not spilling healthy like theirs, but contained and destructive. That look, I was sure, was madness. What could I do? All I could think was *play.* It's all I've ever done, it's all I know that works, it would save me, it would save him. I don't know that I thought that at the time. I just did what I did: I played for him. I think too I prayed for him, me, I don't know. I put every faith in the music's calming him because, as I said, he was still but not calm. I somehow knew then, though I don't think I made the actual thought, that something was about to end, it was the last time, I couldn't let him come again. Something."

No telling, Savannah, how many times she's had to live the experience this week—for the police, whomever, but she carries the nightmare, the least thought must trigger that night, and surely all the years of Fatso. She's so frail there's nothing to her, but she's all dignity and kind and it seems unfair that she has to bear that memory. She told it as if she had to, as if the telling would take her to some realiza-

tion she hadn't perceived yet. The telling was like a lament; she'd lost something that she didn't know she'd had. I hated to interrupt because I wanted to know every detail, but I did because I didn't want her to suffer. She was suffering. Stupidly I said, "He won't. He won't come again," more to myself than to her; and she let out a little cry, painful, but quickly recovered her decorum. She was Miss Kellogg again. She's wonderful. I never admired her more than at that moment. She clings to form. Form saves. It saved her from an emotion she might have regretted later just as her playing had saved her from Fatso that night.

"*I* thought *He won't come again.* I didn't count then on how he comes to mind so frequently. Surely that will go. It must. But that night, I told myself *He won't come again* in terrible confusion because I felt—it confuses me that I could have—relief. I couldn't bear the tension; and I felt terror, not for me, that was there too but it was something else, but for him; yet I was *afraid,* oh, yes, afraid because my playing did *not* calm him. Nothing changed. His face still had that stiff look, but he was seething, struggling. I felt his emotion. Then his eyes moved. That frightened me most of all. They moved as if they couldn't get out of him; something terrible was going on in him. Then they settled on my hands, and he bent forward, swayed a little, staring at my fingers. I have to confess I didn't trust my hands then but I didn't want him to notice, I didn't want to betray him or myself, I was afraid. But he was somewhere else, I don't know what he was seeing, and just then he started up, stood. I stopped playing. I can't say I was waiting for something to happen, but *Now* went through my head *Now,* but—actually there was nointerval—he turned and streaked out, *ran.* I let out a cry—his name; it burst like a breath I couldn't hold, I felt I'd been holding it in from the minute I was aware that my playing was not calming him. My cry was partly relief, but mostly desperation for him because something had *not* happened, something was going to happen, the thing was in him, it hadn't happened, but it was going to—"

She looked prophetic, Savannah, cold still, as if she were seeing it before it happened. The imagination can stun like that and release you from the body an instant. But to what fire! Remember Macbeth stunned by the witches' prophecy to ecstasy, where terror and beauty are one.

"—but not to *me.*"

There was no relief in her words, but a strange lament, perhaps for the García woman, perhaps that it had happened at all, perhaps—surely—for Fatso. "Oh, that poor boy! I should have helped him I keep thinking there was something I could have done, that somehow I failed him, my resources went dead because . . . I was afraid it would be me, Cory. There was a moment when I looked at him and saw that—what?—*distraction* and I was so *sure* it would be me."

"No, nothing could have stopped him, Miss Kellogg. You know how one-track-minded he could be. He could go blind with an idea, talk it out uninterruptedly, not let you get a word in, as if you weren't even there; and then he could be so calm and reasonable and *calculate* his questions, leading you to his answers. His mind was extraordinary. It's a crime so few knew him. He could have used it for so much."

"Yes, yes, such a waste. We do waste so many." Instantly, the teacher in her, forlorn, emerged.

"No, don't make yourself guilty. *I* have to fight that too because I knew him, knew him better than the rest of town. If I'd only been here! If anybody could have saved him . . . But I neglected him, let him go. I console myself by saying we're all guilty, and maybe we are, but some of us get involved, and when you get involved . . ."

I'm not dumb, am I, Cory. I can learn, can't I?

"You must believe your own words, Cory. If nothing could have stopped him . . ." She sought sea, her gaze blank. "Yes, it would be comforting if we could all accept that . . ." Her mouth made a half-smile. Nostalgic she looked.

"I miss him." Her murmur quivered.

It half-mystified, Savannah. She has such contained emotion in her, and such empathy, that it makes me wonder what in her life there was that created a kind of bond with Fatso even before the murder.

Before he could reply, she stood—with that manner she had of terminating an interview—and smiled, recuperating her usual gentility. She said, "There was nothing more. The rest—as much of it as they know—was in the papers. You— I hope you do get to see him. If he's rejected you, it's surely because he cares most for you, and the ones you care most for in one way or another hurt you more . . ."

Something in her heart, Savannah, nobody would ever know.

"And it must be only temporary. He'll come round to wanting to see you." She held out her hand. "I hope when you're in town you'll come again and tell me what's . . . transpired." Her hand was long bone, dry, but warm, and the fingers gripped quick and strong.

"I'll come whenever I'm here."

At the door she said, "The town . . . It's not the same now."

"Nothing is. For you, me, Joey, a few others. But I don't believe the town knows that."

"It's probably good it doesn't." She smiled.

"Yes."

He shut the gate and waved. She was still in the doorway.

There's Fatso's brother to consider, Savannah, José García, Joey. He's going to be a brilliant young pianist if he goes on practicing as he is and doesn't get discouraged by his family and by his situation. Right now he's living in his mother's house with a sister and her family, a situation which will last until the succession of his mother's house is settled (one of the brothers is holding out, claiming to collect for supporting his mother on military allotment). After Fatso's letter, I rented his house and made an arrangement for Joey's keep with the sister, Theresa, living in the mother's house. I gave her the choice of a fixed amount, not high, or nothing; otherwise, I told her, I'd rent a room in Fatso's house to somebody while Joey was living there. Of course, she went the money route. I suppose she had to, she must need it. So his situation for the time being is set up. He goes on with Miss Kellogg. She's gone tooth and nail at getting him auditions, early as it is. He won't be ready for a school of music or university for some time, but she has every confidence he can get in and train under special tutelage and make it with one of the great masters. That's a big dream, but she's staking her faith on it and the boy is possessed—you wouldn't believe it—with all the passion of the three-letter athlete transferred to his hands! Thank God we've convinced him not to accept any sports scholarships.

Now he passed the old cemetery and before turning down Third stopped to view the dump. Its enormous dark primitive arch high over the dead end still evoked for him the hellish fires of night burning inside that gate, which once seemed to impose some dark meaning on that harmony of low land and sea. Always before that gate, he had felt tiny. He did not feel so small now, but that entrance was so fraught with memories of Fatso that he could not escape the sense of doom he associated with it, though he knew that crude arch, the dump itself, was merely one more of the town's myriad attempts, illusory and futile, to separate the fair from the foul in the world.

The García house looked smaller, too small to bear the enormity of what had happened there. Peeling, mangy as an old dog relaxed in the October sun it looked, surrounded by dry earth, not a shred of grass, the porch boards buckled. Winters of ice and snow had taken their toll. The place wouldn't last much longer. He went around to the back, knocked on the kitchen door and waited. He was about to give up when the woman came, the heavy one, Theresa, wrapping herself in blue chenille, her face heavy with sleep.

"Oh, it's you." She resented his managing Fatso's affairs. She'd once given him a piece of her mind. "Couldn't find my robe."

"Sorry to get you up."

"I been up once. I s'pose you want Joey."

"I stopped by just on the chance . . . I can see him at the school. But you can tell him it's my grandfather's, Tom's, birthday. I've asked a few people in, and I'd like him to stop by tonight."

"I'll tell him, but it's Halloween and all, and you know the gangs—

"Well, if he's free—"

"You takin' him? You are, ain't you?"

"Taking him?"

"Don't shit *me*. You gettin' Joey away from Greenport."

"Whatever Joey does is up to him."

"And gonna leave me flat with this fuckin' house and no keep? You think *that's* what Fatso'd want?"

"Fatso wants what's best for Joey."

"*I* know what's best for my brother. Who you think you are?"

"I'm just doing what Fatso asked me to do."

"*What Fatso asked me to do* my ass! I'm his *sister*! You hear? And who the fuck are you? Cory Moorehead. What's in it for you, Cory Moorehead? Je*sus*!"

She slammed the door.

He went back to the car.

He couldn't blame Theresa. She was hard up; the family had always been; she was trapped by the family's refusal to sell the house and divide the money. But she didn't think Where'd Joey be *then*?

Yes, he would take Joey from Greenport. What was there for Joey here at the end of the world?

He would have plenty to tell Savannah. After today he would not have to write it. He would never have to write it out to her again.

But at Brown he had written himself out to her, letters he had been mailing for over a year, describing his failure to see Fatso, his visit to Miss Kellogg, the fire, his mother's death, as if the letters were not only necessary as a kind of immediate and self-imposed therapy, but as if she and only she were necessary as his therapist. But she did not answer; she had never answered. There had been only that first letter from her. There had been that one spontaneous letter right after her June graduation, six months after his own graduation. There had been that farewell long before he started writing to her from Brown. She had *left the litter,* disappeared, ten days after graduation: *I'm going now. Remember, not good-bye—there is no good-bye for us. We have been such friends, Cory, more than friends. I wouldn't hurt you for the world if I didn't have to, ever, but your heart is suffocating me. I can't move in it. I knew one day I would break out of it as I do now.*

If I am driving myself away from you, it is because I am being driven too. I can't help that. You showed me my skin is too small for me. Maybe I'll never get near anything in the city, but I want to reach out. So forgive me if we can't go on with our old world as it was. We never can, can we? I'll carry it with me everywhere. Once he dared to reason that she was *letting him talk*; then that she wasn't *listening,* that life had changed for her, that she was caught up in somebody else's world; then that she was holding out till some strategic moment; then that she was indifferent because they had drifted too far from each other. But he knew better than that. He knew Savannah. Out of the blue and in the midst of a correspondence or apart from one she could have written *I've found my man and the little cottage*; she could have written *Fuck you, Cory Moorehead.* Whatever, she was there, or someone was, she was *receiving,* because he had sent all the letters to Black River Falls and no letter had ever been returned.

And there was no telephone listing in her name.

But why? Where was she? Wherever she was, she refused to answer his letters.

But, Christ, you leave me desperate, Savannah. Why? What are you up to? What's happening in your life that keeps you from writing? All right—so we had a bitter farewell, long ago now; but we're friends, more than friends. We both know that. Nothing could really break us up. We will always be important to each other no matter what.

Though she was not with him, he had lived through everything with *her*: they had graduated six months apart. They had gone from each other in fury and lament, he to the Island and she to Black River Falls. He had shared Fatso's tragedy with her, the impossibility of seeing Fatso in Riverhead and then his recent visit to Fatso in Ossining. She knew Joey and Miss Kellogg, though she had never seen them, and she knew of his arrangements for Joey's future. He had kept her up on Brown, on his visits home, on his mother's hysterectomy, on his mother's death in the fire.

She knew more of the intimate him than anyone alive.

Which meant: he couldn't let her go.

He waited for the letter which he still believed would come.

Which meant: he couldn't let her go.

But he *had* let her go.

At Brown—after over a year of unanswered letters—on a freezing day in dead winter, February, the message came, but not from the postman; it was Western Union with a telegram from a Dorothy Brewster, SAVANNAH GOSHEN NEEDS YOU CALL COLLECT and the woman's number.

Savannah needs you. It was that simple, so matter-of-fact and isolated and insignificant on that carelessly glued strip of paper that no one would ever guess the words had such deep roots in him. She needed him. He could hardly stand it. For a moment he ached with his own breathing and the joy at a message at last, and the fear for her created a thudding that for a moment obliterated his lonely, yes, lonely room. He said, "Savannah, Savannah," undressing, almost unable to see, groping.

When he called, Dorothy Brewster said, "You're the only one she ever really talked about. I knew you were at Brown. She mentioned it enough. She was so proud of that. That's why I called you. I had to call somebody. She needs you."

Need.

"I'm sorry. I know you don't mean to confuse me, but you're not telling me why. Where is Savannah? What's she done?"

"Can you come?"

"I'll be on the train in an hour."

"It's a long and complicated story, but she needs help. She stays in her room on Fourteenth, she has problems, she's very disoriented. Since you're on your way, I'll tell it all when you get here. Take down my address—"

He checked the time (3:20) and calculated the next train from Providence to New York (3:55)—he couldn't make it—and the next (4:55). Four hours to Grand Central. Ten minutes to Savannah.

"She locks herself in. She won't answer the door either. The last time I saw her she was on the bed, dressed, sitting in a pile of letters, and swearing. I think she was talking to them . . ."

Dorothy Brewster was short and sluggish with penetrating dark eyes, roving and rather desperate, a strange contrast to a slow-moving body that sank comfortably into the cushions.

"Savannah I practically adopted." She smoked like Savannah, her open mouth letting the smoke run up the side of her face and into her hair. "I'd been divorced two years, I was lonely, the place was too empty . . . You know the story. I ran into her in Saks. She'd been in the city a couple of months. She'd graduated not long before. She was just wandering, she said, and I watched her—and she *was*. She kept looking back. I mistook the reason, thought *the girl wants to talk*; so I followed her and we ended up over coffee, and she did talk. We met a few times after that. She talked a lot about Wisconsin and you and some others, and in no time I'd taken her home and she stayed. I've always been given to lame ducks."

"But now?"

"Gone. For months she lived with me until she, we, got so bad we couldn't put up with each other. She wanted to live alone. She had to live alone. She stormed out. But it wasn't just that. The aloneness—here, and in that room too—got to her. She's sick."

"Sick! What do you mean sick?"

"I mean she's so disoriented and confused she steals things—"

"Steals!"

"Yes. She picks up things in the stores. She's suffering from kleptomania."

"Savannah?"

"She can't help herself. And I can't help her. God knows I've tried." Helplessness cracked her voice. "She doesn't need me. She never did. She needs you. Here's the address. I'm glad you're here. I can't tell you how glad. You'll go straight to her?"

"It's all right, Dorothy. I'll be there in a few minutes."

"Oh, but *don't* tell Savannah I got you here—please. She'd never forgive me. When she's angry, she's a nightmare."

A nightmare? Not Savannah! What could have happened to her?

He went down Fourteenth Street past the wrought-iron railing, up the long steps, and groped down the almost lightless corridor to Savannah's room. He touched the number, 1-C, and closed his eyes and stood listening.

"I know you're there, you!"

The voice was raucous, deep, a lash—but Savannah's, yes.

"You!"

He knocked.

"Leave me alone, you."

He knocked again. Maybe it was the knock, not Dorothy's, that made her still for so long.

Then he heard sounds like springs, chafed cloth or wood and knew she was close, against the door, listening too. Now he could hear her breathing, husky.

"Savannah, it's me."

The husky sound ceased abruptly.

"It's Cory."

"No."

"Let me in, Savannah."

"What're you trying to do to me!" she said.

"Please let me in."

"Go away. Go away."

He waited, but she didn't move; all was stillness but for that breathing.

"I'm not going till you open the door, Savannah. I'll sit here day and night."

"Please don't do this to me!"

He heard her struggling with her breath a long time.

"Open, please, Savannah."

"Noooo," she cried, but he saw the knob move and then the latch sounded. She opened the door a wedge wide enough for only her face.

"Savannah." He took her face in his hands. It was pudgy, her eyes puffy and worn dark from crying or no sleep, whatever the misery, the problem, was; and the hair unkempt, flat, slept against, little tails; but they were her eyes, Savannah's, soft brown and large, hers. Anywhere he would know them. "Oh, Savannah."

She closed her eyes.

"It's another *thing*," she said. "It's not real." And her breath broke. Her mouth opened as if she were going to cry out, and he knew the teeth, the spaced teeth, his Wife of Bath teeth. He thrust the door open and clutched her—"Savannah"—and kissed her neck, kissed.

"It's you," she said. "It's Cory."

He smiled. "Old me." He shut the door.

Dark. The room was so small that two could scarcely move around. Even shoved against the wall, her bed left a narrows between it and the bureau.

The bed was littered with letters. She crawled back into the middle of them.

They were his letters, piles of his letters.

He had to sit on the bed to talk.

"Well, this is it." Her hand made a directionless flight. "Great, isn't it." She laughed the same nearly hoarse laugh ending in that gulp which used to make him and Rod laugh at UW. Yet Savannah stared at the blue spread, thinned to white strands in places, and plucked a thread and broke it.

"Sixty-five bucks," she said, "but it's a place. Home."

She looked up, perhaps because, as she leaned forward on her hand, his moved and nearly touched hers. He wanted to touch her but she made her eyes do the touching first. She laughed pointlessly, and he laughed too, so happy at the very sight again of her big square teeth stained from too much chain-smoking, the brown eyes, dimples, dark short hair with the frizzy ends. For a moment they were back at UW in the Campus Grill. In a minute she would thrust her elbow forward, shove her face heavily forward on her hands and talk between distorted lips as the smoke drifted up into her eyes and hair.

"I could listen to you read forever," she'd say. "Some day you'll write words like those." In a minute Charlie would come kick them out. "Okay, Charlie, hold your horses," she'd say. Then they would begin the trek to their rooms, sometimes walking until just before dawn, then to class, or home for a quick pick-me-up nap before class or a plain morning's sleep-though.

Sitting on the bed, she was fat now, a prominent bulge over her ribs deepened by the tight belt. Maybe she was eating out of that desperation that was driving her. An instant later, balling the thread between her thumb and forefinger, she said, "How is it with you?"

Quick, he told her about Brown. All the time he was making circles about his presence here. He did not know when she would break, when he would say why it was he came. Dorothy had said, *When she's angry, she's a nightmare.*

They were silent. He could hear time going in her breathing, all those months he'd not been with her measured in her breath.

"Savannah," he said.

"And your grandfather? He's alone now?"

"He has plenty of company, a dog and a raft of cats."

"But not you."

"I don't miss his birthdays. In October. Halloween."

"October," she said. "In Wisconsin it's so cold in October. So much snow. You remember—in Black River Falls—I went through the ice? God, it looked so safe and Rod grabbed my head, you grabbed this arm. Ha! We ran all the way back to the house. Jesus, it was cold! I was freezing. I can feel it—" She shivered, laughed a hard laugh, her eyes on the wall beyond him.

"And you, you're going to—"

"Teach."

"You'll be good at it. But you'll be kind and gentle and tender with them, won't you? *He* was all those things, Cory. I saw them in him. I wanted to be close, to touch inside him so I could have some of him—of you, yes—inside me. You understand? But I couldn't. Oh, it's why *you'll* be good because you do get inside; only sometimes that's not good: *I* can't get you out. You get under the skin, deep as a disease, Cory. I feel that now."

"Because I'm here, Savannah."

"Oh, Cory, don't be hurt, please."

He touched her neck then. "Savannah." But she curled back into herself taut.

"I'm afraid, that's why. I *do* want to be touched, only Rod taught me, without realizing it, how difficult that is. I thought I could get to him if I couldn't get to you . . . It would be so easy after all the sex agony of not wanting to stop. I thought I did too. But when it was over, sex, he was the same. I had nothing of him, really nothing, and I didn't touch him at all. That wasn't the way to him or to you. I don't *know* the way, Cory. I look, I feel for it, but— Please don't be hurt. It's just that you bring him back. He's on your hands too, you know."

"Yes." But he wanted to bleach them clean so she could see they were his hands, not Rod's.

"You were aware even the night it happened, weren't you?"

"I saw—"

"You sensed it before you saw, didn't you? We can't help sensing each other, can we?"

"You're sure of that, Savannah?"

Rod was here. If he reached, his hand would touch Rod sitting innocently between them.

"Dear Cory, pulling the old cryptic again. The time's gone for that," she whispered. He looked up. He could suddenly hear the clock, and she caught his eye. "I know you've got to go," she said. Fearful for an instant and lost, she hunched forward and her breath caught. "That damned treacherous clock! Sometimes at night I have to get up and go out so I won't hear it. I want to run, but outside is so big, it drives me back. And here I keep thinking of UW. I *do* live it all over again, Cory—you and Rod, beer on the table. I trace the initials. I hear every word of the lovers whispering under the arch across the room and smell beer and the lake and the stale men's john and then go to the Grill and you read Shakespeare—Christ, how you read it!—in all that grease and coffee . . ."

She looked at the clock again.

He got up.

"No," she said without moving, staring at the place where he'd been sitting, staring at the emptiness. Her voice was so agonized that when she turned to him her face shocked him. She stood up.

"If you have to go so soon, why'd you come at all?"

She was crying silently, and quivering. She was so close, but with Savannah he could never say the words.

"I came, that's all," he said. She was so close her breath was on him, and he trembled.

"Because Dorothy called you! She *did,* didn't she? That bitch! She *promised*! And now you know everything, don't you? Don't lie!" She threw her hands up, almost touching him, as if to hold back something he couldn't see.

"Yes, then. I went to her flat first. I made her tell me everything. She had to."

"That's a lie too. Oh, no, Cory, you wouldn't lie, I know. But—God-damn her!" She sank helpless onto the edge of the bed and began to cry. "All *right*! If you want to know, I *take* things. I go uptown and walk through the stores and I take things—little things. My God, Cory, I don't even *want* them, they're things I can't even use, and I don't know why I do it. I've got a job, there's plenty to do in New York. I . . . I'm a kleptomaniac."

"You're lonely, Savannah."

"*No*, I'm not, no. There's Dorothy, and there're men I know. And women. No." She stared, vacillating. "Yes, you're right. But it's not that either."

"And it will get worse because you owe Dorothy money and now you know you can depend on her."

"She told you *that*? Yes, she paid the fine, a hundred dollars."

"And it will go on and on. You know that, don't you, Savannah? You'll call Dorothy and Dorothy will get you out and I'll come and then one day we won't be able to get you out."

"What can I do, Cory? I don't know what to *do*."

"Go home, Savannah." He sat her down, and sat close. "Please, Savannah, go back to Wisconsin."

He could hear her then: *I want a houseful of kids. I belong in a kitchen. I'm not cut out for the university at all. Just give me an apron and kids and a backyard to look out into while I work.*

"Go home? I can't ever do that. Not until I make something of me. To fail like this! To admit that . . . no, no, I can't go back."

"It won't be easy to admit you failed, Savannah, but we all fail somehow. Only, Savannah, you'll be able to live then."

"*Savannah*," she said. "Say it that way again." And he knew she hadn't heard the rest.

"Savannah," he said.

"Yes," she whispered. Her nostalgia overwhelmed her, she smiled, her eyes closed. He watched her hands come up to his face, fearing them. When they touched his cheeks, the sudden shock of her fire in them made him tremble. "Again," she said. Her breath was on her hands, and his own suddenly held the soft flesh over her ribs. "You won't go?" she whispered. "Don't." Her lips touching his neck pained him. *I came for this, I did.* And he thought quickly, *Help her, help her*, all his blood pounding.

"Savannah," he said.

"Don't—" She held him taut, close, whispering, "Don't move, don't, don't—," her face jammed close, her voice wistful. She was crying.

He cupped her head in his hands and rolled her over on her side close against him and still she did not open her eyes. He said, "Savannah, promise you'll go home, promise," and she smiled and propped her hands together against his chest like a comforted child.

After a while she said, "Light me a cigarette and put out the light," and then, "You must go in the dark so I can't see you—quiet." She rolled over on her back and smoked while he whispered that she must go back, must, promise. After a while she stubbed the cigarette. She lay against him. He held her until she fell asleep. He had no way to tell her part of him had died and another part wanted to live forever.

In the middle of the night he got up and dressed and left a note, *This is all I have left of my scholarship and GI Bill this month. You promised to go home. Please go, Savannah, till something can be worked out.* He laid all the money he had on the dresser, and kissed her and left.

Walking along Fourteenth Street, he realized he had left thinking he could have something of Savannah at last, but even in that moment with her he had failed. He could not know what or *who* during all those months in New York had happened to Savannah, whose love she had had, whose love was on his hands. He still did not know what they could be together; so what he had, counted for a lie. She was as far away as if he had reached into the New York sky and watched it grow farther away and deeper the closer he got, and he was afraid the way you are afraid when an impossible dream becomes suddenly possible, when there is no ready dream to replace it and you might fall forever.

A hundred times since, in his head, he had gone down Fourteenth Street past the wrought-iron railing, up the long steps, and groped down the lightless corridor to Savannah's room.

Back at Brown he had waited for several days, to give Savannah time, before he called Dorothy Brewster: Yes, Savannah had given up her room, but she hadn't called or written Dorothy a word. "And she won't," Dorothy added. He said, "She'll take her sweet time, but she will." "And if I know that girl at all," she said, "you'd better put your faith in eternity." "I'll put it in Savannah, Dorothy." "You're lucky to have faith in anything," she said.

Still Savannah had not written him, but he kept writing to her address in Black River Falls. He had to sustain something in her and in himself. He couldn't let her go. He was sharing his life with her, trying to. She was the only person he could share it with, the only one who had known Rod, the only one he could share Fatso and Joey and the town with, all that the town could not know. Because the letters were not returned, somebody was forwarding them, he assured himself, so she must be receiving them. . . .

Now, since it was lunch time, thinking Theresa might not tell Joey about the gathering for his grandfather, who would surely wonder why Joey wasn't there, he decided to drive to the high school to find him.

How naked the streets were, and empty. You could feel the threat of deep winter in the cold October air. The trees were stripped, the gutters laden with dead leaves, and the town looked shriveled, shrunk closer to the ground. Without the green town and harbor fused, flat, gray. Only the masses of orange pumpkins catching the sun outside the grocery stores gave life to the bright but colorless day.

Before he could spot Joey in the school cafeteria, the boy had risen and was already crossing the hall.

Cory couldn't believe. *Look at him. How proud Fatso would be!* For the boy moved with ease, with dignity, not hurrying, his dark wavy hair rising and falling gracefully with his motion, a walk as graceful.

He thought of his momentary encounter with Theresa, of the faces of that family, of Fatso.

Where did the grace come from?

"Cory!" Joey gripped his hand, smiling, revealing the slightly spaced teeth, which, so unlike his brother's, made his face with its fine thin nose and sensual deep red lips attract, dynamic. Those candid eyes stared straight into him, dark, deep—Fatso's, exactly—but in an appealing form and with charisma. He had grown taller, slim, straight, his head high suggesting a natural pride.

José María García.

Who he was.

Part was Miss Kellogg. She had helped him emerge from the chrysalis.

"I almost didn't recognize you, you've sprung up so."

Joey laughed. "Half a head. *I* can't believe it. I had to hang my bedroom mirror higher."

"Never thought I'd have to look up to you."

"You!" Joey poked him. "I knew you'd come today."

"You couldn't have."

"Because it's Halloween."

"You remembered!"

"You wouldn't forget Tom's birthday. Especially now, without your mother."

Joey's directness was a discretion. They could talk about feelings without shame.

"It's a miracle how Gramp has cleaned up the place. I've got Clarence to tear the chimney down. It won't cost much and I'll feel better because it's dangerous; kids play around it too much."

Gramp had bit by bit carted away charred wood, the remains of two-by-fours, caved-in debris that filled the cellar, till only dead coiled wires remained and the partial cinderblock foundation which German had worked on, the fuse box, the crippled gas furnace, the charred water boiler standing tilted forlorn as a defeated soldier, and the cement blocks from the back and front stoops. The cellar steps stood almost untouched like some perverse invitation to descend.

The truth was that it evoked too much history, standing barren as a testimonial to what lived in his and Gramp's memory, which would die too. And more: the fire had left only that image too phallic, as if all could go but that irrationality; it haunted with that passion she had given herself over to, that fire she had followed to the end, which had lured and blinded Gramp so that he blundered and the fire turned on him like his own inner fire, leaped up and enveloped him and left him with those hands as a visible testimonial to its power.

"You'll both feel better when everything's leveled," Joey said.

Joey's sensibility startled.

"Yes."

"And you—the music? I haven't seen Miss Kellogg this visit. It's a quickie visit. I have to go right back for classes. I get my M.A. degree in June, then back to Wisconsin in the fall. I've got a job. They know me there. They want me back. I hope to do the Ph.D. in minimum time—"

"Your letters, they save my life, Cory. And Santi's."

"Fatso's?"

In prison saved.

"Yes. I send them to him. He lives for your letters because he lives for me. How can he? Everything's for me. And him in that cell, my brother, who since a kid had all the freedom in the world. The dump was his, and the town, and the ocean. I have all this freedom because of *him,* but *he* didn't have anything like this freedom as a kid; he never could study—"

"But he made his freedom. He worked to be independent so he could learn. He wanted to know."

"*You* know more than I do, though I see him once a month, because he can talk to you about things I don't understand. He does—did, didn't he?"

"Yes."

"Sometimes I think—it's terrible to think it, I know—but sometimes I do: I think he killed Ma for me, I mean so he could give me now what he could, so I could go as far as I could. That's what he wanted. You think that's crazy, Cory?"

"No, but I don't think you can say. Fatso—Santi—had his own obsessions. They led him to that moment . . . to your mother."

It was possible Joey was at least partly right. *Sometimes,* he had written Savannah after his visit to Ossining, *I think the irrational tricks the mind with an obsession which is its disguise to blind you to where it's really taking you. I don't mean the way it does with dreams, to soften feelings, to solve problems, to avoid pain, because the irrational doesn't do that—it leads you right into agony, it intensifies pain and intensifies joy, maybe they're even the same thing. It held out a lure to Fatso. It hypnotized him, maybe. He was blind to everything else.*

"It's useless to worry about that now. What's important is that, whatever else he's experiencing, you're his joy, and that goes a long way to making something worthwhile to him. He doesn't feel useless up there."

Cory could tell Joey nothing. His and Fatso's history was too complex to explain even to himself and Fatso. He knew they themselves did not know how far they had gone.

"I wish he could hear me play. Maybe . . . if you could write him you heard me . . . could you come this afternoon? Miss Kellogg wouldn't mind. I'm sure she wouldn't." The plea in his dark eyes was Fatso's.

I can learn, can't I?

"I've been wanting to hear you."

His eyes shone—"Hot damn!"—and his teeth.

"*You've* been listening to my grandfather."

"Shades of Tom." He mimicked *"Hot damn! "* and threw back his mound of hair and laughed.

"Maybe we could tape you for Fatso. I don't know the prison rules. We'll have to find out."

"Wow! At three. You won't have to stay. I practice three hours."

"And at eight at my grandfather's?"

"*I'll* be there before."

"Because I'll have a big surprise for him."

"I love surprises!"

The bell sounded for afternoon classes. "I've got to go. Math. I wish I could master it." He rose, dumped his lunch tray, and called back "Three o'clock."

Watching him go, he thought, *He's Fatso made over, as if something driving through his parents had insisted on remolding the same stuff, and succeeded—in the new jaw, the slightly spaced even teeth, the physique slightly taller and narrower, a form which attracted people and responded to them but which was also endowed with Fatso's capacity for obsessive inner concentration. Yes, he thought, it's the same stuff, but it was the structure, Fatso's form, that made all the difference. You accepted or turned against it, and the world accepted or turned against it as if it were deliberately formed to determine your own and others' reactions, to challege you to choose a path or simply let go and be carried in the current.*

He parked the car behind Bohack's grocery, but did not go in. He crossed the lot to the police station on Main and then went down to the corner and stood surveying Front Street, bright but with an absence of green to frame and soften it. He saw himself, a sudden boy at the far end of the street running through the years to arrive at this moment. He saw Fatso bent, intent, driven; saw Gramp pulling his makeshift cart, his mother emerging from Grant's; saw the Zimskis and old Emil and Jimmie-the-whisper and Al biking his way to the Oyster Factory; saw his young cousins streaming out of the Arcade; saw Cash the cop, Whit, the new mayor in front of his cigar store, Doc Kaplan, Dr. Spurling; saw blacks from Third, fishermen in and out of the bars, and tourists—

Then the October street, so suddenly peopled with them, with faces, was as suddenly as empty as the hollow pumpkin faces everywhere waiting for night and candles to bring them to life.

He walked the waterfront piers to the train dock and then back to Claudio's and Preston's, and back on Main he cut through the alley by the hardware store and behind the laundry to "Fatso's fish factory."

He halted at the long low building, trying to catch the busy sounds from inside.

But the town was dead, unreal to him because Rod was dead, because his mother was dead. They had taken the town with them. It had all died into his imagination. Now only Gramp was real in this town that had died, but when he was not in Gramp's presence he too lived in that other town alive only in his imagination.

Where Fatso lived.

Santi.

Santiago.

Because Fatso is someone else now, Savannah.

In spring, some weeks after his call from Dorothy Brewster and his February visit to Savannah on Fourteenth Street, a letter came from Joey: "My brother says he'll see you now if you'll go."

Because of my mother, the fire, Cory thought. *His own mother must always be on his mind.*

On a sunny weekend in late April, having secured visiting rights, he drove upstate to the prison complex at Ossining. Everywhere forsythia blazed in fountains of still yellow fire and the trees were unfurling their first yellow green leaves. The brisk air incited. Such a live day! But the drive was eternal and he was apprehensive, the more so the closer he got to the prison.

And I had reason to be, Savannah.

Because he couldn't believe. Behind the glass, he was led in. García, the guard called him. Cory froze. *Who?* Bones. Bones stood there. *Jesus, no!* He and Fatso gazed an instant, but forever. Fatso! His hair was shorn, and if it weren't for the teeth . . . He was so skinny that his head and teeth seemed to have grown enormous. Though his flesh was reduced to almost nothing, his arms looked tough, wiry, all muscle and tendon. *He's shrinking.* "Fatso?" he whispered. Fatso must have seen his mouth move. He came straight to him and sat. Yes, his, Fatso's eyes—they were pits deep, dark, smoldering.

"Fatso." Suddenly those early days flooded. He felt a strange joy, smiled and reached with both hands, forgetting the glass. Alerted, the guard moved. Only their voices could touch.

"Santiago," Fatso said. "They don't know Fatso. Fatso's not on the record. Listen— Time's short. We talk fast here."

"Everything's taken care of, Fatso—"

"Santiago."

"Yes, Santiago. When I leave Brown, Joey's going with me. The house is rented. At the right time, if and when he needs money for his education, we'll sell it—"

"Don't waste words. I know. Joey tells me. But you—I talk to you, day night I talk to you, all the time here I talk to you, Cory Moorehead. You're the only one who knows the Fatso from then; it's hard for *me* to remember him though I see him every day, *this* me."

"You're awful thin."

"Who could escape this head, jaw, these teeth? How? Only, yes, by concentrating till you reach the end of thinking. Then something will happen. That. I work at that. I wait for that."

"But you have to eat."

"Words, eat words, Cory Moorehead, yes. But words are worms. You eat words till you become words too. You can do that—*think* yourself into things till you *become* things, you become the *sub-*

stance of things, you *move* with the substance of things; then you become the *moving* in the substance, the *motion itself—"*

"But that's theory."

"No! *You* know better. You know men animals insects flowers trees. *You* told me your sensations, how you identify with them to the point where—"

"Yes, but it's to discover, to feel the relationship and find out how much more we are so we can come back and—"

"Back! Never! You wouldn't talk like that if you'd gone far enough: because then you *couldn't* stop—*I* couldn't, I *can't*."

"But you've got to stop to test what you've learned, put it to use in the world."

"You must *get* there first, see the whole thing, know what it *is*." He flung his arms up. The guard braced. "You wouldn't want to come back. I *know*."

"Maybe in philosophy and the arts and religious experience, but in ordinary life no man."

"You're wrong. Listen— I was *there*. My feet— *Listen!* I have to tell you because it was you, yes, long ago, you— I don't know how to tell you: as if our meeting was beginning long before, eons before, that day in Tom's; as if we were fine single threads in time going on and on till the moment we crossed in Tom's—you understand?—and the two became a single thread—yes, we did—and we were going somewhere. It was coming. It had been coming a long time. It was always coming."

Coming here. To prison. All I could think, Savannah, was that his education, mine, had led him to this, all his brilliance (it was! is) confined for life in a cell, in a complex, in walls, stone—cut off. Despite what he had done, the pity of it, the waste . . .

"I was *there*, Cory Moorehead. I set my foot there."

"There?"

I was cold. The longer he talked the colder I felt. Something in me said I don't want to hear. But I couldn't move. I did want to hear. I had to know. I was fascinated. His eyes made me, and his voice—

"Yes. Listen— It was the music—"

He halted, his eyes concentrated—listening?—and then broke his gaze.

"I can't remember every detail. They say you can, after, but don't believe them because what you *did* isn't what *happened* to you, no. Do you see that? Because I don't know how I got to Miss Kellogg's or *why* I went there. I don't remember going in. I can't remember a detail, a word we said, nothing but the hands. But I was moving all the time; *something* was moving, all the time *moving*; it was moving *before* I got there. *Music.* I thought it was in the music, I could feel it coming, I felt it when it entered me, it carried me. Maybe that sound, something in that sound, was already carrying me to Miss Kellogg. I was immersed in it, *immersed.* I didn't want it to end, I was *in it,* I didn't want to get out, I didn't want to break *where it was going,* I had to go with it—I mean the moving wasn't just *inside* me, I was *inside* it— Then it was the hands: I couldn't take my eyes off the hands, the hands were *making* the music but the music was *moving* the hands, the music was coming through the hands, music, musics clashing, too many, and I wanted to hold the music, I would grip those hands and *feel* it, I *would.* Where was it *coming from?* The hands stopped. The music stopped. All the musics stopped because her hands stopped. But the *sound* didn't stop. I *heard* it the way I used to hear it begin to come in the stillness and silence of the dump. I heard the sound, I *felt* it, I felt it in my hands, going through *my* hands my head my body me. It was all around me, it filled the dark, I could hear the dark beating. Where was it going? I wanted to *know.* And I wanted to go. *Where?* The dark moved. The silence, *it* was filled with sound. What *was* it? I had to know what was in my own hands head heart. I could hear my blood. I knew it was coming through blood, but from *where*? I had to go there, I had to touch where it was coming from; and my hands *did;* they touched the blood, mine, hers, her neck, moving and moving. I could feel the moving, I was *in* it. I had to know what the moving was, where it was going. I'd go with it, I held and held and held—"

Fatso never took his eyes off mine, Savannah. I couldn't move. I don't think I've ever been so afraid. Nothing in the war ever scared me like listening to him. I didn't want to hear it, but I was afraid he'd stop. It wasn't only as if I were frozen there watching Fatso strangle his mother, but I was doing it, and at the same time I felt he was strangling me, as if I were strangling myelf—I was Fatso and I was his mother. Later I thought: he never blinked once.

He stopped, but stared still. His hand moved; it broke the spell.

"Fatso, you don't need to confess anything to me."

"Confess! Don't be a fool! You came for this, you know you did. It's for *this* I asked you to come—because it's yours too—to take you to—"

"Take me—?"

"*There—I* told you. Because—listen—I was somewhere else. Don't ask where. I don't know, I can't name it, but I was moving with it, and I *knew* I was somewhere I'd never been before, *nobody'd* ever been before. It was moving alive all around me but I couldn't see it yet. I heard a baby cry. I saw it lying in the dark high ahead, red with blood, reaching out to me. I moved—but it disappeared. Where? I wanted to follow it. I was seething, *thrilled* but *afraid.* Remember *Is this a dagger that I see before me?* The dark must be *filled* with things never seen, never even imagined before, and the ground too. I stood listening. I could *hear* the silence seething. I'd never been so elated. I was where I wanted to be, longed to be, where I belonged. Any minute I *knew* I'd see into that dark, my eyes would be that dark, and I could take the next step and if I took that I could keep going straight to the heart of it, I'd know it, I'd never have to turn back. And I did feel it. The dark moved, things moved—"

And if you'd seen him, Savannah, you'd have thought he was somewhere else, transfixed. I thought: How will I get him back? But I didn't want him to come back yet. I wanted to see it, hear it, too. It scared me, but fascinated. I didn't want to come back.

"But noise broke it. The dark broke. *They* brought me down, voices. *Words* brought me back. They cut me off. I tried to hold the noise back. I didn't know where I was. Then it was the dump. I was standing in the dump, but it was all changed. It wasn't my dump. It was all closed off and neglected, a mess. I could hardly recognize it. 'You, Fatso.' It was Cash the cop, with the new one, Eddie. 'Okay, Fatso' Cash said. 'Come on, boy.' I went with them. *It* was gone, but I'd been on the edge. Next time I'll see it all—I will—all. And listen, Cory Moorehead— I'm not sorry. I'd do it again. I'll get there again, I don't care how. I'd never been so alive."

His eyes, those eyes, in that ghost body looked so alive, Savannah, but he wasn't Fatso. He never once looked at me as if I were Cory. The old camaraderie he once had for me was gone. He was alone. He knew he was alone. He even wanted to be alone. There was a perverse vanity about it, and I understood that, terrible as it was, because he was convinced that nobody, nobody, had ever walked that terrain—and perhaps nobody has walked his particular terrain. Who can know? But he was living in another landscape. I know him. He must spend most of his time trying to imagine what's beyond where he'd been. He may never think of anything else, except that for him it's not imagined, it's real; it's more real than I was who was sitting right there. I must have looked like some relic out of a world that he no longer really lived in. The peculiar thing was that we sat there staring into each other all that time as if each couldn't free himself from the other. It's trite to say it was like looking into a mirror, but that's exactly what I mean to say, Savannah: actually the pane of glass was between us; it separated as factually as the distance he was looking at me from, like a self he had made an object of to examine at a distance, reasonably. Yet everything he said bound me closer to him with an emotive conviction that I could never deny but that he no longer felt for me, as if he had let me go and I him. I can't know what he was thinking of the Cory Moorehead he had known, but something—because he had asked me there—he had had to tell me, his friend, his mentor, his colleague, his conscience even—his maker and . . . destroyer, whatever self or selves I was to him. If only I could have thrust my hands through the glass or in some way touched him to wake him to something inside him that surely must not have died and could still be stirred, or said something to him to break through that undeviating reason that had imprisoned him in his obsession. The pursuit had converted all his emotion into that obsession itself and led him to prison. I wanted to say something to break through, but—and you of all people will never believe this—I couldn't find the words, Savannah. I couldn't think of a single word to reach him.

The guard moved. He said something. Fatso turned.

"Santiago, I'll see you again." he said. He smiled, thinking to evoke a response from Fatso, but Fatso could not smile. For the first time it struck Cory he never had, or could. *Laugh,* yes. His throat could laugh noisily, but the formation of his teeth prohibited any possible smile.

"No. Don't come back. I don't need you. You sent me out to look without daring to yourself. I had to tell you where I went. Now you know. There's nothing else to say."

The guard came up behind him.

"Good-bye, Santiago."

Silent, Fatso got up and turned and followed the guard and did not look back.

Cory went out to the car. He could not wait to leave. He could not drive away fast enough. *What am I running from?*

Fatso's voice pursued. He heard it. He took it with him. *It's inside me now.* Then he knew it was what he wanted, what he had come for. He wanted to castigate himself, didn't he? It would always be there, what he did—what he did inadvertently. It would be there when he was too proud. It would humble him. As a boy, whenever he was quick, superior, snotty, Gramp recited to him "*Pride goeth before a fall.*"

But I'll hear Fatso's voice all my life, Savannah. It comes. It haunts. All the time he was talking, he scared me with my own thoughts, with his face too because the Fatso I knew, whom nobody else knew, was gone. He had become somebody else. Maybe he was Santiago; but, worst of all, he did seem to be speaking from another place, in a voice speaking through all that was left of that cadaverish body. Moments come when I ask myself how education and experience could lead to this, the worst thing, to be a voice that will never be heard.

Only when he was back in his room in Providence did he realize how exhausted he was. He sank onto the bed and closed his eyes. Rod. His mother. Now Fatso.

It's too much. I'm too young for all this.

Then he thought of Gramp.

And he was ashamed.

Now, walking down Fatso's streets, Cory was sure that any minute Fatso would round a corner with his quick, determined pace, head bent, eyes staring at the pavement ahead. Why *wouldn't* he expect Fatso? This was what he had come home for. After all, it was not only Gramp's birthday but Halloween, the eve of All Saints' Day, and what more appropriate than encounters with all his ghosts. How else could he lay them to rest?

It was Ma's ghost which was most difficult. Because of the fire he had not been able to see her. He, Gramp too, had yearned for a last look at her; but as that was impossible, they felt they had not seen the end, it was still coming. Here, for both, she was everywhere. But there was a joy in that sadness, as if she insisted, wouldn't leave, like ghosts of earlier times who had earthly secrets to reveal before leaving.

As if by revelation (it was lunch hour and there was a slight flurry of people going into the corner cafe and Paradise Sweets and Helen's and Meier's and farther up The Diner since Mitchell's and Claudio's were closed for the winter), German's familiar red pickup parked at The Diner and German went in. No more brown-bagging it and no more kitchen since he was rooming at the Manaton House. Cory had expected he'd show, and show he did, his truck impeccable: German kept his vehicles as some men kept women, as elegant appendages; he was jealous of his possessions—car, guns, tools especially.

German was on a stool at the counter. He saw that German had spotted him at once in the mirror. He saw too the mouth mutter and the undisguised drop of his jaw quickly recover in a smile forced, then his perfect teeth flash friendly.

"Some surprise!" German was heavier, a slump of stomach against the counter—beer for sure. "German," his mother used to say, "has legs like toothpicks and can't carry his weight. His legs get so tired they ache."

"Hello, German."

"You out to see your grandfather?"

"It's his day."

"His?"

"Halloween's his birthday."

"Ah. I'm bad at birthdays."

"There'll be cake after supper, a couple of people. Consider yourself invited."

"We'll see. I'm not much for cake."

"German," she used to say, "can't stay away from my desserts. Cream puffs! I make a baker's dozen and they're gone before the day's over."

"How's your grandfather doing?"

"You know Gramp. He always says, 'You can't kill a Verity.'" Cory could hear Gramp's chortle. He laughed.

And German laughed, brittle.

"You haven't seen him?"

"Now and then. When I pass. You know how it is. You drift—work, the Legion, my club . . ."

And "some woman," the Polacks had been quick to tell Cory. Why not? German had his right. Free. How had the fire affected German? There was no knowing, but surely he'd suffered, was suffering, that loss? Cory didn't want to believe he may not be.

"And you— You winding it up at Brown?"

"At the end of spring semester."

"Going to top it off brilliant? Your mother said you would."

"She always exaggerated. You know mothers."

"She saw you clear enough." German stared into his coffee.

"Well, you try to live up to expectations."

"Yes. It's tough. She had her standards."

The skin was dark, deep, under German's eyes. He had a worn look, encroaching crow's-feet, and as always he strained his lids wide open and blinked as if trying to clear his vision. "Sometimes," his mother used to say, "German has the briefest blackouts. His circulation's cut off and he stares, sometimes even slips off the chair but he doesn't know it's happened. It's like being dead for an instant, the doctor told me."

"I thought you'd be in Detroit or Carbondale or Scranton. You always talked about them and family."

"Yeah. I've been back to see Ma and the sisters. Well, the water gets you, I guess. Maybe you just sit things out. One place is as good as another for that."

"I'm not so sure. Some places are like people you never want to leave."

German laughed, then said with sudden seriousness, "I've never had that pleasure."

"There are few joys like it."

"Maybe someday I'll have that luck."

"I hope you will, German. Well, I'd better wind this up or I won't get to all my chores, and I've got somebody arriving on the train at six."

"But you haven't had a thing. Have a beer."

"Drink one for me. And don't forget. If you have time, consider yourself invited."

"Yes. Well—"

"See you."

"Be good, Cory."

Now the day was stained. His clothes were rank with greasy-spoon odor. But the odor evoked. *Shades of the Campus Grill.* Savannah had never let him forget: *"Fair is foul, and foul is fair?"* Still the meeting tarnished. German was evidence of a world gone, and his grandfather was, but German was the residue and his grandfather the essence. How did you balance them out? Or were they the same thing? Was everything?

Over the sea far small white puffs of cloud, looking clean and cold, seemed to stand still, making the sky too blue. The sun made the water hard gray, molten, and laid the town too hard bare, stripped.

He went back to the parking lot and drove out Main to the back road—aware as he passed a block from Gramp's house that the dead chimney was jagged and lower, so Clarence was really going at it—and down Manhasset to Stirling Cemetery.

He had not entered it since his mother's burial. He knew he would enter it once more, the last time, only for his grandfather's. The day would come but he hoped, foolishly, never, because he did not believe in the nothing that was there though he sympathized with old Emil's talking to the dead because it consoled. You crossed the river of the dead as easily as Charon. The little meander of the crick, which ended in a still pool just below the slope of the family plot, caught a bit of blue sky into the earth. Well, you're all here. Rodney. Estelle. Mary. In the vacant plot between Mary and Estelle would lie *Thomas.* The great granite stone *Mary - Thomas* spanned their graves. Ma, more loyal than his wife and for longer, was where she'd wanted to be, beside her father. Only Gramp's loyalty outdid hers. Eternal it seemed.

But there were other presences, family and family buried beyond them, generations; and there were presences. He felt them surround, move with him across the lots and back to the car.

It was but a few minutes to Gull Pond. In Fatso's house a form moved past a window. He drove over the wooden bridge onto the beach overlooking Shelter Island and the sea beyond. Despite prison, he would leave the Fatso he'd know interred here; but he would carry the ghost, he would carry his guilt, and Fatso's presence itself would be visible in Joey. He could never—did not want to—escape that presence, his responsibility. You had guilt and you had guilt and you had guilt; in between you had some joy, but mostly you had guilt. But he would lay that ghost with the others.

And one of those others—it came to him now—had never touched this soil, but had touched him deeply. He would lay his ghost too.

Dalton.

One month at Brown someone had stolen the rent money he'd left in an envelope on his bureau as he did every month. Shortly after the first his landlady came up to his third-floor room and rapped. "You're always so prompt about your rent . . ." "But I left it in the same spot!" Useless. It was gone. He paid her. Too proud to borrow from friends or home, he left the library twice a day and went back to his room, where he hoarded the cheese and bread he had to feed on all month long.

He was sitting on the bed, munching. The sun, high, struck the wall of the house and it glowed and reflected bright cream in the narrow long two-story window of the enormous house next door, denying him the view of the staircase and part of the interior which he could see at night. All the houses here, in a section once prosperous, now decaying or turned rental, were too close together. The house had become a kind of terror to him. He had been awakened one night not long after he'd moved in by a woman's cries and shouts, screams. He sat up. A shaft of light cut the ceiling over the foot of his bed. He got up and went to the window. A woman was standing on the staircase, her back to him, bent over the railing, screaming at a man below. He could hear her every word of accusation: that hussy, filth, filth, all night long, the lies. . . . He was embarrassed for her. He did not want to hear. He did not. He went back to bed, but it went on too long. Why didn't she stop? And of course it occurred frequently, irregularly. He came to expect it, it disturbed his sleep, he was too constantly alerted, he couldn't study in his room—he would have to tell the landlady he must go, and he would, he'd decided, as soon as his GI check came and he could find a cheap room. But the stolen rent set him back; he had to endure. Meantime, he had developed a certain empathy for the woman—he'd never heard a word of the man's arguments—who was forever at home, never out of her robe; who displayed a certain elegance of form and manner, a beautiful if aging head. He had come to expect the argument. He had come even to feed on it as if in installments, though with dread at what it was doing to his sleep, feeling insidious, even guilty, for watching yet attracted by her human exhortations, the tension between that beauty, perhaps love, and that cursing of such filth as he had never heard before from a woman's mouth, and a woman with such a contradictory facade. She was a lush. Whether she had driven her husband from her because of it or whether she had begun her retreat to alcohol because of his adventures, he never found out; but he could not forget the few times he had been home and seen her come to the front door, gracious in her long robe, with a charming smile and manner, a flight of musical laughter escaping her when the delivery man came up the porch steps with a basket full of liquor.

He was thinking then of her whom he wanted to escape, of all the traps in the self and outside it, when someone knocked on the door.

"Dalton!"

"I knew you'd be knocked for a loop. I got fed up with BU, chucked the books, and decided I'd drive over to Brown and surprise the hell out of Cory. You thought I'd died the good death, didn't you?"

"Holy cow! I can't believe this. Look at you!"

"What's wrong with me?" But flattered, he laughed. Cory knew he'd revealed in his tone and his look too his admiration. Dalton had flowered: He held himself with mature confidence, his form slimmer and more graceful than ever. He was groomed. His head, classic with its high cheekbones and strong chin, was not merely handsome but authoritative.

"What was ever wrong with you! Come into this humble abode and sit down. Cheese, anybody?" He laughed to conceal his embarrassment at the opened loaf and the sliced cheese, at the bare, almost simple poverty of his room. "Wow! Savannah should see you now!"

"She has."

"Has! When? Where is she? She doesn't write me a word. She doesn't answer a letter. She's not written to me since the one letter I got after she graduated."

"Whoa, whoa, Cory. She never wrote me either—answered, I mean, my few niggardly notes from BU. But I ran into her in Black River Falls, pure luck because she was there to rent her mother's house, her house now. She's in Madison."

"Madison!"

"Back to the womb, working in the registrar's office. If I know her, with her determination these days, she'll *be* the registrar before she's through."

"That doesn't sound like my Savannah."

"Oh, she's yours all right. If it weren't for you, she said, she wouldn't be back in Wisconsin, she wouldn't be working at the university, she wouldn't be determined to make a success of it. You always did challenge her, Cory. Remember? She fed on it too. You saved her, she said. She wouldn't tell me how. And you won't, I know."

"She saved herself, Dalton. It was *her* will."

In a tiny room shabbier than this, dark, depressing. It overlay this one; it for a second obliterated Dalton. *Savannah trapped in it. No. In herself trapped.*

"I don't know the story, but, knowing Savannah, I doubt that. Something gave her the motive to summon up her will."

"She was broke."

"Come on, Cory. Don't play the innocent behind that innocent face."

"Go ahead, call me stupid. You know how I loathe ignorant innocence. How do I know her motives if she doesn't write?"

"She won't. She didn't say, but that part of Savannah, even I know. What she wants she'll joke and kid and gibe about, but she won't beg, not our Savannah. She has character—plenty, more than she ever showed us on campus. She won't waste life on what won't be. She—you know it, Cory—puts a value on herself. The home slavery she once offered, the house and kids, was a fiercer dedication than you or Rod or I knew. She's not compromising. She'll wait. He—the right man—will have to go to her. The right man—"

"O*kay*, the right man. So she won't write. Who's been doing all the writing? Who's kept her up to the minute on everything. Whose letters are . . . the bond? What more—?"

"So get up tight! More? I'll tell you *when* we have lunch. I'm taking you, it's my day. I'm your—what is it?—amphytrion, cicerone, whatever."

"Poor student you! Get a windfall? Pick up on a rich bitch?"

"A birthday present from the old man. He's actually come round to thinking I'm going to make it in business if I keep up. He likes the publicity, highest awards and all that."

"You don't mean it! Je*sus*! Congrats."

"You see, we Black River Falls people have plenty of will. How's it with you Rhode Islanders?"

"Prick."

"Now you sound like Savannah. Let's go. You pick a place."

"There's a great little French place downtown with the best onion soup."

"Great."

"A graduate student with a car!" Cory circled the old Ford coupe. "How'd you make it from Boston?"

"It wasn't easy. I fed the radiator all the way."

"Your father must really have come round."

"I told you, he's sold on me."

"Some doing! Now you *know* you have charisma."

"Fat chance! Hard work! That's his doctrine. *You* know, our prewar training: if you work, buy a house and pay it off, have ten thousand in the bank when you retire, you've got it made, the world'd go on forever. But *they* didn't have The Bomb. It just may not go on forever."

"Well, maybe till we get our degrees anyway."

"Then?"

"I've a good offer from Wisconsin—teaching and maybe working for the Ph.D."

"You'll be with Savannah!"

Savannah. He didn't believe. All through lunch he could hardly contain. Since they were together, he almost proposed they call her at the registrar's office and surprise her; but instantly dismissed it. Dalton's presence might have left him tongue-tied. He was excited by Dalton's presence, reveling in that voice from *then*, inundated by a host of images which his imagination could hardly sort out. When lunch was over, though he didn't want Dalton to go, he felt ashamed because he couldn't wait to be alone. He had to call Savannah; he had to hear her voice, speak to her.

When Dalton said, "I suppose I've got to get back?" Cory said, "I'll ride down and get you through the traffic hazard,the thousand islands they call that maze—no signs, just choose a direction and pray for your life."

They followed Benefit Street and descended on the thousand islands. "It's like riding the crack-the-whip at the carnival. I'd hate to have to walk across there at five o'clock quitting time!"

"You see, at Brown you take your life into your hands every day. What price knowledge!"

Dalton nodded, mute, gone serious suddenly. "It was all too quick, Cory. We didn't have time for anything."

"Well, Boston's not far. Now that we've broken the ice . . ."

"Have we?"

Dalton looked genuinely pained at going.

"We haven't done anything," Dalton insisted.

They entered the sudden dark of the overpass.

"It's not Boston. Providence never was a very exciting city."

"But you're here."

"That doesn't add much to the city!"

"But you're why I came. I thought of coming a thousand times. I'm ashamed I didn't show before, and you so close." He lay his hand on Cory's knee.

"I think often of what we had."

What we had.

Left, beyond the darks, the sunstruck dome of the capitol burned bright and clean.

They broke suddenly into light.

"You'd better let me out on the side there if I'm going to walk back, Dalton."

Dalton pulled over.

"Well—"

"I can take you back, Cory."

"No. It's a great hike."

"You're sure?"

"Yes."

"But I want to."

"You've got a long trek."

"It can wait. Cory?"

Dalton was too intense. The hand was gone, but the voice insisted, and his eyes.

"No," Cory said.

"We could go to your room."

Cory tried to slough it off with a chortle, false. "That St. John of the Cross cell!"

"We could, Cory."

"You'd better get back, Dalton."

"You're sure?"

"I'm sure."

"I don't know when we'll see each other again."

"I'm sure."

"It may be the last time." Now Dalton's voice came quick with despair.

"Maybe," Cory said.

"The last chance." Dalton's eyes were keen on him.

"Yes. I'd better get back. You be careful, Dalton, and don't get into trouble. It was great to see you . . ."

"Yes," Dalton said, but did not move, his head poised, his hand in his lap, firm over his groin, waiting, almost sure of himself now. But Cory slammed the door and stood there waiting for him to leave. For too long Dalton waited too, smiling, appealing, as if Cory would change his mind; then, shrugging, Dalton waved and drove off.

Cory flagged and stood on the curb, following the car till it disappeared. He turned away, indifferent to the city, besieged, because offended—no, hurt and confused and then disappointed in himself, yes, in what it was in him that attracted or tempted, which caused him to ward off others. Would that always be the case? And he innocent? *Was* he? You were responsible for all that was in you, so you had to accept that responsibility too. *Dalton.* For a moment he went furious, thinking Dalton insidious to insinuate, to sever, destroy *what we had. Why?* Because of study, because lonesome with not much money for dating, because of nostalgia . . .? Dalton was always one to preen and parade his body, perhaps thinking he was playing it safe in another city, just one time and with an old friend who would be tongue-tied of course. Thinking all that aroused his fury again; but then thinking *Wisconsin, loneliness, desire,* and yes *affection* too, and *sure he would understand, he's in the same boat* at Brown, he felt suddenly steeped in compassion and some resentment against his own sympathy. But the proposition riled such a tumult in him that he dared not call Savannah. He had barely time anyway though it would be earlier in Madison. He did not call until late the next morning.

"This is a voice out of your wicked past, Savannah Goshen."

"Cory! *Cory*!"

"And why in hell have you been so silent all this time?" But he kept his voice gentle. "Have you any idea how long it's been?"

"Oh, Cory." Her voice broke. "I can't believe this."

"It's what *I've* been waiting for, Savannah. Why, oh why, haven't you ever answered one of my letters? I've written ever since the day I saw you in New York. You've kept me mystified. If it hadn't been for Dalton—"

"Dalton!"

"Yesterday. He came over from Boston, but I'll tell you all that, or write it, later. *You tell me.* You've got a lot of explaining to do."

"Oh, Cory, it's *you,* it's really you, that voice—" She laughed. "I could listen to it forever."

Transported an instant—"I can smell the greasy spoon"—he laughed. "But why, Savannah?" He could hear her trying to control her breath, the chokes, sobs.

"I couldn't, and especially after New York, Cory. When I got back to Wisconsin, I was too ashamed, so ashamed I couldn't write you. Don't think I didn't want to every day, but I didn't want pity or support. I— It was *because* of that, of you, that I got hold. I *wouldn't* live that image of me I'd left with you. I was determined that if you ever did find out, ever did see me, it would be a strong Savannah, different anyway, so you'd see what was underneath, what I hope was always there waiting for someone to challenge it. You always did challenge me. Rod always said so, didn't he? It kind of bothered him that you always picked up my weak points—you *did,* Cory—but the challenge always worked. I *did* something about it. I *passed* math, for instance. Remember?"

"Yes. But how would I know what'd happened to you if you didn't write. Besides, who *wanted* you to change? I didn't. I knew *my* Savannah, not Rod's, not Dalton's, but mine."

"And how'd I know you had your vision of *your* Savannah. You'd never tell me—you never did—and I wanted you to. I always did. I waited for that. In fact, that's why I decided that after New York I'd never write. You'd have to. And not only that, but *you'd* have to come to me. Oh, not out of pride or to make you *prove* anything, Cory, but because I didn't want to spend my whole life in a useless love, yes, useless, because I knew I could never have you—"

I could never have you, Cory.

"—and no matter what, it simply made no sense to spend my life pining for what I couldn't have, so I buckled down, I got hold—the way you told me to in New York—and went back to Black River Falls and remade the arrangement about the house, a good one, and came back here, the terrain of all my dreams—to *remould* my dreams. I found myself a little nook and got a job with the U—and for what?—to live the same dream of hope by rejecting it, challenging myself to forget it, only to keep it present by being here in Madison: Cory forever with me, me waiting but knowing the waiting would be useless because the move would have to come from him and that, that, I told myself, was impossible. It would never happen."

"But it did."

"—and then that with time you'd forget, be so involved with study . . . I don't know . . . and with your . . . future—"

"Stop, Savannah. Don't. I'm here."

"Yes, and, Cory, I can't believe. I'm talking—you know me—to keep talking."

"Don't you think *I* know that? I know my Savannah."

"Yes. It's half the trouble. Half."

"And the other?"

"It's too . . . entwined, twisted. I don't know how to unravel it. *You* must, if you can, if you want to. I'm here, always have been, but can't say, won't say I will be because life doesn't let you choose. You choose but *it* intervenes, it bucks you."

"You wait."

"Wait! Jesus! The agony of filling time until you—if you can—put behind you, forget—"

"—until the right moment, Savannah."

"If it ever comes. It may not *ever*. It's a bet, and time goes, and you die. Endings, remember?"

"Or die if you don't wait?"

"Cory—?" He waited long. He listened to the stillness, some breath. "I don't know what you're saying. You listening?"

"I'm still here."

"Cory, I don't think *you* know either. In the heat of the moment I'm apt to say anything and make some terrible blunder when I'm excited—you know that better than anyone—but not now, not this time. We have to know what we're doing. We always have, but there are things unsaid—yours, mine, Rod's even—and even if they remain unsaid we have to have an understanding about them—I've thought it a long time—even if that understanding is only with ourselves, each within himself, but reckoned with, maybe without a word to the other but some gesture to let the other know that it's *done*, we've decided something. We'll know when it happens, but until then . . ."

Wisdom, he thought, startled at a maturation in her words, at a fiber too, hard too, in a certain—protective?—firmness in her tone.

"You *have* thought." Nothing but thought, he wanted to add, humbled, shamed almost, by what he and Rod had done to her. *Ours*. Intended or not, for better or worse, we've made her that— and, in whatever way, always *mine*.

"Of nothing else but." She—with *his* words—struck, and added, "though I wanted to think of anything else but. But how avoid your own life, what you want most in this world? Don't *let* me, Cory. My big mouth always did get me into trouble."

"You, Savannah! I've found you." He was startled at his own exuberant almost giddy realization. White she stood, with that small waist, wide hips, dainty ballerina shoes, her head shaking her short hair as she laughed throaty with those Wife of Bath teeth. He laughed aloud into the speaker, "I won't lose you now," thinking *Rod, won't lose Rod either*, thinking *You, Rod.* For suddenly they were both there behind that white figure, Rod and he; he saw himself sitting at

The Rathskeller table flailing words at them, and overwhelmed by the sight she'd conjured up he said, "No, I won't let you go, I need you, we'll always be—"

"Don't, Cory. Wait. Give it time. Don't—in the heat of this—say anymore. You know how we are. Wait. You may be sorry. You mustn't be—ever. We've been through too much. No mistakes. Not anymore. Understand, Cory, please. You don't know—can't—at this spur-of-the-minute call because of Dalton and UW and *him*." Rod he knew she meant. "Will you—wait, I mean? Take time. Think."

"Savannah, Savannah—" She sobered him as suddenly as she had spontaneously thrust him giddy. "You know I will. We're not ourselves now, or maybe we are, too much ourselves. But you're right. We'll wait."

"You've got Brown to contend with first."

"Maybe. We'll see what gives. I'll—oh, Jesus, when don't I?—write. You *did* get all those letters?"

"Yes, surely all. I've kept them, my treasures, every one."

He envisioned her on the bed *then*, in New York, sitting among all his old letters to her.

Savannah.

"I'll call when I can."

"Poor student." She laughed. "*Lis*ten to the working girl talking. Not poor now."

"I can call sometimes—extra lunch money, GI money!"

"Call collect."

"Not my style, sorry."

"Well, think about it. In a pinch anyway. Write it down—my home phone, my address here too. If Ada answers—"

"I'll take care of Ada."

"You don't know Ada! Oh, Cory—"

He waited. "Yes?"

"Nothing. Just *Oh, Cory*. Shall we leave it at that, till whenever?"

"Whenever, no. Tomorrow. I'll write you tomorrow—where I left off last time, and about Dalton. You'll want to know."

"Yes. All."

"All. Till tomorrow, Savannah."

"Cory, you sound—"

"Don't tell me! Exultant. Or a reasonable facsimile thereof!"

"Idiot."

"At last?" he said.

"We'll see how long your idiocy lasts."

"Tomorrow, then," he said.

"When wasn't it tomorrow?"

"Don't, Savannah."

"Tomorrow then."

"Tomorrow."

And the next day, euphoric still, feeling an old world somewhat restored, he did write. He wrote everything that had happened since the last letter *in your notes toward the life of,* wrote *Dalton, who brought us together again,* but did not write *and who left, denied.*

You were there all the time, Savannah, sitting between us, so real I wanted to say, "Don't you see her, Dalton?" I wanted to touch you. And I'm ashamed to say I couldn't wait for him to leave to make that phone call to you. But he didn't leave. We meandered through the whole afternoon. We covered part of the city, finally drove up to Prospect Park and sat at the base of old Roger Williams' statue, looking out over the city till dusk came, when he had to drive back to Boston for classes in the morning.

But he did not tell or write her their farewell.

Ended.

Now, here in Stirling Cemetery, he laid Dalton's ghost with the others, though he knew ghosts would unexpectedly rise, unpredictably appear at will; but, as with the others, he would reckon with his.

Let be.

Far, west, a dark blanket rimmed the horizon, moving almost imperceptibly. The lowering sun turned its edge crimson. All the gravestones cast long shadows, and wind soft as a whisper made the webs cast by the trees quiver on the earth around him. The place was too alive.

There was a feel of early snow in the air.

If it were coming, he hoped the six o'clock train from New York would get here before the snow. He had plenty of time to stop for Joey's practice session; it would be his last chance to see Miss Kellogg.

After what I've told you about his brother Fatso, you'll be startled at Joey, Savannah. He has all the beauty that was denied Fatso, and even more talent. Miss Kellogg is certain he has a touch of genius and that he will go far. I've promised Fatso I'll do everything I can to get Joey away from his family and to foster his talent. I owe Fatso that. He insists, and rightfully, that I do. Oh, he takes the responsibility for what he did, but he knows nothing is done in a vacuum, even when the responsible ones—if they no more than gave him birth—are completely unaware of their guilt or what guilt is. And Fatso's proud that, even from where he is, he can play a part in Joey's life. His life, he calls it. And it is, it's part of his, though to Fatso it means more than that: there's power, there's even the fruit of madness, the irrational, behind it, which has partly brought the help about. Fatso will insist on that. It's his (our, as he would have it) life. And who's to say he's wrong? Here we are, you and I, doing his bidding, and willingly, because I—he insists I cannot escape from this, and I cannot—both by accident and will brought it about. It started years before, the day of the Joseph story from the Bible, but (Fatso has worked it all out) even before that, at his birth and before, in an unending chain he has dreamed—dreams, still—of tracing to its origin because he wants to see, experience, be the source; and he's certain he will, he'll keep trying, because once he felt close, he was almost there. It was Miss Kellogg who from the very beginning befriended him and without knowing it nurtured the impulse in him through the music which may be the making of his brother. He relates to the music, to what's in it, what it led him to, its very reflection of the irrational that it comes from and that it carries us to, that source he insists he will reach.

On the sidewalk in front of Miss Kellogg's, Cory stopped to listen. Joey was playing. Outside was very quiet, dead even, and the music seemed to come from a far place, alive but contained. He thought of Fatso, and for a moment he understood how the walls should be removed so the music could break free, spill, resound, and transport them.

On the porch he stood a moment too, watching. Through the diaphanous curtains Miss Kellogg had seen him and nodded and raised a hand—for *silence*, of course. *Wait. Don't interrupt.* How she respected Joey and music, the artist work! Then she made her frail flight on tiptoes across the room to let him quietly in, signaling him to sit between the front windows, some distance from the piano. She was a hawk, vigilant, with almost invisible motions—toes, fingers, head, supremely eyes—following Joey's. The piece was obviously difficult.

Something he saw of Fatso in the boy's concentration, its *fierceness. It* was the one-mindedness, the blinding out of the world, that bound Fatso and Joey. Both pursued music. But Joey had drive, direction, *control.* Was *that* the difference? Because Joey was working within *form*, the music had form, he was guided by form, he was mastering form, and with form mastered he could interpret form and within his capacities create. But Fatso? Where was the form for Fatso? Music moved Fatso. Music led him, *lured him*—it must have—to some point where the *heard* music did not so much cease but faded into the music, the *silent* music, till he was transported to an invisible realm whose form nobody knows. He could not step outside of it, not see it from outside, and he could not control it. He gave way to the madness within the invisible form—if it has form!—and struck without control. Or *was* his striking out at that moment control? Had his will and *the* will in him—had his mind and his blood—become one perfect coordination? Did Fatso for a moment sense an ultimate form? Was something in him moving in perfect coordination with all of nature outside of him? Cory experienced something now of that movement, how for a moment you could *enter* the music and be carried, your control lost in a greater motion so that you did not know who or what you were or knew *more* of who or what you were than you had known outside of that experience. Was it that Fatso felt?

Was it, Fatso?

Since his phone call to her office, he had written to Savannah the whole history of Fatso. *You know—must—more of my life than anyone. It's your life now, part, a great part. We have chosen that. So you see, I—no—we are bound to Fatso's brother because of Fatso just as you and I are bound inescapably, as we would be if we never were to see each other again, by Rod. In a way I've become a father, too young and inept but a father, to Joey as you'll become a surrogate mother to him. And maybe we have acquired a brother in place of Rod because that's what Fatso and I are too, what our lives have made us, brothers. This is a chance for me to make restitution—as if I could! but some?—for Rod. Joey makes Rod visible. That's a certain joy, pain too, but I think I need that. It keeps my thought clear.*

His thought cleared now, restored, for the music ceased. Joey sat there a moment, still, his hands raised before he let them rest on his knees, yet without moving, as if to let the music wash away and somewhere cease. He was racked too, but he had something of an intuitive performer's presence, though the polish must come. Then he turned with utmost seriousness to Miss Kellogg. When she said nothing, he smiled and nodded at Cory, though distracted with a student's expectation. But Miss Kellogg did not reveal.

She said, "That's his challenge. I've started him early on the 'Goldberg Variations.' It's going to take some time to master even part. If that doesn't get him in . . ."

"Don't even think that," Joey said, stricken.

Her hand brushing his arm appeased him.

"Getting that piece down to perfection is all we'll think about tomorrow and tomorrow and the day after."

So he was her monopoly now. Her life. Fatso's brother. Whom Fatso had brought her.

"We must be ready for Ruzinski. I've written him. Has Joey told you that?"

"Yes. I was more excited that he was!"

"You *think!*" Joey clamped his hands nervously.

"He said if the boy has as much promise as I indicate, it would be a crime not to audition him. Ruzinski! Imagine. He's one of the great teachers, and he takes few pupils."

"I know I shouldn't tell on her, but *she* said she'd see me to the end. She won't die till she sees me there."

"Joey!"

"The university has practice rooms," Cory said. "Something can be arranged. If not, we can make a private arrangement. There'll be money enough for that. But *Ruzinski* ! Oh, what you've done, Miss Kellogg! I'll write his brother."

"No. I'll *tell* him," Joey said. "He expects me next week, but—do you know what he said?—he's going to stop seeing me."

"Stop?" Cory said.

"So that's why you've been so upset lately?" Miss Kellogg said.

"Some. But yes. You know why? He says it might affect my career if they find out my brother's a jailbird. Why *would* it, Miss Kellogg? What's that got to do with my playing?"

"People . . ." Her eyes wandered to the window, the harbor. ". . . are sometimes strangely . . . rigid . . . and cruel."

"They were to him." Joey resented.

"Indifferent," she said.

"More," he said.

"Indifferent is bad enough," she said.

"Yes." Again Cory wondered what past had determined her thinking, for such ample, strong sympathies belied those fragile bones.

When Joey was gone, what would fill her life?

Joey would fill his and Savannah's. *He's as good as he is talented, Savannah, and you'll love having his youth and fire and intensity around. The only thing I'd prefer having is Gramp, but when I asked him if he wouldn't like to leave the Island and live with me when I finish the M.A., his eyes actually opened wide, they didn't quiver, and he said, "You know better than that, boy. I've lived here and I'll die here and be buried here with my people. I thank you, but this old man's got along this far and he can go the rest of the way alone, so don't you worry. Somebody's got to look after this property. Besides, you and yours—oh, you'll have them one of these days soon; you don't know how quick it happens—will have to have a place to come to. We couldn't ever leave the Island, could we? What'd the place be without a Verity on it?" I heard Mrs. Swithins' words in Virginia Woolf about what makes a view so sad . . . and so beautiful: 'It'll be there, when we're not.'*

"Well, I'll leave you both to your preparations." Cory did not wait. He took Miss Kellogg's hand. "What you've done! Who else could have?"

She smiled. "Many. I just happened to be in this place at the right time. Besides, it's Joey who's done the work."

Joey was too loyal for such judgment. "Oh, no, it's you who've suffered. I haven't missed one move of your eyes or hands. Cory, you don't know what she puts up with!"

She laughed. "If such pleasure were all I'd had to put up with in my years of teaching . . . well, Cory, I hope your career gets on. I know it will. As for Joey, I'm glad to know he'll be in the most sympathetic hands when he leaves me."

She accompanied him to the door. For the last time? he wondered, as if Joey were her last student. When she'd moulded Joey, Cory knew what she'd do, simply go on to another pupil. Wasn't music her fate? Without it her life would be death. How long could such frailty, nearly bone, last?

"Good-bye, Miss Kellogg." He took, before she could offer, her hand, dry and warm but firm. "See you at Gramp's, Joey."

Now under the encroaching clouds, the air itself seemed dust, gray all the buildings, the stripped trees forlorn in their isolation, the streetlights pale in the half-light and the road pale, the harbor a dark shadow against the graying sky. Everywhere windows began to light up, the houses closing in against the night, town huddled close to this flat land, shrinking under the immense darkness. He was afraid it would disappear and live only inside him. He wanted day. He wanted to press the dark back and *see.* Mine. The town *was.*

This town is a person to me, Savannah. I love it. The town is my grandfather. My grandfather is the town. And everything's in him. All the family. History. There's no past for us, men, unless it's in what lives. Think of a town, the world, with an objective past, millions of artifacts and no people!

Since Dalton, since finding her, he had inundated her with letters.

But you don't write. Why?

Over the phone she'd said, "Because I'm waiting for the word. If it comes—when it comes?—you'll know it."

"I'll know it when *I* find it," he said.

"Oh, you'll find yours, but will it be mine?"

"Why wouldn't it be?"

"Yes, why?"

"You mystify me, Savannah."

"I mystify myself."

"But why?"

"Yes, why?"

"If we knew!"

"You even sound mystified."

"Then I sound right." She laughed.

He saw her face now in the distant dark, but hazy. He longed for it. He did not believe it could turn vague, though he saw clearly the widely separated teeth, the flicked hair. But it was as thin as a veil, misty. He wanted it fully defined.

Now, with the lights town emerged, defined itself: On Front Street most of the stores were being closed. There was the supper rush of cars enlivening the streets and the late rush at the A&P and Bohack's. Helen's bar and Meier's and Frank's and The Diner and the gas station glowed, and the marquis of the movies went on and both hotels lit up lower Third. Always the lights attracted. Nights he would go down street and street, and days he would follow again and again the lanes and field paths to Mill Pond and the Sound, and all the beach paths, the woods, always with the feeling that there was something behind it all, under, that he would one day perceive, understand, and know with the wholeness of revelation. He longed for that. He was waiting for that. He had been waiting, it seemed, long before his own life. Was there a time even before memory that memory could discover?

Sometimes he felt he was caught up in a terrible dance with an anonymous partner who came unseen, whom he could no more resist than one could resist a silent music, not the song or the music but a madness beyond the actual notes, a rhythm which the composer had unknowingly released when he released his own passion channeled into notes restraining that other passion yet releasing it. He no more knew what it was, or who, than the composer who unknowingly released inklings of that madness beyond the controlled madness he composed, which was his but made of what he could not even know. He knew now that without knowing it, the composer, like him, was listening even against his will for that madness, wanted to know what that madness was composed of, how it moved, worked, and captivated. If he could know that, he could know himself, know others, and have a sense of the meaning of the dance.

What was in him waiting to be created?

I would find it, Savannah, whatever it is. It would be worth finding no matter what the cost.

"I haven't any idea what you meant in your letter," she'd said, "because you're always so abstract, and you know *me*—if you can't touch it, it doesn't exist. Oh, I know, Cory. It's there. Whatever you want, it's there; but *you* want to make it concrete too. I know you're not looking *out there*, but maybe you're overlooking it here."

"What does that mean, I've got it under my hand?"

"You *know* that's what I mean, but *you* have to realize it. Besides, *I* don't know what *it* is. I can't tell you. The only way I'll ever know is to share what *you* find, and you don't tell me in terms that I can understand, concrete terms, Cory."

"That's because *I* don't."

"Oh, I think you understand more than you say. The question is how much you'll share with me. That will tell me everything."

"Everything?"

"All I need to know. I'm waiting."

He'd laughed.

But she *had* waited.

Fall had come, and the leaves dying. All Providence had turned a delirium of redyellowgoldbrown. After a sullen day at Brown, bucking the wind from his rooming house toward the John Hay, tempted by the fires of blown leaves, he walked in the gutter, kicking up leaves, reveling in the brittle crunch, laughing aloud as he used to when he'd lived with his father and that Louise and that Anthony on Benefit Street. He could laugh freely now, remembering that boy, himself, going along the street kicking up leaves with a furious pleasure till he came to the house across from the tenement house he lived in. He had halted then because looking up he had seen a face in the window. He halted now. He stood long in the gutter, startled that all this time in Providence he had not once gone back to that wooden house with the high brick wall along the sidewalk. A sudden sick feeling, a strange nostalgia, came over him so strongly that he knew he had to go there this instant. He could not explain. *Go.* Instead of going to the library, he went down the hill to Benefit Street and turned right and ascended along the left side so he could see that house on the opposite sidewalk. How many years had it been? He had been five then. Would it still be there? Would he recognize it?

He could close his eyes and see it.

The farther up the street he went, the more run-down the houses, the more sad the facades of those two- and three-storey buildings, still austere in their decaying dignity.

There. He recognized the house at once. Yes. The configuration was fixed in his head forever. He halted, suddenly afraid. His eyes went straight to that window. But no face! Nobody. The window reflected the sullen day, gray as dust, dirty. But no, no face. Abruptly he was no longer five. But the fear lingered because the *face* evaded. Always the hazy face faded, fled. Why? Where was it? Did he imagine it? *Had* he always imagined it? Had it been only in his head? Was it inside him?

His father.

He had come for his father.

He wanted to know what his father was.

Always the father in the back of his mind lingered. And always that face. Was that face his father's face? He knew that face was not his father's, but he knew that his father's face was *in* that face, behind that face; that that face encompassed his father, his fathers, his natural father and Pete and Reggie Webb and German and Gramp and all the other fathers that made him; that that ghostly face had led him all the years since, lured, was still luring him. The face was not *nothing,* it was real, it was real in him. Hadn't it lived in him all these years? Wasn't he standing here on Benefit Street staring at a real house on this sullen day, breathing real air? Surely that face had made him realize that the face must be in his father too, in all his fathers, in everybody. Was it what Fatso and Rod and Joey too had been looking for in him? Was the father the brother and the son too? The face was always there waiting to be pursued. Come or go, it always lingered on the periphery of his mind. He pursued. He would pursue. He was certain it was somewhere in the world. Here. He did not want to miss it. He had to *know* it. He would. The face was in him. There was some reason. The impulse was in him. He had to track it. He had always to be vigilant.

He saw himself running madly through the labyrinth of his own mind, bewildered, lost, insistent. Turbulent, he turned his gaze from the empty window and made his way up to Prospect Park and stood at the iron railing at the edge of the cliff, under the statue of old Roger Williams with his hand raised in peaceful greeting over Providence, and looked out over the capitol, downtown, the thousand islands, and the far harbor. The wind was rabid—it tore, riled, making the sky a restless blanket of dark mounds and layers of gray. Here, high above the city, the sky seemed too close, the cloud shifting and reshaping. Prepossessed, he stared till he saw that face he remembered hazy in the dust and grime of that window, *black* or *white* he could not tell. He saw it spread enormous in the dusky sky; saw it coming down, pressing close. Whose face? If only he could see it clearly! For he yearned, he could not escape yearning; and he insisted because he needed to know. What else did you have to go on but knowing? Even *knowing*, you could not go on alone. He felt the largeness of the sky, the surrounding gray. He blinked, trying to sharpen that face into form. But the face shifted, spread, re-formed, defying his imagination. Now it veered, neared and neared, almost taking shape—eyes vague but eyes, a kind of mouth thick, broad forehead, something resembling short hair, stringy, thin . . . *Not* a man's head. "You!" he cried aloud. "You!" He laughed loud. "Savannah!" He closed his eyes, trying to see her face, but he could not see it whole. It frightened that he could not define every feature; but he read into the clouds the separated teeth and that hair short and wiry which she shook like flicking a fly off. *Savannah.* He gazed till it vanished. *You put the face there,* he told himself, *but you couldn't unless it was there in you.*

He did not tell or write her that, not yet, perhaps one day. She would understand. She would always understand, and if she did not, such was her compassion that she would live with it unconsciously, accept, knowing that one day it would make sense to her. She would accept because it *meant* to him, because it was the core and substance of his life he could not escape. She would not ask *why* he could not escape. He could not tell her, he did not know, and she was surely aware of that; otherwise, he would surely tell her. He might come one day even to telling her *he would put me in a home* because it was the source of his greatest shame; it was to him blasphemous that his father did not want him, would *shed* him, rid himself permanently of him, *give him away,* make him in essence illegitimate or disowned. He thought of his squadron commander—his major, Bernie Whitehouse—who had turned his plane around on D-day because he could not lead his men, *sons,* to their death. He could not tell that either, but not from shame of his major, no, but from both pride and shame, pride in his major's love for his men, so different from his own father's, and a shared shame for the judgment the world made of the coward, who could not tell his reason either, just as he could not tell of his father's intentions. The world would pity, but there was a mean side to pity, it could lack feeling. He feared pity. He believed the major had not.

In his delirium he raced back to Brown, kicking up leaves, exultant in his decision. *After all this time waiting for a sign, Savannah.* He laughed. Not a sign, no, but admission, yielding. You fool you, Cory Moorehead! Why had it not come sooner?

He called Savannah:

"Hello," she said.

Without preliminary, he said, "Savannah, I don't want to be without you."

Apprehensive, he could not fathom the long stillness.

She was crying.

She said, "Say that again."

"I don't want to be without you."

"Oh, Cory—"

"Savannah—"

"Don't say another word, please. You call me later, at home?"

He knew. Words. She could not wield yet.

To the Blue Room he had gone then and joined his classmates George and Billie and Truman for coffee, and had it not been for his almost instant captivation by Professor López-Morilla's seductive labyrinthine conversation, his intensity underscored by his deep Spanish rhythms, he would not have been able to bear the slow time.

So, night come, he called again:

"At last," she said. "You said it *at last,* Cory. All the time since you left the campus—in that apartment in New York, in Black River Falls and here in Madison—I've dreamed of those words. For a minute I thought you'd say something when you came to New York; when you didn't, I thought they'd never come. I came back to Madison out of nostalgia and faced the city without you. Maybe without even admitting it to myself, I've been waiting for you here."

Then he told of that projected face, of his life in Providence with his father and that Louise and that Anthony, but not *put me in a home.*

"I don't want to be without you, Savannah. You know that. You've always known that."

"I knew it, but you didn't. I imagined that the longer you were at Brown, the farther away you were, the easier it would be to forget."

"Forget!"

" People do. It ' s the easiest thing in the world for some people. "

"Not when you've lived what I've lived. You know—what you don't know!—more than we can say. You feel me more than anyone. You're the closest to me—and, yes, Rod—"

"Yes."

"I can never forget that. I don't *want* to, Savannah."

"And I don't want you to, I won't let you, I won't let myself, because without him . . ."

"Say it: we might not have happened."

"That. And more."

"More."

"It's too much to say."

"Bit by bit we'll say it, and one day, all."

"One day, yes."

"We have a lifetime."

"I hope it won't take that." There was that hoarse throaty laugh. He closed his eyes. The Union. At that oak table. Under the arch. Across from him. In white. There she was.

"Savannah . . ."

She said finally, "I'm waiting, Cory."

"It's a gamble."

"Yes. But I don't want to gamble with anyone else."

"Savannah . . ."

"Yes?"

"I don't think I can be complete without you."

"Oh, Cory, that's what I'm for."

"You! You'd give—"

"What I won't give. I'm not exactly cut out for this nun's life."

"Well, it's too easy for me to become a monk in a cell, closing out the world, when it's the world I love."

"It's because you have to have a still place to gather it in, don't you?"

"Yes. *You* keep me in it."

"I want to, Cory. I will."

"You're sure you can bear that?"

"I can bear anything."

"You know me. It won't be easy."

"Anything, I said."

That had been two weeks ago.

Then had come that letter, the second letter she had ever written him: *Save this for the times that always come between people, the bad moments, the hard days, when we remember things and the past plays hell with us, batters, and we need something realistic to set us right again, talk plain sense into us in other words, because no matter what happens to us, between us—even if nothing ever had happened between us—I'll love you, Cory. Though I don't believe in destiny, you seemed from the very first moment I saw you in the Union my destiny. When you came to New York you proved how much you cared for me or you wouldn't have come right away. That day something might have happened, and even when it didn't I thought This is my treasure, what he's left me, the hours spent beside me in that bed, holding and loving me. I thought What more can I ask of him? I thought What can I do for him? I felt I owed you something for that demonstration of love. So I did what you asked—I went home—and that saved me. I didn't know it saved me for this, for you at last, for what I dreamed of, Cory. No, not the dream of the little cottage and the man and kids in the country. That I'll always have. You have to have a backup even when you realize the life you really want must be the one you're choosing all along as I chose to come back to Wisconsin because you urged me to and then chose to come back here to Madison because I wanted to be where we had been, at first to indulge my memories, then to face them and put them in their place, though always in the back of my mind I must have thought I'm waiting for Cory. And I was. Oh, I knew the hazards. I know them. I don't want you to think I don't. I say this because I love you, Cory, and want you to know I go into this "gamble" with my eyes wide open. I've asked myself a thousand thousand times since you went back to Greenport, Why would he want you, Savannah Goshen? And there are plenty of reasons—good, dubious, bad—and Cory knows them; but I had to spell them out for myself, see them, and make sure you saw them too because sooner or later, sometime when we were together, in one way or another, you would have to admit them—not to yourself, you've done that I'm sure, but to me so as not to mislead me because you'd never betray intentionally, I know that, not just me but anybody, as you didn't—you didn't, Cory—Rod or Fatso or your stepfather German or Dalton or your mother or your grandfather anymore than your mother or grandfather would betray anyone, I gather from all you've told me. I know some of what's in you, a good bit, though there's a mountain more I don't know but want to. I want your life, Cory. I want to know every moment you want to tell me but only what you want to tell me because there are always the private sacred moments and love doesn't intrude, I've learned that; it waits for what love gives and doesn't ask more, I won't. That goes for me too. I'll give of my life all I can. What I want you to know is that I have no illusion about the complexity of our love and want to be sure you don't because, apart from what you love in me as simply me, whatever I am, you love me too for this place, what happened to us here at the university. That includes all that happened there on Long Island too and how it affected you while you were here, and all that happened to me here too, and that means Dalton, but mostly Rod, because he was more than your brother. He wanted to be more than your brother. He couldn't be more than your brother. He didn't fool me—I think he knew that, though we never uttered a word about it—and he didn't intend to. He couldn't articulate that because he knew you didn't realize he wanted to be more than your brother, and I think he didn't precisely because you weren't aware of or perhaps fully aware of or perhaps repressed by (and of course you'd be) being brothers. So I served to be you because I was nearest to you—he could get at you that way, get near you that way, supplant you and yet be you with me, maybe even knowing—maybe even intentionally—that he could give me part of you. It wasn't something I realized the instant Rod took me after your grandmother, his "Ma's," death, but little by little as he and you suffered little agitations. Petty antagonisms became frequent enough to point to the heavy undertone that was growing between you. I don't have to remind you of the culminating incidents. But I was always at the center—I should have realized that from the moment I tracked him down as your brother, and I might have, but there was Dalton: I was so lured by Dalton, sex, and involved that for a time it blinded me to what was happening with Rod and why. So in a crucial way I was at the heart of it and to blame for a good bit of what happened. You feel—you shouldn't, I've urged you not to, though I know you suffer what you suffer and that's that—you're responsible for Rod's death; but you have to remember that you share that with me because it was through me that the tension was brought about. It's possible that nothing might have happened. Rod might have gone on, even gone away. It's possible that the confrontation between you was merely postponed because he came to me after his grandmother's death. We'll never know that. Whatever, for a time I was you to Rod, as close as he could get to you—with distance that is clear to me now—just as I might have been, after Rod, as near as you could get to him, had it happened in a different way between you and me: as it* will *happen, Cory. For me Rod was as near as I could get to you. As far as he could be, he was you. We have to face that because it's one of the reasons for our being together. We can't deny it. It's a bond and it's a bond finally we don't want to disavow. We can't. We'll lose more than we gain. In a peculiar way we owe that to Rod, who did not realize what he was doing for us. We have to be realistic, Cory. We can't deny memory. We can't deny our life.*

He hadn't mentioned the letter when he'd called her again because she'd know the call *was* the answer:

"I want you to come. We can't wait till the semester ends. We've wasted so much time. Can you?"

"Can? You know I will."

"I want you to meet somebody."

"Meet? Oooooh! *Him*. Your grandfather. But—"

"Not here."

"Greenport! You want me to go to Greenport."

"You have to know it."

"Oh, I want to. I've always wanted to. When I was in New York, I'd even thought of going myself alone when you weren't there—I never would but *how* I've thought it—just to see what you both talked so much about."

Both.

He laughed, exulting now: because they must begin *here.*

"Because Greenport's you," she said.

"And I want it to be you, yours," he said. Because, after, all their lives, it would be theirs. "Listen— Halloween's his birthday. You'll be his birthday present. Take the train from Chicago—will you? The Greenport train leaves from Penn Station. It's three hours to Greenport. I'll steal time from classes, you from work—"

"Will I!"

"Listen—" He gave her the schedule. "There's an afternoon train that gets into Greenport at six. I'll meet you at the depot."

All the week he had tried to repress his exultation, to concentrate, and all this day he exulted in the surprise—he wouldn't tell him—he would give his grandfather Savannah.

It was near time.

Now true dark settled. With the trees stripped of leaves and the streetlights exposed you could see Front Street arrow white and deep into the night toward Southold. Now down the sidewalks came the first ghosts, ghouls, skeletons; kids of all ages and sizes were out early, impatient with their *trick or treat.* Far cries came, hoots, gang talk, laughter. The street was almost cleared of parked cars.

The red pickup was parked outside The Diner.

German.

For a moment Cory halted, pondering those massive shoulders, that blonde head, huddled over the counter. What was German's life like now? He must be lonely and feel isolated because this town was not easy with outsiders. Why did he stay? He'd said he hated this town, the Island; said he missed Detroit—never Pennsylvania, always Detroit. Despite everything, he felt close to his sisters and his brother; said he wanted to go back there; said he *would,* he *couldn't wait.* He cursed the place sometimes, his mother'd said. So why, German? What would keep him here and make him bear the loneliness and isolation? The promise of another woman? Surely it wasn't grief. He wouldn't want to stay where *she* had been. He was not the type to mope over things; surely he wasn't that passionate or morbid. Or was it mere apathy? German had little ambition. Though he envied learning and what it reaped, he resisted it; he rejected the discipline and work required to garner it and forge a way. He waited. He liked to wait. He expected his windfall. He felt he deserved it, but that there was some kind of injustice aimed at him. Yet he implied that if he sat it out, vigilant, a time would come when he could seize his day and win. He'd show *them* that sitting and watching *with wits* was also a way.

Cory faltered. He would ask again. He even thought *I'll insist he come.* Though he could never really like him, he wanted to be fair to German, because there must be something he didn't understand about German. His mother had loved him, hadn't she? German had behaved like the best of sons to Gram when she was dying of cancer, hadn't he? He had always been polite and pleasant with him, Cory, and what's more real buddy-buddy with Rod, hadn't he?

Perhaps because he was anticipating this moment with Gramp, his neighbor Edie, Joey, Mrs. Doyle and her daughter, and Savannah; and perhaps because German looked so isolated hunched over the counter drumming up talk with the waiter, having to eat out now, to depend on the regulars for a little life, to drum up company to be able to stand a town he claimed he hated, he felt sorry for German. Yet he would not cross the street to ask him to Gramp's again. There was something hurt in German that made a hard streak in him, and that roused a responsive hard streak, a stubborn *no,* in Cory.

He went on to the parking lot.

You could feel snow in the air.

The depot made a nest of light in the dark, pitch now. Only three cars and the town's taxi were waiting for the six o'clock train. The harbor and town seemed infinitely small, a few lights on Front Street and the lights on the docks reflected in the water, the night so dark that the few pinpoints from windows on Shelter Island seemed tinier but brighter in the dark.

Far up the rails he saw that bright white eye of the train pressing down on the town. The train whistled three times, the rails gleamed and the great thing, shooting yellowish breath, throwing sweat off its undersides, trundled thunderously in, reverberating the ground. It was as if at last *he* let go, *his* breath, *his* pounding. He laughed, watching the engine and the first cars ease close to the harbor's edge and lie still, the windows alive with the reflected lights.

Then from the last car she descended and stood an instant—in a long dark coat, wearing spikes, which made her deceptively tall. She set down her suitcase. She waved. The coat parted. White! He laughed loud. He might have known. The girl in white. And he ran.

"I can't believe this," he called out. *Here* in Greenport. He'd never have believed the real Savannah and the real town would come together.

"Cory." They clutched, kissed, held.

"It's unbelievable! You're here in this town, mine, in this life and not in that other."

"Oh, your voice, Cory, your voice. I can feel it vibrate. I've waited for that voice, all this time I've waited to hear you." Her hands went under his jacket to his chest. "I could listen to your voice all my life."

He laughed. "That may be your punishment."

"Isn't one's hell another's paradise? Oh, Cory, *I* can't believe this either."

He took her bag. At the car he turned, flung his arm out to scoop in the waterfront. "*This* is Greenport."

She gazed, taking in the harbor and Front Street. "It won't exactly dent the universe, will it?" She shook her head and laughed that guttural. Those teeth! He felt an overwhelming comfort. In the car he took her head in his hands and kissed, kissed. He said, "These lips" and she said, "Don't complain. You can't change them. Do it again," and laughed—that guttural. He smelled cigarette in her hair. "You haven't changed any of your habits, I see." "Nerves. Did you expect me to?" "No, it would ruin you." "I was already ruined." "You!"

Here and there ghosts appeared again, glittering gowns, kids clumsy in high heels, boxed scarecrows, skeletons.

"What fun! *I* used to. A domino I made once," she said.

All along the streets front doors and porches were lit up. From dark places everywhere pumpkin faces. lit up by candles flickering bright, stared out at you, slit eyes and nose and mouth and wide ear-to-ear smiles.

"Look at the pumpkins! Their mouths look like—" He broke into a long laugh.

"What's that funny?"

"They look like Gramp laughing with his false teeth out."

"I can't wait to see."

"Don't be shocked."

"At what?"

"He's old."

"I know."

"He's burned."

"I know."

"He can't see well."

"But gets along."

"He can't hear much."

"But he's got his radio."

"He's poor."

"Who isn't! Look at us. You." She kissed him. "You fool, you. I know all that. And he's got you, only you."

"Yes."

"What more could he want?"

"That's your line, not his. There's plenty he could use, but *he* doesn't think so. He's got about all he needs, more. What's that?"

At the foot of Monsell Place at the edge of the crick, the building loomed, in the dark a blaze of windows reflected like layers of light in the depths.

"The hospital. A landmark. At night it always tells us where we are."

"And where are we?"

"I'll show you tomorrow."

"The world of Cory Moorehead?"

"The universe of Cory Moorehead."

Now he realized: all day in his itinerary he had been preparing the way for her.

He stopped at the empty lot.

"Here?"

"It's where the house was."

Slowly the dark in dark, the well of the house, became visible, and the dark of bricks to be hauled off. It was strange not to see the dark chimney lone against the sky.

"They're from the chimney. Clarence has just torn it down."

For an instant they sat. She said nothing but her hand brushed his cheek.

"Oh-oh, he's got company."

The outside light over the door was on, the entry door was open, and five or six kids were just emerging. You could see his grandfather's shadow cast on the entry floor from the kitchen light behind him. Then the door closed him off.

"Trick or treaters. He's always ready for them. They know he always is. They love Tom."

You could see through the front room the light in the kitchen.

"I know that house," she said.

"You do?"

"From everything you said. I could move around in it."

"You'll have to. There's nowhere else to go."

She laughed. "It's the only place in the world I want to be."

"Come on, then, while nobody's come yet."

"Who's coming?"

"Not many. There aren't many *to* come—for his birthday—and for you."

"Me. They know that?"

"No."

"Does he?"

"No. You're the surprise, his birthday present."

Her head fell against him for a moment. Then she said, "I can't wait to meet him."

"You ready?"

"Ready."

As they approached, they could see the back of his head through the front window. He was sitting as always at the kitchen table.

Cory went in first. The cats, comfortable over the floor, raised their heads but made no moves.

Gramp looked up, squinting. The table, set before he'd left, was exactly as he'd left it except for the bowl of tea rimmed with tiny Japanese men and women acting out their lives.

"Is it you?"

"It's me."

"You've been long enough."

"Maybe I had a good reason."

Gramp laughed. Like those pumpkins! "See. I told you, Savannah."

He drew her into the room.

"Many happy returns!" she said.

His grandfather cocked his head, squinted, stared.

"This is Savannah, Gramp."

His grandfather gripped the wide wicker arms and drew himself up to standing.

Savannah gripped both his hands.

"I know you," she said.

"You do?"

She kissed his forehead.

"Mr. Verity. Thomas Tilton Verity. Tom Verity. Gramp," she said.

He laughed. "Somebody been telling tales?"

"Cory can tell them," she said. "He's got the imagination, and the voice. I wonder where he gets them from."

"You do?"

"I think I know."

"You do?" He laughed. "You say *Savannah*?"

"Yes."
"That all?"
"Savannah Goshen," she said.
"Goshen?"
"Yes," she said.
"Goshen."
"Yes," she said.
He smiled, reminiscent.
"Nice name, Goshen," he said.

Tom

"*Uh*-oh."

Tom dropped the toy fire engine. He had cut his finger on the metal ladder.

Pal, sniffing at a hole, halted and turned his head to inquire.

"Useless as a fart in a gale of wind," he muttered. Mostly he was his own company.

He stared at the sudden blood. "Still alive then." He laughed. And licked. "It works for animals. And ain't *we* animals?" And laughed again, and sucked.

The dump, the pond, trees and fields all the way to the Sound were stripped by winter, stark under bright morning sun. But cold.

The fire engine he set in his cart with the scooter wheel and a split vase he could seal like new for Mrs. Doyle, who liked a bright thing—maybe the glitter spoke to eyes as bad as his—and a perfectly good tennis ball, a lead soldier in need of paint, a music box with no mechanism. A good haul. He couldn't expect more the way people ransacked the dump ever since the war. Funny. And the country prosperous because of the war.

All the war years Fatso had picked up junk for him and kept the shop loaded. No end to work. He liked it that way. *Work for the night cometh when no man can work.* He hadn't had to teach Fatso that. Passing Third, he took in the low house with the long porch. The Garcías'. How Fatso'd worked! He hated to think of the boy in a cell up in Ossining. Confined. Nobody should be. He himself knew *confined.* In the hospital. In bandages. Months and months confined.

But Fatso— Killing his *mother*. You couldn't understand. *He* knew that. The fire.

Thirty-odd years, and to this day he did not know that moment; all the details stood out sharp but against nothing, a nightmare that changed all his days in one instant.

"Come, Pal."

Pal dashed, a slick gleam of black in the stark sun, halting to sniff a tree and raise his leg to wipe out an earlier claim.

He pulled his cart past the old cemetery, adjacent to the dump, thick with old stones, thick with old trees too. The stones were bold with sun and cast sharp shadows.

Why'd the town set the cemetery smack beside the dump? Blasphemous that seemed.

Ben. All the others. But buried in the new cemetery

And Mary.

At the other cemetery almost on a bet you could hear Emil's nasal whine across the flats, having a heart-to-heart with one of the graves or, worse, poor Bud Frome from just down the street, half-crazy with shifting his tidbit on the stock market day after day, who had gone full crazy when his wife died and went every afternoon at four sharp, a regular date, "to talk to my honey," he'd say.

Tom needn't go to Mary's grave to talk. All his days he talked to her. And Stell now. They were never far. And sometimes *that. It.* He'd stopped calling it *Him, God* the day he'd preached his last. But *You*, yes. Quitting preaching was his way of castigating himself because he'd felt *some reason for the fire, that punishment beyond my clumsiness. It's up to me to take it into my own hands. Who else? Because what's to blame's in you; it came from them, your own. You got to accept it, like them. You're responsible. Or not worthy.* Because who ever told you a man deserved a thing in this world just by being born?

His feet stirred a few dead leaves. Dry for December.

At the fork of Main and First, the World War I soldier pointed his bayonet toward the Sound—forever. You could see the Revolutionary War obelisk a block away. Wars and rumors of wars, yes. No wonder all the churches. The spires stood in plain sight: Episcopal, Presbyterian, Baptist, Methodist, all within two blocks; but St. Mary's and the Synagogue the other side of town, as if the others had something against them.

He crossed at the Episcopal and downed the block to his corner, facing the hospital. Too familiar. But memory removed the great red brick building. He saw that private house the hospital once was, saw the high second-story room, white, white; saw the white sheets over his body; saw his own arms raised, white too, all white bandages; and for a long time only the sight of white ceiling and walls till he could move his head and see out the window nothing but endless sky and then gradually when he could be raised and when he could sit up by himself the view of the creek and Sandy Point and far sea and sky forever.

He never had to think *fire*. It came quick. A sight, a sound, and flame would suddenly leap, surround. An instant he'd be back on the barge galley bungling by pouring that grease or kerosene, he didn't know which, on the stove, the blaze leaping over him, his clothes afire, arms flagging fire, him running up the steps, wind turning him a living flame ready to leap overboard when a voice out of the fire spoke and hands threw a tarpaulin around him, rolled him, smothered the fire, saved him, his body singed, scorched, burned third-degree. In the hospital bed he lay wrapped white, all but his mouth to eat, his eyes to see nothing but that white, and his ears to hear, keep hearing that voice like God's *Give me your hands, Tom,* Nate Coon's voice, or Nate God's—the same, was it?

As quickly, he'd be standing in *now*. Here he was, with these hands, this cart, his junk.

And Pal panting.

And this winter wind. Its cold breath stirred. Lucky he had good lungs in this barrel chest! He could sure bellow. But which Verity couldn't? He laughed for the family fame: you could hear a Verity a mile away.

Deaf, *he* missed hearing the sea.

His brother Gill, deaf and blinder than he, with glasses deep as telescopes, had been the loudest. Gill had ended up caretaker of a property on the jut across the crick from the hospital, living in the cottage with some wandering hens kept for eggs and the nanny goat he'd kept for milk, that would wind on its chain round and round the iron stake till it couldn't move even to get to its food, poor creature. Some womanizer Gill had been! Weekends at the cottage Gill and a couple of his young pals would live it up with city girls on vacation picked up in the Wyandank or the Stirlington or one of the bars on Front Street. Summers you could hear their shouts and laughter from clear over the crick. You couldn't scold Gill. He'd squint shut as a mole. "Oh, shit, Tom." It was his way. He missed Gill. Gill was almost the last to go. Of his nine brothers and sisters Bertie and he alone were still here. His own ten children had scattered over the country like the tribes of Israel. His didn't want him after the fire, no. But she did, Stell did, Stella-for-star. She was always there.

But the house was gone. The sight of empty space when he rounded the corner still startled, a year since the fire. For a while he'd looked to the standing chimney as evidence they'd all lived there, but Cory'd had the chimney removed. Now when he looked up for the house, the chimney, for instants it was hard to believe he wasn't mad. Where was the house? Where Stella Mary Momma and Poppa his kids his brothers and sisters horses goats his grocery? At times he'd swear fire was actually alive, fire was conscious, fire had gone after him as if it hadn't finished its job on the barge, as if it had been waiting all the years for the right moment to take everything. And fire did, almost. *All but Cory and my place,* he thought as his house in the rear came into view. *It's Cory's because he's what's left—and whoever would be after.* He was guardian of the place for Cory.

That possession had stunned German.

"You?"

The day the house burned down German had gone to stay at the motel on the Sound; the next day he'd taken a room at the Manaton House on First.

"Plenty of space here with me."

"Cory'll need the space," German said.

"He won't be needing two bedrooms," Tom said.

German did not reply.

Truth was German had always hated this house because it was makeshift, hated it because it wasn't his, hated the low lintels he had to duck under because he was so tall, hated him too, or resented. Oh, Tom knew. No place needed two men to run it. German, he had to admit, was right. A husband had his rights, didn't he? German was as independent as he was. He'd never come in if he didn't have to; he'd come to the door, give his message, go. He was always polite, he'd grant that to German; but it was the formality, the sense of duty, that told. German resented, he held back, he bit his lip and kept silent. Tom knew German had priority, but German had come to the wrong family, the wrong woman. Stell'd had her terms. Oh, she'd never spoken them to him, her father, no; but he knew her man was doomed to have *him* like a shadow forever there, and he doomed to be there, for he could no more leave her for long than she could him. At thirteen she had laid hands on his flesh`and tended his third-degree burns with washing and salves and bandages and knew his body like her own. Since, he could no more imagine breathing without her than he could imagine not moving inside the circuit the generations of Veritys had traveled.

So at noon a few days after Stell's funeral it was a startle for Tom to look out the front window and see German—he'd gone back to work the morning after she was buried—in the burned rubble, kicking through the char, turning up objects.

The fire had left next to nothing of her. But German and Cory, who'd come from Providence by the first train and taken the ferry from New London, had had to identify. The horror had sobered German at once. He had felt responsible. "It was my day, Pearl Harbor. If I'd taken her with me . . ." You couldn't deny the immediate horror and in the next days the grief in German's face, the puffed flesh, the filled eyes, the unblinking stare, his staunch silence.

German was inching over the black remains.

He wouldn't go out. It might embarrass German.

German seemed to be systematic, working in restricted areas.

What was he after?

Whatever, it was a fool's errand! He wouldn't be finding anything there.

German was gone within the half hour, but late afternoon after work he was back—with a rake this time—and worked the time the sun stayed. Neighbors passed, curious, but perhaps out of respect did not meddle. And German raised no eyes to confront. Social as he could be, he preferred to be very private.

He was sure tearing at the foundation.

Stell said he always went too hard and fast at a thing, why he passed out sometimes. That plate in his head cut off his circulation.

Day was low now.

Tom went out.

"German, come in and wash and have something to wet your whistle. You'll make a mess of your truck."

German's truck was his passion.

"*You* keep booze?"

Tom laughed. "A bit here for emergencies."

German's doctor said Scotch was the only drink he could touch with what ailed him. German loved his beer and whiskey, and together. Trouble was they didn't love him, but German could sure tank up at the Club. Rebellious, taking it out on her, he'd hurt himself.

Tom was surprised when German actually came in. He'd expected the usual excuse. So it was clear: German had his feelers out.

"There're plenty of towels, German, and fresh soap."

As usual German was silent, and as usual his eyes averted. Bloodshot they were. From alcohol. Or grief. Or alcohol because of grief. Well, he *looked* struck. Silently German washed. When he ducked back through the low doorway, he was startled, then smiled, at sight of the Scotch Tom had set on the table.

"*She* saw to it I had some. *You* know." He found a clean glass. "That'll set you straight." He chortled, feeling sinful by association, bad as brother Gill.

"Sit, German."

He did. That alerted. He gulped down his Scotch and poured another.

"You comfortable enough at the Manaton House?"

"It'll do."

"Staying here'd save you eating money, and it'd give you a place till you decide . . ."

"Decide?"

"Well, you never liked the town. You always talked about Detroit."

"Things change. I might set up here one day."

"When'll that be?"

"When things go right for me."

"I see."

"A piece of land. I could build."

Out front you could see through where the house had been. The emptiness defied imagination. You knew history had died. You had to trust memory.

"You're good at that."

But *she* hadn't been able to get German to lift a finger to work on the house. "And you a real carpenter and cabinet maker," she'd say. "Not till it's in my name," he'd kept repeating, and he'd stuck to his guns.

"Land's high here because of the beach," German said. "This town may be at the end of the world and hell in winter, but it's peace for who wants it and summers it's the paradise people dream of."

"You got a spot in mind?"

German turned his head and stared out at that emptiness.

"What's wrong with right there?" His mouth was already relishing a sight. Or triumph.

"Where Stell's house was?"

"Ours."

"Ours?"

"Hers and mine."

"Oh, you'd have to talk that over with Cory."

"Cory!"

"The house was always the boys."

"How do you figure that?"

"Stell always looked after her boys. She'd never change that."

"But word of mouth doesn't count. You know that. What judge'd stand for that?"

"It's no matter for a judge."

"This may be."

"Stell was too smart for—what'd you say?—word of mouth."

"How do you figure that?"

"With the problems this family had with her mother's property, you think she wouldn't put her wishes in writing?"

German abandoned that emptiness. This time he looked straight at him. "You mean a will?"

"Her will, yes."

German's breath broke. It was no laugh, no chortle, but a little choke of triumph.

"Nothing survived that fire; every paper in the house was burned to bits."

"Her will wasn't in the house."

German's eyes froze. His lips thinned. The face went stone. Tom might have been that Medusa.

Before German could ask, he said, "She kept it here, German."

"In this house?" German's face went dumb.

"She put it in my strong box sometime back."

Resentment gave German his form again.

"Why didn't *I* see the will?"

"We all knew it'd go to the boys—to Cory, since Rod . . ."

"Cory." The fury, or hate, bit. "You'll have to prove it to me," German said.

"Nobody's keeping it from you, German. I think you know that."

"Cory!"

"He'll be glad to let you see the papers anytime, I'm sure."

German broke, bolted up. The cats scurried into the other rooms. German swerved and in his rage forgot and struck his head on the low lintel. "Jesus H. Christ!" He ducked out of the kitchen and slammed the outer door.

The way German behaved sure implied it would be the last of him. It needn't be. He could have stayed here. He and Cory felt responsible for him, for her sake; she'd have wanted German here if he'd chosen to stay. But German had become all surface. He'd loved her once, maybe did yet; but even with her alive he'd turned to things—*got the gimmes* she'd have said—and wanted, *wanted*. How'd he expect to get them—by gift, inheritance, assocation? Lured he was, and falsely, by the judge's friendship, imagining somehow he'd get into that world. Not by a long chalk. German didn't, surely never would, know this town. Rigid, resistant, the old families. Rich or poor didn't matter so much as *old*, settlers' families from way back, gentry or swamp yankees, a pride even lack of money hadn't quite overcome.

He was surprised German had crossed his threshold, but he wouldn't have if it hadn't been for his truck . . . He wouldn't soil that truck for anything or anybody.

Yet Tom pitied German because he was the alien. Cory and he and the town somehow had let German know that, couldn't help it. But Tom pitied because he too they pitied: because *cast aside* by the family, by the town's pity, by shame. Ignored. After the fire they'd avoided him, offended by *scars*, by *crippled*, by *poverty*, by that *eyesore* his makeshift cart.

"Why, Pa, go ahead and do whatever's easiest for you," she'd said.

Stell.

Stella-for-star.

You got used to moving in a fixed orbit.

Courteous the old-timers were, and kids, a word to him now and then. In his ordinary passage down the streets, he was Tom, as natural to town as any neighbor's child or cat or dog or the bronze soldier or the town hall.

Sometimes his own eyes were filled with the curse of himself, the sight of his own young self and what he knew he had had and what he'd had beyond his own knowing. Handsome he was. His looks were legend all along the North Fork. Lord, you gave. Because God gave to some abundantly. To Tom Verity He gave abundantly. But God gives not perfectly. Oh, no. Deceive not yourself. God gave the eyes. The family eyes were not perfect. All the children were cursed, but he did not know he was to be the most cursed, as if one had to be chosen to represent the rest, a model whose fate you had to turn your face from and be glad your curse was not his. Tom could deceive himself too, but not for long: to see well he had to squint his pinkish blue and stare. Why his eyes? Why his brothers' and sisters' eyes? No man knew. Family sin, they said, your mother and father were first cousins, they said. And that was so, though Cory would now smile gently and talk genes till Tom'd ask why deficiencies then and why in some? Where'd they come from? How? A gift, his eyes? Why give a perverse gift? Was God perverse? Would I be perfect with perfect eyes? Cory could not say yes. Where would imperfection then lie? Oh, Tom knew. Because his eyes were the sign. He had been blind to his own self. But he had learned: imperfection turned you inward. I was an ignorant proud peacock who didn't know my own ignorance or pride—till Alice Wilson.

There ahead was the Wilson land, midway in the block between that bordering on the hospital and the next, where his own place was. The Wilson house fronted Main; its lot ran back a block to the sidewalk he stood on.

He knew that house, every room; after school, Alice had often taken him there. "Tom Verity, from my class, Momma." And her momma, "Oh, Alice!" as if her momma didn't know a Verity when she'd seen them all her life; you couldn't miss one. Yes, Alice had taken him room to room. And Alice sweet, innocent, respected Alice ran her fingers over his neck and his chest and down his shirt and leg to startle and excite and please, all this after he had had to quit school young as he was because *bad times* for the family. By then he'd met Mary, the dark, the brown-skinned, brown-eyed Mary, who would resist, resist, so still, so staring, her eyes filled with a seething which made Tom seethe. Mary would quietly, unperturbedly say no, so he burned; and rather than burn, to make Mary burn if he could, he would go back to the school for Alice every chance he could. He would not stay away from Alice a minute till somehow time meandered and habit imprisoned and their bodies drove till before supper, after, in day, in dark, they would meet for a minute. Where? "In the stable, Tom." His hands could roam; he could almost *have*; he could madden, be maddened, till madly she said, "I'll have the duke of the town, you, Tom Verity, I will." And she gave, gave, and then refused so as to madden till he could not stand the madness and she laughed and still denied him. When he could stand Alice's denials and the wait no more, could stand Mary's denials and the wait no more, in desire and fury and vengeance too on Mary, he took his father's tilbury and he and Alice went the thirty miles to the JP at the county seat in Riverhead, and married. But *nothing*, no, because though only a few minutes too late, Alice's vigilant momma arrived with Tom's father, who, little as he was, would, he said, thrash Tom to within an inch of his life if, license or no, he dared touch that girl, already broken in had he known it—*ruined,* their folks would have said.

"Did you forget, boy, everybody on the North Fork knows the Verity tilbury? And don't you go pleading *law* to me because this lady is law and I'm law. You understand, boy?"

And Mrs. Wilson: "Don't tell *me* you're married, young lady. You're *not* married, and you're not *going* to be married till your father and I say so, and that's final."

No marriage.

Nothing.

Because *annulled.*

Tom burned. *Better to marry than to burn,* the Book said, though when he'd conquered his frustration, fury, secretly he exulted. *Saved!* Because it was really for Mary's flesh he burned, had burned from the moment of her deep eyes, dark, the beautiful bones shaping her square face (in private the family called it a *squaw's* face), and her strange beauty inherited from the blood *tainted* Indian on her mother's side. Pride caused her never to associate with Indians if she did not have to or with the town niggers or Polacks or Jews or the Puerto Ricans who came as cheap labor to pick in the potato fields, and to bring the children up not to, but not to be unkind to them either. Tom clung to Mary as to a wall holding back a passion overwhelming beyond all his imaginings, sure it would break through. But, citadel that she was, she resisted. "When we're married, Tom," she said, smiling. She was proud too of her self-assurance. Through Alice's forbidden notes smuggled to Tom; through her few escapes from the house after raging to see Tom, pounding on doors or windows; through the futile attempts to keep her at her aunt's in Patchogue from which she periodically escaped back to town, appearing at his job distraught; through it all, Mary kept placid.

Her placidity triumphed.

But not without blight.

They came out of the church to the news that Alice Wilson was dead. Not to mar the service, people had held back the news. "Her father found her hanging from a beam in the stable," Minna Doyle said. "She'd used the horse's reins. It was Follett's neighing that got her father to the stable."

But Tom and Mary were too young, too self, too passion for the sign. They were too deep in passion to hear the cry out of the dark or see that dark form against the sun.

But it came. The form would hang, dark. The Wilsons sold the house to Jeff Rounds and moved; and Jeff broke up the lot, sold the back piece with the stable facing Sterling Place to Angus Rhodes. It would be years before Tom, farming, failed; then went as cook on the skimmer and oyster boats, and fished, and sometimes scalloped, and failed; then rented from Angus the by then renovated stable and set up in the grocery business, and failed.

It was in that store on certain afternoons at dusk during the war-to-end-all-wars, when not a customer came, that there was such silence that you could hear the quietest wind or even the waves strike the

Sound shore far off; and something hanging dark would blotch the clear sky or the Doyle yard across the street and hang in his mind what he had never seen hanging there; and it would strike him with wonder how he had come to be on Wilson ground and in the old Wilson stable refurbished, its shingles darkened deep brown by time.

It struck now as he passed the spot on the block where his first store had been: no store, no stable, no building now. The place had turned garden.

Perhaps it was merely the haunt of his happiness with Mary that made him think what that happiness had cost Alice or, if he dared think too much, what that happiness had cost him. But he *was* driven to think too much because he felt Mary so much; he maddeningly felt Mary, maddeningly could not *not* think of her.

Because his very happiness was a desperation and an agony:

Because she wanted him, *him*, but only when *passion*.

And passion besieged. There was no time she could set, no time he could plan on, expect. She released the passion in him, but it was not hers to control, or his. What roused her, what roused him, was not Mary of the dark eyes, the brown hair, the high cheekbones, no *thing* to touch, not *flesh*, not skin, heat, bones, wet. What roused them was a fire like a distant volcanic motion reverberating through them which flared, released not at her will or his but at *its own* as if she were a victim of that torrent and he a victim of that torrent in her, a torrent which might erupt while they were eating a roast or picking over apples in the cellar or walking Moore's woods or the beach or brushing each other *Mary! Oh, Mary!* or clutching in dark by the outhouse, *Tom! Tom!*

She took him to madness. She struggled speechless, only the deep moans and the quick cries uttered as if through some ritual she made him enter blood itself and drew him down into the oblivion of that torrent till only the torrent itself mattered, the madness.

After, the world was too sudden, stark, but beautiful because he knew he could touch something invisible in it—he had touched it in her flesh.

But it left him alone.

She left him alone.

Because from the beginning Mary was indifferent.

He did not understand her indifference. It was the source of his silent festering. It was her nature to be placid and passive before him. He accepted that because he could not imagine life without her. He could not imagine living without that invisible encounter with their very selves and everything around them which she somehow took him to. He did not understand it but he lived in it. He thought maybe it was her bit of Indian blood, some latent primitive instinctive blood rite, that was responsible; though the minute he thought, he knew better. Simply he could not explain that mystery in her; but he did not want to lose that mystery, did not want to lose her. Nor did he want to hurt her; that would hurt him more.

Oh, she was always kind to him, always soft-spoken and gentle. She did not like indoors or housework. She did what she had to, but in good weather lived in her garden. Under her hand a rage of asters, zinnias, mums, nasturtiums, peonies, purple irises, roses glutted the yard and morning glory wound over the trellis and possessed the fence. Any day, as early as she could, indifferent to weather, she would put on her sneakers and a cap over her short-cropped hair, almost boyish, and walk the beach. She would spend all day roaming the beach and low sand cliffs of the Sound, swimming, sitting on the enormous boulders, munching on the lunch she would pack in her basket, picking berries, and in winter wrapped warm to struggle against the cutting wind off the Sound. She was at home in the fields and the woods and with her hands in the earth; the house was alien as if it were too small to contain what was in her.

She was near to him, but forever far.

He endured the distance for the heights she carried him to, but he chafed at the indifference in their daily lives.

And the babies she carried indifferently as if they too were something indifferent passing through her, hers but not hers, though she did her duties—tended, cooked, cleaned.

What saved at first was that, to earn a living, he had gone to sea: so he came home a visitor to the madness of his random weekend or once-a-month or every-two-month returns. He lived for that passion. From the beginning she was quickly pregnant and after the first, Llewellyn, it seemed her belly was always round, bearing; and it would go on—it had.

But there was a fury in her because he was distant, at sea, and an agony of desire in him repressed till those escapes when he could release himself to all madness.

She persuaded him to give up the sea. He could do something in town, must. His absences were unbearable for her and the children, she said. What child wanted a father who was a stranger?

So he had taken this building (strange, when he thought, that Mary had driven him to this building, where Alice . . .) and on more faith than capital he set up his grocery store, the first in the neighborhood.

Ma loved *her Tom*, and he was all for Ma, a tyrant who with an unrelenting will ruled him and his brothers and sisters, and Pa, who stood for her bombardments and never raised his voice to her no matter how mean she was; and *mean as a snake* she was. It was Ma and the relatives who all during the war with the Kaiser helped herself and charged everything, she and all his family running up bills they never paid, offsetting the few faithful customers who never flagged with their payments even through the war. Times got so bad he had to move the store into the front room of their house. Still almost nobody paid till finally the year after the war Tom had to go back. "Not to sea again!" Mary cried. Back on the boats, yes. But he was lucky—he was an ace cook, a true chef—when he was hired on Commodore Vanderbilt's yacht, his moment of elegance. Even Mary loved his dress uniform, though she fussed: he was far, he came home too infrequently. "You're a good provider, Tom. Even in our worst times the kids have been warm and never hungry. But I want you here." He was at sea for two they'd lost, the baby girl dead at birth and four-month-old Ellsworth choked to death on his own phelgm. At home later, during the great plague of *black* diphtheria, fearing for his fourteen-year old, he sent her to his sister Jane in Bristol. "Sent Dorothy straight into the middle of it, you did, Tom," Mary said. She never forgave him Dorothy's death. The memory of Dorothy was always in her heart, pricking. "You're at the Commodore's mercy. No matter how kind and generous he is to you, you're his because you must be ready to go whenever he wants you. The children are growing, Tom, they need a father. We've got to do something."

So for Mary he went on the bunker boats, shorter trips, and ended up on that barge, not knowing he was moving toward the moment of fire waiting for him in the galley of a barge that was carrying him back to his Mary.

After the fire, during which she had gone so long dormant, after his return from the hospital, his hands still bandaged, *she* was all fire, and he was. On that night and for as long as his hands were bandaged (because she *wouldn't* see them and *wouldn't* tend them, "Let Stell"), they flamed like their first night of fire; and late in life—Mary was forty-three—conceived their tenth. *My ten tribes of Israel*, he called them. Of the seven remaining, in turn his William his David his Richard his Benjamin his Martha his Lila abandoned him as Mary had abandoned him, divorcing him because *Oh, Mary!* she shuddered at the touch of those hands. She *could* no more, could not bear. "I can't, Tom, I can't." They were all ashamed of the patriarch fallen, of those hands, of his poverty.

Except for *her*.

Stella-for-star.

Who had bathed and salved and wrapped his hands. Who had tended his body. Who had revived his spirit.

On a night of moon, after the divorce from Mary, he went the long way around town to the little church on Chapel Lane and stood there and raised his hands to the sky—the moon made them bone white—and talked to Him:

". . . and you said Give me your hands, Tom, and I gave them to you, and you took them. Then I knew I'd preached with too much pride, so after a time I left the pulpit to humble myself as you had humbled me. Oh, that was pride too, showing myself doing penance before the world, which pitied my hands and my burnt body and my life. And that was not enough—oh, endless is the way!—it needed my hands to drive Mary from me because she was all to me, to prove I could live even without love, yet loving. I thought you demanded that, and then I thought it was death you wanted of me, though I'd escaped the fire; and I did near die, for I could neither eat nor drink nor take rest, thinking on her, and on them, my children, that these hands drove from me too, all but one daughter. And when the love that left me was given to me in her, I was afraid—how she might leave husband and children and cling to me. And I told her. But would she listen? She was my daughter and did *I* ever listen? In my blindness I looked to you as the cause of everything, knowing you were and were not. I had to go through the fire I made myself before I knew, and even then I didn't know till I saw in her what was the fire I must go through: because I loved too much. It was that—you can love too much. It lacked but my knowing, and my knowing took all these years."

What would life have been without her?

But you took her!

Oh, what is it you require of me?

How often he had wanted to shout that out to God! At such moments he was not humble. He blasphemed. Would he never learn? Because God had humbled him, yes; God had kept humbling him till he was sure he was chosen to be humbled by Him, by Something, It. *Was* there something greater than God? Once It had set on him, like a hound it kept the scent, pursued and made him the inevitable scapegoat, or could not stop, or was convincing him he deserved it? He could almost believe, even make out, some pattern, a design. From his birth—and on Halloween to boot, soul or fool that he was—it seemed he was branded by error. They'd named him after the 1876 presidential candidate Samuel T. Tilden, and someone in town clerk's office had misspelled the name recorded as Thomas *Tilton* Verity.

Humbled. By fire. As if this family were married to fire. And by water. Fire fed by air, fire that took yours back into air, and water that sent you back to silt, made you earth again.

But, humbled, he knew. When fury passed, restored to sanity, he knew: *not* God but Tom, because the fire was within. It's in you, Tom. It was, when he thought, in all of us. In all things? Yourself released it. Whatever you did that let your fire out to meet the greater fire, *you* did it, Tom. *You* failed to use your head and contain your own fire. But that's what your life was, bungling into the pits in your own self, pits you learned to cry out from or crawl out of, yet carried in you still. Blame yourself, Tom—that's hard—but yourself, yes. God doesn't do; men do. Hadn't he said that to—who was it?—Fatso, yes, who hated the Joseph and his brothers story. Poor Fatso! He'd met the fire in himself too.

He would go to the woods and talk; that was his place. He didn't fear what was *there.* After the fire, dark was his comfort.

Fire.

Now he stood in his own yard and stared into the charred remains, black and ashes, of the house gone, the earthen cellar naked and the unfinished cinderblock walls exposed, loose blocks and holes. It was all before him: that day last December, the Pearl Harbor parade at eleven, and the long quiet darkening December afternoon and . . . the far voice calling him out of the deep . . . It called louder and louder. Then a sudden banging bolted him out of sleep on the daybed, his eyes filled with fire, and he shouted "Nate!" *Not the fire, it couldn't be, it couldn't happen, no, not twice, never.* He threw up his arms and saw his hands already burned, *so not the fire, no, but what?* The window, the sky filled with fire. Then someone struck the door. A voice shouted, "Mr. Verity! Mr. Verity!" and suddenly in the doorway stood a woman. "Mr. Verity." She reached to help him up. She was big. It was Edith, she had him, she was lifting. "What, Edith?" But his eyes were on fire, he was seeing fire—how could that be?—and then it struck: It's *out there.* "Mr. Verity, you've got to get out of the house before the smoke gets too thick. You've got to have air. No, let *me.* Hold on." His throat was choked with words. He *could* not. He fell against her. She held. "Stell's house is on fire." He heard the high timbre in her voice. She was strong, Edith. "The house?" choked out of him. "Yes, on fire," she said. As he and Edith emerged from the entry, he heard sirens, clanging, shouts, the whack of water from the hoses thick and long and white uncoiled under the headlights. Blue lights were flicking on the patrol cars that blocked off the street; and the faces, he couldn't tell whose, were bright with fire against the dark that walled them in.

He would fall.

"Stell," he said. "She's not in there?"

"There's nobody," somebody said.

The sight was too big. He was almost without breath. He was panting. The oldest Raynor son brought a chair and pressed him down onto it. "Best you be still, Mr. Verity."

But he couldn't down his heart, his heart was throbbing in his head, his head would break.

He was moaning—for them, Ma Pa sisters brothers cousins in-laws three hundred years history this place this earth theirs. Going. By fire.

Thank God Stell wasn't home. Thank God Cory. And German.

The fire blinded. He couldn't keep that other fire out; it was all over his hands clothes flesh eyes. His blood surged. His head reeled—*Nate*!—and he had all he could do to keep his arms from flailing. He could hear himself moaning; he couldn't stop, he couldn't stop the thunder.

The flames made thunder, and the water.

The roof collapsed.

Ours.

He saw men flagging and shouting, but heard nothing but roaring.

Edith was still standing by him, her gaze flat, filled with fire like all the eyes. The Foster boy stayed close.

Then, high on the ladder, the figure in glowing yellow oilskin flailed at the wreck and shouted.

Firemen went as near to the house as they could, but flames and smoke and heat drove them back.

The second story walls collapsed.

On the upstairs floor the brass bed stood alone against the dark sky. The frame glittered here and there through the char.

The firemen were gathering.

Something.

"Mitch?" Edith called.

She left Tom's side.

Tom turned to the Foster boy. "What?"

Edith was talking to the men.

Her hands went to her mouth, clamped her lips, then covered her eyes.

"What's happening?" Tom said to the Foster boy.

One of the men in yellow put his arm around Edith.

The crowd was trying to get closer, but the police held them back.

The blue lights flicked and flicked.

Edith came, slow.

Her breasts were heaving.

"What?"

She came close. Her face was wet.

"Edith?"

She gripped his shoulders and sank down on her knees, her mouth close to his good ear.

"It's Stell." It wasn't her voice.

He felt her wet face against his temple.

For an instant he didn't understand.

Then he knew.

Stell.

He bolted up, but sank.

Stell was straight ahead. *StellStellStell!* The words choked. "Stell!" She didn't hear. She had her back to him. Her clothes and arms and hair were afire. She was struggling with the air. She was trying to put the fire out. She was running. *Don't run!*

He started after her—

Wait, Stell!

"Tom—"

He couldn't move, hands held him.

Something struck him down.

It could have been a second later that he woke crying, "Stell, wait!" Everything was white, walls and ceiling and sheets. *No.* Where was he? *When? Nate?* He raised his hands: burnt. The fire *had been*—long ago. Then he'd had a nightmare; he'd dreamed the house was burning, and Stell. What was he doing *here* if it wasn't the fire? *Nooooo.* Then he heard his own voice crying "Stell Stell Stell." A face came. Stell? Mary? A form, white too. "There, Mr. Verity, there—" Her hand was on his head, smoothing his hair. "Who?" "I'm your nurse, Mr. Verity." "Nurse? I don't need— Where am I?" "You're in the Greenport hospital." But *when*? She said, "You're going to be fine, Mr. Verity. You just rest." "Stell Stell Stell." His chest ached. Then he tried to bolt. "Where's the fire?" The window was all sun. "It's morning, Mr. Verity. You'll be fine." Finefinefine! "Fire," he cried, "there's a fire!" She said, "Here, Mr. Verity. I want you to take—" *I want you to tell me, tell me—* "Tell me!" he cried. Was she crazy? Maybe *he* was.

But it *was* a fire, the house was burning, he *saw.* And then Edith. And the Foster boy. Engines. Town. They'd sat him in a chair. He saw Stell. She was on fire. She was running. He went after her. He shouted. He shouted "StellStellStellStell" to that girl nurse working at his arm. "Now, Mr. Verity, there. You'll sleep a while. There."

Then he woke. It was still day. Quiet. Then it was Cory. "Is it you, Cory?" He knew where he was. He remembered. It *had* happened. He hadn't dreamed it, but *I'd, oh God, give anything, go through fire again, God, if I could bring Stell back. If only, God, you—* His wet eyes blinded him. Then he remembered: "Cory, I passed out." "Don't talk, Gramp." *Cory.* Did he know? They had taken him the two blocks to the hospital. "Cory, the fire! Your mother—" Cory's face came down. He kissed him. "Don't say a word. Don't," Cory said. "I don't know how long I've been here. How long, Cory?" But he knew what he'd see when he got out: nothing.

Ashes.

Ay, who had promised us more?

Then it was Edith with Cory. She was there. "The nurse'll dress you, Mr. Verity. We're going home."

"Home? Home!"

He was frenzy. They must know what he was seeing.

"I'll be in when the nurse is through. We'll go together."

She and Cory supported him. It was a long slow way down to her car.

They went home.

All that remained was a dark crater.

Now he stared into that void.

Nothing.

With no Stell, nothing could come of it.

Oh, my daughter.

She went into the dark. And what she took with her!

He was glad the chimney was gone, too dangerous for kids who sneaked in and played there despite his warnings. No fire or flame—his life's death, fire. Now Cory'd have to have the cellar filled. Or maybe he himself'd start hauling barrels full of dirt. Loose cinder blocks lay akilter, the cellar walls a shambles. What had German wanted there? Oh, he hadn't missed German's shenanigans. Stell hadn't either. "What do you suppose, Pa?" Oh, it was on their tongues, *money,* but they hated to say. Saying condemns who says, and you can't take words back. But German—he'd see German times when Stell was not at home raise the cellar door and go down; and always he knew German was doing whatever secret thing he was doing because always and only at those times he pulled the door down shut after him. He would stay long and emerge dusty and self-conscious too if you could judge by the way he kept his head averted, never a glance in his direction. At first German must have gone down when he knew or thought he was not there to catch a chance glimpse of his activity, but with time German had grown bolder and gone down even knowing he was in his house, banking on his being half blind. But he was no mole yet and he had a nose for things.

Greedy, German had grown.

And brash.

But why?

Oh, *she*'d understood German had never had a thing. Poverty he came from, poor miner his father, dark and depressing his world, and not much chance to shake it. The war got him out of it, saved him. Saved? But money. How much greed?

"He thought," Stell had said, "he married a rich widow, Pa. What's so bad is he should know better. Something changed German on the spot. He's been suspicious for so long, thinks I'm hiding something from him. Why would I? How can he even think that, especially after coming to the house every day after Reggie and Ben were gone, and knowing Ma, and Ma buying him a second-hand Ford, and with us living as carefully as we did, and especially after how good he was to Ma, surely not doing it for what he could get out of her, or me."

He didn't say *But change comes* but thought it, thought *with time you get ideas you maybe didn't start off with,* but did say, "In this world a body has to watch himself, and his."

"I know, Pa."

Though he didn't keep an eye on German—Why should he? German was Stell's problem—squinting, he didn't miss much, but it was best to keep a close tongue in your head.

Now in the gutted cellar, shadows were stark. The ground was throbbing with sun. A winter day to envy. Bright and cold. His limbs told. Stiff.

Weather promised a bright Christmas.

He hauled his cart to his shop and unloaded. In no time his collections from the dump and this or that yard or what people brought him filled the space German had left when he'd taken his equipment and the wall of tools he'd kept arranged as perfectly as a display in Wash White's Hardware.

You had to know the terrain better than a roach to be able to get in and out and meander through and under things, but in all this apparent disorder *he* could put his hand on a common pin. What you couldn't see at long range, you remembered. Had to.

Today was the twenty-second. Three days till Christmas. Only two and a half left to work in.

Feed the cats. Or he'd not get much done with them pushing pressing purring at his legs.

He went through the entryway into the kitchen.

Pal was a frenzy of wagging, saliva ahang from his mouth.

"All right, you first." Pal drove his nose into the pan, almost overturning it. "*Steady!* You're not starving to death, old boy." Pal gulped, looked up, and nudged his thigh gratefully.

"You! You won't do, Pal. You're getting gray. You know that?"

And slowing down.

Well, who wasn't?

The cats rocked his arm as he set the food down.

"Keep that up and I'll fall flat on my face, then where'll you be, eh?"

They wouldn't touch spilled food.

When the five were settled, all rhythmic tails, he heated and poured tea left in a pan, added his milk—he'd put nothing in his stomach till it growled, then only soft stuff because it all backed up on him—and sat beside them at the table in the wicker rocker he'd just repainted dark green, his bucket close by, smoked a Marvel, then went back to the shed.

The little fire engine—his cut from it was now a hard dry streak, fine—had a wheel missing and the ladder once straightened would need a new catch to hold it in place when raised. In the vice he managed to straighten the ladder fine. Then he carefully emptied a jar of metal odds and ends over a newspaper and spread them. He pressed his face close. It was some time before he found a tiny metal cylinder that might do the job. In the vice he bent it, inserted it in one side of the fire engine, several times tried to bend it with pliers but they shot free—"Shit and two makes eight!" he muttered—before he finally took a hammer he could hold to and gently bent the cylinder in place before the hammer slipped free. There! Some kid'd have a great time with that.

A tap and rattle at the edge of the shop startled.

"Momma says don't swear."

Two abrupt little forms materialized against the bright sea of light out the shop door.

He squinted.

Ricky! Tim!

He laughed. "She ever tell you not to eavesdrop?"

"Said that too."

"You sure scared me."

"We did?" That tickled them.

"What you doing so far from Fifth Street?"

"Ma got tired of us whining, she said."

They were eight and seven, but nearly the same size. Facing each other, they were mirrors, blonde and creamy with eyes a blue glitter, all moving bones he couldn't ever keep track of. They crawled between things, under, around. "Watch you don't hurt yourselves."

"You finish my catcher's mit?" Tim was everywhere searching.

"T-ain't Christmas yet."

"Aw, Tom, have a heart."

"Well, let's see—" He found his way through the labyrinth to the far wall. Two cats, settled in after their orgy, leaped. "You, Jezebel!" The boys darted after, but she and the Whore of Babylon scooted behind boxes. The shop seemed to have erupted broken bikes, scooters, wagons, benches, sawhorses, and everywhere tools. Despite that clutter, he knew his place—that chair in the center and the long table where those thousand thousand days he'd bent to work, murmuring his thoughts and sometimes when he missed and struck his hand muttering that cussword.

The catcher's mit, with new leather strips, hung on the wall.

"About two stitches of this waxed thread and you'll think you're a Brave."

"Yankee!" Tim flared.

"Sure."

"Here's my bat!" Rick jerked it free.

"Finished last week. Where've you *been*?"

"School wasn't out yet. Ma kept us in to do homework."

"So much of it?"

"Yeah. Mr. Verity, what's your name?"

"*Tom*, stupid!" Tim said. "Ma *said* she bought the fixed-up chair from Tom."

He made pin money to buy materials he needed to repair the year's broken toys.

"Tom," he said.

"What'd I tell you, dope."

Tom slid his hand into the thimble strap with the quarter fixed and sewn into the leather palm and pushed the needle through several times and hitched the thread taut with his mouth. His eyes quivered, nerves maybe, working too many hours in no true light to repair the heap of toys.

"Can we take them home now, Tom?" Tim said.

"*Mr. Verity*, Tim! Ma says you don't call grown-ups by their first names."

"Can we, Tom?"

"Tim!"

"Oh, shit, Rick."

"*Who* says don't swear?" Tom said. "Of course you can take them. They're all yours. That's your Christmas."

"Wow!"

"But it's a little late in the season for baseball."

"We can practice for next year."

"Bye, Tom."

"*Hey*, Rick," Tim said. "Ma said be sure 'n thank Tom . . . I mean Mr. Verity."

"Thanks, Tom," they chorused.

Tom laughed.

"Merry Christmas, boys."

They scooted lickety-split.

He set two bike wheels into the frame and screwed them on. As long as the sun held bright, he took advantage—squinting close up he managed fine—and painted the last two frames a lively red. By Christmas morning for sure they'd be dry. A curio box he glued, then sanded and shellacked the music box he'd picked up at the dump today and set it on a shelf to dry. He had a loose music box mechanism that played a pretty tune; a little wedging and some glue and it'd fit this one fine. Maybe for the little Hicks girl.

Shadows were filling the room.

You could go blind, Tom.

As if you weren't!

He chortled.

Outside the shadows were long. Dark as ghosts. Sometimes they were. With his eyes they were all dark. You had to be close to them. But the ghosts were inside you. Course, he was glad in his young days the whole family swore they'd seen his aunt Stella appear under the apple tree in plain day, white as the blossoms themselves. *If there's a heaven, I'll come back to tell it.* Well. But he'd been glad then. Faith in a good place wasn't a bad belief.

Some tea might give him some gumption.

His tea reheated on the gas, he poured it and sat and cupped his hands around those tiny figures in the made-in-Japan bowl.

Of a sudden the cats bolted.

Some noise?

This time the ghost was white. It stood in the kitchen door pane.

He squinted: a woman.

StellMaryMa.

She pushed the door open.

"Mr. Verity . . .?"

"That you, Edith?" Since Stell she kept an eye out. That girl!

This time she brought a package.

She wiped the table for him and set it down and opened it, all white tissue.

"There!" She held it close. "Isn't she a beauty."

"Why, who'd ever—"

That old doll she'd taken to make new clothes for. She was the perfect seamstress, for some years fleshed out her husband's salary full-time with both her needle and the Singer.

She'd done the doll up proud. The dress was powder blue, and the bonnet, both trimmed with white lace and set off with narrow red ribbons. And white booties!

"She looks better than store-bought!"

Edith laughed and set the doll back into the box.

"It'll make some child happy."

"I got one in mind," he said.

"You have everything you need, Mr. Verity?"

"An old man don't need much, Edith."

Mostly what you needed just about nobody could give you. But something they could.

"Is Cory coming for Christmas?"

"It'll be a last minute surprise if he does. It costs. Summer he'll be here for sure."

"Well, if you need a thing, call over the fence."

"I'll do that. Thanks for the doll. Family all right?"

"Driving me wild, but what would I do if they didn't?"

He nodded at that. She closed the door.

Edith never dropped in for long. And never forgot. For Stell. For him too, but for Stell. No, she'd never forget, Edith. Always on her side of the fence ready to do.

She took over when Stell died.

Took over for Cory before he got here.

Took over for German because he'd taken the fire bad. Fainted, they'd said, out of it, and blamed himself he wasn't home when it happened. Cried. Well, German had his grief and guilt to bear too.

And took over for him, blind as a bat and deaf as a coot, but, worst, dead to the world. Passed out. In the hospital. But for Edith, he would have missed Stell's burial. Cory was afraid he'd collapse at the grave. What Cory didn't say—oh, *he* knew his Cory—was that Cory couldn't bear the thought of losing *him* too. But Edith knew what might have killed him long ago; and Cory knew too and had feared for him: he had had to see Mary lowered into the ground. You had to *see*, you had to know, you had to be sure. You wanted to know where they were. Placed. You could go to them. *Stell* understood. She must have seen Reggie forever floating somewhere in the ocean, and Ben . . . she'd never known.

Sometimes, the way the cats had come to the door and hung around and then moved in on him, he could believe they were his people come back to home ground.

People said cats smell. But nothing could be cleaner than his cats. And Pal. Albert had given Pal to him trained. Next to godliness, those animals. *He* must be far from it. If anybody smelled, he did. Oh, not his body. He'd wash himself down, but if he didn't empty his bucket and rinse it out . . .

Tea finished, he gazed into the dregs, but roused himself. Day was low now. Work. He'd be at it till late this night. Those kids depended.

Outside, the shadows were deep. In the shop he turned on the raw bulb he'd rigged to hang low over his worktable, weak in the late afternoon light. He turned a scooter upside down and hung it over the corner edge to give it some wheels—if he could put his hands on those cotter pins.

Languid, Magdalene raised her back and rubbed it against Pal. Pal chafed her head affectionately. She rose on her hind legs and set her paws on his back, but they slipped off because Pal abruptly moved to the doorway and stood, alerted.

"What is it, Pal?"

The sky was losing light. On the corner the delicatessen neons had gone on. The yard was sunk in dark, her cellar submerged. Only the trees' high branches still caught falling sun. The shorn bushes and the lilacs stood dark.

In the yard he saw nothing but shadows.

"What, Pal?"

Pal went right up to a shadow and stopped, then returned wagging, satisfied, and continued rubbing his nose against The Whore of Babylon.

Then the shadow moved.

Old, you *saw.* The least shadow and somebody might *be.*

Before dying, was there some ground you traveled where in day or in dark shadows came at will out of your memory and stood there?

The shadow was thin as a stick.

Who?

He could not determine.

Then feet and legs inched into his orbit of light.

"Hello!"

That child. In clothes dark as her skin.

Stell's. She *was.* If anything ever was.

The girl had never come so close.

She held her old doll.

"Far from home, ain't you?"

She shook no.

"Well—" He laughed. "Maybe not so far." Fifth Street. "I forget town's small and you're young. I'm working. You want to watch?"

Not to press her, he went back to the cotter pin, maddening to find thehole and insert the pin and then pry the ends apart with a screwdriver and wedge them back with the hammer to secure the wheel, then spread them flat. He muttered to himself as if she weren't there.

She came out of the dusk and stood on the edge of dim light, watching.

"You ever leave your girl home for her afternoon nap?"

She shook no.

"She must get pretty tired."

No.

"Don't *you*?"

No.

"Or lonesome?"

Because she would come, stand, and stare long—at that house, at where it had been. She'd pay no heed to whoever passed. Or him. And why? He didn't understand. Something went on in that little head.

Let be.

She gazed.

"Are you lonesome?"

She turned her head and eyed him aslant, a ponder.

Finished, he rose and went outside, halting beside her in the little alley between the shop door and his back entry.

"She must have a bunch of friends?"

Her head went no.

"You must."

She clutched her doll close.

"It's all right for you to come here? Your family doesn't care? It's getting dark. Won't they worry?"

She didn't answer, but dropped her head and cocked it toward the house.

"You miss her?"

Her head quick faced him. Her dark eyes, wide opened and rimmed with bright white, were like a bold question.

"Stell," he said.

Sudden, his own grief erupted.

Her mouth opened.

"Stell was my girl." He felt himself trembling.

He thought he heard her throat.

Her eyes were suddenly wet. She was very still—no child of his could ever be so still—but her tears moved.

Her head brushed his jacket.

He put his arm around her and drew her close. And she yielded. Her head rested there. He felt her breath struggle. Her chest heaved. Her trembling could be his own. Then her throat broke.

"It's all right, all right."

How long had she kept whatever it was bottled up?

Her chest heaved against him, and settled, slow.

Sometimes kids had more to bear than we know.

Her tears bathed his hands.

He took out the handkerchief always ahang from his back pocket—it wasn't clean—and tilted her head back and wiped her face.

"Emmy," he said.

Hearing her name startled her.

"I've got a surprise for you. You can come in." She looked around at the cats dispersed and comfortable, and at Pal standing like a host. "Pal and the cats won't hurt you. They love company. Smile at the little lady, Pal."

She lowered her head without shifting her eyes from Pal, and *she* smiled.

The package was on the table just as Edith had left it.

"No use waiting till Christmas. Open it."

She would not set her doll down.

When she turned the tissue back, she bit her lip, and looked up.

"It's yours."

She gazed at the doll.

"Yes. Take it."

She did not take her eye off the doll.

"Don't you think your doll'd like a playmate?"

She gripped hers.

"You could name her for my girl."

She shook *no no no* violently. Her face was fierce. *No.* She held her doll up with one hand, the other struck its breast with the forefinger till he caught her meaning.

"You mean *that's Stell*?"

"Estelle," she whispered. Barely a breath he heard. It was the first word he'd ever heard from her.

"*Course* you'd like to name your own child, but I'm thinking there's a beautiful name you *could* give her. How about Star—like Stella-for-star—because Stella means a star."

The beauty of the word must have struck because as quickly as he said *star*, she smiled. Her eyes shone.

"Star."

"Hold her. She'll want to get used to you and Estelle."

She hesitated, but for only a moment, then drew Star out of the box and stood her and Estelle face to face on the table to introduce them, and looked up at him and smiled, then sat with one on each thigh.

"There. You've got a regular family now."

Pal barked.

He laughed. "See. Even Pal says so."

But Pal kept it up.

"Oh-oh." He eyed the front room window—through the far window, headlights. "Something amiss?" The lights cut off.

He let Pal out again.

Presently he came wagging in.

Something familiar then.

Before Tom reached the door, a heavy trudge vibrated the entry floor and a man appeared in the doorway.

Emmy bolted from the chair and hid behind Tom.

He squinted.

"Well, German . . ."

German simply stood there. He wiped his hands over his eyes and let his arm fall loose.

His arms dangled.

Drinking.

Or drunk.

I might be deef and half-blind but you can't beat my smeller.

"A long time since I've seen you, German. Sit, won't you?"

"I'm fine." His head was cocked. "What's that kid doing here?"

"Oh, Emmy's an old friend. Ain't you, Emmy." When he turned to her, she clutched both dolls, her face buried in them.

Why was she so afraid?

"Hanging around all the time." German's voice, always big, was too loud.

Tom heard the fury.

What had the girl ever done to German?

"Don't you ever go home?" German's voice pursued.

Why, the child was petrified! Hard against his back, she was trembling.

"Now, German."

"Now, German," German said. His hand covered his eyes a moment.

"Emmy's my guest."

He turned and put an arm around her. She pressed her face against him, the dolls crushed between. She would not look at German.

"Guest!" German said.

German had always before, surely out of respect for Stell, behaved like a gentleman with him.

"Come now. You know German."

She jerked. Her head dug into him.

Something came over German's face. He blinked, and shook his head. He was looking at the old doll.

"That kid." He gave her a bitter look. "*You*," he said, hard.

Her eyes grew big.

She was trembling.

"German won't hurt you."

German reeked.

German swayed.

"A kid that young should be home where she belongs instead of snooping around all the time."

"You don't worry about Emmy. I'll see she gets home all right. Emmy, you can sit in Pal's corner. He'll keep you plenty busy."

No she shook, and grasping both dolls in one arm, one hand dug her fingers into his sleeve and held.

"It's all right, Emmy," he said. "Sit a minute, German."

"Sit! I've *been* sitting—too long."

What was German scouting around for now? Since Stell, he'd almost never come. The last time had been some days after Cory'd left. He'd said, "What do you mean it's not my land? Who kept the house up? I did. Who paid the bills on it? Me. German did." "You know Stella always intended the house to go to the boys if anything happened to her, German. With Rod gone everything, the land and this house, is Cory's. That's long settled." "Cory! That's tough. If she'd wanted Cory to have it, she'd have left a will." "You knew she had a will, German." "Well, if she did have, you'd have to prove it. Anything she had went up in flames. Any fool would know that." "Stell's will wasn't in her place, German." *"What?"* "A long time back she brought me the will to keep here in this house." "You crazy or something? Where is it? Prove it." "Cory can show it to you, German. It's all good and legal." "I'll believe it when I see it." "You'll see it." "Well, I'll be a son-of-a-bitch."

"Yes, sitting too long," German said, "and thinking."

"Too much thinking can be hard on a body."

"No kidding!"

"Sure you won't have a cup of tea? Take only a minute to heat." Tom sat. Instantly Ruth tried to leap into his lap, but Emmy had sunk on the side away from German and latched her arm over one leg.

Ruth whined resentfully when he set her down.

He poured his bowl full and cupped it between his hands and took a careful sip.

"Hadn't seen your truck lately. You been traveling?"

"Traveling! Now where would *I* go?"

"Thought maybe you were visiting your people."

"On what?"

"It take a lot?"

"More than I got. But I'll get there one of these days."

"Stell said you always wanted to go back to Carbondale."

"Detroit."

"Yes, Detroit."

"She had it right."

"Plenty of work there?"

"My brother'll always give me a job, he's a big shot at GM, but I don't want any favors. I'll wait and get it my own way—"

"That's usually best."

"—and right here."

"In Greenport?"

"Greenport."

"Always thought you wanted to leave."

"I do. This fucking town!"

Tom was silent. German was drunk and words would only aggravate him. But he bent Emmy's head. Paternal resentment he felt—for her, and in the town's name. This town was the world, and more—centuries of history, the nation's, the family's, his—all one thing. *We made it.* Since 1636, his family's country, and all they knew at first hand of the universe. *Birdie.* Her bony hand would shake genealogy at him. "Did you know we were thirty-sixth cousins to FDR, Tom?"

He'd laugh. "He must be thirty-sixth cousin to everybody, Birdie."

What we had. *This.*

"Nothing to keep you here."

"Nothing *shit*! I'm not leaving till I get what's mine."

"Yours?"

"Mine."

Tom pushed his bowl back. He stood. Emmy leaped up, and he slipped his arm about her to hold her back. Her hand clutched his.

Alerted, Pal rose and stood by him, looking up, expectant. The cats merely turned their heads, curious.

"And what would that be?"

"What'd that be! Je-*sus*! As if you didn't know."

"Me?"

"Yes, you."

"How'd I know?"

"Because you, you and that son of hers, got it. And me nothing. Not a pot to piss in."

"It's his by rights."

"It's my land. Mine. I got the rights, I paid the bills, it was my money supported her."

Money. Stell had said *If I put it in his name, in five minutes he'd turn the place into cash, Pa.*

"The property, halfway to the Sound once, was in this family centuries. We all depended on that house. It's family, German."

"Family! You think Cory won't kick you out when he needs money?"

"Cory'd never do that."

"You just wait."

"Stell looked out for her father, German. She wrote me in a life lease on the property."

"I'll be goddamned if she did!"

Tom said, "If you'll excuse me, it's time I was getting back to work, German."

"You think you're all so fucking smart, shutting German out, don't you? But German'll be back. I'll get this place yet."

"I'd let it be, German, and get on with your life."

"I'll find a way, I'll find it, there's a way. You can destroy papers, burn them, but—shit!—you won't be able to keep this place up for long, and when you can't—"

"I'll manage."

"You will, eh?"

"As long as I have hands, I will."

German turned clumsily and struck his head on the outer frame.
"Jesus H. Christ!"
Outside, his feet struck the ground unevenly.
Tom heard him pitch against the wall of the shop.
Emmy flinched. Her eyes darted up at him. They were full.
"Everything's fine." He caressed her head.
Dark came too early down.
He squinted.
It was the shortest day of the year, and the darkest.
He could not see German, but he heard him moving in the dark.
"I'll have this place yet," German said.
"I'm still here," Tom said.
"I'll get you out," German said.
"I'm still here," Tom said.